PRIMAL BONDS

THE DARKTIME NOVELS

A FADA SHAPESHIFTERS TRILOGY

REBECCA RIVARD

WILD HEARTS PRESS

SAVING JACE

A FADA NOVEL

The Darktime Trilogy begins with a heart-pounding romance between a black panther shifter and the woman who saves him from a fae assassin.

"There is sex and suspense and everything you could hope for in a shifter book." ~Paranormal Romance Guild

Winner, Reviewer's Choice Award for Best Paranormal Romance

PROLOGUE

OF GODS AND SHAPESHIFTERS

They say Dionysus is a wild, untamed god, beautiful in the way of all gods. He loves wine and women, and his rites are dark, tempting, addictive. It was Dionysus and his followers, both fae and human, who created the first fada during his infamous bacchanals. By some mysterious magic, the fada were shapeshifters, a mix of fae, human and animal genes—and a touch of the god himself.

The first fada lived in the Mediterranean Sea, water shifters who could change to dolphins, seals, otters, even sharks and other fish. They were dark, ruthless, and as untamed as the god who'd first given them life. From the Mediterranean, they spread throughout the world's rivers and seas.

Centuries passed, and then one day, a tiny clan of Arab fae from North Africa's Fertile Crescent got together and created the earth fada, shifters who could change to land-based animals like cougars or bears or deer. Dionysus found it amusing to provide the spark of life to this new creation. The North African fae gifted the quartz and its special energy to earth fada alone. But like most fae gifts, it came with an edge—with the right incantation, a fae can control an earth fada through his or her quartz.

Fortunately, that knowledge is known to only a few North African fae.

When an earth fada reaches a certain age, he or she is taught the secret of the quartz. They vow to guard the secret with their lives. Because if the fae ever learn the earth shifters can be controlled through their quartz, they're doomed.

CHAPTER 1

THIRTEEN YEARS EARLIER: THE DARKTIME

Jace Jones slogged through a cold December rain on Baltimore's west side, dog-tired after a rough two-month assignment in South America. All he wanted was a shower and a six-pack.

His best friend Adric was pacing the street in front of Jace's den. "Takira had her cub."

Jace's exhaustion fled. That was bad. His sister wasn't due for another month. He'd hated to leave her, but you didn't say no to your alpha.

"She's okay? It's too early—"

"She's fine, and the cub is, too. I just came from their den."

Jace raced down the stairs to his den, Adric behind him, and tossed his backpack on a chair. "Your uncle? He's expecting me to report."

Adric's uncle, Leron Savonett, was the Baltimore alpha. An abusive, out-of-control alpha who didn't deserve the title. Sending Jace out of the country when his sister was heavily pregnant was typical behavior for Leron—keep families and friends apart.

Adric's face hardened. He was Jace's age—barely in his twenties—but the past few years had left him with an old man's eyes. "Leave him to me."

"Thanks, man." Jace stopped only long enough for a shower, then rushed across town.

He'd missed the clan's winter solstice celebration. It was early Christmas morning. The streets were empty except for a few hard-eyed humans for whom December twenty-fifth was just another day.

Takira's mate let him into their tiny apartment. Silver was a half-blood fae, beautiful in the way of all his people. Right now his stunning face was drawn. He looked as exhausted as Jace.

"How is she?" Jace demanded.

"Fine. Tired, but fine."

Takira was in bed, a tiny bundle in her arms. She looked weak and way too thin for a woman who'd just given birth, her skin an ashy brown, but she smiled proudly up at Jace.

"She has her father's chin." She touched the infant's sharp chin. "And his pointed ears." She grinned at her mate.

Silver's spare features softened. "She's got a lot of her mom in her, too—and I thank the gods for that."

Jace kissed his sister's cheek and stroked a finger over the cub's soft black curls. "She's beautiful."

"Do you want to hold her?"

He gulped. It had been years since he'd held a baby. He and Takira were earth fada. Their Baltimore clan had been decimated by a bloody civil war. The two of them had lost both their parents by the time they were in their teens.

The Darktime. That was what the clan called the bloody civil war that Leron Savonett had sparked when he'd set out to become alpha no matter what the cost —and the gods knew, the cost had been tremendous, year after year of killing and dirty deeds.

Things had become so bad it was all they could do to survive. Food was scarce, which meant the few cubs that had been born were sickly or died.

His lungs clenched as he stared down at the infant.

Takira kissed her tiny nose. "Meet Uncle Jace, sweetie."

"Hello, love." He lifted the child from his sister's arms. "She's so light. Can't weigh much more than a feather."

Takira chuckled weakly. "She's a newborn, idiot."

"Mm," he said, all his focus on the precious bundle in the crook of his arm. He pressed a kiss to her soft forehead. Her scent was milky-sweet, not a whiff of the graveyard stench that emanated from most night fae. He detected a hint of silver and iron, though—silver from her fae blood, iron from the human.

My niece. I'm an uncle.

It struck him like a punch to a gut.

The cub gazed unseeingly up at him with wide, catlike eyes. Then she gave an adorable little stretch like the unfurling of a flower before settling back into the tightly curled position of a newborn.

Jace swallowed hard—and just like that, his heart was hers.

"Her name is Merry," Takira said. "Because it's Christmas—and it's a happy name." As followers of the old gods, the fada celebrated the winter solstice, but their Jamaican mom had made a big deal of Christmas, too.

"It's perfect," he said. "She's perfect."

"I just wish Mama could've seen her." A tear leaked from the corner of Takira's eye.

Jace's chest squeezed. "She would've loved her, and Dad would have, too." Their father had been a mix of Cherokee and Scottish, with a deep, fierce love of family that he'd passed on to his two offspring.

"Yeah." Takira smiled through her tears.

Silver hovered protectively nearby. He touched Takira's shoulder. Their eyes met, and Jace guessed he was sending reassurance through the mate bond. Takira rubbed her cheek against Silver's palm.

Merry's tiny brow furrowed.

Jace rubbed a finger over it. "Don't worry, little one. I've got you safe."

"Thank you," said Silver.

Jace gave Merry a last kiss and handed her to her father. Night fae were stunning, with pale skin and black hair. Silver might be half-human, but he looked all night fae—mesmerizing as a glittering cobra. Jace could barely tolerate being in the same room with him; the man made his skin crawl. Night fae were the energy suckers of the fae world. They fed on dark thoughts and emotions.

How the hell had Takira fallen in love with the man, and worse, taken him as her mate?

Still, Silver's expression was tender as he looked down at his new daughter.

Takira moved restlessly. "You can't tell the alpha. He thinks I lost the baby last month. Promise you won't tell."

"The alpha doesn't know?" Jace pulled a chair up next to the bed. "How the fuck did you manage that?"

Takira flicked a glance at Merry, then lifted her chin. "I lied."

"The hell you did. With a cub inside you?" He scowled. Fada couldn't lie, not without making themselves violently ill. And since she was pregnant, the cub would've been affected as well.

"I had to." His sister's expression was fierce. "It was the only way to save her."

"She was sick as a dog after," Silver interjected. "That's why she's so thin—for two weeks, she could barely keep food down. But she had no choice. Your friend Adric told us that Savonett was going to force Takira to abort the baby. He doesn't want the clan to be saddled with a fae bastard." His mouth twisted.

Anger flared in Jace. "When you were seven months along?"

At his sister's nod, he snarled. "Someone needs to put that SOB down."

It was Leron's fault their parents were dead, too. Oh, he hadn't killed them directly—just sent their mom to almost certain death in an overseas skirmish, and then dragged their dad into clan politics. Leron was a vile, power-hungry excuse for an alpha.

"She's a fada," Takira said. "I know it. We all have a few drops of fae in us, just like we all have some human. But she's going to be able to shift."

"How do you know?"

His sister touched her quartz. "I can feel her drawing on my energy already."

He nodded.

"We're going to hide her," Takira said. "Only you, Adric, and Marjani"—she named Adric's sister—"will know about her. For now, Marjani's covering for me —Leron thinks I'm still in Florida on a mission. I'll go back to work in a few weeks."

"Maybe you should just run," Jace said, but even as he spoke, he knew it was hopeless. The alpha was too powerful—and fada trackers were the best in the world.

"He'll hunt us down," she returned. "You know he will. The best thing is to hide in plain sight."

Jace nodded. "I'll back you up any way I can. And you know Adric will."

"I know." Takira grabbed his hand. "Promise me something. If anything happens, you'll keep her safe."

"Of course. You don't even have to ask. You know I'd die for her."

"Say the words." Her gaze desperately searched his.

He clasped her hand between his. "You have my vow. I will keep your daughter safe no matter what it takes."

And between the five of them—Takira, Silver, Adric, Marjani and Jace—they were able to keep Merry a secret for four years. And then one bleak January day, Jace stopped by his sister's apartment to find it had been trashed, the small family gone.

Jace, Adric and Marjani had torn Baltimore apart looking for them—and then extended their search up and down the East Coast. But Jace never saw Takira or Silver alive again.

CHAPTER 2

THE PRESENT DAY

Jace should've known better than to stop for a drink at a local bar.

Grace Harbor wasn't his town. Normally a Baltimore earth fada wouldn't be welcome this close to Rock Run river fada territory. But he'd been visiting the quartz mine his clan was excavating just north of Grace Harbor, and when a couple of Rock Run men had invited Jace and the other miners out for a beer, he'd figured why not? It wasn't like he had anyone to go home to.

For a Thursday night, the bar was packed. Some of the other fada had hit on the humans, but Jace made it a practice to stay far away from humans—especially females. He'd downed a couple of beers, caught a few innings of the Orioles game on the TV behind the bar, and decided to call it a night. Outside, the air was still warm from the June sun as Jace made his way to the parking lot in the back to get his motorcycle.

The night fae was waiting for him, lurking in the narrow space between the bar and the next building. The only warning was the acrid scent of metal and decay. Then a tall, pale man stepped out of the shadows, buzzing with a dark excitement.

Invisible tentacles slid over Jace's skin, seeking to entangle him in a net woven from his darkest fears. *Death...loss...betrayal...*

Night fae liked to play with their prey. A scared, panicky victim was catnip to creatures who fed on negative energy.

Jace's growl came from the depths of his cat's wild, primal soul. He drew on his quartz's energy, resisting with everything he had. A silent, deadly battle commenced—five minutes, ten minutes...

He was losing. Sweat beaded on his forehead. His quartz's song grew fainter. He thought of Merry and threw everything he had into fighting back.

It wasn't enough.

The night fae's teeth flashed in triumph. The shadows shifted and a knife jumped into his hand. He lunged, slashing open Jace's belly.

It was like taking a red-hot poker to the gut.

Jace grunted and doubled over. When he forced himself upright, the bastard stabbed him a second time right below his navel. Digging deep and twisting.

But the fae had made a fatal mistake. He'd let himself get within reach of a man whose animal was a jaguar.

Jace's claws shot out. He struck at the night fae, ripping out his throat in a single, savage blow. The man gurgled and staggered back into a brick wall. He slid to the ground, twitching, his expression shocked.

Jace waited, breathing hard until the man's heart went silent. He was dead.

A hand to his belly, Jace crouched on the asphalt, hurting so bad he could barely think. The motherfucker had stabbed him with an iron knife, poison to both fada and fae. Worse, the blade must've nicked a small artery, sending the poison directly into Jace's bloodstream.

His vision hazed. He set his jaw and hauled himself upright. For a few seconds, everything went black. He swayed on his feet, gazing down at the leather-wrapped hilt sticking from his abdomen.

Get it...out.

Gritting his teeth, he grabbed the hilt with both hands and jerked the knife free.

The iron blade hurt even worse coming out than it had going in. From far away, he heard himself groan. He let it drop to the ground and used the last energy in his quartz to heal the nicked artery. The spurting blood slowed to a trickle.

The parking lot was blurry. He shook his head and forced himself to focus.

The night fae was sprawled at his feet, his blood seeping onto the asphalt. Jace could still see his mocking smile as he thrust the knife into Jace's belly.

The bastard wasn't smiling now.

Thunder grumbled in the distance. Jace's skin prickled. The parking lot appeared empty, but he sensed more night fae nearby.

And there was no fucking way he could ride a motorcycle.

Taking a bandana from his pocket, he pressed it to his wounds and limped around the corner of the building. The movement sent a dizzying jolt of pain through him.

He leaned against a loading dock, breath sawing in and out, and closed his fingers around his quartz, drawing what energy he could from the vibrating crystals. The stone warmed in his hand. Given time, it would refill with energy, but time was something he didn't have.

From the parking lot, he heard two men speaking in hushed tones. His heart rate ratcheted up. He couldn't tell if they were night fae, but his skin still tingled, so he forced himself to keep going, dragging himself around a chain-link fence.

He zigzagged, slow and awkward, through town, trying to throw off any trackers. He was fading fast when he arrived on a dark, quiet street. At some point, he'd lost the blood-soaked bandana, but maybe that was a good thing—if someone was following him, it would draw their attention and hopefully, grant him a little more time.

He'd left Grace Harbor's small business district. Mind working, he considered the long line of attached Formstone houses.

He couldn't run much further. He had to go to ground before he passed out altogether.

Two doors down, a plump, gray-haired human sat on a concrete stoop, cigarette in hand. She glanced his way and did a double take.

He peeled his lips, showing his canines, and snarled lowly, his cat rising at the sign of a threat.

"Easy now." The female came to her feet and backed up. "Tim?" she called through the screen door. "You there?"

Jace didn't wait to meet Tim. He lurched off down the sidewalk. Thunder crashed and he scented the rain close behind. That was good. It would wash away the blood, hide his scent.

About halfway down the block, he came to a break between the row houses. Limping into it, he followed a strip of asphalt to its exit in an alley behind the houses.

He was almost back where he'd started, the bar a hundred yards to his left. He cursed and headed the opposite way. He was staggering now, the single streetlight hurting his eyes. A few doors from the end of the alley, his legs gave out.

Hide. Dark. Den.

But his den was thirty-some miles south in Baltimore. He crawled into the nearest backyard, instinctively seeking a dark corner, and collapsed against the concrete steps.

The iron crawled through his veins like a troop of fire ants. He took a few short, ragged breaths and tested his quartz. The tiny crystals were nearly depleted. Instead of humming their customary song, they were barely vibrating. Too weak for him to draw on the quartz's energy to heal himself.

Too weak even to signal for help.

If the iron didn't kill him outright, the night fae would find him.

Merry.

He told himself his niece was safe with her adopted family. But there was so much she didn't know...

Adric will watch over her. Make sure she has what she needs.

Even so, regret lanced him, the pain worse than anything the night fae had inflicted. He leaned his head against the concrete and prepared to die.

CHAPTER 3

*E*vie almost didn't see him.

She was on her way home from a late shift at the restaurant when thunder rumbled. She picked up the pace, jogging the last few yards down the alley to her backyard. The lavender her mom had planted was about to bloom. Purple spikes shivered in the rising wind, their scent perfuming the air.

A crash of thunder made her jump. She sprinted down the gravel path bisecting the tiny garden. Suddenly, every hair on her nape lifted. She skidded to a stop, straining to see in the light cast by the single bulb over her back door.

There. A man huddled by the stoop, his eyes glowing an unearthly green in the gloom. His chest shuddered, and the chunk of quartz hanging from a leather cord around his neck caught the light.

Earth fada. With those glowing eyes and the quartz, he had to be.

Keeping her gaze on the fada, Evie bent and scrabbled in the garden for a weapon. Shapeshifters didn't just turn up at your back door. Whatever this guy wanted, he was trouble—and she didn't need any more trouble in her life.

Her fingers closed on a small rock. She straightened and raised it threateningly. "Get the hell out of my yard."

The man stared back at her, unblinking. Then his lips curved. The prick was *laughing* at her.

Anger seared through Evie. Anger, and fear.

Her kid brother Kyler was in the house. At least, he was supposed to be. She had to get this man—this fada—out of here.

"Did you hear me?" Her fingers tightened on the rock. "I want you gone. *Now.*"

His eyes closed. The small smile faded, and he rested his head against the concrete foundation. "Can't."

"What do you mean, you can't?"

He slid sideways, boneless as a rag doll.

What the—?

Evie froze.

Several seconds ticked past. The man didn't move.

She eased closer. That's when she smelled the blood.

She darted a look around. There were three homes to one side of their row house and six to the other. Most times you couldn't move two yards without a neighbor popping out to see what was up.

Where was nosy Mrs. Linney when you needed her? Or Kyler, for that matter?

"Hey." She nudged the shifter's shin with her toe. "You okay?"

When he didn't move, she dashed up the steps, yelling for her brother. "Kyler! Open up, damn it." She hammered on the door. "It's me, Evie."

No answer.

She set her jaw. Would it kill the dude to be where he was supposed to be for once? She dropped the rock and dug in her backpack for her keys, her eyes on the motionless fada.

Her fingers closed on the key ring. She shoved the house key in the lock and pushed open the door. The kitchen was empty, but the light was on. She dropped her backpack on the nearest chair.

"Jesus. Wake the neighborhood, why don't you?" Kyler sauntered into the kitchen, tall and thin and full of sixteen-year-old attitude until he saw her face. "Evie? What's the matter?"

"Outside." She jerked her chin at the backyard. "A fada. He's hurt —bleeding."

"For real?" Kyler pushed past her and vaulted over the railing to the injured shifter.

Evie followed. "Hurry. I have a bad feeling about this."

Somehow, she *knew* she had to get the shifter inside—and soon—or he was dead. The fada were the killers of the magical world—assassins and mercenaries. If this man was injured, someone dangerous was after him.

Kyler slid his hands under the fada's shoulders and head. "Grab his legs."

She hurried to obey. Rain poured down, drenching them to the skin.

Kyler looked at her. "Ready?"

"Yep."

"One, two, up," he said, and they lifted him.

Evie staggered, struggling to keep her end up. "Damn, he's heavy."

"I've got him." Kyler moved his hands lower on the shifter's back, taking more of the weight, and together, they maneuvered his limp body up the stairs and into the kitchen.

Her brother raised a dark brow. "Where should we put him?"

"The floor, I guess."

They laid him on the ratty vinyl. Swiping the rainwater from her face, Evie peered down at the unconscious man. His face and shoulders were wet, but the dark stain spreading across his T-shirt wasn't from the rain.

While Kyler locked the back door, Evie scrubbed her hands in the kitchen sink and squatted down for a closer look.

His thick lashes were spiked with water drops. She couldn't help noticing that the man was freaking gorgeous—shiny black hair, broad cheekbones, a body that was all hard muscle. But then, the fada had a few drops of fae blood, and with it a touch of the fae's beauty.

Easing up his T-shirt, she sucked in a breath. He had a deep slash across his lower abdomen, and another small but deeper wound directly above it.

Kyler whistled. "Somebody cut him good."

She nodded grimly. "Get me something to clean it with. Hot water, but not too hot."

Kyler nodded and filled a bowl with warm water. Meanwhile, Evie found a couple of clean kitchen towels and knelt next to the fada, dabbing at the blood. From what she knew about first aid, the wounds weren't life-threatening. Neither was spurting blood, which meant the knife or whatever had cut him hadn't hit an artery. And the blood seemed to be clotting.

The biggest danger was probably infection. Hopefully, he'd be out of here before she had to worry about that.

She wrung out the cloth and dabbed at the gashes again. She'd heard some-where that whiskey disinfected a wound, but the only alcohol in the house was a six-pack of cheap beer.

"D'you think we should pour some beer on it?" she asked Kyler. "You know, to kill the germs?"

"*No.*" The earth fada's eyes opened. The intense green had faded to hazel. "Use...my quartz."

Evie didn't know much about shifters, but everyone knew earth fada had a special connection with their quartz. This man's looked like an ordinary rock to her, but what did she know?

She reached for the pendant.

"No!" He grabbed it himself. "Don't touch. Only...me."

She jerked her hand away. "Gotcha."

The fada's fingers toyed with the quartz, and it started to glow the same green as his eyes had. His lips moved, and the blood stopped seeping. His wounds closed a bit, too.

"Wow," said Kyler.

The fada's head dropped back to the vinyl. "Can't."

He released the pendant. The quartz lost its glow and turned back into a plain, smoky gray with a touch of purple. Pretty, but nothing out of the ordinary.

Evie swallowed. "So what should we do?"

His eyes shut. "Nothing."

She sat back on her haunches. "Look, you are *not* going to die in my kitchen. You got that?"

He grunted.

Kyler dropped to the floor on the other side of the shifter. They met each other's eyes over his body.

"Maybe I should call 911," she said.

"What good would that do?" he asked. "Fada use their own healers. A human doctor would probably be useless."

"But they could clean the wounds. Stitch him up."

Outside the storm had worsened. Wind whipped through the trees and rain drummed against the kitchen windows. Thunder boomed, shaking the house.

She and Kyler stared at each other. Neither moved to take out their phones.

Her shoulders slumped. It had been a long day. Before working her shift at the restaurant, she'd gone to her biology class at the community college. In between, she'd rushed home to make sure Kyler had supper. Now she was exhausted, out of ideas.

Hopelessness rolled over her. "He's going to die," she said dully. "And take us along with him."

Kyler's throat worked. "There's nothing we can do."

The earth fada roused himself to growl, "Fucking fae. He's messing with your minds—you have to fight it."

"What do you mean?" Evie asked.

The fada's hand was on his quartz again. The muscles of his neck strained with effort. The glow infused it again.

"Touch me," he gritted.

"Touch you?" she repeated. *What was the point?*

"*Now.* Anywhere."

She and Kyler glanced at each other and then Evie shrugged. "All right."

She took the earth fada's hand while Kyler touched him on the shoulder. Nothing happened.

Evie blew out a breath. Why bother? She was so tired, her clothes and hair soaked from the rain. If she could only lie down...

Then something odd happened. The hand touching the earth fada warmed. She frowned down at it. The heat moved up her arm to her shoulder, and she and Kyler were enfolded in its warmth.

Her brother's mouth slackened. "What the fuck?"

"Night fae," the fada rasped. "Don't...talk. He—hear you."

Evie's stomach did a complete flip. "A night fae? That's who's after you?"

She'd only seen one night fae in her entire twenty-six years, but one had been enough. He'd been coming out of an after-hours club in Baltimore, tall and loose-limbed with black hair and pale skin. She'd stopped and stared. He was rock-star sexy in a tight black shirt and leather pants.

Then he'd turned and caught her looking—and smiled, a cold show of teeth. Darkness washed over her, powerful and seductive. When she'd shuddered, his smile had widened.

Evie had sprinted out of the alley, his mocking laugh echoing in her ears.

The earth fada gave a terse nod. "Afraid so."

Evie shut her eyes. What had she done?

For the most part, the fae kept to themselves, considering humans as somehow less—which was fine with her. You did *not* want to attract the attention of a fae. You especially didn't want to attract the attention of a night fae.

She looked at her white-faced brother, the brother she'd promised her mom to protect, and stifled a moan.

The rain eased. Gravel crunched.

The night fae was right outside.

Evie grabbed the fada's hand with both of hers and prayed. Hard.

CHAPTER 4

*J*ace swam out of the darkness. A female appeared.

Dreamlike, he wondered if an angel had descended to save him from the night fae—an edgy blond angel in jeans and a black muscle tee.

Then she threatened him with a rock, and he jolted awake.

Fucking wonderful. She was going to bash his head in. A female, and human at that.

His mouth twisted wryly—and he passed out. The next thing he knew, he was on a vinyl floor blinking up at a fluorescent light.

He tensed. There were two humans now, the edgy blond angel and a lanky teenager with short brown hair and suspicious eyes.

He had to get out of here. He tried to roll over, but the female was messing with his stomach. He readied himself to fight her off until he realized she was cleaning his wounds. That wouldn't be enough, not against iron. He tried to use his quartz, but he was too weak, the crystals barely vibrating.

He let his head drop back to the floor.

An earth fada's quartz was almost a living thing. With rare exceptions, his crystals' unique song had been with him ever since he'd bonded with his own personal quartz as a cub. To have the song fail now was hard, like watching a family member do a slow fade into death.

And there was nothing to stop the iron burning a path through his veins, poisoning him slowly and inexorably.

His gaze fixed on the female. She was striking, with a face he could've stared at for hours—warm brown eyes topped by dark, definite eyebrows and high cheekbones in a narrow, intelligent face.

Her mouth moved. She was scolding Jace, telling him he'd better not die in her kitchen.

Inside he chuckled—if he were himself, he could take her out with a single swipe of his claws. But she had spirit. He liked that. Reminded him of Takira.

He inhaled, testing the humans' scents. They were tense and afraid, but they seemed to want to help.

And his cat liked the blonde's smell. It relaxed, easing them both. When the female touched Jace's stomach, the cat damn near purred.

Okay, that was strange.

Then every hair on his body stood on end. All the sass went out of the female. Even her hard-eyed brother drooped.

Night fae. Jace had brought trouble straight to these people's door.

"Think," he managed to say. The female leaned closer to listen. "Happy thoughts."

He used the quartz's last trace of energy to protect them, then slid back into the darkness.

～

"HAPPY THOUGHTS? YEAH, RIGHT." Evie met Kyler's eyes. "Better do what he says."

The doorknob rattled and she froze. She darted a glance at the deadbolt. But somehow either she or Kyler had remembered to lock it in the rush to get the injured fada inside. Fortunately, the door was solid wood, and the shade on the back window was down. He couldn't see into the kitchen.

Because she *knew* it was a man. She could almost picture him on the top step —tall, dark and coldly determined, sending feelers out.

A night fae.

She stilled, her breath shallow. Dread filled her. As if she could fool the fae when she knew he could sense them. But the earth fada was somehow shielding them. The dread lessened.

Across the unconscious man's body, Kyler had his eyes screwed shut. Her wannabe badass looked scared to death, his face pale, his lips pressed tight.

Her heart clenched. That frightened, vulnerable expression took her back seven years to when Kyler's dad had died and all they'd had left was their mom.

Their mother had tried her best, but those first few months, she walked around like a zombie. Evie's dad had left before Evie was two, but Kyler's dad had been an anchor for all of them. His sudden heart attack was just too unfair. Meanwhile, the money was running out. Her mom's part-time job and food stamps only stretched so far.

Kyler had tried to act tough, but one night their mom had snapped and thrown them outside, ordering them not to come back until bedtime.

Kyler had slipped his hand into Evie's. "What are we going to do?" he'd asked in a small voice.

Evie had taken a deep breath. "Why don't we walk to the playground?"

Fortunately, it was summer, and there was another hour of light. She and Kyler rode every piece of equipment on the playground at least three times, and by the time they went home, their mother had calmed down and let them back in without any fuss.

The rattling stilled. But the fae was right outside.

Evie didn't know how she knew, but she would've bet her pitifully small bank balance on it.

Happy thoughts, Evie. Happy thoughts.

Kyler's tenth birthday. Yeah, that had been a good day.

Things had been better by then. Their mom had a job at an upscale restaurant, and Evie was working at a pizza place after school and on weekends. They lived paycheck to paycheck, but at least they had food in the house.

She and her mom had pooled their money to buy Kyler the latest video game console and a couple of games. Evie had baked Kyler's favorite cake—chocolate banana, but hey, he'd asked. Now she tried to visualize his expression as he blew out the candles, then tore open his packages.

He'd learned not to expect much. That made his grin when he'd seen the console even more special. His face had lit up brighter than the ten candles on his cake. "This is the best birthday ever!"

Now Evie smiled. She squeezed the fada's hand more tightly.

More footsteps, but they were moving away. The ominous presence receded.

Evie expelled a breath. She *felt* the night fae moving down the alley, testing other doors.

She stiffened. There must be blood on the back steps. Had the night fae seen it, or had the rain washed it away in time?

Happy thoughts, damn you. Don't think about the blood. Not now.

Things went quiet—and then, whatever had been shielding them abruptly failed.

The earth fada was unconscious again. The ominous feeling increased.

Evie's spine iced. The night fae was coming back.

She and Kyler exchanged a look.

"Don't stop," she mouthed. "Happy thoughts." She set a finger on either side of her mouth and mimed a smile.

His lips twitched. "If you could see what you look like..."

She made a face at him and they both smiled. Weakly, but it worked. The ominous feeling slid past her without latching on.

She made another face at Kyler, and he caught on and made one back. They took turns making silly faces at each other. A laugh escaped Evie, and she froze until she realized the best thing was to make the night fae believe they didn't know he was out there.

Kyler made a monkey face at her, and she returned, "Yo mama."

He chuckled.

And the night fae was gone.

She let out a shaky breath. "Better wait another couple of minutes," she said in a low voice.

"Yeah." Kyler glanced at the unconscious man. "What are we going to do with—"

"I have no freaking idea. What's he doing in Grace Harbor anyway? This is Rock Run territory."

The local fada were water shifters who changed to dolphins, sharks and other water-based animals. The nearest earth fada clan was thirty-five miles away in Baltimore.

"We can't just throw him out," Kyler added. "The night fae could come back."

"I know." Evie pinched the bridge of her nose. Their narrow row house consisted of two floors, with the first floor taken up by the kitchen, living room and a tiny half bath. The upstairs consisted of two bedrooms and a full bathroom, but they couldn't carry an unconscious man up a flight of steps to one of the bedrooms. "I guess we'd better move him onto the couch."

"Sounds like a plan." Kyler rose to his feet.

It took them a few minutes to work out the best way to transport the injured man into the living room until Kyler had the idea of putting him on a sheet. They each took an end, Evie at his head.

"One, two, up," her brother said.

This time Evie was prepared for his weight. Bracing herself, she bent her knees and lifted her end of the sheet—and she still staggered.

She gritted her teeth. "Got him."

They maneuvered him past the kitchen table, Evie walking backward. She turned into the living room and almost banged his head against the wall.

"Almost there." Kyler strained to take more of the load.

The couch backed up to the wall dividing the living room from the kitchen. They maneuvered until they were parallel with the cushions.

"Lift him a little higher," Kyler said. "He's sagging in the middle."

Evie gripped the sheet and obeyed.

"Good grief," she muttered as they eased him onto the couch. "What does he have, concrete for bones?"

The man lay sprawled where he'd landed, his breathing shallow, a leg dangling off the couch. Evie slid a small pillow beneath his head while Kyler pulled off his sneakers. He wasn't wearing any socks. Kyler arranged his legs so both feet were on the cushions.

Evie pulled up the hem of his T-shirt and flinched. The cuts on his stomach had turned an angry, puffy red.

"That doesn't look good," muttered Kyler.

"Can a wound get infected that fast?"

"All I know is their biology is different from ours."

She frowned. "But I thought they healed faster than humans. Plus, he did something with that crystal to heal it. He shouldn't be getting worse."

The earth fada moaned.

Evie laid a hand on his forehead. His skin felt clammy. "Shh. You're okay."

A pulse at the side of his neck jumped erratically. She set two fingers on it.

"It feels really fast," she said to Kyler. "Is that normal for them?"

He moved a shoulder. "Fuck if I know."

The fada's eyes popped open. They were a bright, feverish green again. "Salt."

"Salt?" she asked. "Are you thirsty?"

Kyler stood up. "I'll get him some water."

"Yes." Their patient moistened his lips. "But...iron—poison. Need salt. Clean." He indicated his stomach.

"You want me to clean it out with salt?"

A short nod. "Salt. And warm water."

Kyler returned with a glass of water. Evie took it and lifted the fada's head enough so that he could drink. His eyes closed but he greedily gulped the water down.

She handed the glass back to her brother and helped the guy resettle his head on the pillow. He lay there, eyes closed, panting raggedly. His light brown skin had an unhealthy yellow tinge. And were those red streaks spreading from the wounds out across his belly?

"What was he saying about the salt?" Kyler asked.

"He said clean it out with salt and warm water."

The fada's eyes opened. "One part salt, four parts water," he said in a clear voice. "And *now*. Or I...die."

CHAPTER 5

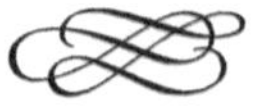

Jace could guess who was behind the attempt to kill him—Lord Tyrus. Nothing else made sense.

Tyrus was the only surviving son of the night fae prince, but more importantly, he was Silver's half-brother. When Tyrus had learned that Silver had mated and sired a daughter, he'd put out a contract on the entire small family to ensure his father had only one heir—himself. The assassins had gotten first Takira, then Silver, but a Rock Run fada had saved Merry.

Prince Langdon, Tyrus's father, hadn't wanted it known that he'd spawned a mixed-blood granddaughter. But when he found out Tyrus was hunting Merry, he cast a special ward to protect her. Any night fae who tried to harm her, even Tyrus, would meet their end.

Thank the gods Merry had a new set of parents now, a Rock Run couple who loved her like she was their own daughter. When Jace had finally tracked her down, years after Takira's death, she'd been adopted by the man who'd saved her from the night fae and his mate. As far as Merry was concerned, Rui and Valeria do Mar were her parents now, the Rock Run base her home. Jace couldn't bring himself to take her away from the only family she'd ever known.

The pretty blond female frowned down at Jace, and his mind spun away from his niece.

The pain was a raging fire in his belly now. While he was unconscious, the small amount of healing he'd done seemed to have been reversed, another symptom of iron poisoning.

"Salt and warm water?" The female's low, practical voice came from down a long dark tunnel.

All he could do was tell her what to do and hope it worked. Because if not, Jace would die, and probably the two humans as well. He'd somehow eluded Tyrus's henchman, but the night fae lord was smart—and brutal. He'd track Jace down and snuff these two like flies.

Fortunately, his rescuers followed directions. The boy returned with a pitcher filled with the salt solution. The female knelt on the floor next to the couch and then, to Jace's surprise, touched his cheek.

He squinted in her direction and her face swam into view, pinched with concern. "I'm Evie, by the way, and this is my brother Kyler." She indicated the skinny dark-haired teenager.

Her fingers were cool—or was it because he was so hot? He moistened dry lips and then croaked his name. "Jace."

"Nice to meet you, Jace."

His lips twitched despite himself. It was so human, to introduce herself at a time like this...but sweet.

Her fingers brushed his forehead, and he tensed, anticipating what was to come.

"Try to relax," the female—Evie—murmured.

She smelled like fresh soap; she must have washed her hands again. He could've told her there was no need. The iron would kill any germs, and if not, the salt solution would do the rest.

That was, if the iron didn't kill him first.

"Relax," Evie repeated, and to please her, he smoothed out his forehead.

"Okay." She wet a clean rag with the salt solution and dabbed at the wounds. "I'm going to clean this out for you."

"No," he said, and she stopped and looked at him, her brow furrowed. "Pour it into the cut," he said. "You have to...rinse it out. Poison." He rolled onto his side and dug his fingers into the couch, knowing what was to come.

"Okay," she said. "Take it easy."

He drew a slow breath, but there was no way he could relax. "Just do it," he said between clenched teeth.

Her brother handed her a folded bath towel. She tucked it under Jace's stomach to catch the overflow, and then set her fingers on either side of the lower cut and gently pulled it open. "You pour," she told Kyler.

"Good," Jace said. "That's good. Clean it out."

The kid tipped the pitcher and salt solution poured into the wound.

Jace's whole body bowed in pain. God's cat, it was like getting stabbed all over again. He tightened his jaw and rode it out. Because screaming, especially in front of two humans, would be the final humiliation.

And then, mercifully, he passed out.

When he came to, Evie was stroking his forehead. "There, there," she said in a motherly voice at odds with her edgy appearance. "It's all over now."

He stared at her through slit lids. "Thanks," he managed to say.

She looked down at his stomach. "Did it work?"

He frowned, checking inwardly. The fire in his blood had subsided to a simmer. "Think so."

"Can we do anything else?"

"Water."

"Just plain water?"

He gave a single nod.

She removed her hand from his forehead, and he grabbed for her, latching onto the hem of her shirt. "Not you. Him." He jerked his chin at the teenager.

Her dark brows lifted. "You want me to stay?"

He nodded again. He knew he was being unreasonable, but both cat and man wanted her to remain close.

"Okay." She took his hand. "Kyler will get you the water, then."

His fingers folded on hers. "Thanks," he whispered.

When the water came, she put an arm beneath his shoulders to support him while he drank greedily. It was ice cold and wonderful.

He finished the glass, and she laid his head back down on the cushion and pressed a wet rag to his forehead. He closed his eyes in relief at the coolness. How did she know exactly what he needed?

The storm had slowed to a drizzle. From far away, he heard Evie tell her brother to go outside and make sure there wasn't any blood. Smart woman.

"The rain must have washed it away," Kyler replied.

"Get the hose out and wash it down anyway."

"'Kay." He heard Kyler's footsteps move into the kitchen.

Evie touched Jace's arm. He pried opened his eyes to see her holding another glass of water. "You need liquids—you're burning up. Unless that's your normal body temperature?"

He shook his head. "Water...good."

"That's what I thought." Again, she slid an arm beneath his shoulders and held the glass to his lips.

After drinking his fill, he rested his head against her shoulder and let his eyes close again. She'd changed into a dry T-shirt—gray with a purple star in center. She stilled and then to his satisfaction, remained where she was. She was a sturdy little thing—the arm around him had a lean strength—but the spot between her shoulder and her breast was soft and comforting. He inhaled deeply, filling his nostrils with her sweet, womanly scent.

His breath sighed out. Tomorrow he'd be embarrassed at how weak he was acting, but right now, he didn't fucking care. Because he needed this.

"Do you want any more?" The glass nudged his lips.

When he shook his head, she lowered him carefully to the pillow. His cat whined, but both of them were too weak to do anything about it.

Evie came to her feet. He watched through slit lids as she stretched. The hem of her T-shirt rode up to reveal a tan strip of skin above her waistband.

She glanced down and caught him looking, and her eyes flickered. She unhurriedly brought her arms down and straightened the shirt.

"I'm going to see how Kyler's doing. You'll be all right for a few minutes, won't you?"

He nodded. His cat wasn't happy, but the man told the cat to suck it up.

She touched his shoulder. "Try to rest. I'll be back as soon as I can."

He listened as her footsteps moved down the hall to the kitchen.

He drew a slow breath. With Evie out of the room, the effects of the iron seemed worse. He touched his abdomen. The salt had neutralized the iron so that it wasn't still feeding into his bloodstream, but he felt like he'd been run over by a frigging semi.

He'd live, as his soldier mom used to say, but he was in for a rough night while his body worked to eliminate the small amount of iron that had entered his bloodstream. The best thing was to sleep and let his body's natural healing abilities take over. That would also give his quartz time to reenergize so he could call for help.

He trusted that Evie and her brother would do their best to keep him safe—and trust didn't come easily to Jace. Even so, he instinctively sized up his surroundings, noting the exits.

The living room ran the length of this side of the narrow house. He was on the single couch, which backed up against an inside wall. The two windows behind him faced the alley, their blinds closed. An air conditioner hummed in one window, which was good, even though his animal preferred fresh air.

Closed windows meant that he couldn't be scented from the outside. Fae didn't have any better sense of smell than a human, but they could be working with a fada.

On the other side of the living room, two more windows looked onto a narrow front porch. If he lifted his head, he could see the front door to the left of the windows. The room itself only had a few pieces of furniture. Other than the couch, there was an easy chair, a sturdy oak coffee table, and a bookcase filled with books, DVDs and other knickknacks, and crowned with a large green fern.

Evie returned. She sat on the edge of the couch, careful not to bump him.

"Is there anyone we should call?"

Jace considered that. He shared a den in Baltimore with a handful of other unmated men. They were friends, but they didn't keep tabs on one another. He wouldn't be missed until tomorrow morning at the earliest.

Adric was alpha of the Baltimore clan now. He'd be pissed off when he found out Jace was hurt and hadn't tried to contact him, but the night fae clearly didn't know where Jace had gone to ground. In fact, calling for help might lead the bastards straight to this house.

"No," he told Evie.

"Not even your mate?"

"No mate," he said firmly, and then wondered why he'd told her. As a fada, he couldn't tell a lie without making himself violently ill, but that didn't mean he had to answer the human's questions.

"That's good."

He watched, fascinated, as she pinkened. His clan was mostly brown skinned. He hadn't known someone could blush that easily.

"I mean," she added, "no one will be worrying about you then."

"No," he agreed. "No one will worry." And for a moment that seemed so fucking sad. He tightened his jaw. Hell, in another minute he was going to be tearing up like a girl. "I'll leave in the morning." By then he should be well enough to slip away without anyone being the wiser.

"Okay, sure." Her relief was clear, but she hurried to add, "If you feel up to it, I mean."

"I'll leave," he repeated grimly.

Evie took out her phone. "You mind if I play some music?"

"Go right ahead."

She tapped the screen and set the phone on the coffee table. Music filled the room, a soothing mix of nature sounds, flutes and drums that sounded like something he'd heard coming out of a yoga studio in downtown Baltimore.

His lids drifted shut.

"Go to sleep," Evie said. "You're safe. Kyler didn't see anyone outside."

He nodded. No sense explaining that a night fae could blend into the shadows even better than a fada. Because the night fae was gone for now—Jace's skin would've been crawling if he were near. The assassins' orders would've been to get in and out quickly, standard operating procedure.

Besides, the remaining night fae—because he suspected there had been three altogether—had to remove their fallen comrade before he was found by a human, or worse, by one of the local fada. The Rock Run alpha would be furious to find a night fae in his territory—dead or alive.

Evie grabbed a laptop and sat in the easy chair at the foot of the couch. She folded her legs tailor-style and frowned at the screen.

Jace studied her profile through half-open eyes. She was...fascinating.

Thin but sturdy, with clearly defined muscles on her upper arms. Her platinum hair was cut short as a man's and she had those strong dark brows, but her cheek had a soft curve that could only belong to a woman. She wasn't wearing any makeup, but her earlobe was pierced by a delicate gold hoop from which dangled a silver disc.

Evie touched the screen, scrolling through a document.

"What are you doing?" he asked.

"Writing a paper for my biology class." She started typing. "It's due next week."

"You're in school, then." He swallowed a touch of envy.

No one in his clan had been to a human college, but it wasn't unheard of. As a teenager, Jace had already been studying the clan's quartz technology, and he'd have loved to major in physics and IT at one of the local universities.

But the clan had been in the midst of the Darktime, the bloody internal war that had come to a head in his late teens. He'd been too busy surviving to even think of going to college.

"Yeah. I just started back, but I'm going to be an LPN." She slanted him a grin. "I just thought of something—you're my first patient. You *can't* die on me. That would be too effing wrong."

He stared, entranced, at the dimple that winked to life in her right cheek. Just as quickly, it was gone. He wanted to keep watching her, but his eyelids drooped.

Outside, rain was falling again, a soothing patter against the windows.

"I'll do my best," he muttered and slid into sleep.

EVIE GLANCED at the sleeping shifter. His color looked a little better now, and he seemed to be breathing normally.

Relieved, she turned her attention back to her paper. When you worked two jobs and went to school, you learned to focus whenever you could snatch the time. In fifteen minutes, she had the first couple pages written.

Kyler returned to report that he'd washed down the whole area behind the house, even the alley as far as the hose could reach. "Of course, Mrs. Linney came outside and asked what I was doing washing the steps in the rain." He flopped down on the floor and took a gulp from a can of soda.

Evie shut her laptop. "You didn't tell her—"

"Yeah, right." Kyler gave her the kind of look only a teenager could give. "She'd broadcast it to the entire frigging block. I told her I spilled my soda and you'd be pissed off if I left it until morning. Ants, you know. And then it started raining harder again, so I probably didn't need to bother."

Evie gave him a thumbs-up. "Quick thinking, squirt."

"I hate it when you call me that," he grumbled, but she could tell he was pleased at the compliment.

Jace muttered something and both their gazes shot to him. He sighed and moved his head against the pillow before curling up on his right side.

Kyler lowered his voice. "What are we going to do with him?"

"Hell if I know. He says he'll leave in the morning."

"Good. The dude's trouble. I mean, what the fuck do the night fae want with him?"

"Who knows? But it doesn't matter. Tomorrow he'll go back to Baltimore or wherever he came from, and we can forget he was ever here." Her heart pinched at that, which was crazy. Shifters didn't mix with humans, except for the occasional hookup—and hookups weren't her thing.

Kyler glanced at the curled-up fada. "Wonder what his animal is?"

"A cat."

"He told you?"

"No." But she'd bet a night's worth of tips she was right. "Look at how he moves. And his body—that's a cat's body if I ever saw one."

Kyler glanced at Jace's long, powerful body and shrugged. "If you say so." He took another slug of soda. "It's kind of cool having a shifter in the house—especially a Baltimore shifter. I've never seen one up close before."

"Me either. I wonder why he was in Grace Harbor?"

They contemplated the sleeping man for another minute, and then Kyler finished his soda and rose to his feet.

"Are you going out?"

"I was thinking about it, yeah." He paced to the front windows and twitched aside a curtain to peer out at the dark street.

Evie took a moment to choose her words. Kyler was so easy to set off these days.

"Do you think you should? That night fae could still be out there."

He glanced over his shoulder. "Why would he care about me? But I guess I should stay here in case he comes back. I don't want you here by yourself."

Evie blinked. Was this the brother who just that morning had growled that Evie wasn't his frickin' mom and he didn't have to answer to her if he didn't want to? But all she said was, "Thanks."

Kyler returned to her side of the living room. He sat down, his back against the wall, phone out.

She frowned. "You're not going to tell anyone about Jace, are you?"

"No, Evie," he said with exaggerated patience. "I'm just letting Ben and the other guys know what's up." Ben, who lived three doors down, was Kyler's best friend.

Kyler sent a flurry of texts, and then settled down to play a game.

Evie glanced again at Jace. He looked okay, so she went back to her paper. By eleven o'clock she had a rough draft done. Shutting the laptop, she massaged her forehead.

In the kitchen, Kyler was making popcorn. He returned with two large bowls and handed her one.

"Thanks," she said, digging in. "I only had time for a sandwich tonight."

"Thought you might be hungry." Her brother popped a handful of popcorn into his mouth. "I'm going upstairs," he said, crunching his way through it. "Shout if you need me—or if you want me to sit with him."

"I will. And Kyler?" He halted in the doorway to look over his shoulder. "Thanks, dude. For helping tonight, and for staying in with me."

His narrow face split in a grin. "Hey, it was an adventure. Too bad I can't tell Ben."

She nodded. "Maybe in a few weeks, but for now, we'd better keep this quiet."

With Kyler in his bedroom, she took a quick trip upstairs to brush her teeth and grab a sheet and pillow from the hall closet. "Don't stay up too late," she told Kyler.

He grunted in response.

Back downstairs, she shut off all the lights except the one in the hall and curled up again on the easy chair.

She had fallen into a light doze when something made her open her eyes. Jace was staring at her, his irises glowing that odd feral-green again. Her skin prickled. She glanced around the room for a weapon.

Then his breath sighed out and she reminded herself he couldn't hurt anyone right now.

She rose to her feet. "You okay? Would you like some water?"

"Yeah." He swiped his tongue over his lips. "I'm so damn thirsty. And I need to take a piss."

"Water first." She hurried into the kitchen and returned with a large glass, which he drained in a couple of gulps and then handed back to her.

"Can you walk?" She glanced at him doubtfully as she set the glass on the coffee table. "I can get Kyler. He's upstairs."

He eased his legs over the side of the couch. "I can do it." He set his feet on the floor and used the coffee table to push himself to standing.

He only took a couple of steps before he winced and grasped his belly. "I could use some help here," he said ruefully.

She was already moving the coffee table out of the way. "Put your arm on my shoulders," she said as she slid an arm around his waist.

Together, they shuffled into the hall and turned right toward the bathroom. Fortunately, it was only a few steps further. Evie flipped on the light and helped him inside.

Jace gripped the sink and dragged in a breath, head down. He was flushed, his temples beaded with sweat.

She bit her lower lip. "Will you—I mean, do you need any help?"

"I'm okay," he muttered.

"Okay, good." She backed toward the door. "I'll be in the hall if you need me."

"I won't. But thanks."

She shut the door and walked a few feet down the hall to wait. The toilet flushed and then she heard water running, followed by a long silence.

She rapped on the bathroom door. "Everything okay in there?"

"Yeah." The door opened and he limped out. "Just moving...slow."

Evie's eyes widened. He'd washed his face and taken his shirt off. Her gaze went to a hard chest covered by wiry black hair, and then she jerked it back to his face.

The look he gave her made her cheeks heat. The man might be injured, but that considering expression told her he was recovering fast. They stared at each other. A heartbeat passed, then another.

He spoke first, indicating the shirt balled in his hand. "It was bloody. Where do you want it?"

She swallowed. "Just drop it next to the sink and I'll take care of it."

"Thank you." He tossed it into the bathroom.

She hesitated and then reminded herself she was a nurse. Well, almost, anyway.

"I'll help you back to the couch," she said in her most professional voice and slid an arm around his back.

He shook his head. "You don't look strong enough to hold up a kitten," he said, but let her take some of his weight.

The man was all muscle. Beneath her hand, his waist was taut, the skin hot from his fever. She tried not to notice how good he smelled—warm, sweaty male.

Down, girl.

Sure, the man was sexy in a dark, dangerous way, but he was hurt, for God's sake. And even if he wasn't, he was a fada—and a Baltimore earth fada at that. Everyone knew they were a murderous clan. She was surprised any of them were still left alive.

The last thing she wanted was to have anything to do with a Baltimore shifter.

No, she'd make sure Mr. Jace No-Last-Name left as soon as he was able, then pray she never saw him again.

Back in the living room, Jace sank down on the couch. He closed his eyes and bent forward at the waist, his breath ragged. It was clear he was hurting.

Evie turned on the lamp next to the easy chair. "You're hot. I'll turn up the air conditioner." With that done, she shoved her hands into her back pockets, feeling helpless. "Are you hungry? I can make you some chicken soup. Or—"

"I don't think I can eat anything right now," he said without opening his eyes.

"Yeah, right." She flushed, recalling he'd taken a knife in the belly. "Maybe something that digests easily? I have popsicles." Her mom had given them popsicles whenever she or Kyler were sick.

"A popsicle." His hard mouth edged up. "Okay, sure."

"Be right back." She hurried to the kitchen and returned with an orange popsicle. It would put more liquids in him, and maybe the sugar would give him some extra energy.

While he ate the popsicle, she rinsed his T-shirt out in the bathroom sink and hung it up to dry before getting a popsicle for herself. When she came back, he was reclined on the couch, still sucking the popsicle. A cat's paw was tattooed in black and gold on his upper left arm. He saw her looking and his face shuttered, so she didn't ask, just curled up on the easy chair again.

The cuts on his abdomen were still an angry red, but they were starting to close. "I think you're healing," she said.

He nodded. "It's going to be a rough night, but this helps." He indicated the popsicle. "Feels like my fucking belly's on fire."

"I wish I could do more."

"You did good. I just need to rest now, give it time to heal."

She wrapped her arms around her legs. "What happened, anyway?"

"Some bastard night fae stuck a knife in me."

"The one that was outside?"

"No. The guy who stabbed me is dead."

She gulped. "Oh."

He regarded her from beneath thick lashes, as if expecting her to cringe from him. But she knew that sometimes, you don't have a choice.

Jace's eyes closed. Silence fell while they sucked on their popsicles.

"Iron," she said. "It was an iron knife? That's why you're feverish?"

He nodded. "You know what iron does to a fae?"

"Sure." Everyone knew that iron was a fae's Achilles' heel. They couldn't even stand it against their bare skin. "It's like poison for them. But you're a fada, aren't you?"

"Yeah. But we have some fae in us. Iron doesn't affect the fada as bad, but it's still poison to us. And the knife was probably cold-forged—formed into a blade at room temperature. That makes a difference."

"Salt neutralizes the iron?"

"Yeah, but don't ask me how. It just does."

She opened her mouth to ask why the night fae had stabbed him, and then closed it again. It was better she didn't know.

"That's right," he said, seemingly reading her mind. "The less you know, the better." He slid down on the couch until he was prone again. "I'll be all right, now. You can go to bed."

She shook her head. "I'm staying right here in case you need me."

His brow lifted—and then he smiled. A quick but real smile that lit an answering warmth inside her. "You don't have to," he said, "but thanks." And with that, he curled up on his right side, closed his eyes and fell back asleep.

She finished her popsicle, and then set a pitcher of ice water on the coffee table within easy reach of her patient before curling up on the chair again.

She was too wide awake now to sleep, so she took out her phone and checked her messages, and then downloaded a book to read, but her gaze kept flicking to Jace. He was a beautiful man: big shoulders, six-pack abs and long, strong legs. And inked—besides the cat's paw, an intricately rendered tat of a snarling black jungle cat stretched across his upper back.

Kyler came downstairs in a pair of gym shorts and she jerked her gaze back to her phone.

"You sure you're all right?" he asked.

"I'm fine."

He yawned and scratched his stomach. "Okay, but holler if you need me. I'm all grown up—you need me, you call for me."

He frowned down on her, and for a second, she was reminded of his father, even though Aaron had been shorter and square-faced, while Kyler had a narrow, sharp-boned face. But those dark eyes and the frown were all Aaron, who had been just the same when it came to protecting his family.

"I will." She crossed her heart. "Promise."

"G'night, then." Kyler gave another huge yawn and went back upstairs to bed.

Evie shut off the light and snuggled up on the chair again.

Kyler had made her proud tonight. All spring, he'd argued with her about every little decision. Some nights he slammed out of the house and didn't come home until after midnight. She didn't know what she was going to do with him when school let out next week. He'd tried to find a job, but so far, no luck.

But tonight, he'd really come through. His dad would've been pleased.

She smiled. She'd have to remember to tell Kyler that in the morning.

She glanced at her sleeping guest one last time. His face had gone slack, his lashes dark crescents against his cheeks. Curled up on the couch like that, it was hard to believe he was as dangerous as people said.

Her eyes drifted closed and she fell asleep.

Two hours later she jerked awake to find Jace thrashing in his sleep.

"No," he muttered. "Mary—" He bolted upright.

She fumbled for the switch on the lamp next to the chair. It came on and he hissed, an angry cat-sound.

She blinked against the sudden light, trying to see him. "You all right, dude?"

He ignored her to chug water from the pitcher she'd left on the table, then fumbled with the zipper of his pants.

She rose to her feet. "Jace? What are you doing?"

His gaze swung to her and she took an involuntary step back. His eyes were that strange bright green again. His growl raised fine hairs all over her body.

"Okay." She raised her palms. "Take it easy."

He snarled and dragged off the pants. Bright bits of color danced over his skin —and then a huge black panther was crouched on her couch.

CHAPTER 6

*J*ace was hot. So fucking hot.

He groaned and thrashed on the couch. His belly was burning. But the heat seemed to have spread everywhere.

He turned onto his side and then onto his back again.

"No…Merry—"

He dragged a hand over his face—and was thrown back seven years into his worst nightmare. Adric had finally tracked Merry and Silver to their latest address. It had been over a year since Jace had last seen any of Takira's family. His sister had turned up dead, and Merry's fifth birthday had come and gone while she was on the run with Silver.

The call from Adric came just after midnight. Jace rushed to the site—only to find a burned-out house. The bitter scent of ashes and death filled the air.

Adric had been waiting in the shadows. His throat worked. "I'm sorry, bro."

Jace had backed away, shaking his head. "No. No. There must be some mistake."

"No mistake. I tracked them both here." Adric's eyes were bronze holes in his face. "It burned down last night. The neighbors said no one got out alive."

"Leron," Jace had rasped. "I'll kill him. I'll fucking tear him to pieces." He'd turned to stride off, but Adric's hand clamped on his arm.

Jace tried to shake him off. "Let. Me. Go."

"No. I won't stand by and watch you commit suicide."

Jace's mouth had twisted. "What the fuck do I have to live for?"

His friend blew out a breath. "I can't answer that for you, but I do know I need your help to take Leron down. And we will. We're close, Jace. But if you go after him now, you could blow it all to hell."

"You ask too damn much."

"I know," his friend returned quietly. "But it's not for me. It's for the clan."

Jace had stared at the house's charred remains, the desire for revenge raging through his veins. He'd fisted his hands, dropped back his head and roared his fury at the moon. The local dogs had joined in, an eerie, mournful howl.

When he'd turned back to Adric, he knew his eyes blazed a feral green. "Fine," he bit out. "But promise me he'll die. No mercy."

"No mercy," Adric had agreed.

Now Jace writhed on the couch, his soul as dark and bitter as that burned shell of a house that he'd believed had contained his niece's remains.

An unfamiliar scent recalled him to the present—a female. *It's only a dream.*

With an effort, he forced his eyes open and looked wildly around until he recalled he was in some human's home in Grace Harbor.

Evie. He grabbed onto her name like a drowning man would a life preserver.

She'd left a pitcher of water on the table. He fumbled for it and, without bothering to pour the water into a glass, drank deeply. His cat was to the fore now. It wrinkled its nose at the chemical taste of the water. But it was cool and wet. The burning eased, but he was still too hot.

He had to shift; he'd heal faster in his cat form. He sat up and reached for his zipper.

The female was staring at him, eyes wide. He hesitated. He distantly recalled that he hadn't shifted already because he didn't want to frighten her. Humans tended to get edgy around a 250-pound black jaguar.

His cat rubbed at his skin, frantic to get out. He could feel his eyes had gone night-glow, signaling his animal was in control.

The female backed up and his chest rumbled. *Didn't she know he wouldn't hurt her?*

The hell with it. He dragged off his pants and let the shift take him—and almost didn't make it. Energy danced over his skin, and for a few frightening seconds he thought he'd get stuck between man and cat and die, his organs unable to adjust to a half-shifted state.

His quartz. A quick check told him it had recharged to about forty percent. He drew deep, pulling energy from the slowly vibrating crystals, and completed the shift. He lay on his side, weak and trembling. So much for his big, scary cat.

But the female took another step back. The cat instinctively leapt off the couch to stop her. She froze and babbled something, and he scented fear, sharp and acrid.

No. He nudged her hand. *It's all right.*

She sucked in a breath.

He rumbled low in his chest but held still.

"Okay," she said in a strangled voice. "Okay. I'm the good guy, all right? The one who's trying to help you."

He huffed a breath and waited, his head against the back of her hand.

At last she understood. Her hand turned and she stroked his head.

Ah... He pushed back against her hand, rubbing his scent onto the skin. Then he got his head between her hand and hip and that was even better.

He breathed in her spicy feminine aroma and rubbed his head against her hip, taking her scent on him and marking her with his. His chest was rumbling again.

"Are you *purring*?" She let out a high, nervous laugh. But to his satisfaction, she relaxed.

He pushed her hip, herding her toward the couch.

"You want me on the couch?"

He gave her another nudge.

"Okay, but you must be thirsty. Why don't we get you some more water first?"

That seemed like a good idea, so he followed her to the kitchen and watched as she filled a large bowl with water and set it on the floor. When he lapped it up, she gave him some more.

Then he went to the back door and waited. He needed to keep voiding the iron in his system.

This time she guessed immediately what he wanted and unlocked the door. He paused on the small concrete landing to test the air. He could smell his own blood, but just a trace—the kid had done a thorough job. There were other scents —a dog, a nearby car engine that had only recently been turned off—but he couldn't pick up the noxious, graveyard odor of a night fae.

He padded down the stairs, pissed on a patch of grass next to the driveway, and then came back to where Evie waited in the doorway to let him in.

Back in the living room, Evie got the sheet from the easy chair and sat on the couch. He figured she wouldn't want him on the couch with her, so he lay down on the floor in front of it. The jaguar wanted to stay close for two reasons—his animal liked how she smelled, and it feared the night fae would return. Or another shifter might show up, one who'd scented Jace's weakness. This way, Jace would be between Evie and any danger.

Evie curled up, her head on the pillow he'd been using. He could see her watching him in the darkness, and then she sat up and patted the cushion on the other end. "That floor's got to be hard."

He didn't need a second invitation. He heaved himself onto the couch, circled once and then settled on the cushions at her feet with a contented sigh.

Evie lay back down. He could tell from her breath that she was awake, and he felt a twinge of guilt at disturbing her sleep. Well, tomorrow he'd be gone and her life could get back to normal.

But he'd been right to shift. The fever had broken, and even though the shift had drained more energy from his quartz, he could hear the tiny crystals humming a healing song. The quartz had recovered enough energy to aid in his healing now, although he was still shaken from the nightmare.

Merry's fine, he reminded himself. *She's safe at Rock Run.*

But if he died, what would happen to her? Sure, Rui and Valeria had given her the family Jace couldn't, but they were river fada, not earth fada. Someday Merry would probably want to return to the Baltimore clan, to be with her own people, and Jace wanted to be there to ease her way. Not everyone in the clan would welcome a mixed-blood with open arms.

And only another earth fada could teach Merry the secrets of her quartz. Yes, Adric would instruct her if Jace died, but by tradition, it was Jace's right as her only living family.

Evie nudged him with her knee. "It's all right," she murmured. "Go back to sleep."

He edged closer, waiting until her breath smoothed out and she went boneless with sleep, then laid his head on her thigh. Even through the blanket and her jeans, he could smell her. Summer and lavender.

He inhaled deeply, imprinting her scent on his mind.

SOMEONE WAS at the back door. *Rat-a-tat-tat. Rat-a-tat-tat.*

Evie jolted upright, because it was barely dawn, and there was no good reason for someone to be knocking on her door so early.

Jace-the-panther was already off the couch and disappearing around the corner into the hall. She hurried after him into the kitchen to find him with his nose to the door.

She crept up next to him. He stepped back, indicating with a twitch of his head that she should open the door.

"You know who it is?" she whispered.

For answer, he nudged her hand in the direction of the doorknob.

"Okay, then. If you're sure..." Sliding the bolt to the left, she cracked open the door.

A lean, good-looking man stared back at her. The tips of his spiked black hair were bleached blond, and he had a gold stud in one earlobe. She couldn't see a chunk of quartz, but he had a telltale lump beneath his T-shirt.

A warning chill tightened the back of her neck as he looked her over with cool bronze eyes. But his words were polite enough.

"Peace to you and yours," he said in the traditional fae/fada greeting. "Sorry to bother you this early, but I believe you have one of my men here." His gaze flicked to Jace, who had edged the door wider so he was standing beside her.

Evie kept a firm grip on the doorknob, her every instinct screaming not to let this stranger inside. "Peace," she returned. "And you are?"

"Adric. Jace's alpha."

"Lord Adric." Her fingers clenched on the doorknob. Even in the human world, the Baltimore alpha's reputation was known. People said he'd killed his own uncle and driven his cousins out of the clan. In Baltimore, he had as much power as the mayor, and even the gangs left him alone.

The alpha inclined his head.

Jace leaned into her. Not pressuring her, just reminding her he was there.

She glanced down and he rumbled in reassurance. It was clear he wanted her to let his alpha inside. And the longer she left Adric standing there, the more likely one of her neighbors was to see him, which would only complicate things.

Besides, the alpha could've easily pushed his way in. The fact that he hadn't was a good sign.

She forced her fingers to release the doorknob. "Why don't you come in?"

"Thank you." He didn't seem to hurry, but he was past her almost before she knew it.

She shut the door behind him, but didn't bother bolting it—because what was the point?

Adric crouched next to Jace, a hand on his shoulder. "You okay, bro?"

Jace nuzzled the alpha's hand.

"You're hurt?"

While Jace rumbled what Evie took to be a yes, she eyed Adric. Like Jace, he was all muscle in jeans and a camo-print T-shirt that strained over his shoulders. Average height, but with a powerful build that reminded her of the ex-Army ranger in her biology class.

But damn, the guy was young. From what she'd heard, she'd have expected the

Baltimore alpha to be older, in his mid-forties at least. Sure, the fada lived way longer than humans, and so aged more slowly, but this man didn't look much older than Evie herself.

Adric glanced up at her with those odd metallic eyes. World-weary eyes. Eyes that had seen too much, too soon.

And suddenly Evie didn't have trouble believing the stories. This was a man who'd killed, more than once.

But his concern for his injured friend was clear. He rose to his feet. "Can you shift?" he asked Jace.

Evie raised a brow. So the fada couldn't always change forms? Last night, Jace had made it look easy, but then she'd never seen anyone shift before.

Jace-the-panther twitched a soft black ear.

Adric bent to examine Jace's quartz. "Better not," he agreed.

Evie would've loved to know what the man could learn from the quartz, but whatever it was, he wasn't sharing.

Adric turned to her. "I know he's hurt. I followed the trail to your house. I have a man cleaning it away, so no one else can follow it."

"There was a storm, and we hosed down what we could."

The Baltimore alpha nodded. "I know. But he dripped blood all the way down the block. Thank the gods the storm came when it did. If whoever was tracking him had picked up his trail—" He shook his head. "What happened, anyway?"

"It was a night fae."

The alpha tensed—an almost imperceptible tightening of his neck and shoulders. "You're sure? It wasn't a fada?"

"No. The night fae followed Jace here, but he didn't seem to know which house Jace was in. Jace protected us somehow."

"Good. You don't want to know what a night fae can do to you."

"I can guess." Evie rubbed her arms, remembering the darkness that had slithered out of the night. "He stabbed Jace with an iron knife."

"Iron?" Adric shook his head. "No wonder his quartz is so drained."

Evie nodded. A glance at the clock above the stove told her it was a little after seven. "Look, why don't you sit down and I'll make some coffee. That's if you drink coffee?"

Jace snorted.

The alpha's mouth quirked. "I would fucking kill for a cup of coffee. I've been out all night tracking him. When we didn't find a trace of him in Baltimore, we came up here."

He took a seat while Evie started a pot brewing. She tried to act normal, but it was unnerving having a creature who was basically a human cat seated at her kitchen table.

Jace-the-panther had settled on the floor next to the table and was watching her as well. She filled a bowl of water and set it next to him. She and Adric watched as he greedily lapped it up.

"We did what we could," she told the alpha. "He wouldn't let me call for help."

"We?"

"My brother and me."

"Ah." He waved a hand. "Relax, love. I'm not here to cause trouble—I just want to take him back home."

She nodded but remained near the coffeepot as the water heated and started dripping through. She did *not* want to sit at the table with Adric, and if worst came to worst, she could always use the hot coffee to protect herself.

Kyler's footsteps sounded in the hallway above.

Evie briefly closed her eyes. She didn't care what she'd promised last night— she didn't want her brother involved in this. But it was too late now.

Adric rose to his feet with a feline grace as her brother entered the kitchen, barefoot and clad only in a tank top and loose gym shorts.

Kyler's eyes bugged at the sight of Adric and the big black cat. "What the fuck?"

Evie inserted herself between Kyler and the bronze-eyed shifter. "This is Lord Adric," she told him. "The Baltimore alpha."

Kyler's mouth dropped open. "No shit."

"Good to meet you." Adric stuck out his hand.

"This is my brother, Kyler," Evie said. "He helped me with Jace last night."

"Wow." Her brother pumped the alpha's hand. "It's an honor to meet you, my-my lord."

"Call me Adric."

"Okay, sure." Kyler glanced down at Jace, who had risen to his feet again. "And that's Jace? He's a...panther?"

"Yeah," Evie said.

"Actually, he's a jaguar," Adric said. "A black jaguar. You can see the spots if you look close."

"Wow," Kyler said again.

A lean, furry body brushed Evie's hip. Jace had moved closer. It was almost as if he were protecting her.

Adric's brow raised. A look passed between the two fada, but all the alpha said was, "I'd still like to hear what happened last night."

"Yes, of course," she told him. "Please, sit down."

While Adric sat back down and Kyler got himself a tall glass of milk, Evie set milk and sugar on the table and handed Adric a mug of coffee before pouring another for herself. She and Kyler took seats at the table across from Adric, while Jace lay on the floor near her feet, his gaze on his alpha.

Adric dumped a hefty amount of milk into his coffee and then drained the cup in a couple of gulps. Evie went to refill his cup, but he rose to his feet. "I've got it."

She and Kyler exchanged a look. It was so surreal—the freaking Baltimore alpha making himself at home in their kitchen.

Adric sat down and leaned back in his chair, one big hand wrapped around the mug, seemingly at ease. But his eyes were watchful.

Evie cupped her own mug and tried to imitate his calm.

"So," he prompted, "a night fae, huh? And how did you get involved?"

"I found him—Jace—outside. In my backyard. I didn't know he was hurt until he passed out."

"He passed out?" Adric scowled at Jace. "How the fuck did the asshole get close enough to hurt you that bad?"

Jace's growl was low and vicious. Evie blinked, but Adric just shook his head.

"Go on," he told her, and she explained what had happened after she'd found Jace on her doorstep, with occasional interjections from Kyler.

"I don't think the knife went in too deep," she finished, "but he was getting worse until we cleaned the cut out with salt water. Thank God he was able to tell us what to do."

"You say he shifted in the middle of the night?" Adric glanced at Jace.

His eyes were closed, his big black head resting on his paws, but his ears twitched.

"Yes," Evie confirmed. "I think his fever spiked. He was restless and moving around, and the next thing I knew, he'd changed to a jaguar."

Adric shook his head. "You should've had her call me," he told Jace.

The big cat huffed in disagreement.

"Stubborn ass," his alpha returned. He looked at Evie. "He hasn't shifted since?"

"No. But he seems better—he's definitely moving easier this morning."

"Right. Okay, let's talk about the night fae. Did he get a look at you?"

"No," Evie said. "He was right outside the door, but he couldn't see us. The window blind was down."

"So he didn't see you, and he doesn't know for sure Jace was here?"

"No on both counts."

"That's good. And night fae can't scent any better than a human, so I know he didn't follow Jace's trail here. He was trolling the neighborhood, seeing what he could find."

"But I could swear he could somehow feel us on the other side of the door."

"He could." Adric took another gulp of coffee. "Night fae get off on dark energy—fear, anger, pain. He could sense you all right, but he couldn't be sure one of you was Jace. And from what you said, Jace used his quartz to tamp down your energy. The only way to hide from a night fae is to sit quietly and slow your breath and heartbeat."

"And think happy thoughts," Evie said.

"Is that what Jace told you?" The corner of Adric's mouth twitched. "I suppose it didn't hurt—but if Jace hadn't been here, all the happy thoughts in the world wouldn't have helped you. He was trying to keep you from panicking."

Evie exchanged a glance with her brother. *What if Jace hadn't recovered enough to protect them?*

She felt another rush of last night's dark fear. This time it was mixed with anger. That the night fae had dared mess with their minds...

Adric's calm, businesslike tone recalled her to the kitchen. "Sounds like you're safe enough. We'll make sure there's nothing to trace Jace to you or your house." He finished his coffee and came to his feet, and Evie and Kyler rose with him. "And now, I believe we'll be on our way." He came around the table and held out his hand to her. "I owe you, Evie Morningstar."

She stiffened. How did he know her last name? In fact, now that she thought about it, she hadn't told him her first name either.

"No worries," he said with a hint of amusement. "I just wanted to know what I was walking into."

"Of course," Evie replied faintly as she shook his hand. His fingers were warm and strong—perfectly normal, in fact. It was easy to forget he was one of the most dangerous men in America. "You don't owe us anything. We couldn't let him bleed out on our doorstep, could we?"

"Some humans would've." Adric was turning toward the door when he drew a deep inhale and swung back around. "What the fuck? You're fae?"

Evie took a step back. Kyler put an arm out to steady her.

"What are you talking about?"

"I smell silver." He leaned closer and took another breath. "It's you, not your brother."

Jace had gotten off the floor and was growling lowly. One side of his mouth peeled back to reveal a sharp white canine.

"You're a fae," Adric said. "It's faint, so maybe you're a mixed-blood, but I know a goddamn fae when I smell one. What clan? And I want the truth, woman."

CHAPTER 7

*F**ae.*

Jace snarled, low and savage. He was operating at a primal level, his animal close to the surface while he was healing.

To his jaguar, the fae were the enemy. They'd tried to kill him last night. They'd been behind Takira's death, and they'd almost killed his only niece.

His lip peeled back. Now he could taste as well as smell Evie's scent, allowing him to separate the different notes. She definitely had some fae in her: he detected a hint of silver. The only reason he hadn't noticed before was that his own body had been emitting a metallic odor as it rid itself of the iron in his system.

Evie paled but held her ground.

That gave his animal pause. The cat shook its head, confused.

"What clan?" Adric asked again. His voice was softer now. Menacing.

"Look," she said, "I'm not fae, okay? D'you think if I were a fae I'd be living like this?" Her gesture encompassed her shabby surroundings. "And why does it matter anyway?"

"It matters," Adric returned grimly.

Neither Jace nor his cat liked the alpha's tone. He had to shift. The energy drain on his quartz was still considerable, but he needed to be able to speak.

He focused inward, drawing on the tiny crystals. Normally, he had the strength to change forms with ease, and he enjoyed the buzz of energy it brought. But today, the energy was weak—more a prickle than a buzz. It increased and he almost had it, and then it faded.

"Jace," Adric said, "are you sure—"

Jace barely heard him. He sucked in a breath and tried harder.

And then his friend was beside him, adding his quartz's energy to Jace's, and the prickle strengthened to something close to normal. Through sheer force of will, he wrenched himself back to man and immediately doubled over, gulping oxygen.

Evie's eyes narrowed. "Get out of my house," she said, low and mean. "Both of you."

"As soon as I get some answers," Adric replied.

Jace came upright. The man was in charge again, and things didn't add up. "Leave it, Ric."

The alpha stiffened, but Jace was a lieutenant, directly below Adric in the hierarchy. More than that, he was an old friend. Adric was wrong, and he needed to hear it.

"She had nothing to do with this," Jace said. "It was pure chance I ended up at her house. And when the night fae came, she and the boy could've told him I was in here with them. Instead, they were nearly caught. There's no way she was working with him."

He turned to Evie. She had an angry flush on her cheeks, but that was better than seeing her pale with fear.

"I'm sorry," he apologized. "As you can see, we don't like the fae."

"Don't fucking trust them, either," Adric muttered.

She blew out a breath. "I am *not* fae, damn it."

"No?"

But her scent held the freshness of truth. Whatever she was, she believed what she was saying. Adric scented it too, because he relaxed.

And at least she wasn't night fae—she didn't have that graveyard stench. So she was sun fae or ice fae. Still an enemy, but not the dark hunters the night fae were.

Adric gave her a small smile. "If you would just get Jace's clothes, we'll be on our way."

Evie's gaze flicked at Jace. "Fine," she said coldly, and jerked her head at her brother. "Kyler—"

"No—you go. I'll stay here with the two of them."

She opened her mouth to argue, then glanced at the teenager's tight jaw and nodded her head.

While Evie went into the living room, Jace and Adric stood quietly, hands open and relaxed to show Kyler they meant no harm. It was funny, really. Like the kid had a prayer of a chance against two shifters. But Jace respected that Kyler had stepped up to protect his sister, and he knew Adric did,

His alpha examined the lanky teen. "How old are you, anyway?"

Kyler balled his fists. "Sixteen. Why?"

"No reason."

Jace slid Adric a look. What was he up to? But his friend just stood there, his gaze moving around the kitchen, noting the scuffed and peeling vinyl floor, the cheap plastic blinds on the window and the fact that the table and chairs were clearly secondhand.

Like Evie had said, if she were a fae, would she live like this? Even the most down-on-their-luck fae usually had something to sell—a ward or a spell, or a Gift that was valued in the human world. Her fae blood really must be just a trace, probably less than most fada.

Evie reentered the kitchen and thrust Jace's pants and shoes at him. "Here."

He took the pants and pulled them on, leaving the top button undone in deference to his still-healing wounds. To put on the running shoes, he had to sit on a chair, because there was no way he could bend over to lace them, and he was damned if he'd ask anyone for help. He shoved his feet into the unlaced shoes and stood back up.

Evie shot a glance at his bare chest and then met his eyes. She pinked up and pressed her lips together.

So he hadn't imagined her interest last night. He'd been too hurt to do anything about it, but he'd planned to return when he felt better. For this woman, he would've made an exception to his rule about human females.

Now that was blown to hell. She just wanted him and Adric out of here, and frankly, he'd think twice—make that three times—before getting involved with a mixed-blood, especially one who didn't even know what strain of fae ran in her veins.

But as he looked at her set face, regret twanged through him, a single harsh note. Just once, he would've liked to touch those soft cheeks of hers, smooth a finger over those strong dark brows. Taste her pretty lips.

Adric had his wallet out. "Here's something for your trouble." He held out a handful of bills to Evie.

Jace tensed. "No," he started to say, but it was too late.

Evie's eyes flashed. "Get out—now. Both of you." She pointed to the back door.

"Okay, okay," Adric said. "Just trying to show our appreciation."

"I don't need your appreciation," she gritted. "I did it because I'm a fucking nice person, got it?"

"Got it," Adric said mildly. Jace could tell he was trying not to laugh. He tucked the money back into his wallet and glanced at his quartz. "Luc's here."

Jace held out a hand to Evie. She hesitated, jaw tight, but took it.

"Thank you." He squeezed her hand. "And you, too, Kyler. I won't forget this."

"Fine." The kid shook his hand, then jerked his chin at the door. "Now leave."

He moved closer to his sister so they stood shoulder to shoulder, expressions hard. But beneath the anger there was fear, and that made Jace's heart twist.

Because he'd stood like that with his sister, too. More than once.

With a regretful nod in their direction, he followed Adric out the door.

CHAPTER 8

Outside the sun was rising over the alley. The storm last night had cleared the air. It promised to be a bright, cloudless day, the kind that made Jace itch to run free as his cat, far away from humans and buildings and roads.

Luc was waiting in a jeep. Luc was another lieutenant, although unlike Adric and Jace, he was a wolf, with his animal's narrow, hard-boned face and amber eyes. When Adric's cougar uncle had been alpha, he'd appointed only other cats to top positions. But Adric was too shrewd for that. If a man was good, he was good—didn't matter what his animal was. In fact, out of his four lieutenants, two—Luc and another man, Zuri—were wolves. And the fourth was a female, Adric's sister Marjani.

Jace approved. The clan was the stronger for it. Diversity at the top meant everyone was represented when Adric met with his lieutenants. What they lacked were older, wiser heads. All five of them including Adric were younger than thirty-five turns of the sun, but that was because most of the elders had died during the Darktime.

Adric rode shotgun with Luc, while Jace eased himself into the backseat. He leaned against the door and stretched out his legs, trying to get comfortable. That last shift had been a bitch, and now his body, especially his injured abdomen, was protesting.

"Damn," Adric said as Luc put the jeep in drive. "Woman's a wildcat, isn't she?"

"Leave it," Jace said. "She's part fae, remember?"

"Sure, dude." Adric shot him a look. "She's not for you, you know."

"You think I don't know that?"

"All I know is there was something going on in there. Your cat was protecting her—from me."

Jace closed his eyes. "She saved my life. I owed her. End of story." And it wasn't a lie—it just wasn't the whole truth.

"What the hell happened, anyway?" Luc asked as he pulled out of the alley.

"Night fae," Jace replied without opening his eyes. "Son of a bitch stabbed me with an iron knife."

Luc snarled. "Tell me he's dead."

"He is."

"What the fuck were you doing in Grace Harbor?" Adric asked. "I thought you were in Rising Sun, examining that new vein of quartz."

Jace opened his eyes. It was clear the alpha wasn't going to let him rest until he answered a few questions.

"I went to Rising Sun first." On a normal day, Jace wouldn't have been at the mine; he was the clan's chief tech, not a miner. But the miners had found a new vein of high-grade quartz and he'd wanted to see it for himself. "By the way, those crystals just might work in the clan's smartphones."

Every fada had a Gift, and Jace's was to work with the tiny crystals in quartz. He'd designed a quartz smartphone that had promising applications, but they were still working out the bugs.

"No shit?"

"Yeah. We'll have to run some tests, but it looks promising. I asked the miners to send some to the Factory for testing."

"That's good news." Adric permitted himself a rare smile.

Jace nodded. "Anyway, after work, I went out for a drink with a few of the guys. Some of the Rock Run men were there, too. Tiago do Rio invited us."

That got Adric's attention. Tiago was the youngest brother of the Rock Run alpha and a high-ranking member of the clan in his own right.

"Do Rio, hmm? Think Rock Run had anything to do with it?"

"Why the fuck would they help a night fae?"

"Because Tiago's big brother Dion would love to stop our mining. He hates having us on his mate's territory." Lord Dion wasn't just the Rock Run alpha, he was mated to Cleia, the sun fae queen.

"And he's not happy about us mining so close to Rock Run, either," Luc added. "They may have figured out that you're the guy who developed the smart-phone technology."

Jace considered that, but it didn't compute. "I don't like him any better than you, but if Dion wanted me dead, he wouldn't hire a fae. He'd do it himself."

"True," said Adric. "And we signed a contract with the Rising Sun fae. If Dion doesn't honor it, his mate would have his balls on a platter."

Luc snorted and Jace grinned. "She would." Dion might be a big, dominant man but Queen Cleia was one of the most powerful fae in the world.

"Which leaves us with Lord Prick." It was their code name for Tyrus.

"That's my guess."

A muscle ticked in Adric's jaw. "God's cat, I'd like to take him out. But the prince would wipe the floor with us if he found out we killed his only living son."

Jace nodded. They'd discussed this before, and the answer was always the same. It wasn't fucking worth it. The only consolation was knowing it was a stalemate. They couldn't take out Tyrus, but the reverse was also true. Prince Langdon had kept his son in check for the past six years—although Tyrus had apparently slipped the leash.

Thankfully, Merry was protected by Langdon himself. The night fae prince had woven a protection ward deep into the crystals of her quartz. If anyone—fae or not—tried to hurt her, they would die. Instantly.

"The bastard will go too far one of these days," Luc muttered. "And then, he's dead."

Adric growled in agreement.

Luc took the I-95 ramp south toward Baltimore. They bumped over something in the road and Jace tensed against a jolt of pain.

"Sorry, bro." Luc eased the car onto the interstate. "Couldn't avoid it."

"Hang in there," Adric added. "We'll have you home in less than an hour."

Jace nodded, tight-lipped. "I need you to do something for me—call my niece. Rui and Valeria should know what happened."

"Of course." Adric tapped his quartz. "Merry? How are you, love?"

"Uncle Ric!"

Jace's mouth curved at her excited response. In the days after they'd first found Merry with the Rock Run fada, she'd been terrified of Adric, especially after he'd tried to steal her back from the couple she thought of as her parents. But the alpha had a soft spot for cubs, and it hadn't taken long before she adored him like all the clan's young.

"Don't be worried," Adric said, "but Uncle Jace got hurt. He's going to be okay, though."

"Uncle Jace?" The brightness went out of her voice, which made Jace want to kill the night fae assassin all over again. "He's okay? You're sure?"

"Absolutely. He's here with me right now."

"Why didn't he call me then?"

"Because he's using all his energy to heal."

"Oh. That's good, then. Can I talk to him? Please?"

"Of course." Adric removed his quartz and held it over the seat so Jace could speak into it.

He leaned forward. "Yo, Merry. I'm okay, like Uncle Ric said. I won't be able to see you tomorrow, though. But I'll come and see you in a couple of days."

"Promise?"

"Promise."

"Okay, then." Her relief came through the quartz. "I hope you feel better soon."

He smiled even though she couldn't see him. "I feel better just talking to you. Now, is your dad around?"

"Yeah, we just had breakfast."

"Tell him Uncle Ric wants to talk to him. And Merry? Love you."

"Love you too."

Jace sat back. His belly was throbbing, which meant he was healing, but he'd had enough talk. He leaned his head against the seat and listened as Adric told Rui do Mar about the night fae attack.

Rui was also Dion's second-in-command. He understood immediately that Merry could be in danger. Wards could be broken. Yes, it would be suicide to kill Merry, but that didn't mean Tyrus wouldn't send someone after her. If the assassin died, Tyrus would chalk it up to collateral damage.

"Thanks for the heads-up," Rui told Adric. "I'll let the alpha know. We'll keep her safe."

"I know. That's the only reason she's still with you."

"Try and take her," Rui retorted, "and you won't live the week."

Adric ignored that to say, "We'll keep you informed."

"You do that."

"And do Mar?"

"What?"

"Give Rosana my love." He tapped the phone, cutting off the other man's growl.

Jace's mouth twitched. Rosana was the youngest do Rio, a sultry black-haired beauty about twenty-two turns of the sun. Adric singled her out every chance he got: dancing with her at the sun fae's big midsummer celebration each year, bringing her small gifts.

And Rosana encouraged him.

It drove the Rock Run men insane, especially Tiago and Dion. Jace didn't know what Rosana's game was, but Adric did it to tweak the older alpha.

Adric and Luc fell into a low-voiced conversation. Strategizing. Jace tried to listen, but his eyes closed, and all he heard was the healing hum of his quartz.

The next thing he knew, Luc said, "We're here."

Jace sat up. They'd arrived in Baltimore. Adric hopped out and opened Jace's door, holding out his hand. Jace took it, because frankly, he needed the help.

The clan lived in small dens scattered around the city. Most of them lived underground, with a house on the surface as camouflage. Some of the dens were connected by underground tunnels, although not Jace's.

After his parents died, the brick house on his lot had fallen into disrepair, but Jace had fixed it up and rented it out to a single mom and her kids. The mom was grateful to have a landlord who kept things in good repair, and in return, she ignored the odd hours he and his den mates kept—and the big cats, wolves and bears that could be seen in the backyard from time to time.

Adric slid an arm around Jace's waist. When Jace tried to shrug him off, he growled, "Let me help, you idiot."

"Asshole," Jace returned, but gratefully accepted the alpha's strength as he limped around back to where his den entrance was concealed in a small shed protected by a *look-away* spell.

Suha, the clan's head healer, was waiting in her usual colorful tunic and capris. A slender, black-haired woman whose animal was a deer, she had a doe's soft brown eyes and calm ways, except where it came to her patients. Then the woman could out-hardass Adric.

She greeted Jace with a careful hug and a kiss on each of his cheeks, then set her hands on her hips. "Don't you know better than to mess with a night fae?"

"He messed with me, babe. And I'm the one who's still walking around."

She rolled her eyes. "Inside with you."

Adric touched his quartz and murmured the words that dissolved the *look-away* spell. The den was two flights down. Jace could no longer keep up the pretense that he wasn't in pain. He shuffled down the stairs, gripping the rail like a lifeline. Adric stayed on his other side, taking as much of his weight as he could.

By the time they reached the bottom, sweat had beaded on Jace's forehead. He leaned against the stone wall as Adric opened the door to his den and then helped him into the small foyer.

Jace's parents had carved the den out of the bedrock long before he was born. Both of them had been soldiers, but his dad had been an engineer at heart. In his downtime, he'd built this big, solid home for his mate, their two cubs, and assorted other members of the clan. Even in the Darktime, everyone knew they always had a bed at the Jones' den.

He limped into the living room, a large, comfortable space with exposed stone walls and furniture that dated to his parents' time. The floor was covered with worn throw rugs and large pillows for their animals to curl up on, and the mantelpiece held a collection of quartz that his soldier mom had brought back from her tours overseas. Other than replacing the pillows, the only thing Jace had added was the big screen TV on the wall. He'd had to rig up a solar-powered electricity system, but it was worth it.

Now the only thing that greeted him was Tigger, a testy orange tomcat who'd moved in last year and never left. That was strange. Jace glanced around, nostrils flared, testing the air for his den mates' scents. With four men besides himself calling the den home, it was rarely empty.

"Everyone is out looking for you," Adric said. "They should be back soon—I sent word we found you. But I had people searching in a fifty-mile radius."

He grunted. "Call out the effing cavalry, why don't you?"

"Shut up and get into bed."

Suha had gone down the hall to Jace's bedroom. She didn't have to ask where it was. She'd patched up his wounds more than once.

With Adric's help, he hobbled after her and lowered himself onto the edge of the mattress. Damn, he'd swear these cuts had been seared into his gut by Hades himself. This morning he'd thought they were almost healed, but now they felt worse than ever.

Suha placed a small, blunt-fingered hand on his shoulder. "Lie down before you fall down."

He gritted his teeth and obeyed. But it was good to be home in his own bed. His muscles softened.

Suha scanned the wound with her quartz as he stared at the ceiling. His dad had left the stone walls bare in here, too. The stone was dotted with mica, giving the dark gray rock a pretty shimmer. He could almost hear the walls humming.

"Not bad," Suha murmured. "They're healing, especially the shallow one, but deep inside, they're still open. And you're spiking a high fever."

Her voice seemed to come from far away. He dragged his gaze back to her face.

A fever. That's why he felt so odd, as if he were floating above the bed. He dug his fingers into the sheets to ground himself.

Adric got a chair from the kitchen for Suha and set it next to the bed. "The humans cleaned the cuts out with salt water," he told her.

"Within a half hour," Jace added.

"Thank the gods for that." Suha frowned at her quartz. "But the iron had already spread into your blood. That's why you still feel—"

"Like shit," Jace finished for her. "But I'll heal."

"With help." She fixed him with a stern look. "Now relax and breathe."

Jace scowled. "I don't need your energy. Save it…" He trailed off as he lost his train of thought.

"I'll be the judge of that," the healer returned. "Close your eyes and breathe. Picture your body filling with healing energy…a warm, golden light."

"I'll help." Adric moved to Jace's other side, but Suha shook her head.

"I know you're strong, but you're burnt from being out searching all night. Save your energy for yourself. I've got this."

Adric nodded but remained where he was. He gave Jace's shoulder a squeeze. "You heard the woman. Close your eyes and let her do her stuff."

He obediently closed his eyes and focused on the warmth in his belly. At first it seared, the unhealthy fire of last night, but even worse. He went hot, then cold. The humming of the walls grew louder, became an irritating buzz that made him want to clamp his hands to his ears.

He moved his legs restively. "Hot."

"I know." Suha murmured something to Adric and a minute later he returned with a damp cloth. Suha placed it on his forehead, and Jace gave a hiss of relief.

The burning changed, became a pleasant glow that infused his wounds with healing energy. The buzzing in his head receded as his own quartz's crystals hummed louder in response, until his whole body was vibrating with an unearthly music that was both sound and magic.

He drew a deep breath and released it, and let himself float in the soothing sea of energy.

Time passed. Ten minutes, then another ten.

Adric touched Jace's shoulder, ignoring Suha's directive to add his energy to the mix.

Jace slit his eyes. His friend squeezed Jace's shoulder, his normally sculpted, arrogant face soft with concern.

Suha shook her head at Adric, but allowed him to braid his energy through hers. They all knew that he couldn't remain idle when any of his people were hurting. The vibrations swelled to an ocean of sound, peaceful and yet energizing.

More time passed as the energy ebbed and flowed, washing the pain away. His eyelids grew too heavy to lift.

"There," Suha said. "That should do it. You're going to have a couple of scars, but that can't be helped." She touched his cheek. "How do you feel?"

He forced his lids to open. Suha's pretty oval face hovered above him, her large doe-eyes narrowed with concentration.

"Great," he murmured. "Sleepy, but great. Thank you."

"Good. I want you to stay in bed for a few days, got it?"

He nodded.

"He'll be fine," Suha said to Adric.

He briefly closed his eyes, and Jace realized how worried he'd been. "Thank you," he told the healer.

"You'll stay with him?"

"Only until his den mates arrive, and then I have to get home to Marjani. But I'll check back later."

"How is she?"

Adric shrugged. A year ago last spring, Marjani had been kidnapped and raped by a den of feral water fada. All the ferals were dead, and Marjani's body was healed, but it was going to take a long time before her mind was whole again. It clawed at all of them, but Adric had taken it extra hard—because how do you get over your sister being hurt like that?

Jace knew the answer: you didn't. It was always part of you. The regrets, the what-ifs, the fucking helplessness. Because if you'd only known your sister was in danger...

"About the same," Adric said at last.

Suha pressed her lips together. "I'll come by to see her later."

"Thank you." The alpha's face was naked with the love and hurt he felt for his sister. "I thought she was getting better, but she hasn't been outside in over a week. I can't—" He spread his hands.

Jace roused himself to say, "Tell her...I need a visitor."

"That's not a bad idea," Suha said. "Tomorrow, maybe." She squeezed Jace's hand. "You be good now, you hear? When I say stay in bed, I mean it. You don't want a relapse."

"Yes, ma'am."

A slim black brow winged up. "And don't think I don't know when someone's being evasive. Say the words."

He scowled, but she simply gazed back until he muttered, "All right. I'll stay in bed. For the rest of the day."

He caught Adric's smirk and scowled at him as well, but his friend returned, "Listen to the healer, Jace. I need you at full strength to help get the bastard that did this. Now, are you hungry?"

And Jace realized he was. Starving, in fact.

"Just liquids today," Suha said. "Broth, a yogurt smoothie. We don't want to stress his digestive system yet." She gave them both a kiss and let herself out.

With her gone, Jace took a nap while Adric went out to a diner to pick up some food. Yogurt wasn't his usual fare, but it was about all he could handle right now. At least it was strawberry. He sipped the smoothie and watched enviously as Adric wolfed down his own two ham-and-egg sandwiches in rapid succession.

Jace's den mates returned. They wandered in and out of the room to see how he was doing. Sam, a burly redhead whose animal was a Bengal tiger, was first. He was followed by Beau, a slow-moving, slow-talking bear, and Horace, a cougar who was one of the clan's best trackers. They stood over Jace, shaking their heads and needling him about being caught off-guard by a fae until Adric told them to get the hell out and let him rest.

The last to arrive was Zuri, who'd been directing the cleanup in Grace Harbor. A fellow lieutenant, Zuri was a tall, dark and charismatic wolf who pretty much had to beat women off with a stick. Along with Adric, he was Jace's closest friend.

Zuri got a second chair from the kitchen and set it next to the bed. "Everything's calm." He propped his long legs on the foot of the mattress. "I followed Jace's trail myself from the bar to the human's house, and I couldn't scent a thing."

"And the woman and her brother?" asked Adric.

"I have Kara watching the house." Zuri named a young female who had recently arrived from their sister clan in Jamaica. "She's good at blending in with humans. Even if they see her, they won't know she's one of us."

"Excellent," Adric replied.

Jace nodded, relieved. He'd been going to ask that Adric see to Evie's protection. "The woman—Evie—she's good people. I'd hate to see her and her brother get hurt because they stuck their necks out for me."

Adric and Zuri exchanged a look.

"You don't usually go for human women," said Zuri.

He growled. "Who the fuck says I'm going for her?"

His friend raised his hands, palm out. "Nobody."

Adric snorted and got to his feet. "Look, I have to go. I could use a shower—bad—and I told Marjani I'd bring her some breakfast." He lifted the takeout bag. "She doesn't remember to eat sometimes. Feel better, okay?"

He squeezed Jace's shoulder and with a nod to Zuri, left.

Zuri stayed another few minutes and then started yawning until Jace told him to go to bed, he'd be fine. The other men were either in bed or in the living room watching TV.

Jace looked at Tigger, who had stretched out between his open legs. "Looks like it's just the two of us."

Tigger yawned and kneaded the sheet, narrowly missing Jace's balls with his claws, and then settled his head on his paws. A minute later he was snoring.

CHAPTER 9

"And don't come back." Evie slammed the deadbolt shut behind the two fada.

Kyler was studying her as if she had two heads.

"Damn it," she snapped, "I am *not* fae."

"Part fae." He leaned in to sniff her. "You smell human to me."

"Very funny." She shoved him away, but he just chuckled. "Of course, I do. If I were fae, wouldn't I know it?"

"Maybe. But one thing we do know—if you have fae blood and I don't, then it's not Mom."

She scraped both hands through her hair. "Drop it, Kyler."

"So it's Fane."

She heaved a sigh. "And God knows where he is."

Her dad wasn't the type to leave a forwarding address—if he even had an address to leave. Fane Morningstar came and went as the spirit moved him, and Lord knew, that wasn't often; she could count on her fingers the number of times she'd seen him in the past ten years.

It wasn't that she didn't like her dad. Everyone liked him. He was tall and blond, with a laidback way of moving and talking as if time moved slower for him somehow. He always had a smile for you, and she'd never once heard him raise his voice.

If her mom asked difficult questions, like how long he was staying this time, the man just...disappeared. Evie had learned early not to count on Fane. You just enjoyed him while he was around, and then did your best to forget him when he left.

"If anyone has fae blood, it's Fane," Kyler said. "There's that picture we found. You know, after Mom died."

"Yeah." Evie set her jaw and started tidying the kitchen, picking up the bowl and coffee cups and setting them in the sink.

They'd found the photo tucked in a cigar box along with other mementos. In it, Fane had an arm slung around their mom's shoulders, and they were both grinning at the camera. It had to have been taken over twenty-five years ago.

The last time they'd seen Fane, he'd looked exactly the same, right down to his wide grin and unlined face.

"What are you going to do?" Kyler asked.

"Make pancakes." She took a box of pancake mix from the cupboard.

Her brother blew out a breath. "About this fae thing."

"Nothing." She measured a cup of the mix into a bowl, added milk and broke an egg on top of it. "Even if it's true, what does it matter?" she asked as she stirred the batter. "It's not going to change anything. If I do have some fae in me, it's probably something like one-hundredth. It's not like I can work magic or anything."

Kyler placed his hands on his narrow hips and shook his head. "My sister, a fae."

She pointed her fork at him. "This is between you and me, got it? You tell anyone, and you're toast."

He grinned and raised his hands. "Okay, okay. Don't shoot me with a fae ball, sis."

"Very funny. I mean it, Kyler Ferris." She gave the batter a vicious stir. "Just get the plates out, will you?"

"Hey, don't be so touchy. At least you have a dad to visit you. I don't really even remember mine. I probably wouldn't know him if I passed him on the street."

Evie bit her lip. She ached to hug her brother, but she knew from experience he'd shrug her off. Their eyes met.

"You'd know him."

"Yeah, sure." Kyler opened the cupboard and took out two plates.

After breakfast, Kyler went to school and Evie finished cleaning up. She double-bagged Jace's bloody T-shirt and then, recalling what a good sense of smell the fada had, threw it into a dumpster on the next block. Meanwhile, she washed and dried the sheet he'd used.

In a short while, there was no trace that Jace had spent the night on her couch. She'd almost believe she'd dreamed the whole thing, except she didn't have that good of an imagination.

How was he doing? She bit her lip. He was the kind of man who'd do too much, too soon.

Not my business, she told herself. He had his friends to take care of him now. The best thing was to forget they'd ever met.

Her mind turned to what Adric had said about her being part fae. He'd seemed so certain.

If only there was some way to get hold of her dad. But the last time she'd seen him was two years ago, right before her mom died. She wasn't even sure how he'd heard her mom was sick, but he'd arrived in time to say goodbye. Her mom had been alert enough to smile at him, and Evie would always be grateful for that.

Fane had stayed through the death and, to Evie's surprise, had even taken charge of the arrangements, including paying for the memorial service and cremation. On the third night he'd said, "You seem like you're doing okay, Evie love," and the next morning he was gone, leaving only a glittering stone on her night table...which turned out to be a diamond worth close to ten thousand dollars.

Trust her dad to give her a gift that caused even more trouble. She'd been afraid a jeweler would ask awkward questions, so she'd pawned it instead. But the pawn shop had given her five thousand for it, and she had to admit the cash had helped.

Evie shook her head and took out her laptop. She had homework to do.

That afternoon she ate an early dinner with Kyler, and then headed to the Wine Bar, an upscale restaurant on the water where she was a server. Grace Harbor was a small, historic city bordered on two sides by water—the Susquehanna River to the north, and the Chesapeake Bay to the east. This time of year, the streets were filled with boaters and weekenders. It was Friday evening, and the restaurant was packed.

She should've been too busy to think, but Jace kept popping into her head at odd times. That curious smile as he'd been hurt and bleeding next to her stoop. His broad shoulders and cat-like grace. The way his eyes changed from hazel to green...

"Excuse me." The man at the table before her spoke. "Miss? Is that our food?"

Evie blinked. She was standing in the middle of the restaurant, a plate in each hand. "Sorry about that," she said with a smile, and slid the plates in front of the man and his date.

He closed his mouth on whatever he'd been about to say and gave her a brief smile back. She smiled at the woman he was with as well, because it was low class —and bad for tips—to flirt with a guy in front of his date. "Can I get you anything else?"

"No, we're fine." They each waved a hand, eager to assure her there was no problem. She'd always had a gift for soothing people's feathers, making them smile. It was why she was such a good waitress.

But was there more to it than that? Her mom had said Evie's way with people came from Fane.

Damn it, she was *not* going to think about it. Fae or not, what did it matter? It wasn't like she could do anything useful, like change straw into gold. Now that would be a real Gift.

She got off work a little after eleven. She'd taken her car this time, because after last night, she was wary about walking home after dark. Now she came out of the restaurant to find a light rain falling—and she hadn't brought an umbrella.

She grabbed her keys and her backpack and jogged to where she'd parked her ancient blue compact under a street light—just in case.

At least it was a warm rain. Evie swiped the water from her face and started the car. The ignition sputtered and went dead. The car had been her mother's, and it had grown cranky with age. It especially didn't like wet weather.

"C'mon, hon." She crossed her fingers and tried again, and this time the engine ground to life.

The half-mile drive home took under five minutes. She drove slowly, the black lampposts casting a warm yellow glow on the rainy streets. Grace Harbor had once been a workingman's town, with crabbers, fishers and a herring cannery. But these days, it had a funky, small-town vibe with mom-and-pop stores alongside art galleries, antique shops and upscale restaurants like the Wine Bar.

She passed a couple of her neighbors out for a stroll, umbrellas lifted. It was hard to believe that just last night a man had almost died right in her backyard.

She parked her car on the concrete pad behind the house, took a thorough look around, and then sprinted up the steps to her back door.

Kyler wasn't home yet, but there was nothing unusual about that. His curfew on the weekends was midnight, and he usually came home the last possible second. That wouldn't have bothered her, but the last few weeks he'd started pushing the curfew—coming home at twelve-thirty or one and daring her to object.

Tonight was one of those nights. She started texting him five minutes after midnight.

At least he replied, telling her not to worry.

Too late, she replied. *I'm worried and I want you home. NOW.*

She could see he'd viewed the text, but he didn't reply. She sat on the easy chair, fuming, as she finished her paper. Because she *was* worried about him, especially after last night. What if that night fae came back? Her whole body went cold, just thinking about it.

It was almost one o'clock before Kyler sauntered in the front door, red-eyed and smelling of pot. He flopped on the couch and regarded her through slit eyes.

"Go ahead. Tell me what a bad boy I am."

She clenched her jaw so hard her teeth hurt. "You're only sixteen, Kyler. Too young to be out after midnight, and too damn young to be smoking weed."

"Go to hell, Evie." He rested his arm over his eyes. "You're not my mom."

Her stomach sucked in. For a few seconds, she was blinded by hurt and anger.

"No," she said as calmly as she could, "but I'm responsible for you until you're eighteen. If you get arrested, it's on my watch."

"Don't worry about it. I'll tell them it's me, not you."

"You think I care about that? I care about you, asshat. And I promised Mom I'd take care of you, damn it."

He raised up on his elbows to glare at her. "Fuck your promise. If taking care of me is so hard, then forget it. Mom never should've asked—"

"Oh, for Chrissake." She rubbed the bridge of her nose. "I didn't mean it like that. You know I didn't."

"Yeah, sure."

"But I mean it, Kyler. From now on, you'd better be home at midnight, or I swear I'll—" She halted because she didn't have anything to threaten him with, and they both knew it.

Kyler levered himself off the couch. "Okay, okay," he grumbled. "Don't get your panties in a twist."

She watched as he stalked out of the living room, his thin body rigid, his T-shirt a little too small. He'd grown six inches this year so that she was barely able to keep him in clothes.

She blew out a breath and rested her head on the back of the chair.

What am I going to do with him this summer?

CHAPTER 10

*J*ace spent most of Saturday in bed.

Tigger kept him company. Jace wasn't sure who'd first let the tomcat in, but within a week he had the run of the place. He'd adopted Jace, wisely zeroing in on the alpha of the small den. Jace had christened him Tigger, just to yank Sam's chain, because Tigger was basically a mini-Sam— an orange tiger-in-miniature.

Jace did sleep for a couple of hours. When he woke up, Zuri brought him some beef broth. They talked a little, and then Zuri left to run some errands. With the coast clear, Tigger jumped on Jace's bed and settled against his leg. A short while later he was purring.

Touched, Jace stroked the cat's fur. Tigger didn't usually share anyone's bed, preferring a perch on the living room couch where he could survey both the kitchen and the front door. He was clearly offering support to an injured den mate.

The afternoon passed slowly. Jace took another short nap. When he awoke, his head was clear for the first time in twenty-four hours. He stared at the ceiling, stroking Tigger and thinking.

Frigging woman. Because he couldn't get the tough little human out of his mind.

He knew damn well she needed help. It couldn't be easy, raising a kid who wasn't much younger than her.

Jace knew something about that himself. Yeah, Takira had been older than him, not younger, but only by two years. During the Darktime, the alpha—Adric's uncle Leron—had separated families as punishment or simply to keep them from conspiring against him. Jace's own mom had been sent on a military mission to South America that had kept her away for a year. While she was gone, his peace-loving, half Native American dad had been killed in a bloody spate of fighting.

By the time Jace was fifteen, he and Takira had been on their own save for the small pack they'd formed with Adric, Marjani, and some of the other young members of their clan. At fifteen, Jace was already bigger and stronger than his sister, so he'd been her protector as much as she was his.

And then Takira had fallen for Silver, a half-fae, half-human who turned out to be Prince Langdon's illegitimate son. Langdon had kept Silver a secret—the night fae frowned on mating with anyone but another pureblood—but somehow Tyrus, his only other living son, had found out. Maybe even from Adric's bastard of an uncle.

Remembering, Jace's fingers tightened in Tigger's fur. The cat hissed and Jace released him. Tigger shot him an outraged glare and then stalked off, stiff-legged, to the foot of the mattress before lying down again.

The Darktime. It had been like a virus attacking the clan, a killing fever that swept through the ranks, sucking in even good men and women until no one knew who to trust. Darkness and hatred had ruled.

But the day Jace had heard that Takira had been raped and murdered had been the day he'd truly understood darkness. A familiar acridness coated the back of his tongue. If only he'd known that Tyrus had targeted Takira and her small family...

Jace had been with Adric, planning a strike against Leron Savonett. That small, well-planned attack had turned the tide, eventually leading to the battle that finally took down the vicious alpha. Jace had rushed to Takira's den with the news that she no longer had to hide Merry. But they were gone. The next he'd heard, Takira was dead, and Silver had taken his daughter and gone into hiding.

He dragged a hand over his face. What the hell made him think he could help Evie and Kyler? Better he stayed away. If Tyrus was stalking Jace, he was a danger to them.

He threw off the sheet, earning another irritated hiss from Tigger, but Jace was going to go insane if he spent any more time staring at the ceiling.

He limped into the living room and sprawled on the couch. One by one his den mates woke up from their naps and joined him, taking seats on the chairs or the large pillows strewn on the floor.

When Adric returned it was after six o'clock, and the four of them were eating

Chinese take-out—soup for Jace—and watching the Orioles. When Adric entered, everyone except Jace rose to their feet. They hugged and nuzzled each other—their animals needing the touch—and then Adric took Sam's seat on the couch next to Jace.

Sam didn't even blink. Adric was the alpha, but more, he'd earned their loyalty a hundred times over. The man would die for them, and nearly had.

Adric looked Jace over with a professional eye. He wasn't a healer, but like all of them, he'd done his share of field medic work. "Should you be out of bed?"

Jace growled. "Don't start."

"It's your funeral," he said, helping himself to a plate of ginger garlic chicken. He watched the last two innings of the baseball game with the rest of them, and then jerked his chin at the other men. "I need to talk to Jace and Zuri."

The room cleared immediately. Adric spun a chair around so its back was facing Jace, and sat down, arms draped over the back, while Zuri took a seat on the opposite end of the couch.

Adric scrutinized Jace. "You sure you're all right?"

His nape tightened. "Why?" He set his empty soup bowl on the coffee table. "What is it?"

"I've been thinking. That night fae was waiting for you, right?"

"Far as I could tell."

"So, d'you think it was Lord Prick?"

"I didn't see him," Jace said, "but who else could it be? The man was right outside Evie and Kyler's door. We could feel him out there, trying to sense where I was. I protected the three of us the best I could, and then I passed out. Somehow she held him off. Hell, maybe thinking happy thoughts worked."

"Could be the fae in her. If I had to choose, I'd say she was sun fae, and if there's one thing the sun fae are good at, it's being happy."

Jace nodded slowly. Sun fae were rich, sexy, hedonistic—the fae world's version of a Hollywood elite. Evie might not have the wealth, but she had a sun fae's magnetism. Hell, even with a knife wound to the gut, he'd wanted to fuck her.

"But if it was his royal prickness," Adric continued, "then why? He targeted you for a reason."

"Merry," Jace said, tightlipped. "He can't get at her because she's too well protected. That ward of her grandfather's keeps the night fae away from her, and Rock Run has adopted her into their clan. You'd have to be touched in the head to fuck with Rui do Mar." The river fada who was Merry's adopted father was also Rock Run's most feared assassin. "No." Jace shook his head. "The only way the night fae can strike at her is through me."

"Merry, yeah—but why you? Sure, you're her uncle, but it's Silver's line he's worried about. And if he really wanted to hurt Merry, he'd go after Rui and Valeria."

"True." Jace rubbed his forehead. "But then why?"

Adric was out of his chair and pacing. He could never sit still for long.

"Think about it, Jace. You're the key to my whole strategy for getting the clan back on its feet. You're the one who knows the quartz technology inside out. Yeah, we've got others who can do some of what you do, but no one has a grasp of all the pieces like you do. If you die, the project could be set back years—and who knows what would happen in the meantime?"

"Hell." Jace met Adric's eyes. "You think someone's trying to sabotage the project."

"I do."

Zuri's brow creased. "But why would the night fae care?"

Adric and Jace spoke as one. "Because he's not working alone."

CHAPTER 11

$\mathcal{M}$onday morning, Jace woke up feeling almost like his old self.

Suha had returned on Sunday to nag him to take it easy. He nodded and obeyed, because the healer knew her stuff—and he did need the rest. Suha's healing combined with the energy from his own recharged quartz to speed things along.

Zuri had brought Jace's bike home, so just after dawn, he slipped out of the den, Tigger on his heels. Somehow Suha got wind of it, though—he'd swear the woman was part Seer—and he found her waiting in the backyard.

The healer set her hands on her hips. "Where d'you think you're going?"

Tigger perked up—he had a crush on Suha. He butted her calf, marking her with his scent.

She ignored the lovesick tabby to glare at Jace. "I haven't cleared you to work, Jones."

Uh-oh. She'd used his last name. Not a good sign.

He attempted a winning smile. "I'm fine. See?" He lifted his T-shirt to show her. The cuts had healed, but as she'd predicted, they'd left behind two raised red scars. Normally fada healed quickly and cleanly, but not when iron was involved. Jace would bear the night fae's marks the rest of his life.

"I'll be the judge of that." Suha removed her crystal and ran it over his belly. "Not bad," she conceded. "But you nearly died, Jace. Iron poisoning is no joke, and you suffered some internal damage. I want you to take it easy this week."

"I am taking it easy. I'm only going to the Factory to test some of the new quartz. Those new smartphones are losing their charge too quickly."

The Factory was the name Adric had given their combination test lab and manufacturing plant. Right now, it was just a big room in a building they'd rescued from the wrecking ball, but Ric liked to think big.

Suha nodded. The clan had been informed about the basics of what they were doing—produce quartz smartphones to Jace's design, and then sell them to the other earth fada clans.

"So?" she returned. "They can survive a few days without you."

"But I can't. If I stay in another day, I'll be climbing the walls. Even Tigger is sick of me." He nodded at the tomcat, who'd tired of trying to gain Suha's attention and was investigating an interesting smell near the fence. "Please?"

The healer cast her gaze skyward. "Don't blame me if you have a relapse."

"I won't." Jace planted a kiss on her cheek. "Relapse, that is."

And they both knew Suha would come running if he did.

THE FACTORY WAS ONLY about a mile away in a blighted section of West Baltimore. The building had once been a grocery store, and the sign outside still read Allen's Stop-and-Shop because that was as good a camouflage as any. After they'd cleared out the display shelves and cash registers, they'd been left with one large room for the tables, computers, and equipment used to manufacture the smartphones, and a storage room in the back.

Jace felt a familiar pride as he entered the Factory. This was his baby; Adric had given him free rein to set up shop, directing the small crew to not just manufacture smartphones for the clan, but to refine and improve the technology. The beauty of quartz was that it produced a strong current when fed by an earth fada's natural energy. It was also strong and waterproof.

Adric was even considering selling the phones to water fada, whose biology tended to short out regular electronic devices, although none of them were sure they wanted to put such a tool in their rivals' hands. They'd have to work out the energy issues, too. Water fada didn't require quartz for life energy like the earth fada did, but on the other hand, they couldn't work with the crystals from an early age like Jace's people could.

And after that, who knew? If Adric could work out a deal with a human communications company—and figure out a way for humans to operate the quartz—the sky was the limit. They might one day sell the phones to select humans as well. The military would love a waterproof phone that could hold a charge for several weeks. Right now, though, you had to have at least a few drops of fae blood to operate a smartphone.

But there was one big problem; the technology burned the quartz up. It wasn't reusable like an earth fada's own quartz, and low-grade quartz didn't work at all. The clan desperately needed a new supply of high-grade quartz like the vein they'd located on the border of Rising Sun Fae territory.

Resolving all the issues would take years, but Jace was up for it. During the Darktime he'd used his Gift with crystals to design weapons. It was a pure joy to use his Gift in a positive way.

Now he took a deep, satisfied inhale, breathing in the familiar scents—the sandiness of ground quartz, the oil they used to reduce dust, the metallic odor of machinery. A couple of people were already at work—an engineer known as Frog for some damn reason, and a pretty, dark-haired tech named Dina. They glanced over their shoulders and did a simultaneous double take.

"Jace?" Dina came to her feet. "Shouldn't you be in bed?"

"Suha gave me the green light."

Dina inhaled, testing his statement for truth, and then shrugged. "Okay, great. I have an idea as to why the energy is getting sucked out so fast." A cougar who'd inherited her mom's Italian coloring—and brains—Dina was even more single-minded than him.

He pulled up a chair and the three of them hashed out her idea. A couple of other men came in a few hours later, and they all traded ideas before breaking off to test them.

They were eating take-out pizza at their work stations around one o'clock when Adric walked in. Jace removed his goggles and rose to his feet. "Hey, Ric. What's up?"

"Meeting. Zuri and Luc are on their way." Adric helped himself to a slice of pizza. "What the fuck?" He frowned at the broccoli and spinach.

"Dina thinks we need more greens," Jace said.

"We're cats, not cows," Adric muttered. But he took a large bite and then smiled at Dina. "Actually, that's not bad." He took another bite.

Dina beamed. Like all the unmated women, she perked up around the alpha, even though everyone knew Adric wasn't ready to take a mate. Not that the man was deprived. He had his pick of the clan's women, who were happy to hook up with the alpha even for a night.

A minute later, first Zuri and then Luc entered, following their practice of arriving separately at meetings for security reasons. Adric gulped down his pizza and jerked his head in the direction of their underground war room.

Dina, Frog and the rest of the Factory crew looked curious, but they knew better than to ask questions. Adric shared information on a need-to-know basis, having learned the hard way that the less people knew about your business, the better. Sometimes it even saved your life.

Zuri and Luc grabbed some pizza and the four of them headed for the storage room. There, Adric opened a trap door and they all passed through a ward set to allow only Adric and his lieutenants through before climbing down a ladder.

The war room had been carved by Adric and a couple trusted stoneworkers from the bedrock beneath the Factory. Adric was a Gifted tracker—he hired himself out to the fae for outrageous sums—but what he really liked to do was work with stone. He could make a rock practically sing with joy as he used a combination of chiseling and magic to transform it into art.

A thin vein of white quartz twisted through the rock walls. The quartz had been magically engineered to soundproof the room. Combined with the ward, it even allowed them to speak a fae's name freely without attracting his or her attention.

They seated themselves around the large table Adric had carved from a single large rock. Like Camelot's famous table, it was round. This way, Adric said, each of them could see everyone else—and everyone's ideas had equal weight.

Adric spoke to Jace first. "I hear you're cleared for work, just nothing too strenuous."

Jace scowled. "Suha snitched on me."

"Of course. You're not going out on this one, bro. But I wanted your input." He looked around the table, addressing all three of them. "On Saturday night Zuri went back to the bar in Grace Harbor where Jace was attacked. He asked some questions, but no one knew anything."

Jace nodded. No surprise there. "The assassin 'ported in. I don't know about the other two, but they must have blended in somehow or I'd have seen them myself."

"They probably used a glamour," Adric said. "Made themselves look like someone else—someone who fit in. Maybe even a river fada."

"But a glamour only fools the eyes—not the nose."

The alpha shrugged. "So they didn't get too close. You weren't going to scent them across a crowded bar." He looked at Zuri. "Tell him what you found out."

"I didn't discover a damn thing inside the bar," the tall, dark wolf said, "but I thought I'd sniff around the parking lot, see if I could pick up anything. That's where I ran into Rui do Mar, who was having a look around himself. I figured we should coordinate our efforts. Grace Harbor is their town, not ours."

"Do Mar knows Tyrus's scent," Adric inserted. "You know what he did to the prick after he tried to kidnap Merry."

"Tracked him to his lair in France," Jace said, "and beat the shit out of him. Almost killed the bastard."

Officially, Rock Run remained quiet about the attack on Tyrus, because if it became known that Dion's second-in-command was the man who roughed up his son, Langdon would've been forced to act. This way, the prince could pretend nothing happened—and Tyrus wasn't going to broadcast that a fada had overcome him so easily.

"Anyway," Zuri said, "Do Mar was pissed as hell that a night fae dared attack a fada practically in Rock Run's backyard. He promised to let Dion know, and then we went over the parking lot with a fine-toothed comb. Not only does do Mar have Tyrus's scent memorized, the man's animal is a shark. He can detect a few particles of blood in a fucking ocean."

Jace nodded impatiently. None of this was news to him. "And? He picked up Tyrus's scent?"

"Yep. Do Mar was sure—said he'd never forget it. And he recognized the scent of the man you killed, too. Tyrus's chief enforcer."

Jace was on his feet. "That sonofabitch." He spun to look at Adric. "I'm going after him."

"No fucking way."

Jace slapped his palms on the granite table. "Damn it, Ric. You're my alpha, but this is my family. Don't ask me to choose between the two."

Adric's snarl made Jace's spine tighten. The other two men moved uneasily. "Sit. Down."

Jace's claws pricked out, but he grabbed onto his patience and obeyed.

"First," the alpha held up a finger, "you're in no condition to take on a toddler, let alone a fae. Second," he held up another finger, "if we do this, we have to be smart about it. You're a smart man. Use that brain of yours."

Zuri murmured agreement, while Luc looked on, his wolf-gold eyes watchful, but Jace knew he'd be a hundred percent behind whatever Adric decided.

"Fine," Jace spat out. Adric might be right, but Jace was sick unto death of Tyrus targeting his family. "But this time, he's dead. The man's not going to rest until every last Jones is wiped off the face of the earth."

"If it's you he's targeting," Adric returned. "I'm not as sure as you are. Is it you he wants, or would any of my lieutenants have done?"

"Does it matter?" Zuri asked. "Either way, I vote we put the man out of his misery." His lips peeled in a show of canines.

"I intend to," the alpha returned. "When he tried to kill Merry six years ago, I had no choice but to let Rock Run go after him. We weren't strong enough."

They all nodded. At that point, Adric had only been alpha for a few months and the clan was still reeling from the Darktime.

"But things are different now." Adric's smile was deadly, his cougar a shadow on his face. "We're a hell of a lot stronger than we were six years ago. If Tyrus wants a fight, he's going to get a fight. I'll bring it right to his fucking lair."

They all rumbled agreement.

"But we have to be careful," Zuri said. "If Prince Langdon finds out, we're all dead."

"Agreed." Adric looked at Jace. "Thoughts?"

His mind was already ticking along: analyzing, examining patterns. "We find out everything we can about Tyrus. Where he lives, who he hangs out with, what he fucking eats for breakfast. Then we figure the best way to take him out so that it doesn't rebound on us."

"My thoughts exactly," said Adric. "I don't care if it takes a month or two. In fact, that might be good. He's a fae. He'll think we're too stupid—or afraid—to come after him."

Zuri fingered his quartz. "The night fae compound is in Virginia, but Tyrus spends most of his time at his lair in France. We'll have to catch him outside. The night fae guard their lairs with triple wards."

"So we catch him outside," said Jace. "Drag him into the noonday sun and keep him there until his fucking skin fries."

"First, we need more intel," Adric said, "including exactly where his lair is."

"Do Mar will tell us," Jace said. "He has as much skin in this game as we do."

"Good." Adric looked around the table. "Well? You in?"

They nodded as one. "Fuck yeah," Luc said.

"You're elected, then," Adric told him.

Jace made a sound of dissent, and Adric slashed him a look. "We need you here to work on the smartphones."

"They'll keep for a few weeks."

"Do you really want to be out of the country if he sends someone after Merry? We're not even a hundred percent sure he's in France."

Jace blew out a breath. Adric was right; he'd rather stay close for now. "Fine," he said, even though his animal was scraping against his insides, coldly eager to go hunting.

Adric turned back to Luc. "Take Nash with you."

"Nash Savonett?" Luc lifted a shaggy black brow. "You sure?" Nash was Leron's youngest son.

Adric nodded. "He's shaping up to be an excellent tracker, and he's earned it.

It's been six years, and he's proved his loyalty to me. It's time we gave him a chance to work his way up the hierarchy."

"What about Kane?" Jace asked. "He's not going to be happy if you pass him over for his younger brother."

"Then he can prove himself the way his brother has. He works hard, but he plays both sides. I don't trust him with a covert job like this."

Zuri cleared his throat. "There's one more thing. You were right, Jace—you heard a third man that night you were attacked. Do Mar doesn't know who it is, but he had the scent of an earth fada."

CHAPTER 12

Adric loped across the broken-down Westside neighborhood he called home. A third of the houses were boarded up or turned into squats for junkies. But there were families here too—a tricycle was overturned on a small, neatly-kept lawn, and two women sat on a stoop, a toddler between them.

A man with a gangster tat on his neck strutted down the sidewalk, all broad shoulders and attitude. Then he got a closer look and continued past, eyes down. Adric was the most dangerous predator around, and everyone knew it.

Adric rented the house above his den to a pair of baby-faced drug dealers barely out of their teens. The older one leaned against the porch rail, arms crossed, a cigarillo hanging out of his mouth.

"Wassup, bro."

Adric jerked his chin. The drug dealers were camouflage—no one would guess the Baltimore alpha lived here—but he was thinking it was time he cleaned up the neighborhood like Jace had.

The teenager's flat brown eyes tracked him as he headed around the house. He pulled up the trap door concealed beneath the back porch and loped down the two flights of stairs to his den. As he entered the living room, the motion triggered the quartz wall sconces he'd installed when he and Marjani had first moved in.

The den had belonged to a family who had been completely wiped out in the Darktime, but Adric didn't think about that. Not anymore. It was his home now, the first since his parents had died and he and Marjani had been sent to live with their uncle. Leron's den had never felt like home.

The wall sconces cast a warm amber light over his sister, curled up on a rug in front of the fireplace. She was in her cougar form again. She'd turned on the fake fire—also quartz-powered—and was gazing into it, eyes slit. The flickering firelight turned her pelt a soft gold, but it couldn't conceal her weight loss or that her fur was patchy with ill health.

Adric blew out a breath. Sometimes an entire day went by without his sister taking her human form.

"Did you eat today?"

Her head lifted, turned. Cool blue eyes examined him as if he were an annoying insect.

He clenched his hands, feeling helpless. "You have to eat, Jani."

She tilted her head, considering that.

His claws pricked his palms, his cat wanting to slash something. He drew a slow breath and retracted them.

"You can't go on like this. You didn't go out the whole weekend. Jace asked for you. He almost died, you know. Would it have killed you to pay him a visit?"

That got through to her. She'd always liked Jace. Her furry gold brow knit, and she yowled a question.

"He's fine," Adric replied. "He was back at work today."

She set her head back on her paws. Discussion closed.

He let out a growl of frustration. Marjani was one step away from becoming feral, lost in her animal—and forever lost to him. Because he'd have to put her down if she became truly wild. He couldn't have a feral cougar with her intelligence roaming Baltimore.

He fingered his quartz, tempted. He was one of the rare fada with two Gifts. He was a tracker, one of the best in the world. But he had another, secret Gift— the ability to hypnotize others with his quartz.

Marjani was one of the few people who knew about his second Gift. He could hypnotize her, compel her to forget what had happened last year. But she'd made him promise that he wouldn't.

"No," she'd snarled when he'd suggested it. "This is me. My life. I need to deal with it. You can't make everything better, Ric—not this time."

For Marjani, he'd break a sworn vow, even if the backlash killed him. But she was the one who'd extracted the vow, and that was what stopped him.

He dropped onto the rug. It was a plush orange shag like something from the sixties, one of his few indulgences. He'd installed it as much for Marjani as for himself—a reward for the times they'd shivered all night in some boarded-up house, or crouched in the chilly rain because Leron had ordered them to stand watch.

He sat cross-legged and stared into the fire. The fake flames danced, bright flickers of warmth. Even in the summer, their cats craved heat.

"I need you, Jani. I need all four of my lieutenants. There's something I'm not seeing. Lord Prick was behind Jace's attack, but it looks like he might've been working with one of us."

He swallowed something acrid. He'd done some terrible things to end the Darktime, including assassinating his own uncle rather than challenge him to a duel for alpha. But he hadn't been able to risk losing. Leron had been out of control, and Adric was the only one strong enough to take him. It was either kill Leron, or see everyone he loved die.

When he'd first taken over as alpha, he'd cleaned up the last pockets of resistance and declared the Darktime over. Most of their elders were dead, and the ones that weren't either swore allegiance to Adric—or were executed. That should've been the end of it. He'd turned his attention to rebuilding his ragged, war-torn clan, believing he had the full support of his remaining clanmates.

But six years later, he was still fighting an underground conflict that he suspected had been instigated by his own cousin, Corban Savonett. Marjani's attack had been carried out by some rogue river fada—but the rogues had been working with some of Adric's own people.

Corban had never accepted Adric as alpha. He believed that as Leron's oldest son, he should've been made alpha after his death, but the fada didn't work like that. An alpha had to earn the title. And strength wasn't enough; an alpha needed his people's respect, too.

Corban had challenged Adric anyway, and lost. But even though Adric had made his cousin a high-ranking sentry, a position just under his four lieutenants, Corban hadn't given up. Instead, the bastard had struck at Adric's weak spot—Marjani. His sister was strong—a hard-ass soldier—but they'd drugged her and smashed her quartz so she couldn't fight back.

Adric's fingers curled. If he'd had any proof that Corban was behind it, he'd have slit the bastard's throat, but his cousin was too smart to get caught. He hid behind others, and every single one of them had either died or killed themselves before Adric could question them.

He gazed broodingly at Marjani's silent form. He questioned his decision to let Corban go every day. Every single fucking day.

But—"I couldn't execute Corban without proof," he told her. "I swore when I became alpha things would be different." Plus, Corban and his brothers were still a power in the clan. Adric had been afraid that if he pushed too hard, he'd set off another clan war.

So instead, he'd sent Corban out of the country on a job for the ice fae, after first forcing his cousin to swear he wouldn't come back until the job was complete. Corban was to capture a rogue ice fae and return her to her king for justice. Corban would be lucky to come back alive, and they both knew it. A powerful ice fae could literally freeze you where you stood. They fed on the energy of motion, meaning they could stop your heart, your lungs...or simply lock your muscles in place until you died of starvation.

Marjani's head swung toward Adric. His breath hitched. She was listening.

He hurried back into speech. "If only we knew what the fuck happened to Corban. But he's gone missing. I can't even raise him through his quartz. He could be dead—but I don't think so."

And why wasn't the ice fae king more concerned? Sindre had listened to Adric's explanation with an inscrutable expression and then said, "The agreement is void, then."

Adric had inclined his head, relieved Sindre wasn't demanding he send another man out on what amounted to a suicide mission. But it was damned odd. Sindre was an old, cold fae, and the fae had a thing about honoring a contract. The king should've been out for blood, but instead he'd given up with barely a protest.

Marjani rose to her feet, gave herself a shake and padded out of the room.

"Jani?" he asked, but she didn't acknowledge him. Disappointed, he scrubbed a hand over his face. He was so damned tired.

But a short while later, she returned, a woman once again. She paused a few feet away and gazed down at him with shadowed eyes. She'd put on gray shorts and a T-shirt. Once, she'd worn bright, colorful clothes like Suha. And just the other day, he'd come home to find she'd given herself a buzz-cut.

But she was up, and the eyes gazing down at him were the rich brown of her human form. For now, that was enough.

She stuck her hands into the back pockets of her shorts. He'd thought she was too thin as a cougar, but this was shocking. Her arms and legs were bony brown sticks.

His breath whistled in. He rose to his feet, trying to conceal his dismay.

Marjani didn't seem to notice. When she spoke, her voice was rusty from disuse. "Tell me what you know."

CHAPTER 13

Monday evening found Jace on his way up to Grace Harbor. Suha would bitch that he was doing too much, but Merry was worried about him, and if Jace could ease that by visiting her, then he would.

He reached the Grace Harbor exit and tried not to think about Evie. But his jaguar was more basic. It perked up, flexing its claws and vibrated its throat in an instinctive mating vocalization. A picture of Evie formed in his mind—shiny blond cap of hair, big dark eyes and that tight muscle tee cupping small but perfect breasts.

"Yeah, yeah," Jace muttered. "But we're here to see Merry, remember?"

The cat settled. The cub came first. But after...

Jace headed west until he reached the narrow dirt road that led to Rock Run. Two minutes after he crossed the line into Rock Run's territory, two large men on motorcycles appeared on the next hill. They zoomed down the incline toward him, leaving a cloud of dust in their wake.

Jace stopped his bike at the top of the hill. He was in a lush old-growth forest, the Susquehanna River visible over the treetops to the north. The big river undulated in the late afternoon sun, a wide ribbon of bronze and gold. To his left, Rock Run Creek snaked through the greenery on its way to the Susquehanna.

The Rock Run men skidded to a stop a few yards way: Tiago do Rio and Chico Nobrega. The alpha had sent his own brother, and Nobrega was Tiago's best friend and a Rock Run sentry.

"Peace to you and yours." Jace raised a hand in greeting. "I came to see my niece."

"Peace," Tiago returned. "But this isn't your scheduled day." Both men were dark, good-looking Latinos, but Tiago was a younger copy of his brother Dion—big, broad and arrogant with a mane of black hair tied back with a leather thong and blue eyes so light they appeared almost silver.

"Do Mar knows why I couldn't come on Saturday," Jace returned.

And if Rui do Mar knew, then Dion knew, which meant Tiago was giving him a hard time for the hell of it. Jace's jaw tightened, but he kept his posture relaxed, nonthreatening. He'd put up with worse to see Merry.

Tiago's gaze raked over Jace. "I hear you ran into some trouble the other night."

"I did. You wouldn't happen to know anything about it, would you?"

It was Tiago's turn to tighten his jaw. "Is that what you think?"

Jace shook his head, because this wasn't worth a pissing contest. And if Rui was correct, an earth fada was to blame, possibly one from Jace's own clan. He was still reeling over that piece of information.

He gave Tiago the same response he'd given Adric. "If you wanted to take me out, you'd do it yourself, not hire a fae."

Nobrega's eyes creased with amusement. "He's got a point, Ti."

Tiago's tension eased. His mouth quirked. "If you think I'd dare harm a hair on that pretty head of yours, you don't know your niece. She'd have my effing balls. Come on, then." He turned his bike and roared off toward the base.

"Pretty head?" Jace muttered. But he followed at a matching pace.

Nobrega fell in behind, hemming Jace between the two of them. A not-so veiled threat.

They were deep in the forest now, passing through huge old oaks, beeches, sycamores and maples. The path narrowed until they were nearly brushing the vegetation on either side: lush fiddlehead ferns, tiny pawpaw trees, a stand of mountain laurel. Jace had never seen the inside of the Rock Run base—Dion had drawn the line at that. Instead, he met Merry in the woods at the edge of the river fada's territory. It suited them both. Sometimes they ran as their jaguars; sometimes they walked as humans.

Tiago stopped near an ancient tulip poplar with a double trunk that twisted its way through the leafy green canopy, one trunk mirroring the other in a slow, ponderous dance. Jace pulled up next to him. "Thanks for the escort," he drawled as he set his bike's kickstand.

Tiago gave him a thumbs-up. "Anytime."

Merry was waiting in a clearing with Rui do Mar. She was thirteen-and-a-half now, all arms and legs in shorts and a tank top in her new favorite color—lipstick red. It was obvious she was a quarter fae; she had the sharp chin and pointed ears. But she had Takira's hazel eyes and crinkly black curls, and sometimes she did something that was so like her mom that it took Jace's breath away.

Merry spotted Jace and her face lit up. She sprang across the clearing, graceful as a leggy young deer, while her adoptive father followed at a slower pace.

Jace enfolded her in his arms. "Hey, baby."

"I was so worried about you, Uncle Jace." She hugged him back and pressed her face into his chest.

He ran his hand over her head. Her cheeks were wet when she lifted her face.

"Yo, none of that." He looked helplessly at her dad.

Do Mar was a large man with shoulders the width of a door and the cold eyes of his shark. Jace was never going to warm up to him, but the man would stop a bullet for Merry. The Rock Run second stared back with his usual stony expression, but a muscle jumped in his jaw.

"I told her you probably used up one of your nine lives," he said, "but that means you still have a couple left."

Merry rolled her eyes at her dad. But the joke worked, because she stopped crying.

Jace reached around her to clasp the other man's hand. "Thanks for letting me see her."

Do Mar tugged one of Merry's curls. "She asked," he said simply and then added, "I'm going to stick around today. Just in case."

The two of them exchanged a look over her head. The first year, either Rui or Valeria had always been there when Jace visited, but over time, they'd trusted him to be alone with Merry. That trust hadn't been easy for them, and Jace appreciated it. But he didn't fault Rui for sticking close today. Hell, if the shoe were on the other foot, he'd do the same.

Merry gave a last sniff. Jace swiped the backs of his fingers down her cheek. "I'm hard to kill, you know that."

Her slim dark brows snapped together. "No, you aren't. You almost died. I felt it—here." She touched her neck, where a shard of his own quartz hung next to hers. Six years ago, he'd broken off the piece to save her life at a time she'd been dangerously weak, and she'd kept it even after she'd found her own.

"But I didn't. Now give me a smile." He slung his arm around her narrow shoulders.

She crinkled her nose at him and then giggled when he waggled his brows at her. They started walking, following a path along the creek. Do Mar trailed at a distance, allowing them privacy but keeping them in sight.

"School's out," Merry said, "so I went fishing with Mama Ria this morning. I used my jaguar to scare the bass into her net."

"Poor bass."

"She says she catches twice as much fish when I come along."

"I'll bet she does." He squeezed her shoulders.

This. This was what he wanted for Merry—a safe, happy life with people who loved her. It tore him up that he couldn't give it to her himself. Cubs were everything to the fada, and he was her only living relative.

For two long years, he'd thought Merry was dead—and then she'd turned up at Rock Run. At first, he'd have done anything to bring her home. When Valeria and Rui had refused to give her back, he and Adric had tried to kidnap her back. But in the end, Jace hadn't been able to go through with it. Merry barely remembered him. Valeria and Rui were her parents now.

Adric hadn't wanted to leave Merry with the river fada. The clan needed their children; they'd lost so many in the Darktime. But he'd allowed Jace to make the final decision, and Jace had left her with Rock Run, even though it had gutted him to do it.

It had been the right thing to do. She had a whole family now—Rui and Valeria had had two more children since adopting Merry—and the powerful Rock Run Clan behind her. All Jace could offer her was a den with five males and a place in a dirt-poor clan that might never fully accept a mixed-blood, whatever Adric might say.

Merry wrapped a wiry arm around his waist and rested her head on his shoulder. "I've been practicing with my quartz."

"Good girl. You can show me what you learned next time."

She nodded. She understood that the lessons between them were private. When she was younger, she'd run to Valeria with every new skill she mastered. Some things were instinctive, like soaking up energy from vibration of the crystals. But there were tricks to using the energy—how to focus it to heal yourself, or turn it outward to make a shield—and for those, she was sworn to secrecy.

When she turned sixteen, he'd teach her the final, dangerous secret, but Adric had to be present for that.

Merry slanted him a grin. "Do you know how to tell a smallmouth bass from a largemouth?"

"Uh—count their teeth?"

She bumped her hip against his. "No, silly."

And she proceeded to give him a lesson about something called a maxillary, a large flap on a bass's upper jaw, which apparently extended further on the largemouth than the smallmouth. There was something in there about vertical and lateral stripes, too—Jace didn't catch which belonged to which. He was just enjoying being with his niece.

He stayed an hour, and then reluctantly took his leave.

Do Mar sent Merry into the base. The two of them watched as she trotted off.

The air snagged in Jace's chest. He made himself say the words, because do Mar deserved to hear them. "You're doing a good job with her. Her mother—Takira—would've been so damn proud."

"My mate deserves the credit. Without her..." Do Mar grimaced. "I was in a dark place, that first year after I brought Merry home. I don't know what would've happened to her if not for Valeria."

Jace nodded. He didn't know the details, but he'd heard do Mar had gone into a bad place for a while where his best friend was a wine bottle. Jace didn't judge; he'd been tempted a few times himself.

"I know, and I've thanked Valeria, too. But you're Merry's dad, a good one."

Do Mar slanted him a fierce glance. "I love her like she's my own daughter."

"I know. I should've thanked you before this."

"No thanks necessary. She is my joy." The other man swallowed hard. "I want you to know she's been under close observation. She will not be outside our wards without at least two guards as protection. So even if her grandfather's ward fails, she is safe. This, I promise you."

"That's good to know." It sucked, to know that his niece was safer at Rock Run than with him in Baltimore, but he'd made his peace with it. "You'll keep me informed if anything changes?"

"Of course."

After that, Jace should've gone back to Baltimore. He was tired and his wounds were starting to protest all the running around he was doing, but both he and his jaguar needed to make sure Evie was okay.

So Jace joined the sentry assigned to guard Evie and her brother. Suha was going to bite his head off, but if she had her way, he'd still be in bed.

The sentry reported that everything was quiet. "The woman went out for groceries—I heard her telling her brother—and the kid's at the high school shooting hoops with his friends." He jerked his chin in the direction of the schoolyard on the next block.

"I'll look around anyway." Jace took a stroll through town to satisfy himself there was no hint of the night fae or the mysterious earth fada. Everything seemed quiet, but he still wasn't satisfied. Grace Harbor might not be big, but it had a population of over ten thousand—plenty big enough for a man to hide in. If something happened to Evie or her brother, he'd never forgive himself.

He waited with the sentry in the shadow of the warehouse across the alley until Evie pulled up in a rusty blue car. His chest rumbled in a purr, his jaguar happy just to be near her.

He watched as she gathered her groceries and headed up the back steps. She paused on the stoop to glance around, and his whole body snapped alert. Both man and cat wanted to go closer...to talk with her, fill his nostrils with her scent. Find out if her skin was as soft as it looked.

But it was best he stayed away. The Darktime had left him scarred, bitter. He'd lost too many people—his parents, his sister, good friends. Even his niece was being raised by another man. And he'd killed—because he'd had no choice. Those grim years were a part of him, however much he wanted to forget them.

He liked women, enjoyed the release of sex, but other than that, he walked alone—and he could count the number of people he trusted on one hand.

No, Evie wasn't for him. He'd guard her, make sure he hadn't accidentally dragged her into whatever had sparked the attack on him. Nothing more.

Because on top of everything else, he didn't do humans, and he especially didn't do humans who were part fae.

The sentry sent him a curious look and Jace forced himself to turn away. He faded further back into the shadows. He waited until Kyler was safely home, and then headed back to Baltimore.

But the next night he was back.

CHAPTER 14

*E*vie stopped her car on the pad behind her house and turned off the ignition. The ancient compact shuddered and then went ominously silent. She muttered something dark. The car wasn't long for this world. Somehow she'd have to find the cash for a new one.

It was Saturday night, nine days since she'd found Jace bleeding in her backyard. Not for the first time, she wondered how he was doing—and then scowled and told herself he was fine, and probably back doing whatever it was he did.

She grabbed her backpack and got out of the car. The house was dark except for the light she'd left on over the back door. Kyler must still be at Ben's house. At least she hoped that was where he was, because he hadn't bothered to check in with her—again. He'd been pushing her all week, "forgetting" to check in and then coming home way after his curfew.

"School's almost out," he'd said. "All we're doing is taking finals, and I'm allowed to go in late."

"You'd do better on your tests if you had a good night sleep."

"Relax," he returned in a tone that had Evie tightening her jaw. "I've got practically a four-point average." And he did, so what could she say?

Now she glanced at her phone—it was after midnight. He should be home, damn it. And he hadn't left a message either.

She sighed and slung her backpack over one shoulder, flipping her keys so that the tips stuck out between her knuckles. If someone attacked her, she was going to be ready.

Evie was almost at the steps when her nape tingled in an eerie repeat of last Thursday. *Someone was watching her.* She gripped her keys and glanced around.

Across the alley, a pair of luminous green eyes stared at her, unblinking, from the shadows.

Her heart kicked into a gallop. "Jace? Is that you?"

Please let it be him.

He stepped forward. She blew out a breath. It *was* Jace.

He crossed the alley in a few long, loose strides. An atavistic tremor went down her spine. This was the real Jace—and he was nothing like the injured, feverish victim of last week.

No, this man was dark. Powerful. Raw-boned. A panther in a T-shirt and jeans.

She squared her shoulders and lifted her chin, because damn it, she'd saved the man's life. She refused to let him spook her.

He stopped a few feet away. "Hello, Evie."

He was bigger than she remembered, but then, last week he'd been hunched over nursing his injuries. Now she realized he was a good half foot taller than her with the lean, hard build of a soldier. Another shiver went down her spine—but this one had nothing to do with fear.

She swallowed. "You're better?" She glanced at his stomach, although the wounds were covered by the shirt.

"Suha thinks I should still be in bed, but yeah, I'm much better."

"Suha?" Evie felt a pinch of jealousy, which she immediately stomped on. Why should she be jealous? She barely knew the man.

"Our head healer. She knows her stuff, but she's one tough mother, you know?"

Evie pictured an older, somewhat overprotective woman and smothered a smile. "Seriously? You let her boss you?"

"Better than listening to her nagging. She's so calm and reasonable—and she makes you feel like a shit if you don't take her advice. But we're lucky to have her. We lost our last healer in the Dark—" He halted.

Evie flashed on those stories about the murderous Baltimore shifters and glanced away, somehow sure she didn't want to know.

"Anyway," Jace said, "I came to see how you are."

"Me?" Her eyes narrowed as she recalled how he'd acted when Adric had accused her of being part fae. The man had *growled* at her. "Aren't you afraid I'll bewitch you or something?"

"No." Shame flashed across his face. "I'm sorry about that. You helped me, and you didn't deserve that in return."

She shrugged. "I would've done the same for anyone." And he *had* stood up for her with Adric. From what she knew about the fada, the alpha was king, so that meant something.

He stepped closer, a slow, graceful ripple of his muscles. "Would you? Have done the same for anyone?"

Her mouth dried. "Yes."

Their gazes snagged and Jace smiled—not with his lips, but with his eyes. The corners creased in a way that made her stomach flip. "You have a good heart."

She smoothed her hands down her pants, painfully aware that she was still dressed in her server uniform—straight black slacks and a white button-up shirt. And she probably smelled funky; it had been a busy night at the restaurant.

He fiddled with the hoop in her left earlobe. "But you should be more careful, living alone with only a young kid like your brother."

"I've known most of the neighbors for years. We look out for each other."

"Yeah? That's good. I'm glad you have someone, at least."

As if on cue, Mrs. Linney's stoop light went on three houses down and she stepped out her back door dressed in flip flops and an outsized neon-green nightgown. Jace immediately stepped back from Evie and tucked the quartz pendant out of sight beneath his T-shirt.

Mrs. Linney lit a cigarette and peered at them over the top of cat's-eye glasses. "'Evening, hon. You're out late."

"I just got off work."

"Ah..." The older woman blew a perfect smoke ring and then narrowed her eyes at Jace. "Don't I know you from somewhere?"

Evie concealed a grin. Not much happened on their block that Mrs. Linney didn't know about.

"No, ma'am," he responded. "I don't believe so."

"This is a friend of mine," Evie said. "Jace—" She realized she didn't know his last name.

"Jones." He nodded politely to the older woman. "Good to meet you."

Evie glanced from him to her neighbor's curious face and made up her mind. "We were just on our way inside," she told Mrs. Linney. "Tell Mr. Linney I said hi."

She grabbed her backpack and headed up the steps, Jace following. Inside, she flipped on the kitchen light and shot him a rueful smile. "That's our version of a neighborhood watch. I swear the woman never sleeps."

"I don't mind. For all she knew, I was some strange man looking for trouble."

"I do feel safer knowing she's keeping an eye on things." Evie opened the refrigerator. "Want a beer? Or I have ice tea if you'd rather."

"Beer, please."

She got out two cans and handed him one. He glanced curiously around the kitchen while she took a sip of her beer. It was ice-cold, just what she needed. She leaned against the counter and let out a breath, tired to her very toes.

Jace frowned. "You work too hard."

She moved a shoulder. "It's the weekend. I run my ass off but I make a ton of tips."

"When will you graduate from nursing school?"

"In two or three years. I just started."

He shook his head. "It's too much."

"Maybe, but it's worth it." She set the can on the counter. "Why are you here, Jace? I thought you lived in Baltimore."

"I do, but I come up pretty often. My niece lives near here, and the clan is mining across the river."

"Mining what?" she asked curiously.

"Quartz. This whole area sits on a thick vein of quartz. That's why radios and cell phones sometimes can't get a signal—the quartz blocks it."

"But what do you do with quartz other than wear it around your neck?"

"We make things with it." He took a gulp of beer, clearly done with the subject. "Anyway, I wanted to let you know we had someone watching you and Kyler all week, and there's been no sign of the night fae."

"You had someone watching us?" She frowned, not sure how she felt about that.

"Just as a precaution. You don't know the night fae."

She recalled the cold, malevolent presence that had come to her door and decided to be grateful. "I have to admit, that guy creeped me out. In fact, that's why I drove to work—normally I just walk or ride my bike."

His brows knit. "At midnight?"

"It's a small town."

"Your brother should pick you up at night."

"What would he do against a night fae?"

"Nothing. But there are human predators, too."

She rubbed her nape. "Look, I'm careful."

Jace pressed his lips together but let it go. "Well, you don't have to worry. He must know I'm back in Baltimore."

"You know who it was?"

"Yeah, but it's better if you don't know. Besides, saying a fae's name aloud can draw their attention."

"Right." Evie recalled hearing that somewhere, although with the fae you never knew what was real and what was myth.

Jace finished his beer and set it in the kitchen sink. "How long have you lived in Grace Harbor?"

"Since I was eight. My mom and dad bought this house." Or rather her dad had—right before he left for good.

"But it's just you and your brother?"

"Yeah. Mom passed a couple of years ago, and who knows where my dad is?"

His eyes flickered. "I'm sorry about your mom. That's too young."

Evie swallowed. "Yeah." That's what she thought, too; your mom wasn't supposed to die before you were out of your twenties. "It is."

"So your dad's the one who's part fae?"

"I guess. If I'm part fae, it must've come from him."

She'd had a week to get used to the idea. She supposed it could be true. Fane was tall and blond like the local sun fae—and gorgeous, even if he was her dad. He could be a mixed-blood. Her mom had never really gotten over him, although she'd made a good life with Kyler's dad.

And Fane had a way of knowing things, like that her mom was on her deathbed.

"I'm sure it's just a trace," she added. "I mean look at me—no magic, no Gift."

Jace prowled closer. "You're beautiful like the fae."

Evie's pulse sped up, but she rolled her eyes. "Yeah, right." He was the one who was beautiful—a spare male beauty with high cheekbones and a firm, knowing mouth, his eyes a brilliant mix of gold and green and brown framed by those impossibly thick lashes.

"And your brother—Kyler?" he asked, just as if he weren't standing so close. "He hasn't seen or heard anything?"

"Not that he told me. He's at a friend's house right now—but you already know that."

He shrugged but didn't deny it. "I was standing guard outside the restaurant most of the night, but yeah, I checked in on Kyler a few times."

Those beautiful eyes were fixed on her mouth, making her lips tingle. She had the curious feeling they were having two conversations, one aloud, one silent.

"So there's no one else out there?"

"Just me tonight. We're pulling off the guard after this."

"Thank you."

Another silence. "So we're alone," he murmured.

"Yeah." She crossed her arms. "Should I be scared?"

His brows drew together. "Never. I'd never hurt you, Evie."

His scent filled her head. Warm and masculine. A bit spicy. Already she recognized it; she could be in a pitch-black room and she'd know it was Jace.

"Because I helped you."

"You know that's not the only reason." He was just two feet from her now.

Desire fluttered in her belly. Her fingers flexed on her arms. She itched to pull him closer. To run her lips over the golden-brown skin of his throat...taste him.

His nostrils flared. She had the uncomfortable feeling he could scent her reaction to him. But damn, it had been a long time. She didn't have time for a relationship, and she didn't do casual, especially with Kyler at such a tricky age.

She uncrossed her arms and gripped the counter behind her. *What had he said?* "Don't be scared." She gave a jerky nod. "Got it."

They stared at each other, and abruptly, the silent conversation became audible.

Jace's throat worked, the sound loud in the sudden hush.

Her heart pounded in her ears. She drew a jagged breath.

He stepped closer. Slowly, carefully, he framed her face with his palms. "I want to kiss you."

She set her hands on his chest. "Not yet."

"No?" His mouth brushed her cheek.

She shook her head. "I need to know one thing."

"What?" His warm lips moved to the side of her neck. His body radiated warmth. An answering heat slid through her, a slow, hot river that pooled in her belly.

"Who's Mary?"

The muscles under her hands went rigid. He pulled back. "How do you know about her?"

"You said her name—twice. When you were hurt."

"Oh." He relaxed. "My niece. Her name's M-E-R-R-Y like in Christmas. There's no one else, if that's what you're asking." Those warm lips were against her ear now. "Only you. I can't stop thinking about you. It's like you're under my fucking skin."

"I know—I mean, I can't stop thinking about you either." Her eyes drifted shut as his tongue traced the outer edge of her ear. "I'm busy," she said. "I don't have time—"

"I know." His teeth closed on her earlobe, and something dark and delicious flashed down her spine. "And I don't...you're a human—and a fae."

She stiffened, and then shrugged. Because how could she be insulted? She didn't want to get involved with him either, did she? "Yeah. Me and you...we don't—"

"Mix." He sucked at the turn of her shoulder.

She opened and closed her mouth—and stopped thinking.

His mouth moved up her neck, leaving rivulets of pleasure in its wake. Her head fell back. From far away, she heard herself moan.

"You're so soft," he said against the vulnerable underside of her throat. He rubbed his cheek against her and the rasp of his stubble was so damn erotic. She slid her hands up to his shoulders.

He stepped closer, his cock hard and powerful against her belly. Her leg bent of its own accord so that she could hitch herself up against him. That was better —now she could feel him right against her sex.

He slid his arms around her and fit his mouth to hers. His lips were warm and dry and tasted of beer and mint. He licked at the seam of her mouth, but when she opened to him, he didn't move his tongue inside, just lapped at the edges. Tiny tastes interspersed with little bites. Quick bursts of pleasure that had her digging her fingers into his shoulders.

"Jace."

"Mm?" His tongue moved inside, played with hers.

She sucked on it and he groaned. One hand came to her nape, holding her in place while the other gripped her ass, pulling her tight against him.

The kiss went on and on. The playful sensuality turned urgent. A pulse beat between Evie's thighs—there, where he was pressed, big and hard, the zipper of his jeans rasping over the seam of her pants.

He raised his head and they both dragged in a breath.

Evie pushed against his chest. "I—we have to stop. Kyler..."

Jace's lungs heaved. His heart slammed hard and fast beneath her palms. He nodded, his gaze on her mouth.

"He's going to be home any minute."

"Okay." He brushed his lips over hers and stepped back. He picked up her beer and offered it to her. As she took a gulp, he said, "We're going to finish that someday," with a little half-smile.

Something about that silky self-confidence made her womb clench. But hey, if it weren't for Kyler, Jace would be taking her up against the counter right now.

"Maybe," she returned. Now that he was a few feet away, common sense had returned, cool, pragmatic. Sometimes she hated how damn sensible she was.

She tilted her head. "Why *are* you here, Jace? Not for this." She waved a hand between the two of them.

"Don't be so sure about that." His gaze raked up and down her body. "But I did have another reason. Suha says the reason I healed so fast was because of you and your brother. If you wouldn't have flushed the iron out of the cuts so fast, I'd be dead. We take those things seriously. I owe you my life."

Her jaw tightened. She did *not* like where this was going. "No, you don't. Not the way I think you mean it. Like I told you guys last week, I would've done the same for anyone."

His face set. "Yes, I do." She went to say something and he raised a hand. "Let me explain. Here, I brought you this so you can contact me." He fished a quartz from his pocket and held it out to her.

She eyed it without touching it. It was a clear rose pink, flat on one side and a conglomerate of crystals on the other side. "A quartz? But what good is that to me?"

"It's a kind of a smartphone. If you need me for anything, you just tap it."

"A smartphone? But it's just a rock—a chunk of quartz."

"It's quartz engineered to be a phone. You tap here." He touched a small depression on the flat side and an orange light glowed on in the center. "Then just talk into it. It's set to contact me directly."

He tapped the depression again and the light turned off.

"How does it work?"

He moved a shoulder. "A mix of engineering and magic. It doesn't work for humans, but with your fae blood, you should be able to operate it. Try it and see." He offered it to her again.

When she still didn't take it, he took her hand and pressed the phone into her palm. "Please, Evie. We want to help you, me and Adric both. He—we—would've said something last week, but we wanted to give you a chance to cool down."

She pressed her lips together. "I don't need help."

"I thought you'd say that. But you don't have to use it, just keep it on you."

She stared down at the quartz in her palm. It was warmer than she'd expected.

"Try it," he urged. "Just once, so I know you understand how it works. You never have to use it again—but please, keep it with you at all times."

She blew out a breath. "If it will make you happy..." She touched the depression and the orange light came on.

"Speak into it." He tapped his own quartz.

She brought it to her mouth. "Earth to Jace," she said, and then jolted when her voice came out of his pendant.

"That's all you have to do," he said.

She shrugged and put the quartz into her back pocket. "Fine. But don't expect me to use it."

"I thought you'd say that, but you're wrong. You need help. You're trying to do everything yourself, and that's hard. I bet you're working two jobs and going to school."

"One and a half. And it's not forever."

"And your brother—where is he, anyway? Shouldn't he be home by now?"

She stiffened. "That's none of your business," she said evenly.

Jace expelled a breath. "Hell, I'm no good at this. But I want to help, Evie."

"I appreciate that, but it's not necessary."

"I had a sister," he told her. "Older than me, but just by a couple of years."

"*Had* a sister?"

He nodded, jaw rigid. "She was around your age when she died."

"I'm sorry. That sucks." The anger left her as quickly as it had come. She couldn't imagine life without Kyler. "So this is because I remind you of your sister?"

He huffed a laugh. "Hell no. Well, maybe. You may be a human, but you're tough. Nobody pushed Takira around—and she would've done anything for me, just like you and Kyler." He scraped a hand over his short black hair. "But I'm not looking for sympathy. I'm just telling you why I'd like to help."

"Thank you, but we're fine. Really."

"All right. But if you change your mind, I mean it—I'd like to help you, Evie."

She could've sworn she saw a flicker of pain in his eyes, but why would he care if she accepted his help? He was only there to repay a debt because apparently, his sense of honor demanded it.

He turned toward the door. "I'd better be going. Thanks for the beer."

"No problem." She chewed her lip. "Jace?"

Ask him, you chicken. Ask if he wants to see you again. Because her body was still humming, and she was afraid that when he left this time, it would be forever.

He swung back toward her. "What?"

The back door slammed open and Kyler burst inside. The two of them leapt away from each other.

"Evie?" He turned on Jace. "You *are* hitting on my sister. I didn't believe him."

Jace's head whipped around. "Believe who?"

"That guy outside. The one from your clan."

"My clan? I'm here alone." He turned to Evie, suddenly all soldier. "Use the phone. It will go to my quartz, but if I don't answer, it will route to Adric next. Tell him to get up here. Stat. And you, Kyler"—he stabbed a finger at her brother —"lock the door and don't open it for anyone but me or Adric."

Her brother's mouth dropped open. "What the fuck's going on?"

"That's what I'm going to find out. But I need you to stay in here with your sister. Can you do that?"

Kyler looked from him to Evie and then jerked his chin. "Yep."

"Good man." Jace clapped Kyler on the back.

To Evie he said, "You'll call Adric?"

"Yeah." She showed him the quartz phone already in her hand. Behind her, Kyler grabbed the baseball bat they kept in the pantry.

"Lock the door," Jace repeated, "but if someone breaks in, swing first. Your only chance is to take them by surprise."

Kyler tightened his grip on the bat. "I'm on it."

And then Jace was out the door.

CHAPTER 15

*J*ace hadn't meant to let Evie see him. He'd been there every night this week, blending into the shadows, and she'd never even suspected. But tonight, he'd known his eyes had gone night-glow in the dim light. He could've lowered his lids when she'd turned toward him.

Instead, he'd stared back. His heart had given a jubilant thump, his animal thrilled that she'd sensed him when she hadn't the night before or the night before that. And before he knew it, he was crossing the alley to her.

Talking to Evie, having a beer in her homey little kitchen, was a balm to a man who'd been raised on war and bloodshed. He'd reveled in the unaccustomed sense of peace, like lying in the grass on a summer day and watching the clouds drift by. And kissing her was even better. He could get addicted to this woman: her spicy mouth, that sexy dimple, the taut body that was a perfect fit for his...

Then Kyler burst in and jolted Jace out of his pleasant haze. Because he'd come up here alone, and if a man from the clan was outside without his knowledge, it meant trouble anyway you looked at it.

Now he halted on the stoop, scanning the area with his night vision. Behind him, he heard Kyler shoot home the deadbolt.

Good man.

The other fada had disappeared. So he didn't want to be seen. Jace's skin prickled.

A scrape of gravel. He narrowed his eyes. There—across the alley, right where he'd been standing.

The shadows near the wooden fence coalesced, became a large animal. A shaggy black wolf.

No. It couldn't be.

The wolf darted around the corner and disappeared.

Jace threw off his clothes and shifted to jaguar. As his animal, he could run faster and his senses were more acute, but he lost precious seconds in the shift. He shot out of the yard and around the corner in the wolf's wake. Tracking it in a sea of small-town scents wasn't easy, but he caught a wild, distinctive scent to the left and turned in that direction.

Two houses down, a dog's indignant yapping changed to a terrified whine. Jace swerved in its direction and bounded over a chain link fence. The dog was pressed against the back door of a small white house. At the sight of Jace's 250-pound jaguar, it whimpered and then peeled back its lips in a last, pitiful defense.

Jace ignored it to soar over the fence on the opposite side, hot on the wolf's trail.

He still couldn't quite believe it was Corban Savonett. The man was supposed to be dead. But Jace had known that scent since he was a cub.

When last heard from, Adric's cousin had been in the Himalayas tracking a rogue ice fae female—and then he'd disappeared, his quartz winking out along with him.

But it made sense. Corban was a sly SOB. If he couldn't beat Adric in a fair fight, it was just like him to try and take out his lieutenants.

Jace pounded after the huge black wolf. His jaguar was fast, but he hadn't regained his full strength yet. He began to flag, but then something odd happened —Corban slowed down, too.

The fur rose on Jace's nape. *Too easy.* With Corban's head start, he should've been able to easily shake Jace off.

Trap!

He swerved just as another earth fada appeared beside Corban, a cougar Jace didn't know. The two of them turned as one and charged Jace.

He went airborne, bounding sideways over a white picket fence. He was in a backyard with a wood playset. He ran up the slide and along the top bar and then launched himself onto the garage roof, hoping to confuse Corban. Wolves relied heavily on their sense of smell, especially at night.

Corban and the cougar raced into the yard, but Jace was already soaring off the other side of the garage. He hit the asphalt at a full run.

He considered his options. His main priority was Evie and Kyler, but even if he led Corban and his henchman away from their house, Corban knew where they lived. And Corban wouldn't give a damn about collateral damage, especially two humans.

Jace would have to stand and fight.

He headed for Susquehanna River and the small park that would be empty at this time of night. Thank the gods he knew Grace Harbor from his visits with Merry. For the first couple of years, this had been the only place the Rock Run fada had allowed the two of them to meet. Neutral territory, but close to the base.

Now Jace knew the perfect place to take a stand.

He reached the park and sprinted toward a stream that fed into the Susquehanna, Corban and the cougar right behind. He ran onto a footbridge that spanned the stream and whipped around to face them. The bridge was too narrow for them to both attack him. They'd have to take him on one at a time.

They skidded to a halt a few yards away. Two sets of gold eyes gazed at him. All three of them were panting hard.

He caught a good whiff of the cougar's scent and mentally raised a brow. A female—interesting. But then, Corban never seemed to have trouble attracting women, although why any female would align herself with a prick like Adric's cousin was a mystery to Jace.

Corban snarled a warning. *Surrender—or die.*

Jace curled his lip. Like the wolf would let him leave alive anyway. *Go fuck yourself.*

Corban gathered his muscles and leapt. Jace rose to meet him and they collided with a crash that would've broken the bones of any creature who wasn't a fada.

And damn, it hurt. Jace's breath left his lungs. Pain ripped through his almost-healed knife wounds. Suha wasn't going to be happy.

Then he stopped thinking and went for Corban's jugular. The wolf jerked right, but Jace got a mouthful of fur and blood.

Corban went for Jace's throat, silent and deadly. Meanwhile, the cougar had somehow slipped past Jace and was snapping at his hind legs.

Two against one wasn't fair, but then Corban had always fought dirty, even back when they'd been cubs and he was several years older and nearly twice Jace's weight.

But Jace wasn't a cub anymore—and he'd learned some dirty tricks of his own.

He slashed at the cougar's face with a hind leg, claws extended. She yelped and jumped back. Jace dodged Corban as he lunged a second time for Jace's throat. He slid past the wolf and then turned and sank his teeth into Corban's hind leg.

His jaguar's long, curved canines were powerful enough to pierce a skull. He sliced through muscle above the hock and crunched against bone.

The wolf's furious snarl split the night. He struck wildly at Jace, biting whatever he could reach—Jace's face, his shoulder.

Jace released Corban's leg to go for a killing bite to the neck, only to have the cougar leap on his back. Sharp canines sliced into his nape. He ignored the pain to slam her against the bridge's metal railing. She released his nape and fell to the wooden planks, unconscious.

Jace turned toward Corban, but the coward was racing off as fast as he could on three legs. Jace looked after him, chest heaving, itching to chase him down but knowing it wasn't worth it. From the amount of blood he'd left behind, Corban wouldn't try anything else tonight.

Meanwhile, Jace had Evie and Kyler to protect, and on top of that, he was bleeding from several places himself.

He hissed a cat's version of a curse after the wolf's retreating figure and turned to the cougar. Adric would want to question her.

Shifting back to man, he tapped his quartz. The alpha answered immediately; Evie must have gotten through to him. "On my way," he said over the muted roar of a motorcycle.

"We've got a situation here." Jace explained what had happened.

When he got to Corban, the alpha snarled. "I *knew* the bastard wasn't dead—that would be too fucking simple. I want to talk to that female. I don't care how you do it, but make sure she doesn't leave."

"That's what I thought. But your cousin—what if he goes after Evie and her brother? He knows I was there."

Jace didn't have to spell it out. They both knew Corban wouldn't give a damn if innocents got hurt, especially humans.

"Fuck. What the hell were you doing there, anyway? No, don't answer that. You can explain when I get there."

"I'll meet you at Evie's house. I'll bring the cougar with me."

"I'll be there in twenty minutes." Adric ended the connection.

The cougar's eyelids fluttered. Jace knelt on the bridge to check her for injuries. Other than a gash on her head, she was all right. In fact, his injuries were worse.

He wrapped his hand around her quartz; lightly, but she felt it all right. She tensed and opened her eyes, her upper lip twitching in an attempt at a snarl.

"Shift," he ordered. "Now."

She growled weakly.

"Maybe I'm not being clear. You don't have a choice." He tightened his grip on her pendant.

She jerked in pain. Deep within, he sensed its panicked vibrations, echoing its wearer's terror. You didn't touch anyone's quartz without their permission, and even then, only a close relation or a lover could wrap a hand around it without causing a deep, visceral discomfort.

He was being a bastard, but he didn't fucking care. The fada who'd kidnapped Marjani had smashed her quartz to bits. This woman might not have been part of that, but she'd attacked Jace for no reason other than Corban's say-so. Worse, she was a threat to Evie and Kyler.

The cougar whimpered. He let up on the pressure but kept the quartz in his palm. "*Shift.*"

Deep within, a single point of silver glowed to life, then another and another. Jace added a small portion of his energy to hers. He was the stronger, but his quartz was still being drained of energy to heal him, both from his earlier iron poisoning and now the cuts Corban and this female had inflicted during the fight. He'd give her an energy boost, but she could drain her own damn quartz to shift.

Silver and blue and purple sparkles spread over the cougar's fur, and then a naked woman was curled up on the bridge, chest heaving, her hair a wild tangle around her shoulders.

Jace released her quartz and grabbed her arm. "Don't even think about running. Understand?"

She growled, but nodded. He rose to his feet, bringing her with him.

She was tall and curvy. Jace took in her body with clinical detachment; shifters were used to seeing each other in their skins. He was more concerned about getting a naked woman back to Evie's without some asshat human calling the cops.

The woman touched the side of her head. "Hurts."

She was telling the truth, and yet he sensed the lie beneath. She wasn't as injured as she was pretending.

He hardened his jaw. "What's your name?"

She pressed her lips together. Names had power in their world.

He jerked her close and slid a finger over her quartz.

Her eyes flashed angrily. She knocked his hand away and wrapped her own fingers around the quartz, protecting it. "Nika," she gritted.

"That's better." He took a firm hold of her upper arm. "Let's go."

Their mad dash through Grace Harbor had taken the form of a large circle. They'd ended up just a few blocks from Evie's house.

Jace hurried the woman through the night, keeping an eye out for both the cops and Corban, although Jace was pretty sure the wolf would have to go to ground. Even with the help of his quartz, that leg of his was going to take a few days to heal.

They reached Evie's house without incident. Jace marched his captive up the steps and tapped on the back door with his free hand. "Evie? It's me, Jace."

She did a double take when she saw him standing there naked, bloodied, and with a tall, curvy, and very naked female. "What the—"

"I'll explain—just let me in, please."

She hesitated another few seconds and then stepped back. "Come in."

"Thanks." Jace strong-armed his captive into the kitchen. "Do you have any rope?"

Evie started to nod, then her eyes widened. "You want to tie her up?"

"She attacked me, Evie. I promise I won't hurt her—I just want to keep her quiet until Adric arrives."

The shift had healed both his and Nika's superficial cuts, but he was still bleeding from the claw marks on his face, shoulder, and thigh, and Nika's face had a deep gash from the blow he'd struck with his hind claws. Evie's gaze flicked to the blood on Jace's face to Nika's, and then she opened the door to the pantry.

"I think I have something in here..."

While he was gone, she'd changed into a purple tank top and loose gray shorts that stopped halfway down her thighs, exposing a length of strong, shapely legs. He eyed her calves as she rummaged in the pantry for rope and silently wished Nika back beneath whatever rock she'd crawled out from under.

"Is there anything I can do?" Kyler asked. To the kid's credit, after one quick look at Nika, he'd kept his eyes on her face.

Jace nodded. "Get her a towel or something to cover up with."

"Right." The teenager jogged upstairs and returned a minute later with a large beach towel and a pair of gym shorts for Jace.

Jace wrapped the towel around Nika and pulled out a chair. He twirled it to face him. "Sit."

While she obeyed, he dragged on the shorts. His own clothes were still outside where he'd dropped them, but he wasn't going to open the door until Adric got here. He didn't think Corban would try anything until his leg healed, but he wasn't going to take any chances with Evie and Kyler.

He snagged a paper towel. "Give me your quartz," he ordered Nika.

Her claws slid out. "And if I say no?"

He locked gazes with her. He couldn't risk Nika changing to her cougar. With her teeth and claws, she could do serious damage to a human within seconds. "You don't want to play games with me."

She snarled but gave in, conceding Jace the silent contest. As he'd suspected, he was several degrees dominant to her. She scowled and dragged off the quartz, setting it on the towel. He wrapped it carefully and stowed it in his pocket.

Nika wound the beach towel more tightly around herself and slumped in the chair.

Good. She wasn't going to try anything without her quartz. She wouldn't even attempt to escape. An earth fada could survive without a quartz, but no one would do it willingly. It was like having a vise around your chest. You couldn't breathe as well, you had less energy. You could make do with another quartz, but finding the perfect match, a quartz that resonated with you on a magical level, could take weeks.

Jace leaned against the counter and examined his captive. She had red hair and unusually pale skin for an earth fada.

She stared back impassively. "You have sent for Lord Adric?" It was the longest sentence she'd said yet. For the first time, he realized she had a foreign accent—Russian or some other Slavic country. Where the hell had Corban found her, anyway?

"Yeah." Jace glanced at the kitchen clock. "He should be here any minute."

Fear etched her face.

"I see you've heard of him."

"Of course." She smoothed her expression, but he scented her rising dread. "He is well known."

Jace nodded. Earth fada weren't as prolific as the water fada; there were only a dozen clans scattered around the world. The Baltimore clan had come to Maryland about fifty years ago by way of Jamaica and the Persian Gulf. Adric might be the youngest alpha, but his reputation as a ruthless SOB had quickly spread.

"You entered Adric's territory," Jace said, "and attacked one of his own people. I'd say you were asking to meet him."

She moved a shoulder, her gaze on the floor.

"And Nika?" He leaned closer. "Everything you've heard about him is true."

She remained silent but a fine tremor went down her spine. He grinned evilly and came upright to find Kyler eyeing him with a mixture of horror and respect. He winked at the lanky kid over the top of Nika's head.

Evie exited the pantry with a ball of clothesline. "Will this work?"

"Perfect." Jace took it and turned to Nika. "Put your hands behind the chair."

The cougar bit her lip. "Please. There is no need. I will not run—I swear it."

Jace inhaled. She had the scent of truth. Beside him, Evie tensed and he caught a whiff of fear.

A spike of anger lanced through him—not at Evie, but at Corban and the life he, Jace, led. He knew damn well any headway he'd made with Evie tonight had evaporated the minute he dragged a naked and injured woman into her kitchen. His stomach hollowed.

And things were about to get worse, because he was going to have to convince her to leave town. Corban Savonett was a coldhearted bastard and Jace's scent was all over Evie. If Corban couldn't take down Jace, he'd go after her next. Grace Harbor was no longer safe for her or Kyler.

Evie dragged a hand over her cropped blond hair. "I know she attacked you, but she's hurt."

Jace swore under his breath but dropped the clothesline on the table. "All right," he told Nika. "But one false move and I'll smash your quartz into a hundred pieces. Are we clear?"

Her throat worked. She dropped her head so that her tangled red hair hid her face and gave a jerky nod. "Yes." She touched the bump on her head. "Hurts."

Jace didn't trust her worth a damn, but the pitiful-me act worked with Evie. "Can I give her a glass of water?"

He sighed in defeat. "Sure. Why not?"

While Evie got Nika water, Kyler handed her an ice pack for her head. Jace hooked his foot around the bottom rung of the nearest chair and dragged it in front of Nika. He dropped onto the seat and crossed his arms. Not speaking, just making it clear she wasn't moving an inch without his say-so.

Nika pressed the ice pack to her head and stared down at the floor. At least she was smart enough not to challenge him directly.

Evie touched his shoulder. "Jace?"

"What?" he rapped out without taking his gaze from his prisoner.

"You're hurt."

"I'll live." But now the adrenaline had worn off, he was feeling every single one of the bites and cuts Corban and Nika had torn out of his hide. Shifting had caused most of them to scab over, but a gash on his thigh was oozing blood. The worst was his abdomen, where it felt like the deeper of the knife wounds had torn open again.

"This is getting to be a bad habit." Evie's tone was dry. "You bleeding in my kitchen."

He barked out a laugh and glanced up in time to see her lopsided grin. The hollow feeling eased. "Clean it up then," he grumbled. But his cat twitched its tail in delight.

Evie dampened a clean washcloth and used it to dab at the cuts on his face and shoulder. When she got to the gash on his thigh, she sucked in a breath.

"Just clean it," he said. "I can heal it."

"Sure you can."

When she was finished, he ran his quartz over his thigh. The wound tingled and started closing up. The knife wound was trickier, but he sent a burst of energy into it and hoped it would hold until Suha could work her magic.

Nika watched, the ice pack to her head.

Evie sent him a look from where she was washing her hands in the sink. He could practically hear her urging him to help the injured woman as well. With a sigh, he rose to his feet and ran his quartz over the gashes on Nika's face and head. Just a few quick pulses, but it would ease her pain as well as speed up her healing. Without her quartz, her ability to heal herself was even worse than the average human's, since all her energy was now being directed to merely staying alive.

Kyler took a seat on the other side of the table, while Evie remained standing. The kid raised a shaggy brown brow. "So we're waiting for Lord Adric?"

"Yeah. Tell me," Jace said, "what did that guy say to you, anyway? The one who was outside?"

Kyler glanced at his sister.

She cocked a hip against the counter. "Tell him, Kyler."

"He said that you were just fucking with Evie. That you eat little girls like her for breakfast."

Evie rubbed her hands over her arms. Kyler had told her the whole thing while they waited for Jace to return. If it wasn't so serious, she would've laughed.

She rolled her eyes. "I know you guys are shifters, but does he have to go all Big Bad Wolf? Besides, you're a cat."

Jace's mouth twitched. Score a point for Evie. She had a feeling Jace didn't smile much. She liked that she could make him laugh, if only inside.

Then he replied, "Actually, he *is* a wolf," and she gulped.

Because she'd only been joking to hide her fear, and now it was creepy. How long had the other man been outside? And what if he'd gone after Kyler?

Her brother folded his arms. "Fuck this wolf-and-cat thing. Is it true?"

"*Kyler*," she hissed, but Jace calmly met his eyes.

"What happens between me and your sister is our business. But I would never hurt her. He was just trying to pull your chain."

"So where's the wolf-man now?"

"I don't know." Jace jerked his head at the woman wrapped in the towel. "We'll talk when the alpha gets here."

Evie nodded. The woman hadn't moved from her slumped position, but of course, she could hear every word. Evie didn't know exactly what had happened, but it was clear the woman and the missing man had attacked Jace. That was why she'd let Jace back in her house, and allowed him to hold the woman until his alpha arrived—but that was as far as it went.

What the hell was going on? Evie fingered the quartz in her pocket. She'd been so damn worried. Each minute with Jace gone had seemed like an eternity. She'd hated that the only thing she could do was to call Adric and then wait for him to drive the fifty minutes up from Baltimore.

Jace trained his gaze on his prisoner. He appeared relaxed, long legs stretched before him and an elbow resting on the chair back, but it was the coiled energy of an animal prepared to spring.

The woman slid a look at Evie. Her pale blue eyes were flat. Not angry or cold, just flat, as if Evie were too insignificant to worry about.

Evie wasn't sure if that was good or bad. "Well," she said, "I don't know about the rest of you, but I'm hungry." She'd been too busy to grab more than a snack tonight.

Kyler brightened. "Works for me."

She rolled her eyes. "Why aren't I surprised?"

"Hey, I'm a growing boy."

But the tension in the room dropped several notches.

Evie got out sandwich fixings and went to work. A few minutes later, she had four thick tuna sandwiches topped with slabs of melted cheddar. Jace inhaled appreciatively as she handed him a plate. "Tuna. Great."

"I figured you'd like it."

"Why?"

She smirked. "You're a cat, aren't you?"

His mouth twitched again. "A jaguar, not a house cat."

"Here." She handed him a plate for the red-headed woman, who was eyeing Jace's sandwich hungrily. "I made one for her, too."

He shook his head, but passed it on to her. When the Baltimore alpha arrived, he found the four of them eating tuna melts.

Evie opened the door at Jace's request and Adric strode in as if he owned the place. He nodded hello to Evie and Kyler and then eyed the woman, who straightened up and set her plate on the table behind her.

"This is her?"

"Yep." Jace rose to his feet. "Name's Nika."

A small woman with a shaved head slipped in after Adric, Jace's clothes under her arm, and Adric jerked his chin in her direction without taking his eyes off Nika. "This is one of my lieutenants," he said.

The newcomer set the clothes on an empty chair and stuck out a hand. "Marjani. I'm also his sister—and you must be Evie."

"That's me." Evie shook her hand. Marjani was a female version of Adric—a lithe cat of a woman with smooth butterscotch skin, large dark eyes and a perfect oval face. But her body was scarecrow-thin and her eyes had hollows beneath them so that Evie wondered if she'd been sick.

"You're the humans who saved Jace's life." Marjani looked from Evie to Kyler. "Thank you. He's like a brother to me."

Evie moved a shoulder. "We didn't do much."

Marjani touched Evie's arm, and then moved to where Adric and Jace were staring down at Nika. The redhead moistened her lips and kept her gaze on the alpha. Adric and Marjani stepped closer, and Nika shrank into herself.

Evie's stomach tightened. She could almost see the teeth and claws come out, two predators homing in on their prey. She swallowed and glanced at Jace, who had stepped back, allowing Adric to take over. He gave a slight shake of his head, and she forced herself to remain silent. This was between the fada.

"So. Nika." Adric set a hand on the back of her chair. "You're new around here, aren't you?"

She jerked her head in assent.

"I thought so. But we're going to get to know each other, won't we, love?"

Nika's throat worked. Her gaze darted from him to Marjani and then back to the floor.

"She's not from around here," Jace said. "I think she's from Russia or Eastern Europe."

"And you say she was with Corban?"

"Yeah."

Adric shook his head. "You're bullet bait to him," he told her. "Someone he can throw at me to save his own ass."

She raised her chin. "He says you lie. That you can do it without harming yourself."

"Do you scent a lie?"

Her nostrils flared. Then she shook her head. "No," she admitted. "But maybe I would not."

"Corban is the one who plays with the truth. And the man's a fucking coward, too. Look how he left you behind to take the heat."

Nika pressed her lips together.

"You know the rules," Adric said. "You come into my territory without permission, you're mine. I could slit your throat right here and no one would say a word."

Kyler moved uneasily, but Adric sliced him a look, and he kept his mouth shut.

Nika merely nodded. "As you say."

The alpha turned toward Evie. "Can I trouble you for some clothes for Nika here?"

"Yes, of course." She hurried from the room. The redhead was several sizes larger than her, but she found an oversized T-shirt and a pair of yoga pants that she thought would work. When she returned to the kitchen, Jace had taken the opportunity to get dressed in his own clothes as well.

Nika shed her towel and pulled on the shirt and pants, unconcerned with her audience. Evie elbowed Kyler, who had his gaze locked on the woman's full breasts. He reddened and dropped his eyes.

Adric was holding the paper towel with Nika's quartz. Her eyes went to it, but she didn't say anything. The alpha unwrapped it without touching it. He cocked his head, and Evie had the odd impression he was listening to it. He gave a nod and then wrapped it up again before tucking it into his pocket.

"We'll take care of her," he told Jace. "You two"—he nodded at Evie and Kyler —"go with Jace."

The two men exchanged a look.

"What do you mean?" Evie asked.

"Jace will explain. But my cousin is a coldhearted SOB. If he thinks he can hurt me through you, he will."

She passed a hand over her face. None of this made sense. "Why would hurting me hurt you?"

"Jace is one of my top men—a lieutenant. And it's clear he's interested in you, or else he wouldn't have been here."

Jace was a lieutenant? But it fit; he had that air of calm, confident power.

"Come on." Jace set a hand on her back. "We can talk upstairs. You too, Kyler."

As they moved into the hall, Adric said to Nika, "I'll ask you one time. Where's Corban?"

Silence.

Evie glanced back to see the alpha dangling his quartz in front of Nika's face. Then Jace moved to block her sight and hustled her toward the stairs.

She dug in her heels. Yes, Nika had helped attack Jace, but Evie couldn't help feeling a little sorry for her. "What's he going to do?" she demanded.

He propelled her forward. "Don't worry," he said in an undertone. "He won't hurt her. She'll tell him what he needs to know."

"But—"

"Upstairs. The less she knows, the better."

Evie nodded and led the way to the front bedroom—her mom's. Evie still didn't think of it as hers. The walls were still the same deep plum her mom had chosen, and she had her mom's colorful orange, blue, and purple Boho quilt on the bed. Even the sturdy fruitwood dresser had been passed down through her mom's family. The only furniture Evie had added was an inexpensive table which held her printer and a stack of books and papers.

Jace closed the door and turned to face her and Kyler. "I'd like you to come to Baltimore with me for a few days—hide in my den until we track down Corban."

"But why? What's going on?"

He scraped a hand over his short black hair. "We're not sure," he admitted. "But we're afraid Corban is behind the attack on me last week, which means he's working with the night fae. And that's twice now my trail has led right to your door. Until we know what's happening, you're not safe here."

Evie sank down on her bed. "This is insane. I have work. And Kyler—"

"Is out of school for the summer," her brother inserted. "Maybe we should listen to the man."

"You want to go?" An hour ago, he'd been ready to punch Jace out, and now he was all for leaving with him.

He moved a shoulder. "You didn't see this Corban. I did. He's one scary motherfucker."

Jace crouched before Evie, his hands on the mattress on either side of her. The claw marks on his face were healing rapidly, but they'd come dangerously close to his eye. "I'm sorry, Evie. Corban knows I was with you, and he scented you on me. He doesn't play by the rules—and he likes to hurt women. Do you want to take a chance he won't come back?"

She grimaced. "No, of course not."

"It's Saturday night," Kyler said. "You don't have to be at work until Monday evening. We could go for a couple of days at least."

Evie stared at the marks on Jace's face and went cold as she realized that both Corban and Nika must have been out there, watching Kyler come home from Ben's. They could've grabbed him, torn him to pieces...and she'd never have known why.

"Please," Jace said. "I promise, you can leave whenever you want. But this house is too hard to protect. He could come at you from either side." He jerked his chin at the windows overlooking the street. "Even climb in through the windows. Climbing up here would be nothing for a fada."

Evie glanced at Kyler and made up her mind. "All right."

Because she trusted Jace. If he'd wanted, he could've hurt her and Kyler ten times over by now; but instead, he'd been outside the house, guarding them. He'd lost sleep to make sure they were okay, and damn it, she was touched. Yeah, she was tough, independent—and proud of it—but she wasn't stupid enough to think she could take on a fada. If Jace believed they were in danger, then they probably were.

"Thank you," Jace said as if she were doing him a favor and not the other way around. He stood up. "I'll wait in the hall while you pack. Make sure you bring enough for a few nights."

Kyler followed Jace into the hall. "I can send my friend Ben a text, right? Tell him we're going to be in Baltimore with friends?"

"Sure. Just don't give him any details."

Evie took out her own phone. She'd taken the biology final last Tuesday, and her summer class didn't start for another week. The only people she needed to contact were her bosses at the restaurant and the coffee shop. She'd been so busy the last few years that she'd lost touch with her friends from high school. Her only uncle lived in Canada, and she hadn't seen him since her mom's funeral. Evie could disappear for a month and no one would notice except Kyler and her boss and maybe Mrs. Linney.

Lord, that was sad.

It was rare for her to have a Sunday off, so she'd been planning to surprise Kyler with a trip to the beach two hours away in Delaware. But Monday she was due to work the evening shift at the restaurant and then Tuesday morning at the coffee shop. She texted her boss at the restaurant saying she might not make it in on Monday, but decided not to contact the coffee shop yet. Surely they'd be back home by Tuesday—because she really couldn't afford to lose more than a day or two of work.

She pocketed her phone and went to her dresser.

CHAPTER 17

*A*dric removed his quartz pendant and pulled up a chair in front of Nika.
She squared her shoulders and set her hands on her thighs. "What are you going to do?"

Her voice was calm although he knew she was afraid. Interesting. She'd been giving a good imitation of a completely cowed submissive, someone low on the dominance scale, but a fada that low would be trembling with the effort of fighting an alpha.

"You know where my cousin is," he murmured. "Tell me, love."

He swung his pendant in front of her face. Back and forth, slow and steady.

Nika moistened her lips. Her gaze flicked to the pendant and her right hand fisted.

She wanted his quartz, even though it wouldn't do her any good—the tiny crystals within were aligned to his unique frequency, vibrating with him on a primal level. But with her quartz removed, her body would be craving the magical energy it was being deprived of.

He focused on his quartz. Deep within, the heart flared a fiery mix of bronze and blue that even he found mesmerizing. He dragged his gaze away and back to Nika's face.

Back and forth.

"Tell me," he said again. "Where's Corban?"

On Nika's other side, Marjani was careful to keep her gaze on the woman's face, not the glowing quartz. At least something good had come out of this. It was the most animated he'd seen his sister in months. But then, she had even more reason to hate Corban than he did.

Back and forth.

Nika followed the movement with her eyes. The flickers in the quartz were mirrored in her pupils, twin blue flames in the black.

"Talk to me, Nika. All I want is information. Tell me what I want to know and I'll let you live."

Her mouth compressed, but her gaze remained on the swinging quartz.

In the Darktime, he would've forced the information from her and then smashed her quartz before dumping her on the streets of Baltimore—if he didn't just slit her throat. Nika might not be the meek mouse she was pretending to be, but she was no match for a man of his strength.

But the Darktime was over, and he had little taste for hurting a woman, even one working with Corban. Of course, raiding her mind for information against her will wasn't much better. But the clan came first.

His first question was simple. Get her to answer one question, and the next one was easier. "Where did you meet Corban?"

Her jaw clenched tight. Dislike and fear came off her in waves, a bitter, unpleasant scent. He didn't think all that fear was for him, either. No, she was afraid of Corban, too.

Back and forth.

He repeated the question. "Where did you meet Corban?"

When she still didn't answer, he drew deeply on his Gift. Hypnotism: his dirty little secret. Most earth fada could hypnotize others if given enough time and opportunity, but he could do it so quickly and thoroughly that it was akin to compulsion. He was sure other people suspected, but only his top people knew for sure, because if his Gift ever became general knowledge, he could lose the clan's trust. How could his clanmates know what was true and what he'd planted in their minds?

Panic flared within Nika. He kept up the dark, steady pressure—and felt the moment her will collapsed in on itself.

Something deep inside her howled in fury, but her mouth opened. "In Iceland." The words were slow, a little blurred.

Adric raised a brow. Iceland was the ice fae's home territory.

"What were you doing in Iceland?"

"My alpha, he sent me to the ice fae."

"Why?"

She shrugged, her gaze on the moving quartz. He drew more energy from it. The flickers coalesced into a vivid cobalt fire.

"Tell me, Nika."

"I am to work for them. The ice fae, they pay the clan good money."

"And Corban? Why was he in Iceland?"

"He works for them too."

"Who? Who is he working for?"

She swallowed and then whispered, "The king."

Adric considered that. He hadn't heard from Corban since he'd disappeared soon after leaving for the Himalayas to track Sindre's rogue female. For the first three months, Adric had kept tabs on his cousin; as alpha, his quartz was linked to everyone in the clan. But then the link had been abruptly cut. As far as everyone knew Corban had died, but Adric suspected he'd smashed his own quartz so that he could go into hiding.

It had been left to Adric to explain to King Sindre why the Baltimore fada hadn't completed the job they'd been hired to do. The ice fae king was a tall, striking man with long blond hair and the ice-gray eyes of a predator. He'd been waiting at the entrance to Adric's den. A clear message: the king could find him anytime, anywhere.

Adric had apologized and offered to send another tracker, but Sindre had simply scrutinized him with those frosty eyes. Adric's hand had gone to his quartz. Ice fae fed on the energy of motion. A powerful fae like Sindre could suck the energy out of your very molecules. The only way to resist was to shield your-self—either with iron, or by putting up an energy barrier.

"Very well," the king said at last. "I'll find the woman myself. It seems she is too clever for even a fada tracker."

Now Adric realized his cousin must have struck a deal with Sindre. He narrowed his eyes at Nika. "Where is Corban now?"

"He ran away."

"Yes, but where is he staying?"

"Nowhere. We flew in last week. By now he's already gone." Nika surfaced enough to shoot Adric a triumphant look. "You must travel to Iceland to find him."

Adric swore under his breath.

"Sounds like him," Marjani muttered. "Strike and run."

Adric shook his head. He tried to get more information from Nika, but she didn't know much else. She did tell him which flight they'd been booked on, but Corban wasn't stupid—he'd take another flight under a different name. Adric would send a man to check the airport anyway, but he knew it was a waste of time.

Like hell, he'd chase Corban to Iceland. That was exactly what his cousin wanted. Adric's fingers tightened on his quartz.

Nika twitched and he focused on her again. He was going to have to bring her out of the trance soon. His own energy was being drained at a rapid rate, and if he pushed Nika any harder, he risked damaging her brain.

But first, he had another question. "What about the night fae? Why are they working with Corban?"

"The night fae?" But her eyes flickered.

"*Tell me.*" He threw everything he had into extracting that last bit of information, but he'd lost her. She'd thrown up a barrier he couldn't penetrate.

"I do not know."

It might be the truth—and it might not. Because "I don't know" could mean anything, or nothing.

He ground his teeth. "Then who?"

But she'd regained control of her mind. She closed her mouth and refused to say anything else.

The last thing he did was erase Nika's memory of how he'd hypnotized her. She'd remember that she'd given him information, but blame herself for being weak.

Sometimes Adric was an even bigger bastard than his cousin.

Nika's breath sighed out. Her chin fell to her chest as she slid into a deep sleep. He grabbed her shoulders to keep her from falling off the chair.

"Let's get out of here," he told Marjani.

"What about her?" She jerked her chin at the sleeping woman. "You're not bringing her back to Baltimore, are you?"

"No fucking way." Nika was hiding something, and he was damned if he'd bring her into their den, or anywhere near the clan, for that matter. "We'll leave her on Rock Run territory. Let them deal with her."

Dion wouldn't hurt Nika for no reason, but he *would* keep her captive while he tried to figure out why Adric had left her on his land.

Marjani's brows shot up. "I like it. And her quartz?"

"You hang onto it." Adric handed the pendant to Marjani and lifted Nika in his arms. His scent would be all over her. The river fada would know he'd left her there deliberately—what they wouldn't know was why.

They'd driven up in one of the clan's jeeps. After he laid Nika on the back seat, his sister took the wheel while he put in a call to a high-ranking sentry, directing the woman to send some men to the Baltimore airport on the off-chance they could catch Corban.

Next he contacted Zuri and brought him up to date. "Corban still has friends in the clan," he said. "If he's hurt bad enough, there's a chance he'll go to ground in one of their dens. Start with his old den. I want someone we trust to visit every single one of the bastard's friends. He's gone too far this time. He knows damn well an attack on Jace is an attack on me. I want him, Zuri."

"If he's in Baltimore," the lieutenant replied grimly, "I'll find him."

His last call was to Bryah, a tough young sentry itching to prove herself. He'd left her and another sentry searching Grace Harbor for Corban while he was occupied with Nika and Jace. "Find anything?" he asked.

"Only some traces of blood, sir. We followed his scent as far as the bay and then we lost him. We ran along the shore for half a mile in each direction but there was no trace of him. We crisscrossed the town after that. I can tell you he was up here for a day, maybe two. He could be hiding somewhere, but my guess is he left by boat."

"Unless he was 'ported out," Adric muttered. His fingers tightened around his quartz. He'd swear Corban had the DNA of a fucking weasel, the way he wriggled out of tight spots.

"You think he's working with a fae?"

"It's a possibility."

"I didn't pick up a fae's scent."

Adric nodded. That was useful intel, although not conclusive. "You did good," he told Bryah. "Go back to Baltimore. Zuri could use you in the search down there."

Marjani drove west along the Susquehanna River. Rock Run owned several thousand prime acres along the shore, including the mouth of Rock Run Creek. The river fada's underground base followed the creek; its actual location was a closely kept secret. Adric had gotten inside once, but the sun fae had wiped his memory of the details, and he'd never been able to get past the wards again.

Adric felt the familiar clench of possessiveness. God's cat, he wanted Rock Run's territory for the clan. It had everything—forests for their cats and wolves and bears and deer to run free in. Fresh water to swim and fish in. An underground base that was perfect for a growing clan.

Once, he'd plotted to take Rock Run's territory, but he'd set that plan aside. Rock Run had three times the people, and now that Dion had mated with the sun fae queen, it would be suicide to go up against them. Queen Cleia could literally incinerate a man where he stood. No, his clan was going to make the money they needed from selling the new quartz technology, and then they'd buy their own chunk of prime forestland.

And Jace Jones was crucial to that plan. He was the brains behind the smartphone project. Kill Jace, and the clan could kiss their plans for new territory goodbye—and Corban knew that as well as Adric.

They reached Rock Run's border. The road narrowed to a strip of asphalt and gravel. To their left the terrain was thick with trees; to the right, the Susquehanna rushed by just yards away, the rising moon casting a shimmering gold trail on its wide black waters.

"Here?" asked Marjani.

When he nodded, she stopped the jeep. Nika was still unconscious. Adric set her in the grass beside the road.

Marjani followed with Nika's quartz. "She's stronger than she's pretending," she said as she unwrapped it. "You know we have to do it."

"Fine." He dragged a hand over his spiked-up hair. "Do it then."

His sister's eyes flashed the chilly sapphire of her cougar. She found a heavy rock, set the quartz on the road and smashed it into several jagged pieces.

Nika jerked and slipped further into unconsciousness.

The quartz shards sparkled like dim stars, still sharing energy with Nika. Scooping them up, Marjani walked onto the narrow beach and tossed them into the river. The last piece, she placed on Nika's chest where she'd be sure to find it.

"She'll be all right," Marjani said, as if he were arguing. "That's more than Corban allowed me."

The sparkling pieces were carried rapidly downriver. One by one, they winked out of sight as they sank beneath the water.

A dolphin's fin appeared upriver. A Rock Run sentry coming to investigate.

"Let's get out of here," Adric said, and they jogged back to the jeep.

But he glanced over his shoulder as the dolphin shifted—and felt the shock clear to his bones. It was Rosana do Rio, the only sister of the Rock Run alpha—and the woman he'd wanted for six long years.

"I'll be right there."

"Damn it, Ric," Marjani growled, but he was already moving down the road.

Rosana strode onto the beach. It was too dark to see her clearly, but her image was emblazoned on his brain: a heart-shaped face, a cloud of wavy black hair, and eyes the rich blue of the ocean. Her irises turned a bright, night-glow silver, and their gazes locked.

His heart thundered in his ears. He stopped a yard away. "It's been a while." A year, in fact.

They'd danced at Tiago's mate ball. She'd melted into him for that single dance, and he'd murmured in her ear, trying to entice her to come to him later. But when the dance ended, she'd pulled out of his arms, saying, "I can't do this," and walked rapidly away.

Now he hungrily took in her naked body. She was a man's wet dream—slick from her swim, with high breasts and sleek thighs. Her hair tumbled in damp ringlets over her shoulders and beneath his heated gaze, her nipples beaded. But she kept her chin level and met him look for look, a proud and arrogant do Rio to her very toes.

But she wanted him. He gave a slow, deliberate inhale, letting her know he scented her need.

She glanced from him to Nika. "You're on our territory." Her voice was naturally husky. The woman could read a fucking menu and sound sexy.

"I brought you a gift."

"A gift?" A delicate black eyebrow winged up.

He indicated Nika. "She attacked one of my men in Grace Harbor. I figured your brother might want to question her."

"Grace Harbor isn't our territory."

He shrugged. "Close enough." Which she knew as well as him.

Upstream, another dolphin was making a beeline for them. Adric stepped closer, fingered a wet black ringlet. "I have to go."

He prided himself on his control. He'd never have made alpha without it. But then Rosana moistened her full lower lip and his control broke with an almost audible snap. With a growl, he speared his fingers into her hair and dragged her up against him.

She went stick straight—and then she gripped his shoulders and opened her mouth. Adric sank into her. There was no other word for it. He went deep and mindless. One hand tangled in her hair while the other smoothed over her firm ass, urged her up against his aching cock. His tongue sought hers and they tasted each other. One slow, sweet kiss.

His heart slammed against his rib cage. His head swam with her scent—fresh water and green grass layered over something that was all woman...a fragrance that could only be Rosana do Rio.

A furious snarl sounded from the river. A young, hard-driving *tenente* named Davi rose from the water, his gaze lethal.

Adric raised his head and resolutely set Rosana from him.

Behind him, Marjani had backed up the jeep. She shoved open the passenger-side door. "Get in, you ass."

He ignored her to touch Rosana's cheek. One last stroke of her downy skin.

Her throat worked. She captured his hand—and set it firmly against his chest. "Goodbye, Lord Adric."

"Rosana—" He was close to begging...and he'd never begged a woman in his life.

Davi strode toward them. "What the fuck's going on?"

"It's all right." Rosana slapped a palm on the *tenente*'s chest. "Go," she told Adric.

His cougar gnashed its teeth at seeing her touch another man. But Marjani was right. Rosana do Rio wasn't for him—and not just because he was alpha of an earth fada clan and she was a river fada. No, there were other, darker reasons he couldn't allow himself to take Rosana.

With a mocking salute to Davi, he hopped into the jeep. The Rock Run man growled and started toward them, but Marjani slammed her foot on the gas pedal and they sped off in a hail of gravel.

His sister shook her head. "God's cat, Ric. You have to get over this obsession with her."

"I don't want her." It was a lie, and his stomach lurched in response. "Not for more than a fuck," he amended.

Marjani snorted and he scowled at her. They drove in silence until she reached the main road. Then her eyes creased with amusement. "Dion's going to go insane trying to figure out why we left Nika here."

It wasn't a smile, but it was the closest she'd come in a long while. Adric blew out a breath—and wrenched his mind away from the sexy Rock Run female.

"And then he'll give up," he said, "and have his mate 'port her back to Iceland or wherever the hell she's from."

"Either way, she'll be taken care of. Smart."

"Exactly." Adric smirked and tapped his quartz. "Zuri? Any news?"

CHAPTER 18

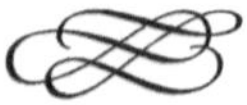

"So," Kyler said, "are you going to sleep with him?"

"Jesus." Evie's fingers tightened on the steering wheel. "You're my brother, not my dad."

"You're all I have."

Her heart pinched. "Ditto, squirt."

"I just want you to be careful."

"I will. But I like him. I really like him." She slanted him a look. "Would it be so bad?"

"Nah, he seems like an okay dude. A hardass, but not like that guy I talked to—Corban. He was cold right to the bone. That guy would slit your throat and smile the whole time."

A chill inched up Evie's spine. Right then and there, she decided to stay with Jace as long as necessary. She and Kyler were in over their heads. They couldn't even go to the cops; the fada policed themselves. Yeah, there were rules—the fada weren't supposed to mess in human affairs. There was even a human-fada treaty between the US and the American fada. But everyone knew that in reality, the fada did whatever they damned well pleased. The authorities turned a blind eye to everything but the most blatant violations of the treaty.

"Jace and Adric will get Corban," Kyler said. "You'll see."

"I know." She didn't doubt that for a second.

"And it's okay with me." He waved a hand. "If you two...you know."

She compressed her lips, trying not to laugh. "Thanks."

"Like I said, he's an okay dude. But that doesn't mean you're more to him than a piece of ass." And with that brotherly warning, he put his ear buds in and leaned back in the car seat.

~

JACE PULLED his bike into the shed. As he eased his injured leg over the seat, he stifled a groan. Damn thigh had stiffened up during the hour ride south. But what worried him was the way his knife wounds were burning. He slid a hand under his shirt and grimaced when he touched blood. Just a few drops, but he'd definitely ripped something open.

Behind him, Evie's car wheezed to a stop and let out a couple of explosive pops. He made a mental note to have Sam go over her car. He was the clan's best mechanic; the engine would be purring by the time he was through with it. It was the least they could do after dragging her into what was shaping up to be a clan war.

Besides, Jace *wanted* to help her. The woman carried too much weight on those tough little shoulders. As a fada, he never understood why the humans didn't rally around their single parents—female or male, raising a cub alone was a damn hard job. Evie wouldn't accept his money, but he figured she wouldn't say no to Sam tuning up her car, especially after she saw that nothing made the tiger happier than to be elbow-deep in an engine.

Evie and Kyler exited their car, backpacks in hand. As they walked toward the shed, they glanced around, taking in the freshly painted house and the neat, fenced-in backyard.

"I'll show you around in the morning," Jace said. He was proud of his block. He'd worked hard to make it safe for his human neighbors. The rats had been chased off, and he made sure that the landlords kept the houses up to code. In return, when a house fell vacant, he helped the landlord find a responsible tenant. Adric might tolerate drug dealers on his block, but not Jace.

It had paid off. The yards were well kept and blooming with flowers, and a group of elders had started a community garden on a vacant lot. The woman who rented his house had tubs filled with tomatoes and zucchini on the front porch, and as soon as morning came, the street would ring with the shouts of children unafraid to play outside.

"I'd like that," Evie said.

He walked toward them, intending to take her backpack, and then winced as his leg protested. Evie hurried up and slid an arm around his waist.

"You're hurt."

He grunted, but set an arm on her shoulders. If she wanted to plaster that sweet little body against his, he was all for it.

"Where's your den?" Kyler asked.

"Here." Jace touched his quartz and murmured the words that dissolved the *look-away* spell.

"Wowzer." The teenager's jaw slackened as the stairs appeared. "That's frickin' cool."

"Your den is underground?" Evie peered down the two flights.

"Yeah."

He'd never taken a human into his den. Ever.

And his cat was calmly satisfied. As far as it was concerned, everything had worked out just as it should. Except that Evie was in danger. The cat didn't like that, but that was all the more reason to keep her close. And her brother, too, because the cub was essential to Evie's happiness—and besides, the cat liked him.

"Sick." That was Kyler. "Ben would never believe this."

Evie's scent was wary, but interested too.

"What's the matter?" Jace asked her.

"It's so...dark."

Ah. He'd forgotten she didn't have a cat's night vision. And maybe she was a little cautious about entering a fada's den?

He led the way down the stairs, leaving the two siblings to follow or not as they wished—and then held his breath, not sure what he'd do if Evie changed her mind. Because both man and cat wanted her here, had a deep, primal need to protect her.

He glanced over his shoulder. "There are quartz lights built into the walls. Our motion will turn them on." The lights glowed on as he spoke—tiny blue and silver crystals set into the dark gray stone in irregular patterns.

"They're beautiful," Evie breathed, and started down the stairs after him.

He sent her a smile. "Thanks. They were my mom's idea."

Evie trailed her fingers down the wall. "They're like stars in the night sky."

"That's what Mom said."

When they reached the bottom, he touched his quartz to the lock in the heavy oak door. It swung open and he ushered his two guests through the small foyer into the living room. They looked around curiously, taking in the exposed stone walls, the quartz wall sconces and the colorful pillows scattered on the floor.

Evie fingered a beautiful rose quartz that his mom had brought back from Brazil, and then peeked into the spacious kitchen. "Wow, this is a big place."

"My dad built it." He watched as Kyler wandered into the kitchen and then back out again. "Five bedrooms, because he and my mom were always bringing someone home."

Her mouth curved. "They sound like nice people."

"They were." He felt the familiar tug of grief that his parents had died so young. Fada normally lived for hundreds of years, but his mom and dad hadn't even reached their seventies.

Were. Her dark eyes met his in shared compassion. "But you don't live here alone, do you?"

He shook his head. "I have four den mates, although right now Luc is out of the country. And there's Tigger—thinks he runs the show."

On cue, the tabby leapt off the back of the couch and strolled over to sniff Evie. Introductions over, he butted her leg, completely ignoring Kyler.

"A cat?" Evie broke into a smile and to Jace's disgust, crouched down to coo over Tigger. The damn housecat got all the attention. But he had to admit, Tigger had his uses, because when Evie stood back up, her wariness was completely gone. It was hard to be suspicious of a guy with a fat tabby for a pet.

"Let me show you the security system." He and Sam had installed it themselves. It ran on crystal power, and was keyed to each of his den mates' individual quartzes, as well as Adric's. "We can work it with our quartz," he said, "but you just have to key in this code." He showed them the sequence on the touchpad next to the door and then made sure they both had it memorized.

"That will keep out a fae?" Evie asked.

"We worked iron into the lock. We have to be careful not to touch the lock itself, and I guess you should, too, since you have some fae in you. Kyler, it shouldn't affect you at all. Between this and the *look-away* spell, nobody can get in here without my permission."

She touched his arm, her face solemn. "Thank you."

"You're safe," he added. "The night fae aren't interested in you, and I'm not leaving you or Kyler alone for a minute until we find Corban. He'll have to go through me to get to you."

"Where are your roommates?" Kyler asked.

Jace inhaled, checking for scents. "Beau's in bed—he's a bear and likes his sleep—and the other two are out. Adric has them sweeping the city for Corban."

The teenager stifled a yawn and nodded.

"The bedrooms are through here." Jace led the way into the hall, where the five bedrooms were arranged in a semi-circle around the living room and kitchen. "We have two bathrooms, one at either end of the hall." He pointed them out. "Kyler can take the extra bed in Beau's room. Don't worry about bothering him, he's used to it. And Evie, you can have my room. I'll sleep on the couch."

"Your friends won't mind?"

"It's my den. But no, they don't mind. They're used to it—we have packmates staying over all the time."

He ushered Kyler into Beau's room. A single fae light winked on, enough to show the huge lump curled up on the bed. His animal was a brown bear, and even as a human he was huge.

Beau cracked open an eye. "A human?" Bears had an even better sense of smell than cats.

"Yeah. Name's Kyler. He and his sister need a place to stay."

"Help yourself, bro." Beau waved a massive hand at the spare bed.

"Thanks." Kyler set his backpack at the foot of the bed.

Jace left them to it and opened the door to his own room. His dad had left the walls uncovered. Three fae lights glowed to life, casting a soft yellow hue over the worked gray stone.

It was a plain, masculine room, save for the colorful Native American rug at the foot of the bed; the room of a man who lived alone. Other than the large oak bed, the only furniture was a chair and a nightstand with another of the large chunks of quartz his mother had brought back from her tours overseas. This one had come from Morocco, where his mom still had a few relatives, her family having migrated from North Africa to Jamaica several centuries ago. It was a piece of art—an oblong tower of white calcite encrusted in places with silver crystals and a darker gray mineral running through the center.

"I thought it would be damp," Evie said, "like a cave. But it's warm. And I love the rug."

"My great-grandma wove the rug. Dad was part Cherokee."

"It's beautiful." Evie crouched to trace a finger over the red, green and black pattern.

"Our cats don't like the cold, so we have heating coils set in the floor. Actually, the wolves don't either. The bears don't give a shit, but they're in the minority."

She gave a gurgle of laughter and rose back to her feet. "I can't imagine anyone telling Beau what to do."

"You don't. But like I said, he doesn't care. It takes a lot to rile Beau."

"I like him already." The fae lights drifted toward her and her eyes widened. "Are those what I think they are?"

"Fae lights? Yeah. I did a sun fae a favor and she gifted them to me."

She stretched a hand toward one of the glowing balls, and to Jace's surprise, it floated down and slid over her palm as if welcoming her.

"I can feel it." She turned awed eyes on him. "It's warm and a little tingly."

"Tap it, and it will shut off."

She obeyed and the light winked out.

"You can leave it on while you're sleeping if you want—it will sense how much light you need and power down."

"Wow." She tapped the light a second time, and it glowed back on and wafted its way toward the ceiling.

"You can put your stuff in there." He indicated the closet. "Feel free to take a shower if you want."

She nodded. "I really appreciate this. I hate to put you out—"

Her gaze went to the large unmade bed in the center of the room. It was a tangle of sheets and the red print bedspread he'd bought because it didn't show dirt. He hadn't expected to be bringing anyone home.

She glanced at him and he just knew her mind had gone the same place as his: the two of them nestled in the sheets, bodies joined.

Not tonight.

He'd brought her here to protect her, not fuck her. You didn't take advantage of a woman like that. And his knife wound—the deeper one—was throbbing.

But he could almost taste her nipples in his mouth, feel her fingers digging into his shoulders, her body moving with his.

She dragged a hand over her hair, ruffling the short blond strands.

"I'll be fine," he said.

"What?" Her pupils were big and dark, the irises a rich brown shot with gold.

"Sleeping in the living room. I can change to my jaguar and curl up on a cushion."

She stepped close and his lungs seized. She touched his cheek. "Your jaguar is beautiful. I'd like to see him again sometime."

His animal preened. The cat loved to be admired.

Jace smoothed down her ruffled hair. It was silky soft, like a kitten's fur. "You will." It was a promise, even if she didn't know it.

He brushed his mouth over hers. Their lips clung, and then he stepped back. "I'll help you make the bed."

She touched her mouth. "All right."

He grabbed a spare set of sheets from the closet, and together, they stripped off the old sheets and put on the new ones. And damn if that wasn't almost as intimate as touching her. His cock was painfully hard.

He balled up the dirty sheets and tossed them into the closet. "If you need anything, I'll be in the living room."

She nodded her thanks, and he closed the few feet between them. "Good night," he said, and swayed closer. Not to kiss her again. He just wanted one last whiff.

But she turned her head and their mouths met, and then she was in his arms.

Heat flashed up his spine. Fuck his injured belly, and to hell with what was right or wrong.

They twined around each other. It was as if the two hours between their last kiss and this one had never been. They picked up right where they'd left off: his tongue in her mouth, his hand on her ass. She pressed herself against his aching groin, making sexy little moans that vibrated through him like a tuning fork.

He wrenched his mouth from hers and dragged in a breath. "I didn't bring you here for this."

"I know, but—" She set her lips to his throat and sucked. Heated sparks danced over his skin. "It's okay. I want this—I want you. But you're hurt."

"Not that hurt. And Suha's going to stop by. I'll be okay by the time she leaves."

"Yeah?" She nibbled his ear, and his eyes slit with pleasure.

He nudged her chin up, gave her a last, deep kiss and then resolutely set her from him. "Later. I'll come back after your brother's in bed."

"All right." Her lips were moist and reddened from his kiss.

His gaze fixed on her mouth, his mind painting a lurid picture of those moist lips on him. He almost grabbed her again, but instead he reached blindly for the doorknob. "Later," he repeated.

Her dimple flashed. "Sure."

She took her backpack and set it on the bed to unpack it. The three fae lights floated down to circle her head like a faerie crown.

His brow creased. Fae lights sensed when the user needed them, but these three acted as if Evie was some kind of a lodestone.

He'd never seen a fae light do that, even around another fae.

～

EVIE SHOOK OUT HER CLOTHES—A couple of T-shirts, a sleepshirt, and a pair of cargo pants—and hung them on hooks in the closet. The underwear could stay in the backpack, which reminded her that she still had on the plain black panties and white sports bra she'd worn to work that night. She hadn't planned on anyone else seeing them.

Not that Jace seemed to care; she had a feeling he was just fine with bare skin.

She did a little happy dance. This was really happening—her and Jace. Even it if was just for a couple of nights, she intended to squeeze every last ounce of enjoyment out of it.

She headed for the bathroom to wash up. The fae lights trailed after her, casting a warm glow over everything.

The bathroom was jaw-dropping—two sinks, a walk-in shower carved from speckled gray stone, and a black jacuzzi taking up one corner. Plain white towels were stacked on a small table, and the shelves were scattered with razors, shaving soap and other masculine paraphernalia.

Back in the living room, she found Jace and Kyler had been joined by a large man with curly cinnamon hair and pale gold eyes. The fae lights had trailed her down the hall. They spread out across the room as Jace turned to smile at her.

"There you are. I want you to meet Sam."

The big redhead held out a blunt-fingered hand. "A pleasure."

Evie's hand was swallowed in his. His grip was firm, but it was clear he was holding his enormous strength in check. "Thank you."

"I was telling Sam what happened tonight," Jace said.

The other man nodded. "Adric already sent word to me and some of the other soldiers. We're searching Baltimore for that bastard cousin of his. I just wanted to make sure you have things under control."

"We're fine," Jace replied. "Beau's in his room, and I have Kyler here as backup."

Her brother straightened his shoulders and gave a short, unsmiling nod as Jace's quartz buzzed.

"It's Suha," Jace said.

"I was just on my way out," said Sam. "I'll let her in." With a nod to Evie and Kyler, he headed for the door.

Jace limped to the couch and sat down, his injured leg stretched out on the cushions. "I'd better sit down, or she'll yell at me."

Evie suppressed a smile. She was looking forward to meeting the woman who could make a badass like Jace scramble to please her. Then Suha entered and Evie's eyes widened. This was no motherly healer—in fact, she didn't look any older than Evie—and she was pretty, with a dancer's grace. Her flirty yellow summer dress made Evie feel like a bag lady in her tank top and sweat shorts.

"You must be Evie." The healer gave her a warm smile. "Nice to meet you. And you too, Kyler." Tigger gave an imperious meow and bumped her shin. "Yeah, yeah, I see you." She scratched the tabby behind the ears and he rumbled with pleasure.

Kyler stuck out his hand. "Hello. I'm Kyler." He winced. "Right. You know that."

Evie met Jace's eyes and tried not to laugh, but Suha just smiled and shook his hand. "Peace to you and yours."

"Peace." He gazed down on her, a silly grin on his narrow face.

The moment stretched until Suha gave her hand a tug. Kyler's cheeks reddened and he released it like it was a hot coal.

The healer gave him a wink, like the two of them were in on a joke, and Kyler's embarrassment faded. Right then, Evie decided she liked her.

"So." Suha turned to Jace. "I hear you had a run in with Corban and tore something open inside. I suppose you had to chase him down yourself."

"There was no one else."

Suha rolled her eyes. "Let me have a look."

"Should we leave?" Evie asked.

"That's up to Jace."

Jace leaned back on the cushions. "It's fine with me if you stay."

Evie and Kyler helped move the coffee table so Suha could pull up a chair next to Jace. Evie sat on the other end of the couch while Kyler sprawled on a nearby chair, his long, knobby-kneed legs stretched out before him.

Suha removed her quartz and lifted the hem of Jace's shirt. His knife wounds were seeping blood.

Evie bit her lip. "He wasn't bleeding a couple of hours ago."

Suha muttered something that sounded like "stubborn ass" and ran her quartz over his abdomen. The stone began to glow with warm, healing colors—pink, yellow, peach.

Jace's eyes closed. He was quiet, but fine lines of pain radiated from around his mouth.

Evie stroked his ankle, wishing there were more she could do to help. His breath sighed out and Suha gave her an approving nod, so she kept doing it.

Suha moved to the gash on Jace's thigh. It had scabbed up, but it was still nasty looking. The healer ran her quartz up and down it, and then went to his nape, where she clucked at the puncture wounds. "An inch to the right, and you'd have been paralyzed for life."

Evie gulped and met Kyler's eyes, but Jace just shrugged.

Suha moved back to Jace's abdomen. Several minutes passed. Evie scooted closer and took Jace's hand. His lips curved, although his eyes remained shut.

Kyler got up to wander around the room, examining the TV and the colorful chunks of quartz on the mantelpiece. He crouched down to examine the fireplace. Instead of logs, there were several large amber-and-brown chunks on the firebox floor.

Tigger strolled past him and the teenager held out a hand. The cat ignored it with a lordly disdain, continuing past to the kitchen. A moment later, they heard the crunch of kibble.

Kyler sat down with his back against the wall and took out his phone. He swore under his breath. "I can't get a signal."

"It's the quartz," Jace said without opening his eyes. "There's a streak of it in the bedrock. It messes with the signal."

"Can I charge it?"

"Sure. I rigged up an outlet for the TV. There's one in the kitchen, too."

"That's lit. At least I can play games." Kyler got a cord to charge the phone, and then sat down in the chair again, eyes half-shut. It was past two o'clock, and he'd been up early to apply for a job at a local pizza place.

Evie opened her mouth to tell him to go to bed, and then closed it. He'd only snap at her, and it wasn't like they had anywhere to be in the morning.

Suha continued working on Jace, moving from his thigh to his stomach to his nape. A trio of fae lights drifted down to circle Evie's head. She felt that curious tingle of energy, and the hand holding Jace's warmed.

She blinked, and looked again. The gash on his thigh was visibly healing like a fast-motion video.

When it was just a thin red line, Suha shot Evie a look, her brow furrowed, and then sat back. "There," she told Jace. "You can run a frickin' marathon if you want. But for God's sake, can you go a couple of weeks without letting someone take a chunk out of you?"

He propped his elbows on the couch and winked at her. "You're the best."

"Yeah, yeah." But she grinned back at him before turning to Evie. "And you—you're part fae."

She shrugged. "That's what they say."

"But no one told me you're a healer."

CHAPTER 19

A healer? Evie frowned. "Because I'm not. Am I?"

Suha fingered her quartz. "I drew on your energy to heal Jace, and I can only do that with some of the stronger members of the clan—or another healer."

Evie shook her head. "I wish it were true, but when my mom had cancer, I tried to heal her. I put my hands on her and prayed she'd get well. I even tried sending healing energy into her—you know, like faith healers do. But it didn't work."

But damn, wouldn't that be something? She'd wanted to be a doctor or a nurse as far back as she could remember. When her mom got sick, Evie had found out everything she could about the treatments, gone to every appointment. Maybe if she knew enough, she could fix her—but it hadn't worked.

And in the end, all she'd been able to do was hold her mom's hand and promise she'd take care of Kyler.

"I'm so sorry." Suha touched her hand. "But even a trained healer can't save everyone. And it's possible you hadn't come into your Gift yet. With fada, it can happen anywhere from the time we become teenagers to our late twenties."

Evie's gaze slid to Jace. He was looking at her with an unreadable expression.

"I—" She scrubbed her hands over her face. Her brain felt sluggish, too tired to take in one more shock.

Jace jerked his chin at Kyler. "She needs to eat. Get her something from the kitchen—apples, peanut butter. Suha too—a healer burns through energy fast."

"I'm on it." He rose to his feet and headed for the kitchen.

Suha indicated the glowing orbs hovering around Evie. "The fae lights are drawn to you. Trust me, they're not like that for just anyone."

Evie swallowed. "They aren't?"

"No. The only time they get that close to me is when I'm healing someone and about to run out of juice."

"Huh." She glanced at the lights. "Still, even if I have some fae blood, it's probably just a few drops."

Suha shook her head. "If you have a fae Gift, it's probably more than a few drops."

Kyler returned with a plate of sliced apples, a jar of peanut butter, spoons and four sandwich plates, and set everything on the coffee table.

"Eat." Jace scooped some peanut butter onto a slice of apple, set it on a plate and handed it to Evie, while Suha helped herself.

Evie realized she was hungry—starving, in fact. She downed the slice and helped herself to another. "But how can I heal people without a quartz?" she asked Suha.

"Fae healers use their hands. You probably felt your palm heating when you were touching Jace."

She nodded slowly. "I did. But that doesn't mean I healed him."

"You helped."

She rubbed her forehead. "If you say so."

"Look," Suha said, "you're tired. Why don't I come back tomorrow and we can talk some more?"

"Thanks—I'd like that."

Suha ate another couple apple slices and came to her feet. "I'm off then."

"Not by yourself." Jace made to stand up. "I'll walk you home. Corban would love to get his hands on our healer."

Suha raised a brow. "He has to catch me first. Besides, you're the one he wants, not me. Beau can take me."

"On my way," a deep voice rumbled and Beau shambled in. The man was *big*, with wiry black hair and shoulders as wide as a door, but he had a sweet smile. Jace sank back onto the couch as the bear-man slung a massive arm around Suha's shoulders. "How's my girl?" he asked her.

"Good." She slid an arm around his waist and raised her face for his kiss.

Kyler's face fell, but he smiled manfully. "Nice meeting you, Suha."

"You, too," she said with a kind smile.

"Don't wait up," Beau said as the two of them headed out. "I'll crash at Suha's place tonight."

Kyler let out a gusty sigh, and then helped himself to some more food. Not much interfered with his appetite. "If you're a healer," he said to Evie between bites, "you didn't get that from Fane."

"Fane's your dad?" Jace asked. "So you know who he is."

"Sure, but he never said he was fae."

"But he never seems to get older," Kyler said. "And he's tall and blond and looks like a fucking model."

"Sounds fae to me," Jace said.

"He couldn't help our mom," Kyler added. "I mean, the dude's a flake, but he wouldn't have just let her die—not if he could've healed her."

"He loved her in his way. He's just...Fane." Evie moved a shoulder. "He comes and goes as he pleases."

"He's your dad," Jace growled. "The man should've helped you out."

"He did. After Mom passed, he gave me a diamond worth thousands of dollars."

Kyler snorted. "Only Fane would give you a diamond instead of cash."

"It saved our butts," she shot back.

Jace shook his head. "That's just like a fae. Throw some fucking glitter at a problem and hope it goes away."

"That's Fane." And it was true, but it hurt to hear it from Jace, because if the fada were right, she was fae, too. And besides, she loved her dad—she'd just learned not to count on him.

She blew out a breath and decided to think about it in the morning. "I'm for bed." She crossed the room to drop a kiss on Kyler's cheek. "Night, squirt. You should go to bed too. It's late."

He gave a big yawn and for once, didn't argue. "'Kay. See you in the morning." He gathered the empty plates and carried them into the kitchen.

"'Night, Jace." Evie gave him a smile that she hoped didn't look as forced as it felt. Jace had closed down. Apparently, the fact that she might have more than few drops of fae was a game changer for him. "Thanks for everything."

"Don't thank me." He rose to his feet. "It's my fault you got dragged into this." They stared at each other across the coffee table, and then he said, "Have a good sleep."

Her heart sank. So he wasn't coming. "You, too." She turned blindly toward the bedrooms.

∽

Jace sat on the living room couch as Evie and Kyler got ready for the night and then retired to their separate bedrooms.

Adric called to check on him and to report that they were still looking for Corban. "According to Zuri," he said, "the bastard never got on the plane. It was to Costa Rica, by the way."

"Who the fuck does he know in Costa Rica?"

"Hell if I know. But he's been gone for over a year. Maybe he met someone, or maybe it's someone he knew from the Darktime—one of my uncle's contacts. Leron used to send him on secret missions. But then again, maybe he just wanted to hide in the fucking rain forest. Anyway, I've got every tracker in the clan out looking for him. If he's still in Baltimore, we'll find him."

"Good. And Ric? When you question him, I want to be there."

"You got it. But meanwhile, you're the best protection Evie's got."

"That's the only reason I'm not out there with you right now."

Adric ended the call and Jace glanced toward his bedroom. Evie was probably in bed now—his bed. Jace's cat was awake and swishing its tail.

The woman. She waits. Go to her.

Jace remained stubbornly on the couch.

Why *had* he let Evie see him tonight? As he'd crossed the alley, he told himself that all he wanted was to make sure she was okay. His clan wasn't rich. Hell, they were hanging on by their fingernails, with every spare penny going toward rebuilding the homes and businesses that had been destroyed during the Darktime. Anything left over was invested in this new venture with the smartphones.

But Jace had some cash set aside. He could help Evie if she wasn't so stubborn about not taking his money.

He sure as hell hadn't planned to kiss her. But she'd looked so damn brave, clutching her keys like she had a prayer of chance against a man who had six inches and sixty pounds on her. And holy singing crystals, that had been some hot kiss. He'd been seconds away from stripping off her clothes and taking her right there in the kitchen.

But what the fuck was he thinking? She was a human and a fae, and he had a policy about not mixing with other races. Look where it had gotten Takira.

The wall sconces sensed the lack of motion and dimmed, but Jace barely noticed. He was recalling how happy his sister had been with Silver.

"So he's part night fae," she'd said. "He's not his genetics any more than we are. Who knows how much fae we have in us? You have a powerful Gift yourself. Does that mean you have more fae than me?"

"But a night fae," he'd growled. "Mate with anyone but one of them."

"Oh, Jace." His sister's dark eyes were knowing and a little sad. "You don't choose your mate—you just *know*. He's the one. And he's a good man. If you'd just meet him, you'd see."

"Is this what we've been fighting for all these years? For the right to mate with a fucking fae?"

"He's half fae." She'd lifted her chin. "And I thought we were fighting for the right to live our lives however we choose—instead of as Leron's pawns."

"You're right." Shame had tightened Jace's stomach. "Forget I said that. Go with your Silver."

"You'll come to our mating ceremony?"

He'd crossed the room in two strides and wrapped her in a hard hug. "Try and keep me away."

His sister was thin. Food had been scarce for a long time. Her stomach shouldn't have bumped against his.

He'd stepped back and ran a hand down her tunic. "You're—"

"A baby." A smile split her face. "We're having a baby. Can you believe it?" There hadn't been a cub born to the clan for three years.

Now grief swamped him. He dropped his head into his hands. If only he could go back and unsay those words to Takira. Because what had happened hadn't been either her fault or Silver's. All she'd tried to do was make a family with her mate and daughter.

It had been Leron and Tyrus who'd smashed his sister's happiness like a fragile glass.

Jace heaved himself off the couch. *Fuck this.* Takira wouldn't say he was honoring her by staying away from Evie.

She'd say Jace was being an ass.

CHAPTER 20

s Evie exited the bathroom, she heard Jace in the living room on his quartz phone.

She said goodnight to Kyler and then went into Jace's bedroom. The fae lights brushed over her as if saying hello, and then spread themselves across the ceiling before dimming to a soft glow—which was pretty effing awesome when you thought about it. Maybe Jace would let her take one home.

She left the door slightly ajar and changed into a striped cotton sleepshirt. Jace came down the hall and she tensed in anticipation, but he went into the bathroom and a short while later the shower came on.

She set the quartz phone he'd given her on the night table next to a pretty chunk of amethyst and sat cross-legged on the bed. Waiting for Jace—who probably wasn't going to come.

She combed her fingers through her damp hair. *What was so bad about being part fae?* Sure, the fae could be selfish, unpredictable creatures—look at Fane. But Evie wasn't like that, and if Jace couldn't see that, then to hell with him. She scowled in the direction of the bathroom.

A fae light brushed against her chest, right over her heart. She felt as if she'd been hugged.

She gave a wry smile. "You're trying to make me feel better. Thanks."

The fae light pulsed a bright yellow, and then dimmed again. Evie held up a finger, and another light—this one a soft pink—floated down to balance on her fingertip.

She stilled, afraid to breathe. It weighed no more than a soap bubble, a globe of miniscule stars. But unlike stars, the tiny points of light were in constant motion, turning in hypnotic spirals so that she had the unsettling sensation of falling endlessly into the center. The colors changed, the pink changing to a shimmering copper and gold and then back again.

The shower turned off. She dragged her gaze from the fae light and it wafted back to the ceiling.

She smoothed the sleepshirt down over her thighs and looked at the door. Several minutes crawled past, but still no Jace.

She blew out a breath. He wasn't coming, and she was tired. Time to go to bed. She gave her pillow a few hard punches and went to lie down.

A tap sounded on the door. Her heart leapt. "Come in."

Jace slipped into the room along with a few more fae lights and closed the door behind him. He'd changed into a white ribbed tank and brown shorts that hung low on his hips. His short black hair was damp from the shower, and stubble shadowed his jaw. He leaned against the door and stared at her—all hard muscles and honey-dark skin.

God, the man was beautiful. She moistened her lips. "Hello."

"So," he said, "you have more than a few drops of fae."

She lifted her chin. "So what? If I'm fae, then I'm one of the good ones, right? Being a healer is a good thing—like Suha."

He took a step toward her, then another. Lithe, catlike steps that made her heart slam against her rib cage. He was a predator, a man who literally had teeth and claws, but she trusted him with her life—and more, with Kyler's life. And when her heart sped up, it wasn't because she was afraid.

He stopped beside the bed. His gaze raked down her body, dark...hungry. Heat curled through her belly.

"Later," he murmured. "We'll talk about it later."

"Fine with me." She held out a hand. His fingers closed around hers, but instead of joining her in the bed, he drew her to her feet.

"You're not too tired?" He caressed her upper arms, and even that slight touch sent sensation jolting through her.

She pressed a kiss to the hollow of his throat. He smelled of soap and warm, spicy male. "Not anymore."

His pulse pounded beneath her lips. "God's cat, I want you—since the minute I first saw you." He gave a short laugh. "Even when I thought you were going to bash my head in with that damn rock."

Her mouth curved. "Really?"

"Yeah. I thought I was dying and you were a fucking angel. But what about you?" He leaned back so he could meet her eyes. "I'm an animal, Evie. The jaguar's part of me. Can you handle that? Because if not, tell me to get the hell out of here."

She fisted a hand in his tank. "Jace?"

"Yeah?"

"Shut up and kiss me."

He blinked, and then his cheek creased in a smile. "Yes, ma'am."

Powerful arms enfolded her. His mouth came to hers in a slow, bone-melting kiss. First, warm lips slid over hers. Then he teased the seam of her mouth with his tongue. When she opened to him, he slid his tongue inside, tasting her in leisurely sweeps that had heat licking through her.

She moaned and rose onto the balls of her feet to get closer. Big hands gripped her hips, urging her up against his erection. He dragged up the hem of the sleepshirt and then stilled as he palmed her ass.

"No panties?"

She ran her lips over the stubbled edge of his jaw. "I never wear panties to bed."

He squeezed her bottom, his mouth a wicked curve. "I like how you think, woman." A long finger delved between her cheeks, stroking into her cleft from behind.

He touched her clit from below and pleasure stabbed through her. She tightened her grip on his shoulders and rested her forehead against his chest while he played with her—sliding his finger into her, stroking over her most sensitive flesh. Her arousal ratcheted up, became an aching need.

She wriggled against his hand. "*Jace.*"

"Mm?" He brought his hand to his mouth and sucked her cream from his finger, his gaze locked on hers.

She shook her head. "I—"

"I know." He traced his lips over each of her eyebrows. "I know." And somehow, she felt that he did. They were in this together, each of them helpless against the other.

He took her mouth in another hard kiss. His tongue swept between her lips, demanding a response. Heat curled through her belly and lower, between her thighs. A pulse beat deep in her core. She sucked his tongue deeper and twined a leg around his hip, pressing her bare flesh against him.

He groaned low in his throat and ground himself against her. Electricity danced up and down her spine: hot, bright pricks that stoked her desire even higher. His hands moved to her breasts, now pinching her nipples, now caressing them.

He dragged his mouth from hers and regarded her from beneath thick black lashes. A flush painted his broad cheekbones, and the hazel of his irises was spiked a brilliant jade.

She curved a hand around his cheek. "That green in your eyes—"

"That's my cat."

"That's what I thought. When you're a jaguar, your eyes are green."

"The jag wants you too." His voice was guttural, and she knew both cat and man were present at this moment. His lids lowered, and he studied her warily, as if expecting her to change her mind and send him away.

She stroked his neck, his shoulders. "I'm not afraid of your cat. He's beautiful."

His jaguar had fascinated her from the first night. After Jace and Adric had left, she'd googled black panthers and found out that they could be either jaguars or leopards. A black panther still had the jaguar or leopard markings, but they were hidden by the extra black pigment. Even when Adric had first accused her of being fae and the jaguar had snarled at her, she'd still found the cat gorgeous in a savage, primal way. But even then, Jace's cat had seemed to want to protect her— he'd put himself between her and his alpha, and she guessed that for a shifter, that was a huge deal.

"He thinks you're beautiful, too. And sexy as hell." Jace angled his head against her palm, inviting her to stroke him more deeply. She obliged, combing her fingers through the short strands of hair on his nape.

"I was afraid you wouldn't come to me," she confessed.

Teeth scraped over her throat, sending dizzying waves of delight through her. Her fingers dug into his shoulders.

"I couldn't stay away."

"I'm glad."

He bent her over one strong arm and sucked at the base of her neck. She made a sound of sheer pleasure. "Jace..."

"Mm?" he said against her throat.

She set her lips against his ear and whispered, "Take me to bed."

His muscles locked. His nostrils flared, as if drawing her scent to his very heart —and then he snapped into action, scooping her up and setting her on the mattress. She scooted back against the pillows and watched as he dragged off his tank top.

He crawled onto the bed, part cat, part man—and in one smooth move, had her on her back, his thighs straddling hers, his hands on either side of her head.

He had a soldier's body, hard and roped with muscle. Her breath sucked in at the sight of all that smooth male flesh. She smoothed her hands down his chest. "You are one fine man."

"Yeah?" He nuzzled her neck.

"Oh, yeah." She trailed her fingers over his ridged abdomen. The muscles twitched under her hands, and she smiled inwardly. She loved that she affected him as much as he did her.

She came to the scars on his belly and frowned. "I'm sorry you got hurt again." She traced a finger over the longer, shallow mark.

He moved a big shoulder. "I've been hurt worse. I'm just sorry I dragged you into all this shit."

She nodded. And yet a part of her whispered that it wasn't all bad. Because if Jace hadn't come to her door, she wouldn't have ended up here with the sexiest guy she'd ever met pressing her to the mattress.

Jace tugged at the hem of her sleepshirt. She lifted her upper body, and he pulled it over her head and dropped it on the floor.

He sat back on his heels, taking her in as if she was the most delicious treat. Her nerves tingled. It was like he was touching her with his eyes, searing her with his gaze.

When she reached for him, he shook his head. "Let me touch you."

"All right." She set her hands back on the mattress and waited to see what he would do.

He started by feathering his fingers over her rib cage—light, delicate touches that sent a quiver over her skin. Next, he moved to her breasts, cupping them in his large hands.

"Beautiful," he breathed as he brushed his thumbs over her nipples.

She smiled up at him. She was average and she knew it—nothing special. But Jace made her feel like a freaking sex goddess.

Her nipples puckered and his eyes darkened. "Fuck, you're hot." He pinched them, and she sucked in a breath as pleasure shot from her breasts to her womb.

She traced her fingers up and down his wrists. He was strong, with those hard, heavy bones she'd noticed right from the first. His forearms were corded, the backs of his wrists covered with fine black hairs.

She slid her hand up his arm to the tattoo on his upper arm. The cat's paw itself was black, with touches of gold fire at the claw tips. She outlined it with her finger. "This is something to do with your cat?"

He grunted, and something about the way his face tightened told her he didn't want to talk about it. Then he swooped down to nip at her throat and everything else flew out of her head.

His fingers went to work again on her breasts, stroking and pinching until she was writhing on the bed. He bent down and sucked each nipple until they were both a wet, rosy pink.

She dug her heels into the mattress and tried to lift her hips toward him, but her legs were closed, her thighs pinned between his. She pushed at his chest, but he took her hands and pressed them to the mattress on either side of her head.

She moaned. "Please, Jace."

"Please what?" His lips moved against hers, soft and warm. "Do you want me to kiss you?" He teased the seam of her lips with his tongue.

"Yes." She lifted her head and tried to deepen the kiss, but he just gave her a quick peck before sitting back again.

"Maybe you want me to touch you here..." His fingers moved down her abdomen, leaving tiny flames in their wake, driving her to madness.

"Yes," she rasped.

"I like to take things slow." His voice was warm and a little rough. It stroked over her nerve endings like coarse silk. "That's okay, isn't it?"

Her head moved from side to side against the pillows. "Yes. No. God, Jace."

He chuckled, and then—finally, blessedly—he moved so that his knees were between hers. She gave a whimper of relief and bent her knees, opening to him. He slid a finger over her curls, and she lifted her pelvis, straining toward his touch. His finger slid lower, brushing over her most sensitive flesh so that she clenched her jaw at the pleasure of it.

He played with her, sliding his finger in and out of her, teasing her clit, until she was wound so tight, a single touch would've set her off, and then he lifted his hand.

"*Jace.*"

"Hm?" He brushed his fingers over her again.

She narrowed her eyes. "Stop teasing."

He nipped her ear. "You do know that I'm a cat?"

"So?"

"We like to play."

She gasped as he touched her again. "Oh," was all she could say as he slid two long fingers into her and then out again.

He nuzzled her collarbone. "You know you like it."

She angled her head so that he could kiss her throat. "If I say yes, are you going to tease me more?"

"Yeah." He nipped her skin. "But remember, I can scent a lie."

She raised her hands in mock surrender. "Then yes. Do your worst."

"Oh, angel." His breath rasped in. "I'm going to make you scream."

He brought his hands back to her face and lowered his body onto hers, keeping himself propped on his forearms. His legs came between hers and she automatically widened her thighs. He was still wearing his shorts. His hips settled against hers, his cock hard and thick against her through the thin layer of material separating them.

"So soft." He cupped the base of her skull in one big hand and nuzzled her cheek. "Everything about you is soft. Your hair, your lips. Your skin." He moved his mouth to her ear, sucking the hoop with the silver disc into his mouth, tonguing and nipping the sensitive lobe. "Soft. But strong where it counts."

"Mm." She wrapped her hands around his shoulders, exploring the round, hard muscles. His quartz lay between them, smooth and warm against her breast bone. It felt almost alive, like a bird's egg.

Jace lifted his head. The pendant hung from his chest, the smoky gray and purple infused with a faint green glow.

"May I?" She reached for his quartz but didn't touch it, recalling how he'd recoiled the night he'd been stabbed.

He shook his head. "It hurts if anyone but a close relative touches it...or my mate, if I ever take one."

"But it doesn't hurt when it rests on my chest?" she asked, and ignored how her heart constricted at the thought of his someday taking a mate.

"No. And don't ask me to explain why—it's not logical. Magic has its own rules."

"Why is it glowing?"

"Is it?"

He looked down, frowning, and then shrugged. "Thing has a mind of its own. Now, where was I? Oh, yeah—I was talking about how soft you are. Here and here." He pressed a hot kiss to each of her nipples, and then licked the undersides. "And here."

Her legs writhed beneath his. She reached down and tried to push off his shorts.

His hand went to his waistband. "You want these off?"

When she nodded, he murmured agreeably and got out of bed to remove them. He grabbed a handful of condoms from the nightstand drawer and dropped them on the table next to the amethyst before crawling back on top of her.

She touched his chest. "Jace?"

"Mm?" He smoothed a hand down her belly.

"I should tell you it's been a while."

His thumb brushed over her clit. A quick, light touch that made her muscles tense. "I'm honored then."

"You should be." Her mouth quirked. "I don't take my clothes off for just anyone."

He stilled and stared down at her, eyes shuttered. "I am."

But she sensed his withdrawal. So this was just sex. She kept her smile—but inside, her stomach twisted, even as she told herself that was all she wanted, too.

He lowered his mouth to hers and she kissed him back hard, wrapping her hand around his nape. He met her kiss for kiss, sweeping his tongue into her mouth. Tasting her. Teasing her.

She felt hot, unbearably aroused. Her hips moved restively against his, and she sucked his tongue deeper.

His groan vibrated deep inside her belly.

When he lifted his head, they were both sucking in oxygen. They stared at each other without speaking, and then Jace pressed a kiss to her collarbone.

"Your skin is like strawberries and cream," he rasped. "And fuck, I want to eat you."

He didn't wait for her response, just headed down her body. When he reached her mound, he pressed her thighs apart. "Beautiful."

She pressed her palms on the mattress, her thighs rigid in anticipation.

He pressed an open-mouthed kiss to her clit. Sensation zinged up her spine, tightened her nipples. He feathered his lips over her needy sex, licking and teasing her until she thought she'd go mad—and then he swiped his tongue up her moist center.

"Oh, God," she said on a moan. "No....no."

"No, what?" he asked against her pussy.

Her head moved back and forth on the sheets. "I mean yes."

"Yes to this?" His tongue slipped over her, circling her clit. Light, sure touches that had every muscle in her body constricting.

She threaded her fingers through his hair. It was almost dry now, the strands silky thick. "Yes."

"Or maybe you like this better?" He opened her with his thumbs and dipped his tongue inside her.

Her core contracted. She muttered something incoherent.

"Can't make up your mind?"

She shook her head, unable to form words. She only knew that she wanted more, so that was what she said: "More—please."

He gave a throaty chuckle against her inner thigh. "I like a woman who begs." He rewarded her with more licking and sucking.

The tiny flames danced up and down her body, gathered at her center.

He nibbled at her belly. "I'm waiting, Evie."

Heat spiked through her. There was something so sexy about the way he said it, low and firm. Her hands fisted in the sheets. "Please, Jace. Please. Kiss me. Suck me."

He murmured something rough and dark. He slid a long finger into her and at the same time, set his lips to her tender, aching flesh—and sucked. Hard.

Electricity arced through her. Her hips bucked and he pushed her back down onto the bed. She dug her fingers into the mattress and whimpered his name. Her thighs tightened on his arms, and then she pressed up against him.

"That's it," he murmured, stroking a finger into her wet opening. "Come for me, pretty Evie."

She cried out one more *please*, and then the fire at her center exploded in a series of rapid, molten bursts.

Jace gave a last, voluptuous lick to her pussy. She lay on the mattress, too pleasured to move, and watched as he fitted a condom on himself.

He came back over her body. She was still feeling the aftershocks. He worked his way up her body, kissing her as he moved: her stomach, her nipples, the sensitive indentation of her throat.

He settled between her thighs. His tip nudged her center, blunt and so good. She raised her hips to take him in and he thrust into her in a leisurely glide.

She moaned as her body stretched to accommodate him. It was too much. It wasn't enough. And then she was completely filled.

"Yes," she said hoarsely. "Just like that."

He buried his face in her neck. "You're so tight," he gritted against her skin. "So fucking hot."

He pulled out and thrust in again. Every nerve ending in her body shuddered with wonder. She dug her heels into his ass. "More."

He lifted his head and gazed down at her, his eyes a gorgeous swirl of green and gold and brown. His canines looked sharper, as if he were truly half cat at this moment.

Her jaguar man.

"More of this?" he asked in guttural tones, and thrust back in—hard.

"Yes." Her breath sawed in. "Please, yes."

She gripped his head and kissed him. He kissed her back, and then took her hands and, threading his fingers through hers, pinned them on either side of her head, holding her in place while he continued moving in and out of her. Slow, deep strokes that she felt clear to the base of her spine.

It was erotic, sensual. Perfect.

And then slow wasn't enough, and she canted her hips toward him, tightening delicate inner muscles around his thrusting cock.

"Holy fuck," he muttered, and they moved together, fast and hard. "That's it. Take it, Evie."

He released her hands. "With me," he said. "I want you with me." One arm wrapped around her shoulders while the other cupped her hip so he could thrust into her at a new angle.

Oh. My. God.

Pleasure and pain fused into one glorious burst of sensation. She heard herself cry out, and then she shot over the edge. He pumped into her a few more times, and then groaned out her name and followed her.

❧

JACE RESTED his face in the turn of Evie's neck, lungs heaving. He felt as if he'd been run over by a steamroller like a cartoon coyote—but what a way to die.

He inhaled deeply, steeping himself in her summery scent—fresh, sexy, and all Evie.

Her breath huffed out, a warm puff against his temple, and he gave her a last kiss on the lips before rolling onto his back. He curved an arm around her, tucking her close to his side. She murmured something and set a hand on his waist. A minute later, she went lax with sleep.

Poor baby was exhausted. A wave of protectiveness washed over him.

It's just sex, he told himself. *She doesn't want more, and neither do you if you're smart.*

Then he dragged in a breath. Because who the hell was he kidding? His cat was already acting possessive and the man was halfway in love with her.

Still, Evie wasn't his mate. He didn't feel the mate bond—not even a hint. Not that he was sure what it felt like, but everyone said you just *knew*. And yet... the cat was so content in her presence. He'd never felt that around any woman—fada, human, or fae.

The fae lights had drifted closer to Evie. There were six of them in the bedroom now. The woman was a fucking light magnet. They hovered near, tinting her face with a warm glow. Her dimple flashed in her sleep.

He recalled how she'd looked when he'd come into the room—impossibly beautiful, her hair the color of sunlight, her eyes a deep topaz beneath her dark brows.

He smoothed a thumb down her cheek. How had he fooled himself into believing she had only a few drops of fae? The woman practically glowed, just like the rest of her kin.

But she wasn't just fae, she was human, too. A mixed-blood, just like Silver.

"Fada don't mix with other humans or fae." Leron had pounded that into all of them, until Jace had believed it. "Humans are weak, easy to break, and the fae would sell out their own mothers for a handful of jewels. And you'll have cubs who can't take an animal form."

Jace had shuddered. The cat was part of him, clear to his soul. Being without it would be like cutting out a vital, irreplaceable piece.

That had clinched it for him. He was pretty sure he'd muttered that to Adric, when he'd given his friend the news about Takira's mating. "Her cub probably won't even be able to shift."

Gods, he'd been so fucking self-righteous.

And Leron had been wrong because Merry *could* shift. She was a beautiful black jaguar, just like him.

He tucked Evie closer and stared at the ceiling as one by one, the fae lights winked out until the room went dark.

CHAPTER 21

*E*vie came awake in slow increments. She was curled on her side, a big arm draped over her waist.

Jace. Her lips curved.

No covers except a sheet tangled around her legs, but he was spooned around her, and his body generated plenty of heat.

She was pleasantly sore in places that hadn't seen any action in way too long. She might even have a couple of slight bruises where he'd gripped her hip at the end, but who cared when she felt so good? She curled her fingers around his hand where it rested on her stomach and opened her eyes.

Without windows, there was no way to tell the time, but she guessed it was close to morning. Above her, the fae lights glowed on, painting the room with the muted colors of dawn—rose, a soft yellow, a pale sky-blue.

"Nice trick," she murmured.

Lips tickled her nape. "Who're you talking to?"

Her cheeks heated. "No one."

The arm on her waist tightened. "The fae lights?"

"Yeah," she admitted. "They seem almost alive. I thought about morning and they came on."

"It's you. They're somewhat self-directed, but I've never seen them as responsive as they are to you."

"Really? Huh." She stretched out a hand on the mattress. A shining ball the color of sunlight slid over her palm, sending a tingle up her arm. "So why does that bother you?"

He released her waist and rolled onto his back. "It doesn't."

"No? It sure seemed like it did last night."

"It's like we said in your kitchen—we don't mix. Fada, humans, fae—" He moved a hand.

"Wow." She sat up and swung her legs off the bed. "So I have two strikes against me. Maybe I'd better just leave."

"No—wait." He grabbed her wrist. "Don't be mad."

She pinned him with a look. "Let. Me. Go."

He released her and sat up. "Just listen—please? I'm sorry. But you said yourself that we don't mix."

She had. And she'd be wise to remember it.

She sank down on the edge of the mattress. "What?"

"I told you about my niece Merry. Her mom—my sister—was killed by some of our own people. But the night fae helped." He blew out a breath. "Because she had a baby girl who was a quarter fae. I know you're not a night fae, but the baby was part human, too, and it caused problems for Takira in the clan. Things were so bad then, anyway—people went a little crazy. After Takira died, a night fae went after her mate and the cub. Merry was the only one who survived."

"Oh, Jace." She closed her eyes. "I'm so sorry."

He jerked his head in acknowledgment. "Merry has to hide from the night fae. They have a thing about keeping their bloodlines pure. She'd be dead now if not for the Rock Run fada."

"Oh, God." Evie's heart squeezed. She could only imagine how she'd feel if it were Kyler.

"It was almost nine years ago, but—" He looked away.

She touched his thigh. "You still miss her. Your sister."

"Every fucking day. You asked about the tat." He indicated the cat's paw on his shoulder. "It's in honor of Takira. Her jaguar was gold and black."

She swallowed, and then scooted closer. Just touching him—thigh to thigh with her shoulder against his.

He slanted her a look. She'd thought he had a hard face, but now she knew him better, she saw there was something soulful about it, too—as if the hardness were a mask he wore to hide whatever was beneath.

He's sad. Underneath, he's sad and lonely. Evie didn't know how she knew. She just did. He was still grieving—for his sister, his parents.

"If both her parents are dead, why doesn't your niece live here?"

"When things went south, Takira took her family and disappeared. Merry was just four years old and she had to go into fucking hiding. And Takira"—his breath rasped in—"I never saw her again."

"I'm so sorry." She threaded her fingers through his.

"Anyway, after Takira was killed, Merry's dad took her and ran, but the assassins found him, too. Merry was about five by then. Somehow she ended up in Grace Harbor with the Rock Run fada." He shook his head. "I thought she died with her father. By the time we found her again, two years had passed and she thought of the woman who'd adopted her as her mom. I..." His throat worked. "I couldn't take her away."

Evie nodded. She understood, even agreed—but her heart hurt for him. To be forced to make such a choice...

"It's for the best," he said. "She's got a family—a mom and a dad and a little sister and brother. And I get to see her every week or so. At least I know she's alive, and happy."

His hand clenched around hers. She brought it to her mouth and kissed it, heart hurting for him. "How old is she?"

"Thirteen. She's frickin' smart, too—and even prettier than her mom." His voice rang with pride. "Her animal is a jaguar, like all the Joneses. And she's all black like me—another black panther."

"She sounds awesome."

"She is." He didn't speak for a while, and she was about to say something when he grated, "For two years, I thought she was dead. *Two fucking years.*"

"Oh, Jace." She hesitated, and then did what came instinctively—took him into her arms.

"Takira should've come to me, damn it. Why didn't she come to me?" His voice was a harsh whisper against her neck. "Why did she run like that? She had to know I'd help her, no questions asked."

"I don't know." She stroked his nape, heart breaking for him. "But if things were as bad as you say, maybe she thought it was better you didn't know."

He pulled away and stared down at his hands. "Or she just didn't trust me."

"Oh, Jace. Why would you say that?"

He lifted his head, his expression bleak. "Because I told her straight out not to mate with Silver."

"Oh." She swallowed hard. "I see."

"I was a fucking ass. But I came around. I could see how much she loved Silver, and he would've done anything for her. And when I found out she was having Merry, I was so happy for her. She was such a cute cub—still is. So when Takira disappeared like that with no warning, what was I supposed to think?"

"Maybe she was protecting you. If you didn't know where she was, you couldn't be forced to tell anyone."

His eyes flashed cat-green. "I wouldn't have given her up to anyone."

"Not even your alpha?"

"No." His fingers curled on his thighs. "Fuck. Maybe. It's hard for a fada to say no to his alpha. And our alpha then was the mother of all bastards. He might've dragged it out of me—I was younger then, not much older than Kyler."

"That has to be it. It's the only reason that makes sense. She didn't hide Merry from you—you knew her up until she was four. If your sister ran without telling you, it was to protect all of you, not because she didn't trust you."

He scrubbed a hand over his face. "Maybe you're right. I guess I'll never know." He pulled her toward him. "I want you, Evie. Come back to bed —please?"

That please arrowed straight to her heart. She cupped his face. The kiss they shared was soft, special. She knew he wouldn't want pity, but she ached for him. "All right. Just give me a minute." She pulled on her sleepshirt and headed to the bathroom.

When she returned, the room was awash with early morning light. Looking up, she realized that the ceiling had slits reaching all the way to the surface. An air circulation system was running as well, but the slits let in sunlight and additional fresh air.

Jace had used the other bathroom, but he'd beat her back to the room and was reclined against the headboard, an arm behind his head. Even at rest, his biceps bulged. His stomach was ridged, the scars thin pink lines that somehow made him even sexier. Nearly hidden beneath black chest hair were flat brown nipples, and lower down, his cock nestled in another patch of dark hair. It was already at half-mast, but as she watched, it lengthened into a full erection.

She swallowed, her mouth literally watering.

His hazel eyes gleamed in the dawn light. "Come here." He beckoned with one hand.

She pulled off the sleepshirt and climbed on top of him. His thighs were large and hairy between hers, his penis a hard stalk between their bellies. She set her hands on his shoulders and gave him a long kiss. Pouring all the understanding in her heart into him.

Because sometimes sex was just sex, and sometimes it was more—a way to share your deepest self with someone. To say, *You're not alone.*

The kiss transformed, went from compassionate to heated.

She raised her head and looked down at him through lowered lids.

Jace's mouth quirked. The sadness in his eyes had retreated, replaced by something hot and a little wicked. He rocked his hips, his meaning clear.

She began to move, sliding up and down on his erection, not taking him inside, just teasing them both as the underside rubbed against her pussy.

Jace's fingers tightened on her hips but he allowed her to take the lead. When she stopped, he cupped her breasts, pinching the nipples into sensitized points before reaching between their bodies to swirl his thumb over her swollen little nub. Unhurried, tantalizing strokes.

She closed her eyes and let him tease her. Tiny shocks reverberated up and down her spine, and her inner thighs tightened as she began the slow spiral to climax.

But she didn't want to hurry things, so she moved his hand away and leaned forward to rub her lips over his. He tasted of mint and morning. She gave him a leisurely kiss and then started to move down his body.

He went to roll her onto her back but she stopped him with a hand on his chest. "Stay there. I want to taste you."

His indrawn breath was all the answer she needed. She moved down his hard, flat stomach and circled his erection with her fingers. He was long and thick and a little sticky from her juices.

She lapped at him. Delicate licks that made his thighs go rock-hard.

"Fuck, you look hot," he said, and slipped a hand around her nape. "Take me, Evie," he said in a stern voice that made her insides melt. "Now."

She tightened her grip on him and obeyed. He tasted dark, salty.

She glanced up to see him watching her with smoky eyes. She smiled and sucked him deep into the pocket of her cheek.

"Yes," he said between gritted teeth. He tightened his grip on her nape, guiding her to please him. She continued working her mouth up and down him, loving that she could excite him like this. When she got tired, she scraped her teeth lightly over the cap, and his groan told her how much he liked it.

She palmed his balls. They were cool and tight. She rolled the sacs between her fingers.

He let her suck him a few more times, and then stopped her, saying, "I want to be inside you."

"Mm." She licked him one more time—a leisurely slide of her tongue up and down his heavily veined erection that had him muttering a curse.

When she lifted her head, he reached for her. "Give me a kiss."

She straddled him again and fitted her mouth to his. He framed her face with his hands and stroked his tongue over hers, firm and self-assured. A man preparing to take his woman.

He kissed her until she was panting for breath and squirming against him, and then he lifted her away from him. She gave a groan of protest and his mouth quirked.

"Easy, angel. You'll get what you want." He flipped her onto her stomach and smacked her bottom. "Raise your hips."

JACE WATCHED as Evie obediently propped herself on her forearms, her pretty round ass lifted to him. She was all smooth pale curves. Her scent filled his head, tart with arousal.

He'd never told anyone the whole story about him and Takira, and it had left him churned up inside. Scraped raw—but with the promise of peace. Maybe not today, but someday soon.

Now he just wanted to forget. Seeing Evie in such a graceful, submissive posture triggered the dominant male animal in him.

Lust punched through him. He wanted to fuck her long and hard, hear her make those sexy little moans that went straight to his dick.

He wanted to fuck her soft and slow, until she was begging to come—and then he wanted to make her scream.

He covered her body with his and speared his fingers in her short platinum locks. His cock was hard enough to drive spikes. It nudged against her ass, but he ignored it to nibble at her nape.

She made a sound of pleasure and arched her back, pushing that heart-shape bottom up against his erection.

His heart smacked against his ribcage. Every muscle in his body strained to take her.

He grabbed a condom and rolled it on, even while his animal grumbled at putting anything between him and that lush pink perfection. He probably didn't have to. Fada didn't spread diseases to humans and vice versa, and it was rare that a fada impregnated a female who wasn't his mate. But it could happen, and he didn't want to take the choice from her.

Evie's breath shuddered in. She glanced over her shoulder at him, her pupils so dilated her eyes appeared almost black.

He placed himself at her center and thrust home. Her body clenched around his, tight and hot.

Yes. Fuck, yes.

He withdrew almost to the tip and thrust in again. Taking her slow and hard and perfect.

She made a high, needy sound and he curved his body over hers, scraping his teeth over her nape, tonguing the turn of her shoulder.

She gasped his name. "Please. I need..."

He took one of her hands and brought it to her clit. It was slippery and swollen with arousal. "Touch yourself."

She rubbed herself, shuddered.

He cupped her chin, drawing her head back so her spine arched.

"Harder," he told her. "Make yourself wet for me."

She shook her head, and he knew it was more that she was dazed than that she was saying no, but he nipped her shoulder anyway. "Evie." He put all the force of his dominance in his tone. Fada males liked to master their women in bed, and his animal craved this. But he would've backed off if he couldn't tell it was exciting her as much as him.

At his tone, she squeezed around him like a hot fist, and he nearly came out of his skin. *Holy Mother Goddess.*

He felt her fingers move beneath his as she began playing with herself in earnest.

He dragged in a breath, his muscles shaking with the need to drive into her harder. "That's it." He set both hands on her hips as he rocked slowly out of her and then back in. "Touch yourself. Just like that. Make yourself come."

He couldn't see her touching herself, but he could picture it. The visual filled his head with a dark heat.

Lost in pleasure, he didn't even question why it was so important that she submit to him. He just pumped in and out, teeth gritted at how good it felt.

His quartz brushed over her back, and that felt good, too. Somewhere in the back of his mind he thought, *That's fucking odd.* Because even a casual touch of his quartz by the wrong person could send a shock of pain through him. But as he'd told Evie, magic had its own logic.

Just before he came, his quartz heated against his chest. He glanced down to see that the smoky gray and purple was shot through with emerald.

And suddenly, he just *knew.* She was his mate.

Damn, he was an idiot.

He growled in helpless surrender—and then thrust into her, hard and deep until he touched her womb.

She moaned and twisted under him, saying his name over and over, and then changing to *please please please.*

And in the end, she screamed.

CHAPTER 22

*J*ace tucked Evie close to his side and stared at the ceiling. What the hell was he going to do?

He could deal with her being a mixed-blood. He felt a stab of shame that he'd taken Leron's twisted prejudices as his own. If nothing else, he'd seen with Merry that a fada who was one-quarter fae and one-quarter human could still shift—and be the best niece a man could possibly ask for. If Takira were here, she would've slapped him upside the head.

Leron was dead, and it was time to bury his prejudices along with him.

Not that this was a done deal—the female always had the right to refuse a mating. But Evie wanted him, was maybe even a little in love with him. Hell, just the fact that she'd had sex with him was proof. He'd known she wasn't the type to sleep around even before her confession that it had been a while.

But would she want a fada for a mate? Because the prejudice wasn't all on his side. It was a huge step from taking a fada as a lover to joining his clan, and as his mate, she wouldn't have a choice. He was too important to the Baltimore fada, and besides, he didn't want to live as a solitary.

And yet how could he walk away now? Might as well ask him to rip out his heart.

Court her, said the cat and conjured up a hazy scene with candlelight and wine and Evie in a skimpy red nightgown.

His lips quirked. But hell, yes—wine, flowers, chocolate...whatever it took. And a job for that brother of hers, because the two of them were a package deal.

Jace wanted to ease her burdens, let her focus on what she really wanted to do, which was become a healer. His mate was strong in a way both man and cat approved, but that didn't mean she couldn't use a helping hand.

He pressed a kiss to her mussed blond head, and with a fatalistic shrug, accepted that this was his new life: Evie at the center. And he guessed he'd gained a teenage brother, too. His existence had just gotten a hell of a lot more complicated.

A family, the gods help him. With a mate that was part human, part fae—just like Silver. Somewhere in paradise, his sister was laughing her ass off. He let out a breath—and grinned.

Evie nuzzled his jaw. "You're thinking too loud."

"Sorry." But there was more proof; she was picking up his emotions.

She wriggled closer so that she was plastered against his front. He smoothed a hand down her back, heart full.

She smothered a yawn. "Damn, you tired me out."

"Sleep, then." He patted her bottom.

"Mm," she said.

He listened as her breath slowed, deepened. A few minutes later she was asleep.

He could've lain there all day holding her. Maybe even gone back to sleep himself—and there was almost nobody he trusted enough to fall asleep around. And yet last night he'd curled himself around Evie and slept deeply, untroubled by nightmares and more relaxed than he'd been for years.

Wonder filled him. This was what being happy was—this warm, contented feeling.

His cat settled its head on its paws and purred...and Jace dozed.

He was awakened by the buzz of his quartz. He silenced it and, easing out from under Evie, slipped into the hall, closing the door behind him.

It was Adric. "Just wanted to check in. How are things?"

"Okay on this end." He wasn't ready yet to talk about this thing with Evie, even with Adric. "Corban?"

"At least someone had a good night." Adric's tone was amused. Not much got past the alpha—he might not know that Jace planned to mate-claim Evie, but it was clear he'd guessed Jace hadn't slept alone. "Me, I'm on my way back to my den to catch some sleep. I'm sorry, bro—we didn't find Corban. The prick's disappeared into thin air."

Jace's contentment fled. "Fuck."

"He's here in Baltimore—I'm sure of it. But I can't narrow down his location. He's got a new quartz that I can't track him through, and he's smart enough to hide his scent." His friend expelled a breath. "Anyway, I called Beau, and he's on his way back with Suha. She wants to talk to your Evie anyway. Seems she might be a healer."

"Yeah." Jace didn't even argue that Evie wasn't "his." Because she was.

"Beau's under orders to stick with you for the next few days. I don't want you going anywhere alone until we find the bastard—got it?"

"Damn it, Ric, I don't need a fucking babysitter. I took on Corban *and* his little friend, remember?"

"Humor me," his friend drawled. "If nothing else, it's safer for Evie and Kyler."

"Fine." Jace dropped his head back against the wall. "Get some sleep. I'll report in later." He ended the call.

Fear crawled up his spine. Because now that he was wide awake and not stupid from sex, he realized that mating with Evie increased the chance that Corban would go after her. Tyrus, too. Jace's stomach bottomed out at how difficult it would be to keep her safe. That brother of hers as well.

Claws pricked his fingertips. Inside, his animal gave a jaguar-roar, ready to take on the world for its mate.

Evie appeared in the hall, dressed in the striped sleepshirt. It was so old it was practically see-through in places.

The roar faded. A word came through loud and clear. *Mine.*

And he would die to protect her.

"Morning." She gave a stretch that had the shirt riding up until he could see the notch at the top of her thighs. "Is it okay if I take a shower?"

He swallowed hard and for a few seconds, forgot all about Corban and Tyrus.

"Sure," he managed to say. "Towels are on the shelf." He ran a proprietary hand down her hip and tried not to stare at where the threadbare material clung to the hard points of her nipples. "I'll get breakfast started."

"Thanks." She came onto her toes and kissed him.

He watched as she slipped past him. That shirt barely covered her ass. Damn, he wanted to follow her into the bathroom, bend her over the jacuzzi, and—

He heard Kyler moving in his bedroom and pulled himself up short.

Shower. And breakfast.

And that shower was going to have to be alone. He muttered a curse and headed down the hall to the other bathroom.

When Evie emerged from the bathroom, the den smelled of breakfast.

A couple of fae lights trailed her to the kitchen. Jace was at the stove, barefoot and shirtless, a pair of shorts hanging low on his hips and a shaft of sunlight illuminating gleaming brown shoulders. Fried ham sizzled in a skillet while he cracked eggs into a bowl. As he beat the eggs into a yellow froth, the muscles under his jaguar tattoo flexed so the cat appeared almost alive.

Heat curled through her. It was insane. She'd just had sex with the man, and already she wanted him again.

Kyler had his back to her, taking plates from the cupboard, and Tigger was supervising from a perch on a kitchen stool. On the counter, an old-fashioned French press was slowly filling with coffee.

Jace poured the eggs into a second skillet. He and Kyler were talking something over in a serious tone. Evie paused, not wanting to interrupt. Jace was good with her brother, treating him like he was an adult, and Kyler was eating it up. She felt a pang of guilt—Kyler needed an adult male in his life.

Not your fault, she told herself. But she ached for her brother.

"You have to step up," Jace said as he added red bell peppers, cheese, and chunks of ham to the skillet. "Your sister needs you. You're not a kid anymore."

Whoa. They were talking about her? She frowned, not sure how she felt about that.

"You think I don't know that?" Kyler set three plates on the sturdy plank table. "I've been working my ass off to get a job, but no one wants to hire a sixteen-year-old."

"Maybe the clan can find you some work."

Kyler's face lit up. "Seriously?"

Jace nodded. "I'll talk to the alpha."

Evie frowned and moved forward. "That's nice of you, Jace, but we're not going to be here that long."

Jace twisted to smile at her. She had a feeling he'd known she was there all along. Guess you couldn't sneak up on a shifter.

"Morning, babe." His gaze moved appreciatively down her body, lingering on the band of skin left exposed by her green cropped tee. "I'm making Western omelets. Sound good?"

"Sounds wonderful. But about finding work for Kyler—"

"Why not?" Her brother rounded on her. "You know I need a job."

"No way you're going to drive to Baltimore every day." *And work for the Baltimore fada.*

Kyler started slamming forks onto the table beside the plates. "Damn it, Evie, when are you going to stop treating me like a five-year-old? People have been working for the Rock Run fada for years and nothing's ever happened to them."

She set her jaw. "We'll talk about it later."

"It's not up to you, Evie. This is my life, my decisions."

Jace laid a hand on Kyler's shoulder. "Apologize to your sister," he said sternly.

Her brother went stiff. "What?"

"You don't swear at your sister and you don't raise your voice to her. She's doing the best she can. She deserves your respect."

Kyler flushed. "Sorry," he mumbled. "I didn't mean anything."

"It's okay," she said.

"No, it's not," Jace replied. To Kyler he said, "I know you didn't. But if you want to be treated like an adult, you need to act like one."

His shoulders slumped. "But I've applied for every frickin' job in Grace Harbor, and no one's hiring. I'm either too young or they already have someone."

Jace squeezed his shoulder and released him. "That's a bitch, and I'm happy to help—but only if it's okay with your sister."

They both turned to her, Jace so clearly deferring to her that she couldn't get mad at him for interfering, Kyler with his jaw set but his eyes pleading.

"Please, Evie? I don't have to take it. Maybe they'll have something I can do in the morning when you don't need the car."

She sighed. She hated being the bad guy all the time. But she wasn't sure they should get in any deeper with the Baltimore fada. Yeah, she was trusting Jace to protect the two of them, but they wouldn't need protecting in the first place if someone wasn't trying to kill him.

Her gaze flicked to the still-healing claw marks on Jace's face. "We'll see," she told her brother.

His face fell. "Which means no."

"It means we'll see," she returned.

But it was Jace's expression that made her flinch. His eyes shuttered and she felt his withdrawal like a physical thing. "Give your sister some time to think it over," he told Kyler. "Pushing her is just going to get you a no for sure."

Evie shoved her hands in her pockets. She'd hurt Jace, and that was the last thing she wanted to do after he'd trusted her enough to share his sister's story. But her brother came first.

"Need any help?" she asked.

"You could make toast." He handed her a loaf of bread and a knife. "Butter's in the cooling unit." He indicated a steel door set into the stone.

She nodded and set to work.

An awkward silence fell, each of them focused on their task until Jace set a platter of omelets on the table. "Breakfast is served."

"Thank you," Evie and Kyler said at the same time, but before they could take their seats, footsteps pounded down the stairs. The front door banged open and suddenly the kitchen was filled with lean, heavily muscled males.

The newcomers sorted themselves into Sam plus two other men, their faces grim with tiredness. They revived at seeing Jace, though, unashamedly hugging him and asking how he was doing.

When he turned to Evie and Kyler, the shuttered look was gone. "Meet the rest of my den. You already know Sam, and these other two are Horace and Zuri." To his den mates, he said, "This is Evie and her brother Kyler."

"Morning." Sam was already pulling Evie into a hug. "You slept good?"

"Yeah." She couldn't help glancing at Jace. Sam's brow shot up, but he didn't say anything. Instead, he cast a hungry eye at the omelets and all but licked his lips.

Jace waved a hand at the table. "Help yourself. I'll make some more."

"Thanks, man." Sam bumped fists with Kyler and took a seat. A moment later he was tucking into his breakfast.

Next was Horace. He had dreadlocks, deep brown skin and an easy smile, and Evie liked him immediately. "Welcome to the den," he said and gave her a kiss on the lips that had Jace growling.

"Enough already. Give the woman some space."

Horace winked at her, and then shook Kyler's hand. "Hey, bro, wassup?"

"Not much," he replied, and the two of them fell into a conversation while Horace set to work making another pot of coffee.

That left Zuri. As he stuck out his hand, Evie couldn't help widening her eyes. He was gorgeous, the kind of man women went stupid over—tall and broad shouldered with a shaved head, a narrow black mustache and a soul patch beneath his full lower lip.

"So you're Evie."

She gave him her hand. "That's me." Instead of shaking it, he brought it to his lips for a kiss—but the whole time his dark eyes scrutinized her coolly.

"Zuri's one of Adric's lieutenants," Jace said from the stove where he was frying some more ham.

That figured. The man had an edge to him. She gave him a polite smile and resolved to stay out of his way.

"Ric said you couldn't track down Corban," Jace said.

The other lieutenant scowled. "Bastard's gone to ground. We're not even sure he's still in Baltimore."

"Ric thinks he is. Sit down and eat. You need fuel."

Zuri squeezed his nape. "Might as well—the trail's cold for now."

The men helped themselves to the omelets on the table while Evie handed around steaming cups of coffee and Kyler manned the toaster. It was obvious Jace's den mates were tired and upset that they hadn't been able to find Corban. But except for Zuri, they went out of their way to be nice to her and Kyler, acting as if nothing would make them happier than having the two of them as guests for the next month. And even Zuri wasn't rude, just quiet.

Jace took a seat at the head of table with Evie and Kyler on either side and passed her the platter with fresh omelets. Evie took a bite—and closed her eyes in bliss. The man could cook. The omelet was amazing, a perfect blend of flavors.

She opened her eyes to find Jace's gaze on her mouth, his irises a smoldering jade.

She gave a tentative smile. "It's really good."

He leaned closer to murmur, "It's a pleasure to feed you."

Her heart leapt. She'd been afraid she'd ruined things between them, but it seemed he was ready to play again. A glance at the men told her they were focused on their own food, so she slid the fork between her lips—very slowly. When she was done chewing, she licked her tongue up the tines.

Jace's eyes narrowed on her lips. "When I get you back to bed...," he muttered in a voice for her ears only.

Her stomach flexed in anticipation. Their gazes locked, and sound receded as they stared at each other.

Kyler made a gagging sound. "Right here. Trying to eat."

"Shut up, squirt." Evie batted a fae light at him. He slapped it away and there was a blue flash.

"Jesus, Evie." Kyler shook his hand. "That smarts."

Evie gulped. "Sorry—I didn't think it would...what happened, anyway?"

"It felt like I touched a live wire."

All four men were staring at her like she'd grown an extra head. She set down her fork. "What?"

Jace shook his head. "It's just that fae warriors use fae balls as weapons. A light shouldn't flash like that."

Kyler chortled. "Evie Morningstar, fae warrior. I *knew* you were going to try to incinerate me with a fae ball."

She pointed her fork at him, narrow-eyed. "One more word out of you and I will." But she frowned at the fae light, shaken. She could've *hurt* Kyler.

"A fae warrior can conjure his or her own fae balls." Jace squeezed her knee, seemingly reading her mind. "Your Gift seems related to the lights, but unless you can form your own, Kyler's safe."

"We'll just be sure not to make you mad," Horace said straight-faced.

She rolled her eyes, and he winked at her. Evie grinned back. Sam and Horace, at least, had accepted her into their circle. She wasn't sure why she cared since she wasn't going to be here that long—but she did.

Breakfast over, Horace got to his feet and gave a long, bone-cracking stretch. "God's balls, I need a shower. And then I'm going to sleep until afternoon."

"Me too." Sam and Zuri followed him while Evie got up and started to clear the table.

"I'll wash if you dry," she told Jace.

Kyler helped carry the dishes over to the sink, and then tried his phone again. It still didn't work, but he went into the living room to play a game, leaving her alone with Jace.

"Thanks," she said. "For offering to help out Kyler. I'm just not sure..."

"It's okay. I understand. You could always take money from me, you know. As a loan," he added when her spine went rigid. "We don't know how long this is going to go on. I feel responsible for the fact that you can't work."

She unclenched her muscles. Maybe she *was* being too stubborn. If the shoe were on the other foot, she'd want to help him. "All right. But only if it's a loan."

"It's a deal. Of course, you could always pay me back another way." He set down his dish towel and wrapped his arms around her where she stood at the sink, elbow deep in soapy water.

Her heart kicked up. "What do you mean?"

"I think you know." His lips brushed over her neck.

She chuckled and then caught her breath as he nibbled his way to her earlobe. She rinsed the last plate and set in the dish drainer, and then clucked her tongue. "That's bad, paying a man in sex."

"Maybe I like bad girls." One hand squeezed her breast while the other wandered lower to her shorts.

Her nipples prickled. Heat slid over her, thick and sweet as molasses. "In that case, what are your terms?"

"What are you offering?" His cock nudged the small of her back.

"Depends." She twisted her head to kiss his throat and then started in on the silverware. "Pretty much anything is up for negotiation."

"Anything? Oh, angel, you don't know what you're saying."

"No?" Somehow her wet hands were around his neck and his fingers were working their way into her waistband.

"If your brother wasn't in the living room," he muttered against her ear, "you'd be bent over the table right now, taking me."

She gulped. She'd almost forgotten Kyler. She turned her head and gave him an open-mouthed kiss. "And I might even let you."

He slid a finger into her damp panties for a quick, teasing touch. They both heard the front door open. "Anybody home?" Suha called.

CHAPTER 24

$\mathcal{E}$*vie didn't trust him with her brother.* Jace was still reeling from the blow even as he stepped back from her with a growled, "Later," and turned to smile at Suha.

It clawed at his soul. Didn't she know he'd protect Kyler with his life?

But how could Jace argue Evie was wrong? From what she'd seen of his clan so far, they were dog-eat-dog, like in the Darktime.

His first instinct had been to withdraw. The mate-bond was fragile—a gossamer-thin thread that either of them could still break. It would hurt like hell, at least for him, but it was still possible.

Then his stubborn side asserted itself. Evie was right—and she was wrong. Things had changed under Adric. The clan wasn't like that anymore. Maybe the world didn't know it, but that was because a bad reputation was the best protection as they worked to rebuild themselves.

Damn Tyrus and Corban anyway. A cold anger burned in his stomach. But he refused to let them ruin this for him. Evie was the best thing that had happened to him in a long time, and he wasn't going to give her up without a fight.

He'd just have to be crafty. He was a cat—cunning and patient. Changing Evie's mind would require both, and meanwhile, he had her in his den. What better place to show her the rock-solid bonds that were at the heart of a clan?

Suha took out her quartz to scan Jace. She nodded with satisfaction. "You look good, babe." She gave Evie a sidelong grin. "I'm not going to ask why."

Evie shot Jace a guilty look and then her dimple flashed. He just looked back, straight-faced.

"Nope," Suha said, "don't want to know."

Beau had stopped to say hi to Kyler, but now he shambled into the kitchen. "Hey, girl." He lifted Evie off her feet in a hug.

Suha smacked him on the shoulder. "Take it easy, you ass. She's not used to bears."

But Evie just grinned and hugged him back. "I don't mind."

Beau set her carefully back on her feet. She was flushed and a little mussed and Jace wanted to eat her up.

Suha shook her head and shooed Beau out of the kitchen. "Go do your man-stuff. Evie and I need to talk."

The bear wrapped a huge hand around her nape and nuzzled her ear. "Are you trying to get rid of me, woman?"

"Yeah," she said, but her eyes closed in pleasure.

"All right," he said, and grabbed a mug of coffee before heading back into the living room.

Jace glanced at Evie. "Want me to go too?"

But she shook her head and asked him to stay, so he got the three of them a fresh cup of coffee and pulled up a chair next to hers at the kitchen table.

Suha took the seat across from them. "So," she said, "have you had a chance to think of any questions?"

Evie took a sip of her coffee. "No offense, but I'm not even sure I'm a healer. Like I said last night, I wasn't even able to help my mom."

"Even if you had the Gift of healing, you'd need training. What do you know about the fada?"

"Well," Evie said, "everyone knows you're part animal—and that you're magical in some way. And you earth fada have the quartz"—she nodded at Suha's pendant—"which is important to you in some way."

Suha nodded. "Fada are a mix of animal and human genes, but every fada has at least a few drops of fae blood, too. We don't have the full range of fae Gifts—ours tend to be related to our animals. The most common fada Gifts are hunting and tracking, but we also have a few healers in every generation. Some of us are born protectors—they guard the most vulnerable, like nursing mothers and cubs. Jace is Gifted with crystals. He can do amazing things with quartz."

Jace nodded. "But I had to train under another crystal engineer to fully utilize my Gift. Just like Suha trained as a healer."

Evie blew out a breath. "I wish you were right, but I really don't think I'm a healer."

Suha held out her hand. She had a nasty black-and-blue mark on the back. "Why don't you see if you can make this bruise disappear?"

"Sure, but why didn't you just heal it?"

"Lesson One: Don't waste your Gift. Because every time you call on your Gift, you burn energy. The bruise will heal on its own in a few days. Not that healing it would be a big deal, but what if someone gets hurt bad, and I need every bit of energy? Like Jace when he was stabbed by the night fae—I almost didn't have enough juice to draw the poison from his body. The alpha had to step in and help me. And iron poisoning is a serious thing—he could've died."

Evie's fingers tightened on her mug. "You didn't tell me."

He shrugged. "Things worked out."

"He wouldn't. And not because he's a fada and you're a human." Suha rolled her eyes. "It's because he's a man."

"Guess that's the same with every race," Evie muttered, and the two women exchanged a very female grin.

Suha set her bruised hand on the table. "Give it a try. You can touch the bruise if you want. The key is to picture it healing."

"How do I draw on energy to heal you?"

"You just do. Picture the bruise healing, and the energy will come."

Evie nodded. She stared at the bruise, and Jace could sense her gathering her concentration into herself. Nothing happened that he could see, except a couple of fae lights drifted over to brush across her shoulders.

Evie tried again, this time touching the bruise. Jace felt her whole body go rigid, but still nothing happened.

"Try to picture it whole, unbruised," murmured Suha.

"Okay." Evie's dark brows furrowed.

"Breathe," said Suha. "Slow and easy."

She dragged in a breath and glared at the bruise as if it were an enemy and she an invading arm. When it remained unchanged, her shoulders slumped. "I'm sorry," she said, sitting back. "I can't."

Jace set a hand on her back. "Maybe she's an amplifier," he said to Suha as he massaged her in slow circles.

"A what?"

Suha lifted a brow. "You just might be right. An amplifier works with a healer," she told Evie, "adding their energy to the healer's—but they can't heal on their own."

"Last night," he said, "you were able to add your energy to Suha's."

"And the fae lights?" asked Evie.

"Who knows?" The healer shrugged. "There's something about your energy that draws them, and that enhances your own."

Evie's face fell. "So if this is true—that I'm a—whatever you call it—then I'm not going to be able to heal people on my own."

"Amplifiers are valuable, too," he said.

"Yeah?" She seemed unconvinced. But then, for someone like her it would be a dream come true to have the Gift of healing. Jace hated seeing her so disappointed. He wanted to pull her onto his lap and tell her it was all right, that she was perfect just as she was.

"I'm sorry." Suha squeezed Evie's hand. "To be a healer is an amazing Gift, one I thank the Goddess for every single day. But think about it—you can still help heal people. Any Gifted healer would pay to work with you. We get stretched to our limits, especially when sickness sweeps through the clan, or when we're under attack."

Evie's chin lifted. "I wouldn't charge. I might not have much money, but I'm not going to take payment for helping to heal someone. If you need me, just ask."

"That's good of you," Suha responded, "but it's only fair that you get paid. Look at me—anyone in the clan can come to me for healing, and I'm happy to help however I can. But in return, the alpha pays me a salary. How would I live otherwise? Healing is my calling—but it's my job, too, just like the doctors and nurses in your world. And sometimes, people give me something extra—food, a piece of pottery, a hand-knit sweater. It would be wrong to refuse, don't you think? When they're only trying to thank me."

Evie nodded slowly.

"So if I call on you to help me—and I will—you'll accept payment for it, or else I won't feel right asking. You'll need to be trained, of course. Energy work can burn you up if you don't know what you're doing."

"Leesa," said Jace. The woman was a deer like Suha, and one of the few elders to survive the Darktime. Leron Savonett had simply ignored her—to him, deer were the bottom of the barrel.

Suha nodded. "Leesa is our only amplifier. I'll call her later if you're up for it."

Evie wrapped a hand around her coffee cup. One thumb rubbed the surface. "Thank you," she said without looking at Jace, "but we're probably not going to be here that long."

Suha's brows shot up. "I see. Well, let me know if you change your mind."

<h1 style="text-align:center">CHAPTER 25</h1>

Corban Savonett hailed a cab in the Baltimore Inner Harbor.

"Druid Hill Park," he barked.

The cabby was a young male with the black hair and features of a south Asian —Pakistani, perhaps. His gaze went to the bloody gash on Corban's neck, and he opened his mouth to say no.

Corban was already inside. He gazed back steadily.

The cabby shut his mouth. "Yes, sir."

Corban dropped his backpack on the seat and tried not to look as weary as he felt. He'd taken a stolen motorboat to Baltimore and then abandoned it near the aquarium. He'd lost a lot of blood before he'd been able to seal the gash on his neck, and he hadn't had any energy left to deal with the chunk Jace Jones had taken out of his thigh. He was no healer, and his quartz was drained from the demands he'd put on it to track Jace Jones to his human girlfriend's house.

His lip curled. Figured Jones was chasing human tail. The man was weak, just like his sister. Takira could've been a high-ranking sentry, but she'd thrown it all away for her mate and that mixed-blood cub of hers.

The cab bounced over a pothole and pain jolted through Corban. A hiss escaped him and the cabby muttered an apology.

Corban ground his teeth. Damn Jace Jones anyway. The man should be dead by now. It had been two against one, and Corban had always been able to whip his ass.

But the scrawny kid had grown up. Corban should've realized that when the night fae assassin had failed to kill him, but he'd chalked it up to bad luck.

The ride to the park took fifteen minutes. The cabby let him out at an entrance near Jones Falls Expressway. "No charge," he said.

Corban jerked his chin in acknowledgment. He hadn't been planning to pay the guy anyway.

The street was dark and deserted, the nearest streetlight dangling brokenly from its pole. The only sound was the low-grade hum of traffic on the expressway.

The cabby eyed him in the rearview mirror, his scent an acrid mix of fear and perspiration.

Smart man.

Corban toed off his shoes and left them on the floor of the cab. His switchblade was already concealed in his hand. In one swift move, he hooked his left arm around the cabby's throat and at the same time, pressed the blade's catch. It sprang open and he touched the point to the cabby's cheekbone just beneath his eye.

"Don't move or I'll take your eye out."

"Easy, there." The cabby slowly raised his hands. "I don't want any trouble. I didn't even charge you for the ride."

"You're a fucking prince among men. Now give me your shoes."

The man's throat worked. "My shoes?"

Corban pressed the knife deeper. Just enough to nick his cheek. It was a bluff —the last thing he needed was the attention that cutting the cabby would bring— but the man said, "Sure, sure. But you have to let go first. I can't reach them."

"Open your door."

"Okay. Here I go." The man unlocked the door and pushed it open.

"Here's how it's going to go down. I'll let you go, and you toss your shoes out the door."

"That's all? You just want my shoes?"

"That's all."

"Okay, sure. No problem."

Corban released the cabby but stayed close, breathing down his neck.

The man took off his shoes and tossed them out the door as directed. His hands were trembling, and his breath was coming in fearful huffs.

Corban sneered. Humans were so easy to scare.

"There." The cabby met Corban's eyes in the rearview mirror. "My shoes, just like you asked."

Corban shoved open his door without answering. The moment his feet touched the sidewalk, the cabby pulled shut his door, hit the gas and sped off.

Corban swore and jumped back, barely avoiding being sideswiped. The cab kept going down the street, the back door still open.

Corban pushed his feet into the man's leather loafers. They were shiny brown and with that just-bought smell. He wiggled his toes. They fit good, too. He'd got the better of that bargain.

Adric was a legendary tracker. Corban didn't think Adric could follow Corban's scent through his shoes, but he wasn't a hundred percent sure. Better to be safe.

His destination was a quarter mile away near Jones Falls, the large creek that ran through Druid Hill Park. He hobbled toward it as fast as he could, careful not to brush against trees or bushes.

He reached the boulder that covered the entrance and sank down on it, heart pounding with the effort it had taken to get here. But every minute he spent above ground was dangerous. He shoved the boulder aside, uncovering the entrance to a small, hidden den, lowered himself partway down the rickety metal ladder and with his last ounce of energy, set the boulder back in place before descending the last few feet to the floor.

The den was basically a dirt cellar with a water supply and a toilet. Corban had dug it out in secret, so that not even his father had known about it. No lighting, which meant it was pitch black. Corban paused, waiting for his eyes to go night-glow. When he could see again, he limped his way to the two musty wool blankets stacked in a corner. Sinking onto the blankets, he eased off his pants and examined the back of his thigh. The wound had scabbed up, but it needed to be cleaned. With grim determination, he rose back to his feet and went to the sink.

It had been a couple of years since he'd been here. The spigot gave a groan and a pop, and then rusty water gushed out. He let it run until it was clear, and then found a clean T-shirt from his backpack and used it to rinse the dried blood from his neck and thigh.

He was too drained to change to his wolf. He rolled himself up in a blanket and allowed himself a smile. Adric would never find him here.

Then he passed out on the dirt floor.

After Suha left, Evie and Jace took a walk to Druid Hill Park along with Kyler and Beau.

"Should be safe enough," Jace said. "The night fae won't be out on a sunny summer day—their skin's too sensitive to light. And Corban's gone to ground."

"And the day Savonett gets past the two of us," growled Beau, "is the day I slit my own throat."

So the four of them headed up to the surface. The way out led through the big shed. Evie had only caught a glimpse of it last night, but now she could see it was filled with motorcycles and a car with most of its insides removed. There was a huge workbench at one end, and a mix of human tools and those which looked like they were quartz-powered.

Kyler's eyes bulged. "Wow," he breathed with a reverence usually reserved only for his favorite games.

"Sam's the mechanic," said Jace, "but we all like to mess with engines."

"Sick." Kyler ran a hand over a cobalt-blue fuel tank. "If you need any help, just yell."

"I will." Jace opened the outside door and inhaled, testing the air. "Seems clear, but wait here a minute." He moved forward. Evie was reminded again that he was part cat. There was something very feline in his walk—loose and easy, each step precise, graceful.

Beau ambled out behind him. He tipped his head back and inhaled deeply. "No sign of Savonett or a night fae," he agreed.

Jace nodded and motioned to Evie and Kyler to join him. Kyler and Beau walked on ahead, leaving her and Jace to follow.

Evie couldn't get it out of her head—she was part fae and she apparently had some kind of Gift. An amplifier, whatever that was supposed to be. But it felt right—she'd felt the heat in her hands and had somehow *known* she was helping to heal Jace.

When Suha had offered to get her training, she'd lit up inside—until she'd realized she couldn't accept. Jace hadn't said anything, but when she'd refused, he'd removed his hand from her back.

But he must know this was only temporary. He'd said himself they didn't mix.

She sighed. What she really wanted was to talk this over with Fane, because if it was true that she was part fae, why hadn't anyone told her?

Jace had said that speaking a fae's name attracted their attention, but it hadn't worked to call Fane in the past, except maybe that time right before her mom died. Still, as they walked down the driveway, she turned to Jace and deliberately said her dad's name aloud.

"Do you think Fane could help me?"

He raised a brow. "Your dad?"

"Yeah. Fane." She repeated it a little louder. "I have some questions—like what kind of fae am I? And why the hell didn't I know?"

Jace slipped an arm around her shoulders. "Maybe he's trying to protect you. If you're mostly human, you don't want to be in the fae world. You'd be at the bottom of the food chain, powerless against the stronger fae. And those pricks eat their young."

Her mouth twisted. "Or maybe he doesn't want to admit he has a mixed-blood daughter."

He tightened his grip but didn't say anything. She winced inwardly, recalling his niece Merry was in a similar situation.

She blew out a breath and set Fane from her mind, because when had he ever come when she needed him? Meanwhile, it was a gorgeous day and a hot-as-hell guy had his arm around her. If she was only going to have these few days with him, then she was going to squeeze every last bit of enjoyment from it.

Jace's neighbors were seated on their marble stoops, chatting to friends and enjoying the morning sun. The houses were small, each on a tiny piece of land, but they were neat and well-kept. Everyone they passed called out a friendly hello to the two fada. Jace and his den mates were clearly well-liked.

A tiny girl in a pink dress with her hair in tight cornrows pelted down the sidewalk, her mother a few yards behind. "Up, Mister Jace." She raised her arms imperiously.

"Chantelle." He released Evie and swung her into his arms. "How's my girl?"

"I los a toof." She pointed to the space where one of her front teeth used to be. "Mama says the toof fairy is gonna bring me a dollar."

Jace smiled at her mother. "Morning, Kari."

"Morning," she returned and then shook her head at her daughter. "Chantelle, don't bother Mister Jace. He's got visitors today." She gave Evie an apologetic smile.

"Oh, I don't mind," Evie said.

"Good," said Jace, "because me and Miss Chantelle are old friends, aren't we?" He dropped a kiss on her small rosebud of a mouth.

Chantelle pursed her lips and kissed him back. "See, Mama. He likes it."

"Hmm," he said with a wink at Kari. "Which little girl I know likes to fly?"

"Me, Mister Jace!" shouted Chantelle. Jace chuckled and tossed her gently into the air. The child erupted in helpless giggles as he caught her with large, sure hands. "Again, Mister Jace! Please."

He tossed her up and down a few more times before shifting her to his hip with the ease of a man used to kids. And right then, a piece of Evie's heart broke off and landed at his feet. He was just so damn adorable, this tough, inked shifter with a tiny girl in a pink dress clinging to him.

Evie gulped and looked away. Jace pulled her close with his free arm and introduced Kyler and her to Kari, before handing Chantelle back to her mom so they could continue on their way.

Evie slid an arm around Jace's waist while the other two walked ahead. He slanted her a sheepish look. "Those are my tenants. Chantelle's dad isn't in the picture, so I help out where I can."

Evie pressed a kiss to his jaw. "You're my hero."

"It's nothing."

"No," she said. "It's something. Trust me, I know."

He squeezed her shoulders. "I'd like to pound some sense into your dad."

She shook her head. "It wouldn't do any good. Some men just aren't meant to be fathers."

"I can't understand it. Cubs are so fucking precious."

"That's what I think." Their eyes met and she looked away, afraid of what he would see in her face.

He's not for you.

Suha had warned Evie away from him in the nicest possible way, pulling her aside to murmur, "Promise me you won't hurt him."

Evie had drawn back, affronted. "I won't."

"Not intentionally, no." Suha's dark gaze was knowing and a little sad. "But

Jace—he's a dominant male, and so you might think he can't be hurt. But he can. You're special to him, Evie. The Darktime left him different. He was always a serious kid, but losing his sister—that ripped him to pieces. He was so dark for a while there that I thought we might lose him. An earth fada can will himself to death. The quartz—we use it to heal ourselves, but it can be used the opposite way. To turn on ourselves."

Evie had swallowed.

"But he came out of it. It helped when they found his niece."

"He told me about her."

"He did?" Suha's delicate black brows had winged upward. "That proves my point right there. He feels something for you. Just—don't hurt him."

Evie had glanced at where Jace was arguing basketball with Kyler and Beau. "I wouldn't," she'd said.

Suha had moved a shoulder. "If you don't want him, say so now. Don't let it go any further."

Now Evie pressed a hand to her breastbone. Because maybe she would hurt him. But if she did, it wasn't going to be one-sided.

Jace glanced at her. "Everything okay?"

She rose on her toes and kissed him. "Yeah."

The rest of the day passed in a happy blur. They walked with Jace and Beau to the park and around Druid Lake, and then headed back to the den, where they sprawled out on the grass drinking iced tea under a big maple. Beau remained standing, one arm propped on the wooden fence that circled the backyard, relaxed but alert, his deep brown eyes continually scanning the area. The men got into a conversation about motorcycles while Evie pillowed her head on her arms and gazed up at the rustling green leaves. It had been a long time since she'd just laid on the grass without anything to do.

Jace traced a finger down her jaw to the hollow of her throat. "Sleepy?"

"Mm."

He nuzzled her ear. "Take a nap if you want. I'll be keeping you up tonight."

Her lips curved. "Is that a promise?"

The answer was a sexy growl that made her abdomen tug.

Sam woke up and wandered outside, yawning. Jace sat up and murmured something to him, and he nodded. Before she knew it, the tiger had his head deep in her car's engine, and when she objected that she couldn't pay, he'd shrugged a big shoulder.

"I'm not asking for money. I need something to do, and I'm sure we have some spare parts in the shed."

"But—"

"Let him," Jace said. "The man's a genius with engines, and he really does like to play with them."

"All right," she said, "but I'm making dinner tonight."

"Works for me," was Sam's reply. "I'll trade a few spark plugs for food anytime."

Kyler joined him, and the two of them spent the rest of the afternoon with their heads under the hood, joined an hour or so later by Horace. There was a lot of shaking of heads and muttering, but by the end of the day Sam literally had the engine purring.

Zuri appeared with Tigger in the curve of one arm. He set the cat down and took over for Beau on guard duty. To Evie's amusement, Tigger stalked around the perimeter of the backyard as if he were on duty too before settling on a branch of the maple. Meanwhile, Horace and Beau went out for groceries, and a short while later Suha, Adric and Marjani showed up with beer and wine.

That night Evie and Jace made fried chicken, biscuits, and sweet corn for everyone. Somehow the whole group fit around the kitchen table. Evie took in the hard-eyed soldiers bantering with one another as they downed her fried chicken, and felt like pinching herself. Two weeks ago, she hadn't even known Jace existed, and now he had his hand on her thigh under the table, his pinky teasing the edge of her shorts—and the Baltimore alpha was seated a few chairs down, grinning at something Kyler had said.

She wanted to gather up the day like the gift it was and hold it close so she'd never forget it.

But the best part was yet to come. This time, Jace didn't even wait for Kyler to go to bed, just stood up as Adric and Marjani left, pulling Evie to her feet along with him.

"Good night, everyone." He nodded to his den mates, who were sprawled around the room, Kyler in their midst, watching the basketball playoffs. Even Tigger was watching, curled up on Suha's lap.

Kyler just gave them a wave before turning back to the game. "Night, you two."

Jace set a hand on the small of Evie's back and steered her down the hall. The moment they were in the bedroom, he backed her up against the door, framed her face with his hands and kissed her, hard and deep.

Evie's head swam. She gripped his waist and hung on as her heart pounded in her ears. He moved his mouth to her neck and nipped the beating pulse, sending a jolt straight to her sex.

"Goddess, I want you." A harsh growl against her skin.

She drew a serrated breath. "Me too."

"Show me."

He didn't need to ask twice. She slid her fingers into his hair and dragged his mouth down to hers. Kissing him with all the hunger in her heart. Sucking his tongue into her mouth. Nipping his lips. Sliding a hand down his back to squeeze one of his firm buttocks.

His breath sped up. His hips moved, pressing into her belly. She could feel him, thick and ready.

He removed her arms from his neck and pressed them against the door, her hands on either side of her head. "You're mine, Evie." His eyes seared into hers, dark gold touched with the green of his cat.

She wet her lips. "You said we don't mix." But a part of her cried, *yes*.

"I'm an ass. Now say it." He nipped her jaw, and pleasure jolted straight to her clit. "I want the words. Just for tonight."

"Or else what?" Her chin jutted.

Because that had hurt, what he'd said about the two of them not mixing. She might have her own doubts, but not because he was a fada.

But you agreed, a little voice reminded her.

He lifted a single black brow. "Are you teasing a cat?"

She moistened her lips, but she was damned if she'd back down. "Yes."

"Oh, baby," he crooned in a dark voice that made her inner thighs clench. "Then you better be ready to play." He captured her wrists in one hand and held them above her head, while with his other hand he undid her shorts. "Or else what?" he repeated. "Maybe I'll keep you against the door until you beg to come."

She slid him a look from under her lids. "Maybe I'd like that."

He chuckled and skimmed his fingers under the waistband of her panties. She was wearing her only sexy underwear—black satin with a touch of lace and a bra to match.

His heated gaze took in the black lace against her cream-colored skin. "Did you wear these for me?" When she nodded, he murmured, "Good girl. Now say it, Evie."

But as soon as she opened her mouth, he covered it with his as if afraid to let her speak. Her heart lurched as she realized he didn't expect her to say it. He kissed her as if he were aching as much as she was, his tongue curling over hers, taking her deeper by slow degrees. Meanwhile, his fingers slid deeper into her panties, teasing her sensitized flesh until she was breathless and aching.

She wanted to touch him. Her hands jerked in his grip but he wouldn't let her go. He kept them pressed to the door above her head and continued kissing her until she was dazed, her legs like limp noodles.

He lifted his head, his expression hard and a little wild, and she knew his cat was inside, looking out. He squeezed her bottom. "You're a bad girl to wear these tight little shorts. All day, I kept looking at your ass and picturing what I was going to do to you when we were alone. I swear my cock was hard the whole fucking day. And this shirt..." Long, work-roughened fingers stroked her belly. "The way you keep flashing me. It's enough to drive a man insane."

She laughed up at him, but God, he was making her hot. "I wasn't flashing you. All you could see was my stomach."

"You think that isn't bad?" He released her wrists and jerked up her T-shirt to expose her breasts. "I wanted to taste you, lick you, and then move up your stomach to your hot tits." He pinched her nipples through the black satin...and then his mouth was on her and he was sucking the points to hardness.

She cupped his head, holding him close. His mouth was warm and wet. Each hot suck shot straight to her womb.

She moaned, and he gave a sexy rumble in response. From her breasts, he moved his way lower, trailing a searing line of kisses down her abdomen until he reached her mound.

"Mine," he growled against her panties. He pursed his lips and blew a hot stream of air into the satin right above her clit. "Say it."

She whimpered and pressed her palms against the door, her body straining to him. "God, yes. Please."

He stilled. Slowly his eyes turned up to hers, so that she felt like prey. Sexy, not-even-going-to-try-to-run prey. Then his lips curved in a wicked smile. "But I'm still going to tease you...because we both like it."

He came to his feet and swung her into his arms. The world spun and Evie nipped his shoulder. "I do. Like it, I mean."

His answer was a fierce kiss. When it ended, she was on the bed with him kneeling over her.

The first thing he did was to strip off her clothes. He dropped them next to the bed and sent his own after them. "That's better." His gaze stroked down her body where she lay with one knee bent up, lingering on her nipples, which tingled eagerly, and then continued down to the tuft of dark blond hair between her legs.

"You're darker here." He traced a fingertip through her curls.

"Because I'm a natural blond. This—" she touched the hair on her head —"gets bleached by the sun. That doesn't, unless I sunbathe naked." She slanted him a wicked smile.

"Damn." He pressed her bent leg down and straddled her. "Now I've got a picture in my head of you spread out naked in the sun like a fucking sex goddess." He traced a finger around her nipples and then down her breastbone. "Would you burn?"

"No—I don't burn. I just get a little darker."

"Beautiful," he murmured as he stroked her flank. "This afternoon in the sun, you sparkled like someone sprinkled silver dust on you. I wonder if you have some sun fae in you. You should talk to Queen C about it."

"Sure. I'll just drive up to Rising Sun and knock on her door. If she even has a door..."

"Adric knows her. He could talk to her."

She shook her head. "If the sun fae wanted me, they'd have done something a long time ago."

"Maybe. The fae have their own way of looking at things, though. And time moves more slowly for them. She may be planning on doing something, but by the time she gets around to it, you'll be fifty years old. You should think about it —the sun fae can help you train your Gift, if you don't want to ask Leesa."

"All right—I'll think about it." She trailed a finger down the hard muscles of his abdomen. "But right now, I have better things to do."

"I like how you think, woman." His eyes glinted with his cat: golden brown with shards of green radiating out from the pupils.

She slipped her arms around his neck. "You promised I'd see your jaguar again."

"Mm." His chest rumbled, and she grinned.

"Are you purring?"

"Yeah," he said with a sheepish smile. "The cat likes you."

"So I can see him?"

"Sure." He backed off and crouched on the mattress. Color cascaded over his skin, bright bits of green and gold and copper that reminded her of the inside of a fae light. They spread out until his body glittered, indescribably beautiful.

And then suddenly, his form was more cat than man, and then a black panther stood on the foot of the bed. He was big and brawny, with powerful legs and long, sharp canines. This close, she could see the roseate pattern on his pelt— large, irregular black spots surrounded by a dark walnut that blended in to make him appear all black from a distance.

She drew in a breath, awed and the tiniest bit afraid, even though she *knew* it was Jace.

He settled next to her and nudged her with his head. "You want me to pet you?" He rumbled and nudged her harder, so much like Tigger it was impossible to be afraid. "Okay," she said with a chuckle and smoothed a hand over his head. His fur was velvety soft over the hard bones of his skull. "You're beautiful."

He pushed his head harder into her hand, and then crept even closer so he could rub against her jaw. Marking her with his scent.

She turned her head and their eyes met. His irises were a pure green now, but she saw the man there too, his gaze alive with intelligence.

She stroked a hand over his jaw. This time his purr was loud and clear.

He came up over her, and rubbed his head over her chest. Her already sensitized nipples hardened. Her breasts felt achingly full.

Then he moved down her body and rubbed his head against her mound, too. Her breath sucked in. "*Jace.*"

He gave a badass growl and came on top of her again, a paw on either side of her head. His fur glittered, and she watched as he changed back to man. This time it was a quick shift—less than thirty seconds.

"I want you," he said in a gravelly voice that was half cat, half man. "Now."

"Yes." Her arms were already around him. Her hips rocked off the bed, touching his erection where it hung, hard and heavy.

His fingers speared into her hair, holding her still as he trailed love-bites over her neck. Her insides clenched. Something unexpected in her liked being held down like that—firm and yet gentle at the same time. His to tease however he wished.

His other hand went to her pussy. He dipped a finger into her, and then trailed the moisture around her tender nub. Pleasure swirled through her. "Yes. There."

"That's it, angel. Take it." He continued to play with her, but when her sex tightened, he took his hand away.

She moaned his name, and he said, "You can come when I'm inside you."

"Get on with it then," she said between her teeth.

His cheek creased. "You're so damn cute."

For answer, she reached down and squeezed him. His smile disappeared. She worked her hand up and down him, toying with his balls, learning the feel of him. His cock spurted with pre-cum and she rubbed it over the slick cap, enjoying how his eyes slit with pleasure.

His hips gave an involuntary jerk and she squeezed harder. "Fuck," he muttered. He removed her hand and grabbed a rubber from the night table. He worked it over his erection, and then crawled back on top of her. She reached between their bodies and guided him to her entrance. They both watched as he slowly entered her.

Her breath hissed out. He paused, and she met his eyes. She knew what he wanted.

"Please. I want it. I want you."

He slid in another inch. "That's it, Evie. I love it when you beg me."

"Please," she said again.

He slid deeper, and then withdrew again. He continued moving in and out in tantalizing increments until at last he was fully seated in her.

She rotated her hips in slow circles, pleasuring them both.

His jaw clenched. "That's it. Take me, baby. Tease me."

His hand was in her hair again, the other hand on her ass as he began to move in her, holding her in place for his firm, perfect thrusts. From somewhere far off, she heard herself making sounds of arousal, soft at first, and then louder as her pleasure increased.

It was so good. Her chest constricted. Because she'd found him, but she couldn't keep him.

"Mine," he said, and she nodded, throat tight.

Because she *was* Jace's, for as long as he wanted her. It was crazy, but it felt *right*.

But even if she waited until Kyler was grown up, they were from such different worlds. How did she know it wouldn't just be her mom and Fane all over again?

Sensation stormed through her, searing her nerves. And then she was convulsing around him in an explosive orgasm that both shot her high—and cracked her heart.

CHAPTER 27

Corban hurt. His injured leg throbbed, and his head pounded in time.

He'd tried again to heal his thigh, but his quartz had been pushed too hard. He'd have to heal the old-fashioned way, which was too damned slow. Every hour he was incapacitated was another hour that Adric had to track him.

Morning came. He couldn't see the sunrise, but he noted it with a fada's internal clock. He got up to pee and downed several cups of water before curling up in the blankets again. The day passed with agonizing slowness. He was hungry, but all he had to eat were a couple of nutrient bars he'd brought from Iceland. He rationed them out—one in the morning, one that evening—and ignored his hollow stomach.

He considered calling one of his brothers, but he was wary of letting even them know his location. Kane could be trusted, but Nash was Adric's man now. And even if they didn't betray him, they might inadvertently lead someone to his lair.

No, it was safer to remain incommunicado.

Tomorrow. Tomorrow I'll go out hunting. The park had rabbits and other small mammals. His wolf salivated hungrily.

Outside, night fell. He forced himself to move his injured leg. The pain made his chest seize, but it was getting better.

He gritted his teeth and forced himself to exercise the torn hamstring: stretching it, bending the knee.

Midnight came and went. He wrapped himself in a blanket and dozed, tormented by fevered dreams. Nika, furious that he'd left her behind to face the music. His father telling him what a weak excuse for a man he was.

But the worst were the black shadows that slithered out of the walls to wind chill fingers around his limbs. His nostrils twitched. *Metal and decay.*

He jerked awake to find Tyrus staring down at him.

The night fae lord was dressed in black from his overpriced duster to his hand-made leather shoes. Tall and thin, he loomed over Corban like an elegant crow, his eyes dark coals in his pale face.

"Get up." He planted his toe in Corban's ribs.

Corban had already thrown off the blanket. He rose to his feet, ignoring the pain that stabbed through his leg. *Never let them see that you're weak.*

Even standing, he had to look up. He was tall for an earth fada, but the night fae had a good six inches on him.

"Jones is still alive." Tyrus's tone was icy with scorn. "And Adric took your woman prisoner. What the fuck am I paying you for?"

"Kill him yourself then," Corban snarled. "Your assassin failed, too."

Tyrus struck. Long white fingers wrapped around Corban's throat, rattlesnake-fast. "You dare argue with me, fada?" He gave Corban a shake.

Corban growled. His claws slid out and he took a swipe at Tyrus, but the night fae grabbed his wrist and shoved him back against the wall.

Stunned, Corban stared at Tyrus. The man must have the Gift of wayfaring. Only a fae who could move at an inhuman speed could've evaded a fada so easily.

Fear coated his insides.

Tyrus held Corban pinned against the wall. His gaze snagged Corban's. He froze, ensnared by the unholy red flicker in the night fae's pupils.

Energy hummed over Corban's skin—cold and black as the slithering shadows of his nightmare. His bowels iced.

"No," he said, but the sound was swallowed in the darkness.

The energy increased, braiding itself into ropes. One rope twined around his skull, while a second spiraled around his chest and a third licked up his injured leg.

Blackness. Endless as a nightmare. He was small, helpless, cowering before his father.

"Stupid cub." A hand clouted him in the head. His ears rang. A single tear slid down his cheek, and his father hit him again, disgusted.

"Stop your blubbering, you little coward."

Corban tried, but the tears wouldn't dry up. They ran down his cheeks, hot and damning.

The blows fell again and again, until Corban's face was on fire and he was woozy with pain. They didn't stop until Corban forced the tears down into some-where so deep and tightly guarded, they never escaped again.

The rope around Corban's chest constricted. Panic clawed at him. He was forced to take short, shallow breaths, unable to fill his lungs.

"I own you," Tyrus said, soft and cold. "We have a contract."

Despair washed over Corban. He fought the urge to turn his head and offer submission to the night fae in the way of his wolf.

But he'd been raised by a bastard. Despair and hopelessness were mother's milk to Leron Savonett's son.

Rage rose up in him. All the rage the sniveling little boy had had to hide. It blew away the despair, replacing it with a red-eyed fury. His head pounded, and his vision clouded.

His switchblade practically leapt into his hand. He released the blade with a snick and pressed it into Tyrus's belly. "Get. Your. Hands. Off. Me."

Surprise flashed over the other man's face. He released Corban and took a step back, but his silent assault continued—only now, he was feeding off Corban's anger.

Gods, the man was a sick fuck.

If only Corban had a blade of iron, he'd end this for good. A knife straight to Tyrus's black heart. Because Tyrus's death would serve Corban's purpose almost as well as Jace Jones' death. Prince Langdon would never believe the clan wasn't behind the attack, and he'd be on Adric in a flash.

But without iron, Corban would only make Tyrus madder, and he needed Tyrus to get him to Jones and his pretty little human. Jones was the key to the smartphone tech. Remove him from the equation, and Adric would be back to the beginning. And then Corban would wait until Adric showed up—and kill him as well.

With both Jones and Adric gone, Corban would be the strongest man in the clan. Nothing would stop him from taking over his rightful place as alpha. Some of the lieutenants might squawk, but they'd accept him—or die.

Corban took a fighter's crouch, the knife loose and easy in his right hand. He knew his eyes were pure gold now, his wolf running the show. And with the wolf came calm.

The dark ropes of energy loosened. He sensed Tyrus' confusion.

"Enough," Corban gritted. He might not be able to kill a fae with a steel blade, but he could hurt the man.

The fire in Tyrus's eyes faded. "You're stronger than I believed." He tilted his head, scrutinizing Corban as if he were an interesting problem.

"So this was a fucking test?" Corban remained in the crouch.

"A test?" The night fae lifted a brow. "No. But you've proved you can still be of use to me. Come here." He beckoned with a single long, sharp-nailed finger.

"Why?" he returned without moving.

Tyrus pressed his lips together. "I can heal you. Then I'll take you to the jaguar's lair."

"Jones? He has a *look-away* spell concealing the entrance." Corban knew approximately where Jones lived, but the spell kept him from determining its actual location.

"A child could break that spell. Now come."

Corban stared at him for another moment, and then nodded. What did he have to lose?

He crossed the few steps between them. The night fae set his hand on Corban's chest, and muttered a few words in an arcane fae language.

Corban's entire thigh lit up with an eerie blue flame. Pain seared through him. A shriek escaped his lips. He cursed and shoved Tyrus away, and then fell to the dirt floor where he curled up in agony and waited to die.

And then the blue flame was gone as abruptly as it had appeared.

Corban dragged in a breath. Then another. When his body stopped quivering, he sat up, panting softly. His hand went to the back of his thigh. He froze, and then twisted so that he could see the back of his leg. The ugly gash was gone, the scar rapidly closing over.

Tyrus was already moving up the ladder. "Come. Dawn is only a couple of hours away."

Corban took a cautious step. The pain was completely gone and he could move with ease. He released one last breath and then pulled himself up the ladder after Tyrus. At the surface, Tyrus strode into the woods without looking back, confident Corban would follow.

Corban paused to tap his quartz. It was time to call in the only man he still trusted in Baltimore: his middle brother, Kane. Born a year apart, he and Kane had formed an alliance against their dad. When their youngest brother Nash came along four years later, they'd protected him as best they could. Maybe that had been a mistake, because Nash had grown up weaker because of it—he was firmly in Adric's camp.

But Kane had stuck by Corban, supporting his bid to be alpha until Adric had won the challenge and forced both brothers to swear allegiance to him or die. It wasn't an easy thing for a fada to break such a vow, but it could be done if you were determined enough.

Still, the effort had made Corban violently ill for a month, especially since he'd smashed his quartz at the same time. But he'd had a new quartz ready and he'd holed up in a cave in the Himalayas until he'd recovered.

"What in Hades is going on?" Kane hissed into the phone now. "The alpha has everyone out looking for you."

"Fuck that. Are you still with me?"

There was a fraught silence, and then his brother expelled a breath. "Of course. But—"

Corban named an intersection near Jace Jones's den. "Meet me there now."

His brother understood immediately. "You have a way to get past the *look-away* spell?"

"Yeah."

"It still won't work. He's got a den full of soldiers."

Corban glanced after Tyrus, who had disappeared in the woods. "I have a night fae with me. Lord T."

"So it's true. You're working with the fae." Kane's tone was gruff with disapproval.

"For now." Sometimes you had to deal with the devil if you wanted to win. "You in?"

Kane bit out a curse. "I'll be there in ten minutes."

CHAPTER 28

$\mathcal{J}$ace curled his body around Evie's and played with her breasts. Two nights with the woman, and already he couldn't imagine waking up without her.

She mumbled something in her sleep. Good, she wasn't awake.

He angled his head so he could bite her nape. A light, teasing cat-bite.

Her breath sighed out. He slid his hand down the curve of her rib cage, stroked her stomach. His fingers were inching lower when his quartz buzzed. He swore under his breath but rolled onto his side and answered in a sub-vocal voice so as not to wake her.

The news from Adric chilled him. Luc had reported in from France that he'd finally found Tyrus's lair, but Tyrus had left for Paris soon after.

"And he didn't take a car," Adric said. "He was running. The man's a fucking wayfarer."

"No." Jace's stomach dropped. "But it makes sense—the way he pops out of nowhere..."

Wayfaring was a Gift only the most powerful fae had. Some—like Queen Cleia of the sun fae—could 'port from place to place. Others could shadow your footsteps so that you never knew you were being followed, and still others could move freakishly fast. Dressed in his customary black, Tyrus would blend into the shadows. If he was a wayfarer, you'd never seen him rushing by. You'd just feel the chill as he passed.

"Luc and Nash are on their way home."

Jace nodded. "You think he's coming to Baltimore?"

"Yep. But why—what the fuck does he want?"

Jace raked a hand over his head. He didn't like this, not at all. "He hasn't tried anything for six years—and Merry's still protected by her father's ward. So what changed? Why go after me now?"

"Hell if I know. But be on guard. Don't let anyone in the den until we know more."

"Got it."

Adric cut the connection and Jace rolled onto his back. His cat was growling lowly, its tail twitching in agitation. Bloodthirsty visions rolled through Jace's mind, the jaguar's way of communication: *Kill. Protect. Mine.*

The cat wanted to stalk and kill Tyrus—but the night fae lord was Prince Langdon's only surviving son. If Jace killed him, Langdon would descend on the clan like a nuclear holocaust. It would be the Darktime all over again.

No, Jace told the cat, and it snarled but retreated further into his mind.

But that wasn't all. Just as he was turning back to Evie, his phone buzzed again. This time it was Merry. Evie was stirring so he slipped out of the room to take the call.

"What's up, babe?"

"Papa Rui wants to talk to you," Merry said.

"Okay, sure." Something was up—Rui almost never asked to speak to him, letting Valeria do most of the communicating.

Do Mar went straight to the point. "You know that female your alpha left on our territory—Nika? She's gone."

"What do you mean, gone?"

"That's what's fucking strange. Dion and I questioned her, but we couldn't get much out of her other than that she's from a Russian clan and that she came with Corban Savonett to Grace Harbor—which I'm sure you already know. Dion told her we'd better never find her making trouble in Rock Run territory again, and then Cleia was going to 'port her back to Russia. But when the guard checked on her an hour ago, she was gone."

Jace scraped his fingers over his hair. "How is that possible? Your wards—" Queen Cleia herself had made sure that Rock Run's wards were practically impregnable.

"I assure you, the queen is looking into it. There's no scent, no sign that anyone was inside. Only a powerful fae could've 'ported in and out of here without anyone knowing."

"Hell. I knew she wasn't all she seemed." He expelled a breath. "I'll inform my alpha. Thanks for letting us know."

"*De nada*. You won't be visiting next weekend." It was a statement, not a question.

"No. Not until we know what's going on."

"I think that's for the best. Here, Merry wants to say goodbye."

Do Mar returned the quartz to Merry, who said, "I heard what Papa said."

"I'm sorry," Jace told her. "I won't be coming to visit, but we'll talk. I promise."

"Is it because of that earth fada lady?"

He hesitated, but Merry wasn't stupid—she'd figure it out for herself. "Yeah. It's for your own safety." Because if he wasn't careful, he could bring this right to her door.

"Okay."

Jace grimaced. Damn, he hated that Merry was so accepting—so fucking adult. She was only thirteen. She should be whining like a normal teenager.

"Love you, sweetheart."

"Love you too." She cut the connection.

Jace remained in the hall, hand wrapped around his quartz, still reeling from the bad news. First Tyrus, and now Nika had escaped. Who the hell was she, really?

And why were his instincts screaming a trap was about to be sprung?

He tapped his quartz. "Adric? There's something you should know." He relayed the news about Nika.

Adric swore under his breath. "Fuck. The fae who can get past Cleia's wards can probably be counted on one hand."

Jace nodded. "The prince," he said, meaning Prince Langdon, "and the ice fae king." Sindre, whose name was coming up too damn often these days. "Those are my best guesses. And possibly my Lord Prick, but if he could teleport, he wouldn't be running to Paris."

"Agreed. Thoughts?"

"That we need to increase security. Corban knows where I live, and if he's working with the night fae, the *look-away* spell won't keep him out of my den." He glanced over his shoulder at the room where Evie was sleeping. Powerful fae or not, they'd have to step over his cold, dead body to get to her.

"I'll put the clan on high alert. No one goes anywhere alone, and the young and the old should be guarded twenty-four/seven. We'll increase our patrols through the city, too. But it's too damn large of an area to protect."

"We could gather the vulnerable in one place, but there's something to be said for keeping the dens scattered around the city."

They'd had this conversation before. On one hand, the small, scattered dens that earth fada preferred made it easier to eliminate them one den at a time. On the other hand, there was strength in remaining spread out. It had saved the clan in the Darktime—even a crazed alpha like Leron Savonett hadn't been able to wipe out all the pockets of dissent.

"What do you suggest?"

Jace was already running scenarios in his mind. "So far, Corban has focused on me, but it's you he really wants. I'm just a means to get to you."

"So I'll draw him out of hiding."

"No fucking way. That's just what Corban wants. I'll do it."

"No—I'll be damned if I'll cower in my den while that bastard attacks my best people. Besides, Evie and Kyler need you right there."

Jace grimaced. Adric was right. While he trusted that his den mates would guard Evie and her brother with their lives, neither he nor his cat was comfortable with leaving them for any length of time. "Then let Zuri do it."

"It's not your decision," Adric said. "Corban wants me, so let him try to take me. I beat him once."

"He wasn't working with a night fae then," Jace returned.

"It's almost dawn. The night fae will have to go underground. Corban will be forced to deal with me alone."

Jace blew out a breath. "You're the alpha."

Something had been niggling at him ever since yesterday when he, Evie and the others had walked to the park. "Remember when we were teenagers and we tried to track your cousin in Druid Hill Park—but we never could?" Corban would disappear for hours, and he was so good at hiding his scent that even Adric couldn't find him.

"Hell. You think he has a lair in there somewhere?"

"Makes sense."

"We went through the park once already, but it's worth another pass. I'll head up there at noon when that fucking night walker will be sleeping. If Corban's somewhere nearby, just seeing me may draw him out. If not, I'll go over every square foot. If he has a lair, I'll find it."

"Don't go alone."

"I won't. So here's the plan—Horace and Sam are to stick with you, Evie and Kyler. I'll tell Beau to stay with Suha—she's valuable enough that Corban may try to strike at her—and I'll take Zuri and Marjani to the park."

"Marjani? You think that's wise? She's so close to going—"

"Feral? I know. Believe me, I know. But then again, this might be what she needs—someone to protect. She's been better ever since I asked for her help with this whole Corban mess. Maybe I made a mistake, coddling her this long."

Jace rubbed his lower lip. "She needed time to heal. But I agree, maybe it's time to bring her back on duty."

Marjani had been one of the clan's best soldiers. What had happened to her could've broken anyone—male or female—but it must have been a special hell for a woman who'd never taken any shit from anybody. To be violated in such an intimate way, made to feel so helpless. Like Takira. Jace swallowed harshly.

Adric was speaking. "I'll contact Zuri, tell him what's up. You bring Horace and Sam up to date."

"I will. And Ric? Thanks—for Evie and Kyler." Because he was wrapping the protection of the clan around the two humans.

"Hey, you'd do the same for me. Besides, I like your Evie and the kid. They're good people."

"They are." He cut the connection.

A moment later, he heard Zuri speaking to Adric. "On my way," he said. Jace glanced in his room to see the other lieutenant was already up and pulling on jeans and a T-shirt.

"I'm going to spread the word about Corban," Zuri told Jace, "to those who don't have a smartphone, and then I'll head over to Adric's."

Jace nodded. Not everyone could use the new technology—it was one of the glitches they still had to work out. "Watch his back. He thinks he's fucking invincible."

"Don't worry," Zuri replied, "I will."

Jace nodded and continued down the hall to wake up Sam and Horace. He brought them up to date with a few terse sentences, before heading for the shower, his plans for making love to Evie tabled. He didn't even want to get near her in this frame of mind.

He knew Corban had to die, but it still left a bad taste in his mouth. It was so fucking senseless. The Darktime was supposed to be over. He was sick and tired of the infighting, of pointless deaths. He wanted to build things—not kill. To be free to explore this thing with Evie and maybe someday, have a cub of his own with her.

His heart squeezed at the thought of a sassy little girl with Evie's bright hair and dark brows.

And if the clan had a problem with a mixed-blood, well, he'd make his own den with Evie and Kyler and any offspring the gods blessed them with. Adric would support him. Hell, Adric had accepted Merry, the only granddaughter of the night fae prince himself.

But if Corban had his way, it wasn't going to end until Adric and every last one of his lieutenants was dead.

Jace slammed the heel of his hand against the tiled wall. Then he stood under the shower head and turned it to full.

CHAPTER 29

It was the fae lights that woke Evie. She'd been on her side with Jace spooned around her, both of them naked. He'd been lazily caressing her, and she had a smile on her lips as she came awake. Then Jace had left the bed, and she'd rolled onto her back and dozed off again.

The next thing she knew, something stung her arm. She swatted it away, but a moment later she felt another sting to her shoulder, and then another to her face. She jolted awake to find the fae lights swarming her—and a tall man dressed all in black staring down at her.

Her heart kicked into high gear. She scrambled up against the headboard, the sheet clutched to her chest.

"Who the fuck are you?" *And how had he gotten in here?* She opened her mouth to scream for Jace.

The man raised a hand. "I wouldn't, if I were you. Your brother..." He cut his eyes at a corner of the room.

She whipped her head around. Kyler was sitting against the wall, knees hugged to his chest, staring unseeingly in front of him.

His face twisted in horror. "*No. No...*"

Her stomach bottomed out. "Kyler! What's wrong?" But he didn't seem to hear her.

Her gaze swung back to the tall man. Dark eyes regarded her from a pale, incredibly beautiful face. *Night fae.*

Kyler moaned again and she launched herself at the intruder. Nobody messed with her brother. "Stop it, damn you." She clawed wildly at his face.

He easily held her off. Those black eyes caught hers and she froze, fingers still curled into claws. The night fae slid a cool finger down her cheek. Fear sliced through her, but she steeled herself to remain calm and bear it. Anything to get his attention off Kyler.

Kyler made an agonized sound. "Evie. I'm sorry. So sorry. I couldn't help it." He came to his knees and looked up at her, his gaze stark.

Help what? But that didn't matter right now. She took a step back and screamed at Kyler, "Run! Get Jace."

Kyler's breath scraped in. But instead of trying to escape, he threw himself at the night fae. "Get away from my sister, you prick."

And ran right past the man. He barely avoided slamming headfirst into the wall. He caught himself with his hands on the stone and glanced around, angry and confused.

Evie blinked. One moment the night fae had been standing in front of her, the next he was gone—and then he reappeared exactly where he'd been, a foot away from her.

Kyler snarled and launched himself at the man again.

"Enough." The night fae's arm lashed out. He grabbed Kyler by the throat and squeezed.

Her brother's eyes bulged. He scrabbled desperately at the man's long white fingers, but the man held on, a slight smile on his lips.

Fury blinded Evie. With an animalistic growl, she grabbed the night fae's wrist and tried to drag him away from Kyler, but the fae shook her off like an annoying insect. When she came right back, he slammed an elbow into her solar plexus.

Pain exploded through her. Her breath left her lungs in a whoosh. She stumbled back, her diaphragm seizing up, and dropped to her knees, opening and shutting her mouth like a hooked fish as she tried to catch her breath.

Kyler's struggles were slacking off. Panic snaked up Evie's spine. Somehow, she found the strength to crawl toward the night fae and wrap her arms around his lower leg.

He glanced down at her and laughed. "By the dark gods," he said in a French accent, "you don't give up."

And then he swung Kyler into the wall like he was a ragdoll. There was a dull thud and her brother slumped to the floor, unmoving.

Evie's breath rushed in as her diaphragm finally unlocked. For a few seconds she couldn't move. She sank onto her forearms, head against the floor, sucking in oxygen.

From the hall came furious shouts and bone-chilling snarls. *Jace and the others. Oh, God, they were in trouble, too.*

Something cool and oily brushed over her back, teased her breasts. Her skin prickled. Suddenly she was aware she was completely naked with a cold-eyed stranger. She pushed herself up on her knees to face him and covered herself as best she could with her hands.

The tall, black-haired fae crouched next to her. Chilly fingers stroked her nape. Fine hairs stood up all over her body. "You know who I am?"

Evie batted his hand away. Kyler moaned and she shot a frantic look at him.

A hand caught her wrist. Squeezed until the bones ground painfully together. "Answer me."

"No," she said between clenched teeth.

"The animals didn't tell you?"

"The animals?"

"The fada. Your lover."

She narrowed her eyes. "He didn't want to draw your attention."

His cruel mouth quirked. "Oh, you have my attention." He drew her to her feet. "I'm Lord Tyrus—and you're part fae."

～

THE BATHROOM DOOR opened as Jace shut off the shower. "Evie?" he asked.

No response.

His nape tingled. He jerked open the shower door. A huge black wolf stared back at him.

Fuck. Jace started to shift but Corban was already in the air. He slammed Jace into the wall. Lights exploded in his head and he slid to the floor.

His focus lost, Jace couldn't complete the shift. He only just managed to yank himself back to man so he wouldn't be caught in a half-shifted state. It was the devil's choice, because he couldn't fight off Corban's wolf as a man, but the alternative was death as a half-man, half-cat.

He was trapped in the shower with the wolf. Claws dug painfully into his chest, holding him down as Corban's teeth sank into his throat. The metallic scent of blood filled his nostrils.

Jace went clawed and lashed at Corban—slicing at his eyes, his muzzle. The wolf hung on grimly. Black spots swam before Jace's eyes. He shoved his thumbs into the corners of Corban's mouth near his molars and managed to open his jaws enough to pry him off. He threw the wolf against the wall and scrambled to his feet.

He swayed, dizzy from the blow to his head, one thought in his mind: *Evie.*

Corban rose to his feet. Somehow Jace got out of the bathroom ahead of him. He slammed the door shut, trapping the wolf inside.

Where the hell were Sam and Horace?

"Attack," he roared. "We're under attack."

The hall remained ominously silent. He gripped the bathroom doorknob, holding the door closed as Corban slammed repeatedly against it, trying to break out.

Jace's chest heaved. The black spots returned, threatening to blot out his consciousness.

Corban went silent. Then the doorknob jerked. He was trying to turn it with his teeth.

Jace clenched his jaw and willed the black spots away. He was aware of blood running down his chest from the gash in his throat. But he had to hang on long enough to sound the alarm. With Sam and Horace apparently down, he was Evie and Kyler's only hope.

He tapped his quartz and said a brief prayer of thanks when Adric responded immediately. "What's up?"

"My den," Jace rasped. "Under attack. Corban is inside. I'm hurt, and I don't know where Sam and Horace are."

He inhaled—and caught a stench of night fae.

"Fuck." He wasn't sure if he whispered or shouted it. He was sliding down a long, dark tunnel. "Night fae. In my den."

Evie. Kyler.

His knees gave out and he sat on the floor with a thump. He swiped a hand over his eyes, trying to clear his vision. *Was that a black wolf padding down the hall? But how?* Corban was still in the bathroom, clawing at the door. The handle started to turn and Jace realized he'd released it.

"Hang on, bro. We're on our way." Adric's voice.

"Hurry," he mumbled.

The wolf in the hall shifted to man, and Kane Savonett loomed over Jace.

"Bastard," Jace mouthed.

Kane grabbed Jace's quartz and he jolted in pain. But that was nothing compared to how it felt when Kane pulled the quartz off him.

Jace's entire body lit with a tooth-jarring agony, and then everything went black.

The last thing he did was to fall sideways so his body would block Corban when he emerged. Even a few extra seconds might save Evie and her brother.

CHAPTER 30

yrus raked his gaze over Evie's naked body. "Get dressed."

"Okay, sure." She grabbed some clothes before he could change his mind. Kyler was slumped against the wall near the bed. She shot him a worried glance as she pulled on her cargo pants.

"Come." Tyrus beckoned to her.

She swallowed. "Why?"

Kyler groaned, and the night fae's gaze moved to him. Evie stepped to the left so that she was between the two of them.

"Kyler?" she asked without taking her eyes off Tyrus. "You okay?"

"Think so."

She darted a look at her brother. He was sitting up, rubbing his head. He blinked at the blood on his fingers.

"What happened?" he asked.

"You hit your head against the wall."

He nodded and then winced. "Fuck, that hurts." He glanced at Tyrus, and his face tightened with hatred. "Asshole," he growled.

She moved back and set a staying hand on his shoulder. "Hush. It's okay."

Kyler didn't seem to hear. "I'm sorry, Evie. He got into my dreams somehow —a nightmare. When I woke up, I was at the door, letting him inside." He glared at the night fae. "Why don't you fight fair, you freaking prick?"

She dug her nails into his shoulder. "Kyler. Shut. Up."

"I'm not afraid of him," he returned sullenly, but to her relief, he subsided.

Tyrus ignored their byplay to focus on Evie. "Come, woman."

"No fucking way." Kyler wrapped wiry arms around her legs. "She's not going anywhere with you."

"No?" The fae's black eyes flashed red.

Evie gulped. It was like something out of a horror movie. She slid down the wall until she was crouched next to Kyler, an arm flung out to protect him. Her brother muttered something and dropped his head on her shoulder, and she had the sick feeling he was only half aware of what was going on.

She glared up at Tyrus. "What do you want?"

"Ah...now that's an interesting question." The red faded. Tyrus sat on the mattress and stretched out his long legs, one ankle crossed over the other. The fae lights had clustered around her and Kyler, leaving him in the shadows. Only his face and hands were visible, a pale glimmer like a new moon in a dark sky. The tips of his pointed ears emerged from midnight-black hair.

He was sharp-faced, beautiful—and he made her spine prickle like a thousand spiders creeping up her vertebrae.

"I'm here in Baltimore," he replied, "because I have a dislike of your new friends, especially Jones and his alpha. It wasn't very smart of you to get between me and my prey."

She raised her chin. "So sue me."

He just smiled. "But now that I know about you, Evie, I find I'm interested in you. Very interested. It's been over a week since I last fed—and the fae in you makes your energy special."

The den was still as a morgue now. Where were Jace and the others? If they were all right, surely they'd have burst in by now. Evie's heart twisted. Jace must be hurt bad, because if he could get to her, he would—that much she knew.

The fae lights moved closer to Evie. They were smaller than she'd ever seen, barely the size of a ping-pong ball, but they brushed over her in a warm caress: *Stay strong.* It was almost as if they'd spoken.

She wrapped an arm around Kyler and lifted her chin. "What do you mean, my energy is special?"

"Taking energy from a human like your brother is like drinking beer or a cheap wine. It serves if there's nothing better. But your energy—it is like a fine champagne. I may even invite some of my friends to taste you."

Her stomach lurched. "No," she said fiercely. "I won't let you. I'll stop you like I did before."

"Can you?" Tyrus raised a brow. "So that was you in the kitchen? I thought it was Jones."

"It was me." *At least part of the time.*

"Yes?" He rose to his feet. "Well, do your best, *ma chère*. I don't think you'll win. But it makes the game more amusing."

The bedroom door opened. Evie's heart surged—and then sank. It was a big, dark-skinned man she'd never seen before.

He eyed her coolly. "This is Jace's human?"

"Yes." Tyrus beckoned to Evie, and she found herself releasing Kyler and rising without intending to.

Panic skittered over her nerves. He was controlling her somehow, forcing her to walk the few feet between them.

A finger traced the curve of her jaw, lingered in the hollow of her neck. "I can set you free, but I need your promise that you'll come quietly."

Her chest jolted in and out. She couldn't get enough oxygen in her lungs. Inside, she was screaming, but all she could do was stare at him mutely.

"Evie? Nod your head if you agree."

She jerked her chin in assent, and he released her. Her breath shuddered in.

Tyrus stared down at her from his great height. "Do I have your promise?"

"Not Kyler," she returned tightly. "Only me."

"*No.*" Her brother's harsh voice tore through the dark room. He had both hands on the wall, trying to bring himself to his feet.

She took a step toward him. "No, Kyler! Stay there—*please.*"

He shook his head and grimly continued, literally crawling up the wall.

"You're bargaining with me, human?" Tyrus narrowed his eyes at her.

She set her shoulders. "Yes. I want your promise—just me, not my brother."

He shrugged. "Done. It's you I want, not him. Now do I have your promise?"

"Yes."

"Say the words."

"I promise to go with you if you leave Kyler here."

"Agreed." Tyrus smiled. A chill, victorious tilt of his lips. "Let's go then." He reached for her.

She took an involuntary step back, unable to help herself.

"Evie?" A soft, deadly question. "You're not breaking your promise, are you?"

She swallowed dryly. Everyone knew you didn't break a promise to a fae. It was the only way to hold them in check. If she broke her promise, who knew what Tyrus would do to Kyler?

"No," she said between numb lips.

He waited, hand out, until she forced herself to step forward again. He swung her into his arms. This close, he was unnaturally cold, and he had the sickly-sweet scent of death. She held herself stiff, her entire being revolting at his touch.

Tyrus rubbed his cheek against hers. "You're strong. I like that. Strong women are so much more fun."

Her fingers curled into claws, but she thought of Kyler and remained quiet. She could endure this if it saved him.

Tyrus followed the large man into the hall. The first thing Evie saw was Jace sprawled unmoving on the floor, a huge wolf the color of midnight standing over him. She made a small, dismayed sound, and the wolf's shaggy head swung toward her. Sharp canines glinted in the dim light.

A fae light wafted over Jace and her breath hitched. What she'd thought were shadows on his face and neck was blood. He was covered in it. She twisted in Tyrus's arms, forgetting everything but the need to save him from the wolf.

The fae's grip tightened. "Remember your promise," he said in silky tones.

She stilled, but narrowed her eyes at the wolf. "Get the fuck away from him," she said, low and mean.

The shifter's burning gold gaze swung to her.

There was a movement behind them, and she glanced over Tyrus's shoulder to see Kyler in the bedroom doorway, hands braced against the frame to hold himself up.

Horror swamped her. She was afraid to speak, but silently begged him with her eyes to stay hidden. When she turned back, the big black wolf had a paw on Jace's chest.

Fury engulfed her. "Damn you!" she spat at Tyrus. "Call the wolf off him. He's hurt—he can't defend himself."

"Quiet." His dark eyes flickered red again.

Evie froze except for the fine-grained trembling of her body. This was how a cornered rabbit must feel. Afraid and hopeless and seething with hatred.

Tyrus jerked his head at Jace. "Bring him," he told the wolf.

The shifter's lip peeled back to reveal sharp white teeth, but Tyrus stared him down. "Bring him. You work for me, remember? And get rid of the boy."

"No!" Evie burst out. "You promised. You said you wouldn't hurt him—that was the deal."

"Actually, I didn't. All I promised was that I wouldn't take him—just you."

Her mouth dropped open. "You...*bastard*." She punched him in the throat without thinking of the consequences, and he staggered back and loosened his grip enough that she dropped to the floor. In an instant, she was back on her feet and flying at him, fingers curved into talons.

She was past caring about herself. She just wanted to hurt him.

Her nails slashed a bloody trail down his cheeks, but he was quick as a rattlesnake. The next thing she knew, her back slammed into the wall, his hands pinning her wrists next to her head. But she was beyond reasoning. She twisted in his grip and aimed a knee at his balls which he barely evaded.

"Fuck," Tyrus said, the earthy curse sounding odd in his cultured voice. He grabbed her chin and snapped, "Stop it right now," and tried to do that mind-control thing on her again, but this time it didn't work, maybe because she was so pissed off she was operating on instinct, not on a conscious level.

"Not until you promise," she snarled back.

"Fine." He jerked his head at the fada. "Don't touch the boy."

The wolf growled, and Tyrus added, "Let me rephrase that. Touch him, and you're dead. Is that clear?"

The wolf curled its lip, but the big man said, "We understand."

Evie halted, chest heaving. "Get inside the bedroom," she told Kyler.

"No." Her brother stared at her, white-faced. "I won't let him take you."

She met his eyes. "Please, Kyler. There's no sense us both going." She mouthed, "Tell Adric."

His throat worked, and then he nodded and obeyed. She saw the bedroom door shut behind him as Tyrus swept her back into his arms, and then the next second, they were in Jace's shed.

Her jaw slackened. How had Tyrus made it up to the surface so quickly?

To the east, the sun was rising. The night fae cast an assessing eye at the pink haze spreading across the sky and then continued out of the shed. So it was only full sunlight that affected him.

Tigger was returning from a night of tomcatting around. He rounded his back and hissed at the fae, who kicked out at him. The cat yowled and leapt out of the way.

Tyrus took off running at an inhuman speed. The streets passed in a blur. He didn't stop until they reached Druid Hill Park, where he set Evie down, took her wrist in a painful grip and dragged her down an asphalt path at a punishing pace despite the fact she was barefoot.

They'd gone about a half mile when he turned onto a dirt path that led into the trees. A few minutes later they reached a small, hidden clearing. Tyrus stopped by a large rock and moved it aside as if it weighed almost nothing.

She glanced at him and gulped. Already, the cuts she'd made on his cheeks were healing over as if they'd been made yesterday, not ten minutes ago.

Tyrus jerked his chin at her. "Get in."

"Down there?" She glanced over the edge. A rusty metal ladder descended ten feet into a cellar. She felt the color drain from her face at the thought of being trapped in the small, dank space with him.

Her mind screamed *no* but she reminded herself of her promise. If she broke it, it wouldn't rebound just on her. Kyler and Jace would be in danger too.

And besides, running wouldn't do her any good—Tyrus would catch her before she'd gone three steps.

He didn't wait for her to make up her mind. He moved with that preternatural speed, grabbing her by her upper arms and dangling her over the ladder. Her heart leapt into her throat and she instinctively scrabbled for footing. As soon as her foot touched a rung, he released her, and she slipped, dropping a good yard before she grabbed the top rung and halted her fall.

"Keep going." Tyrus set his heel on her left hand, his face alight with a vile enjoyment. "Or I'll break your fingers. It makes no difference to me."

That was when it hit her—he didn't care if he hurt her as long as he could still feed on her energy. In fact, he might even prefer it.

Ice skated down her spine. "All right." She tried to drag her hand out from under his foot, but he ground his heel into the bones before releasing it.

Pain shot through her. She half-climbed, half-fell the rest of the way down the ladder until her feet hit the dirt floor.

Above her, Tyrus slid the rock back over the opening, leaving them in the darkness. He ignored the ladder to drop to the dirt beside her, his duster billowing around him like the wings of a massive black bat.

He turned toward her, his pale face the only thing visible in the pitch-black cellar. "Afraid, *ma chère*?"

She nursed her throbbing hand against her stomach and glared at him without speaking.

His thin mouth quirked. "Good. Fear has its own special taste."

CHAPTER 31

$\mathcal{A}$dric cursed and met Marjani's eyes across the kitchen table.

She was already on her feet. "Corban attacked Jace's den?"

"Yeah—with a night fae."

Her face darkened. "Tyrus?"

"He didn't say—but who else could it be? And the bastards took his quartz. I can feel it." As alpha, he was connected to most of the clan in a magical way that was like a mate bond, although weaker. His bond to his top people like Jace was even stronger. He'd sensed the minute Jace had gone dark. There was a hollowness where his friend's strong, steady energy had been.

"I'll come," his sister said.

Adric gulped the last of his coffee to give himself time to think, and she made an impatient sound.

"Stop babying me. I'm fine—and you need me."

He gave in, because she was right; he did need her. "Two minutes."

"I'll be ready."

They met at the front door. Marjani had an iron knife in a protective leather holster strapped to her upper arm, and he knew there was a switchblade in her back pocket and a shiv strapped to her thigh. His sister was a magician with knives. You'd think she had a Gift for it, except he'd never heard of such a thing.

He'd brought a switchblade himself, but if things went south, he was going in as his cougar. His teeth literally ached to sink into Corban's carotid.

As they emerged into the early morning light, Zuri arrived on his motorcycle. He looked from Adric to Marjani. "What's wrong?"

"Corban and a night fae attacked your den." Adric slung a leg over his bike while Marjani hopped on behind.

Zuri's jaw set. Without a word, he swung around and took off down the street, Adric right behind.

The outside door to Jace's den was wide open, the *look-away* spell broken. Adric took the lead as they pounded down the steps. The scent of blood was strong—Jace's mainly, but a touch of Corban's as well.

Adric eased open the front door. The living room was intact, except for a thin trail of blood, also Jace's. The bedrooms were dead silent. The three of them moved into the hall on catlike feet.

He inhaled, sorting through the scents: Kyler, Sam, and Horace were all still present, if injured. He set that aside to identify the three that didn't belong. He didn't think they were still in the den, but just in case, he kept his voice too low for anyone but Marjani and Zuri to hear. "It's Corban and Tyrus all right...and Kane Savonett."

The three of them exchanged a glance. Another traitor, this one living and working with the rest of them for the past six years. Even though Adric had never entirely trusted Kane, it was still a blow.

They all saw the pool of blood outside the bathroom. Jace's blood, mixed with a fair amount of Corban's. At least his friend had gone down fighting. But the bathroom was empty.

A faint groan came from Jace's bedroom. *Kyler.*

"Go check the other rooms," he hissed at Marjani and Zuri as he slipped in through the partially open door.

The teenager was seated on the floor, arms around his legs, rocking back and forth and moaning, the back of his head matted with blood.

Adric's jaw tightened, but he kept his voice calm. "Kyler? It's me—Adric."

He started and scuttled away, wild-eyed. "*No...*"

"It's okay." Adric crouched beside him and stretched out a hand. "You're safe now. I'm here to help. Just tell me what happened."

The teen's whole body shuddered.

Adric clasped his shoulder. "Kyler? Snap out of it. I need you to tell me what happened so I can help your sister."

"Evie." Kyler's wide, shocked eyes focused on Adric. "They have Evie."

"Who?"

"A night fae and a wolf and another man. You have to help her."

"Do you know where they took her?"

The kid shook his head. "But you can track them, can't you?"

"Yes. Now come. You can wait in the living room—put some ice on that head." He rose to his feet and held out a hand.

Kyler looked at it for a few seconds and then took it.

"There you go." Adric placed an arm around the kid's bony shoulders and helped him into the hall.

Marjani stepped out of Sam's room to report that he was injured, but that Suha was on her way over with Beau. "They tore him up pretty bad, but he was able to use his quartz to stem the bleeding."

"Good."

Zuri called from Horace's room. "Ric? You'd better come here."

Adric jerked his head at Kyler. "Take the kid," he told Marjani. "His head got banged up, but nothing too much else that I can see. Get some ice on that head of his, will you?"

She nodded and helped Kyler down the hall as Adric strode toward Horace's room.

"That must hurt like a bitch," Adric heard her say.

"They've got my sister," Kyler returned.

Marjani expelled a breath. "We'll get her back. I promise."

Horace was unconscious, his face ashen, his body covered with multiple bite wounds and scratches. But what made Adric's stomach lurch was the wadded-up pillowcase Zuri had pressed to Horace's inside thigh over the femoral artery.

Zuri met Adric's eyes and shook his head.

"It's bad?"

"He's bleeding out."

Adric briefly closed his eyes. Not Horace, the guy who always had a smile, even in the worst of the Darktime. He hesitated, torn. The longer he waited to go after Jace and Evie, the harder it would be to track them, but he couldn't just leave Horace to die.

"They sliced him with a fucking iron knife," Zuri said grimly. "I can scent it."

A muscle jumped in Adric's jaw. "Salt water," he barked. "And hurry. I'll take over here."

He pressed the heel of his hand to the pillowcase over the wound, bearing down hard. When Zuri returned, he stopped the pressure so Zuri could thoroughly rinse the wound. The artery was spurting blood, but if they didn't neutralize the iron, Horace was going to die anyway.

When Zuri was done, Adric sent a pulse of energy into the wound to try and stop the bleeding, but the wound was too deep for him to heal. Suha was Horace's only hope. Thank the gods she lived close by.

Zuri was waiting with a clean pillowcase. He pressed it to Horace's thigh above the artery.

A minute ticked past, then another. Adric washed the blood off his hands and checked on Sam. When the burly redhead heard how bad Horace was injured, he tried to get out of bed.

"Stay." Adric pressed him back to the mattress. "There's nothing you can do, and we need you to focus on your own healing."

Sam muttered but subsided.

Adric left him to return to Horace's room. The cougar was still unconscious. His scent had taken on a distinctive iron scent, more like a human's than a fada. Adric sent another pulse of healing into him, but the iron resisted his attempts to close the wound.

Zuri ground his teeth. "Where in Hades is Suha?"

"It's only been five minutes," Adric said. But he was beginning to wonder, too. He scraped a hand over his hair. "I've got to go. You and Marjani hold down the fort."

"No fucking way. That's just what they want. I'll go."

"Then I'll have to outthink them." Because Adric was the best tracker in the clan and they both knew it.

But as he turned to leave, he heard Suha's low voice accompanied by Beau's deep rumble. A moment later the healer's light steps came rapidly down the hall, followed by Beau's heavier tread.

"What happened?" she asked as she removed her quartz from her neck.

"Iron poisoning," Adric replied. "The bastards made sure to hit an artery, too." The iron would spread through Horace's blood even faster. Even now, it might be reaching his heart and brain.

"You cleaned it out?"

"Yes, but it had at least fifteen minutes to spread through his bloodstream before we got here—maybe more."

Suha muttered something dark and held her quartz over Horace's thigh.

"I have to go," Adric said. "They have Evie and Jace."

"Okay," she said without taking her eyes from her patient. "I've got this."

Adric squeezed her shoulder. "I'm counting on you."

She snorted. "So what's new?" She blew out a breath. "I'll do my best, Ric, but you know how tricky iron poisoning is." She smoothed Horace's dreadlocks away from his face.

Adric nodded grimly—and then sprang into action. "You stay with Suha," he told Beau, who was staring down at Horace, jaw tight. "Zuri—you're with me."

In the living room, Kyler was on the couch holding an ice pack to his head, while Marjani was pacing restlessly to and fro. Her head snapped around as Adric entered.

"Tell me he's going to be all right."

"Suha's doing everything she can."

It was a non-answer and they both knew it. Marjani slapped her palm against the wall. A sudden, sharp sound that made Kyler jerk.

"What I want to know," she ground out, "is how the fuck they got past Jace's security?"

Kyler made a choked sound. "That was me."

Zuri had stopped to wash the blood off his hands. He entered the living room in time to hear Kyler. All three of them gaped at the young human.

"*What?*" asked Marjani.

"I'm so sorry. I didn't mean to, I swear I didn't. I couldn't stop myself. He—the night fae—made things so fucking bad." Kyler dropped the ice pack to press his fists into his stomach. "So dark. Nightmares—and the only way to stop it was to let him in." Shame reeked from him. "He said it would be all right if only I let him in—but it wasn't. He took Evie, and the earth fada took Jace."

Marjani's glare softened. "We'll find her. I promise."

He shot an accusing look at Adric. "You said we'd be safe here. But we weren't."

His stomach twisted. "You're right, and I'm sorry. All I can say is that I'll get your sister back."

Two young soldiers pounded down the stairs, Ryder and Jamila. Adric ordered them to lock the door after them. "No one else gets in without my say-so —got it? Zuri and Marjani, you're with me."

He squeezed Kyler's shoulder. "I have to go find Evie. Meanwhile, you're on duty with Ryder and Jamila. A soldier-in-training. Help them however you can. Okay?"

The kid swiped a stray tear from his cheek. "Yeah, of course."

Adric headed up the stairs, Zuri and Marjani at his heels. Behind him, he heard Kyler asking, "Is my sister going to be all right?" The heavy front door closed, cutting off the response.

"Don't." Marjani elbowed Adric as they reached the surface. "This isn't on you."

"Like hell it isn't. He's right—I'm alpha, and I promised they'd be safe."

"Doesn't mean you're responsible for every fuck-up in the clan. This is Corban's fault, not yours."

Adric rounded on her. "I'm the one who let the prick go last year —remember?"

His sister scowled back. "You did the best you could with the available evidence."

"Tell that to Evie and Kyler." He shook his head. "One thing I know—this time, Corban's gone too far. I finally have the proof I need to take him down."

Marjani's eyes met his in cool agreement.

"Not even his supporters can argue he wasn't behind this," Zuri added. "His scent is all the fuck over our den."

"Damn right." Adric bared his teeth. "Far as I'm concerned, Corban Savonett is dead." He strode toward his bike. "Evie first. It's what Jace would want."

He knew he was right, but by the gods, it wrecked him to say it—because if Corban had Jace, they had only a small window of time before his friend was dead.

CHAPTER 32

$\mathcal{J}$ace fought his way back to consciousness. He was in motion, being jolted around inside an enclosed space. He opened his eyes to find he was in the trunk of a car speeding down a pot-holed street. He braced his hands and feet against the inside of the trunk and tried to think.

His body was one big ache, but worse, there was a huge, echoing silence where his quartz should be. The bastards had taken it.

Hell. He couldn't even shift. Even if he were completely well, the shift would be slow and laborious without his quartz to draw on. But injured as he was, there was only a small chance he'd make it through.

And Tyrus had Evie. He'd been unable to open his eyes, but he'd been aware enough to realize Tyrus had taken her. Gods, he'd been guilty of a huge miscalculation. Trusting his defenses to keep the night fae out. But he'd never thought Tyrus would go for Evie instead of him.

At least Kyler was safe. He'd heard the bargain she'd made. A mama bear didn't have anything on Evie Morningstar. His chest clenched. *I should've told her I love her.*

He pushed that thought aside to take inventory. He had various assorted bruises and cuts from his fight with Corban, but the worst was the gash on his throat. When he touched it, his hand came away bloody.

Somewhere nearby, his quartz murmured. He also scented Kane, and to a lesser extent, Corban. So this was probably Kane's car, and Corban had Jace's quartz because there was no way he'd let his younger brother take charge of it.

The car stopped and he heard the brothers quarreling. "Why the hell would you sign a contract with a night fae?" Kane demanded.

"Tyrus wants Jones—and I want him gone. Adric has sunk every penny the clan has into the new smartphones. Take Jones out, and Adric's back to the beginning. It will prove once and for all that that I'm the stronger."

Jace shook his head. Corban would never understand that people didn't follow Adric just because he was strong. They followed him because he was a natural leader, one who always put the clan first. Not a weak prick who would use a night fae against his own people.

Kane growled. "You're going to get us both killed."

Hope sparked in Jace. So Kane wasn't a hundred percent in?

But Corban snarled and the younger man said, "It's your funeral," and shut up.

Car doors opened and slammed. Jace tensed, preparing to fight.

The trunk popped open and Corban stared down at him, Jace's quartz in his fist. It was the first good look Jace had had of him in over a year. He was leaner, his face lined with exhaustion as if the months away had been hard on him.

"Get out," he snarled. "We're taking you to your woman."

"My woman?" Jace froze in the act of launching himself at Corban.

"That human-fae mixed-blood—your scent is all over her. Now get out." Corban squeezed Jace's quartz, and pain slammed through him as if Corban had reached into his chest to grab his heart.

Jace set his teeth and obeyed. There was no sense in resisting if it would get him to Evie, but he was weak from loss of blood. He only made it a few steps before he stumbled and dropped to one knee. His body wanted to stay folded in on itself, but he forced himself back upright. They were in a parking lot in Druid Hill Park. To the south he could see downtown Baltimore, the skyscrapers hazy in the simmering heat, the humidity already on the rise. On a nearby path, an early morning runner loped past, earbuds in place, oblivious to their tense little tableau —or pretending to be.

Evie was nowhere in sight. "Where is she?" Jace demanded.

"That way." Corban motioned at Kane, who started down the path after the runner.

Jace nodded and focused on putting one foot in front of the other. Corban fell in beside him.

Jace shot him a look. "Tell the night fae to let her go—she has nothing to do with this. You know what perverted bastards they are."

The wolf shrugged. "I have a contract."

"On me, yes. But what did she ever do to you?"

"Nothing, but Tyrus wants her. And he wants you gone because you're one more thing standing between him and Merry." Corban's lip curled. "And because he's a night fae, and if he can't get at Merry, he wants to make her suffer."

Jace stared at him, chilled despite the heat. It made sense. Tyrus couldn't kill Merry because of the ward, but he was a night fae. He'd enjoy making her suffer, and what better way than to kill off the people she loved? Which could mean that Valeria and the babies were in danger, too. He didn't count Rui—it would take a hell of a lot to take down the shark assassin.

Jace had to contact Rui, warn him his family might be a target. He raised a hand to his quartz before he recalled that Corban had it. His fingers curled into his palm.

"*Move.*" Corban gave Jace's quartz a warning squeeze.

Jace sucked in a breath and obeyed. The trek was less than a mile, but it seemed like hours, each step an agony, as if he were pushing through quicksand. The only thing that kept him going was a grim determination to reach Evie.

At last they stopped in a clearing. Jace scented both Evie and Tyrus. The wound on his throat was bleeding in earnest now. He licked dry lips and blinked woozily in the rising heat as Kane uncovered the entrance to an underground den.

Corban pushed Jace toward the ladder. "Down there."

"Jace?" Evie peered up at him, her eyes huge.

"Coming, angel." Jace started down the ladder, but his hands and feet felt like they belonged to some other man. His foot slipped off the rung and he tumbled the rest of the way down, banging his head against the side of the ladder before hitting the earth floor with a jarring thud.

He wavered for a moment and then crumpled to the ground.

The next thing he knew, Evie was running her hands over him, her breath coming in jagged sobs. He wanted to reassure her, but he couldn't speak or even open his eyes, his whole being focused on simply breathing.

"Oh, God." Evie patted his face. "Please don't be dead. Please don't be dead."

Behind his eyes, the darkness shifted. He slit his lids. Evie was crouched next to him, her scent filling his head and bringing a measure of calm. On the other side of the small space, Tyrus and Corban were speaking in undertones, and he could hear Kane on the surface pacing agitatedly back and forth near the entrance.

The cat peeled its lip. *Attack. Kill.* Claws scored Jace from the inside.

Not yet, he told it.

The jaguar subsided, tail twitching angrily. It hadn't given up, and Jace agreed. To save Evie, he'd shift even if it killed him, but first he needed more intel.

"Jace?" Cool fingers touched his cheek. "You okay?"

"Yeah." He moistened dry lips. "You?"

A jerky nod. "I'm fine. And you're going to be okay. Just hang on, got it?"

He forced his lids to open more fully. "Okay."

Evie's shoulders slumped in relief. She dragged off her T-shirt, leaving her clad only in a bra and pants, and dabbed at the blood on his throat and chest. Tyrus loomed behind her, watching them with avid eyes. Sick bastard.

Fresh blood welled from the wound on Jace's throat; the fall must have ripped it open even further. Evie wadded up the shirt and pressed it to the wound. "Heal yourself, damn you."

He pointed at his chest where his quartz should be. "Can't."

"They took it?" Evie twisted to glare up at Corban. Her eyes lit on the quartz and she lunged for it, but he jerked it away and backhanded her across the face. She stumbled and made a hurt sound that was like a blade to Jace's heart, but came right back up.

Jace grabbed her arm. "It's okay."

"No, it's not." She pressed a hand to her cheek and he realized she was holding the other hand to her stomach, favoring it. It was red and swollen.

Fury blazed through Jace. He shook with the need to take down both men. That they *dared* hurt his mate. But on its heels came a cold-eyed determination. He would bide his time, and wait for his chance—and then all three men would die.

"It's okay," he told Evie again and mouthed, "Trust me."

She removed her hand from her face and gave a short nod.

Corban turned back to Tyrus. "Give me the diamonds. I'm outta here."

The night fae's gaze raked over Jace. "He's damaged. I'll be fortunate if he lasts the day."

Evie snarled and Jace tightened his grip on her.

"Nothing in the contract said how long you get to play with him," returned Corban. "He's here, and my part is done. You've got his woman, anyway—that will make it even sweeter. Now, my payment?"

Tyrus tossed a small black pouch at Corban. He snatched it in mid-air and checked the contents. He frowned. "There's one extra." He removed a glittering stone from the bag and thrust it at Tyrus. "Don't play your fucking fae games with me. You'll pay what we agreed—no more and no less."

The night fae regarded him coolly. "Consider it an advance."

"For what?"

"I want you to lay down a false trail. I don't want your alpha finding us."

"Adric's not my fucking alpha."

"Pardon." Tyrus inclined his head mockingly. "Lay down a false trail for the Baltimore alpha. I'll leave at dusk—but I don't want to be disturbed before then. I don't care how you do it."

"Or," Corban returned with a smirk, "I could lead Adric here and let him drag you into the sunlight. How long would you last, I wonder?"

Tyrus struck. One moment he was eyeing Corban coldly, the next he had Corban up against the wall, a knife to his throat. Jace felt the dark hum of Tyrus's energy, sucking at Corban. The whole thing was done in a creepy silence.

"What the fuck?" Kane started down the ladder, but Tyrus bared his teeth at him, and the other man froze.

The night fae turned his gaze back to Corban. "Do we have a deal?"

Corban glared back, hate in his eyes, but growled an assent.

Tyrus released him and stepped back, but kept the knife out. Corban shoved a few things into a backpack and headed for the ladder.

"You forgot something." The night fae held out a hand. "The quartz?"

Corban shrugged, and then to Jace's horror, tossed his quartz to Tyrus. The night fae's cold fingers wrapped around it, and Jace felt an answering chill clear to his soul. Terror touched him, black and stark. Anyone who held his quartz could hurt him—but a fae who knew the secret could *control* him. It was the earth fada's Achilles' heel, the price exacted by the fae who'd created them. Those fae had feared the water fada's independence and had ensured Jace's people would have both greater power, and a greater weakness.

"You fucking SOB." Jace struggled up on his forearms to glare at Corban. "You...give our secrets to a fae? This is the kind of alpha you'd be?"

Corban's jaw worked. "Shut the fuck up."

Kane was crouched at the surface, mouth slack with dismay. "Corban. Think about this, man. You'll have every earth fada in the world gunning for you."

Corban swung on him. "Only if they find out."

Kane shook his head. "I don't like this."

"You don't have to like it."

Kane's throat worked, but he nodded and backed away from the opening.

A shadow fell over Jace. Corban stared down at him, his face dark with loathing. "You're just like your sister. Bringing mixed-bloods into the clan."

"At least I didn't betray my alpha and sell secrets to a fae."

Corban's heavy black brows snapped together. "Make sure you kill him for good this time," he told Tyrus as he aimed a kick at Jace's stomach. "I swear the fucking cat has nine lives."

Evie threw herself forward to block the kick, but she was too late. It landed squarely on his still healing knife wounds. Jace grunted and fought to remain conscious as Corban swarmed up the ladder.

The rock dropped back over the entrance. He and Evie were alone with Tyrus.

CHAPTER 33

$\mathcal{A}$dric spent a precious few minutes tracking Tyrus. The night fae's noxious scent covered Evie's but he caught a hint of her as well.

"He's headed north," he told Marjani and Zuri.

The three of them jumped on the bikes, Marjani still behind Adric, and accelerated down the quiet street. He deliberately didn't call any backup. Any more men and they'd risk spooking Tyrus, and then they'd never find Evie. The same applied to Corban and Jace.

As alpha, Adric could use Jace's quartz to pinpoint his location to within a hundred yards. However, with the quartz removed, that ability was gone. Still, he had the sense the quartz—and possible Jace—were moving in the same general direction as Tyrus.

He refused to think about the fact that his friend had been bleeding right up until they'd apparently put him into a car. The only good thing was that if he was still leaving a trail of blood, Adric could follow the scent.

But Evie first.

"Faster," Marjani said in his ear. "If he takes her out of the city, we'll never find her."

He shook his head. "Sun's too high. He'll have to go to ground until tonight."

"You hope," his sister returned.

Zuri zoomed up beside them, and they wove through the early morning traffic, ignoring red lights and stop signs. The trail led into Druid Hill Park.

They pulled into the nearest parking lot. Zuri inhaled. "Jace is here, too."

Adric's heart leapt. Maybe when they found Evie, they'd find Jace, too. "He said something to me early this morning about Corban having a lair in the park. Let's spread out to search."

The three of them loped into the woods to shift. They needed their animals' heightened senses to track Evie and Jace.

Adric completed the shift first. He took off north without waiting for the other two, his Gift for tracking on hyperalert. It was like a sixth sense that let him know if he was on the right or wrong path, and it also sharpened his regular senses.

Behind him, he heard the other two finish their shifts and spread out to the east and west.

He crossed an asphalt path and scented the night fae. A few yards later, a drop of blood. *Jace.*

He changed back to man so he could alert Marjani and Zuri through his quartz, and then back again to his cougar to continue following the scent. When the trail left the path to go into the trees again, he overran it for few seconds, but his Gift soon alerted him.

Wrong.

He doubled back and met Marjani and Zuri arriving different directions. He jerked his head to the right and they all darted into the trees. Zuri had his nose to the ground, but Adric and Marjani were using their cougars' sharp vision as much as their noses.

They were on the right track. There were multiple signs that men had come through these woods, and recently: a broken twig, a partial shoeprint, a short blue thread caught on a wild rosebush's thorn.

He scented Jace's blood and a hint of sweat—the acrid odor of a man pushed to his limits.

Where the fuck are you?

He drew on his quartz and frowned. The connection he had to Jace's quartz was fainter, as if a barrier had been thrown up between the two of them. Then the connection broke.

Adric's heart punched. *Damn you, you're not dead. You're not.*

He halted. His cougar couldn't communicate in words, but he yowled a warning: *Danger.*

The scent trails split, with Tyrus's going in one direction and Corban, Kane and Jace's going in the other. Adric didn't hesitate—the important thing was to find Tyrus, and hopefully, Evie. He loped after Tyrus.

Something was balled up on the ground. Adric's breath caught, but it was just a bloody T-shirt covered with Jace's scent. When he investigated more closely, he realized it wasn't even Jace's T-shirt.

He snarled. Corban was messing with him—trying to confuse the trail.

But that didn't mean Jace wasn't close. Adric slowed down, slipping from tree to tree, eyes peeled and ears pricked.

The woods went silent. The fur on his nape bristled. Zuri and Marjani sidled up to stand on either side of him.

A black wolf burst out of the trees. Corban.

Go! Adric hissed at the other two. He could hold off Corban while they rescued Jace and Evie.

Marjani tore off. Zuri hesitated, torn between obeying his alpha and protecting him.

Adric had never demanded unquestioning obedience from his lieutenants—he wanted men who could think for themselves—but now he put all the force of his dominance behind his growl. "*Go—now.*"

Even then, Zuri might have stayed, but protect the vulnerable had been their creed since they were cubs, and Jace and Evie needed him more than Adric did. He turned and sprinted after Marjani.

Adric planted his paws and snarled at his cousin. *Bring it on.*

And then Kane slunk out of the shadows.

CHAPTER 34

$\mathcal{E}$vie crouched over Jace, instinctively trying to protect him as the tall, hard-eyed shifter—Corban—closed them into the darkness with Tyrus again.

Jace groaned. She ran her hands over him, furious tears pricking her eyes. What kind of coward kicked a man when he was down?

And what did Tyrus mean, Jace might not last the day? Icy shards pierced her chest.

No fucking way. She was *not* going to let Jace die.

She squeezed his hand. "You're going to be all right—I promise."

He muttered something unintelligible.

"Jace? Can you hear me?"

This time he didn't even answer. Her fear spiked.

To her left, Tyrus rustled and she guessed he was sitting down. All she could see were his eyes, a strange blue-black glow in the gloom. Better than that terrifying red, but not much.

Gradually, her eyes grew accustomed to the dark and she could make out Tyrus's outline. He'd settled onto his coat, his back against the wall. Jace's quartz was suspended from his fingers, a weak green light at its heart.

If Jace had his quartz, he could heal himself. She had to get it back.

Black tendrils teased at her arms and face, but Tyrus seemed tired. The sun was fully up now—this must be when he slept. She slapped at them, but her hands went right through them. Then the tendrils brushed over her breasts.

Oh, no. Hell, no.

She sat on the floor with a thump and crossed her arms over her chest. "No sex," she rasped. "That's not part of the deal."

"No? Not even if I tell you I can heal the fada?"

"What do you mean?"

"I'm a healer in my clan."

Her mouth dropped open. "You're kidding."

"A fae can't lie, Evie." A cold smile curled his mouth. "Of course, a healer knows precisely the right places to cause pain, too."

The tendrils snaked past her. Jace jerked and then whined, the sound of a hurt animal.

Evie's heart clenched. "Stop it!" She lunged at Tyrus, only to realize too that that was what he'd wanted.

Strong hands clamped on her arms, forcing her to her knees between Tyrus's thighs. She tried to strike at him, but he simply tightened his grip.

Her fingers curled helplessly at her sides, but she raised her chin and snapped, "Get your fucking hands off me."

He trailed cool fingers down her throat, teasing her breasts above the bra. She shuddered and jerked back.

"Should I hurt him again?" A soft, malevolent murmur.

She briefly closed her eyes—and surrendered. "You heal him first," she gritted. "Or I'll—I'll—" She stuttered to a halt, because she hadn't a clue of what to threaten him with.

"Or you'll what?" Tyrus nuzzled her ear. "Fight me, Evie."

Her spine went rigid. *Run*, her brain screamed, but he had her trapped.

The darkness latched onto her like a many-armed octopus. Sucking at her... feeding on the fear and anger, and it *hurt*. Like no pain in the world. Icy-hot agony that slithered over her skin, drank from her soul, caressed her most secret parts—rape without the physical act.

"Fight me." A dark breath against her throat.

She bared her teeth at him and he chuckled. She shouldn't fight him, she knew she shouldn't, but she couldn't help it. It was instinct, a trapped butterfly battering its wings against the glass.

Her hands came to Tyrus's chest. She dug her nails into him through the silky material of his shirt and his head dropped back, eyes slit with enjoyment.

Her stomach bottomed out. Whatever she did, she was fucked. Hopelessness swamped her. Her only consolation was that he'd forgotten Jace to focus on her.

Block him.

But she couldn't. It wasn't like in the kitchen when she'd had Kyler to help her, and Jace had been intermittently shielding them as well. This time Tyrus was totally focused on her, and he was strong, relentless. All she could do was endure.

He fed on her for what felt like an eternity but was probably only a few minutes, and then released her. He sat back, replete.

She slumped on the dirt floor, breath scraping in and out of her lungs.

A bone-chilling growl filled the small space. "Let. Her. Go."

She lifted her head to see Jace's eyes glowing green with fury. He was struggling to sit up.

"It's okay," she whispered.

He didn't seem to hear her. The growls continued, his cat pushed to its limit.

Evie forced herself to crawl the few feet to him. She felt old, wrung out, each movement of her arms and legs an effort. The whole time, she felt Tyrus's gaze on her, but he said nothing.

When she reached Jace, she set her cheek against his, still on her hands and knees. Her breath shuddered out. She was shaking, her fingers and toes like ice. She inhaled and tried to calm herself.

"Don't try to get up—please. It's okay."

His gaze swung to her. His jaguar stared out of his eyes. She touched his face. "I'm okay."

His head tilted and he rubbed his cheek over hers, catlike. The prickles of his night-beard were comforting—a welcome antidote to the smooth, cold tentacles.

"Come. Here." Guttural tones that she had to strain to understand.

She lay next to him, careful not to jar his injuries. He slid an arm under her, and she nestled her head into his shoulder. Seeking safety, even though she knew it was just an illusion. Tyrus wasn't going to let them go.

Gradually, she grew warmer and she realized how cold Tyrus had left her. Her shivers ceased, and she sensed Jace calming.

When he spoke again, his voice was that of a human. "Kyler?"

"Back at your den. I made Tyrus leave him behind."

He exhaled. "Thank the gods."

She nodded, although she wasn't sure how much control Tyrus had over the black wolf, who must've been Corban. And on top of that, Tyrus had fed on Kyler, too. She swallowed and burrowed closer to Jace.

Kyler's okay. He has *to be.* If they got out of this alive, she'd never bitch at him again.

Jace set his mouth to her ear. "Hang on," he said in a faint voice, each word clearly an effort. "I got word...to Adric before...they took us. He'll come...save you. And I'll keep that...prick away from you...until then."

"*No,*" she returned in an urgent, equally low tone. "Don't try anything. He can't hurt me. Not really." Not like Jace, who was rapidly growing weaker. She knew he had to be hurt bad—he hadn't even been able to get off the floor to help her when Tyrus was feeding on her.

Jace's only reply was a grunt.

She drew in a breath. "I can get your quartz."

"No." His grip on her tightened. "I don't want you...anywhere near...him."

She didn't reply, but she'd made up her mind. Jace needed his quartz to heal himself. They couldn't count on Adric finding them in time.

Tyrus shifted position. She sat back up so she could keep an eye on him, but Tyrus was only settling back against the wall. Why the hell didn't he go to sleep? But he seemed wide awake, although relaxed, sated from his meal.

Tyrus spoke. "You and the fada—you love him?" He sounded curious, but she didn't trust his reasons for asking—and she was damned if she'd tell him before she'd told Jace himself.

She moved a shoulder. "I haven't known him that long."

Jace tugged on her hand. When she leaned closer, he murmured, "I love *you*," the words a warm tickle in her ear.

She blinked. Heat crept into her chest, chasing away the last of the chill. "I—" She halted and shook her head.

"You feel it." Jace brought her hand to his heart. "My mate," he mouthed.

"You're telling me this now?" she whispered back.

He gave her a crooked grin. "Didn't know myself...until a few hours ago." He sobered. "Wanted you to know...in case..."

She shot a glance at Tyrus, but he was holding Jace's quartz by the cord and examining it.

"You are *not* going to die," she told Jace.

He pressed a kiss to her hand and then released it. He opened his mouth and tried to speak, but couldn't.

She squeezed his fingers. "You're not going to die. I won't let you."

"Mate bond," he said at last. "Not complete. But might help. The two of us... together...stronger."

She nodded. She did feel calmer, and she could swear there was a fine thread connecting her to Jace. Her heart filled with wonder. Could this be the mate bond? She touched a hand to her sternum, right where she felt the connection, and Jace nodded as if he'd heard her question.

Tyrus closed his fingers around Jace's quartz. He touched it to the hollow of his throat and muttered something in a language Evie didn't recognize. "Sit up."

His dark eyes focused on Jace—and Jace jerked upright. He snarled, and Tyrus said, "Quiet," and Jace's mouth clamped shut as if a switch had been flipped.

Evie started. *What the fuck?*

Tyrus's mouth curved. "The possibilities are so interesting. I could order you to do anything. Kill that niece of yours, even."

Fine hairs raised all along Evie's spine. "You wouldn't."

Jace's throat worked. His expression was murderous, but whatever Tyrus was using to control him wouldn't allow him to speak.

"No?" the night fae said. "I can't kill her myself—she's protected by a ward. Anyone who touches her dies himself. But if Jones does it for me..." Tyrus released the quartz and let it swing from his fingers.

Whatever had been holding Jace upright released. He flopped forward like a marionette with its strings cut, but came right back up with a snarl. He lurched at Tyrus, but the night fae touched the quartz to his throat again.

"Stay where you are."

Evie had worked out what Tyrus meant. Her stomach dropped. "He would die, too."

"Exactly. It would kill two birds with one stone, yes?"

Jace strained against the invisible bonds, the cords of his neck quivering with tension. But it was no use, and he was dangerously weak. All too soon his shoulders slumped. He sent Evie an anguished look and leaned back against the wall.

Evie took his hand and racked her brain for ideas. But she kept circling back to the one sure thing: *Steal back Jace's quartz.*

Tyrus's eyes drifted shut, but she'd bet her last dollar he wasn't sleeping. Still, if they were going to fight back, it had to be now, before the night came again. Daytime was when a night fae was weakest.

Beside her, she sensed Jace gathering his energy. She felt that spark of amazement again. So this was the mate bond? This deep *knowing* of another person? Even as faint and new as the bond was between them, she felt connected to him in a way she never had to any man.

Then her heart sank. Jace was going to attack, weak as he was—and even though he believed he couldn't win. She could *feel* his uncertainty—and his determination.

She gripped his hand. "Not yet," she whispered.

"Can't." He subsided, his expression bleak. "Can't...shift."

"That's bad, right?"

He grimaced in assent.

She glanced at Tyrus. How the hell was she going to steal back the quartz? If only she had a weapon... But even if she did, she wasn't sure she could hurt Tyrus. He moved so freaking fast—and he was fae, practically unkillable.

Jace had gone silent again, his breath coming in shallow pants. Then his lips moved. "I'm sorry," he said in a nearly inaudible voice. "For dragging you...and Kyler into this. If I hadn't...come to your door...Tyrus would never have..." He trailed off.

"Stop it," she hissed back. "This is *not* your fault."

His throat worked. "Shouldn't have...brought you to Baltimore. But seemed... like the right thing to do."

"Oh, Jace. Don't do this to yourself—I agreed to come, didn't I? They would've gotten to us even easier if we stayed in Grace Harbor."

His eyes flicked to Tyrus, his expression stark. "But when I make a mistake, people die."

Her heart contracted. She knew he was thinking of his sister. "No one's going to die," she said fiercely. "Now stop talking. Rest."

His lips quirked. "And think happy thoughts, right?"

Her cheeks heated. "You heard that?"

"Yeah."

"It worked, didn't it?"

"You." He reached for her hand and brought it to his chest. "I'm thinking about you. You make me happy."

Emotion welled up in her. She brushed a kiss over his lips, too full to speak, and then settled next to him, cross-legged, a hand on his thigh. "Rest. I'll watch Tyrus."

He nodded and shut his eyes.

Silence fell. Tyrus's eyes had closed and his breathing changed. She was almost sure he'd fallen asleep. He'd set Jace's quartz on the coat beside him. The fae were so arrogant and sure of their superiority, it probably didn't even occur to him that Evie might try to steal it back.

She rubbed her palms over her upper arms. When Jace had sat up, the T-shirt she'd pressed to his throat had fallen to the floor. When she'd kissed him just now, her hand had touched the wadded-up material. The shirt was soaked with blood.

There was no more time. Jace needed his quartz—now.

She forced herself to wait another five minutes to allow Tyrus to fall more deeply asleep. That was when she realized something was digging into her ass.

She slipped a hand into her left pocket and caught her breath. A fae light had somehow shrunk to the size of a marble and hitched a ride. She rolled it between her fingers. It was soft and warm, and made her hand tingle. Nice, but probably not any help.

She left the tiny light hidden in her pocket. No point in letting Tyrus know about it. And knowing it was there comforted her, made the dark seem less threatening.

Let's go, Evie. She crept across the floor. If Tyrus woke up, she'd say she was getting a drink of water. It wasn't a lie; she was dry-mouthed with fear.

The quartz had stopped glowing. She brushed her hand over the dirt where she'd last seen it, keeping a chary eye on Tyrus.

When she couldn't find it, she inched closer. Tyrus's darkness reached out for her, but a quick glance told her he was still asleep. Heart in her throat, she scrabbled around in the dirt until her fingers touched a smooth, oblong shape. She snatched up the quartz and slipped it into her bra before rising to her feet and continuing to the sink. She gripped the edge, waiting for her galloping heart to settle.

Behind her, Tyrus stirred. She shot him a look. His eyes gleamed at her in the darkness but he didn't say anything. Hands shaking, she took a metal cup from a hook and filled it with water. She drank deeply, then refilled the cup and returned to Jace, aware of Tyrus's gaze on her the whole time.

Kneeling next to him, she slid an arm under his shoulders and lifted him so he could drink. He drank greedily and she realized with a pang that she should've gotten him water sooner. He'd lost so much blood.

But at least she'd retrieved his quartz. She turned her body so that Tyrus couldn't see and slipped it into his palm.

Jace stilled, and then his fingers closed on it.

Her neck crawled. Tyrus was still watching her. Any minute he'd figured out she'd stolen back the quartz. "Hurry," she whispered to Jace.

His chin moved in a slight nod. He didn't move or show in any way that he was drawing on the quartz, but she saw the glow brighten between his fingers. She set her hand over his to cover it.

A minute passed, then another. When she flicked a glance at Tyrus, his eyes were closed again.

Jace's breath altered. It was deeper, more powerful. He nudged her hip. "Help me," he mouthed.

Of course. She mentally smacked her forehead. She was an amplifier; she could help Jace heal himself.

Tyrus might have weakened her, but nobody got the best of Evie Morningstar. She set her hand on Jace's stomach and focused with everything she had.

CHAPTER 35

Jace hurt in every bone of his body. But that was nothing to the pain and fury he felt when the night fae went for Evie, and he was too fucking weak to help her.

He ached to get her out of here. If he thought it would do any good, he'd humble himself, plead with Tyrus to let her go. But he knew Tyrus would refuse. It must be a rare treat for the prick to be able to feed on another fae's energy, even a part-human like Evie.

At least Jace had had the chance to tell her he loved her, that she was his mate. The bond had sprung into being. He had to believe that was a good thing, that together, they were stronger than either was alone.

Evie moaned, and Jace cursed Tyrus, dark and vicious. The wound on his neck spurted blood, and he blacked out. He came back to consciousness to find he was trying to sit up, attempting to get to Evie.

Another harrowing minute ticked past before the night fae released her. She crawled back to Jace and huddled next to him, her body trembling.

He might have gone for Tyrus anyway but the fucking fae had his quartz. The pendant wasn't alive. It didn't know it was being used to control Jace. It just called mindlessly to him and he was forced to obey.

Fury condensed in Jace, cold and grim. Tyrus's plotting made sense now, but he'd miscalculated one thing.

Jace would never harm Merry. He'd kill himself first.

But first, he had to save Evie. He tucked her close to his body, comforting her the only way he could. Tyrus dozed off and Jace forced himself to relax and conserve his energy. He must have drifted off again, because he didn't realize Evie had left his side until she was lifting his head, urging him to drink.

He eagerly gulped the water. It was cool and good, soothing his parched throat. "Thank you," he rasped.

Then she slipped the quartz into his hand. He went rigid with shock—and admiration. How the hell had she managed to steal it back?

Hope surged. Maybe they had a chance after all.

He gripped the quartz and drew on its energy with everything he had. The crystals' song was high-pitched, agitated. Drawing on the quartz so hard was dicey —he risked blowing it out— but he had no choice.

The first thing he did was close the wound on his throat. Replacing the blood loss would take hours, but he could stem the flow. Next, he pushed energy into his body—a quick-and-dirty fix. It would take the place of the blood he'd lost, but only for a short time. But he only needed a few minutes to take Tyrus down.

And he *would* take Tyrus down. Failure wasn't an option.

Sweat beaded on Jace's temples. He drew harder—and hit a brick wall. He hated to ask Evie for help—she was already drained from Tyrus—but he might only have a few minutes. Night fae usually slept in the day, but Tyrus was running high from feeding on them.

"Help me," he whispered, and Evie gamely added her own energy to his. Pride filled him. His mate had a spine of pure steel.

Tyrus started awake. His eyes gleamed red in the darkness. "You stole from me." His tone was surprised—and cold as only a fae's could be.

Jace swore under his breath. "That's enough," he told Evie. It would have to be.

"You're...okay?" She collapsed onto the floor without waiting for an answer, her chest working.

Jace's heart lurched. He lifted her onto his lap. "I love you," he said. "So fucking much." Her mouth curved but she didn't speak. He rubbed her back, terrified that between him and Tyrus, they'd drained her too deeply.

But Tyrus didn't care.

Dark energy slipped over the two of them. Soft at first, like the damp brush of fog, then they were enveloped in chilly tendrils. Jace burned with guilt and shame.

He'd failed his sister.

He'd failed Merry.

And now he was going to fail Evie.

The tendrils multiplied like a ball of squirming maggots, enveloping Jace in a slimy darkness. He had the urge to flail at them wildly, but that would only play into Tyrus's hands. The more negative energy Jace put out, the more Tyrus had to feed on.

Evie wrapped her arms around his waist. "We can beat him," she whispered fiercely against his neck. "Happy thoughts, right?"

He buried his face in her hair. He didn't know about happy thoughts, but he knew one thing—this woman was his heart. Warmth flared in his chest. He brought her hand to his mouth and kissed the palm.

A trembling smile bloomed on her lips. She curled her fingers as if capturing his kiss for safe-keeping. "Love you."

Their eyes met. The blackness receded, but hovered nearby. Testing for weaknesses.

Jace gathered himself for a fight.

The tendrils returned, insidious, relentless. This time they burrowed deeper, sucking at their energy. Evie shuddered and Jace snapped.

Enough.

"Run if you can," he told her and set her on the floor behind him.

"No," she said, but he was focused on Tyrus now.

He crouched on all fours, man and jaguar united. "You fucking SOB. Can't you see it's too much for her? Feed on me, damn you."

Tyrus's eyes bored into him. Icy claws of dread clamped on his nape, but he ignored it to prowl closer.

Something black and sharp bored into his heart. Tyrus was feeding in earnest now, but a feeding night fae did nothing to relieve the pain. Instead, he somehow made it double and then redouble, so that Jace was lashed with regret: so many people dead...so many ways he'd fucked up, let down those he loved.

"*No.*" He hunched his shoulders as if the lash were a physical whip, and grimly bore it.

Beside him, Evie swallowed audibly. "Jace..."

She was curled up on the floor, gasping for breath. Tyrus hadn't let up on her. She was being sucked into the darkness with him.

Fuck that.

His growl was low and primal. He had enough energy now to shift. One chance to save Evie. He'd have to make it count.

The cat was a hundred percent with him. *Kill. Save the female.*

Jace dropped the quartz pendant over his neck and set his mouth. The shift was agony. His skin burned, and his bones popped and cracked, twisted beyond their capacity. An involuntary groan tore from his lips.

"*Jace.*" Behind him, Evie gasped and pushed herself up on her hands and knees. "What are you doing?"

He ignored her to focus on drawing enough energy to fuel the shift. Lights exploded behind his eyes. A fireball of pain scorched through him until it was all he could do not to scream.

He folded his fingers around his quartz and squeezed, sucking every bit of energy he could. *Now.* He wrenched his form from man to cat—and then collapsed on the ground, weak as a kitten.

Evie sobbed out his name. "Jace."

He pushed himself to stand on wobbly legs, and snarled at the night fae.

Tyrus stalked toward him—and Jace struck.

A jaguar's bite was twice as strong as a lion's. He could kill an animal by sinking his teeth into its skull. Jace went for Tyrus's spinal cord, determined to end this.

But the night fae was incredibly fast. In the blink of an eye, he was on the other side of the small room. Still, Jace had him on the run. The dark feeding stopped as the other man focused on surviving.

Evie scuttled into a corner, smart enough to get out of the way. Something glowed in her hand—a fae light. She held it up, casting a light over their battle.

Tyrus raised a hand and muttered a phrase in an ancient fae language. The air gathered into a sharp point and flew at Jace. It would've taken out his eye if he hadn't flung himself to the side, but instead, it sliced open his cheek.

He leapt for Tyrus and again, the fae evaded him. Jace's jaguar rumbled angrily. They circled each other, breathing hard.

Tyrus raised his hand and muttered another spell. This time, the air formed itself into a rope that wrapped around Jace's throat like a noose. He clawed furiously at it, but it was some magical material that repelled his attempts to dislodge it. The noose tightened. His vision darkened at the edges. He made one last, desperate attempt to sink his teeth into Tyrus but the other man easily pushed him off.

"No!" Evie dashed between them, the fae light in her hand, and shoved it into Tyrus's face.

The room seemed to explode. Tyrus's body lit up with an eerie blue fire that danced up and down his limbs, burning through his clothes. The scent of scorched flesh filled the air. He shrieked and stumbled backward.

Jace blinked, temporarily blinded, but he could hear Tyrus moaning to his left. He growled and moved toward him, the cat in ascendance. The fae was slumped against the wall, hands to his face.

Jace pounced, slapping his paws on Tyrus's chest and ripping open his throat. The sickening taste of metal and decay filled his mouth. He gave Tyrus a hard shake, and the body flopped lifelessly in his grip. He let Tyrus fall to the dirt floor and stood over him, still partially blinded. He was quiet, but was he dead? He cocked an ear and heard the faint beating of the fae's black heart.

Evie was moaning. "Ohmigod. Ohmigod."

The rock over the entrance shifted, and shadows moved down the ladder. Jace growled, still unable to see clearly, until he recognized the scents as Marjani and Zuri.

Tyrus's breath rattled in.

"He's not dead," Evie breathed. "Oh, God."

Jace's vision cleared enough to see Marjani thrust an iron blade beneath Tyrus's rib cage. A single expert stab to the heart, one of the only sure ways to kill a fae.

Tyrus grunted and then went limp.

"Now he is," Marjani said.

CHAPTER 36

*A*dric ignored Kane to focus on Corban. He and his oldest cousin were evenly matched, his cougar as large as Corban's wolf. He'd beat Corban once before in a fair fight—the duel for alpha, with the clan's lieutenants and top soldiers as witnesses.

This time, it wouldn't be fair, and his animal was coldly pleased. Fuck the rules. Corban needed to die.

Adric crouched low, ears back, and bared his teeth. Kane circled uneasily, his gaze darting between Corban and Adric.

Adric's tail twitched. *Traitor.*

Kane's eyes cut to his brother. Corban growled, and Kane whined. Then he made up his mind and ranged himself next to Corban.

So be it. Adric would take them both on.

Corban's muscles bunched, preparing to attack. Adric struck first, darting in and sinking his teeth into Corban's ruff. The wolf's blood filled his mouth, hot and salty.

Corban shook him off and snapped at Adric's leg. Adric danced away. Kane sidled closer for a sneak attack, and Adric snapped, tearing a gash in Kane's muzzle.

The battle started in earnest then. The two wolves came at Adric from either side, but he twisted and leapt straight up, and they crashed into each other.

He came down and ripped into the nearest nape with his teeth. It was Kane.

He gripped his vertebrae and gave him a vicious shake. There was the sound of snapping bones, and the wolf grunted and went limp, his head at an odd angle.

Regret twanged through Adric. He'd grown up with Kane, the other shifter just two years older than him. But there was no time to mourn.

He released him and turned toward Corban, but the bastard had run, leaving his brother to distract Adric while he escaped. Corban was already disappearing into the trees.

Adric shot after him, but the wolf had a good head start, and Adric was bleeding from wounds he hadn't known he had.

His cougar's blood was up. It urged him to give chase, but the man knew it could be a trap. And even if it wasn't, Corban was leading him out of the park and away from Evie and Jace. He slowed, but his cousin did, too. Then the air around Corban shimmered and twisted.

Adric halted and watched from a safe distance as the wolf disappeared. A fae had 'ported the bastard out.

Adric let out a furious snarl. And he scented silver, not a night fae's unpleasant scent, which was one more layer of mysterious to this whole hellacious business.

He shifted to man and started limping back toward Kane. The wolves must have chomped on his leg, too. He had to pause a minute to pulse some healing energy into it. He couldn't afford to be at less than full strength.

That done, he contacted Beau, bringing him up to speed with a few terse sentences. "Put out a call to the nearest soldiers," he finished. "Corban's gone rogue. Their orders are to kill him on sight."

"If he's still in Baltimore," the bear replied. "A powerful fae could 'port him anywhere in the world."

"I know." Adric gripped his quartz and willed his pounding anger to subside. "Meanwhile, get a healer to Druid Hill Park ASAP. Jace is hurt and Kane is dying."

"Evie?"

Adric expelled a breath. "I don't know, but I'm hoping she's with Jace."

"I'll tell Kyler."

Adric gave Beau his current coordinates and returned to where Kane lay on the ground, breathing shallowly. Adric knelt beside him. "Shift." It was his cousin's only chance at healing.

Kane closed his eyes and changed to his man. He remained motionless, his head at that odd angle, his narrow face ashen. His lips twisted. "Can't feel...my legs or arms."

"Fuck." Adric sat back on his heels, his chest tight with a mixture of pity and anger.

Kane moistened his lips. "Sorry...I—he's my brother."

"Fuck that. I'm alpha. You swore an oath to me." *And we were family.*

Kane's gaze slid from his. "I know." To break an oath was a terrible thing. It must have torn his cousin up inside. Probably he hadn't even used his full strength against Adric—his wolf wouldn't have allowed it.

Kane's eyes closed, his only movement the shallow rise and fall of his chest.

Adric glanced around. "Where in Hades is that healer?" But he knew it was already too late.

His cousin did too. "There's something...you should know. Our dad...Leron... he let the night fae in. The Darktime."

"What?"

"He knew...he couldn't win alpha...in a fair fight. So he invited the night fae. They were happy...to feed on our misery. To make it worse."

"God's balls." Adric scraped his hands over his face. But it made sense; he'd seen it himself. Too often, the night fae had been conveniently near at the clan's worst moments, ready to feed off their anger and despair.

Blackness filled his head. The guilt of assassinating his own uncle was a weight he carried with him. Always. But at that moment, he would've gladly stuck a knife into Leron's black heart all over again. So many men and women dead or hurt to feed that prick's ambition...and the young, innocents who'd never even had a chance to live.

And now he'd killed his own cousin.

Tipping back his head, he let out an anguished growl that iced the blood of every animal within hearing range.

Kane's mouth quirked in an ironic smile. "You're better...alpha. Leron would...have hated that." His breath sighed out and his eyes blanked.

"Damn you," Adric bit out. But he closed his cousin's eyes before rising to his feet. Then he called Beau, telling him to send a couple of soldiers to remove Kane's body from the park before some human stumbled upon him.

The chase through the park had led him close to where they'd left their clothes. He dressed and grabbed Marjani and Zuri's clothes as well and started off at a trot to Zuri's coordinates.

It was only then that he realized he could no longer sense Jace's quartz.

~

Evie's stomach roiled. She pressed a hand to her mouth and tried not to lose her supper on the dirt floor. She was not some girly-girl, damn it. She didn't fall apart at the sight of blood. But she could smell Tyrus's scorched flesh, and he was sprawled like a broken doll just ten feet away.

She wrapped her arms around herself. Jace paced toward her, his mouth stained with blood. She shrank against the wall. His stride checked and she *felt* his hurt.

Her heart constricted. She unpeeled her fingers from where they were digging into her upper arms. "I'm sorry." She stretched out her hands to him. "It's okay. I know you had to do it." She was babbling. She clamped her mouth shut.

He remained where he was and her stomach sank. Sparkles danced over his fur and she realized he was trying to shift. The sparkles brightened, and then dimmed, and she realized he was having trouble.

"No," she whispered, knowing he was forcing the shift for her. "Don't..."

But then the bits of colors intensified and cascaded over his body. She squeezed her eyes shut against the brightness, and when she opened them again, he was a man and the blood was gone.

"Evie?" He opened his arms to her, eyes wary. Powerful, naked, and *hers*.

She stepped forward and his face lightened. They met in the middle, hugging and kissing each other. Jace framed her face in his hands. "You're all right?" He kissed her eyes, her mouth, ran his hands over her back.

"Yes, yes. But what about you?" She pulled back to examine his throat and chest. His original wounds had closed up, but there was a bloody slice across his cheek and he had a nasty rope burn around his neck. She touched it with her fingertips and felt all over again the icy fear that had gripped her as Jace had struggled against the magical noose. "I thought you were going to die."

"Cat, remember?" He shrugged a big shoulder. "Nine lives, although I may be down to four or five at this point."

She made a sound that was half-laugh, half-sob. "Oh, God." She laid her head against his chest, and for a long moment, they just held each other, forgetting everyone and everything else. His heart thumped loudly against her cheek and she realized he was as affected as her.

"What the fuck did you do with that fae light, anyway?" he asked.

"I don't know. I just wanted to distract him." She was shaking. He squeezed her tight.

The cellar was filling with people—Marjani, Zuri, and a couple shifters Evie didn't know.

"A healer's on the way," Zuri told Jace. "Can you get to the surface?"

Jace nodded and guided Evie to the ladder. She stared at it, not sure her legs could carry her to the top. The adrenaline that had fueled her desperate attempt to save Jace had dissipated, leaving her feeling like a wrung-out dishcloth.

Jace swung her into his arms. "Hang on, angel."

"Y-you c-can't!" she protested through chattering teeth, but he stopped her mouth with a kiss and carried her one-handed up the ladder while she clung to his neck.

A lean blond man lifted her from Jace's arms and set her on the ground beneath a large oak. Jace sank down beside her, his back against the oak.

"I'm Tommy," the blond said. "A healer."

She nodded. "Evie."

"Good to meet you. I've been hearing all sorts of good things about you and Jace." While he talked, he ran his quartz over Evie. He frowned. "You're dangerously weak."

"The night fae fed on her," said Jace, "and then I took more energy to heal myself. It was the only way."

"I'm fine," she said between chattering teeth. "Jace is...the one...who's hurt."

Jace shook his head. "Evie first."

"You're outvoted," Tommy told her. He gently pressed her shoulder, encouraging her to lean against the oak trunk next to Jace. "You won't feel yourself for a few days," he said as he set his quartz over her heart, "but I can give you an energy boost."

She nodded and gave in, letting her eyes drift shut as her chest warmed with a healing glow that spread throughout her body. She soaked it up like rain on parched earth.

Tommy moved the quartz to her bruised left hand. She'd almost forgotten it in all the excitement, but now that the adrenaline was fading, it hurt like a bitch. But within a few minutes, the bruises disappeared.

"That should do it." Tommy smiled at her. "But take it easy for the next few days."

She tentatively moved her fingers, amazed to find it barely hurt. "I will," she replied, "and thank you."

He nodded and turned to Jace.

Evie rested her head against the trunk and watched, tired to her very toes. She was aware of people coming and going, and intense, low-voiced conversations, but it seemed to be happening far away.

Adric appeared and dragged off his own T-shirt so that she had something covering her. He'd been in a fight himself—his face and chest had been clawed—but his wounds were already closing up. He crouched next to her, bronze eyes concerned. "You okay, love?"

She nodded jerkily. "Kyler? He's...all right?"

"Yeah. A little shook up, but he's fine. Suha and Beau are with him, along with two soldiers."

Relief flooded her. "Thank you," she rasped.

He squeezed her shoulder. "No thanks necessary. I'm just sorry the two of you got caught up in this."

"At least it's over."

"I hope so," the alpha muttered.

Jace roused himself enough to ask about Corban and Kane.

Adric shook his head. "Kane's dead. Corban took off like the rat he is—left his own brother to take the fall."

"No surprise there," Jace said.

"We'll get him," Adric returned grimly. "He's a dead man." He lifted a brow at Evie. "That was you who took Tyrus out with a fae ball?"

"I guess." As if sensing their interest, the fae light wafted onto her lap and glowed a little more brightly. She stroked it, not sure herself exactly what had happened. "I don't know anything about a fae ball—I just used this light. He— the night fae—was hurting Jace. He was fighting with magic, strangling Jace with some kind of magical rope."

She swallowed, recalling her horror as Jace had clawed desperately at his neck, unable to stop the rope from constricting. "I couldn't just stand by and do nothing. I thought about how night fae can be burned by the sun, and—" She spread her hands. "I only wanted to distract him. I never thought it would set him on fire."

Jace's mouth curved. "She was fucking awesome."

Adric squeezed her shoulder again. "Whatever you did, good work." He turned to answer a question from one of his soldiers, and Tommy sat back.

"That should get you home," he told Jace. "But both of you need rest. Go back to your den and stay in bed the rest of the day. Healer's orders."

Jace stood up and gave a bone-cracking stretch. "Sounds like a plan." He bent down and before Evie knew what he was doing, swung her into his arms. To Adric he said, "She's had enough. You have any more questions, you can ask them later."

The alpha inclined his head.

"I can walk," she said, but Jace fixed her with a glare.

"Let me take care of you, okay?"

Evie blinked. She couldn't recall any man ever saying those words to her. She opened her mouth to argue—she could take care of herself, damn it. But although Jace's expression was stern, she saw the worry way back in his eyes.

"Okay," she said and rested her head against his shoulder. Because she *was* a little shaky, and if it made him happy, why not?

Jace headed into the woods with a ground-eating stride. She had the feeling he would've walked all the way back to his den butt-naked, but someone must have called for backup because a jeep pulled up as they emerged from the trees at the park's south end.

A pretty black-haired woman rolled down the window. "Need a ride?"

"Dina," said Jace. "Right on time."

"Anything for you, boss." She gave Evie a friendly smile and hopped out to open the back door.

Jace helped Evie into the jeep and then donned the shorts Dina tossed him. Sitting next to Evie, he pulled her onto his lap. She snuggled against his chest and heaved a sigh.

"That's it." He stroked her nape. "It's over."

She nodded against his shoulder and burrowed closer. He smelled sweaty and a little earthy, and all male. She tongued the ridge of his collarbone, tasting the salt.

His eyes creased in the smile she thought of as all her own. "What was that for?"

"Just because." *I love you.*

"I like it." He dropped a kiss on the top of her head. "Do it whenever you want."

Jace said they were mates, but she knew from Suha it wasn't a done deal. The woman had to accept the bond.

Her chest constricted. Because it wasn't just her—she had Kyler to consider, too.

CHAPTER 37

*A*dric stared down at Tyrus's badly burned body. Marjani was explaining what had happened, including the fact that it was Evie who had somehow fried Tyrus with a fae ball.

Adric didn't give a flying fuck that the man was dead, but—"The prince can't know we did this."

Tyrus had been Langdon's last living son. The night fae prince was going to be out for blood, and if he found out the Baltimore clan was involved, the Darktime would look like a warm-up compared to what he'd bring down on them.

"Agreed," said Marjani.

He eyed her. He didn't need anyone to tell him that she'd struck the final blow. The knife work had her signature. "You okay?"

She stared back with chocolate-colored eyes shot with the chill blue of her cougar. "Yeah."

"Good," he said, although he wasn't so sure she *was* okay. But what was done was done, and she'd only done what she'd had to. "We've got to make him disappear—completely. Call the engineers and tell them to bring explosives." Marjani needed something to do, something human to keep her cougar at bay.

While she started making the calls, Zuri organized the soldiers to bury Tyrus in the soil beneath Corban's lair and clear the surrounding area of any trace of him. No one could know he'd been here.

Adric climbed the ladder to check on Jace and Evie. Tommy, a young male who was training with Suha, was working over Jace. Jace's wounds were partly healed, but his quartz was blown out, explaining why he'd gone dead to Adric. He'd have to find a new one.

Evie sat close by, dressed only in a bra and bloodied pants. Her face was smudged with dirt, her gaze hollow. Adric knew that expression; it was that of someone who'd been pushed to her limit.

He stripped off his T-shirt. "Here. Put this on."

She nodded and lifted her arms like a child. He dropped it over her head. He wasn't a big man, but she was swamped by the gray cotton. A delicate blond fairy, all the glow stripped from her.

He muttered something dark.

Jace curled his fingers over hers and the thousand-yard stare left her eyes. She glanced at Jace. The look that passed between them made something deep and unacknowledged in Adric constrict. So his best friend had found his mate.

He was happy for Jace, of course, but a part of him cried out, *Why not me?* And then he thought of Rosana and clenched his right hand.

While the healer worked on Jace, Zuri walked over to ask about Corban and Kane.

"Kane's dead," Adric told him. "Corban got away. The bastard sacrificed his own brother to save his hide."

Marjani had come up in time to hear that last part. She shook her head. "He's gone rogue."

Adric nodded grimly. "I've got a kill order out on him."

"It's worse than you think. He didn't just help Tyrus kidnap Jace. He sold Jace's quartz to him."

Adric's gut tightened. "He gave him the secret?" He glanced down at Jace, who nodded.

"Fuck." Even knowing Corban as he did, Adric found it hard to believe. Earth fada swore to guard the secret of the quartz with their lives. As it was, most fae treated the fada as their pet mercenaries and errand boys. If the secret of the earth fada's quartz became general knowledge, they could turn the earth clans into slaves.

"I'll let the other earth alphas know." This was no longer simply a battle for supremacy between Adric and Corban; it was a full-out war. Every earth fada in the world would be on the lookout for Corban now, with orders to execute him on sight.

Adric glanced at the dank cellar where Tyrus's body lay. "Thank the gods the man's dead, or I'd have to kill him myself."

"But did he tell anyone else?" Marjani spoke before he could. "His father?"

Adric grimaced. He was still reeling from the information that Leron had invited the night fae into Baltimore. The idea of Prince Langdon having that kind of power over the clan made his stomach churn. *What did the prince know?*

An hour later, it was done. Tyrus was in a shallow grave beneath the dirt floor, and every trace of his scent was removed from the area.

Just to make sure, one of their explosive experts—a woman barely out of her teens—set off a charge after everyone was out. The rest of them watched from a safe distance as the earth rumbled and shook, and then collapsed inward.

Adric didn't kid himself that this was the end of it. Langdon would eventually track down his son's remains, and he might even suspect the earth fada—but he wouldn't have proof.

And if he went after the clan anyway, well, Adric would cross that bridge when he came to it.

Two grim-faced fada were guarding Jace's entrance. Jace stopped to talk to them, but Evie pushed past them to run down the steps to the den.

Beau opened the door for her. She barely noticed him saying hello, her gaze searching the room for Kyler.

His face lit up. "Evie!" He bounded off the couch toward her and then halted. "You're okay?" He rubbed his hands nervously over his shorts.

She gathered him into a hug. "I'm fine." Her vision blurred, and for a few moments, she just held him tight. Then she swiped a hand over her eyes and pulled back to look him over. "What about you? You're okay? The wolves—they didn't hurt you?"

"Nah." Kyler knuckled a tear from his cheek and she pretended not to notice. "They left right after you. But you...that prick didn't—"

"I'm fine," she repeated, because he didn't need to know how close Tyrus had come to breaking her. "Jace was with me." She nodded at Jace, who had come up behind her.

"Thank you." Kyler stuck out a hand to the earth fada.

Jace ignored his hand to pull him into a hug. "Hey, it was a team effort. Your sister smacked the bastard with a fae light."

"You did?" Kyler's gaze swung to her. "Seriously?"

"Yeah. Don't ask me how."

Kyler looked back at Jace. "He's dead? You're sure?"

"Yes."

"Good," Kyler said, low and vicious. "Because I was the one who let him in. I'm sorry, but I couldn't help it. I—"

"You did?" Evie knit her brow. "But why?"

"He got to me." His Adam's apple worked. "He—showed me things. Of you, dead—all of you. And—and—" He pressed his knuckles into his eyes. "I'm sorry. So sorry."

"Oh, Kyler. It's okay—you don't have to talk about it." She took a step toward him, but Beau was there first, dropping a massive arm around his shoulders.

"You have nothing to be sorry about. The man was a fucking fae lord—one of the strongest night fae around. It could've happened to anyone."

"But it didn't." Kyler's eyes were stark in his narrow face. "It was me he got to. Me who let him in—and not just him, but the wolves. And Horace—he's hurt bad. Suha's still with him. Sam's hurt, too, but not as bad."

"Horace is hurt?" Evie's stomach tightened. She met Jace's eyes.

"Fuck," he said, and strode toward the bedrooms.

Her brother hung his head. "If he dies, I'll never forgive myself."

Evie's heart hurt for him. It could've easily been her—she knew all too well how strong Tyrus was. "It's not your fault. I know. He tried that crap on me, and I...I couldn't break away."

"Really?" Kyler shot her a hopeful look. Then he shook his head. "But at least no one got hurt because of you. I'm the fucking weak human."

Evie swallowed and tried to think of something to say, but Beau just gave him a shake. "Enough with the self-pity," he growled.

Kyler flushed. "Sorry," he mumbled.

Beau gave him a squeeze and then released him and headed for the kitchen. "I could use your help here," he said over his shoulder. "Suha's going to be starving when she gets done with Horace, and your sister and Jace could use some food, too."

"Kyler," Evie said. "Horace is going to be okay. Suha's good at what she does."

He nodded, and then gave a little shrug. "I'd better help Beau. You don't want to mess with a bear."

"Yeah." She watched, bemused, as he hurried after Beau. *What had just happened?* But that rough male compassion seemed to be exactly what her brother needed.

She left the two of them debating whether to make breakfast or lunch and headed after Jace.

Horace was on his back, the cover drawn up to his waist. Evie sucked in a breath. He was so still, his cheekbones tinted a fevered red. Suha hovered over him like a benevolent witch in a lime green tunic, her quartz glowing. On the other side of the bed, Jace had pulled up a chair and had Horace's hand clasped between his two palms. His jaw was set. He looked like he was trying to heal his friend through sheer willpower.

Evie touched Suha's shoulder. "Can I help?"

The healer shook her head. "Almost done," she muttered.

Evie set her hands on Suha's back anyway and concentrated on sending her energy.

The healer visibly perked up. A minute later she sat back. "There," she said with satisfaction. She put a hand to her sacrum, massaging it. Her pretty face was drawn, but she winked at Evie. "Thanks for the boost. He's going to be all right."

Tears stung Evie's eyes. She met Jace's eyes across the bed. The relief on his face made her heart twist. "Good," she said. "That's good."

Horace's eyes opened and he glanced from Jace to Evie. "You're all right," he murmured. "I thought—"

"No fucking traitor is going to take me out. Or a fae, either."

"Yeah." Horace's mouth curled in a shadow of his usual smile. His gaze moved to Evie. "Sorry, love. Tried...to stop them."

She touched his hand. "I know."

"Don't talk, you ass," Jace said tenderly. "Save your breath to get better. We're fine, and that motherfucking fae is dead. Here." He slid an arm under Horace's shoulders and held a glass of water to his lips.

The other man drank thirstily before sinking back onto the pillows. Then his eyes popped open, and he clutched Jace's wrist. "What about...Corban and Kane?"

"Kane's dead," Jace assured him. "But Corban got away. Adric said a fae 'ported him out."

"Lord Prick?"

"Nah. We're not even sure it was a night fae."

"Well. Two...out of three...ain't bad.'

"Horace needs to rest," Suha inserted. "You, too," she told Jace and Evie. "The two of you look like you're running on fumes. If a night fae fed on you, you need to recharge. That's the alpha's order, by the way."

But they waited until Horace's eyes closed before slipping out of the room.

"Shower first," she said. "I can still smell that night fae on me." Residual fear rippled up her spine. She had a feeling she was going to have nightmares about Tyrus for a long time.

Jace's fingers spread across the small of her back, large and warm. "It's over, angel."

"Yeah. And the good guys won, didn't they?" She gave him a crooked smile.

"You go ahead," he told her. "I have to call Rock Run."

"I'll wait."

She listened as Jace patched into the Rock Run Clan's landline and asked for Rui do Mar. "You didn't hear this from me," Jace told him, "but Tyrus is dead."

He wrapped an arm around Evie's shoulder and she leaned close, nuzzling his neck. She couldn't hear Rui's side of the conversation, but she could guess the river fada was relieved.

"Yeah," said Jace. "I think he planned to go after your family next."

Rui's growl came through the phone. Jace held it away from his ear.

The other man spoke and Jace nodded. "You're welcome. Tell Merry I love her and I'll be up to see her in a couple of days." He ended the call and brushed his lips over Evie's. "How about that shower?"

He nudged her into the bathroom, locking the door behind them and stripping off his shorts. She had time to remove her shirt, and then he pushed her up against the stone wall. Hot and aroused, and yet his fingers on her face were so gentle, fresh tears welled up.

She blinked them back. "I don't know why I keep crying."

"Reaction. It hits everyone a little different. Me, I'd like to rip Corban's head off. We'll find him, I promise you."

"I know." Because these men weren't going to let a threat like Corban walk around alive for long.

Jace set his forehead against hers. Concern poured off him. "Don't ever do that to me again—go off with a fucking night fae. My heart can't stand it."

She was tired and hungry, but at his touch, a slow burn started in her belly. Her fingers slid into his hair. "It's not like he gave me a choice."

"I don't care." He brushed away her tears with his thumbs. "Promise me anyway." He didn't wait for an answer, just slanted his mouth over hers. His tongue swept inside, tasting her deeply. She sucked on it, and he groaned, a primal sound that made her insides tingle.

His mouth moved to the turn of her shoulder, his night beard an erotic scrape against her skin. He bit her—a sharp nip that made her nipples pebble. "I'm mate-claiming you."

Yes, shouted her heart. But practical Evie said, "What does that mean?"

His gaze bored into hers. "That you're mine—forever. Any objections?"

"I—" He was moving at the speed of light. She felt like she was on a carnival ride, whipping dizzily through space. Her fingers dug into his shoulders, seeking equilibrium.

But he seemed to want her dizzy. Green fire flashed in his irises. "Mine." The word was intensely possessive—but his hands moved over her as if she were the greatest treasure on Earth. Tracing the line of her collar bone...cupping her breasts...teasing her nipples through the satin bra until her knees turned to jelly. She would've slid down the wall if he wasn't holding her up.

Kisses seared her throat, the tender skin of her cleavage. Need washed through her, rich and intoxicating.

Her head fell back against the wall. If it were only her, she'd take the chance—jump on the ride with Jace and see where it led. But it wasn't only her.

She caught his wrists, stopping those clever fingers as they started down her abdomen. "I want to say yes—you know I do—but I have Kyler to think about."

Jace didn't hesitate. "He's mine, too. I always wanted a kid brother."

God, she loved this man.

"But—"

He lifted his head. "What are you afraid of, Evie? Because I'm not sure this is only about Kyler."

"What do you mean? Of course, it is."

"Is it? Or are you afraid that someday I'll leave you—that it's just for a few years like your mom and dad?"

She opened her mouth to say no, and then swallowed. "How do you know it isn't?"

"Because we're mates. I'd cut off my hand before I'd leave you. Say yes, and you'll see."

"Jace—" She shook her head, unable to bring herself to say the word.

He blew out a breath. "There are no good choices here, Evie. I hate like hell that I dragged you into this, but you're a part of it now. And your being part fae means you might not be able to hide in the human world, either. If another night fae finds you..."

She felt her face drain of color.

"I'm sorry, Evie. But I'd die for you and Kyler."

"I don't want you to die for us!"

"I know." He smoothed his fingers over the short hairs at her temples. "But I would, and that's part of it. We brought Tyrus down together, and even then, we needed Marjani to finish it. That's what being a clan means."

She chewed her lower lip. "I can't go back, can I?"

"Afraid not, angel."

"And Kyler will be a member of your clan?"

"Adric will make sure of it. Kyler wants this, Evie. You know he does. He needs something to be a part of."

She stared at him, and then it struck her. This man would have her back until she was old and gray. It would not be her mom and Fane all over again because Jace was committing himself to her, body and soul.

And more, he was right about Kyler. Her brother wanted this—no, he needed this. They both did.

She cupped his hard, beautiful face. "Kiss me."

His eyes flickered green and gold—and then the corners creased in a smile that wrenched her heart. His kiss this time was lazy and sweet. The kiss of a man who knew what he was doing. And when he was done, she felt thoroughly claimed.

She pulled back to scrutinize him. "And you? It works both ways, right? You're mine, too."

"You have to ask?"

She shook her head. Because her heart knew the answer.

His hands went to work again, stroking her to madness. He nipped her lower lip, and then sucked on the small hurt. "Say yes, angel. The woman has to accept the claim."

She nodded. "Suha told me."

"Ah..." His mouth edged up against hers. "I can see you two are going to be a force to be reckoned with."

Her dimple flashed. "Yeah, I guess we are."

His breath caught. Love poured into her. She basked in it like a flower in the sun, and returned it with equal passion.

It was too fast; he was a fada and she was some bizarre human-fae mix. She had Kyler to think about, and how the two of them would fit into Jace's world.

But it felt *right*. One thing she knew was that this man would never leave. As for the rest, they'd make it work.

Teeth closed on her earlobe. "Say yes, Evie."

She wound her arms around his neck. "Yes."

JACE SHUT his eyes in gratitude. *Thanks all the gods.*

He should sit Evie down, make sure she understood what it meant to mate with a dominant fada male. The commitment was deep, intense, unbreakable. He'd be possessive and maybe a little overprotective, but he trusted that she'd let him know when he went too far. Nobody pushed his Evie around.

She *knew*. At some basic level, she knew. She was his, and he was hers—until death and maybe even beyond. The mate bond wouldn't have come to life otherwise.

With her *yes*, it took form in a way that was impossible to put into words. It just *was*—a magical ribbon running between him and Evie. Insubstantial and yet as real and bright as the three fae lights dancing gleefully about their heads.

Emotion swamped him. Love...desire...need. He rested his forehead against hers. "You won't regret it. I'll take care of you and Kyler. Anything you want, it's yours. You just have to ask—"

"Jace." Evie stopped his words with her fingertips. "All I want is you. Yeah, I could use help with Kyler, but only because he could use a man in his life. I'm not looking for anything else. We're in this together."

"Together. Right." He nodded while secretly resolving to help her however he could. But for now, he had a mate-claim to christen. He sucked her middle finger into his mouth, enjoying how her sable eyes darkened to near-black. "Now, about that shower..."

He helped Evie out of her pants and they stepped into the shower. He was still more than a little shaky. He'd have to find a temporary quartz to tide him over while he searched for a permanent replacement.

Evie wasn't much better. As he turned the handle to hot, she yawned and pinched the bridge of her nose. "I could sleep for a week."

He traced a finger down her straight nose, over the slope of her cheek. There were shadows under her eyes. His heart fisted. She might seem tough, but she was much more fragile than he.

No sex, then. Just loving care.

"I'll wash you." He encircled her waist with his arm and nabbed a bar of soap. "You don't have to do anything but relax."

"Mm." She leaned against him, her firm ass up against his groin. His cock sprang to attention, but he gritted his teeth and ignored it to concentrate on Evie. He rubbed the soap over her body in slow strokes, massaging her breasts, running his hand down her abdomen, then turning her around and giving the same careful attention to her back. He knelt to wash her legs and feet, and then stood back up. Squeezing some shampoo into his hand, he worked it into her short blond locks, massaging her scalp for good measure before continuing down to rub her neck and shoulders as well.

Her head lolled back against his chest. Water spilled over her face and her dimple flashed. "That feels so good."

He pressed a kiss to her cheek at the place where her dimple hid. It felt like a secret only he was privileged to know. "I love you."

"Love you too." She turned her head to kiss him.

She rinsed off and then picked up the soap. "My turn."

"You don't have to," he said, but she ignored him to slide the soap over his chest and abdomen. Then she soaped up her fingers and slid them down to where his erection jutted out, washing him with an excruciating care that had him groaning. "You're too tired," he made himself say.

The answer was a very Evie grin. "I'm reviving fast," she said, and gave him a good squeeze.

Heat shot through him, but he grinned back. Loving how nothing kept her down for long. Loving how she could always make him smile. Loving *her*.

He took the soap from her and set it on the ledge. Taking her by the shoulders, he backed her up against the wall and kissed her, slow and deep. She was still smiling; the curve of her lips imprinted itself on his.

Water streamed down his back. Evie twined a leg around his hip and pressed against his front, her nipples pebbled against his chest.

He gulped. "No," he said, although he was having a tough time recalling why not.

She tilted her head and gave him a wide-eyed look that made his breath snag. "Please?"

"You're a witch." He slid the broad head of his cock over her soft, welcoming folds.

Her breath hissed out. "Jesus."

"Is this what you want?" His jaguar rose up, the two of them intent on one thing: claiming their mate. He pinched one tightly furled nipple, and her eyes slit with enjoyment.

"Yes. That's... perfect." She undulated against him, sending a jolt of electricity to his balls.

She was wet and hot and so ready for him. "God's cat," he muttered as he rocked his hips against her, "you're so fucking sexy."

She squeezed his ass. "And you're so...hard." She nipped the sensitive skin beneath his jaw and the jaguar rumbled in approval.

"You like that?"

"Hell, yeah. Mark me."

She nipped him again, harder, sucking and biting at his skin until he knew he'd bear the print of her teeth. When she lifted her head, he held her against the wall and left his own mark at the turn of her neck. Everyone in the den would know he'd claimed her.

Both man and cat felt a primitive satisfaction at that.

He slid his hand down to toy with her clit. She made a murmur of pleasure and he slid his fingers into her folds. She was hot and slick and ready.

He kissed her again while his fingers kept up their slow dance: in and out of her passage, around her tight, swollen bud. Soft, teasing touches until she was writhing in his arms, her breath jerking in and out.

His muscles locked under the strain of holding back. But he kept it up until she said, "Jace," and started chanting "please" over and over.

"Take it," he growled against her ear. "Now." He dragged his fingers over her clit.

Her back bowed as she cried out his name. He kept up a steady, circling pressure until she went limp. "Oh. My. God."

He chuckled and gave her a soft kiss. "Be right back." Exiting the shower, he grabbed a rubber from a basket under the sink, worked it over his erection and returned.

Evie was slumped against the black tile wall, her creamy skin slick, her dark lashes spiked with water. Her nipples were a dusky rose that made his mouth water. She held her hand out to him with a secret little smile that shot straight to his groin.

He stalked toward her and lifted her up against the tiles so he could suck each nipple in turn. She moaned and gripped his nape. Sharp nails dug into his skin, stoking his arousal higher.

His cat purred. It liked a mate with claws.

He set his tip at her entrance and rocked his hips, small nudges until he was full seated. He expelled a harsh breath. She was so tight. So perfect.

Then she squeezed herself around him and his vision blurred.

He wrapped one arm around her shoulders, the other holding her hips to protect her from the hard tiles, and thrust into her. Harder this time.

Pleasure slammed up his spine. She tightened her legs around him and met him thrust for thrust. Her wet body was cool against his, but inside she was a silky hot glove.

On his chest, his quartz warmed, and a distant corner of his mind felt surprise. So it had some life in it after all.

He bent his knees and thrust straight up, hitting a spot deep inside Evie's womb that made her eyes roll back in her head. She gasped and clenched on him, rhythmic tightening that set up an answering pulse in his balls. It was too much. He buried his head in the side of her neck, tonguing the mark he'd made on her, and then joined with her, hard and fast until he came with a muttered curse.

He held himself deep inside, letting the hot, wet pleasure of her sweep over him. Wringing him out, and then filling him again to his very essence.

His breath scraped in and out of his lungs. He let her legs slide down to touch the floor again as he said a prayer of thanks to the gods that had brought him to her door. He'd been only half-alive, his only focus work and Merry. Scarred and bitter from the Darktime, even more than he'd known.

Evie had saved him in more ways than one.

"Mine," he said one last time.

Her arms tightened on him without speaking. But he heard her answer loud and clear through their bond: *Yours.*

CHAPTER 39

eau and Kyler had settled on brunch. Evie and Jace emerged from the shower to find everyone in the kitchen, including Suha and the two hard-eyed soldiers, who were introduced as Ryder and Jamila.

Beau and Kyler were busy putting together breakfast burritos. A pitcher of orange juice and a bowl of ripe strawberries sat next to fresh salsa, and Suha handed Evie a mug of hot coffee as she entered the kitchen.

Jace fussed over Evie, having her sit and then filling a plate for her. When she started to protest, he stopped her with a kiss. "You'll find I take good care of my mate," he murmured against her lips.

"So do I." She tugged him down next to her. "Now eat." She made him a plate and set it before him. Then she noticed the open mouths. Everyone at the table was staring at them.

Suha recovered first. "You're mates—congratulations!" She jumped up and hugged Evie, and then frowned at Jace. "Does she know what that means?"

He wrapped a possessive hand around Evie's nape. "Of course."

Suha set a hand on her hip. "You know it's not binding unless the woman accepts. And she has to know exactly what she's getting into."

"Too late. She's already accepted the claim."

Suha opened her mouth to argue further, but Evie said, "It's okay—I know what it means, and I want it. I can feel him—here." She touched her chest. "The rest we can work out," she said with a smile at Jace, "as long as you all are okay with it. And Kyler, of course." She slid him a cautious look. She hadn't planned on making the announcement in front of five other people; she'd intended to talk to him privately after they ate. "But you seem to like everyone, and—"

"Hey," he said, "of course I'm okay with it."

Suha's face split into a grin. "I guess you do know. And of course we're okay with it. Welcome to the clan." She gave Evie another hug, and then the men were on their feet and hugging her, too.

"Guess we're all one big happy family, now," Kyler quipped as they took their seats again, but the look he shot Jace was wary.

Jace had taken a seat at the end of the table with Evie on one side and Kyler on the other. He dragged Kyler into a one-armed hug. "Yep. You're mine too, bro."

Kyler's shoulders relaxed. He squeezed Jace back and reached for more bacon. "Does this mean I get one of those quartz phones?"

Jace shook his head. "Sorry, they only work for fada or fae. You have to have some magic in your blood."

Her brother's face fell. "Not humans?"

"Not yet. But if we figure out the technology, you'll be first on the list."

Kyler brightened. "That's lit. I can be a test subject."

"It does mean we've always got your back," Beau rumbled.

"Even after what I did?"

Beau's bushy black brows lowered. "Hey, what did I say about that?"

"Sorry," Kyler muttered. "And I'll have yours, for what it's worth."

"Don't worry, we'll whip you into shape." Beau slapped Kyler on the back, nearly knocking him into his plate. Her brother just grinned and started eating again.

Adric, Marjani and Zuri arrived along with a man named Luc, a tall, rangy lieutenant with skin the color of teak who was Jace's fifth den mate. The three of them were somber when they arrived, but as soon as they heard the news, it turned into a celebration.

Adric pulled Evie out of her chair for a bear hug. "Welcome to the family, love. We'll make it official with a mate ceremony, but I'm claiming you and Kyler for the Baltimore clan." He kissed her on both cheeks, ignoring Jace's growled, "Get your own damn woman."

Then it was Zuri's turn. To her surprise, his dark eyes were smiling. "Welcome," he told her. "Jace is a lucky man."

For a moment Evie gaped at him. Then she recovered enough to shoot back, "Thanks. I think so, too."

Jace chuckled. Zuri grinned and gave her a hug that lifted her off her toes.

When she sat back down, Jace squeezed her knee. "They like you," he mouthed.

The noise level increased. Suha toasted Evie and Jace with orange juice, and Marjani brought Luc up to date on everything that had happened. It seemed he'd been in France tracking Tyrus, and was disgusted that he'd gotten back too late to help take the night fae down.

Jace informed Evie that Luc was a wolf, and seeing his cool amber eyes and lean, intelligent face, she could believe it. His expression only softened when he looked at Marjani, but she appeared not to notice.

After brunch, Adric and Marjani left along with the extra soldiers. Jace changed the security code on the outside lock, and then they all took naps, even Kyler.

Jace spooned his hard body around Evie. "God's cat, I'm tired."

"Me too."

But when she closed her eyes, she saw Tyrus's beautiful face and those malevolent red eyes. An involuntary shiver traced up her spine. She opened her eyes and tucked Jace's arm closer around her.

He's dead. He can't hurt you now.

But then she saw his charred, lifeless body and that was almost worse. Because even though she knew it had been him or them, Tyrus might not be dead if not for her. Her chest tightened.

Jace pressed a kiss to her nape. "Want to talk about it?"

"Tyrus. I—"

He squeezed her waist. "You're safe, angel. I promise."

"I know, but—that was my first dead body. Well, except for my mom, and that was different."

"He needed to die."

"I know."

He stroked her abdomen. "Is it what he did before? When I was passed out?"

"That's part of it." She swallowed over the rock lodged in her throat. "I felt so violated. Why the fuck does it bother me that I helped kill him?"

Jace blew out a breath and said, "Because you're a good person. Nobody but a psychopath finds killing easy. Even when you have no choice, it haunts you."

"Yeah?"

"Yeah."

They were silent then, but his hand continued to move over her abdomen in slow, easy caresses. The constriction in her chest eased.

And this time, when her eyes drifted shut, she saw nothing.

CHAPTER 40

$\mathcal{E}$vie pulled her car onto the concrete pad. The lavender had bloomed; several fat bees were buzzing around the fuzzy purple spikes. Other than that, the house was unchanged, its gray Formstone exterior practically indestructible. Was it only Tuesday? It felt like they'd been gone a month.

She nudged Kyler, who was hunched over his phone playing a game. "We're home."

He pocketed the phone. "Looks like everything's still in one piece."

"Yeah." She couldn't help but smile; it was what their mom had always said.

Jace pulled his motorcycle to a stop behind them. Adric was sure Corban had left the country, but Jace wasn't letting Evie out of his sight. "There's still the night fae," he'd said. "We don't know what Tyrus told his lair."

If Jace wanted to stay close, that was fine with Evie—she wasn't an idiot. Besides, why would she want to be separated from her mate?

She watched in the rearview mirror as he removed his helmet and glanced around, a badass fada in sunglasses and a worn leather jacket. Her womb clenched. She still couldn't believe he was hers.

She jerked her chin at the mirror. "You sure you're okay with this?" she asked Kyler. "Me and Jace?"

"Sure. I mean, how many guys have a shifter as a brother-in-law?"

"There is that." They exchanged a grin. "But seriously—we may have to move to Baltimore. I haven't talked to Jace, but I don't think he wants to live up here."

"I can adapt." Kyler reached into the backseat for their backpacks. "Don't forget, I'm not always going to be living with you. This way, I don't have to worry about you."

"Worry about me?" she repeated faintly.

"Yeah," he said as they got out of the car. "It goes both ways, you know."

She met his eyes over the car roof. "Yeah," she said. "I guess it does."

Mrs. Linney was on her stoop, heart-shaped sunglasses perched on her nose and a pink visor on her steel-gray curls. She waved her cigarette in their direction. "Hey, Evie. Kyler."

They waved back. "Morning, Mrs. Linney."

Jace set a hand on the small of Evie's back. She smiled up at him and turned to Mrs. Linney. "I want you to meet my friend—"

"Jace Jones. I remember. How are you, son?"

"Good," he returned politely. "And you?"

"Not bad." She dragged on her cigarette. To Evie she said, "I wondered where you were. I was fixing to call the police."

She grimaced. "Sorry about that. I would've told you but it was kind of sudden."

"Um-hmm." Mrs. Linney eyed Jace. "Well, as long as you're all right."

"We're fine. Thanks for keeping an eye on the house."

They headed up the gravel path. As Kyler unlocked the door, Evie's nape prickled and she was hit by a sense of déjà vu. This was how it had started, except instead of being dark and rainy, it was a sunny morning.

"Inside—both of you." Jace pushed her into the kitchen and turned to face the alley.

A tall man with white-blond hair sauntered into the yard. Jace tensed, but Evie set a hand on his arm. "It's okay. It's my dad." Trust Fane to show up when the danger was past.

"Evie, love." He held out his arms.

She slipped around Jace and down the steps. He was her dad, after all.

Long arms wrapped around her. "I hear you had a spot of trouble."

"You could say that." She rested her head against his shoulder. He smelled of the outdoors, a familiar grassy scent that made her eyes sting. "How did you know?" she asked as she released him and stepped back.

He moved a shoulder. "Word gets around. I came as soon as I could."

Jace came up beside her. "We handled it."

"Did you now?" Fane asked mildly.

Mrs. Linney wasn't even pretending not to eavesdrop. Fane nodded at her. "How are you, Betty?"

She beamed back. "Can't complain. And yourself?"

They exchanged a few words and then Fane set his arm around Evie's shoulders and headed with her toward the house. "Why don't we take this inside?" He quirked a brow at Jace, who was blocking the way. "Do you have something to say, fada?"

Jace shook his head and stepped aside. "Not here," he muttered.

In the kitchen, Evie got beers for Jace and Fane, and sodas for her and Kyler. They sat at the table, Evie and Kyler on one side, her dad across from them. Jace took a stance behind Evie, arms folded over his chest.

Fane studied them with clear blue eyes that somehow didn't give away a thing. As usual, his sharp-boned, handsome face hadn't aged a day. Pretty soon people were going to think he was her brother, not her father. He wore his usual loose linen shirt over skinny black jeans, and his pale hair was tied back with a leather cord so that you could see his ears. With a jolt, she saw they came to a point at the top. Why had she never noticed? But then, she hadn't been looking for proof her dad was part fae.

"Now what's this I'm hearing about you and a night fae?" Fane asked. "And why does this earth fada think he has a claim on you?"

Jace placed his hands on Evie's shoulders. "I'm her mate."

His dark brows shot up. "Are you now?"

"Yes." Jace's tone was that of a man who wasn't going to give an inch.

"This is true?" Fane asked her.

She touched Jace's hand. "Yes."

"Well," he drawled, "that's a complication I didn't expect."

"Why?" she asked.

Fane jerked his head at Kyler. "Why don't you leave us? There are some things it's best a human not know."

Kyler bristled, but before he could object, Evie said, "He stays. I'm not keeping secrets from my own brother."

Her dad's eyes narrowed but Evie simply stared back. Fane rubbed his lower lip and then inclined his head. "You'll promise to guard her secret, then," he said to Kyler. "It's for her safety as much as yours."

"Of course." Kyler folded his arms. "I'm not the problem here—you are."

Fane shrugged and turned back to Evie with a rueful smile, the one that could always get around her mom.

Evie stared back stonily. "I'm waiting."

"So I see." He took a sip of beer. "Where do I start?"

"How about with what kind of fae you are? And why you never told me? And why you left me and my mom—"

"Slow down, love." Fane held up a hand. "The first question's simple—ice fae."

"Ice fae?" Evie blinked.

"Not sun fae?" Jace inserted.

Her dad shook his head. "My father was half ice fae. I was born and raised in Canada. As for your other questions, well, let me tell you a little something about myself first."

Kyler moved restlessly. "Is this going to be one of your stories?"

Fane's blue eyes glittered. "Fae don't lie."

"But you're not pure fae, are you?"

"No, but the fae blood makes it hard for me to tell lies, and it hurts like a bitch if I do." He sat back, one arm on the chairback, long legs stretched out before him. "Do you want to hear this or not?"

"We do." Evie elbowed Kyler and he subsided.

"I'm not that old, as fae go," Fane said, "and I won't live as long as a pure-blood. But I was born in the early 1900s. My father was an ice fae, and my mother was a human. They were mates, and he was faithful to her until she died. But I didn't grow up with the ice fae—they don't have much use for half-bloods. My father was stationed in Newfoundland by the ice fae king. He pays the half-bloods to keep an eye on things for him in various territories around the world."

"To spy for him," Jace said. "Just so we're clear."

Fane moved a shoulder. "The king likes to stay informed."

"Is he still alive?" Evie asked. "My...grandfather?"

"He is."

"But—didn't he ever want to meet me?"

"No." Fane's eyes slid away from hers. "I figured it was better that way—your world is the human world. Why complicate things by letting you know you have a bit of fae in you?"

"I see." Her tongue felt thick. This was a fresh hurt. It was bad enough to have a father who could go for years without seeming to recall her, but she hadn't even known her grandfather was alive—and worse, that he wanted it that way.

"I haven't seen him for years myself," Fane said. "My mother lived into her eighties. After she died, my father went a little crazy. It's hard on the fae, losing a mate. They say you feel like your heart is ripped out."

Behind her, Jace murmured agreement and squeezed Evie's shoulders. Love pulsed to her through their bond. Warmed, she sent a pulse back, still awed at this intimate connection they shared. A connection that told her Jace loved her no matter who or what her father was.

The hurt faded. Because she had Jace at her back, caressing her shoulders, and Kyler at her side, glaring at Fane.

"We lost touch," Fane continued, "but last I heard Father was in Patagonia for some damn reason. As for me, I'm one of the king's envoys."

"An envoy? You're some kind of messenger?"

He nodded. "Turns out I have the fae Gift of wayfaring, which is rare in a quarter fae."

"That's what Jace said the night fae was," Evie said.

"Lord Tyrus? Word is he's dead." Fane glanced from her to Jace.

Evie's chest tightened. Jace gripped her shoulders, asking her to let him handle this. "Is he?"

Fane recognized evasion when he saw it. "The son of the night fae prince," he confirmed. "As you know damn well—and that's why I'm here."

"What d'you mean?" Jace asked.

"I'll get to that in a minute."

Jace rumbled irritably, but Fane just lifted a brow. "You don't scare me, fada."

"Then you're a fool," he shot back.

"No. Just a man who's smart enough to know you won't attack your own mate's father."

That silenced Jace. He gave a terse nod. "Go on."

"You're right that Tyrus was a wayfarer," Fane told Evie, "but his Gift was to move very fast. Mine is different—I blend into my surroundings. Even if you know I'm there, your gaze slips right past me. You never see me unless I want you to."

"So you sneak up on people?" Kyler inserted.

"You could put it that way." Fane gave him a cool, dangerous smile, and Evie instinctively jumped in to draw his attention back to her.

"And you work for the ice fae king?"

Fane inclined his head. "I'm part messenger, part negotiator. The king can send his own messages, but for some things, he needs an envoy who can carry a message back, or cut a deal if need be. Or simply observe and report back."

Evie's hands balled on her lap. "You should never have married my mom."

"I didn't. We weren't married, and we weren't mates."

"Oh." She swallowed. "I didn't know that."

Sorrow flickered across Fane's fine-boned face. "I know I hurt her, and I'm sorry for that. I wouldn't have done that for the world."

"But you did."

"She wasn't supposed to have a child. Usually only mates can conceive." Fane passed a hand over his face. "Hell. That sounds as if I didn't want you, love, but I did. I was so happy when your mother told me about you. Believe that if nothing else. As for why I never told you?" He moved a shoulder. "I intended to get around to it someday. You don't have a fae Gift, so it didn't seem urgent."

Evie scraped a hand over her hair. She'd sort through this later. "So what about me and the fae lights?"

"What do you mean?"

She opened her backpack and lobbed one at him. Fane threw up a hand and it smacked against his palm. They all heard the sizzle.

"Holy mother." Fane swatted the glowing orb away. "Did you make that yourself?"

"No. I brought it from Jace's den." Actually, a fae light had split itself in two, and one half had floated into her backpack while the other half remained back in Baltimore.

"So it's a fae light?"

"Yes," said Jace. "But she used it against the night fae. Not that it killed him, you understand. But it did burn him—bad."

"How about that?" Fane rubbed his chin. "Your great-grandfather is one of Sindre's top warriors. He can make fae balls from the energy in oxygen. If you hit someone hard enough, it's like tossing a grenade at them—and poof." He opened his fingers. "They're gone."

Evie's mouth dropped open. "So you're saying I'm a fae warrior?"

"You're freaking kidding me." That was Kyler. He'd straightened and was eyeing Evie with shock.

"Not unless you can make a fae ball yourself," her dad replied.

She shook her head. "I can't."

"Have you tried?"

"No. It didn't even occur to me."

"If you have the Gift for it, you simply visualize one into being." Fane nodded at her. "Go ahead—give it a try."

Evie looked at Jace, who gave her an encouraging squeeze.

"Try it, Evie." That was Kyler.

With a shrug, she opened her hand and visualized a fae ball shimmering in it. But it was like when she'd tried to heal Suha's bruise—nothing happened, except the fae light drifted across the table to settle into her palm. With a flick of her fingers, she sent it spinning into the air and tried again, jaw set, but still nothing happened.

"Take a deep breath," Fane suggested. "Imagine it forming in your hand."

Evie dragged in a breath and obeyed, but again, nothing happened. She didn't even feel her hand warm like when she'd added her energy to Suha's.

She shrugged. "So much for my career as a fae warrior."

Fane's long fingers touched hers. "Don't be disappointed."

"I'm not, really. I want to be a healer, not a warrior." She thought of the burns on Tyrus and stifled a shudder. She never wanted to do that to anyone again.

"But," said Fane, "maybe you inherited enough of your grandfather's ability to use a fae light in a similar way."

"She's an amplifier," Jace said. "She helped heal me."

"Ah." Her dad looked impressed. "That's a Gift indeed."

Jace released Evie to set both hands on the table. "You won't tell the ice fae about her," he said in a hard voice.

"Do you think they don't already know? I reported her birth to the king. But I won't tell him about her Gift, no."

"Good. Because if anyone comes after my mate, I'll rip your head off your body, Evie's father or not."

"Stop it, Jace!" Evie grabbed his arm and tried to give him a shake, but it was like trying to move a stone wall.

The two men ignored her. "I don't want that any more than you do," her father said. "She's my daughter, after all."

"Then swear it. I want your word that no one will learn of Evie's Gift from you."

"You have it."

"The words," Jace said between his teeth.

Fane inclined his head. "I vow before all three of you that no one will learn of Evie's Gift from me."

The tension went out of Jace. "Good." He came upright again.

"But why would the ice fae come after me?" Evie asked. "It's not like they've cared about me up until now."

"It's not just healers that can use an amplifier," Fane said. "A warrior could use you to make more powerful fae balls, for instance."

"And the night fae would just keep you to feed on," said Jace.

Goosebumps popped up on Evie's arms. She rubbed her hands over them, and instantly, Jace was behind her again, caressing her shoulders.

"That's what Tyrus told me," she said. "That he liked to feed on other fae."

"He didn't realize you were an amplifier?" Fane asked sharply.

"No."

"Thank the gods. Whatever happens, the night fae can't know. They won't hesitate to feed from a mixed-blood. They lump us with the humans and fada," he added with a twist of his lips.

"They'd have to get past me first," Jace growled.

Her father nodded. "Perhaps it's not a bad thing you two mated, then."

Jace folded his arms over his chest. "I take care of the ones I love, fae. Can you say the same?"

"It's fair that you ask, which brings me to the reason I'm here." Fane produced a silver-and-gold pendant suspended from a leather cord and handed it to Evie.

She turned it over in her hands. It was clearly fae made—an intricately crafted cutout of a gold sun cupped by a silver half-moon.

"Fire and ice," her dad murmured. "Sun and moon. A protection charm made by one of the best spellcasters I know. Together, the sun and moon will reflect into the eyes of anyone who might come looking for you, blinding them to your fae nature. Put it on."

Evie's vision blurred. "Thank you." She swallowed over the lump in her throat and slipped it over her head.

Fane shrugged. "I'm a terrible father, but I'll be damned if one of those night fae bastards comes after my only daughter again."

Evie touched the pendant. It was so light she could barely feel it, and yet it hummed with power. "It's beautiful. Thank you."

"Think of me when you wear it—and if I were you, I'd wear it everywhere, even to bed."

She nodded. "I will."

Fane rose to his feet and extended a hand to Jace. "Peace to you and yours, Jace Jones."

Jace's eyes flashed a predatory green, and Evie knew he was wondering how Fane knew his full name. But he shook the proffered hand. "Peace to you and yours...and thanks for the charm."

Evie stood up as well. "You don't have to run off. I can make you lunch. I—"

"Thank you, but I should go. I'm not supposed to be here as it is."

She felt a hint of the old hurt, but it was muted. She rose on her toes to kiss Fane's cheek. "You're welcome anytime."

"I know." He squeezed her shoulders. "You'll be moving to Baltimore?"

"I'm not sure," she said with a glance at Jace, who said, "For the summer at least." He gave Fane the address.

Her father gave her a last hug and then nodded at Jace. "You'll keep her safe." It wasn't a question.

"Like you care," Kyler muttered, but Jace slung an arm around Evie's shoulder.

"She's my mate," he said simply.

Fane nodded. "As for you—" He turned to Kyler, who raised his chin.

"What?"

"That mouth of yours is going to get you in trouble someday. But you're loyal. Evie's lucky to have you." He tossed something glittery into the air.

Kyler snatched it and then stared down at it, mouth ajar. "It's another fucking diamond." He held it up and it caught the morning sun, and for an instant, Evie was blinded. The back door opened and shut, and when she could see again, her dad was gone.

"Ice fae, huh?" Kyler touched Evie's arm, his expression mock-serious. "You don't feel cold."

She knocked his hand away, and then burst out laughing. "Go soak your head, squirt."

CHAPTER 41

*M*erry jiggled Jace's arm. "Where is she? It's after seven o'clock."

"Calm down. She'll be here." He smiled down at his niece, although inside he was almost as jittery. Not because he was afraid Evie wouldn't show, but because he was as excited as Merry. But then, a man had a right to be excited at his own mating ritual.

They were in his backyard. It was mid-July, more than a month since Tyrus's death. The evening sun cast long shadows across the lawn, but the fae balls had blossomed into life, illuminating the crowd. People stood on the back porch and spilled down the driveway, members of the clan rubbing elbows with Jace's neighbors. Some of the cougars and jaguars were perched on the roof.

There was even a family of river fada—Valeria and Rui do Mar, along with their two young children—invited at Evie's request, because Merry wanted them there. Jace had always liked Rui's dark-haired Portuguese mate, but it was a revelation to see the strong, silent shark with a toddler on one shoulder, tugging on his ear, and another pint-sized person wrapped like a vine around his leg.

Jace kissed the top of Merry's head. "You look beautiful, by the way. Your mom would've been so proud of you."

"Really?" She shot him a pleased look and smoothed her hands down the skirt of the flirty red dress she'd somehow talked Valeria into.

"Absolutely. I like that crown-thing you did with your hair."

"My friend Rosana did it." Merry touched the braids wrapped around her head. "Thanks for inviting me to be part of your mate ceremony."

"It was both our ideas. Evie likes you."

"I like her, too. And Kyler."

Jace smothered a smile. Kyler had taken Merry under his wing. He was loving the chance to be a big brother—and Merry hung on his every word. It was good for Kyler. The kid was still beating himself up for letting Tyrus in. He'd asked Marjani to teach him how to handle a knife, and to everyone's surprise, she'd agreed.

"You look good, too," Merry told him. "I've never seen you in a suit before."

He looked down at the slim gray suit and white button-up shirt he'd donned for the ceremony. "I wanted to look nice for Evie."

Merry adjusted the white rose pinned to his lapel. "She's going to love it."

Suha appeared from his den and held up five fingers. "Five minutes," she mouthed.

Jace nodded at Zuri, who began clearing a path from the shed to the flower-entwined arch under which he and Merry stood. Meanwhile, Adric started through the crowd to take his place for the ceremony.

Merry fingered her quartz. "I wish I could remember my first mom. I can remember Silver a little. He did magic tricks and bought me that clown." Jace nodded. Merry's clown was the only thing she had from her old life, since Tyrus's men had torched her house as she escaped with Rui. "But I don't even know what Takira looked like."

Jace's heart squeezed. "She looked a lot like you, sweetheart. You both take after my mom—your grandmother. You have Takira's hair, her eyes. But inside, that's where you're most like her." He tapped Merry's narrow chest. "You have a jaguar's heart. Forget that bullshit you hear about lions—they only rule in Africa. In the rainforest, jaguars are the biggest, baddest cats around."

Adric arrived in time to hear that last part. He snorted. "As long as they don't run into a cougar."

Merry giggled at the two of them, but her shoulders straightened.

Then Jace forgot everything else as Evie stepped into the yard on Kyler's arm. He'd always thought she glowed, but now she shone as bright as the sun. All the air left his lungs in a whoosh.

She wore a simple cream dress with broad straps that left her toned arms bare. Jace had drilled a hole in the rose quartz he'd given her, and it hung around her neck next to her dad's charm. Her only other ornaments were the glittering silver star in her short blond hair and the matching stars on her strappy sandals. Her mouth was painted a bright red, and her eyes were dark and a little mysterious.

She strolled toward him, his beautiful, edgy, sexy-as-hell angel, and he wondered how the fuck he'd gotten so lucky as to get stabbed practically on her doorstep.

Then her fingers wrapped around his arm, and together, they turned toward Adric, waiting to bless their mating. Three fae lights wafted closer, casting a soft gold and pink light over the proceedings.

Adric was smirking as if he'd arranged the whole thing. "Welcome," he said in a carrying voice to the assembled throng. "We are gathered today to celebrate the mating of Jace and Evie. Peace to you and yours."

"Peace," the crowd returned.

Adric spoke a few more words, and then nodded to Jace. The alpha might introduce and bless a mating, but the words were spoken by the couple themselves.

Jace took Evie's hands. Her dimple flashed at him, and he stared back unsmiling, emotion clogging his throat. He cleared it and said, "I take you, Evie Morningstar, as my mate. My light. My heart. You bring out the best in me, and I will love you for all of my days."

They'd chosen a bracelet to mark their mate-day. He slipped it on her. The jeweler had created a striking design of silver vines entwined around a translucent green chalcedony quartz.

Evie bit her lower lip. She firmed her chin and then met his eyes. "I take you, Jace Jones, as my mate. My lover. My panther. My soul. I wasn't looking for you, but somehow you found me, and I will always be grateful. I love you."

Jace removed his quartz pendant and undid the clasp, and she slipped a tiny rose quartz in the shape of a heart onto the cord. The heart had belonged to his mom, an anniversary gift from his dad. It settled next to Jace's quartz with a click, and he could've sworn he felt a jolt of love.

Adric spoke the words of blessing and then formally welcomed Evie and Kyler into the clan. He finished by pulling Evie into a big hug. "Thanks for taking him on." He gave her a smacking kiss on the mouth.

Evie grinned as Jace retrieved her and tucked her firmly up against his side. "He doesn't scare me." She nipped Jace's neck, and then let out a chuckle that ended in a gasp as he bent her backward over his arm for a kiss.

He took his time, exploring her mouth, mate-claiming her in front of his entire clan. When he released her, her eyes were smoky, and he'd almost forgotten their audience. "Later," he murmured with a slow wink as behind them, his pumped-up clan hooted and clapped.

The street had been blocked off for the evening. Sam and Horace, both almost completely recovered, were supervising two huge barbecue grills, and Zuri had cracked open a keg of beer and was handing out mugs as fast as he could fill them.

Jace wrapped an arm around Evie and turned to face the crowd. "Who wants to party?"

EPILOGUE

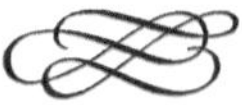

"No," Marjani growled. "He's trying to get you to follow him. It's a trap."

Adric put his fork down. They were in the kitchen eating scrambled eggs and ham. Marjani had surprised him by having breakfast ready when he'd walked in the door that morning—and then she'd told him Corban had sent a message.

See you in Reykjavik.

It was a fucking dare.

"Do you really think Corban's stronger than me?" he asked. It had been six weeks since his cousin had disappeared. Adric had alerted the other earth alphas about Corban's treachery, but it was as if his cousin had dropped off the face of the earth. But if he was in Iceland, that explained why they couldn't find him; King Sindre didn't allow any fada clans that close to home.

Marjani blew out a breath. "Of course not. But he's not working alone. Maybe Tyrus is dead, but that doesn't mean Corban's not working with another night fae. And then there's the ice fae, too."

Adric took a gulp of coffee. Hot as Hades and liberally dosed with cream, it washed away the bitter taste that filled his mouth every time he recalled that Leron had invited the night fae into Baltimore, and then stood by while they manipulated things to get darker and darker, just so they could fucking feed. Like there wasn't enough darkness in the world for them to draw on already.

Holy mother, if Adric ever grew that power-hungry, he hoped his lieutenants would put him down like a rabid dog.

"I need to find out who in the ice fae is helping him—and why. Is it that ice fae woman I sent him to capture last year? Or the king himself? And how does Nika fit into this?"

"Not the ice fae woman. If it was her, Corban wouldn't try to get you to Reykjavik. That's the heart of Sindre's territory."

He shook his head. "Whoever's working with him, I have to go. He's my responsibility." He'd promised the other alphas that he'd take care of Corban, once and for all.

"No—I'll go. The clan needs you right now."

He scraped a hand over his hair. His sister was the one with a Gift for strategy. When she spoke, a wise alpha listened. And she was right—people were still reeling from the recent attacks by Tyrus and Corban, and Kane's death hadn't helped. There were whispers that Adric intended to wipe out that entire branch of the Savonett family, even though Nash himself said that Corban was the one at fault.

The clan was seething. Mistrust. Fear. Anger. Everything Adric had worked so hard to put behind them.

And then there was Prince Langdon. The night fae ruler had been seen in Baltimore twice in the last six weeks, when he normally came to the city only once every five years, if that much.

But damn it, sending Marjani to Iceland wasn't an option. "Absolutely not," he told her. "You're too—" He halted as her shoulders hunched.

"Weak," she finished for him.

His stomach hollowed. "Fuck, I'm sorry. I don't really think that. But I—"

She lifted her chin. "Maybe you're right. But I need to know, and that's never going to happen if I stay here in Baltimore. Everyone treats me like I'm made of frigging eggshells."

"What about Luc?" The lieutenant had loved Marjani for years. He'd waited patiently for her to heal, and these past few weeks, it had seemed Marjani was finally responding. She'd even danced with Luc last week at Jace and Evie's mating.

She arched a delicate brow. "What about him?"

Adric swallowed. He didn't hesitate to meddle in his clan members' lives if he thought it would do some good, but when his sister went all soft and curious, he'd learned to tread with care. "I thought maybe you and him—"

"No. We're friends, and that's all we'll ever be. And while we're on the subject, what's up with you and Rosana do Rio? Do you think I don't know you slip off to Grace Harbor just on the chance you'll run into her?"

Adric's chest tightened. Rosana was his guilty secret, even if he rarely got close enough to talk to her, let alone kiss her again like that night by the river. "Leave it," he growled.

Marjani's jaw set. "Only if you leave off me and Luc."

"Fine." He returned his attention to his breakfast.

They ate in silence until Marjani said, "There's something I'd like to know—why didn't the prince stop Tyrus? He had to know Tyrus was targeting Jace and the clan. You're not going to tell me a man like that doesn't know what his only son is up to."

"Think about it. Jace is one of the last people left who knows he had a half-blood son. Yeah, the prince kept Merry a secret for her own safety—but it benefits him, too. How long would he rule the night fae if they knew he had a child with a human? And worse, that his half-human son then mated with an earth fada—which means he's got a granddaughter who's part animal. You know how pure-bloods think."

Feral blue streaked his sister's eyes. "He'll protect Merry. She's family, and even a night fae feels that bond. But not Jace. It would be better for him if Jace was dead."

"And me," Adric returned with ruthless practicality. "If he knows anything about fada, he knows Jace wouldn't keep a secret like that from his alpha."

"Hell." Marjani scraped a hand over her cropped black hair. "I had to kill Tyrus. He wouldn't have stopped until Jace and Evie were both dead."

He touched her hand. "You did right. He was going to use Jace's quartz to force him to kill Merry—and then the protective spell would've killed Jace. You saved both their lives, and probably Evie's too."

"But the clan. I put all of you in danger. When the prince finds out—"

"He won't," Adric stated. "I obliterated every trace of Tyrus. And if he does, we'll just have to deal with it. I'll track him to his lair and take him out myself if I have to."

She nodded, and he thought that was the end of it.

But in the morning she was gone. Her smartphone was turned off, but the link between them told Adric she was on her way north. To Iceland.

And he literally shook with the need to follow.

But he couldn't, because Marjani was right, the clan needed him in Baltimore, especially with Langdon sniffing around. So he sent Luc instead—and prayed to all the gods that he'd made the right decision.

CHARMING MARJANI

A FADA NOVEL

Against her will, a shifter assassin finds herself falling for a rich, sexy—and treacherous—ice fae.

*"**So many feels** this book delivers..."*
~Uncaged Book Reviews

Winner, PRISM Award (Best Urban Fantasy Romance)

PROLOGUE

Marjani jolted awake, hand on the dagger beneath her pillow.

Someone was hammering on the door at the surface. She waited for Adric to answer it, but her brother must not have come home yet.

The hammering came again.

Damn. It might be important. Adric was clan alpha.

Snatching up the dagger, she threw off the sheet and jogged through the underground den the two of them shared. The amber quartz in the wall sconces glowed on, lighting her way. She took the stairs to the surface two at a time, halting at the thick steel door at the top.

"Who is it?" When no one answered, she tried again, louder. "Hey! Anyone there?"

Shifters had excellent hearing. If a fada waited on the other side, they'd hear her, steel door or not.

She pressed her ear to the cool metal.

Silence.

Her neck tightened. She had a feeling that whoever had knocked on the door was bad news. Dagger ready, she disengaged the lock and eased the door open.

Other than weeds and a scraggly hawthorn tree, the only living thing in the backyard was an oversized rat rooting through a garbage can. She couldn't even pick up a scent. But a folded slip of paper that had been stuck in the doorjamb fluttered to the ground. Snatching it up, she slammed the door shut and threw the bolt.

The note was addressed to Adric in their cousin Corban's distinctive black scrawl. She frowned. Corban wasn't in Baltimore—was he?

She waited until she was back downstairs before unfolding the paper. The message was short, cryptic.

See you in Reykjavik.—CS

Her heart thumped—hard, uneasy beats. She crumpled the paper in her hand.

Corban Savonett. Her oldest cousin…and the man who wanted her brother dead.

For a long time she just stood there, staring into the glowing amber quartz in the living room fireplace. Then she smoothed and refolded the paper, decision made.

Her internal clock told her it was five a.m. Adric would be home soon, and he'd be hungry. Might as well make breakfast.

The food was almost ready when she heard him run lightly down the steps. He poked his head into the kitchen. "You're making breakfast?" He said it as if she'd grown an extra tail.

"Scrambled eggs and fried ham." She flipped a thick slice of sizzling meat. "And good morning to you, too."

"My favorite." He wrapped his arms around her from behind. "Thanks, Jani."

She leaned her cheek against his. She hadn't been much of a sister lately. Adric wasn't this happy because she'd cooked breakfast; it was because she'd done anything at all. This past year, she'd spent whole days as her cougar, curled up on the living room rug and staring into the fireplace.

She swallowed a pang of guilt. "Make the coffee, okay?"

"Sure." While he fixed two large cups with lots of cream, she filled their plates and set them on the battered kitchen table. The den they shared was furnished in early thrift shop. She frowned at her chipped plate. When had that happened?

Adric dug into the food like he was starving…which he probably was. The man was always forgetting to eat. Like her, he was a cougar fada. Hard, edgy, with black hair bleached blond at the tips, and too handsome for his own good.

But lately, he'd lost weight. Their clan, the Baltimore Earth Fada, had had a rough summer, and as alpha, too much rested on his shoulders. His normally lean body looked downright thin.

Not that she should talk. The other day, she'd actually flinched at the sight of herself in the mirror. Was that skinny, big-eyed stranger with the shaved head *her*?

No more. She needed her strength.

She forked up some eggs and gamely chewed.

In her back pocket, the message seemed strangely heavy, as if it were a rock instead of a slip of paper. She waited until Adric had finished his breakfast before handing it over.

"This came for you. About an hour ago."

"What the fuck?" Adric scowled at the note. "The SOB's in Iceland?"

A wolf fada, Corban had tried for years to overthrow Adric and take over as alpha. But he'd crossed a line when he'd shared the secret of the earth fada's quartz crystals with a night fae. Their cousin was a marked man, sentenced to death by a tribunal of earth fada alphas. But he'd disappeared over six weeks ago, and no one knew where he was.

"Looks like it."

Her brother's dark brows beetled. "Where did you get this?"

"Someone banged on the door at the surface. When I went up top, whoever had left it was gone—I couldn't even pick up their scent."

"He wouldn't come himself. He knows it's too dangerous."

"It's a dare," she burst out. "You can't go. He wants to get you out of Baltimore."

Adric fingered the note. "You really think Corban's stronger than me?"

She blew out a breath. "Of course not. But he's not working alone. We know he's formed alliances with both the night fae and the ice fae."

"So he's in Iceland," Adric said. "That explains why the trackers haven't been able to trace him. The ice fae don't allow any fada clans that close to home."

She nodded. The ice fae and their king, Sindre, were almost as reclusive and territorial as the fada. Marjani had seen one, maybe two, in her entire life.

She and Adric went back and forth a little more on why Corban had summoned Adric to Reykjavik. But in the end, they just didn't have enough information.

"Whoever's working with him," Adric said, "I have to go. Corban's my responsibility. I claimed right of execution before the other alphas."

Marjani's heart clenched. They'd lost their mom and dad during the Darktime, when bloody feuds had split the clan into vicious factions. She'd be damned if she'd lose her brother now, when things were finally getting better.

Yeah, Adric was stronger, but Corban would fight dirty. What did he have to lose? There was no way in Hades she'd let that prick anywhere near her brother.

"No," she said. "I'll go. The clan needs you here right now."

Adric speared his fingers through his spiked-up hair.

"I'm right," she said. "You know I am."

"Jani..." He trailed off and shook his head.

"I'll go," she repeated. "I'm your second. It's my job to have your back."

He growled. "Absolutely not. You're too—"

"Weak," she finished. He couldn't have hurt her more if he'd slammed a fist into her stomach. She set down her fork and concentrated on breathing.

"Fuck. I'm sorry, Jani. I don't really think you're weak. But—"

She lifted her chin. "Maybe you're right. But I need to know, and that's never going to happen if I stay here in Baltimore. Everyone treats me like I'm made of fucking eggshells."

And as Adric knew, she had her own reasons for hating Corban.

He forked up a last piece of ham. "What about Luc?"

"What about him?" she asked in a cool voice.

"I thought maybe you two—"

"No. We're friends, and that's all we'll ever be. I've told him that, straight out, but he thinks he can change my mind." She gave a hard swallow and stared down at the eggs congealing on her plate. "I'll probably never mate."

"Jani. You don't mean that."

"No?" She shrugged and turned the subject. "You're the alpha. You're the one who should find a mate—and not Rosana do Rio."

His bronze eyes went flat. "Shut it."

But hurt made her keep going. "You think I don't know you slip off to Grace Harbor hoping you'll run into her? She's the Rock Run alpha's baby sister, asshat. A river fada. You want to start a fucking war?"

"Shut it, I said."

They glared at each other.

Marjani's chin jutted. "Only if you shut up about me and Luc."

"Deal. But you're not going to Iceland, got it?" He picked up his coffee cup, realized it was empty, and set it back down.

"Yeah." It wasn't a lie, because she *did* get that Adric didn't want her to go.

That didn't mean she wasn't.

She got up and poured them both more coffee.

CHAPTER 1

There's no such thing as bad weather, just bad clothing.
~Icelandic saying

Like hell. Iceland was freaking cold.

Marjani wrapped her hoodie tightly around her as she slipped out of Keflavik Airport. It was the end of July, for Goddess's sake. She hadn't expected the bite in the wind.

Her cougar did *not* approve. Back home in Baltimore, the weather had been sunny and humid, and the cat liked the heat.

Oh, well, she wasn't here on a pleasure trip.

Beneath the hoodie, her quartz hummed against her heart. A sheath in her right boot held an iron dagger, and she had an iron switchblade in her front pocket, an iron blade being the most efficient way to kill a fada or a fae. Her left boot held a steel stiletto, and her fishing knife was in a pocket on the leg of her pants. To get through TSA, she'd had to stash her blades in her backpack and check it as luggage, but she didn't go anywhere without them.

Reykjavik was thirty miles away. As she got in the bus line, a burly man smelling of alcohol jostled her. Her cat, edgy at being confined for six hours in a plane full of humans, bristled. Her head whipped around, fangs lengthening, eyes flashing a cougar-blue.

The man squawked and stumbled backward.

She hurriedly reined in the cat. This was ice fae territory. If they found her sniffing around, she was fucked.

Worse, Corban might find her before she found him.

She sent a quick glance around, but all she saw were humans. The nearest ones edged away.

Marjani hunched deeper into the hoodie. She would *not* lose control of her animal. Too much depended on this trip.

The bus for Reykjavik pulled up. She took a seat at the back next to the emergency exit and scanned each face as the bus filled up. Nobody but humans boarded, their salty, iron scent pressing in on her like on the jet.

The seat beside her remained empty. Word must have been passed that she was an earth fada. No one wanted to sit next to the predator in a woman's body.

It was almost noon, local time. The weak sun shone on moss-covered black rocks and scrubby tundra grasses. Houses appeared, colorful concrete boxes topped with corrugated steel roofs. To the north, a white-capped mountain range towered over the rapidly approaching city.

The bus let her off near the city center. She leaned against the bright blue wall of a coffee shop for a few minutes, making sure no one had followed her from the airport. When she deemed it safe, she grabbed a coffee and an egg sandwich and ate standing at the counter, one eye on the door.

After that, she walked the streets for several hours, getting the lay of the land and searching for Corban. But if he knew she was in Reykjavik, he wasn't making himself known.

Sleep dragged on her eyelids. Except for a short nap on the flight from Baltimore, she'd been up for more than twenty-four hours. She checked into a hostel and curled up on the pristine white sheets, the switchblade beneath her pillow, her right hand on the iron dagger's smooth ivory handle. She slept lightly in the way of her cat, one ear cocked for danger. But all was quiet.

When she awoke, it was late afternoon. This time, she donned a wool sweater beneath the hoodie. The iron dagger went into her right boot, the stiletto the left, and the switchblade back into her front pocket.

Five minutes after she left the hostel, she scented silver. Her breath sucked in, but she forced herself to look casually around. A couple of tall, glittering ice fae males strode toward her, pointy ears poking through their long, white-blond hair. She turned and stared into a shop window, heart pounding, watching their reflections as they passed by. Against her side, she held the switchblade, open and ready.

But the men only gave her a quick, uninterested glance before continuing into a nearby pub. She released her breath and continued walking.

Where in Hades was Corban? His animal was a wolf. If he was in Reykjavik, he should have scented her by now.

Her stomach grumbled. Dinnertime. She fingered the meager amount of krona in her pocket and chose a pub that didn't look too expensive.

The décor was cozy, with dark wood and warm lighting. A long bar ran the length of the room, and in the back, a small fire was burning in a stone fireplace. A slim, dark-haired waitress greeted Marjani with a cheerful *hallò* and showed her to a small corner table.

Removing her hoodie, Marjani sat with her back to the wall and surveyed the crowd. It was mostly locals, the Nordic rhythms of Icelandic mixing with English, and everyone dressed casually—jeans, T-shirts, cotton sweaters, even a flannel shirt or two.

The waitress recommended a local ale and something called a lamb boat sandwich.

"Sounds good." Marjani shut her menu.

She touched her quartz, which also served as a smartphone, through her sweater. She'd turned the phone off when she boarded the jet and never turned it back on.

She should probably call Adric, but she'd left him a note. If she contacted him, they'd just argue. And then he'd order her back to Baltimore, because he thought she was too broken to be out on her own.

She didn't want to be forced to disobey a direct order from her alpha. Even if he was her brother.

The lamb boat sandwich turned out to be an upscale sub sandwich—a bun stuffed with slices of fried lamb topped with onions, red cabbage and pickles. She ate slowly, sipping the ale between bites.

Her skin prickled. She sipped her ale and glanced around.

A tall, rangy man with shoulder-length blond hair slouched at a nearby table, drinking a beer. He met her eyes, not bothering to hide that he was checking her out.

Her breath snagged.

Holy singing crystals, he was beautiful, with slanted cheekbones and sky-blue eyes framed by dark eyelashes. His straight nose had a small bump on the bridge, a tiny imperfection that only heightened his appeal, and his black ribbed sweater stretched across a hard chest.

His cheek creased in a smile—and fear wrapped icy fingers around her lungs.

She jerked her gaze back to her sandwich, her stomach tight, heart thudding in her ears.

Fuck, she hated this. A couple of years ago, she might have smiled back, seen where this led. But not anymore. No one touched her. She didn't even let members of the clan get too close.

A shadow fell across the table.

She snarled, her cougar rising to meet the threat. She forced it down. Shifting in the middle of a human pub could be fatal. The fada and humans had treaties about those things. A fada shifting in a pub for no reason would be automatically targeted by the authorities as feral.

She could be shot on sight—or slapped into a cage.

And she'd have to admit Adric was right after all—she was too broken, too close to going feral, to be out on her own.

The tall blond male smiled down at her. Spoke.

Still fighting the cougar, she had to concentrate to make sense of his words.

"I said, mind if I join you?" A surprisingly deep voice, gravel wrapped in silk.

She gave a shake of her head. "Yes."

He lifted a single dark brow. "No, you don't mind, or yes, you do?"

"Yeah, I mind. I don't want company."

His gaze went to the slight lump her quartz made beneath her sweater. "Your accent is American, which means you're from one of two clans."

Fine hairs rose all over her body. He was correct; the only earth fada clans in North America were her own clan in Baltimore and the Navajo clan in Arizona.

But how the hell had he made her as an earth fada so fast?

Her nostrils flared, subtly testing the air. Human—he smelled of salt and iron—but with a trace of silver. The man had fae blood, although it might be so faint he didn't know it himself. Overlaying it was a pleasant grassy scent, as if he spent a lot of time outdoors.

Her cat liked his smell, but the human part of her didn't like that hint of fae. Not on top of the fact that he knew a little too much about earth fada.

Easing the switchblade from her pocket, she released the catch.

"You don't want to use that." He set his plate and glass on her table and took the chair across from her.

"No?"

"No." He leaned back in his chair, resting an arm on the back as if she were an old friend instead of a pissed-off shifter with a sharp blade aimed at his privates. "Too messy."

"How did you know I'm an earth fada?" she asked, soft and dangerous. "Did Corban send you?"

"Who?" His surprise seemed genuine—and besides, her cousin would never ally himself with a human.

She shook her head. "Never mind."

"Don't worry." His voice dropped. "No one else in here noticed—or if they did, they didn't care. Icelanders are used to magical creatures."

She narrowed her eyes. "That's not an answer."

"What was the question?"

Her breath hissed between her teeth. The man was maddening.

"How," she repeated, "did you know what I am?"

He grinned, a flash of white against tanned skin. "It's your walk."

"My *walk*?"

"You didn't walk in here, you flowed—like a dancer...or a cat. Every earth fada I've ever met walks like that."

She made a mental note to clomp out of the pub like a freaking Clydesdale horse. "And that interests you—why?"

"It doesn't. I just liked the look of you. If you want me to leave, I will."

She relaxed fractionally. He was right, she didn't want to draw attention. And his scent had the pureness of truth. He didn't mean her harm.

In fact, all she scented was...interest, of the sexual kind. Was he *flirting* with her?

She scowled, sick of being on edge all the time. Hating that she couldn't have a simple conversation with a stranger without going into fight-or-flight mode.

Yeah, she was jumpy because of Corban, but this wasn't about her cousin.

This was about her.

The too-pretty male arched a brow. "Well? Would you like some company?"

She reminded herself that she wanted to blend in and slid the blade back into her pocket. "Sure. Why not?"

He smiled and extended his hand. "Fane."

"Jani." Shaking his hand, she gave him part of her name.

"Jani," he repeated it in that gravelly voice. "I like it. So what brings you to Iceland?"

"I've always wanted to see the Northern Lights." That was the truth...just not the whole truth.

He sipped his beer. "Not much chance of that in July. The peak time is November to February, although I've seen them as early as September first. They're a sight worth seeing."

"Maybe I'll get lucky."

"Maybe you will." His mouth curved, and for a second, the air was charged with something that made her blink—and then hunch her shoulders. He saw that and continued, "So you're heading north? You have to rent a 4x4 to get up there, though—or take a flight."

"Mm." She ate another bite of her sandwich.

The ice fae court was in the north, near the wild Strandir coast, but Corban had told Adric to meet him here in Reykjavik.

But was Corban actually in the city? What if he was at the ice fae court—or even holed up somewhere else in the country? Iceland was an island the size of Virginia.

Blue eyes regarded her, clear as the sky on a cloudless day. "I'm driving north tomorrow. Want a ride?"

She drew a slow breath. He was being too helpful. Her hand went to her switchblade again.

"Look. I don't know you. If you want to share a table, fine. But why I'm here and how I get around is none of your fucking business."

"You're right."

Those clear eyes seemed to see straight into her soul, to understand what she wasn't saying: Why she was so wary of strangers, even though she was a cougar and a trained soldier.

Why a knot of rage had lodged in her chest, so big and black and tight it threatened to choke her.

What he couldn't know was why she was in Iceland—and what she planned to do when she found her cousin.

CHAPTER 2

$\mathcal{S}$ometimes Fane hated himself.

He'd recognized the young earth fada immediately. Hell, he'd just seen her a couple of weeks ago at his daughter's mate-bond ritual.

Evie had mated with a Baltimore fada named Jace, and Marjani Savonett had attended with her alpha brother. But Fane had used his Gift to blend into the crowd, so no one but Evie and Jace had known he was present.

His focus had been on Evie, his heart full. How had this daughter he barely knew grown up so strong and smart and pretty?

But he'd spared a glance or two for the slim, dark-eyed shifter.

He'd followed Marjani from the minute she'd arrived in Iceland.

His orders had come from the ice fae king himself, a terse message scrawled on magical paper that dissolved as Fane read it: *An earth fada female will arrive today from Baltimore. Watch her, and inform me of her movements.*

No name, but as he'd told Marjani, it was easy to pick an earth fada out of a crowd.

Sindre had *not* suggested Fane meet Marjani. In fact, the king would be displeased to find his envoy had taken his own initiative. And Fane had had enough of Sindre's displeasure to last a lifetime.

But he hadn't been able to resist approaching the sexy little earth fada. Something about her drew him, despite the fact she was almost feral, her cougar close to the surface.

Her shaved head showed off her fine features and catlike eyes. Her skin was a smooth honey-brown—Evie had mentioned that the Savonetts' mom had been from Jamaica—and her lean body vibrated with suppressed energy.

His mind filled with erotic pictures. Marjani beneath him, or maybe astride so he could run his hands over that smooth, beautiful skin...absorb her warmth... take some of that vital energy into himself. Kiss those lush lips that seemed made for a man's mouth.

He saw her hand slide beneath the table, heard the quiet snick as she released the blade. So she had a weapon—probably more than one.

He almost grinned. He was a wayfarer. She might have a shifter's fast reflexes, but he'd bet he was quicker.

When he promised that he meant her no harm, it was the truth. He was a quarter fae, enough that he couldn't lie without making himself miserably ill. But that didn't mean he wouldn't carry news of her to someone who *did* mean her harm.

Sometimes Fane hated himself.

He gave her a crooked smile and set about coaxing information from her.

"Jani." He repeated her name, rolling it on his tongue. The short, sassy nickname suited her. "I like it. So what brings you to Iceland?" He expected evasion, and he wasn't disappointed.

"I've always wanted to see the Northern Lights."

Summer was the wrong time of year for viewing them, which she had to know. But he played along. "Not much chance of that in July. The peak time is November to February, although I've seen them as early as September first. They're a sight worth seeing."

"Maybe I'll get lucky."

"Maybe you will." His mouth edged up. Was she flirting with him? But no, she fastened her gaze on her sandwich and took a bite without looking at him.

"So you're heading north?" he asked, but she didn't take the bait. Then he took a chance and offered her a ride in his SUV.

He realized his mistake as soon as the words left his mouth.

"Look." She settled back in her chair, mirroring him, but with her muscles tight, battle ready. "I don't know you. If you want to share a table with me, fine. But why I'm here and how I get around is none of your fucking business."

"You're right. I'm just making conversation."

When she scowled, he waved an encouraging hand at her. "Now suppose you ask why I'm here. It's called small talk—give it a try."

The corner of her mouth twitched. "Because you live here?"

"Me? No. I visit from time to time, that's all. I love the hot springs. Did you stop at the Blue Lagoon on your way in from the airport?"

"No." She sipped her ale. "Maybe when I leave."

"You have to try the hot springs while you're here. Best part of visiting Iceland."

"So I've heard."

He took a bite of fish. "Iceland has the best fish and chips. Even better than the UK."

"I'll have to try them."

The conversation continued in that same impersonal vein. They finished dinner without him learning much more than he already knew.

But he was pretty sure Marjani wasn't here for Sindre. No, she had another reason.

And he'd bet a handful of diamonds it had something to do with the wolf fada currently being held at the ice fae court in an iron cage.

Marjani paid for her meal and stood up. She jerked her chin at the ladies' room. "Excuse me."

Her walk was free and easy, and he got distracted by her round ass as she headed toward the bathrooms at the back of the pub. But something about the set of her shoulders made him throw some bills on the table and slip out the front door.

He strolled around the back and leaned against a building a few doors down so she wouldn't scent him. A minute later, she came out the back door.

His mouth stretched in a grin. *Got you.*

He had the fae Gift of wayfaring, with two abilities: he could move fast as a striking snake, and he could blend into his surroundings. If he didn't want you to see him, you didn't.

Marjani hitched up her backpack and strode down the alley in his direction. He activated the charm that Sindre had crafted to disguise his scent and stilled, becoming just another shadow against the concrete wall.

Her nose twitched as she passed him. He tensed and held his breath, afraid her shifter senses would pick up the sound.

She glanced around and then continued walking.

He waited until she rounded the corner before heading after her.

CHAPTER 3

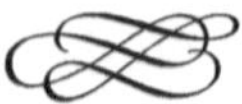

This far north, the summer sun set late. Marjani did a circuit of the blocks around the pub, but there was still no sign of Corban. By then, it was after eleven and she was dead-tired. With a yawn, she headed back to the hostel.

She slept lightly, waking twice when nightmares insinuated their chilly tendrils into her dreams. She was used to that. She stared at the ceiling, listening to the quiet sounds of the sleeping humans around her through the hostel's thin walls. Waiting for morning.

Breakfast was croissants and yogurt. She washed it down with a cup of coffee and set out to find her cousin.

It was a shame she wasn't really a tourist, because she would've enjoyed exploring the small, quirky city. She loved that the stolid concrete buildings were painted in crayon-box colors—red, green, blue, yellow. Even some of the corrugated steel roofs were brightly colored, and the streets were dotted with sculptures and murals. She passed tiny boutiques, funky coffee shops, and cafés that just invited you to come in and sit for a while.

But she didn't catch even a whiff of her cousin.

And yet, the back of her neck itched. She could've sworn someone was following her.

She leaned against the wall of a combination bookstore/record store and looked casually around her. All she saw were locals going about their business. She rubbed her nape and told herself not to be so edgy.

Lunchtime came and went. When her growling stomach became impossible to ignore, she bought bread and cheese and sat on a bench in the Old Harbor to eat. The ocean was a deep, still blue with small boats bustling to and fro. Across the harbor, she could see Mount Esja, its snow-capped flanks covered in plush green moss.

She'd covered most of the center city. Could Corban be in one of the suburbs that spread out to the east and south? If so, she might spend days looking for him.

She was a strategist, a Gift common in cats. Her strat talent had been humming along in the background, fitting facts together along with a heavy dose of intuition—and now she just *knew*.

Corban wasn't in Reykjavik.

She knew her cousin, knew how he thought. After the death of their parents, she and Adric had been taken in by their uncle Leron, Corban's father. It hadn't been a kindness. The man had been one mean SOB.

No one had mourned when Adric had stuck a knife in Leron Savonett one dark night.

His three sons had taken the worst of his abuse, with the eldest, Corban, coming in for more than his share. At times, the five of them had formed an alliance against Leron, covering for each other, helping each other with chores.

But Corban had enjoyed exerting power over his younger cousins. It was as if he had to prove he wasn't the weakling his father said he was.

Adric had protected Marjani as much as he could, but survival had meant predicting what Corban would do next. She could write a whole book on her eldest cousin—his moods, his likes and dislikes, when to approach him and when to stay far, far away...

If Corban was in Reykjavik, she'd know it. Maybe he wouldn't approach her straight on—more likely, he'd jump her in a dark alley—but he *would* approach her. If nothing else, he'd want to know why Marjani had come and not Adric.

Just before sunset, a chilly rain began to fall. Cold and hungry, she pulled up the hood of her jacket. The rain seemed to find its way between the cracks. She walked down to the Elliðaá River, found a quiet corner to shift to her cougar, and caught herself a fat salmon for dinner.

Corban had to be at the ice fae court. She and Adric had suspected for a while now that he was working with the fae—the night fae, for sure, and possibly the ice fae as well. Adric had managed to get the ice fae court's coordinates, just as he had the coordinates of most of the other fae courts and fada clans around the world. Her brother was scary-good at things like that.

That night, she got another few hours of sleep before checking out of the hostel. Her only luggage was her backpack. It was a simple matter to shower and shrug on the pack. By four a.m., she was on a bus to the outskirts of Reykjavik.

At the last stop, she got out to walk until she reached a deserted stretch of road. The rain had stopped, but above, more heavy gray clouds had moved in.

She set her backpack on the side of the road and stilled. Her nape was itching again.

She raised a hand to the back of her neck and cast a look around. Nothing stirred in the scrubby tundra except for a few intrepid rats.

That didn't mean no one was out there. Iceland was a land of magical creatures, its sparse human population meaning the supernatural world had settled here in large numbers. The ice fae were at the top of the food chain, but the island was also home to goblins and elves.

She shoved her clothes and shoes into her backpack, cinched the pack around her shoulders and waist with special straps designed to stretch with her, and shifted to her cougar.

Her quartz heated, lending its energy. Colorful sparks of gold, silver and blue danced over her skin. Warmth filled her chest, spreading throughout her body, and then she *disappeared*, for a time neither woman nor cougar, until the change was complete.

Her cougar snarled and scraped its claws in the hard-packed earth next to the pavement, pissed off at being forced to remain a human for most of the last twenty-four hours.

The cat was increasingly bold. Demanding.

Adric feared she was going feral. She'd overheard him discussing it with Suha, Marjani's best friend and the clan's head healer.

They all knew what that meant—as alpha, Adric would have to kill her. You couldn't have a cougar with a human's cunning and an animal's bloodlust roaming around Baltimore.

Just let me do this one last job. For Adric and the clan.

At least if she died, she'd go out with honor.

She loped north toward the ice fae court, using her quartz as a compass so that she could run through the tundra, avoiding the road. The sun rose, a weak, pale thing, and the sense of being watched eased.

By noon, she'd covered twenty miles, passing like a shadow by tiny fishing villages and farms with shaggy Icelandic sheep and the smallest horses she'd ever seen. She swerved west, coming out on a deserted cliff above the North Atlantic, and made her way down to the beach, where she shifted back to human. Shedding her backpack, she found her fishing knife and strode naked into the icy surf.

Within minutes, she had two fish, which she filleted and roasted on a tiny camp stove.

The taste was fresh and wild. Perfect.

She was licking her fingers when a movement on the cliff above made her bolt to her feet.

It was Fane, looking like a freaking model for *Iceland Magazine* in a silver shirt and worn jeans, long legs braced apart and his golden hair secured with a leather tie. His gaze traveled down her naked body, and his sexy mouth curved.

She ignored the smile to zero in on his ears. A diamond stud glittered in one earlobe, but what made her growl were the pointed tops, obvious now his hair was pulled back. He had more fae in him than she'd guessed.

Without taking her gaze from him, she picked up the fishing knife, flipping it from hand to hand with the ease of long practice. "What the fuck are you doing here?"

"Easy." He raised a hand, palm out, in a placating gesture she didn't trust for a second. "I can explain."

"Yeah, right."

She closed the still-warm camp stove and shoved it into her backpack along with the knife. She strapped the pack on, aware of him watching the entire time. Let him look his fill. One false move and she'd slit his throat.

But he remained on the cliff.

She shifted to cougar and bounded up the cliff, where she snarled right in his pretty face, making sure to show plenty of teeth.

The man was either stupid—or brave. He stood his ground, hands loose at his sides. Not aggressive, but not giving an inch.

She stalked around him, growling lowly.

"I mean you no harm," he said, which earned him another snarl.

She reached his front and paused, tail twitching in confusion. Her cougar didn't know what to make of him, but it didn't scent a threat. In fact, to her cat, Fane smelled somehow *right*, just as he had last night to the human Marjani.

A smile curled over his lips. "By the gods," he said in his smoky voice, "you're beautiful. And you'd rip out my throat in a heartbeat, wouldn't you?"

Her response was a snarl, but inside, the cougar preened itself at the compliment.

He lifted a brow. "Are you ready to listen?"

She gave one last growl and sat on her haunches.

"Good." He expelled a breath. "I don't have much time—I'm supposed to be somewhere else right now."

She stared back unblinkingly.

"Right," he muttered. "You know, I'm risking my bloody neck to help you. And you couldn't give a fuck, could you?"

Another twitch of her tail. Because he was right, she didn't give a fuck.

His hands curled into fists, a crack in his calm façade.

"I can't tell you much, or they'll—" He set his jaw. "It's not important. But the ice fae king knows you're here. Get out of Iceland, Jani. Today. While you still can."

CHAPTER 4

Fane stared into Marjani-the-cougar's turquoise eyes. It hadn't been easy to follow her, but it didn't take a genius to deduce she'd head north toward Strandir and the ice fae court.

He'd shadowed her in Reykjavik as she searched the city. Hovered nearby as she ate lunch alone on a bench, an island of solitude in a sea of tourists. She'd stared out at the water, face bleak, dark eyes haunted.

And damn if he hadn't wanted to sit beside her and try to tease her into a better mood.

He knew a little about what had put that bleak expression on her face. Something bad had happened involving the local river fada. According to his source, the men concerned were all dead. So whatever had happened—and you didn't have to be a genius to guess what a group of men might do to a woman—the SOBs had gotten what was coming to them.

She's an animal, Fane. A mixed bag of genes breathed into life by Dionysus and his wild fae followers.

But she fascinated him, and he had time to burn. He had a day, maybe two, before King Sindre would expect a report.

That night, instead of returning to his own room at a fae-owned inn, he'd waited outside the hostel where she'd taken a room. His patience had been rewarded when she slipped out early the next morning. He'd followed in his SUV, using his Gift to conceal the vehicle, as the bus took her to the edge of town.

When she'd taken off as her cougar, he'd driven north, taking his time so he wouldn't pass her.

But he'd lost her when she headed away from the road and into the tundra, only to catch sight of her again on the cliff. He'd parked and slipped closer—and damn near lost all the air in his lungs at seeing her lithe, honey-smooth body.

Now he squeezed his nape, wondering why he was sticking his neck out for a woman he'd never met. An earth fada, at that.

The cougar twitched her black-tipped tail. She had small, rounded ears and a white patch above each of those startling blue-green eyes. A plume of dark fur started at the inside corner of each eye and continued up her forehead as if drawn by a sooty finger.

In this form, she probably outweighed him, but he'd meant what he said. She was magnificent, all long bones and sleek muscles.

And trouble with a capital T.

"Do you understand?" He placed a hand on her shoulder, and for some reason she allowed it. Her fur was soft, like plush velvet. "You have to leave—today. The king has spies everywhere. You can't trust anyone."

She cocked her head in question, and he gave a mirthless chuckle. "That's right. Me included."

She rubbed her head over his chest—a quick thanks-but-no-thanks—and then gathered those lean muscles and loped off. North.

Bloody-minded female.

Well, he'd done what he could. If she wanted to run straight into a trap, that was her funeral.

He scowled and returned to his SUV. After taking his place behind the wheel, his hand went to his chest. Had Marjani been thanking him—or marking him?

He gripped the wheel and watched as her graceful body grew smaller until it was a dot on the horizon. The thought of that stunning, independent creature caged and at the mercy of the fae court's whims made his stomach turn.

With a low growl, he started the engine and continued north. He'd return to the court a day early. As a mixed-blood, he wasn't privy to the pureblood fae's plans, but maybe he could learn something.

He'd become very good at keeping his head down, doing his job as Sindre's envoy and ignoring everything else. It was the only way to survive as a mixed-blood at the heart of a fae court.

But he had a bad feeling that this time, he might not be able to.

CHAPTER 5

"Well?" Adric Savonett placed his hands on the war room's round granite table and looked around at his three remaining lieutenants—Zuri, Jace and Luc.

Zuri fingered his soul patch. A wolf shifter, he was the clan pretty-boy, his good looks the genetic inheritance of Mediterranean and African globe-trotters who'd met and mixed in the Caribbean. Tall and brown-skinned, he had a shaved head and narrow black mustache to go with the soul patch. Zuri was so good looking, people tended to underestimate him...until he pinned them with his hard black eyes.

"She took a red-eye out of BWI," the lieutenant reported. "She lands in Iceland at 10:50 a.m., their time. That's 6:50 a.m., our time—which would be right about now."

Adric muttered a curse. Marjani had left a note saying she was on her way to Iceland, but he'd wanted to confirm it. Because he couldn't believe she'd take off like that.

She'd known damn well he didn't want her to leave.

He was the fucking alpha—what he said should count. His claws sprouted against the granite table. Like being alpha mattered when it was your sister.

"You want us to go after her?" That was Jace, a jaguar shifter and one of Adric's oldest friends. "We can grab her, bring her back."

Adric's jaw clenched. Gods, he wanted to say yes. He literally shook with the need to follow her.

But Marjani was right. The clan needed him here.

The clan was still reeling from the events earlier this summer when his cousin Corban had brought night fae assassins to Baltimore. By the time the dust had settled, Tyrus, the night fae prince's son and heir, was dead.

Worse, Adric had killed Corban's middle brother Kane. It had been a fair fight. Nash, the youngest brother, had sworn to it, saying Adric had only been defending himself.

But everyone knew Adric had killed his uncle Leron before taking over as alpha. Now they whispered that he intended to take out his three cousins as well.

The clan was seething, afraid Adric was out of control.

Too many unexplained deaths had happened under his watch. Just like when Leron was alpha. Mistrust. Fear. Anger. Everything Adric had worked so hard to put behind him.

All because of his thrice-damned older cousin.

Pushing away from the table, he got up to pace the length of the small under-ground room. They were beneath the Factory, the combination test lab and manufacturing plant for the clan's quartz smartphones. Adric had carved the space himself out of the bedrock, along with a couple of trusted stoneworkers.

"She's on the edge," Jace added bluntly. "If you're not careful, you're going to lose her."

Jace was one of the few clan members who'd dare say it aloud. But then, he'd been with Adric and Marjani since the beginning, when they'd first plotted to overthrow their bastard of an uncle.

Adric closed his eyes. The other man was being polite. They both knew Marjani was the next thing to feral. Most days, she spent more time as a cat than as a human. A good portion of the clan thought Adric should do something about her.

"Ric?" Jace's hazel eyes were sympathetic. He'd lost his own sister in the Dark-time. "You can't let the fact that she's your sister—"

"She's not feral," he gritted. "Not yet."

Because the clan was wrong. Marjani was still rational.

"You haven't seen her like I do," he said. "She made breakfast for me yesterday, and we discussed what to do about Corban. And she was fine at Jace and Evie's mating ritual. You all saw her as her human."

"True," Jace said. "Doesn't mean she should be in Iceland on her own. It's not just that she could go feral—it's that Corban wants her dead. And she might be a hard-ass, but he outweighs her by fifty or sixty pounds. Plus, the motherfucker has nothing to lose."

Luc moved in his seat. The wolves in the clan tended to be taller than the cats, and Luc was no exception. A wild, fierce fighter, he was over six feet of solid muscle, with dark skin and wiry black hair.

"Why the fuck didn't you stop her? You must have known she'd go after the prick." His gold eyes accused Adric.

Adric slapped his hands on the hand-worked granite. He didn't normally explain his decisions, but Luc was in love with Marjani. Had been for years.

"You try and stop her when she's got an idea in her head."

"Don't give me that. You could've done something."

"What? Lock her in her fucking room?"

"At least then she'd be alive!" Luc snarled back.

They glared at each other. Adric's claws pricked out.

"Are you questioning how I handle my own sister?"

Luc's jaw worked. Then he dropped his gaze. "No," he muttered.

Jace spoke into the taut silence. "The question is, what do we do now?"

Adric retracted his claws and retook his seat. "Ideas?"

"We send a man to watch over her," Jace said. "But only one. More than that, and we'll just piss off the ice fae."

Zuri shook his head. "I say we risk sending four or five men. She's not just Adric's sister, she's the clan second, and a damn good one. We can't afford to lose her. And if and when she finds Corban, she'll need help."

Luc growled. "Corban can go fuck himself. I vote we send five men to bring her home, ASAP."

Adric blew out a breath. "Dragging her home isn't an option." She was on edge as it was. When she did spend time in her human form, she'd become a one-woman arsenal, with two or three knives on her at all times. "She needs to do this. Otherwise, we're going to lose her."

Luc set his teeth but nodded curtly.

Adric touched the quartz around his neck, pinging her one last time. But she didn't answer. His claws pricked out again. The cougar was about to explode out of his skin, insistent on going after Marjani. But the cougar also knew that the clan came first.

He made up his mind. "We'll send one man to serve as backup."

Luc rose to his feet. "I'll go."

Adric considered him. The wolf fada looked back, big hands fisted. If Adric refused, he'd have another AWOL lieutenant, because Luc was determined to go, alpha or no alpha. At least if he had Adric's permission, he'd report in regularly.

"All right." Adric jerked his chin in assent. "But you're only there as backup. Unless things go south, you're not to interfere—and that's an order. I don't even want her to know you're there. Pretend you're a fucking ghost."

"Understood." The lieutenant's shoulders released. "I'll catch the next flight."

"The next flight isn't until seven o'clock tonight," Zuri told him. "You won't get there until five a.m. tomorrow, their time."

Adric grimaced. That meant Marjani would be in Iceland for almost a day without back up. But it couldn't be helped.

"Contact me when you're on the ground," he told Luc. "I can use my link to her quartz to give you her general direction."

"Will do." The wolf disappeared up the ladder to the Factory's main floor.

Adric turned to Zuri, his chief of security. "While I have you here, any word about the night fae prince?"

In the past six weeks Prince Langdon of the night fae had been seen twice in Baltimore, when he normally only visited the city once every few years. They all knew why—he was searching for his son, Lord Tyrus.

Baltimore was located between two powerful fae clans—the Rising Sun Fae in northern Maryland, and Langdon's clan, the New Moon Night Fae in Virginia. Adric had kept his dealings with the local fae to a minimum until Corban had teamed up with Tyrus to try and pick off Adric's lieutenants.

Which was why Lord Tyrus was buried deep underground in Druid Hill Park.

"Nothing," Zuri replied. "I have my people on high alert, but the prince hasn't been seen in the city in over a week. Word is he's searching cities up and down the East Coast, not just Baltimore."

Relief washed over Adric. "Then he's not sure where his son died."

"No."

"Good. For now, keep your people on high alert. If the prince shows his face anywhere in the city, I want to know, stat. That goes for any night fae."

"Of course," Zuri replied.

The meeting over, the three of them headed up the ladder.

Up in the Factory, the techies were hard at work on the latest smartphone design. Right now, the Factory was just a small test lab in a former grocery in West Baltimore, but someday, it would be a cash cow for the clan. He hoped.

Jace was the engineer in charge of the quartz smartphone project. Adric listened as the lieutenant brought him up to date, and then told everyone to keep up the good work before leaving with Zuri.

Outside, the two of them squinted against the morning sun. Zuri settled a pair of dark sunglasses on his broad nose.

"Luc will find her. You know he's one of the clan's best trackers. And it's Jani, so..."

Adric nodded. They both knew the wolf would die for Marjani in a heartbeat. "But will she let him catch her?"

Zuri moved a big shoulder. "It's in the gods' hands now."

Adric put on his own sunglasses and they set off, Zuri to meet with his security team, Adric to crisscross Baltimore, checking in with the dens scattered across the city to try and calm the gossip.

All he wanted was for the clan to put the Darktime behind them. For the cubs to be safe and well-fed, and the adults able to afford a treat now and then. A stretch of forest for everyone—young and old—to run and play in.

And his sister back to how she'd been before those river fada bastards had gotten hold of her.

Was that too fucking much to ask?

CHAPTER 6

The journey north took Marjani a week. She remained in her cougar form, traveling mainly at night. At first she followed the Ring Road, staying out of sight of the spotty traffic. The terrain changed from flat plains to arctic highlands, the days slipping by almost unnoticed as they did when she was her cat.

An earth fada alpha was connected to his clan through their quartzes—a magical bond like a mate bond, but weaker. An alpha like Adric could track a clan member through his or her quartz. If Corban were still a member of the Baltimore clan, Adric could've used his quartz to find him, but Corban had smashed his quartz and found another, renouncing Adric as his alpha.

Marjani wasn't alpha, but her quartz hummed a quiet song whenever she turned north, and fell silent if she tried a different direction. That was good enough for her. When the Ring Road veered west, she continued due north.

A steady drizzle alternated with periods of heavy rain. By the third night, she was chilled to the bone, her stomach hollow with hunger. When dawn came, she found a cave and slept huddled near a thermal pool for warmth.

When she awoke, she washed her face and paws in the steaming water. A meal of a few mice barely took the edge off, but she ignored the hunger pangs to set off again.

She only turned on her smartphone once. Adric had tried repeatedly to get in touch with her. She hesitated, and then tapped the off button. He could track her by her quartz, and he'd know if she were seriously injured, or dead.

So he wouldn't worry. Much.

It still hurt, that last conversation. He'd only just stopped himself from saying she was weak—possibly feral. She'd thought Adric still believed in her, even if no one else did. To learn he didn't had been a hard blow.

Maybe you are *too weak to hold off the cougar.*

She shook her head, dislodging the sly voice. But it returned, again and again.

Another night passed. Sometime after midnight, the cat came alert. A plump white sheep had escaped its fence. She swerved toward it, her mouth watering. Already tasting the sheep's sweet flesh.

No.

Marjani-the-human fought a silent battle with the cat. It wasn't worth it. She didn't want to attract attention. She was hungry, yes, but not starving.

The cat pulled up short, snarling at being thwarted. The sheep let out a terrified bleat and galloped off as fast as its sturdy legs could carry it.

Marjani halted, lungs pumping hard and fast. Was this the night she went feral?

Because each time it was harder to say no.

The cougar was a badass with sharp claws and two-inch fangs. No one messed with Marjani when she was in that form.

Yes, the cat whispered. *Let me win. I'm strong. Fierce. No one will ever hurt you again.*

She clenched her jaw and resisted.

Because she was *not* an animal. She was a fada, with the blood of three species in her veins: human, cougar and fae. And she loved her woman form as much as her cougar, even if it *was* weaker.

Another few days passed. Her hunger had forced her to draw heavily on her quartz, depleting the energy in the tiny crystals. She needed food and rest, and the quartz needed time to replenish itself.

The rain had finally stopped when she came upon a river. By then, she was shaky with hunger. She waded in up to her chest and drank deeply before scanning the water for something to eat—fish, shellfish, a water bird...anything. At a flash of silver, she pounced and emerged victorious with a large fish. She settled on the sandy bank and tore into it, devouring everything but the tail and fins.

Replete, she had another drink and then sat on the bank to groom herself. Above her, the clouds had finally cleared to reveal the Milky Way, a glittering band of light flung against the black sky. Her breath snagged. She sank onto her haunches, awed, the crystals in her quartz humming.

As the sun rose, she crept into a hiding place beneath two large boulders and fell into a deep, healing sleep. When she opened her eyes again, the sun was on the opposite side of the sky—although this far north, sunset wouldn't be for hours—and her quartz's energy level was back to a hundred percent.

She was in a bleak highland dotted with steaming volcanic vents and large black boulders. Other than moss, the only green things were the scrubby trees and bushes dotting the riverbank. To the west, stony mountains rose like rugged giants from the ocean, white-capped and harsh.

She caught another fish for breakfast before setting out again, her belly full for the first time since Reykjavik. An hour later, she stumbled upon a dirt track heading northeast in the same direction she was being led by her quartz. She followed the track, hiding whenever a vehicle passed, but for most of the afternoon and evening she was alone in the deserted highland.

Dusk was approaching when her skin tingled. She was surrounded by magic. Powerful magic. She froze, heart slapping against her rib cage.

She'd reached the ice fae court. But where was it?

Dense steam rose from slashes in the ground, wafting over bedraggled clumps of grass and lush moss. The stench of sulfur was everywhere, overlaid by the telltale odor of silver. But the court itself had to be concealed by *look-away* spells, because she couldn't see a trace of it. And probably protected by wards, as well.

She hunkered down in a hollow between two boulders to wait. Sooner or later, a fae would enter or leave, allowing her to get a fix on a portal.

The sun had sunk behind the mountains before her patience was rewarded. A leather-clad fae rode up on a motorbike. Tall and sharp-faced, his cropped silver hair formed a striking contrast to his ebony skin. He halted and muttered a few words in an ancient fae language before flicking his fingers.

A portal opened, a shimmering circle cut out of the very air. He drove through and headed down the dirt track on the other side.

Marjani crept closer. The circle contracted, preparing to close behind him.

No. She leapt through the rapidly closing opening, landing on silent paws next to the track. The silver-haired fae was already thirty yards away, aiming for a black castle rising in the distance out of the otherworldly fog.

Her hackles rose. She didn't like this. It had been way too easy to get in.

But behind her, the portal had closed, the opening erased as if it had never existed.

She was trapped on the ice fae side.

Chill fingers tripped up her spine. She instinctively bared her fangs. But there was nothing to fight, and panicking would only make things worse.

Taking a deep breath, she slipped off the track into the dense white mist and examined the black castle. It appeared to have been carved out of a dead volcano, with a craggy spire at each of the four compass points. A high, crenellated wall surrounded the center, its toothy protrusions like a bear trap waiting to snap shut on an unwary intruder.

Staying concealed in the fog next to the track, she started toward the castle. The ground was uneven, with bogs and boiling hot vents to avoid, so she had to step with care. The stench of sulfur stung her nostrils. By the time she reached the castle, the silver-haired fae had disappeared.

But a round steel door had been left temptingly ajar.

Fuck that. Slipping back into the fog, she slunk west around the rough black wall, picking her way through the tundra, ears pricked and eyes straining.

High-pitched voices came from behind and to the left. She dropped to her belly, hidden by the eerie vapor. The sour stink of unwashed bodies reached her first, then two brown-skinned beings dressed in fur hats and animal skins raced by. They were about four feet high with large, pointy ears and sharp white teeth.

Goblins.

The female seemed to be scolding the male in an odd, chittering language.

This close to the castle, they'd work for the court. She waited, heart pounding, until she could no longer hear them, and then continued creeping along the wall.

She'd gone too far to turn back, even if she wanted to. She'd known when she'd left Baltimore that she might not ever see home again.

It was worth it. Corban had to die. Adric would never be safe while he was alive.

And she had her own reasons for wanting her cousin dead.

Corban was inside the ice fae castle. The weird tingle in her gut told her, the tingle that signaled her strategist's Gift—half intuition, half data-crunching. Her quartz murmured agreement, sensing the closeness of another earth fada, maybe two.

She inched along the wall. A half hour passed. The chilly mist deepened until she couldn't see more than a few feet ahead.

She stumbled into a bog and got mired in the cold black muck. It sucked at her paws, dragging her deeper until she sank up to her chest. She set her jaw and grimly fought her way back to stable ground.

She hung her head, chest heaving, her triumph at getting this far gone. She was moving in circles through the foggy night. King Sindre was an old, powerful fae with the Gift of chicanery. People said he could create illusions as real as a nightmare and use them to manipulate emotions.

If this were a trap, he might keep her creeping along the wall for days until she starved—or gave up.

She growled and set out again. She'd go through Hades itself to stick a knife in Corban's black heart.

The goblins rushed by again, this time in a pack of six. She dove to the left and froze as they passed like an evil wind, chittering to themselves.

When she dared lift her head, she couldn't see the wall—just thick fog in every direction. Dread lumped in her stomach. Digging her claws into the cold dirt, she swung her head back and forth, desperately trying to make out the black castle.

A hint of silver and iron in the air made her lip curl in a silent snarl. Her muscles coiled in preparation. The fog coalesced, moved—and a tall blond man stood beside her.

"Follow me," he muttered without looking at her, his lips barely moving.

Fane? She did a double take and hissed angrily.

His strong dark brows snapped together. "God's balls, woman—don't argue. The *huldufölk* are looking for you." When she gave him a blank look, he said, "The goblins and a few of the king's tame elves. They'll be on you any second. Now come." He strode off.

She hesitated, afraid it was a trap, but Fane was clearly pissed off—at her. If it were a trick, wouldn't he at least try to exert some charm?

And she needed to get inside. Corban was here. She was sure of that.

She loped after him. Fane waited until she caught up, then stooped to whisper, "Shift. Most of them can't tell a fada from a human."

She nodded and obeyed—and then almost didn't make it when the cat blindsided her, fighting to remain in control.

No. I am strong. A picture of claws and fangs flashed in her mind. *I will fight these goblins.*

For several heart-stopping seconds, she wavered halfway between cougar and human. That was bad. If you got caught between shifts, you died, a twisted half-animal, half-human monster.

If she hadn't taken the time to replenish her quartz, she might not have made it. She drew hard on the crystals' energy, determined to complete the shift.

And then she was a woman, crouched at Fane's feet, chest heaving.

He glanced around uneasily. "Bloody hell, can you hurry it up?"

She dragged in a breath. Holy mother, that had been close. But there was no time to think about it. Quickly, she pulled on cargo pants and a long-sleeved T-shirt, not bothering with underwear or shoes.

"Ready." She tucked her quartz into her shirt's neck.

Fane wrapped a wiry arm around her shoulders. She stiffened, but he muttered, "I'm a wayfarer."

"So it was you following me."

A curt nod. "Keep touching me at all times, and they won't see either of us."

He waited until she jerked her chin in assent and then set his palm to a crack in the weathered volcanic rock. The rock melted away to reveal an arched doorway. Together, they stepped through into a large tunnel.

Marjani's eyes widened. Instead of the black she'd expected, the curved walls were a smooth and bluish-white, like the inside of an ice cave. Silver fae lights floated near the glossy ceiling, and bright blue tiles paved the tunnel floor. The temperature was comfortable, like a warm spring day, and the air crisp and clean-smelling.

Fane took her hand and crept forward, following the wall to the west. They passed a double door opening into a huge room at the center of the maze.

"That's the great hall," he murmured.

It was a huge, intricately-shaped hexagon that reminded her of a giant snowflake. At the center, several hundred chic, glittering fae dined at linen-covered tables. Ethereal silver chandeliers floated overhead, and ice sculptures of magical creatures were scattered here and there. From hidden speakers emanated dreamy music, intermingling with the murmur of voices and the clink of fine crystal. Through the tables moved slim, pointy-eared elves, filling glasses and ensuring no one's plate was empty.

Marjani's feet slowed. Other than the few times she'd been to the sun fae court, she'd never seen so many fae in one place. Like sun fae, the ice fae's skin came in every shade from translucent white to deep brown, but their hair was a variation on snow and ice: white, silver, blond, with the occasional shimmering gold or red. And every single one of them was model-beautiful, like Fane.

The clothes were incredible—stylish, fae-tailored creations that would cost a year's pay in the human world—but it was the jewels that made her stare. Ice-cube-sized diamonds. Fiery opals. Blue and purple sapphires, and chunky green emeralds.

With his single diamond stud, Fane was a model of restraint.

"Keep moving," he hissed, and with a start, she realized she'd slowed down to stare.

She sped up, moving silent as a wraith alongside him. To her amazement, no one even glanced their way. It was as if the two of them were invisible.

They traveled another few hundred yards before reaching a short hall with several doors. Fane stopped at the end of the hall in front of a green door and ushered her inside.

"We can talk," he said in a normal tone as he locked the door and dropped his jacket on a chair. "The rooms are soundproof and warded. The fae don't trust each other worth a damn."

He was wearing skinny black jeans and a baby blue shirt that matched his eyes. He raised his arms in a bone-cracking stretch that strained the soft material across his chest. Marjani couldn't help taking in his body, lean and powerful in the form-fitting clothes.

He brought his arms down. "That was too damn close."

"Yeah," Marjani said, still staring at his chest.

His lips edged up and their eyes met.

She looked away first. "This is your room?"

"When I'm at court."

"It's...nice." It was—a small, cozy space.

A walnut sleigh bed with a moss-green comforter hugged one wall, and three sparkling gold fae lights floated overhead, warming the creamy walls. In addition to the plain wood chair that held his jacket, there was an easy chair with a small round table between them. Through a partially open door, she saw a bathroom with a shower and huge oval tub.

He moved a shoulder in a half-shrug. "It suits me well enough."

"You don't live here in Iceland?"

"Gods, no. I spend as little time here as possible. I'm a quarter-fae." His handsome mouth twisted. "They don't treat me much better than they treat the fada. Which is why you'd better talk. Now."

Suddenly he loomed over her. She stared back, not betraying by a flicker of an eyelash that her heart had sped up. The friendly, easy-going man of the pub was gone, replaced by a steely-eyed fae. But she'd been threatened—and worse—by men a hell of a lot more dangerous.

She held her ground and palmed the switchblade.

He blew out a breath. "I'm not your enemy, Jani."

"No?"

"No. In fact, I fucking stuck my neck out for you. Do you know what the goblins would have done if they caught you? They swarm over you like a pack of rats." A muscle flexed in his jaw. "You might kill a few of them, but they just keep coming, clawing and biting until you're half-conscious and bleeding in a dozen places, and then they bind you and put you in an iron cage."

She swallowed. "I guess I owe you one."

He nodded, and she was reminded that it was never a good thing to owe a fae. But somehow, she kept forgetting that Fane had fae blood. He seemed too warm... too *human*. The only fae she'd known had been cold-hearted pricks, with the possible exception of Cleia, the sun fae queen.

"You can start by telling me why you're here."

He was so close she could see all the gradations of blue in his eyes—the navy rim, the silver that streaked his sky-colored irises.

She drew a ragged breath, and his face softened.

"Jani?" He touched her cheek.

She jerked away and he took a step back. She released the switchblade and held it loose and ready at her side.

"I'm not here for that," she said evenly. But inside she was trembling. She edged toward the doorway.

"Fair enough."

But his arm came up, and she dropped into a fighting crouch. "Back off. Or I'll take my chances out there."

"Easy, love. I was just going to invite you to sit down." He pointed to the easy chair. "Let's have a conversation without all this snapping and snarling."

She growled but retracted the switchblade, although she didn't put it back in her pocket. "Okay. Fine."

She needed to know more, and Fane seemed willing to help her. Shrugging out of the backpack, she sat down, the pack at her feet, the switchblade in her hand.

Fane hung his jacket in a small walk-in closet and indicated her backpack. "Want me to put that in the closet for you?"

"No." She pulled it closer. If she had to leave in a hurry, the pack was coming with her.

His mouth curved. "You're a prickly little hedgehog, aren't you?"

"Yeah. You have a problem with that?"

He shrugged. "And yet I found you creeping along the outer wall with a horde of goblins after you."

"They didn't find me, did they?"

He shook his head. "By Hades, I can't tell if you're naïve or foolish."

"Not naïve." Her flat voice made him raise a brow.

"No, you're not, are you?" Sympathy shaded his voice.

What did he know? Shame twisted in her belly. She scowled.

If this model-pretty man dared to pity her, she just might have to prick him with one of her blades. Not to hurt him—at least, not much—but to teach him that Marjani Savonett didn't need anyone's pity.

But all he said was, "This isn't your world, Jani. You might not be naïve, but you don't know how the ice fae court works."

"Then tell me."

He took two bottles of pale ale from a cooling unit and handed her one. "How about I start by telling you why you're here?"

"I'm all ears." Shoving the switchblade back into her pocket, she twisted off the cap and took a sip.

He sat on the wood chair—or rather, sprawled, his long legs stretched out, his bottle of ale in one long-fingered hand. "To spring the big black wolf fada from his cage."

She jolted. "His *cage*?"

CHAPTER 7

Fane could practically see the gears whirring in Marjani's intelligent brain.

Gods, she fascinated him from the top of her shaved head to the tips of her cute little toes. She was so serious, so determined. He wanted to tease her, see her unbend a bit. Make her smile. So far all he'd seen was that twitch of her lips in the pub when she'd tried not to be amused.

Someday, he vowed, he'd coax a true smile out of her...but today was not that day. He was genuinely worried about her. The woman had no idea what she'd walked into.

She recovered quickly. "What's this wolf's name?"

"No idea. There was an earth fada hanging around the court last year. Corban. But I don't know if it's the same guy—I never saw him as his animal. All I know is the wolf in the cage wears an earth fada's quartz."

She worried the bottle label with her thumbnail. "He's black? What color are his eyes?"

"Hell, I don't know. I only got a quick look at him. He's in a tower that belongs to one of the king's top advisors."

Her fine brows drew together. "It must be him. Corban."

"You know him?"

"Yeah," she said flatly. "He's my cousin. But in a cage?" She shook her head. "We thought he was working with the ice fae."

"He was," Fane confirmed. "But things have changed. The only fada in the court are caged or under a *geas*."

A *geas* was an obligation or prohibition, binding to the person who accepted it. Breaking a *geas* was almost impossible, and if you did manage it, you'd lose what mattered to you most—wealth, your magic, even your life. But observe a *geas*, and you gained power, or money, or whatever you most wanted...but especially power.

And power was everything in the ice fae court—especially since Lady Blaer had come of age.

"I see." Marjani rubbed her forehead. He saw with a pang that she had bruised shadows under her eyes, and he could swear she'd lost weight in the week since he'd last seen her. "This...changes things."

"Leave." He leveled a hard look at her. "I'm telling you again—get the hell out of Iceland. You can't save your friend."

"Friend?" The corner of her mouth quirked. "You think I'm here to save that asshole?"

"Then why are you here?"

Her gaze slid from his.

"Tell me." He set his bottle on the small table between them with a snap. "I stuck my bloody neck out for you. You owe me the truth."

"Fine." She leaned forward, cougar-blue mixing with the brown in her irises. "I'm here to slit his throat."

"Ah." He fingered his chin, his mind rearranging things. Part of him was fiercely glad that the wolf wasn't her lover—or worse, her mate. The other part considered why she'd come so far to kill the other fada, risking her own life in the process—and he didn't like what he came up with. He had the bad feeling the black wolf had been one of the men who'd attacked her.

Rage curled through him. He ruthlessly suppressed it. *Not your fight, Fane.*

"Then you'll leave," he said. "The wolf will be dead soon, anyway. For a while he fought to get out, battering himself against the cage until he was bloody. But now he just sits on the floor, staring at nothing."

"I don't know." Marjani watched as the fae lights changed from gold to green, the colors swirling lazily around each other before the gold faded away. "I guess if he's almost dead, there's no reason for me to stay. You're sure?"

"Yeah. But you can't leave now—the goblins' blood is up tonight. No one but the most powerful fae will go outside until morning. You can stay here, and I'll sneak you out at dusk tomorrow."

Her catlike eyes narrowed. "Why are you helping me?"

He gave her a truth. "In the human world, I'm known as Fane Morningstar."

Her jaw dropped. "You're Evie's dad?"

"I am."

"So you knew who I was all along?"

He nodded. "Lord Adric's sister. I was at Evie and Jace's mating ritual."

"The hell you were. We would've seen you."

He spread his hands. "I'm a wayfarer, remember? No one sees me if I don't want them to. Only Evie and her mate knew I was there."

"But we would've smelled you. That silver in your scent—it marks you as fae."

"The king gave me a charm that disguises my scent for short periods of time."

She scowled. "So you can come and go in Baltimore as often as you please without us knowing?"

He moved a shoulder. "Don't worry. The king has better uses for me than to spy on the fada."

Except he *had* been spying on Marjani since she'd landed in Iceland. But that was different—Sindre's envoys watched any fada or fae who entered his territory. And as far as Sindre was concerned, the entire island of Iceland was his territory. In fact, he claimed most of the land north of the Arctic Circle.

She stared back steadily. He had a feeling she knew damn well he wasn't telling her everything.

"Now that you mention it," she said, "I can see the resemblance to Evie. But you're even prettier than she is."

A chuckle rustled in his throat. "I'll take that as a compliment."

"It's not." But a smile tugged at her mouth.

Warmth blossomed in his chest as if she'd given him a gift. He gave himself a shake—because allowing himself to like this woman was a damn fool thing to do —and rose from the chair. "Would you like food? A bath? The hot water is piped in from a geothermal well."

"Both." She made a wry face. "I've been traveling as my cougar for a week, although I did wash in a stream a few times. But you already knew that, didn't you? I *thought* someone was watching me."

He gave a noncommittal shrug. He actually hadn't followed her the whole time because after she'd found the dirt track, he'd known she'd end up at the court.

"Take a bath," he suggested, "and I'll get you something to eat from the great hall."

"Thank you."

The huge, hexagon-shaped hall was large enough to hold a thousand dancing fae, but tonight it held only a few hundred diners. Fane had been a member of the court for sixty turns of the sun, but the ice fae still acted like he was one step up from a servant. For once, he was happy to be ignored. He strolled toward the serving table against one wall, hands in his pockets, just a mixed-blood minding his own business.

"Fane." A large man with a beard and mane of copper hair rose from a nearby table. He was dressed all in black, and unlike the other fae, he wore no jewelry except for a heavy gold bracelet.

Fane muttered a curse. There went his plan to slip in and out of the great hall unobserved.

A pureblood fae, Roald was one of Sindre's top warriors—and Fane's grandfather, although the older man preferred to ignore the connection. Heads turned as everyone looked from him to Roald and back again like a bloody tennis match.

Fane pasted a smile on his face. "Roald. Peace to you and yours." He refused to address his own grandfather as "my lord," although Sindre had elevated him to a lord of the court after Roald had won a particularly important battle.

"Peace," his grandfather returned in his gruff voice. "Come. I wish to speak to you." He strode out the door, not bothering to see if Fane followed.

What now? And why did Roald have to choose tonight of all nights to speak to him, when Fane had a fada hiding in his apartment?

But you didn't ignore a summons from Roald-the-mighty-warrior-Morningstar. Fane headed after him. Once he would have been thrilled by this public acknowledgment from his grandfather. Roald Morningstar was renowned in the fae world—in the six centuries he'd been alive, the man had never lost a battle.

During Fane's first year at court, he'd tried to get to know Roald, but the older man had made it clear he wanted nothing to do with his mixed-blood grandson. So Fane had said the hell with it. As far as Fane knew, Roald didn't even know he had a great-granddaughter, Evie.

But recently, the burly redhead had unbent enough to nod to Fane in the hall. He'd even stopped a couple of times to ask how Fane was doing. Fane had been coolly polite, and that was how they'd left things.

Roald headed for his spacious apartment near the north tower. Fane had to extend his stride to keep up. His grandfather was one of the largest men at court, with long legs and shoulders as wide as a door. He made Fane feel puny, although compared to other ice fae, Fane was heavily muscled.

The door to Roald's apartment swung open as they reached it, a throwaway bit of magic that only the most powerful fae indulged in. Fane had never been past the living room, furnished with severe Scandinavian furniture in white oak. The only touch of comfort was the blue velvet cushions, and Fane suspected those had been introduced by his human grandmother.

He glanced at her portrait, centered over a huge stone fireplace. His grandfather had mated with a human from Norway, a stunning blonde with a wide smile whom Roald had clearly adored. Saga had passed to the other side more than three centuries ago, but his grandfather had never taken another lover. In the portrait, Saga wore an emerald silk dress, her throat and wrists adorned with a fortune in jewels.

An elf couple—two mate-bonded men who'd served Roald as long as Fane had known him—offered them drinks. When they both refused, the slim, black-haired elves bowed themselves out of the room.

Roald folded his arms across his impressive chest and frowned down his beaky nose at Fane. His eyes were a fierce gold—hawk's eyes, a perfect match for his aquiline features.

Fane crossed his arms and stared right back. His grandfather had requested this meeting. Let him speak first.

Roald gave a short nod, as if confirming something. "It's been too long since you were at court."

"The king keeps me busy."

The older man allowed himself a faint smile. "You've done well as his envoy."

Fane had to force his face to remain expressionless. Was his grandfather *proud* of him? "Thank you."

"No thanks are due me. I've done little enough to help you."

That was certainly true. Fane shrugged. "I prefer to make my own way."

"As is right for a man."

Fane shifted his weight, impatient to get back to Marjani. The gods save him from fae etiquette. At this rate, he'd be here half the night before his grandfather got to the point.

"Look, Roald, what do you want?"

His grandfather's dark brows lowered. "Your father should have schooled you in fae ways."

Fane shrugged. Arne had come and gone as he pleased, leaving Fane's raising to his mom. Fane hadn't even known he was part fae until he was an adult.

"So I'm a primitive bastard who doesn't know his arse from his elbow. You think I haven't heard that a hundred times?"

Roald glowered at him. Then he sighed. "You remind me of your grandmother."

"Saga?"

They both glanced at the painting above the fireplace.

Roald's gaze turned inward. "She was a lot like you and your father. A cheer-ful, easygoing woman—but she had pluck. Push her too far, and she pushed right back. But even that was done so tactfully I barely noticed I hadn't gotten my own way."

Fane uncrossed his arms. "I wish I could've met her."

"She would have loved you—her only grandson. I'm sorry she didn't live long enough to see you born." Roald's strong throat worked. "I think of her...more and more, as I age. I wonder if I'll see her when I pass to the other side."

"I—"

"But that's an old man talking." Roald's fierce eyes fastened on Fane again. "I hear you sired a daughter on a human. Is it true?"

Fane went rigid. Evie was his secret. Only Arne knew about her, and he'd agreed that Fane should hide her from the fae world. You never knew when someone would take it into his or her head to use Evie against him.

How in Hades had his grandfather heard? But now that he had, Fane had to tell the truth. He couldn't lie, and evading the question would be as good as admitting it.

"Yes. I do."

Roald sighed. "What is it with this family and humans? I suppose she has no Gift."

Fane moved a shoulder. "She's mostly human."

It was an evasion. Evie might be only one-eighth fae, but she'd turned out to be a Gifted amplifier who could boost another fae or fada's Gift. It was a rare and very valuable talent, one the fae would prize as much as her mate's clan did. Evie was now training with Baltimore's healers to amplify their healing Gifts.

"They tell me she mated with a fada." Roald's voice was heavy with disapproval.

"She did. A jaguar shifter."

"A jaguar." Roald pursed his lips. "What can you expect from a woman? The fada have a certain animal appeal."

Fane stiffened. "She's happy with her mate, and he treats her like a princess."

Roald shook his head, but changed the subject. "I have good news. Your father will be arriving in a few hours. I'd like you both to join me later for dinner."

Harsh words rose in Fane's throat. It was too little, too late. But this was his grandfather—and he hadn't seen his father in years. They never seemed to be at the court at the same time.

"I can't," he said. "Not tonight. I'm sorry."

And damn it, he *was* sorry. He'd thought he was done trying to win Roald's approval, but apparently he wasn't. Still, a formal fae dinner lasted for hours. No way was he leaving Marjani alone for that long.

"The king's business?" murmured Roald.

Fane stared back expressionlessly. An envoy didn't speak of what he did for Sindre.

"Tomorrow evening then," his grandfather said. "I'll speak to Arne when he arrives."

"I'll look forward to it." Tomorrow night Fane would be sneaking Marjani out of the castle, but he'd fit in the drink somehow. It would be the perfect cover if Sindre got suspicious.

"And thank you for the invitation," he added. "Please tell Arne I'm sorry I can't be there tonight. Now if you'll excuse me—"

The other man inclined his copper head. "Until tomorrow."

Fane turned to leave and then halted. "My lord?"

His grandfather had already turned to gaze at Saga's portrait. "Mm?"

"I'd appreciate it if you didn't mention my daughter to the king."

Roald turned his head and their eyes met. "No," he agreed. "It would be best if he didn't know."

"Thank you." Fane nodded to the two elves, who were holding open the door for him.

Back in the hall, he expelled a breath. For six decades, his grandfather had pretty much ignored his existence. So what had changed? Unless he suddenly felt a belated duty to his deceased mate, who after all, had been one hundred percent human.

With a shrug, Fane set the puzzle aside. He had a bigger problem waiting in his room. One he needed to get back to before she took it into her head to come looking for him.

Returning to the great hall, he heaped a large plate with food—cheese, herb-encrusted roast chicken, salad, whole-grain rolls fresh from the ovens. He popped a silver cover over the whole thing, pocketed a couple of apples, and wended his way back through the bluish-white maze to his room.

Stars, he was sick of all the unending white and silver and blue. He yearned for green grass and lush trees and flowers that bloomed longer than a few short weeks.

Back in the room, Marjani was fully dressed down to her boots, but she was slumped in the easy chair, eyes half-closed. One hand cupped the quartz on her chest, a pretty conglomeration of amethyst crystals in a soft gray and purple. The center glowed weakly.

His breath snagged. She looked so exhausted, her beautiful oval face drawn.

The earth fada didn't share the secrets of their quartz with anyone, but he knew it was a symbiotic relationship. A quartz didn't come to "life" until chosen by an earth fada, and the earth fada in turn drew life energy from the quartz's crystals.

But both Marjani and her quartz looked depleted. He grimaced, helpless and not liking it.

He eased the door shut as quietly as possible, but her eyes opened. She straightened, her gaze on the plate. He passed it over and set the apples on the table.

"Sorry I took so long. I ran into my grandfather."

"Your grandfather?" She paused in the act of lifting her fork and frowned. "He's at the court?"

"Yeah, but don't worry. He won't be stopping by. We're not exactly friendly."

He tried to keep the bitterness out of his tone, but the way Marjani tilted her head told him he hadn't succeeded.

"No?"

"He's a pureblood."

"Ah," she said, a world of understand in that single syllable. Everyone knew how purebloods were about tainting their bloodlines.

Fane dropped onto the wood chair and picked up his ale. But he didn't take a drink, just turned the brown bottle in his hands, unsettled by the encounter with Roald.

Marjani began eating with a delicate greed that reminded him of a stray cat that had adopted his family when he was a kid in Newfoundland. A sleek gray female, the cat hadn't been able to look awkward if it tried—just like Marjani.

She was halfway through when she gave a rueful grin and offered him the plate. "I'm starved—sorry. Would you like some?"

He helped himself to some bread and cheese and then handed back the plate, telling her to finish it. "You need it more than me."

"Thanks. I've burned a lot of energy this past week." She touched the quartz, and then flicked him a look and hurriedly dropped her hand as if afraid to draw his attention to it.

Irritation spiked through him. What did she think he was going to do, rip the goddamn quartz from her neck? Then he remembered that she'd been attacked. Maybe some man *had* ripped it from her neck.

He took a gulp of ale.

She ate more slowly now. Her tongue flicked a crumb from the corner of her mouth, and he was reminded again of the graceful gray cat. He half expected her to swipe a tongue over her palm and use it to wash her face.

And why the hell was that arousing? But it was. He pictured her strong dancer's body under his while he licked and nipped at her lush rose lips. Or maybe straddling him, slim fingers wrapped around his cock as she closed those soft lips around the head...

She licked a dab of goat cheese off her finger and he shifted on the chair, so hard it hurt.

He dragged his gaze from her and finished his ale. When he spoke, his voice was hoarse. "Marjani."

She paused in the act of lifting her bottle to her mouth. Whatever she saw on his face made her set it on the small table between them. A steel stiletto jumped into her hand.

At least that was an improvement on the iron switchblade. She could cut him with steel, but with his fae blood, he'd heal fast. Iron, on the other hand, could do some serious damage.

He blew out a breath. "Put that damn thing away. You have nothing to fear from me."

"No?" She cast a pointed look at the tent in his jeans.

He lifted a shoulder. "I'm a man—and a fae. I like sex and I find you attractive. Doesn't mean I'm going to act on it."

She set the tip of the blade on her index finger. A flick of her hand, and the stiletto began spinning. She let it spin for a few seconds and then sent it flipping over the back of her hand. She caught it with her other hand and threaded it through her fingers in a dazzling display.

His mouth quirked. If she thought her little demonstration frightened him off, she was mistaken. But he was sorry if he'd made her uncomfortable.

"I get the point, love." He leaned back in his chair, left foot hooked over his right thigh. "Literally. And if it helps, I already knew you were lethal."

She slipped the stiletto back into her boot. "And you know this how?"

"It's my business to know things. You're Adric's second—one of his top people. No one knows much about you, except that you were at his side as he fought his way to alpha. But I've heard those knives aren't just for show. "

In fact, she was the Baltimore clan's top assassin, but he was too canny to say it aloud. Let her guess how much he knew.

Her smile was full of teeth. "Just for the record, you might want me—but there's no way in Hades you're going to have me."

"As you say." He waved a negligent hand. "Now, how about I tell you a story about a little girl who grew up at court? A beautiful and Gifted girl with more natural power than the court had seen in a generation. She would've been a court favorite except for one thing. She was born of an ice fae father and a night fae mother."

"Go on." Marjani drew up her legs and wrapped her arms around them, resting her chin on her knees.

He stared at a softly glowing fae light, formulating his words. He wasn't telling the story to be clever. He was forbidden to speak of Lady Blaer directly to an outsider.

"Maybe she was born twisted, or maybe it was because she was shunned from a young age. I don't know. Her mother kept her for the first decade or so and then dumped her in Reykjavik and told her to make her way to the ice fae court. The king took her in and kept her close—she was too powerful to do otherwise—but she spent most of her time in the east tower with only goblins for company."

"Holy mother. That's inhuman." Marjani shook her head against her knees. "And you people call us animals."

"They're not my people," he growled. Once, he'd hoped... But not now—they'd made it clear he was an outsider, one of the lesser races. "And yes, they *are* inhuman. They're fae."

She blinked. "Gotcha. So who is this lady and why do I care?"

"I can't tell you her name. But if you listen, you might learn something."

"Can't—or won't?"

"Can't." He waited until understanding dawned on her face before continuing, "A couple of decades passed. In the human world, it was more like fifty turns of the sun. One winter solstice, the young lady broke out of the east tower and appeared at the court—and proceeded to become one of the king's advisors."

"And?"

"She's one of the most powerful fae in the court now. The king is old and she amuses him. He lets her have her way, more than he should. She's so beautiful it hurts your eyes to look at her. Men—including fada—fall at her feet. She binds them to her with sex, and then if they're lucky, she sends them away...even if they don't want to go."

"And the unlucky ones?"

He gave her a stark look. "She keeps them."

"In a cage." Marjani tightened her grip on her legs.

"She's half night fae. She feeds on their pain."

"We go crazy if we're caged. The animal has to be free."

"I'm afraid the black wolf is already halfway there. It's been weeks since I saw him as a man."

She lifted her head from her knees. "But he sent my brother a message. That's why I came."

Fane straightened up. "The hell he did. When?"

"Last week—about ten days ago. He told Adric to meet him in Reykjavik. Dared him to meet him."

"That's impossible." Fane's heart started to pound in slow, hard strokes. "He's not in any condition to send a message. Not without help."

CHAPTER 8

$\mathcal{L}$uc crouched on his haunches, watching the boulders near the dirt track where Marjani had concealed herself.

Finally, he'd caught a damn break. He'd been just missing her all week. His flight had been delayed because of a fucking tropical storm. He'd spent twenty-four hours at the Baltimore airport, then another six in that metal tube that passed for transportation.

By the time he'd landed in Iceland, she must've already headed north, but he'd lost another day in Reykjavik, following her scent all over the city.

He stayed in contact with Adric, but the alpha couldn't get a read on her other than to say she was definitely in Iceland. Finally Marjani had turned on her phone, but only long enough for Adric to confirm she'd headed north. So Luc had followed, increasingly anxious.

He'd thought his luck had turned when he caught her scent near the beach. But it was mixed with the silver of a male fae, which made his wolf want to chew nails. Who was this man who kept crossing her path?

Then a huge storm had blown up and he'd lost both their scents in the deluge. Luc had waited out the storm in a barn with a herd of cranky goats who were *not* happy to share their space with a wolf. As soon as the rain slacked off, he'd resumed his trek north.

If Marjani had mated with him, he could've followed the bond. But she'd refused to accept him as her mate—although he'd asked. More than once.

But he'd finally caught up to her.

As a wolf, his sense of smell far surpassed hers, so after sending the alpha a quick text that he'd found her and she was all right, he took up a vigil downwind and out of sight. Just breathing her in like the lovesick ass he was.

He'd loved Marjani Savonett from the moment he'd first set eyes on the skinny teen with the soft voice and flashing knives. He'd known damn well she was scared —of her bastard of an uncle, that she'd lose Adric like she'd lost her mom and dad —but no one would've guessed it.

Until the night Corban's people had kidnapped her and handed her over to that den of feral river fada. When Luc and his men had picked her up the next morning on a Baltimore street, she'd been bruised and hollow-eyed. He just wished her rapists were still alive so he could cut off their fucking balls and then stuff them down their throats.

A cold-eyed fae with silver hair zoomed up on a motorbike.

Luc crept closer. And then his heart damn near stopped as Marjani dove through the portal after the fae.

He pelted after her, narrowly avoiding plunging into a bog concealed by the unnatural fog. The portal closed as he arrived. Luc tried to leap through anyway. He caught a glimpse of a menacing black castle—and then it disappeared. He landed on the sparse grass, still in the human world.

He threw back his head and howled. He *had* to get to Marjani.

Even at the best of times, he was more wolf than human. Knowing she was inside a fae court without any backup made him half-crazed with worry. If something happened to her, he'd never forgive himself.

He took several paces back and forth in front of the portal before forcing himself to halt. This was getting him nowhere. He had to hide before the ice fae wondered what the big, brown, backpack-wearing wolf was up to.

Moving a few yards off the path, he hunkered down next to a pile of boulders. Around him, the fog thickened until he couldn't see more than a few feet in any direction.

He pricked his ears and heightened his sense of smell. The locals had spoken of the vicious goblins that guarded this area. He had no desire to be set upon and torn to pieces.

The sun set and a cold breeze teased his fur. He hunched his shoulders, thankful for his thick coat, because he wasn't moving from this spot.

Sooner or later, another fae would go through the portal, and this time, Luc would be ready.

Fear congealed in his stomach. *Please let her be safe. Please don't let the fae catch her.*

The fae wouldn't harm her. Not at first. They'd be more likely to force her into some one-sided bargain, keeping her as an assassin...or a sex toy.

But in Marjani's current state of mind, just being held captive might be enough to drive her over the edge.

He growled, low and anxious, still pissed off at Adric. Why the fuck had he let her leave Baltimore?

Something in her was broken, even if Adric refused to admit it. People said she should step down as second, although no one was brave enough to say that to the alpha's face.

If Marjani were Luc's, he'd have tied her to the damn bed if necessary. She was too fragile to tangle with the fae.

But she wasn't his, and he was beginning to fear she never would be. He loved her with all his heart, but the mate bond wasn't there.

He expelled a breath.

Slipping out of the pack without shifting, he worked the clasp open with his teeth and munched through a couple of energy bars and a large chunk of beef jerky.

After that, he settled his head on his paws and dozed, ears pricked. But the night remained quiet save for the occasional squeak and growl of nocturnal creatures.

Just before dawn, he jerked awake as two fae in an SUV drove out of the portal heading south.

The portal remained open. He crept closer. The dirt track wound through the mist to the ominous black castle.

He sniffed, testing the air. He caught a whiff of silver, but that he'd expected. He darted through the shimmering circle.

It closed behind him, but he ignored it as he picked up Marjani's trail. He paced forward, all his senses on high alert.

The high-pitched chatter reached him first. He dropped to his belly and froze.

A sour stench filled his nostrils. Shadows moved. Crept closer.

The fur on his neck stood straight up. He scrambled back up and took off at a run, but it was too late. A manic screech split the air.

He turned to face them, but they were all around him. Ripping at him with razor-like teeth and sharp black claws. Piling on his back until he went down under the sheer weight.

His last thought was a prayer that they hadn't caught Marjani, too.

CHAPTER 9

Fane watched as Marjani climbed into bed fully dressed except for her shoes. The switchblade went under her pillow. He'd bet she had a knife or two hidden on her body as well.

A corner of his mouth lifted in a self-mocking smile. Guess it was up to him to be a gentleman and leave the bed to her. "I'll take the chair," he said and went into the bathroom to wash up. He exchanged his button-up shirt for a T-shirt but left his pants on.

When he returned, she was on her side facing him, the comforter tucked around her so that all he saw was a nose and cat-shaped eyes. He took a quilt from the closet and padded to the easy chair.

"You don't have to sleep in the chair." A quiet voice came from the bed.

He sent her a look over his shoulder. Did she mean what he thought she did?

"It's a big bed," she said. "You stay on your side, and I'll stay on mine."

No, she didn't. With a philosophical shrug, he sat down and settled the quilt around him. "I'm good."

He flicked his fingers and the fae lights dimmed to a soft amber. Marjani's breath slowed, and he thought she'd fallen asleep until she murmured, "Why are you being so nice?"

"I'm a bloody philanthropist. Now go to sleep already."

"Okay." A drowsy mumble. "But...thank you."

He grunted. When he was sure she was asleep, he muttered, "Because I like you. Too much," and then shut his eyes. As the king's envoy, he'd learned to sleep wherever he could.

He was deep in an enjoyable dream involving him and his sexy guest when a whimper jolted him awake. Heart pounding, he scanned the room. Had Blaer found out he was hiding a fada?

Marjani gave another forlorn mewl.

Hell and damnation. She was having a nightmare.

He threw off the quilt and padded to the bed. Sensing motion, the fae lights brightened enough for him to see his guest curled in a tight ball, tears streaking her cheeks.

He stared down at her helplessly. "Hey." He touched her shoulder. "Wake up. It's just a bad dream."

A guttural growl ripped from her throat. Claws sprouted from her fingertips.

He jerked his hand away. "Calm down. It's me, Fane."

Her breath shuddered in. She raised herself on an elbow. The eyes that met his were an unnerving turquoise, and he knew he was face-to-face with the cougar.

The center of her quartz glowed a similar aqua-blue. She touched it and blinked. Awareness dawned.

"I—sorry," she said gruffly. Her claws detracted.

He sat on the mattress. "Want to tell me about it?"

She shook her head. "Excuse me," she muttered and pushed past him into the bathroom. The water ran. He heard a couple of choked sobs that were immediately cut off.

He looked down at his hands and stayed where he was.

When she returned, her face was freshly scrubbed. He rose to his feet. Her eyes met his, red and swollen, the irises back to brown. Daring him to say something.

Lord, he didn't want to care. For the past six decades, he'd done just fine not caring about much at all, and this woman was nothing to him. But his heart constricted at how tense she held herself—shoulders high, feet apart. Prepared to strike if he offered sympathy.

She spoke first. "You can have the bed now."

"I changed my mind. If it's still all right, I'll share it with you."

Relief flashed across her face, but her voice was cool. "It's your bed."

He reached out a hand. "Come here."

She looked from the hand to his face. "Why?"

"I think you need to be held."

Another challenging look. "And why would I want *you* to hold me?"

He set his jaw. "Because I'm the only one here. Now come." He beckoned with his fingers.

She dragged a hand over her shaved head. "I suppose it's the only way we'll get any sleep."

"That's right. Now come here. You can have the outside." He got under the comforter and scooted toward the wall.

She crept under the comforter and lay facing him, her expression neutral. But he'd seen that relief on her face. She wanted this.

Turning onto his back, he slid an arm under her shoulders. When she didn't resist, he pulled her into the curve of his shoulder. She held herself stiff for a few moments and then her breasts heaved.

"You think I'm weak," she muttered against his T-shirt.

He huffed a laugh. "Like hell. You're probably the strongest woman I know."

"Then you don't know many fada."

"Not true. In my work for the king, I've met my share."

"Yeah? What do you do, anyway?"

"I'm one of his envoys. I'm part messenger, part negotiator. I've been to all the major fae courts—ice fae, sun fae, and night fae—and I've also visited a number of fae and fada clans."

"Sounds interesting." She settled more comfortably into the crook of his shoulder, probably not even realizing she'd relaxed. She had a sweet, earthy scent that reminded him of a baby animal's.

He turned so that his cheek was against Marjani's shaved head. Something about the short bristles against his skin was unbearably erotic. He pulled his head back, putting some space between them, and firmly tamped down his desire.

He was offering comfort, nothing more, even if his cock hadn't gotten the message.

"It can be. But..." He trailed off, because what was the use of complaining? He was in for the duration.

But he was sick and tired of being at Sindre's beck and call. He wanted his own life back. He'd spent six decades trotting about on king's errands. Working his way up in the ice fae court—and for what? He was still on the outer fringes, tolerated, but not respected.

Hell, he'd had to hide at his own daughter's mate ritual because no one at court knew he had a daughter—and that was how he wanted to keep it. Instead, he'd observed the ceremony from the back of the crowd, an odd pressure in his chest.

Evie was his only child, and he'd missed too much of her growing up. It was his biggest regret.

Still, he couldn't help feeling happy that his Evie had found a mate. And damn, she'd sparkled in a pretty dress with a star adorning her short blond hair, her face wreathed in smiles as she'd walked toward Jace. He'd stayed for the first toast and then left. Evie was in good hands with her earth fada mate, and Fane was supposed to be in Canada on a job for Sindre. The king wouldn't be happy to know he'd made an unscheduled visit to Baltimore, and he'd be furious to learn Fane had a daughter he didn't know about.

But it was safer for Evie if the ice fae didn't know she existed.

Besides, time passed differently in the fae world. A month could go by and he'd return to the States to find Evie another year older. And frankly, he wasn't good at the commitment thing, even when it was his own daughter.

He inhaled Marjani's fresh, wild scent. "Your dream. Was it about the cages?"

"No. Just something bad that happened to me once."

He squeezed her shoulders. "I'm sorry."

She shrugged and turned the subject. "I'll tell you one thing—I'd pay good money to know who sent that message to my brother. It was in my cousin's handwriting."

"I told you, he's in no condition to send a message. Someone here helped him."

"That's what I figured. So that fae lady you told me about must've been trying to lure Adric to Iceland. Or maybe it was the king?"

"I didn't say that."

"No," she agreed, "you didn't. I'm just glad I came, not Ric."

"Because you can win against a fae where he can't?"

She shook her head. "He's stronger than me. He wouldn't be alpha if he wasn't."

"Then why?"

"I'm expendable," she said in a flat voice. "He's not. You don't know what it was like before he took over as alpha. We can't lose him."

That's when he realized that Marjani had known what she was getting into. This was a suicide mission.

Bloody hell. He tightened his grip on her. "I'll help any way I can." It was a fucking evasive promise, but it was the best he could do.

She should've called him on it. Instead she murmured a thank you.

"You should never have come here." He sounded like a broken record, but he had the bad feeling it was already too late to sneak her back out of the castle—and the thought of this proud, beautiful woman at the mercy of Lady Blaer made him a little sick.

"I had to."

He mentally shook his head. But he supposed to Marjani, there'd been no other choice. That was the kind of woman she was.

She patted his chest. "Don't worry. I'll be okay."

His mouth twisted. Because all of a sudden, he wasn't sure who was comforting whom.

CHAPTER 10

*A*dric Savonett pinged Marjani's smartphone for what had to be the hundredth time.

No answer. Still.

She'd been gone for over a week now. Radio silence on her end, but he'd tracked her through her quartz. From this distance he couldn't pinpoint her exact location, but she was somewhere to the north and east, and Luc had confirmed she was in Iceland.

Safe enough, since her quartz was still alive and humming—until twelve hours ago, when it had gone completely silent.

She's okay. There's more than one reason for her quartz to go silent.

It didn't mean she was dead. The quartz could've been depleted. But most likely she'd reached her goal and passed through a fae portal into the ice fae court.

Then Luc's quartz went silent, too.

Adric's worry ratcheted up. But he was stuck in goddamn Baltimore, holding things together.

He paced barefoot across the living room's stone floor, threading his way through the secondhand couch and battered coffee table that he and Marjani had rescued from a dumpster when they were dirt-poor and never gotten around to replacing. The plush orange shag rug was his only luxury. His cougar liked to stretch out on it and stare into the fireplace.

He stalked down the hall to her room to stare at the neatly made bed. The bedspread, a colorful geometric print, was a painful reminder of the sister he used to have. The one who'd loved bright tunics and leggings.

Until those feral river fada had gotten a hold of her, thanks to Corban and his little band of followers. Now she shaved her head and dressed like a soldier in camo.

He muttered a curse and strode back to the living room where he stared into the glowing amber quartz in his fireplace. Outside, it was a humid night in early August, but his den was carved out of the bedrock two stories below the surface, so he kept the quartz-powered fire burning all year round.

Marjani had loved to sit by the fire.

She's in danger.

All evening, he'd been agitated. At midnight, he'd fallen asleep for a few hours and then got up to pace, his cat clawing at his insides, itching to go to her.

Growing up, he and Marjani had always had each other's backs. Otherwise they'd never have survived the clan war known as the Darktime. But Marjani had been scarred by those terrible years.

She appeared tough, assertive. Only he knew that she still had nightmares about losing their parents and the years they'd spent on the run, hiding from their uncle. She might be a pit bull, but it was protective coating for her soft heart. She wanted to believe that the clan would never again turn on one another like cold-eyed, vicious reptiles.

And because Adric loved her, he did his best not to dispel that belief. His sister might be his most trusted advisor, but she didn't know everything.

Did she really think he'd kill her? No fucking way. He'd lie, cheat and even murder if it meant hiding his sister was a feral.

He squeezed his quartz, willing her to contact him. Damn it, Luc was supposed to have found her by now.

But he'd missed her in Reykjavik—and since then Adric had received only two short communications. In the first, Luc had explained he was heading to the ice fae court's location in northern Iceland. In the second, he'd said he'd found her and was temporarily cutting off communication for safety.

And for the past two days, nothing from either of them.

That made two of his lieutenants lost somewhere in Iceland. The place was a freaking Venus flytrap.

He rubbed his nape and told himself not to worry. Luc and Jani were both strong, capable soldiers.

But she's not herself...

On the surface two stories above, a motorcycle rumbled up to the rowhouse he rented out to a couple of teenage drug dealers as camouflage. Very few people suspected the Baltimore Earth Fada alpha himself lived in the neighborhood.

A minute later, booted footsteps clattered down Adric's stairs.

He stilled.

No one but his lieutenants and a few trusted clanspeople had permission to pass through the ward guarding his den. And they wouldn't come in the middle of the night if it wasn't important.

"It's me," called Jace at the same instant that Adric sensed his quartz on the other side of the door.

Adric ushered him inside and closed the door. "What's up?"

Jace shook his head. Like Adric, his cat genes were evident in his lean, powerful build. He had close-cropped black hair, warm brown skin and his Native American dad's broad face and long cheekbones. He'd dressed in a hurry—his T-shirt was shoved haphazardly into the waistband of his jeans, and he hadn't buckled his short black moto boots.

"Bad news," he said, his mouth a hard line.

Adric's heart sank. He really didn't need any more bad news right now. He gestured for the jaguar shifter to go into the living room. Neither of them sat down.

Jace got right to the point. "Langdon wants to meet with you."

Adric stiffened. Jace had said the night fae prince's name. Clearly, they'd draw his attention.

Hell. This had to be about Tyrus.

"The prince contacted you himself?"

Jace's face sharpened, his cat's fury simmering green in his eyes. "He sent a fucking night fae envoy to our house in Grace Harbor." Jace's mate Evie had kept her house in Grace Harbor, a small city on the Chesapeake Bay, even though she and her teenage brother Kyler lived in Jace's Baltimore den much of the time.

"They're all right?"

Evie was a pretty blond human with a touch of fae, and her brother Kyler, although full human, was smart, scrappy, and—although he'd hate to hear it—loveable. Even though Evie wasn't an earth fada, Adric would've tolerated her for Jace's sake, but the two siblings had earned a special place in his heart when they'd saved Jace from Tyrus's assassins.

"Yeah." His friend growled. "But it scared the shit out of her. The prick wants me to know I'm vulnerable, that he knows where my mate and her brother live."

A cold anger rolled through Adric. "The hell he does." Evie was innocent in all this, and Kyler was a cub—not even out of high school yet.

"His envoy knocked on our front door—at midnight. I scented that he was a night fae, of course, so I told Evie not to open the door. Meanwhile, I changed to my jag and slipped around the house for a better look. Thank the gods her dad gave her that protection charm. At least the bastard didn't pick up that she's a mixed-blood."

Adric nodded.

"But he upset everyone. Even Mrs. Linney. You know how she has her nose in everyone's business." Jace paced across the living room, agitated.

"Hell. I'm sorry." Mrs. Linney was Evie's elderly, chain-smoking, neon-clothes-wearing neighbor. The woman never seemed to sleep—she was better than a watchdog.

"Mrs. Linney came out on her stoop and cussed the envoy out. Called him an ass for waking up the whole neighborhood at midnight."

Adric couldn't help grinning. "The woman has balls."

Jace snorted. "I swear, she's going to give me gray hairs. I don't know what he'd have done to her if I hadn't been there. But as soon as she saw my cat, she went back inside."

"This is why you need to move Evie and Kyler to Baltimore. The three of you are too isolated up there."

"You think I don't know that? But I promised Kyler he could finish high school in Grace Harbor."

Adric scowled, but gave a curt nod. A promise was a promise.

"Anyway, the night fae announced he was the prince's envoy, tossed me the message and disappeared back into whatever slimy hole he crawled out of. Here." Jace handed over an unsealed black envelope. "Read it for yourself."

Adric removed a sheet of paper the same coal black as the envelope. On it was a message inscribed in silver ink.

Prince Langdon requests the pleasure of a meeting with Lord Adric at his earliest convenience. The envoy will return for your response at midnight.

He crumpled the paper and tossed it on the coffee table. "All right. I'll meet with him."

"No fucking way," Jace returned. "You can't. What if he asks you straight out who killed Tyrus?"

Adric speared his fingers through his spiked-up hair. Langdon couldn't find who'd killed his son. The Darktime would look like a warm-up compared to what he'd bring down on the clan.

He met his friend's eyes. "Then I'll have to lie, won't I?"

Jace squeezed his nape. "A lie like that would be like taking a knife to the gut."

"I've survived worse."

"As your lieutenant—and friend—I'd advise against it."

"You got a better idea?"

His friend's dark brows lowered. "No, damn you."

They'd been over this already. They'd known it was only a matter of time before Langdon tracked his son to Baltimore and demanded answers.

"That's what I thought." Adric's smile was thin. "Sending an envoy to your mate's house was just the start. The prince probably knows the location of every single one of our dens. If I ignore this or go into hiding, he'll go after the clan. I knew this was coming, Jace. Ever since Marjani stuck a knife into his fucking psycho of a son."

CHAPTER 11

Marjani stared into space, listening to Fane breath.

She hated Corban. She was here to kill him.

The prick deserved to be in a cage, and she knew damn well if their positions were reversed, he wouldn't lose any sleep over it. The man should've been a serpent, not a wolf.

It did something to you, to know your own cousin had been behind the plot to drug and rape you. Oh, Corban had kept his hands clean so that he could swear to Adric he hadn't touched her—but he'd masterminded her kidnapping by a small den of half-insane river fada. The den had also kidnapped Tiago do Rio, the Rock Run alpha's youngest brother, in an attempt to set her clan against his, the local river fada. If things had gone as planned, both alphas would've been dead, leaving Corban as the Baltimore alpha and the Rock Run fada in disarray.

Somehow Tiago had fought back, even though he'd been drugged himself, and saved them both. But not before the men had had her...

It was her cougar who had kept her sane by stepping in and taking control.

Corban deserved to die—a slow, miserable death. So why couldn't she stop thinking about him, locked in that iron cage and gradually going mad?

Uncle Leron had been right. She *was* weak.

You're soft. His harsh voice rang in her ears. *A female, and a scrawny one at that. You'll do whatever I fucking say, understand?*

Leron had been a wolf shifter, tall and powerfully built. She'd stared up at him, defiant but hollow with fear. Leron rarely beat her like he did his three sons and Adric, but the threat was always there.

She couldn't do anything about her size—she had her mom's slim build. But both her parents had been clan soldiers, and they'd trained her and Adric in fighting techniques from the time they were toddlers. But her parents were dead, and Leron's mate was even more afraid of him than Marjani was.

So Marjani had trained even harder until her body was a finely honed machine, and she was a wizard with knives. She knew the best way to cut a man so that he'd bleed out in less than a minute, and she was never without two or three blades concealed around her body.

And none of that had helped that night in Baltimore when Shania had slipped the aphrodisiac into her drink. A woman she'd thought was a friend—a den mate.

You survived.

She had to focus on that or go insane.

But is it survival when your nightmares make you mewl like a cub?

Her hand flexed on Fane's chest. Gods, she was pathetic, snuggled up to a man she barely knew—and a part-fae at that. But she liked that wild meadow scent of his. Her cat wanted to roll around in it, take the scent on its fur.

Even the thump of his heart beneath her hand was comforting.

You're weak. A female, and a scrawny one at that. You should've been drowned at birth.

She ground her teeth.

Maybe Adric was right—she was too broken to be out in the world. But she'd spent the past year hiding in their den. Sinking deeper and deeper into her animal.

Fada healed more quickly as their animals, so no one had questioned it. In fact, Adric had encouraged her to remain as her cougar.

By the time she was stronger, it was too late. The cat often overrode the human part of her. Not even Adric knew how much. She'd let the cougar remain in control for long days as she'd healed.

Because she felt afraid as a woman. The woman was weak, vulnerable—but not the cougar. If those men had attacked her cat, it would've ripped out their fucking throats.

"You're thinking too hard," Fane murmured. "Go to sleep."

She grimaced. "Sorry."

He sighed. "You can't, can you?"

Her cheeks heated. She mutely shook her head.

He set his other arm around her waist, and she stiffened, but he kept the touch nonsexual. His long fingers spread over her stomach, warm and comforting.

He hummed, low and hoarse, a rough purr like something out of a ratty old tomcat.

She bit her lower lip, trying not to laugh.

He began to sing, and her jaw slackened. He was *good*, his rough voice perfectly on pitch, but with an edge that made it intriguing...and fucking sexy.

Deep inside, parts of her stirred to life. Parts that hadn't shown any interest in more than a year.

The man could bottle that voice and sell it as a love potion.

She didn't recognize the song, but she guessed it was an old folk song. Dark and mournful, about a woman and her dead lover.

Her breath released. Her eyelids fluttered shut.

"That's it," he murmured. "Sleep." He switched to another sad song.

I can't.

She was out before the end of the second verse.

FANE WOKE BEFORE HER. In the night, they had turned so that his back was to her and she was curled up against his side. Marjani came awake as he slid out of bed. She turned over and watched, slit-eyed, as he moved around the room. Not embarrassed, exactly, but not wanting to talk with him either.

He disappeared into the bathroom and the shower came on.

She fingered the amethyst crystals of her quartz, a gift from Adric after her kidnapping. He'd found her a good match, and she loved how the amethyst ranged in shades from deep purple to smoky gray, but she still mourned her old quartz.

The one the river fada had smashed into pieces and tossed into the filthy waters of the Inner Harbor.

Enough. It wasn't her nature to hide. So she'd embarrassed herself—who gave a shit?

Throwing off the comforter, she got out of bed and pulled a sweater over her T-shirt before lacing on her hiking boots. Her blades went back into their usual places—the dagger and stiletto into the leather sheaths in her boots, the switchblade in her right front pocket. The fishing knife she left in the backpack.

The little round table had an inlaid checkerboard, and she found a box of checkers on a shelf beneath the table. She set up the pieces and idly pushed them around, working on a new strategy.

She'd learned the game from her dad and then kept it up. She and Adric had often played matches on the little checkerboard she carried around with her as they shivered during a long, cold stakeout ordered by Uncle Leron.

The thought of her smart, serious dad made her squeeze her eyes shut. Will Savonett hadn't even wanted to be a soldier. If he'd had his way, he would've been a crystal engineer like Jace. His death, along with her mom's, had left a hole in her heart that nothing could fill.

No one should die so young and far from home.

Fane emerged from the bathroom, jolting her back to the present. His blue eyes crinkled in a smile. "Morning."

"Morning."

All he wore were the skinny black jeans from last night. She couldn't help a quick perusal of his bare chest, all lean, hard muscle with dark blond hair curling over it.

That spark of interest heated her insides again. She pressed her mouth into a line and looked away.

Going into his closet, he pulled on a clean T-shirt and an oatmeal-colored sweater with a black-and-white band across the chest in a traditional Icelandic pattern.

"Hungry?" he asked. "I can get us some breakfast."

"Thank you." She rose to her feet. She wanted to be standing for this. "But first, I want to see this wolf."

He stilled. "No. It's too dangerous."

"I'm not asking your permission. Take me to him, or I'll go myself."

He studied her, clearly trying to decide how best to manage her. She raised her chin, because she wasn't going to be "managed."

"I should call your bluff," he said. "You wouldn't get within ten yards of him before you found yourself locked in a cage, too."

She swallowed hard—and reined in her pride. Clashing with him would get her nowhere. In Baltimore, she was a person of power, the alpha's second. Here she was a fada, lower than dirt as far as the ice fae were concerned. But Fane had treated her well. Hell, he'd probably saved her life.

"Please. I have to make sure it's really him. No one has to know. You can conceal me like you did last night, can't you?"

"How do I know you won't try to stick one of those knives into him?"

"I won't. That's a promise." She'd already rejected that as a bad idea. The fae would know a fada was running loose in the castle.

His hand cupped her face. "I have a hard time saying no to you. Why is that, do you think?" His thumb caressed her cheek.

Their gazes snagged. His eyes were very blue.

She moistened her lips. "I don't know," she whispered.

Those sky-colored eyes heated like twin blue flames. "I think you do." He blew out a breath and released her. "I'll probably regret this, but all right. I'll take you to him. We'll go now, while everyone else is at breakfast."

"Thank you." She scraped a hand over her shaved head and then took a step back. "I just need a minute." She dashed into the bathroom to pee and run a brush over her teeth.

Fane was waiting, arms crossed over his broad chest. "I'll have your promise before we leave this room. You're just going to take a look—nothing else. Is that clear?"

"Yes." She instinctively touched her chest over her quartz. "I give you my word."

He looked at her feet. "Better take the boots off—I don't want you clomping around."

"Don't worry." She paced in a soundless circle around him.

His smile was wry. "I keep forgetting you're a cat. Hang on, let me check the hall." He cracked open the door. "It's clear." He beckoned her closer and took her hand. "You know the drill. Stay close to me and no will see you. Don't talk, and be careful not to brush up against anyone."

"Got it."

Together, they strode into the hall.

CHAPTER 12

Fane had lost his bloody mind.

That was the only explanation. He'd worked hard to make his way in the ice fae court, even though he was only a quarter fae. Earned some respect.

Was he going to throw it all away on some fada he'd just met?

He looked at the somber assassin striding alongside him. Apparently the answer was yes.

The wolf shifter was in Blaer's tower on the castle's east side. Fane chose to walk back the way they'd come, avoiding Sindre's tower to the north.

The maze had remade itself overnight, forming new paths, but since Fane was at the court with Sindre's permission, it opened a passage for him, somehow sensing where he was headed. Fane was used to it, but Marjani glanced from side to side, clearly trying to recognize landmarks.

"Don't bother," he murmured. "It's always changing."

They passed a small pack of fur-clad goblins. Marjani stiffened. The goblins sniffed the air suspiciously, pig-like noses twitching, but when they couldn't see anything, trotted on.

They took another few turns before coming upon twin fae lords—Sindre's nephews—blocking the passageway as they murmured to each other in Icelandic.

When Fane was in stealth mode, no one could see him, but he'd adjusted the magic so that he was visible to Marjani and vice versa. He watched her eye the twins, gorgeous in flowing white shirts and black leather pants, their pointed ears poking through long, wavy blond hair.

Most women would've been stunned speechless at the twins' unearthly beauty, but she merely nodded at the small space between the two men and the wall, and mouthed, "You first."

He couldn't help grinning. Perplexed, she tilted her head in a very feline way. He winked and slid through the gap, Marjani right behind him.

A few turns and they were at the east tower. There they had a piece of luck—the door was open. They walked inside.

Blaer might be equal parts ice fae and night fae, but the night fae was dominant. The large circular room they entered could've been decorated by a vampire. A brass chandelier brooded over the center with tiny fae lights flickering where the candles should have been, and a mist curled over the black marble floor. The walls were covered in red wallpaper flecked with black velvet, and the furniture dark and ornately carved.

Marjani exchanged a look with him, part amusement, part horror.

Setting his mouth to her ear, he pointed at the spiral staircase to the left. "The room with the fada is at the top of the tower."

Together, they walked noiselessly up the three flights. But at the top, their luck didn't hold. The door—a thick oak with steel handles—was shut tight.

Fane muttered a curse. He and Marjani might be invisible, but if a door opened, anyone in the tower would guess a wayfarer had just entered.

He placed an ear to the wood. Beside him, Marjani did the same. When he heard nothing, he lifted a brow at her. Maybe her shifter senses had picked up something he hadn't.

She shook her head. "It's quiet," she whispered. "I don't think anyone else is in there."

"Stay behind me," he whispered back. "If I have to, I'll show myself and make up some story. But you can't let anyone see you."

He waited for her nod and then eased open the door.

The top floor was one large room. The skylights had been covered with some kind of magic, so that dim, constantly moving shadows slithered across the floor.

From his position behind the door, Fane could only see the black wolf's cage, but he knew the room held a kitchenette, a couple of plush black couches—and five 10-by-15-foot iron cages. Bright, shiny cages.

In its pure form, iron was a bright white metal, and Blaer's magic kept the cages from rusting. Somehow those gleaming cages seemed even worse, like a cold, sterile laboratory where unspeakable things went on. Blaer didn't even give the imprisoned fada the dignity of a private bathroom, just had a rudimentary toilet and sink in each cage and straw scattered on the floor.

In the nearest cage, the big black wolf lay listlessly on a sheepskin.

He had to be in agony, surrounded by iron like that. To a fae or fada, even cold iron burned like fire. The sheepskin provided some protection, but the surrounding iron would slowly drain the wolf's energy. And each time he touched one of the bars, it would sear his skin, seeping into his veins until his entire body was inflamed.

As the door opened, the wolf lifted his head a few inches, then let it drop back to the sheepskin. His coat was dull and falling off in patches, his eyes rheumy.

Shame filled Fane. Whatever the wolf may or may not have done, this was just wrong. He didn't even want to tell Marjani that Blaer referred to the room as her "zoo."

The earth fada slid past him into the room. He kept a grip on her arm so that she remained invisible.

An open switchblade appeared in her hand. An iron switchblade.

"Remember your promise," he told her. "You get a look only."

She nodded, her gaze on the sick wolf. A shadow slid over him, creeping across his patchy fur like a ghostly creature from another dimension. Marjani's face was expressionless, but the arm beneath his hand vibrated with suppressed tension.

The black wolf's nostrils twitched. Marjani shook off Fane to move closer.

"Corban," she said. The single word held a world of hate.

The black wolf forced himself up on trembling legs. Mad gold eyes narrowed at her.

"I came here to kill you." Her tone dripped with scorn. "But now I just pity you. Killing you would be a kindness you don't deserve."

Her cousin's lips peeled back in a snarl. Fane couldn't tell if he was warning them off—or laughing at them. A thin stream of saliva dripped from a corner of his jaws.

Marjani stopped a few feet away from the cage.

"You think I don't know why you sent that message to Adric? He"—she jerked her head at Fane—"thinks you couldn't have done it without help, but I bet it didn't take much to convince you. Because you'd love to have Ric here, wouldn't you? But it didn't work. You got me, instead." She compressed her mouth. "Goddess, you're an ass. The clan would never have followed you. They don't want more of Leron. We're making something different. Better."

Corban shuddered. His quartz flickered weakly.

Marjani fingered her own quartz. The purple amethyst shimmered blue, and Fane had the feeling she was sending energy to the other fada. But why?

"You've lost," she said, low and hard. "Die with dignity."

A growl rasped from the wolf's throat. Then he lowered his head in defeat. She released the quartz. "Damn you," she said in a shaking voice.

"We have to leave." Fane crossed the room and grabbed her arm.

Then they both froze at the sound of voices on the stairs below.

CHAPTER 13

$\mathcal{M}$arjani's heart slammed into gear. If they were caught, she didn't know what they'd do to Fane. But she'd be thrown into one of those gleaming iron cages.

Fuck that. She'd die first.

Her cougar surged to life, trying to take over. Claws pricked her fingertips and she knew her eyes had gone a feral blue.

"How many?" Fane whispered, reminding her that she wasn't alone. She had him to think about, too. And he knew the court—if she worked with him, they might both get out of here undetected.

Not now, she hissed at her cougar.

It snarled warningly.

Fane jerked, and she realized she'd snarled aloud.

"Jani?" Their eyes met, and she knew he must see the cougar. And then he did something unexpected. Instead of pulling away like any sensible person would, he wrapped an arm around her. "Shh. I won't let them get you. Now how many?"

She gulped. To her surprise, the cougar subsided, soothed by his scent and calm voice.

Quickly, she sorted the voices and footsteps into separate people—a man and two women. Keeping the switchblade ready in her right hand, she held up her left, showing Fane three fingers.

He nodded and put his finger to his lips. Taking her hand, he made the two of them disappear, and together, they crept toward the door.

Marjani sent a last look at Corban. He panted softly, painfully, head on his paws, eyes half-shut.

Waiting for death.

She gritted her teeth, feeling cheated and angry and deflated, all at the same time. She'd come all this way to kill him, hated him for so long. The man wasn't just her enemy, he was her brother's enemy, too.

And he'd proven he would do anything to be alpha, even tear apart their still-healing clan. Just like his father.

She didn't want to pity Corban. He'd made her and Adric's teenage years a living hell. And later, when he couldn't beat Adric in a fair fight for alpha, he'd tried every dirty trick in the book to undermine him. Marjani and Jace had simply been collateral damage.

Corban needed to die. But not like this, weak and maddened from iron poisoning and as mangy as a third-world dog.

The three fae were on the landing below. "The goblins reported activity in the tower." A man's voice.

Fane eased the door shut and pulled her into a corner opposite the door, keeping her tight against his body. He'd put himself between her and the fae, but she peered around him as the man reached the top of the stairs.

Her jaw loosened. It was the tall, leather-clad fae with cropped silver hair that she'd followed through the portal. So she'd been right to be uneasy; he must've known she was there. But why hadn't he captured her immediately?

Behind him came two women. One rail-thin with ebony skin and silver hair who Marjani would bet was his sister; the other curvy with a night fae's black eyes and an ice fae's blond hair. Both wore short dresses that appeared to have been spun from glitter and cobwebs.

Marjani caught a whiff of the curvy blonde's scent and recoiled. Night fae smelled of graveyards and dank basements, and this woman's odor was strong. She had to be the fae lady in Fane's story.

The silver-haired man shoved the door open and strode inside, followed by the woman who looked like his sister.

"Someone was here," he snapped at Corban. "Who?"

The wolf responded with a feeble growl.

With a curse, the man reappeared in the doorway. "He can't tell me anything as a wolf," he told the curvy blonde. "Can you force him to shift?"

She gave him a level look. "Of course."

He nodded and turned back to Corban.

Marjani gulped soundlessly. Fear sheeted up her spine. Only a fae who knew the secret of their quartz could force an earth fada to shift.

How many fae had Corban told, anyway?

The curvy blonde glanced around, black eyes narrowed. A dark, questing energy whispered over Marjani's skin.

She stilled, afraid to even breathe. Beside her, Fane did the same.

Calm. Cool. Emotionless as a chunk of cheese. A slice of bread.

Night fae fed on negative emotion; the blonde must have sensed Marjani's spike of fear. The only way to hide from a night fae was to remain still—and very, very calm. Another hint of fear, and the woman would be on them.

Marjani's fingers tightened on the switchblade.

A frown creased the blonde's unnaturally perfect face. The seconds ticked by.

One. Two. Three.

More tendrils snaked over Marjani's skin, cold and oily. A scream gathered in her lungs, ready to punch out of her chest.

Four. Five. Six.

"Blaer?" Just when Marjani thought she'd break, the silver-haired man appeared in the doorway. "Is something wrong, love?"

The fae lady shrugged. "I thought I sensed something." She crossed to him, her diamond-studded high heels clicking on the marble floor.

The door closed. Marjani went limp.

She scrubbed her hands over her skin, trying to brush away the slimy feel of the tendrils. And then she went stiff. *Blaer?* She recognized that name. Last year, Sindre had hired Adric to find a Lady Blaer in northern India and bring her home. By then, they'd suspected Corban was behind Marjani's kidnapping, but without proof, Adric couldn't accuse him. Corban had too many allies in the clan. So her brother had sent Corban to India to get him as far away from her—and the clan— as possible.

Beside her, Fane drew a slow inhale through his teeth, and then reached for her hand and glided toward the stairs. She kept her switchblade out as they noise- lessly descended the three flights.

As soon as they entered the maze, Fane sped up. She closed the switchblade, shoved it into her pocket and loped alongside him. She couldn't help being impressed. The man moved as swiftly and silently as a shifter.

He didn't slow down until they were a hundred yards from the dark tower and its shiny cages. He continued at a fast walk, long legs eating up the distance as he slipped between the few fae they encountered. She had to trot to keep up.

The maze twisted and turned in unexpected ways, but he always seemed to know which way to go. She tuned into her quartz, trying to use the tiny crystals to orient herself, but it was like being on a spinning merry-go-round with the directions continually changing. If Fane hadn't been with her, she'd have been lost within a minute.

He didn't speak until they were safely back inside his room. "That's the fada who sent you the message?"

"Yeah." She rubbed her upper arms. "It's funny. I thought when I caught up to Corban and finally had my revenge, I'd feel happy—triumphant. The bastard was behind the attack on me, and he's made no secret of the fact that he wants my brother dead."

Fane touched her cheek. "I'm sorry."

She fought the urge to lean into his hand. She was so damned tired. It seemed like forever since she'd had a good night's sleep.

"I thought I'd feel happy. But I just feel hollow." She sank onto the wood chair and stared at her boots. "Guess I could've stayed home in Baltimore. He's going to be dead in a few days anyway."

Fane slouched on the easy chair, face a little pale. "Sometimes I'm glad I'm not a pureblood."

"That blonde with the scent of a night fae—she's the fae lady in your story?"

"She is. Now you see why I wanted you to leave."

"I felt her energy reaching for us." Marjani rubbed her upper arms, recalling the feel of those snake-like tendrils. "Like during the Darktime."

"The Darktime?"

"My clan—we went through a bad time when I was growing up. A civil war. You must've heard about it."

"Yeah." Fane's eyes were sympathetic. "It's just one more story the purebloods tell about the fada so they can justify treating you as animals."

She grimaced. "Sometimes they're not so far off. The bitch of it was that it was started by the clan elders. The ones who should've known better."

"I didn't know. I'm sorry."

"Yeah," she said flatly. "Killing each other off. Going after whole families. And the night fae were behind it—working with the alpha, my uncle Leron."

"I thought you fada have as little to do with the fae as possible?"

"It's...complicated. It was an alpha challenge that set off the Darktime battles. But it turned ugly, and the night fae helped it along—whipping up people's anger, encouraging revenge killings—so they could feed on the darkness. And my SOB of an uncle let it happen. Hell, he encouraged it. To him, it was all about power."

She heard the tremor in her voice and took a deep breath. Now was not the time for her to dwell on Leron. The man was feeding the trees in the dark Appalachian forest where she and Adric had buried him—and she had more important things to worry about, like the fact that Corban had apparently shared the secret of the earth fada's quartz with more fae than they realized.

"Can this Lady B really force Corban to shift?" she asked Fane.

He lifted a shoulder and let it drop. "I don't know. We're not exactly friends. But you heard her—she seemed sure of herself, like she'd done it before."

"Well, right now, he's too weak to shift. I don't care how strong she is, you can't force a shift on a fada that low in energy. If she tries, she'll kill him."

And it wouldn't be an easy death. A fada caught between shifts died in agony, a monster made up of body parts from both the human and the animal.

"I hope you're right. You don't want him shifting and telling her you're in the castle."

Her mouth twisted. "If she doesn't already know."

He straightened. "What do you mean?"

"That man with her? He's how I got through the portal. He was on a motorbike and I followed him."

"Hell. Why didn't you tell me that last night?"

"I didn't think he saw me, but now I'm not so sure."

"That explains why the goblins were out. That was Jon. He and his twin Krysten are Lady B's right-hand people. They're always with her. We have to assume they know you're in the castle." Fane scraped a hand over his hair. "God's balls. I'm not sure if it would be safe for you to leave even tonight."

"Then maybe I should stay until tomorrow night?" Despite everything, her heart lurched at the chance to spend another day with Fane. "Unless," she added, "I'm a danger to you."

"No. She can't enter this room without my permission. But—" He shook his head.

"What?"

"She's not the only problem here. I'm afraid the king will find out you're in the castle. We can only hide you from him so long."

"Then I'll leave tonight like we agreed."

He blew out a breath. "Let's think on it—maybe I can come up with another plan. Meanwhile, I'll get us some breakfast."

Marjani hesitated, and then nodded. Her stomach was still tight from her encounter with Corban, but when you spend half your life hungry, you learn to eat when you can.

Fane left and she bent forward, elbows on her knees, fingers interlinked.

"Damn you, Corban." She closed her eyes, but all she saw was his too-thin body and mangy fur.

No, damn it. I fucking refuse to feel sorry for him.

He'd tormented her and Adric when they'd been forced to move into Leron's den after the death of their parents. As an adult, he'd supported his father right to the end, even when it became clear that Leron was the worst sort of alpha, tearing the clan apart with his petty feuds and killing any who opposed him. Marjani's own parents had been forced to spend years apart, fighting on separate continents as mercenaries to enrich Leron.

At first Marjani had felt bad for Corban. As the eldest, he took the brunt of Leron's heavy hand. Nothing he did satisfied his dad. But Corban had turned around and beat on his two younger brothers and Adric.

Later, after Adric bested him in the challenge for alpha, Corban had pretended to support him while secretly working against him.

She touched the sharp iron dagger in her boot. It had an ivory handle and a sheath of thick leather to protect her from the iron's poisonous effects. The iron switchblade worked in a pinch, but the dagger was her weapon of choice against a fada or fae.

She was a killer, an assassin. She could slip into that creepy tower and slice Corban's throat in under a minute.

You can't, Jani. You might as well send up a signal announcing there's a fada running loose inside the castle.

What a fucking irony. She'd come to Iceland to kill Corban, and now that he was almost dead, she couldn't just leave it be. Because why the hell would she endanger herself for that prick?

Rising to her feet, she paced across the small room.

An earth fada could kill himself with his quartz. You simply directed all the energy into your heart, speeding it up, making it beat harder and harder until it broke. But Corban's quartz was too weak. Maybe he could've killed himself at the beginning, but he'd waited too long.

She'd tried to send him some energy, but without touching him, very little energy had been transferred. She was a soldier, not a healer.

She fisted her hands and brought them to her forehead, breathing hard. She'd promised Fane just to look—and she had.

If she went back later to do more, that wasn't breaking her promise—was it?

Because if she left without putting her cousin out of his misery, she wasn't any better than him.

CHAPTER 14

Fane returned with two cups of coffee and a steel box holding fruit, granola, nuts and *skyr*, the Icelandic version of yogurt. Jumping up, she took the coffee from him while he set the box on the little table. One cup was nearly white with cream, the other black.

She eyed the coffee with cream longingly, but her mama had raised her to be polite. "Which one do you want?"

"Your choice."

"You sure?"

His lips twitched. "I prefer my coffee black. The cream's for you. I had a feeling you'd like it."

"You guessed right." She handed him the black coffee and took a sip of her own milky-brown brew. *Perfect.* Her eyes slit with pleasure.

"Have a seat and I'll make you a bowl of granola."

"You don't have to wait on me."

"Jani. Have a seat."

She sat back down and watched as he spooned the *skyr* into two bowls of granola, sprinkling nuts on top. He handed one to her and took the other chair.

"I heard some people talking," he said. "The goblins have been called off. That's something, anyway."

She nodded. "Do you know how long Corban has been in the cage?"

"A week, maybe more. But in your world, that's close to a month."

"What do you mean 'in my world'?"

"Time runs differently here. Sometimes a day is a day, and sometimes a day is ten days. But I was here a month ago when Lady B threw him in the cage. Before that, he was her lover."

"Her *lover*?"

He nodded. "For over a year. I don't know what went wrong. Maybe she just got tired of him."

Marjani shook her head. "I thought Corban was smarter than that."

"She's a beautiful woman, and when she amps up her glamour..." Fane spread his hands. "She can have just about any man she wants."

She slid him a look. She had to ask, even if she didn't like the answer. "What about you?"

"Me?" He snorted. "I prefer my balls attached to my body, thank you very much."

She nodded, her cat quietly satisfied. For some damn reason, it was feeling possessive about this man.

"I wish—" He shook his head.

She ate another mouthful of granola. "Maybe"—she looked down at the cereal, suddenly bashful—"you can look me up the next time you're in Baltimore."

Then she forced herself to meet his eyes. Because her—bashful? Adric would split a gut laughing.

But Fane was unlike any man she'd ever known. He was older, cultured. As polished as that diamond in his earlobe. Hell, the man even dressed better than her.

Still, he'd been sending some very definite signals. Last night he'd all but said he'd like to fuck her.

"Maybe." He looked back at his granola. "But I don't get there much."

Well, there was her answer. She'd read his signals wrong. But she couldn't leave it alone. "What about Evie? Don't you ever visit her?"

"Every few years or so. She's better off without me."

She frowned. She couldn't understand a father feeling like that. "I bet she doesn't think so."

He finished his coffee and set it on the small table between them. "Trust me, she is," he said in a tone that didn't invite further questions.

She took the hint and fell silent, concentrating on her breakfast. When she finished the granola, she reached for a peach. It was small but perfectly formed. The first bite sent a tart burst of flavor into her mouth.

She gave a hum of pleasure. "That's so good. It tastes like it was just picked."

"We grow them here."

Fane's gaze was on her mouth. Her heart sped up.

"In Iceland?" she managed to ask.

"There's a huge conservatory on the south side of the castle. The king invited a couple of dryads to live here when their trees were young, and they've grown up in the conservatory. They grow things year-round—fruit, vegetables."

She nodded and took another bite of her peach. Dryads were famous for their green thumbs.

Fane was still looking at her mouth. Her lips tingled. She swallowed the bite. "What?"

He leaned forward. "You have peach juice—here." He touched the corner of her mouth, brushing the juice away with his thumb.

"Thanks." His eyes were so beautiful with that dark fringe of eyelashes, like a clear pool surrounded by lush vegetation.

Cool fingers caught her chin.

She stilled. In the past year, no man but her brother had touched her.

The fear was there, but her hunger for touch was stronger. Fane took the half-eaten peach and set it on the table, then stood up, drawing her with him.

She raised her eyes to his. He was a good foot taller than her. He might not be a fada, but the man had muscles. In a bare-handed fight between the two of them, he might just be able to win.

She braced herself for a wave of panic, but her cat gave a happy little rumble. It wanted to rub up against him, roll in his grass-green scent like catnip.

And even the human part of her recalled how he'd held her last night when she'd needed it.

"We have some time to kill." His husky voice vibrated in her body.

"Yes."

He trailed the backs of his fingers over her cheek. "I know something bad happened to you."

She growled, a harsh, feral sound. Knowing her anger was misplaced—she wasn't pissed off at him, she was angry at the men who'd attacked her—but unable to help it.

"What do you know about it?"

"Hey." He stroked her nape. "Fine—we won't talk about that. But I'm going to kiss you, all right?"

"I—" She moistened her lips, and his eyes tracked the movement. "I don't know."

"What do you mean?"

"I don't know," she repeated miserably. "I haven't been kissed for so long. Not in that way."

"Why don't we take it slow? If you don't like it, just tell me to stop and I will. Any time—you just say the word."

All the spit left her mouth. But it was only a kiss. She trusted that when he said he'd stop at any time, he would.

"All right," she whispered.

"Mm." His hum of approval was almost a purr. He gathered her closer, one arm around her waist, while his other hand kept up those soothing strokes on her nape. "You're so beautiful."

She traced her fingers over his high cheekbones, touched his full lower lip. His jaw was covered with dark, grainy stubble. "So are you."

"You think?" He chuckled—and then his mouth touched hers. She stiffened, but he merely brushed his lips over hers, soft and easy. His breath was coffee-scented.

He traced his tongue over the seam of her lips and she closed her eyes. He touched his mouth to each lid, and then continued to her earlobe where he sucked the small gold hoop into his mouth along with the lobe. He gave it a nip, and when she gave a shiver of delight, licked his way up the rim of her ear before bringing his mouth back to hers.

A glow filled her, a warm, easy sensuousness that she floated on like a summer river, afraid to dive deeper.

Afraid even to think about it for fear it wouldn't last.

His tongue slipped into her mouth, sliding along her still closed teeth. She opened them and swayed closer, and he swept inside. Her tongue rose to meet his, and for the first time in forever, she was kissing a man.

Wonder filled her, mixed with the warmth.

He gave a sexy growl that sent tingles up her spine and raised his head long enough to say, "You taste like peaches."

Then he slanted his head and gave her a deep kiss. The kind a man gives a woman he wants to take to bed.

She rose up on her toes to get closer, fingers digging into his shoulders.

The position put her lower belly against his erection. He pressed against her, hard. Insistent.

She stilled. Not pulling away, but not participating any longer either.

He loosened his grip on her and lifted his head. "That's enough, I think." He pressed a last kiss to her forehead and set her away.

Her eyelids lifted slowly, reluctantly.

A smile tugged at his mouth. She felt a slash of hurt—he found this amusing? —until she saw how his eyes had darkened to midnight.

"Best not to start anything we can't finish."

She gulped. She longed to tell him she wanted to finish it—but she didn't. Not really. It was enough for now that she'd kissed a man without freaking out and going clawed on him.

Her mouth trembled around the edges.

"Hey, it's okay." He tapped her nose.

Her cheeks heated. She clenched her fists and blew out a breath. Both Adric and Suha, the clan healer, had told her repeatedly that she had nothing to be ashamed of. It wasn't her fault she'd been kidnapped and drugged, then forced to submit to the four men in the den. They'd even smashed her quartz so she couldn't shift or draw on its energy.

There was no way she could've stopped them. Four against one just wasn't fair.

She *knew* this—in her head, and maybe even in her heart.

But sometimes the shame still threatened to swamp her. She was a trained fada soldier and her brother's second. She'd helped Adric win control of the clan against impossible odds. More importantly, she was a Gifted strategist, someone who could plot things out so far in advance it was almost like she could predict the future.

So how in Hades had she got caught in Corban's fucking trap?

Fane turned away. She sent him a sad look, but his attention was on the white mist forming in his palm.

A fae message.

Marjani tensed. She edged closer, trying to read it, but the black words scrolling over the mist were in a language she didn't know.

Fane's jaw hardened. The mist dissolved, and he slammed the side of his fist against the wall. "Bloody hell."

"Something wrong?" Uneasiness prickled her scalp even though she knew there were a hundred reasons why Sindre might send Fane a message, none of them having to do with her.

Until he turned, face set. "King Sindre requests the honor of your presence."

Her stomach lurched. "Me? He found out I'm here?"

A curt nod.

"But how?"

His gaze slid from hers. "I told him."

"You told him?" She desperately searched his face. "But why? I thought—"

"Haven't you figured it out?" A self-mocking smile curled his mouth. "I'm his spy, love. He sent me to watch you."

"His *spy*?" She took a step back. "You'd give me to them? Put me in one of those fucking cages?" Her voice rose. It felt like all the air had been sucked from the room.

She swallowed and tried to take a deep breath.

But it was too late. Her cougar awakened. Her claws slid out and a furious growl ripped from her chest.

Fane stiffened but did nothing to defend himself. "No. Not in a cage. That's Lady B's thing, not the king."

She stalked toward him. "You're dead," she said in a thick, barely human voice.

He spread his hands. "You can tear me to pieces, love, but Sindre still wants to see you."

The cougar didn't want to hear that. It tried to force the change on her, but she maintained control—barely.

But both of them wanted blood. She retracted her claws and reached for her iron dagger. In the next instant, she had Fane backed up to the wall, the knife at the sweet spot over his carotid.

The iron seared his skin. A blister formed at the point, and the scent of burning flesh filled her nostrils. His throat worked, but he remained silent, gazing back with those fucking sky-colored eyes.

"You didn't have to bring me inside the castle." Her voice was harsh with her cougar's rasp. "You could've opened a portal and let me out."

"Would you have left?"

No, but he couldn't have known that. Not for sure. She glared at him without speaking.

"And besides," he added, "the goblins would've caught you. They were hoping to flush you out. The minute we moved away from the wall, they'd have been on us, and you'd be in a cage right now."

She sneered. "Why should I believe you?"

"Because you can scent a lie."

She scowled. But he was right—his scent had the clean bite of truth.

"This way," he said, "you have a chance. The king is old, and frankly, a little bored. Even a spider eventually gets tired of spinning webs. If you interest him, he won't let Lady B get hold of you."

"What do you mean if I interest him?" She pressed the dagger's point deeper.

Blood welled up, and then the iron seared the tiny wound, sealing it. He had to be in pain, but he didn't blink an eye. The man might be a manipulative, two-faced prick, but he was no coward.

"Talk to him," he urged. "That's all I'm saying."

She bared her teeth. "And if I kill you first?"

"That's your choice, of course. But I'm your only friend in the court."

"My friend?" She sneered. "I'd like to see how you treat your enemies."

His eyes flickered but he stared back calmly until she cursed and released him. Stepping back, she dragged the back of her hand over her mouth in a deliberate gesture.

Wiping the taste of him away.

He had the grace to look ashamed. "I'm sorry. I shouldn't have kissed you."

"You think?" Her look should've fried him where he stood.

Turning on her heel, she strode into the bathroom to rinse her dagger. She shoved it back into her boot and gripped the stone sink, Fane's words thudding in her mind. *If you interest him, he won't let Lady B get hold of you.*

Boredom was a fae weakness, especially with an old fae like Sindre who'd been everywhere, done everything. She'd slit her own throat before she'd be any fae's whore, but maybe she could use Sindre's boredom against him. Play his games for a short while and watch for a chance to escape.

Think, Jani.

But even the most Gifted strategist needed data to work with, and there was too damn much she didn't know. She could guess why Lady Blaer was capturing fada—she fed on their emotional distress—but why did Sindre allow it? And why have her followed? Was it standard procedure, or had he been watching for her— or maybe Adric—in particular?

But anything was better than a cage. To be enclosed like that, trapped and at that fae bitch's mercy...

Her throat closed up. She gulped several breaths and then splashed cold water on her face.

When she returned to the bedroom, Fane was seated on the wood chair gazing down at his clasped hands. He looked...so alone.

Her growl was for herself. She was *not* going to soften toward the prick.

As he rose to his feet, his gaze swept over her. She tensed, wondering if he'd try and take her knives from her. She'd beg if she had to—without the iron dagger, she was helpless against Sindre. Teeth and claws would be useless against such a powerful fae.

But instead, he asked something totally unexpected. "Do you have to wear the quartz over your heart, or can you hide it somewhere else on your body?"

She instinctively brought her hand to where it was tucked beneath her sweater. "Why?"

He expelled a breath. "You didn't hear this from me, understand?" When she nodded, he continued, "Because if Lady B captures you, you don't want to be wearing that quartz. I can confirm this much—she's figured out a way to control earth fada with their quartz. You can hide that one on your body, and I'll get you another."

Marjani fingered the switchblade in her front pocket. Could she trust Fane? She was still reeling at the big fat secret he'd hidden from her.

But it was true that the fada could be controlled by their quartz. With the right words, a fae could enslave a fada. And apparently Corban had been stupid enough to give Blaer the secret words.

"All right. But I want your promise that you won't tell anyone I switched."

"I promise," he said immediately. "Unless Sindre asks me directly. I can't lie to him."

Can't, he'd said. And something else he'd said niggled at her.

"What do you mean, you can confirm this much? What aren't you telling me?"

"Haven't you figured it out?" He eyed her sorrowfully. "I'm under a *geas*, love. I made a bargain with the king."

CHAPTER 15

A *geas.*

Marjani's mouth twisted. Fane was bound to the king...had been working for him all this time.

He'd warned her that Sindre had spies everywhere. Hell, he'd flat out told her not to trust him. But had she listened? No.

She'd willingly come with him inside the castle, slept in the same bed. She'd even allowed the bastard to kiss her.

Holy singing crystals, did she know how to pick men.

His eyes flickered, and she knew he'd seen her contempt. He stared down his straight nose at her. "Do you want another quartz or not?"

"Yes." She swallowed and made herself say, "Thank you."

Because if it kept her out of a cage, she'd be grateful to him even if it choked her.

"We don't have much time. Sindre's an impatient man. But I know where I can get one outside the castle. I'll be right back."

And then he was gone, like the Flash in those human movies. One second, he was there; the next, the room was empty.

She sat down and fiddled with the checkers again. But she couldn't focus.

She gazed unseeingly at the red checker in her hand. *I trusted you.*

She felt again his mouth on hers, his hands on her body. He'd been so gentle with her. Careful.

A black rage filled her head. She slammed the checker down on the board, denting the inlaid wood and scattering the other pieces across the table. A few fell on the floor.

With a growl, she gathered up the checkers and returned them to their box before getting up to pace restlessly to and fro. *Forget him. It's Sindre you have to worry about.*

After what felt like an hour but was really only about ten minutes, Fane slipped back into the room with a quartz about the same size as hers. "Will this do?"

She turned the quartz over in her hand. It was an ordinary milky quartz, not amethyst, but it hummed a weak tune. If necessary, she could probably even make it glow to fool the fae.

"I think so. Yeah."

She undid the knot in the leather cord securing her amethyst and tucked it into her bra before tying a new knot around the substitute quartz. She dropped the cord over her head. "I'm ready."

"Jani?" Fane reached for her. When she just stared at his hand, he let it drop to his side. "I'm sorry."

"Why?" Anger and hurt crammed her throat like sharp gravel. "I'm nothing to you. Just a job for the king."

"That's not true."

She picked up her backpack. "Just take me to him."

He blew out a breath and then opened the door. "Fine."

This time, Fane did nothing to conceal Marjani's presence. She attracted plenty of attention with her shaved head, drab clothes, and hiking boots. The looks ranged from coldly appraising to pity.

She stomped past, deliberately slamming her boot heels onto the bright blue tiles.

A pack of goblins trotted up. They swirled around her, snapping and snarling. She hissed and showed her fangs, and they gave high-pitched laughs like finger-nails scraping down a chalkboard before continuing by.

The maze grew increasingly complicated, crisscrossing itself and turning abrupt corners. At times the pearly walls pressed in so the two of them had to walk in single file.

"I thought the king wanted to see me," she muttered.

"He has a peculiar sense of humor."

"Fucking awesome."

Disoriented, she drew on her quartz, and discovered that she could "see" a pattern in the maze: two lefts and a right, three rights and a left, and so on, always heading steadily north. It was kind of like plotting a path to kings row in checkers.

She memorized the sequence. If she somehow escaped Sindre with her fur intact, she didn't want to get lost in his damn maze.

"This way." Fane ducked through an archway. At the end of a long hall was a huge oak door, leading to what her internal GPS told her was the north tower.

Her stomach knotted. She palmed her switchblade.

"Put that away, damn it." He grabbed her arm. "You can't fight your way out of this. You have to bargain with him."

He was right, much as she hated to admit it. She shoved the switchblade back into her pocket.

"There. Now let me go."

His grip tightened. "I'm not your enemy. Remember that."

"So you keep saying," she spat back. "And yet here I am."

Fane released her. "I'm sorry."

The black rage washed over her again. "Go to Hades," she grated, and pushed past him.

Fane easily passed her with those long legs of his and reached the door first. It swung open on silent hinges, and she stalked into the tower on that wave of anger.

She was in a spacious antechamber. A big bodyguard with long black hair and silver eyes gave her a small bow. No scent, but maybe Sindre had given him one of those charms.

"Welcome, senhorita," he said in a southern European accent. "The king is expecting you. You, also," he said to Fane. "Please, enter."

He indicated an arched doorway. Marjani nodded and continued through the door, Fane on her heels. They were in a huge, high-ceilinged room that took up most of the tower. She blinked.

Because it was snowing.

She shot a look up, but no, a glass-and-steel dome capped the tower. And yet, fat white flakes drifted down to settle on the marbled granite floor and the furniture scattered here and there in intimate groupings.

Silver and blue fae lights floated through the falling snow, augmenting the natural light from the long, narrow windows, and leafless trees around the perimeter stretched gnarled limbs toward the feeble sunlight. The walls held towering bookcases filled with leather-bound books and museum-quality vases and statuettes, and an arched doorway like the one they'd come through marked each of the four compass points.

Presiding over it all was an impossibly beautiful man on an ivory velvet couch, one sinewy arm slung along the back, head tipped to the snowflakes. His white-blond hair spilled over broad shoulders, and he wore pale gray pants and a collarless white linen shirt that hugged his lean torso.

Sindre.

She didn't need Fane's whisper to know who he was. The man reeked of silver and power, the kind only an old, old fae could gather.

Not that he looked his age. She knew the king had seen more than a thousand turns of the sun, but he could've been Fane's slightly older brother. They had the same sculpted features with slanted cheekbones and a straight, definite nose.

He lowered his chin to look at Marjani. She concealed a shiver, because his eyes gave his age away. They were the cold gray of glacial ice, the eyes of a man who's seen entire civilizations come and go.

"Marjani Savonett." Sindre scrutinized her as if she were a butterfly pinned to a corkboard. "Welcome to my court."

The knot in her belly tightened another notch. It was never a good thing when a fae addressed you by your full name.

Setting her backpack by the door, she squared her shoulders and made herself walk forward. "Your highness. Peace to you and yours." She inclined her head. "I apologize if I'm intruding."

Those frosty eyes bored into hers. She forced herself not to squirm.

"You couldn't have entered the castle without an invitation. Who invited you, I wonder?" He glanced at Fane, who remained a little behind her and to the side, feet apart and hands at his sides like a soldier at attention.

"I followed a man in," she said before Fane could reply. "A dark-skinned man with silver hair," she added, carefully sticking to the truth. "He didn't see me. He was on a motorbike."

"Lord Jon?" Sindre asked Fane.

"I wasn't there, your highness."

"No matter." The king returned his gaze to Marjani. "I wanted to meet you, anyway."

She swallowed. "Oh?"

A snowflake landed on her cheek and instantly melted, leaving an icy droplet behind. She brushed it away as Sindre unfolded his long body from the couch and strolled toward her. She clenched her toes in her boots and remained where she was.

He paused a few feet away, smelling of silver and snow.

She had to tip back her head to meet his eyes. He was even taller than Fane, with eyebrows and lashes the same white-blond as his hair. The snowflakes caught on them, forming glittering crystals.

Her fingers twitched. She'd never craved the reassurance of one of her knives so much, even though Sindre would probably freeze her in her tracks—literally— before she could stick a blade into him. Ice fae drew life-energy from the movement of molecules. Even young ice fae could suck the energy out of liquid water, turning it to ice, and the most powerful could draw energy from living things.

"You did well, Fane," Sindre said without taking his gaze from her. "Bringing her to me. I like a man who thinks for himself."

Out of the corner of her eye, she saw Fane give a tight nod.

Her lungs constricted. Was that what he'd done? *Brought* her to Sindre?

Fane shot her a miserable look.

Don't think about it. Whatever Fane had or hadn't done wasn't important now. Not with this beautiful, deadly male eyeing her like a hungry lion would a rabbit.

Her chin lifted. "I brought myself. If Fane helped, he was only doing what I wanted."

Sindre quirked a brow. "I beg your pardon." His voice was soft and silky. Mocking.

She shrugged, out of her depth and sinking fast. Gods, she hated playing fae games. But the rage still burned in her, and it was rapidly being transferred to this mocking male.

She set her jaw. "Are you going to put me in one of those iron cages?"

Displeasure flitted across his face. "You know about the cages?" The falling snow came down harder, and the already cool tower grew even chillier.

"Why? Are they a secret?" She deliberately didn't glance at Fane, but Sindre did.

"A secret? That's a strong word for it." He paced a slow circle around her, his expensive leather shoes kicking up the snow into small white clouds. "But an envoy should know better than to share my private business."

She turned with him. "The man in that cage is *my* business."

"Not anymore. He renounced your brother as his alpha."

Was there anything Sindre didn't know? Fuck trying to talk her way out of this. She might be a strategist, but she had the feeling he was five moves ahead of her.

She slipped her iron dagger from her boot. "Look, just let me leave and—" At a sound behind her, she broke off and whirled around, backing up so she could keep Sindre in sight.

The big, long-haired guard sprinted toward her, an iron dagger in each hand. She gripped her dagger and took a fighting stance.

The king flung up a hand. "Stop. I'll handle this."

The guard halted, and then with a jerk of his chin, sheathed his daggers. But he remained in the tower, standing beneath a twisted gray tree with his arms folded over his broad chest.

She turned back to Sindre. "I swear I'm not here to mess with you or any of your people. That fada you have in the cage? He's my enemy. I'm not here to release him—in fact, I came to kill him."

"And if I'd like you to stay here at the court for a few days? We get so few fada visitors."

"A few days? And then I can leave?"

The king's mouth curved. "It's a deal." He held out his hand for Marjani to shake.

Behind him, Fane gave a tiny shake of his head.

She licked dry lips. Fane had deceived her—and yet, for some damn reason, she trusted him to help her to the extent he could.

"What, exactly," she asked Sindre, "are the terms of this deal?"

The king brought his hand back to his side. "You owe me, Marjani Savonett. You *will* stay for as long as I desire."

Crap, there was her full name again. At least he didn't know her true-name, the one given to her by her parents. But she still felt a pull to obey him.

"I owe you? How?"

"You spent the night in my castle. You ate my food, drank my ale."

Fane made a small movement. "That was my food, willingly shared. She ate and drank nothing of yours. And she stayed in my room."

"But I own you," Sindre returned.

Fane's eyes flickered. But he just replied calmly, "Room and board when I'm at the court are part of the terms."

Marjani's gaze darted between the two men. Was it true? She didn't actually owe Sindre anything?

The king's mouth compressed. He strolled past her, hands clasped behind his back. She stayed in place, gripping the dagger and turning with him in a strange little dance.

He halted. "Name your price. Cash. Land. Precious stones." He flicked his fingers, and a handful of diamonds the size of walnuts showered onto a round marble table.

Marjani's jaw slackened.

"Well?" Sindre demanded.

She wrenched her gaze from the glittering pile. "I'm not for sale."

"No? Then take it and give it to your brother Adric. He's done his best, but it will be a long time before your clan recovers from the Darktime. And meanwhile, you live in your cramped city dens instead of running free as your animals. You have so few young—one or two live births a year at most. If something doesn't happen soon—or if Adric dies—your clan won't survive."

"Damn you," she breathed. Because it was true. Every word of it.

And together, those diamonds were probably worth more than the entire clan made in a year.

She fingered the dagger's ivory handle. "Stay here at the court. What does that mean?"

"You'll be my guest. No cages, I promise."

"And how long is a few days?"

"That's negotiable. A turn of the sun, perhaps more."

"And my duties?"

Suddenly, Sindre was right in front of her. He ran a finger down her cheek. "Take the diamonds. I promise you'll enjoy yourself. And your brother will thank you."

She sent a last look at the diamonds and backed up. Because she couldn't do it, not even for the clan. And Adric wouldn't thank her. In fact, if she sold her freedom for the clan, it just might break him.

"I said, I'm not for sale."

"As you say." Sindre snapped his fingers.

A black-haired female with an Irish woman's creamy skin appeared with two crystal flutes balanced on a silver tray. She crossed the floor with a supple grace that reminded Marjani of a fada, although she didn't smell like a fada.

In fact, like the big guard, she had no scent at all. And why did the guard look so familiar?

Sindre took the crystal flutes from her tray and offered one to Marjani. "Champagne?"

She shook her head. No way was she going to take even a single thing from this man. "No thanks."

With a shrug, he took a sip of champagne, and then set both glasses back on the tray. The woman set the tray on a side table and then gathered up the diamonds, placing them in a drawer that opened in the trunk of one of the leafless trees before going to stand next to the big, expressionless guard.

Sindre strolled closer, his gray eyes glinting like sun on ice. She stared into them, mesmerized.

Why fight him? She wasn't mated. It might even be fun... And he was so fucking beautiful.

Fane cleared his throat. "Excuse me. Frog in my throat."

But the spell was broken. Sindre scowled, and she realized he'd tried to ensnare her with a glamour.

Inside, the cat angrily swished its tale.

"What about power?" the king asked. "You're strong. Smart. You must've wondered why your brother is alpha instead of you."

Her mouth moved in a soundless no, but she couldn't make herself utter it out loud—because it would be a lie. She *had* wondered. She'd been at Adric's side from the start. They acted almost as co-alphas, making most decisions together. But the final say was his.

Sindre pressed his advantage. "You could be alpha instead. Your power would be such that your brother would willingly follow you. In fact, you could allow him to remain as alpha of your home clan and rule over all the earth fada clans. Think about it." Soft, seductive tones. "All you have to do in exchange is stay with me for a little while. No cage—I promise. And then you'd be free to go home and take your place as the most powerful earth fada in the world."

Her palms were sweating. She tightened her grip on the dagger. Yeah, she was tempted—who wouldn't be?

But deep down, she knew Adric made a better alpha than she ever would. He wasn't just strong, he was a natural leader. She might be the one with the Gift of strategy, but he had both vision and the ability to gain people's cooperation. The clan followed him because they believed in him, trusted that he had their best interests at heart.

And he'd earned her loyalty a hundred times over.

"No," she said in a clear, strong voice. "I have all the power I need. Just let me go."

Sindre stared at her for a moment that stretched on and on until Marjani's nerves screamed with the tension.

"All right," he said at last. "I have one last offer for you."

A hush fell over the room. At some point, the snow had stopped falling.

Her gut tingled uneasily. This was it. The offer he'd been leading up to, the one he expected to clinch the deal.

But what could he offer besides wealth and power?

For some reason she glanced at where the man and woman waited by the tree. Their faces were expressionless, the perfect servants. But she could've sworn they were urging her to say no.

Fane spoke. "Your highness?"

"What?" Sindre growled.

"Pardon the interruption, but as you know, the woman is the Baltimore alpha's only sister. It wouldn't do to make an enemy of him."

The king brushed that away with a wave of his elegant hand. "But does he want to make an enemy of me?"

"Still," Fane said. "Lord Adric won't let this go. He recently did a favor for the sun fae, and the queen might ally herself with him."

Actually, that favor had been done over six years ago, and the sun fae had paid Adric well. But Marjani wasn't stupid enough to point that out.

Sindre seated himself on the couch again, his arms stretched along the back like the wings of a large bird of prey. "But if our guest agrees, then how could he possibly be upset?"

Fane opened his mouth to argue, but Sindre cut him off. "Let her answer." His pale eyes turned on her. "I can gift you with a protection charm that would make you impossible to kill. No one could even *touch* you without your permission. Think about it. No one could hurt you, ever again."

She swallowed sickly. "What do you know about that?"

A shrug. "I hear things. Knowledge, after all, is power. Think about it. You'd never be afraid again."

She stared at him. To never feel afraid again. Never to feel helpless. That would be a gift indeed.

Temptation sucked at her, seductive as Sindre's glamour.

Because those feral river fada had stripped her bare in the worst possible way. They'd tricked her into drinking an aphrodisiac, a powerful magical drug. She'd started out fighting them, but in the end, she'd lost all her pride and begged for more.

Suha had explained it was the fault of the aphrodisiac. The drug made you crave sensation—the pleasure of sex, the bite of pain...

"You survived, honey," the healer had told her, over and over. "That's the important thing. No one could've held out against the dose they gave you."

But Marjani couldn't shake the shame. That she'd lost control, begged her rapists for more...she, a soldier and Adric's second-in-command.

"No." She backed toward the exit, dagger out, hoping no one saw the tremble in her hand. "I can protect myself."

"Can you?"

The click of high heels sounded behind her. Marjani spun around as the bodyguard moved to intercept the newcomer.

"It's Lady Blaer," said Sindre. "Let her in."

The guard inclined his head. "As you wish." He ushered in the fae lady with a flourish just this side of mocking.

"My lord." She crossed to where Sindre sat on the couch and placed an air kiss on each of his cheeks before turning to Marjani. "So you found the other fada."

The *other* fada? Marjani glanced at Fane, but he seemed as puzzled as she was.

"You're trying to strike a bargain with her, aren't you?" Blaer's black gaze moved over Marjani.

An icy sweat trickled down her vertebrae.

"And if I am?" Sindre said.

"Perhaps I can help."

"Be my guest."

Anger flared in Marjani. Typical fae, discussing her as if she weren't there—as if she were somehow less than them. *Well, fuck you, too.*

A growl vibrated her chest. Inside, the cat tried to claw its way out. She was tempted to let it, but first, she needed more information.

Blaer's eyes narrowed. "It was you in my tower earlier, wasn't it? If you're here to free Corban, I might take you in his place."

Marjani stared back stonily.

"Not him, then." The fae woman nodded—and went for the jugular. "But what about the big brown wolf?"

Marjani's heart skipped a beat. "What big brown wolf?"

"I didn't get his name. Yet."

Marjani's stomach hollowed. *Please don't let it be Luc.*

She'd been half-expecting him ever since she landed in Iceland. When she hadn't seen him, she'd figured Adric had held him off, that her brother had trusted she could handle this herself.

She should've known better.

Blaer's pink lips stretched in triumph. Meanwhile, Sindre looked on detached, like they were pawns on a chessboard being pushed around for his amusement.

Marjani's fury spiked. Inside, her cougar spat and snarled. Luc might not be her mate, but he was a friend. A good one.

"Look, bitch." She stepped closer to Blaer, crowding her. "It's one thing to cage a man who's turned his back on us. But mess with the brown wolf, and you'll be sorry. We'll hunt you down." She touched her dagger to Blaer's stomach where the poison from the iron would do the most damage.

"Is that a threat?" the mixed-blood fae hissed back.

"Yeah." She let the cat blaze into her eyes. "It is."

"But your clan tried that already, remember? When Sindre hired you to find me. Your brother sent Corban after me, and look how that turned out." Ignoring the dagger, Blaer leaned closer. "Do. Your. Worst. *Fada.*"

"Blaer, *min*," Sindre interrupted. "You don't have my permission to bargain with the fada."

"No?" Blaer slanted him a smile. "I'm only trying to help, my lord. She's worried about that brown wolf. He's a friend, maybe more. You could use him as leverage."

"So I gathered." He raised a blond brow at Marjani. "So what do you say? Will you trade your freedom for his?"

Her limbs locked.

The king's mouth curved. He'd won, and he knew it.

She fingered the dagger. Sweet Goddess, she wanted to thrust it into his conniving heart. "I want to see this wolf first."

"Your highness." Fane again. "Let her go. This is beneath you."

Without taking his gaze from her, Sindre flicked his fingers. Magic hummed in the air. She gasped as frost spread up Fane's legs. He sucked in a breath and locked his knees.

Blaer watched with an avid expression, clearly feeding on his pain.

"Accept the bargain," the king told Marjani. "Or Fane dies."

No. Hell, no.

Fane was nothing to her. The man had been lying to her ever since she arrived. Maybe not straight out, but lies of omission were still lies. He'd let her think he was on her side when the whole time he'd been spying on her.

The ice covered Fane's chest and crept toward his throat. He moved his mouth but the only sound he could make was a croak that raised every hair on her body.

His eyes met hers, desperate and yet stoic.

She swung back to Sindre. "Enough," she gritted. "I said I'll bargain with you. But first, I want to see this wolf."

The king cast a pointed look at her dagger. Without taking her gaze from his, she bent and shoved it into its sheath.

"Happy?" she growled as she straightened back up.

"Very," was the silky reply.

CHAPTER 16

It had been a long time since Fane had been subjected to one of Sindre's punishments. He'd forgotten how much it hurt.

And the king was a master at dragging out the torture.

His feet went cold, and then hot, as if they'd been plunged into an ice bath. Then they went numb. The ice crept up his body as Sindre sucked energy from vital molecules.

It was like being buried alive. His heart and lungs slowed. He couldn't move or speak.

Panic galloped up his spine, and he couldn't even beg for mercy because his fucking vocal cords wouldn't work. He stood there, frozen in place, hoping he wouldn't lose his balance and topple to the floor.

Just when he thought that this time Sindre meant to kill him, the king waved his hand and the ice melted. Now the real agony began as his frozen limbs came back to life. First, his hands and feet pricked like a thousand needles were being driven into them, then the nerve endings lit up like he'd been set on fire.

He put his hands on his thighs and bent over, sucking in oxygen and shaking so hard his teeth clattered like castanets.

"Come." Sindre held out a hand to Marjani.

Fane jerked up his head. "No," he rasped as the king teleported her out of the room, followed immediately by Blaer. "You bloody bastard."

The terms of the *geas* bound him to obey Sindre's direct orders in return for his generous pay—he was a millionaire in the human world—but the king hadn't thought to forbid Fane to follow. Probably figured he wouldn't dare.

What could he do against two fae as powerful as Sindre and Blaer? But he couldn't just return to his room without trying to help Marjani. He felt enough of a coward as it was.

Pushing himself upright, he staggered to the door and leaned against the jamb, lungs heaving.

Gods, he'd never hated himself so much as when he'd confessed to Marjani that he'd been spying on her.

That was the problem with a *geas*. You never knew when it would turn around and bite you in the arse. Back when he'd made the agreement with Sindre, it had seemed like a good idea. He was forty years old and his human mom had just died. He'd been making a living as a fisherman in Newfoundland. His dad had set him up with his own boat, and he had a crew of two, men he'd grown up with. But already his friends had started to comment on how Fane never seemed to age.

And he'd itched to see more of the world.

Then he'd discovered he had this Gift for moving fast...and disappearing. When he'd shown his dad, Arne had invited him to the ice fae court to meet Sindre, saying, "The king can always use another wayfarer."

A fae king's envoy? Fane had jumped at the chance. Hell, it was an opportunity most men would've killed for—and Fane felt a little as if he had.

Only the man he'd slain was himself. As the king's envoy, he'd seen things that had made his blood curdle.

He'd never directly harmed someone, but no one would call him innocent. With each decade, a bit more of him died, until he was becoming as jaded as a pureblood.

But he'd be damned if he'd let Marjani get sucked into this world.

Think. He pressed a hand to his pounding head.

He couldn't ignore a direct command from Sindre, but the king hadn't ordered Fane *not* to help her. So he had to get her away from the king before he could invoke the *geas*.

The black-haired guard opened the door for Fane. A Portuguese river fada, he was under a *geas*, too, along with his Irish mate. The Irishwoman came up on Fane's other side.

"Go after her," she hissed. "Before it's too late."

Fane lurched into the hall and started toward the east tower.

There was no way he could use his Gift to race to Marjani. Even a slow walk was agony, each step spiking pain up his legs. He gritted his teeth and concentrated on putting one foot in front of the other.

The maze was suddenly in a forgiving mood; or more likely, Sindre was too distracted to play his games. Instead of hindering Fane, the path led him straight to Blaer's tower.

By the time he arrived, he was covered in a cold sweat. The three flights loomed before him like a steep mountain. He clutched the banister and started climbing. By the second landing, his heart felt like it was about to explode out of his chest. He halted to catch his breath, and then grimly continued up.

The thick oak door was shut tight. No chance of sneaking in.

The hell with it, then. He shoved it open.

Marjani stood between Sindre and Blaer, staring at the new fada. Fane's stomach twisted. She looked so small and defenseless between the pair of tall, blond fae.

Blaer flicked him a speculative glance, but Sindre's gaze was locked on Marjani, his lean face hungry. Like she was a special treat, one he intended to savor for long hours.

Nearby, the black wolf lay on its side, eyes closed and tongue hanging out of its mouth, panting softly. But Marjani only had eyes for the rangy earth fada crouched in the cage next to the black wolf's. He was naked save for his quartz. Deep scratches and bites marred his teak skin—the poor bastard must have been caught by the goblins—and his face was bruised, his eyes swollen shut.

Marjani bit her lower lip. "Oh, Luc."

At her voice, the man started. "Jani?"

"Yeah."

He pulled himself up to his full height, glaring at Sindre and Blaer from beneath swollen lids before looking back at her. "You're here."

The king set a hand on Marjani's arm, but she shook him off to move closer to her friend. To Fane's surprise, Sindre allowed it. But then, he was a canny man, and patient when it suited him.

She shook her head sorrowfully. "You had to follow me, didn't you?"

Luc's bloodied mouth turned up in a lopsided grin. "You knew I would."

She blew out a breath. "Yeah. But I hoped I was wrong."

"You're all right?" The fada moved as close to the iron bars as he could without touching them. "Those motherfuckers haven't hurt you?" His fierce look included all three of them: Sindre, Blaer and Fane.

"I'm fine. But you..."

The fada's hard face softened. "Don't worry about me." He reached for the bars and then stopped himself from grabbing them just in time. His hands fisted.

"Let her go," he growled at Sindre. "You've got me and Corban. I'll agree to anything you say if you just let her go."

Blaer's dark eyes glowed, lapping up his fear and anger.

"No!" exclaimed Marjani. "Don't make any promises. Let me handle this."

"Actually," the king said, "Marjani and I were about to make a deal."

"Like hell," Luc snarled. His claws slid out and his teeth lengthened so he looked barely human. "Let me out of this fucking cage. Fight me like a real man."

"Is that what real men do?" Sindre asked, interested. "Fight?"

"You win." Marjani whirled to face him. "Let him go. I'll stay here in his place."

"Jani, no!" The fada rammed a shoulder against the cage's iron door. It seared his skin with a sickening hiss, but he did it again and again before giving up to stare helplessly at Marjani. Red stripes from the bars marked his shoulder and arm, and the stomach-turning odor of burnt flesh filled the tower.

"*No.*" Fane was across the room before he'd realized he moved. He grabbed Marjani's arm. "Bargain with him. Make him set a time limit or you'll be here the rest of your life."

Sindre's brows pinched together. "You become tedious, Fane. Step away from her."

He clenched his fists—and then obeyed. Because he had to.

"Bargain with him," he muttered one last time.

"Come, your highness." Marjani crossed her arms and tilted her head to one side. "Surely you don't think a fada can best you in a bargain? What are your terms?"

"A year and a day—in my court."

Her eyes narrowed. "How long would that be in my world?"

Good. She was using that intelligent brain of hers.

"About ten turns of the sun," the king replied.

"And what would my duties be?"

A smile curved Sindre's lips. "To entertain me."

"*No.*" Luc's snarl tore through the room. He slammed against the cage over and over, uncaring of his seared and bruised flesh.

Marjani's chin jutted. "I won't be your whore."

The king inclined his head. "If anything happens, it will be with your full cooperation."

For some reason, that made her freeze. Her lips went white around the edges. "You'll swear to that."

"I will."

Suddenly, Fane couldn't bear it. Sindre had dark tastes—and ways of ensuring an unwilling person's cooperation. A year and a day with him would age Marjani in ways she couldn't know.

He dragged in a breath. The hell with it. He'd break the *geas*. He couldn't live with himself if he stood by while Marjani bound herself to Sindre.

Then Blaer stepped forward and grabbed the quartz around Marjani's neck. Marjani's hand shot out, gripping the fae's wrist.

The two women stared at each other. Marjani's lip peeled to show a single sharp canine. "Let. It. Go."

Blaer squeezed the milky chunk of rock and shot Sindre a triumphant grin. "You don't have to bargain with the animal, my lord. She'll do anything I say."

Sindre shook his head, but remained silent as Blaer tightened her grip on the substitute quartz.

"You're in my power now, fada," she said gleefully. "Drop to your knees."

Marjani stared back. Blaer's brow creased.

Marjani exploded into action, tossing Luc a stiletto at the same time she jerked her head back, ripping the quartz from Blaer's hand. A moment later she was airborne. Her booted feet struck Blaer's chest. The fae staggered backward.

Marjani was right there. She aimed a roundhouse kick at Blaer's solar plexus, dropping her to the floor.

Sindre raised his hand, preparing to freeze Marjani.

Pulling her dagger from her boot, she darted forward and sliced his arm. Blood welled, soaking the white linen. Sindre's breath sucked in. He eyed the slash in disbelief, and then lunged for Marjani.

She danced away in Fane's direction. He grabbed her wrist and somehow managed to summon the energy to conceal them both.

Luc inserted the stiletto's skinny blade in the cage's lock. It released with a click.

"Get Jani out of here," he said in Fane's general direction as he shoved open the door. He leapt at Sindre, shifting in mid-air to a huge brown wolf. He slammed Sindre to the floor just as the king opened his mouth, probably to order Fane to release Marjani.

Fane hustled her toward the door, but she dug in her heels and tried to twist out of his grip. "Let me go, damn it. I'm not leaving without Luc."

A cursing Blaer rose to her feet. Blood trickled from her mouth and her pale skin was bruised from her struggle with Marjani, but a powerful fae like her could heal in minutes from a blow that would've broken the ribs of a human.

Her gaze swung in Marjani and Fane's direction. Dark tendrils slid over his skin. Despair filled him.

Give yourself up—you'll never escape.

They had to leave. Now, while Sindre was occupied with fighting Luc and couldn't order Fane to release Marjani. Because when it came down to it, he wasn't sure he'd have the strength to resist the compulsion the *geas* put on him.

Marjani slashed at him with her dagger. "I said, let me go."

He leapt back just as the blade ripped through his sweater, narrowly missing his stomach. His mouth dropped open. The woman had tried to disembowel him.

Fuck this.

He twisted her right arm behind her back and shoved her into the hall. There, he clamped both arms around her from behind, immobilizing her arms against her body, and raced down the stairs, Marjani fighting him the whole way. Twice, she nearly escaped, but somehow he managed to hang on to her.

He dashed for the nearest exit, and a few seconds later, they were outside the castle by a little-used portal. Still gripping her, he flicked his fingers and muttered the incantation, and then jumped through into the human world.

Unfortunately, to shut the portal required both hands. As soon as he released Marjani, she leapt for the shimmering circle. He rapped out the correct words and made the closing motion with both hands, wayfarer-fast, and then grabbed her by the waist and hung on until it contracted, leaving them on the outside.

Marjani rounded on him. "You asshole." She crouched, her dagger raised. "Let me back in—*now*. I won't leave without Luc."

Jealousy twisted through him. What was the other man to her?

He dragged in a breath. "No."

"No?" She growled and lunged at him with the knife, but this time he was ready and easily evaded her.

"No. The goblins would be on you the second you stepped through. Because you can bet Lady B is sending them after us. You didn't make a bargain with the king, so as far as she's concerned, you're fair game. And she'll have his blessing, because he wants you, too."

She stared at him, both of them panting. High above, the sun peeked out from behind a fluffy white cloud. It was noon—a point in their favor. Goblins were nocturnal; Blaer would have to wake them, buying him and Marjani a little time—as long as they didn't waste time arguing.

"Please," he said. "Your friend—Luc—doesn't want you there. You heard him. He told me to get you out."

"Fuck that. You want to go, fine. I don't need you. Just let me back in."

He set his jaw. So bloody self-sufficient, she was. But a woman didn't get so self-sufficient unless life had made her that way.

"How about if I promise I'll help you get back in? But not right now. You saw what the goblins did to your friend. Their orders will be to bring you back alive, but Lady B won't care if they beat the shit out of you first. Please. Just come with me until we can figure out a plan." He held out his hand.

Marjani's mouth compressed into a tight line, but she put her hand in his. "If he dies," she ground out, "I'll never forgive you. *Never.*"

Still weak and hurting from Sindre's attack, he glared down at her. He'd just thwarted the ice fae king for her, putting his own life on the line, and all she wanted to do was put herself back in the king's power.

And on top of that, now Blaer was after them, too.

It was a hell of a time to realize he was falling in love with the woman.

"At least you'll be alive," he gritted.

CHAPTER 17

*L*uc slammed into Sindre's chest. He fell down and the two of them rolled across the floor.

The ice fae king was strong. He had to be hurting as the iron entered his system, but he didn't show it. Luc strained to reach the king's pale neck and the carotid pulsing so temptingly beneath his ear. But Sindre dug his fingers into Luc's fur, holding him off long enough to mutter a few words.

The air around the king shimmered and he 'ported across the tower. Luc loped after him. As he gathered his muscles to leap, Sindre flung up a hand.

Icy fingers reached inside Luc's chest and squeezed his heart. He dropped like a stone to the floor and lay there, writhing with pain.

Blaer hurried over and grabbed Luc's quartz. He groaned, the pain even worse than what Sindre had done to him.

"Freeze," she hissed, and his muscles locked. He lay on the floor, twitching and humiliated as she yanked the pendant off his head.

"No," he rasped. He tried to make his hand move so he could snatch it back from her. But he couldn't.

"I know the secret," she whispered. "Even the king doesn't know what I know. That it's easiest for a night fae to get to the heart of your quartz."

She chanted the secret words, and dark talons closed around the magic at the center of his quartz. The humming crystals stuttered, and then started up a new, unfamiliar music—a tune that somehow connected him to Blaer.

His bowels iced.

Her lips curved. "You have to obey me."

"*No,*" he said, but it was the last, desperate gasp of a drowning man.

Sindre came up beside her, nursing his injured arm. "Blaer, *min*. Do you really need two? Fane has a point. We don't want to get the earth fada all stirred up. I'll have to fight back, and that might bring the sun fae into this. The queen seems to have adopted the local fada."

Blaer moved a smooth shoulder. "I wasn't planning to keep this one. He's simply bait. The female will come back for him."

"You seem so sure."

"I am. Clan is everything to them—she won't leave Iceland without him."

Sindre's mouth curved. "And when she does, I'll be waiting."

"Exactly."

They exchanged a smile. Then Sindre said, "I'll just take care of this one for you." He 'ported Luc back into the cage and slammed the door shut, then glanced at his bloody arm. "I suppose I'd better have a healer look at this."

The fae lady nodded. "And if I may summon the goblins?"

"I thought you were sure she'll return."

"I am. But it wouldn't hurt to offer her a little incentive."

They headed out the door, ignoring Luc's furious growl.

The last thing he heard was Blaer asking, "And you? What are you going to do about the mixed-blood?"

"Don't worry," the king returned. "He can't go far without my permission."

CHAPTER 18

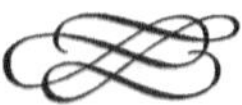

Thrice-damned interfering prick.

Marjani glowered at Fane, moving grim-faced beside her on those long, ground-eating legs. She could've cheerfully slit his throat and walked away smiling.

And why was he helping her, anyway? There was nothing in it for him. In fact, Sindre was going to be out for his blood. And she'd seen how scary a pissed-off Sindre could be.

Her heart clenched—not for Fane, who deserved whatever he got—but for Luc.

Gods, she hated to leave him behind with Sindre and that fae bitch. Luc must know Marjani wouldn't abandon him. Still, that didn't make her feel any less guilty. She'd known Luc would follow her, with or without Adric's say-so.

They covered a mile, then another at a slower pace. Fane wavered, hand to his chest, lips white. He must be running on fumes.

She scowled. "You okay?"

He nodded and pressed on, going slower and slower until he was stumbling forward, feet dragging.

"You have to rest." She grabbed his arm, worried in spite of herself.

He placed his hands on his thighs and dragged in a breath. "My energy. The king...drained me. Almost gone." He nodded at a pile of boulders. "In there...a cavern."

"I'm on it." She wrapped her arm around his waist. "Lean on me."

He tried to pull away. "Too...heavy."

"I'm stronger than I look." She tightened her arm around his waist.

"Stubborn." But he let himself lean on her.

"Yeah, I get that a lot." She headed toward the boulders, half-dragging, half-carrying him.

"There." He indicated a fissure in the boulders. "A cave. Secret."

She snorted. The fissure didn't look big enough for a very skinny elf. "You're kidding, right?"

He grimaced without answering. Okay, now she was definitely worried. In her experience, Fane had a ready response to just about anything. If he wasn't talking, he must really feel shitty.

They had to turn sideways to get through the opening. She pushed him in first, frowning when he stopped to rest his forehead on a boulder.

"Keep going." She nudged him. "You can do it."

He lurched into movement again, eyes half-closed, feeling his way along the boulders. The passageway turned down and tunneled underground. Things went completely dark, and her eyes went night-glow. Not that there was much to see except the rough basalt pressed up against her cheek. Still, it was easier for her; Fane might be lean, but he was still bigger than her.

The tunnel narrowed even more. Fane halted, his cheek against the rock, panting raggedly.

A high-pitched, excited chittering came from far away. The goblins, still distant but moving in their direction. Goose pimples popped up all over her body.

"Move," she said in a hard voice and nudged him with her hip.

He continued to inch sideways, her following—until his shoulders got caught.

She muttered a curse. "You sure you've done this before?"

"Yeah...my secret...place."

"Well, then, you've gained some weight."

That earned her a weak chuckle.

"Okay. When I give the word, blow out your breath—and say a fucking prayer." She managed to turn enough to shove his nearest shoulder with both hands. "*Now.*"

He exhaled with a grunt. There was a tearing sound as his shirt ripped, and then he was through. She slipped after him.

Shortly after that, the passage widened, and suddenly, they were in a small underground cavern. A crack in the ceiling let in enough light to show walls of rough gray basalt. At the opposite end, a turquoise-blue thermal pool steamed gently.

Fane fell to his hands and knees, chest heaving. Marjani almost knelt down next to him, just to give thanks.

"Hey." She touched his back. "You still with me?"

"Don't feel...so good..." He collapsed the rest of the way and curled up on the cavern floor.

Her breath caught. He looked so still, his face pale under his golden tan, mouth a bluish-pink. But his chest was moving.

She gave him a shake. "Damn it, Fane. You better not die on me."

No response.

Dragging off her sweater, she draped it over his chest before sitting cross-legged on the stone floor to take stock.

The cavern was a rough oval shape about ten feet wide and twenty feet long. They had light and fresh air from that crack in the ceiling. But the best part was the thermal pool. The steaming blue water kept the cavern at a comfortable temperature.

And she still had her knives—and her quartz, thanks to Fane.

That was the good news.

The bad news was she was holed up with an unconscious man and no food. She thought longingly of the backpack she'd left in Sindre's tower and everything inside it, including the fishing knife.

At least they had water. She'd done her research and knew Iceland had some of the cleanest water in the world. She glanced again at the pool. The water might smell of sulfur, but it was drinkable. All in all, her cat approved of their temporary den—it was safely underground, easy to defend, and even had its own water supply.

And she could hunt for food, assuming it was safe to go outside. She glanced at the ceiling crack, straining to hear the goblins. For now, it was quiet.

Fane dragged in a breath and pillowed his head on his arm. At some point, he'd lost the leather tie around his hair and blond strands spilled over his shoulders. Her fingers twitched, recalling how silky it had felt when he'd kissed her.

Then she recalled how he'd played her and balled those fingers into a fist. All that time she'd thought he'd been helping her, and instead, the prick had been spying on her.

You were a job to him, nothing more.

Then why had he held her in bed last night without asking for more?

And this morning, why had he obtained a decoy quartz for her—and then helped her escape?

Gods, even after Sindre's attack, he'd come to Blaer's tower. To help her, Marjani.

The man was a fucking onion, with layers upon layers. She had a feeling she could know him for a decade and still not understand how his mind worked. And the bitch of it was, she wouldn't mind sticking around for that long. Fane intrigued her. Inside, her cat hummed agreement.

She scowled and removed her quartz from her bra. For now, she'd keep the other quartz around her neck as a decoy. She didn't think she could stand losing her real quartz again. Once in a lifetime had been enough.

She bit the inner side of her cheek. A part of her would always mourn her first quartz. The pain as the men ripped it from her had been excruciating, like having her heart torn out, and when they'd smashed it in front of her, the agony had doubled and redoubled.

Only a mate or close relative could touch an earth fada's quartz without it hurting. Bad.

And that had just been the start...

She exhaled and dragged her thoughts back to the present.

Time to report to Adric. She hadn't intended to call him until Corban was dead, but he needed to know what was going on with Blaer and her cages. The other earth fada alphas should be informed, and maybe even the water fada clans. This was bigger than Marjani trying to prove herself.

She tapped a slight depression, accessing the quartz's smartphone. Another tap pinged Adric.

He answered immediately. "Jani? You okay? Where the fuck are you? It's been over a month."

For some damn reason, her eyes stung. Goddess, she missed him. The two of them had never been apart for this long. She could just picture him scrubbing a hand over his spiky hair, his hard face a mixture of anger and worry.

He was as much feared as loved. Very few people saw the big heart concealed behind that ruthless façade. But Marjani did.

Adric was only two years older than her, and the two of them were more like twins than siblings, especially after the death of their mom and dad. You tended to bond with someone when you were fighting for survival.

This past year, her brother had been so damn patient with her, gently coaxing her back to something resembling a normal life again. He'd fed her. Talked to her, even though she spent most days as her cat. Asked her advice when her only response was a twitch of her tail.

When she'd gotten so depressed that all she did was lie on the living room rug staring into the fireplace, he'd changed to his cougar and slept curled next to her, knowing that what she needed most of all was touch. And when nightmares left her whimpering and shaken, he nudged her awake and told her stories from their childhood.

Without him, she'd have gone completely feral.

"Jani?" Adric said. "You still there?"

She gave a hard swallow. "I'm fine." She glanced around the cavern and decided her brother didn't need to know everything. "And don't worry, I'm safe."

Then she realized what he'd said. "What do you mean it's been over a month? What day is it?"

"August thirty-first."

"Holy shit. By my reckoning it's only August eighth."

"So you got inside the ice fae court."

"Yeah," she said, still reeling at how much time she'd lost. "And Ric, Luc did, too, but they caught him. Put him in a fucking iron cage. I got him out, but I'm not sure he got away. The last I saw he was fighting with the ice fae king."

"A cage? The king put him in a cage?" Her brother's voice was chillier than Sindre's tower.

She shook her head. "That's the strange thing. The king definitely knows about it, but the person behind it seems to be a lady in his court—a Lady B, who's also the woman the king hired you to track down in India."

"The fae lady I sent Corban after?"

"Yeah. And Ric, it's bad. She knows the secret of our quartzes. She grabbed mine and tried to use it to compel me, but I'd switched it out for a fake quartz. Corban must've told her."

Adric muttered something dark. Only a few fae knew the secret of controlling the earth fada through their quartz—and those fae had been either bribed or threatened into keeping quiet. "What the hell's going on?"

"It's a long story. I promise I'll explain everything when I get back. For now, you need to get the word out to the other earth fada clans."

"Agreed. I'll contact the other alphas as soon as we're done. And Corban?"

"He's in an iron cage, too, completely under her power. I was told they were lovers, but now he's her prisoner. There's no way he could've sent that message to you on his own."

"But it was his writing. The motherfucker tried to sell me out to save himself."

"Yeah. Or she ordered him to send the message." She rubbed a thumb over the quartz's chunky crystals. "He's sick, Ric. Iron poisoning. It's bad—he's almost gone."

"Saves you the trouble of offing him."

She huffed a laugh with zero humor. "There is that."

"Where are you now?"

"Safe in a cavern about three miles from the court. The court itself is in a castle carved out of a dead volcano." She gave him the castle's precise coordinates, knowing he'd file the information for future use. "You can't see it in the human world. It's completely hidden behind *look-away* spells and warded to keep out intruders. The only way in is through portals that the ice fae have to open."

"So how did you get inside?"

She glanced at Fane, curled into a ball and shivering helplessly. Somehow, she couldn't bring herself to tell Adric that the SOB had played her. Her brother didn't need another reason to question her judgment—and besides, Fane was Evie's father, and she liked Evie. Jace's mate might be mostly human, but she was good people.

"Evie's father helped me." It was the truth—just not the whole truth.

"He knew who you were?"

"Yeah. Turns out he's a wayfarer. He was at Jace and Evie's mating."

Adric didn't like that. "And none of us scented him?"

"He says the king gave him a charm that disguises his scent."

"Huh." She could almost hear her alpha brother filing that away for future investigation. "You need to come home, Jani."

"What about Luc? I can't leave without him."

"He's a big boy."

Marjani gave the quartz a look of disbelief. Sometimes her brother could be so damn cold.

"I am *not* leaving him to that night fae bitch. She puts fada in those cages so she can feed on their fear and anger. You should see Corban. He's—broken, just this side of feral. I only saw him as his wolf."

Silence. Then a careful question. "And you? You're...all right?"

Her jaw clenched. She knew he meant well, but it hurt, to have her own brother doubting her control. "What d'you think?"

"You sound good," he said immediately. "I'm sorry."

She unclenched her jaw. After all, Adric had a right to doubt her. She *had* almost lost it last winter. And she was still having trouble with control. "Okay. Okay."

"But I still want you home," he added, and made her angry all over again, especially when he added, "I could make it an order."

"Try it," she snarled.

Another taut silence. Then Adric expelled a breath. "Damn it, I'm your alpha. When I give you an order, you obey it."

"I'm your second for a reason," she shot back. "You trust me to tell you when you have your head up your ass."

A low growl—and then she heard him swallow. "I can't lose you, Jani."

Her heart constricted. Because she felt the same way—if she lost her only brother, she really would go feral.

She softened her tone. "We can't leave Luc here to die in a fucking cage. You know if the shoe were on the other foot, he'd do anything he could to rescue me—or you, for that matter."

"Then I'll send someone else. Please, Jani. I'd come myself, but I can't."

"Why not?" Not that she wanted him to come, but she knew her brother. It must be killing him to stay home while she and Luc hunted Corban.

"We have a situation here."

She got that odd tingle in her gut; her Gift at work. "The night fae are looking for me, aren't they?"

He took a long time answering. "Not you in particular—at least, not as far as I know. But a few days after you left, the prince demanded a meeting."

"Hell." She stared at the steam rising from the pool. "What happened?"

"He hinted that he knows who killed his son. But you know the fae. We danced around the question, each of us trying to gauge how much the other knows. But he's going to come back, and when he does, I'd better be here."

"And if he asks straight out who killed his son?"

"I'll tell him to go to Hades. He has no right to ask anything of me. His son died because he was in *my* territory, fucking with *my* lieutenant and his mate."

"We can't afford to make an enemy of him."

Adric gave a mirthless laugh. "Too late."

"You know what?" she said slowly. "Iceland might be the safest place for me right now. The last place anyone would expect to find me is deep in ice fae territory."

A pissed-off snarl. "I can protect my own damn sister. He's not going to find out who killed Tyrus. I want you home."

"Ric." She pinched the bridge of her nose. This was why she'd slipped out of Baltimore without telling him. "You have to trust me. Anyone else will only get caught. The only reason I got inside the ice fae castle was because Fane helped me." Well, that and the fact that Sindre and/or Blaer had apparently wanted her inside anyway.

At the sound of his name, Fane groaned, a deep, animal sound.

"What was that?" Adric demanded.

"Fane." She frowned down at the sick man as he flung himself on his back, a shudder jerking his long limbs. She touched his shoulder and he jolted upright, staring at her with glassy eyes.

"He's hurt? What the fuck, Jani?"

"Look, I gotta go. I'll report as soon as I know anything."

She cut the connection and zipped her quartz back into a side pocket of her cargo pants before laying a hand against Fane's forehead. It was burning hot.

She cursed under her breath as she guided him to lie back down. "You're not going to die on me, got it?"

Stripping off her shirt, she wet it in the pool and used it to bathe his forehead. His breath sighed out.

"That's it." She dabbed his face and neck, wishing she could do more. But she hadn't been blessed with even a speck of a healer's Gift. "Feels better, doesn't it? Now rest. You'll feel better when you wake up."

She hoped.

CHAPTER 19

Adric clenched his quartz.

She's safe, at least for now. That's good.

Although he hated to admit it, maybe Marjani was right, she was safer in Iceland than Baltimore. Because Prince Langdon had requested another meeting.

No, demanded it. Tonight.

The prince was a night fae, so of course he'd set the meeting for midnight, choosing a bar on the top floor of a fancy hotel in midtown Baltimore.

Adric arrived at eleven, Jace at his side. Zuri took a seat on a metal stool at the shiny black bar, and several soldiers grabbed a nearby table. They'd dressed to blend in—dark button-up shirts and jeans or dress pants, their quartz pendants tucked discreetly into their shirts.

The bar had a stripped-down, urban feel: concrete floors, exposed brick walls and galvanized steel lights hanging like pendants from the ceiling. Running down one wall were floor-to-ceiling windows with a view of Baltimore's Washington Monument, and across Mount Vernon Place, the waning moon peeked from behind the spires of a gothic cathedral dating to the late 1800s.

Adric and Jace chose a table in the corner with a view of the entrance. A pretty redhead in a white shirt, cropped black pants and purple suspenders took their order for a couple of the pricey craft beers.

Adric and Jace nursed their beers as the hour until midnight ticked by. At the bar, two women in tight skirts were flirting with Zuri, and he flirted right back while keeping his back to the bar, dark eyes scanning the room.

Adric looked at Jace. "Any more problem with the night fae?"

"Nah. But I invited Horace to stay with us—for back up. You know how Evie loves him. He's with them right now."

Horace was a cheerful, dreadlocked cougar and a member of Jace's den.

"Good," Adric said. "Let me know if you need more men."

"Will do. But I think the prince was just messing with my head. Still, I'll be glad when Kyler graduates. Evie says she'll sell the house and they'll move in with me for good. She's already after me to redecorate the living room of my den. Says it looks like something you'd find in a frat house."

He grinned at Adric, crazy about his mate and not caring who knew it.

Lucky man.

Midnight approached. Adric scented Prince Langdon before he saw him— silver and decay. The night fae made their homes in elaborate crypts, and their scents held a hint of the graveyard.

Adric's hackles raised. He and Jace exchanged a look and scanned the area.

The prince appeared in a corner a few feet away, coalescing out of the shadows. The night fae were creepy like that. He was flanked by two bodyguards, a male and female—sea fada, by the scent.

"Your highness." Adric rose to his feet and murmured the traditional fae greeting. "Peace to you and yours."

Langdon trod noiselessly forward, dressed in black from his fae-tailored shirt to his Italian leather shoes. His eyes and shoulder-length hair were the same midnight color, a striking contrast to his dead-white skin. His narrow, aristocratic face sported winged black brows in which sparkled several tiny diamonds. More diamonds outlined his pointed ears, and his right index finger was decorated with a square-cut diamond as large as Adric's thumbnail.

"Lord Adric. Peace to you and yours," the prince returned. He had a low, rich voice. From what Adric had heard, women loved it. He nodded to Jace. "And to yours."

The lieutenant jerked his head. "Peace."

Adric indicated the chair across from him. "Please have a seat." The polite words tasted acrid in his mouth, but that was a downside of being alpha. You had to make nice with the fae.

The male guard pulled out the chair and Langdon lowered his tall, elegant body into it. The guards took a stance against the wall, the man scanning the room, the woman keeping her gaze firmly on Adric and Jace.

The pretty waitress bustled up, oozing excitement. She might not know exactly who Langdon was, but she'd guessed he was a fae. "May I get you a drink, sir?"

"You can, love." The prince granted her a small smile that brought a flush to her creamy skin. "Wine." He named a merlot that was no doubt rare and expensive.

"Coming right up. And you?" she asked Adric and Jace. When they shook their heads, she glanced at the stony-eyed guards. "What about your...companions?"

"Nothing for us," the woman said.

The waitress gave Langdon another wide smile. "I'll be right back with that wine." She headed for the bar.

The prince contemplated her very fine ass for a moment before turning back to Adric. "Thank you for agreeing to meet with me."

Like I had a choice. But Adric gave a little nod.

"It's a beautiful night." The prince leaned back in his chair, taking in the dark sky outside the plate glass windows. "Summer is almost over. We'll be celebrating the autumn equinox soon—and then Samhain." He used the Celtic term for Halloween. "My favorite time of the year."

"Yeah?" *Get to the point, damn it.*

The redhead returned with Langdon's wine. When he thanked her in that deep, seductive voice, she backed away as starry-eyed as if he were a Hollywood A-lister.

"In our clan, the little ones trick-or-treat," Langdon said. "Do yours?"

"No. That's not one of our traditions. We honor our dead with a special cere-mony, but that's all."

"Ah." Langdon contemplated the blood-red wine in his glass. "I had three sons, once. But you know that."

"Mm." Adric's nape tightened. He willed his heartbeat to stay steady.

"And they're all dead. I know what you fada say about the night fae. That we're heartless. That we feed on the darkness in others."

Because you do.

"But we love our children as much as you do. I've seen six hundred turns of the sun, and in that time I've only been blessed with the three sons. And now they've all passed to the other side...before their time." The prince's black eyes burned into Adric's.

He felt an unwilling twinge of sympathy. The man was genuinely grieving. But that didn't mean his son Tyrus didn't deserve to be dead.

"Look," he said, "I'm sorry for your loss, but I want you out of Baltimore. This is my town now. Whatever deal you had with my uncle is null and void."

Langdon's eyes blazed red. "You think to tell me what to do? A prince with a lineage going back a thousand turns of the sun?"

Adric bared his fangs. He might be young, but the Darktime had been a crash course in eat-or-be-eaten. "I'm not looking for trouble, your highness. But if you bring it to my doorstep, I'll fight back with everything I have. Are we clear on that?"

The prince took a sip of wine—and changed the subject. "One of my sons had a daughter. Merry Jones."

Jace didn't move, but Adric heard his heart speed up. Langdon's son Silver had mated with Jace's only sister, Takira. Their daughter was Jace's thirteen-year-old niece Merry.

The prince's gaze flicked to Jace, no doubt detecting the lieutenant's agitation with his night fae senses.

"We were told she died in a fire." Adric was careful not to lie. He *had* been told that Merry Jones died in a fire. In fact, he and Jace had believed for years that the girl was dead.

"A fire set by night fae assassins." Jace's voice was a harsh scrape.

Those assassins had also killed first Takira and later, Silver. Only Merry had escaped. And it had been Lord Tyrus who'd set the assassins on them, because Silver was Tyrus's half-brother and Tyrus didn't want any competition for Langdon's throne.

The prince leveled a stare at Adric. "We all know that isn't true. Merry Jones is alive and living at Rock Run. I'm also aware that you see her regularly." He glanced at Jace. "Both of you. I'm sure the Rock Run fada told you about the ward I set, a ward of protection keyed to her quartz. If any of my people try to harm her—if they even lay hands on her without her express permission—they die."

He waited until Adric nodded, then added, "That should be proof enough that I wish the girl no harm. I made no exceptions with the ward except for myself. Even my son Tyrus knew he'd die if he tried to touch her again."

"I know this, yes," Adric said, confused now. Where was Langdon going with this?

The prince's jaw worked. "Tyrus went too far."

"He did. But what does this have to do with Mer—?"

Langdon leaned forward, cutting him off. "You killed my son. We both know it."

"No. I didn't."

Langdon waved that aside. "Oh, you didn't do the deed yourself. But someone in your clan did. I've traced him to Baltimore. He hasn't been seen since. And recently, I received some information from one of your former clan members. Corban, his name is."

Adric went rigid. Because it was Marjani they were talking about—and he had the bad feeling that Langdon had picked up his sudden tension with those Spidey-senses of his.

Damn you, Corban. What have you done?

He set his hands on the table. "Get out of my town. You're not welcome here."

Langdon sat back. "What would the other fae think if I informed them your sister had killed my last surviving son?"

Adric narrowed his eyes. "They'd think it was your son's own fucking fault for sending assassins to off my lieutenant."

Jace growled. After all, he was the lieutenant that Tyrus had targeted. "We know who had your other two sons assassinated," he said. "Tyrus didn't want any rivals for your title, did he?"

A bleak look crossed Langdon's face. "I didn't know. Not until it was too late."

Adric tried not to blink. Had the prince almost apologized for not reining in his psycho son? But Langdon was a night fae and an arrogant SOB to boot. The moment passed.

Cool black eyes scrutinized Adric. "I want access to the girl. Merry. The sun fae queen has set powerful wards around Rock Run. Nobody can break through them. But you"—his gaze shot to Jace—"you meet with her at least once a week."

The lieutenant's hazel eyes sparked a cat-green. Before he could speak, Adric jumped in.

"I'm sorry, but that's not possible."

"Why not?"

"She...passed. Earlier this summer."

"The girl? My granddaughter?"

"Yes." Adric swallowed against the wave of nausea at the big, fat lie he'd just told. "I'm sorry. You should've been informed."

Beside him, Jace went stiff.

Langdon's fingers tightened on his wineglass. "You're lying."

Adric shook his head. "It was in a flash flood. The caverns where she lives with the river fada flooded. They couldn't get her out in time."

From the corner of his eye, Adric saw Jace bow his head sorrowfully. Backing him up without actually lying.

The prince's winged brows snapped together. "Why wasn't I informed?"

Adric spread his hands. "You'll have to ask them. Rock Run doesn't share any more information with me than necessary."

"I'll want to see the body."

"I'm sorry, but that's not possible. We fada don't bury our dead. We cremate them."

Langdon's eyes narrowed on Adric for an endless minute during which he prayed the night fae wouldn't see the cold sweat prickling his upper lip.

At last he murmured, "I see."

He rose to his feet in an abrupt movement and strode out of the bar, his guards at his heels. The few people who happened to be in their path literally jumped aside.

"He gone?" Adric asked between clenched teeth, the lie he'd told tearing at his gut.

Because Merry was alive and well and living with Valeria and Rui do Mar, the Rock Run couple who'd adopted her after Silver's death.

Jace glanced at where Zuri had followed Langdon and his guards into the hall. "Yeah. Zuri says he's left the building."

"Good." Adric got up, stumbled the few feet to a potted plant, and vomited into the dirt.

CHAPTER 20

"Fucking maze," Fane mumbled.

How long had he been wandering the spiraling paths? Hours, maybe days. He was exhausted, his tongue thick from thirst.

Sindre was toying with him, the bastard. The man was a Gifted illusionist. He could conjure up nightmares so real you could touch them.

Fane had to keep moving. To stop—to give in any way—might be fatal.

He set his right hand on the wall. Wasn't there something about a right-hand rule? Touch the wall of a maze with your right hand and at every turn, go right, and you'll eventually find your way out. But you had to do it as soon as you entered the maze, so it was probably too late. And it wouldn't work anyhow on a maze that continually remade itself.

He kept his hand on the wall anyway, and trudged on.

Where was Marjani? Had the goblins captured her while he was lost in this endless white world?

If only he hadn't accepted Sindre's *geas*. But he had, and a *geas* was almost impossible to break.

Even if he did manage to break it, he'd lose everything: his job as an envoy, the money he'd earned since accepting the bargain. Worse, he'd be shamed, known throughout the magical world as a vow-breaker.

The shame wouldn't fall on just him, either. It would attach to his dad, Arne, and maybe even Roald.

Back when he'd accepted the *geas*, ninety-nine human years hadn't seemed that long. But now the years inched by...and he still had thirty-nine to go.

"Sleep," a woman murmured. "You're safe."

"No." He shook his head from side to side. "I'll die. And the king will get Marjani."

"Is that what's bothering you? I'm right here. Safe. We're both safe."

He opened his eyes. Marjani's face swam into view, but he didn't trust his eyes. It would be just like Sindre to taunt him with the one woman Fane most wanted.

"Jani?" he croaked. "It's really you? This isn't some trick?"

"I'm here." A warm hand settled on his chest. "See? You can feel me, right?"

"Thank the gods." He gripped her fingers...and the world whirled away.

He'd walked for another endless day when the wall disintegrated into a chilly white mist that slowly engulfed him. He tried to outrun it, but it was all around him.

No. It's a trick.

He lifted his chin. "Mind over matter, Fane." Because if he could somehow *see* through the illusion, it would disappear.

The fog covered his face. Reaching his arms out in front of him, he stumbled blindly forward until his legs gave out.

So much for mind over matter.

"At least," he told Sindre as the blackness came up to meet him, "you don't have Jani."

He could swore he heard the king chuckle.

"I'm here," she said. "I'm here."

He didn't know how long he was out—an hour? A day? But when he came to, the fog was gone and he was curled up on the stone floor, shivering.

He groaned and wrapped his arms around himself.

"Easy, now." Gentle hands lifted him onto a lap, stroked the side of his face. A woman, but it couldn't be Marjani. After what he'd done, she must be far away by now.

His eyelids seemed to have been glued shut. "Mom?"

"No. It's me—Jani."

He pried open his sticky lids and focused on the woman gazing down at him with a furrowed brow. "Jani?" Relief washed through him. "You're...okay. It wasn't a dream."

"Shh—don't talk. Drink." She slid a hand under his head to lift it, and then set a cup to his lips.

He gulped the water greedily, draining the cup. "More."

"Okay." She set the cup down and started to move him off her.

"No!" Panicked, he grabbed her legs. "Don't leave."

"Just for a minute. You have a fever—you need water."

"No." He tightened his grip on her, not giving a fuck that he was being unreasonable. Marjani was the solid boulder around which the rest of the world swirled. If she left him, he'd be engulfed by the maze again.

"Okay." Cool fingers stroked his hair back from his face. "Calm down."

"Thank you," he rasped and dozed off. When she lifted his head off her lap and set it on something soft, he was too weak to protest. Then he passed out. This time, his sleep was dreamless.

When he next opened his eyes, his head ached and he was hot as Hades, his mouth so dry he could barely swallow. He peered blearily around for Marjani, but she was nowhere to be seen.

His heart slapped wildly against his rib cage.

Had she left him? Or worse, been seized by the goblins?

She murmured something against his shoulder and his heart resumed its normal tempo. She was spooned up against his back, her arm around his waist, her breathing the slow, steady rhythm of sleep.

Relieved, he let out a jagged exhale and then stilled, afraid to wake her in case she left for real. But she had the senses of a cat.

She sat up, yawning, and set her fingers to his forehead. "Holy mother. You're burning up."

Rising to her feet, she stripped off her T-shirt and soaked it in the thermal pool. She had on a plain black exercise bra—of course. This woman wouldn't be caught dead in anything lacy.

As she wrung out the T-shirt, he eyed the strong, beautiful muscles in her shoulders and arms. A wry grin tugged on his mouth. He finally had her stripping off her clothes and he was too damn weak to do anything about it.

She returned with the wet T-shirt and set it on his forehead. He closed his eyes as the ache in his head receded.

"Here. Drink something." She lifted his head—so gently it made his heart clench—and held a cup to his lips. Somehow, he hadn't thought she had it in her.

Not that he deserved her kindness. Hell, if he was Marjani, he'd bang his head on the cavern floor. Hard.

He sucked the water down. "More, please."

She nodded and made another trip to the pool—three trips in all before he'd had enough water. By then the T-shirt had warmed from his skin. He turned it over so that the cooler side lay against his forehead.

Marjani took it and wiped his face and neck before rising to wet it again.

He felt under his head. He was laying on soft wool. He turned his head to look at it.

"You...need your sweater." He tugged at it.

"No worries." She returned to drape the wet cloth over his forehead again, covering his eyes. "It's warm in here, and if I get too cold, I can always shift to my cougar."

He pushed up the T-shirt to look at her. "I...thank you."

Tears leaked from the corners of his eyes. He pulled the cloth back down and lay there, humiliated.

She touched his wrist. "You'd have done the same for me."

"If you believe that..." He trailed off.

Because he would've.

In fact, he'd thrown away his whole way of life for her. If he was lucky, Sindre would release him from the *geas*. If not, he was going to spend the next thirty-nine turns of the sun in a private hell of the ice fae king's making.

Arne was going to be disappointed—he'd stuck his neck out for Fane, arguing that his son deserved a chance even if he was only a quarter fae. And his grandfather Roald would sear him with one of those looks that said, *What do you expect from a mixed-blood*?

His chest tightened, and what felt like a chunk of basalt lodged in his gut.

Marjani sat next to him, legs folded lotus-style. "Rest." She set a hand on his heart. "Right now, you need to get better. Everything else can wait."

He moved his chin, a short up-and-down motion.

She turned over the damp cloth. "Close your eyes."

When he obeyed, she smoothed it over his forehead and then placed her hand over his heart again.

Marjani was safe. That made it all worthwhile.

The tightness in his chest eased and he fell into a deep, healing sleep.

CHAPTER 21

*B*etween them, Jace and Zuri managed to get Adric back to his den before he threw up again. At least this time, he made it to the toilet first.

After rinsing out his mouth, he staggered back to the living room to collapse on the couch. He lay there shaking, his body exuding a rank odor.

Zuri sat on the couch's other end. "I'm staying here tonight. I can sleep in Jani's room."

His glare dared Adric to object, but Adric just nodded. "Works."

Jace remained standing, his brow creased with worry. "I have to go back to Grace Harbor. I don't trust the night fae not to mess with Evie and Kyler, even with Horace there."

"Go," Adric rasped. "But call Merry. In the morning."

Because Langdon would investigate to see if she was really dead.

Unfortunately, they couldn't call her adopted parents, because water fada couldn't use small electronics—their bodies tended to short them out. Meanwhile, Merry was protected by Rock Run's wards, and Adric didn't want to scare her—the kid was only thirteen, after all.

Besides, Rui do Mar, her adopted father, was a scary-ass shark fada. If Langdon wanted Merry, he'd have to get past do Mar, and the shark shifter would die before he let that happen.

"Tell her...get a new quartz," he added. "Throw...the old one in the river. The ward of protection—the prince might be able to trace her through it."

She'd lose the protection, but with Tyrus dead, it probably wasn't necessary anymore.

"Will do." Jace shook his head. "Lord, you're a crazy mofo. I can't believe you told a fae prince a lie right to his face. But you're right. Let him think she's dead—at least until she's grown up."

"The sun fae queen will protect her," Zuri interjected.

"Yeah." Adric hadn't thought of that. But Queen Cleia loved Jace's skinny, serious niece. "Do Mar." He clamped his jaw shut against another wave of queasiness.

Jace understood. "I'll tell Merry to have him contact you."

"Make sure...he knows it's important. The Full Moon Saloon." It was a shifter bar in Fells Point. "Tonight, seven o'clock."

Jace studied him doubtfully. "You sure you're up for it?"

"Yeah." Adric rested his head against the couch's worn fabric. "Just need...sleep."

The rest of the night passed in a feverish haze. Jace left for Grace Harbor, and Zuri contacted Suha. He tried to help Adric to bed, but Adric bared his teeth and he backed off.

And he did it, even though it took him a good five minutes to strip to his boxers and ease himself under the sheets.

Suha arrived shortly after, dressed in a bright, tribal-patterned tunic and leggings. The clan's head healer was a deer fada with short black hair, a pretty oval face, and a doe's calm brown eyes. One look at him, and her full mouth tightened.

"Holy shit, Ric. What did you do now?"

Zuri opened his mouth, but Adric stopped him with a look.

"I told a lie."

That was all Suha needed to know. The healer might be like family to him and Jani, but secrets had a way of spreading through the clan. And right now, the clan didn't need any more upsets.

Her fine dark brows climbed. "A whopper, from the looks of it."

Zuri got a stool from the living room and put it next to the bed. Taking a seat, Suha removed her quartz and held it over his heart, her other hand on his arm.

Zuri hovered on the other side of the bed, his good-looking face grim.

"For fuck's sake," Adric said. "I'm not going to die."

Zuri backed up a step and folded his big arms over his chest. "From where I'm standing, that's debatable."

Suha touched the wolf fada's leg. "Why don't you go get something to eat, babe? The bar on the corner makes killer quesadillas."

"And then get some sleep," Adric growled. "I don't need you standing guard over me. If I need you, I'll call."

Zuri hesitated and then jerked his chin. "All right."

Suha waited until the front door closed behind him and then murmured, "Breathe. Let the warmth fill you."

She moved the quartz in a slow circuit from his throat—which had spoken the lie—to his still-upset stomach, and then back to his heart.

Adric rarely allowed Suha to use her healing Gift on him. Healing burned a lot of energy, and he preferred she save it for the clan members who really needed it.

But he had to admit, it felt good. He sighed with relief as a pleasant heat spread like warm honey throughout his body. His painfully clenched stomach eased.

"That's it." The healer's eyes were half-closed. "Relax. Let your own energy work with mine."

His own quartz hummed in response, accepting Suha's healing energy and using it to counteract the toxins that the lie had released in his body.

His eyelids shut. The next thing he knew it was five in the afternoon, and Zuri was frowning down at him.

"Ric. You all right?"

"Yeah." Adric sat up and swung his legs over the edge of the bed. "Yeah," he repeated, more firmly. He felt a little dizzy, but his stomach had settled. Suha's healing energy had done the trick. It would be a few days until he was back to a hundred percent, but his head had cleared and he was no longer shaking.

From the kitchen came a mouthwatering fragrance. His stomach growled.

"You made me your mom's soup?" Zuri's spicy chicken soup—a Moroccan recipe passed down through his mom's family—was famous in the clan.

"Yep." The tall, brown-skinned lieutenant broke into a rare smile. "But first, take a fucking shower."

Adric rubbed his nose. "I was hoping that smell wasn't me."

∼

By 6:45 p.m., Adric was at the Full Moon Saloon, having showered, dressed and downed a big bowl of Zuri's chicken soup.

At ten to seven, Rui do Mar roared up on a big black bike. Adric nodded to the bouncer to let him in. They'd cleared the bar of everyone but Zuri and a handful of trusted soldiers. Even the owner had been told to wait in his office.

Do Mar was a large, olive-skinned man with short dark hair, a square jaw and hooded green eyes. He strode inside, took one sniff and headed for the dark corner table where Adric waited. The shark shifter could scent a few drops of blood in a fast-flowing river. Detecting Adric's scent in an uncrowded bar must be child's play for him.

"Lord Adric," he said in his Portuguese-accented English as he dropped into the seat across from Adric. "Merry says you wish to speak with me."

No preliminary bullshit with this guy—he went straight to the point. But that was fine with Adric.

"We have a situation. The night fae prince."

"And?" Do Mar lifted a black brow.

"You know his son died."

Do Mar nodded. "We do."

Of course they did. Adric would bet Rock Run even knew that a Baltimore fada had killed Tyrus. But most people believed it had been Adric who'd knifed the man—because that was how he wanted it.

"He asked about Merry," he told do Mar. "He wanted me to agree to give him access to her."

"In exchange for what?"

My sister's life. "That's clan business. But I lied—told him Merry was dead."

Adric caught a hint of surprise in the other man's scent, but his face remained impassive. "I see."

"She got rid of her quartz?" Adric asked, even though he knew the answer. He no longer felt the thin bond connecting him to Merry.

"*Sim*, yes. It was hard, but she trusts you."

Adric's cheek flexed. "I'm sorry." He was Merry's alpha. It was only right that she trusted and obeyed him—no matter that Rock Run had claimed her as an honorary river fada—but he'd hated like hell to give the order. It *hurt* an earth fada to remove their quartz. "It's for her own protection."

"She knows."

"Make sure she finds another quartz—soon. She's still growing. She needs the energy more than ever right now."

Do Mar nodded. "She's already looking for another one. We have a few small deposits within the base."

"Good." The Rock Run Base had been carved out of underground caverns near the mouth of the Susquehanna River, an area rich with quartz deposits.

"There's more," Adric added. "Our best guess is that Tyrus was trying to wipe out everyone connected to Merry. That's why he targeted Jace." He blew out a breath. "And when I met with the prince, he made a point of telling me that all three of his sons are dead."

Adric didn't have to connect the dots. Do Mar bit out something dark in Portuguese. "He wants Merry."

"He didn't say it straight out, but she's his only living heir."

"So he has changed his mind." Do Mar rubbed a hand over his face. "Before, he didn't want his people to know he had a half-blood son with a human. He was happy for us to keep Merry at Rock Run."

"She may be only a quarter night fae, but she's his blood. His only granddaughter."

Their eyes met. Do Mar's shark shone in his eyes, and Adric knew the other man could see cougar-blue streaking his.

"No fucking way," Adric ground out, "am I going to let Merry be raised by the night fae. I wouldn't wish that on my worst enemy, let alone a sweet kid like her."

"Agreed. We will keep a close watch on her. We have one advantage—Dion's mate, Queen Cleia. She loves Merry."

"I'm counting on it." Adric had never thought he'd be grateful the Rock Run alpha had mated with the sun fae queen; it gave Rock Run too much power in their little corner of Maryland. But now he thanked the gods that Merry had Cleia to protect her.

"She's already volunteered one of her best spellcasters to cast a *look-away* spell for Merry's new quartz," do Mar said. "The prince may look for her, but he won't find her."

"Thank you."

"I have no need of thanks," the other man said as they rose to their feet. "You still don't comprehend, do you? Merry is my daughter, here." He touched a fist to his heart. "I would do anything to keep her safe and happy. And my mate—Valeria—feels the same."

Adric nodded—and then stuck out his hand.

Do Mar's hooded eyes flickered with surprise. In all the years they'd known each other, they'd never touched. Touch was reserved for clan members, or at least people you didn't see as an enemy. But Adric could no longer see the shark fada as an enemy, even if he was the Rock Run second.

The other man gripped his hand firmly. "Peace to you and yours."

Adric met his eyes. "And to you and yours."

CHAPTER 22

When Fane awoke that evening, his fever had broken and he felt much better, although weak as an infant.

Night had fallen. The cavern was dark except for a small fire with Marjani crouched beside it, grilling some kind of white fish on a small metal grate. She'd put her T-shirt back on, but her feet were bare. The pool shimmered beside her, the water black in the dim light.

He fingered the thin wool blanket covering him. Where had that come from? He pushed the blanket down to his waist and propped himself up on his forearms.

Marjani immediately crossed to him. "How do you feel?"

"Better, thanks." His voice came out as a croak. He moistened his dry, cracked lips. "But thirsty."

"Hang on and I'll get you some water." Picking up a ceramic cup, she filled it in the pool and brought it to him.

He drained the cup in a few gulps and then turned it in his hand. It was ceramic, the kind the locals kept for everyday use, with no handle and a speckled gray glaze. "Where in Hades did you get this—and the blanket?"

"I made a quick trip outside while you were sleeping. I found a stream to fish in and a little hut with bunk beds and some basic supplies."

He nodded. "The locals rent them to hikers."

"I wish I could've left them something in return, but my backpack is back at the court."

He set the cup on the floor and sat cross-legged, the blanket on his legs. "You're fucking amazing."

"It was either that or go hungry," she said with a shrug. "And I've been in worse situations."

"Yeah, I imagine you have. You're a soldier, aren't you?"

"I was." A shadow crossed her face. "I mean, I *am*."

He'd upset her, the last thing he wanted to do. He pushed the blanket off his lap. "I need—"

"Of course." She helped him to his feet and pointed to a small tunnel behind the pool, where he found the hole she'd dug for wastes. When he was done, he tossed some dirt into it and washed up in the pool.

She was crouched by the grill again. His stomach rumbled at the fish's mouth-watering scent. As he lowered himself onto the cavern floor beside her, she divided the fish into two portions and handed him a plate.

His hands were shaking with hunger. He gripped the plate and gave her a grateful smile. "Thank you."

"You have to eat with your fingers."

"No problem." The fish tasted as good as it smelled. He quickly downed the first couple of pieces, then forced himself to slow down. It wasn't much, but it filled him. His stomach seemed to have shrunk.

He set down his plate. "How long was I out, anyway?"

"Two days. It's around midnight right now."

He gave a low whistle. "No one came looking for us?"

"I heard the goblins the first night, but I haven't seen or heard anything since."

He contemplated the glowing charcoal embers. "The king wants you, then. He wouldn't have sent the goblins after me."

"Why not?"

"He knows I can't go far without his consent. It would break the *geas*."

"Why did you? Accept the *geas*, I mean."

He moved a shoulder. "It seemed like a good idea at the time. My mom had just died, and I didn't fit into the human world anymore. I was a fisherman in Newfoundland—had my own boat with a crew of two. But people were starting to notice how I never seemed to age. Then I found out I had a fae Gift. My dad's an envoy, too. You'd like him—everyone does. Give the man a bottle of wine and a box of crackers and he can make a party. He wasn't home much, but when he was, life was so damn fun."

Marjani rested her chin on her knees, the light from the fire burnishing her profile a rich gold. "Sounds a lot like you."

"I'm afraid so."

Arne had flitted in and out of Fane's life just as Fane had Evie's. Try and talk about anything deep, and Arne shrugged it off with a laugh. His motto was, "Life's too short and time goes by."

Fane blew out a breath. "Anyway, I'd always looked up to my dad…would've done anything to be like him. I was late to come into my Gift, but as soon as Dad found out I was a wayfarer, he brought me to Iceland and talked the king into giving me a chance. Turned out I was good at it. Hell, how many people would turn down an offer to be part of a fae court?"

She shrugged.

He shot her a look. Because Marjani had turned Sindre down—multiple times.

"The king did his damnedest to tempt you, didn't he? And you just kept telling him no. You know how much I admire you for that?"

"Don't." She made a sharp movement with her hand. "I'm—I've made some bad choices myself."

"Yeah? Well, this was the mother of all bad choices." He gave a humorless laugh. "Hell, I was like a fucking kid with my nose pressed to the window of a candy store. The fae are—the fae. Rich, glamorous, sexy as hell—and they wanted me. Fane Morningstar, a fisherman from Canada. The women, well… " He swallowed against the bitter taste in his mouth. "But to them, I was just a shiny new plaything. No pureblood would mate with a mixed-blood like me."

She touched his leg. "I'm sorry."

"Hey, it's not all bad. It's a good job—interesting, and the pay is fucking awesome." His mouth twisted. "Most of the time I don't even have to hurt someone else to do it. And when I do, I tell myself that if I don't do it, someone else will. The king has a half-dozen other envoys."

She took her hand from his leg and straightened up. "That's an excuse. Your actions shouldn't depend on anyone else."

"It's not so black and white."

"For me, it is."

"Well, that's the difference between you and me, isn't it?" He picked up a piece of gravel and tossed it into the pool. It landed with a plunk and sank below the dark, steaming surface. "I can tell you one thing, all the excuses in the world didn't make me feel better about spying on you. A woman I'd come to like. A lot."

She took his empty plate and set it on top of hers. "But you did it anyway."

"Yeah." He briefly closed his eyes. "I owe you an apology for that."

"Would you do it again?" A quiet question in the shadowy cavern.

He took a deep, pained breath. "Probably. Under the terms of the *geas*, I can't disobey a direct order from the king."

"Then don't bother saying you're sorry. Because then I have to respond that it's all right. And it's not. You tricked me, Fane."

He nodded, accepting that. "I'm sor—" He halted and then tried again. "At least let me thank you for taking care of me these past two days. No one would've blamed you if you'd left me outside for the goblins."

"I didn't do it for you," she returned. "I did it for Evie. She's clan now, and you're her dad."

"Ah." He fingered another piece of gravel. "Well, thanks anyway."

"Okay," she added grudgingly, as if he'd argued with her. "Maybe I did do it a little bit for you. That doesn't mean I didn't think about leaving you—because you're right, no one would've blamed me. But you were so sick, and I knew it was because of me."

"You should have left. You need to get the hell out of Iceland. The king is all powerful here. Even the humans obey him."

"How? They're probably watching the airport, and I don't have enough money to hire a boat."

He shook his head. "And you won't leave until you find out what happened to your friend Luc, will you? No, don't answer that. That way if the king asks, I can honestly say I don't know. But the goblins are nocturnal. They hunt at night."

"So you're saying I should wait until morning before I leave."

"Yeah."

She nodded—and then slanted him a look that made him instantly hard.

He swallowed. "Jani?"

"I shouldn't want you," she said, almost to herself. "I was so fucking angry at you when I found out you'd been playing me all this time."

"I'm sorry. So bloody sorry."

"But these past couple of days, I had a lot of time to think." She stared into the fire. "You did try to warn me. Told me I should leave Iceland, more than once. And you wouldn't have been so sick if you hadn't tried to interfere between me and the king."

His fingers tightened around the gravel. "I couldn't just stand by and do nothing. And your friend Luc agreed. He wanted you out of there."

That earned him a growl. "If Luc had his way, I'd be safe in his den, having his cubs."

"You?" He made small, disbelieving sound. "He doesn't know you very well, does he?"

"No. I mean, he *does* know me. But he can't help himself. He's a fada male—he wants to protect his mate—even if it drives me insane."

"All men want to protect their mate. Just like women want to protect theirs."

She looked at him, arrested. "See, that's what Luc doesn't get. That it goes both ways—for me, anyway."

"So what now?"

"I don't know." She looked down at her hands, loose in her lap. "I came to Iceland to kill Corban. After that..." She shrugged and trailed off.

His chest constricted. He'd guessed right; this was a suicide mission.

"I care." He tossed the gravel aside and dared to reach out. When she didn't pull away, he traced a finger over the fine bones of her jaw.

She stilled. "You—what?"

"I care what happens to you. Very much."

She drew a slow breath. "It would just be for tonight. After that, we have to split up—go our separate ways. The *geas* means I can't trust you."

"Okay. Sure." He would've agreed to anything about then. Hell, if she'd asked him for the moon, he'd have grabbed a ladder and started climbing.

"There's something you should know." Her throat worked. "It's...been a while."

He held his breath, afraid to say anything. This woman wouldn't be pressured. She'd have to come to it her own way—or not.

She rose to her feet, cat-supple, and washed the plates before setting them aside to dry. When she turned back, her irises were slivered with turquoise.

And then she flashed him a smile, the first true smile he'd seen from her.

His heart kicked. Her smile was broad and warm and even more beautiful than he'd pictured.

"The water is a perfect temperature," she murmured.

He opened his mouth to reply. But the words died unsaid as she raised her arms, pulled off the T-shirt and black bra, and let them drop to the ground.

CHAPTER 23

*M*arjani drew a deep breath, naked from the waist up except for the fake quartz around her neck. Nervous, but wanting this, her skin buzzing and her heart racing.

Fane stared up at her, a sexy dark scruff covering his cheeks and jaw. Even after being sick for two days and to be honest, kind of smelly, the man was fucking hot.

She'd had two days to think things over. She hadn't exactly forgiven him for spying on her, but she no longer blamed him. Within the limits of the *geas*, he'd done what he could. In fact, he'd tried to get her to leave—more than once—but she'd been laser-focused on getting to Corban.

She could even admit he'd been right to drag her out of the tower. If he hadn't, she'd probably be in a cage right now.

So yeah, she didn't blame Fane, but that didn't mean she trusted him. When she left the cavern, she was going alone.

But for the first time in a long time, she wanted a man—and she'd decided to go for it.

Maybe it was a bad idea. There was no way this thing between them could go anywhere. When she chose a mate, she wanted another earth fada, not a human-fae mix. Someone strong, steady—not this sexy, smooth-talking charmer.

So yeah, this would be a one-time thing—but maybe that was exactly why she should go for it. For once, she was completely free, unhampered with all the expectations that went with being Adric's second. No one but her and Fane would know what happened in this cavern—not her clan, not her friends, and certainly not her brother.

Fane rose to his feet and cupped her face. Clear topaz eyes searched hers. "You sure?"

Desire curled through her belly. "Yes."

His breath sucked in. "Gods, I want you." His mouth ghosted across hers.

A fada craved touch, more than other species. Her cat stretched and gave a happy little yowl. She curled her fingers against her thighs, wanting to touch him back, and yet cemented in place, need warring with fear.

His lips outlined the curve of her cheek. He nibbled her earlobe, tugged at the gold hoop with his teeth. Pleasure trilled up and down her spine, vibrated in her core.

His clever mouth continued moving, pressing kisses behind her ear and up her skull to the coarse black stubble.

"I should shave," she muttered. "It's too rough." Usually she ran a razor over it every few days, but she'd been running as her cougar for over a week.

"I like it." He brushed a palm over the back of her head. "Makes you look like a badass. Goes with those knives you love so much."

She pursed her lips, trying not to laugh—and that was the most wonderful, amazing thing. That she even wanted to laugh right now.

"And that's good?" she managed to ask.

"Oh, yeah." He turned her head to the side—and nipped her nape.

Her breath sped up. It was a dominant, very masculine move. She might be a soldier, but she was also a fada female. She liked a man who wasn't afraid to bite.

He nipped again, harder. "It makes me want to do bad things to you."

A moan escaped her lips. He kissed the small pain away and trailed a finger down the sensitive slope of her neck and across one shoulder.

Her throat worked.

He smiled. "You like that."

"Yes," she rasped.

He traced the arc of her collarbones before continuing to her breasts. He rubbed his thumbs over her aching nipples. "So beautiful," he breathed, his gaze on the dusky buds.

She was flat-chested and she knew it. But Fane's heated look made her feel like the sexiest woman alive.

"Mm." He bent and gave each nipple a hard suck before stepping back and dragging off his sweater. "Why don't we get into the pool? I could use a bath, frankly."

She blinked up at him, dazed with desire. Then her face split in a grin. "I sponged you down yesterday. But yeah, you could."

He stilled in the act of removing his T-shirt. "You should smile more often."

"Yeah?" She rubbed her stubbled head a little shyly.

"Yeah. You look good as a badass, but when you smile, you're beautiful."

He dropped the T-shirt on top of his sweater and reached for the button of his black jeans. He was all hard muscles and tanned skin, his chest sprinkled with dark blond hairs.

Her mouth literally watered. She swallowed noisily, following the trail of those wiry, gold-tipped hairs down to where they disappeared into his waistband.

His lips curved in a wicked smile. She'd removed his shoes the first day to make him more comfortable. Now he slowly and deliberately undid the button of his jeans.

She drew a sluggish breath. The air in the cavern felt heavy, thick.

His smile disappeared. They stared at each other as he slid down his zipper and stepped out of his jeans. His socks followed, and then he stood before her in dark knit boxers tented with an impressive erection.

"Now you." He stepped closer to undo her cargo pants. Dropping to one knee, he helped her out of each leg in turn, leaving her naked except for her black briefs. He caught her hips and nuzzled her belly, rubbing his night beard over the tender skin.

She inhaled in pleasure, taking in his arousal, a hot, salty spice overlaying the grassy green. He pressed a kiss to her mound—and then blew warm, moist air against the material over her clit.

Heat licked up her spine. She grabbed his shoulders and made a low sound, half cat, half human. He nipped and sucked at her sex through the cotton, stoking the heat, getting her good and wet for him.

He gave her a last kiss and lifted his head. "Bath first."

She blinked down at him. "No..."

"Yes. Believe me, you don't want me close to you right now."

And despite her grumbling that she'd been "close" to him for two days, he helped her out of the briefs and rose to his feet.

His gaze tracked down her body in one searing look, and then he dragged her into his arms. "If you knew how fucking much I want you..."

"Same," she managed to say before his mouth covered hers.

It was a deep kiss, involving tongues and teeth. A kiss that demanded she meet him halfway. He'd stopped being careful with her, and she loved it.

She twined her arms around his neck and rubbed her breasts against his bare chest, reveling in the feel of his wiry hair against her nipples. His erection pressed against her belly through the knit boxers. He palmed her bottom and squeezed, muttering hot, sexy things about how he'd wanted to see her naked since the very first day in the pub, how he'd fantasized about her ass.

This time, it was Marjani who broke the kiss.

She walked the few steps to the pool. "Coming?"

His gaze swept over her body again. She had time to see his eyes darken and then she did a shallow dive into the pool, coming up at the opposite end. She swiped the water out of her eyes and watched as he shucked his knit boxers.

His cock was long and hard. He wrapped his hand around himself and looked down at her as he stroked himself.

She moistened her lips, enjoying the view—and then gulped.

Something about the way he stood above her, legs apart, playing with himself...and the bad memories coated the back of her throat, sending fear skittering like a spider up her spine. She set a hand over her jumping heart.

"Jani." He released himself. "Don't."

"Don't what?"

"Don't think." He stepped into the pool and gave her a lopsided grin. "Thinking is way overrated. Ah...that feels good." He sank down on a ledge, the steamy water up to his chest, and stretched his long arms out along the edge of the pool.

She swallowed hard. Gradually, her heart slowed as she realized he was waiting for her to come to him. No coercion here, just a beautiful man who wanted her as much as she wanted him. She let out a breath and removed her hand from over her heart.

You got this, Jani.

If she stopped now, no one would judge her, not even Fane. She'd survived a gang rape. Fane might not know the details, but she knew he had a pretty good idea of what had happened.

But she didn't want to live the rest of her life celibate. Sex was good, a pleasure she refused to let Corban and those warped, feral river fada steal from her.

Fane rested his head against the ledge. His eyes drifted shut.

She frowned. How the fuck could he be so relaxed? Then she shook her head at how ridiculous she was being, and somehow she was moving, crossing the pool in a few strokes to take a seat on the ledge beside him.

She tipped her head back and let the hot water do its magic on her muscles. Fane touched the back of her head, and when she murmured in pleasure, began stroking it. Her tension eased. She moved her head against his palm, seeking more.

He massaged her nape, his fingers gentle, knowing. Something pinched in her chest.

It had been so long...

She turned her head to look at Fane. His eyelashes were a dark crescent on his lean cheeks, and his corn silk hair floated around his face.

"You may be right," she told him.

"About what?"

"That thinking is overrated."

His smile had a self-mocking edge. "Some would say I live my life by that principle."

"I don't believe that."

"You don't know me very well."

"I know you well enough. If you couldn't think several steps ahead, you wouldn't have lasted long in a fae court. Especially this one."

"Are you saying I'm as devious as they are?"

"Yeah." Her mouth quirked. "I think I am."

He threw back his head and laughed aloud. Then he sobered. "Gods. It's been so long since I talked to someone like you."

"Like me?"

"Someone who tells me exactly what she thinks of me. I'm so bloody tired of all the doublespeak. If only I'd met you before I——" He shook his head.

She moistened her lips, equal parts flattered and sad for him. "I wasn't even alive when you signed the contract with the king."

"No." He let his eyes drift shut again. "You weren't, were you?"

She studied his sculpted features, the pointed ear peeking through his wet blond hair. How in Hades had she ended up here, naked in a pool with this man?

She had a fada's prejudice against rich, entitled fae. They used fada—as servants, assassins, bodyguards, or for sex—and then looked down their glittering noses at the "animals."

But she was beginning to see that Fane was almost as much an outsider among the purebloods as she was.

Without opening his eyes, he rubbed a lazy hand over his chest. The water beaded on the curly blond hairs.

She drew a breath, her fingers literally tingling with the need to touch him.

"You didn't find any soap in that hut, did you?" he asked.

"No. And I looked, too."

He slid the rest of the way underwater, surfacing in the center where he scrubbed himself off with handfuls of grit before swimming back to her. He stood up in the pool, his waist level with her eyes. The tip of his cock bobbed above the water.

"Come here." He reached out a hand.

She swallowed—and not in a good way. No, this was an *I'm-not-sure-I-can-do-this* swallow. She instinctively crossed her arms over her breasts.

Fane's eyes flickered and she grimaced.

"Sorry." Cat's balls, she was a mess. But she couldn't make herself uncover her breasts.

His mouth thinned. "Don't."

"What?"

"Don't apologize."

She opened her mouth again and he raised a hand, palm out. "I mean it. You have nothing to be sorry for."

She sank deeper in the pool. "I wasn't always like this," she muttered. "So weak."

"You're not weak."

"How the fuck could you know?" she snapped, and then felt ashamed at how bitchy she was being. She was pushing him away, but she couldn't seem to stop herself.

"I just do." Sitting on the ledge, he curled an arm around her shoulders. When she didn't resist, he eased her onto his lap, cuddling her against his chest. "You're a badass to the core, and I'm happy just to hold you."

She sat there stiffly as strong fingers massaged her nape, stroked down her vertebrae. His erection was there against her hip, but he didn't draw attention to it, just kept petting her.

Her shoulders relaxed. How did he always seem to know exactly what she needed? She set a tentative hand over where his heart thumped slow and even beneath her cheek.

He kissed the top of her head. "Nothing's going to happen unless you want it to. You know that, don't you?"

"But I do want this. I *do*."

"Then we'll take it slow, okay?"

She nodded against his chest. "Thanks," she whispered. "For being patient."

He gave an odd little chuckle. "For you, Jani, I have all the patience in the world."

He nudged her chin with the back of his hand, bringing her mouth up so he could kiss her. She caressed his face, letting herself float on his kiss, a warm, weightless feeling. They explored each other's mouths, tasting all the hot, dark corners, sucking on each other's tongues.

By the time he rose to his feet with her in his arms, she thought she just might be able to do this after all. She wrapped an arm around his neck and let him set her on a nest made of their two sweaters.

Even then, he was in no hurry. He knelt beside her, his fingers whispering over her body: her breasts, her thighs, the sensitive skin behind her knees... A slow, easy seduction.

"You're so beautiful." A murmur in the dim light cast by the flickering fire. His wet hair fell around them, the diamond stud glinting in his left earlobe like a star.

Heat slid through her. Her breasts felt full, sensitized. Then his hot mouth closed over her nipple and she heard herself moan.

He gave a hard suck to that nipple, and then moved to the other, flicking the tip with his tongue, and then drawing it into the wet cave of his mouth. Stoking her arousal with teasing touches and sexy murmurs.

Wonder filled her.

That she wasn't afraid.

That she only wanted more.

Because this, what Fane was doing, was nothing like what those men had done to her. That had been an assault. They'd done their best to break her, and damn near succeeded.

But this, this was beautiful. How a woman and a man were meant to come together, in mutual pleasure.

Fane cupped her face and nuzzled her neck. His hairy thighs were between hers, his erection rubbing against her center.

And it felt *good*. Right.

She drew a breath, and then to her dismay, tears stung her eyes. She *never* cried.

Fane lifted his head. "What's wrong, love? Do you want me to—"

"No!" She dashed the tears away. "Nothing's wrong. It's just so good..."

Their eyes met, and she could've sworn he saw right to the heart of her. "It is for me, too."

He touched his lips to each of her eyelids in turn and then continued his exploration of her body, kissing his way down her breastbone to her belly. He trailed his lips over her mound, and she bent her knees to give him more space.

"Mm." He licked her, long and slow. "You taste so good."

Another lick, and then another.

And the good feelings got even better. Desire fizzed in her veins like champagne. She stroked his hair where it lay wet against her thigh.

Without warning, he sucked her clit into his mouth, and she let out a high, surprised mewl. He sucked harder, strong tugs that sent heat sparking through her. He moved lower for more of those delicious licks before returning to her clit again, learning what made her gasp and buck her hips.

Meanwhile, his long, knowing fingers played over her body—her nipples, her bottom, her inner thighs.

She reached for his head, trying to hold him against her sex, and he pulled back, his breath warm against the heated flesh.

She moaned. "Fane."

"I just want a look at you. You're like a flower." He teased her opening with his fingers. "A hot, wet, gorgeous flower that opens only for me."

She bit her lower lip. Desire climbed in her, but somehow she couldn't let go.

Then he husked, "Open for me, love. I want to see you come." He set his mouth to her clit and with a few self-assured licks, broke the tight hold she had on herself.

"Yes," she said. "*Yes.*"

He inserted two long fingers in her, and that was even better. Her sex clamped around him. Stars burst behind her eyes, shooting down to her toes and to the top of her head. Warming her to her very soul.

Fane stroked her inside with his fingers and outside with his tongue until she shuddered back to awareness with a sigh.

He raised his head. "Enough?"

"Oh, yeah. Too much."

"Never too much." With a sexy chuckle, he crawled back up her body to fit his mouth to hers. She tasted herself on his lips, mixed with his own male flavor.

She felt happy, even triumphant.

Because it felt like a victory.

She wrapped her arms around Fane and kissed him back as hard as she could.

CHAPTER 24

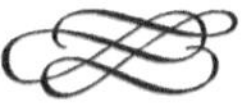

Fane lifted his head from Marjani and rolled to one side. Propping his head on his hand, he traced a finger down her nose and over her plush lips, swollen from his kisses. Her delicate features had a faint flush, her cat-shaped eyes heavy with satisfaction.

His heart swelled, because he'd been the one who put that look on her face.

He toyed with one of her small, pretty breasts. He loved her lean, streamlined body. He ached to bury himself in her, but he'd promised he'd move slowly, and he meant to keep that promise.

That this hurting, complicated woman had trusted him with herself as far as she had was an incredible gift.

He'd hated to see those flickers of fear. The gods knew he wasn't a violent man. A wayfarer didn't have to be. When things got rough, Fane simply…disappeared. But at the thought of anyone hurting Marjani, something dark and ugly balled in his chest.

She turned on her side and set her hand on his chest. "Now you." She tiptoed her fingers lower and encircled his erection.

He sucked in a breath, practically jumping out of his skin with pleasure. But he made himself say, "Only if you want."

"I want." The seriousness on her face made his lungs constrict.

"Then have at it, love." He rolled onto his back, pulling her on top.

"Mm," she purred. She straddled his hips, her eyes sparking blue-green.

He filled his hands with her taut, round ass. "I love it when I see your cougar."

She leaned forward to rub the tips of her nipples over his chest. "The cat wants to eat you up." The movement brought her mound against his cock. She gave another sexy purr and wriggled against him.

Heat sizzled up his spine. He flung out his arms. "I'm all yours."

She straightened up, her gaze on where his erection curved between their bellies. His fingers curled into his palms, but he kept still.

"Your move," he murmured.

She smiled—and did exactly what he'd hoped, wrapping those slim, competent fingers around him.

"That's it," he rasped. "Harder."

She slid her hand up and down his hard length, stroking and squeezing. The pads of her fingers were calloused, the slight roughness oddly arousing. The slit wept liquid and she smoothed it over the flushed cap.

His breath quickened. Remaining still became an impossibility.

With a low, inarticulate sound, he thrust into her fist. She worked him with one hand while with the other she played with his balls. Then she curved over his abdomen and swiped her hot little tongue over the cap.

His entire body clenched. "Holy fuck."

And then it got even better, because she lapped at the sensitive underside, licked her way up and down. It was so good, it hurt—and he wanted it to go on forever.

But of course, it couldn't. His balls drew up tight, and pleasure gathered at the base of his spine. He was close to exploding when she came higher onto her knees and placed his tip at her entrance.

He stilled, recalling they had no protection. Teeth clenched, he gripped her hips and lifted her a little away. "I don't want to give you a baby."

Thank the gods she was fada. No STDs, hardly any risk of pregnancy without the mate bond. But even so, he was careful these days. He'd gotten Evie's mom pregnant, after all.

Her brow furrowed. "But we're not mates."

"I wasn't mated to Evie's mom, either. I'll pull out."

She nodded and eased down on his dick. His mind went blank as wet, silky heat enclosed him.

When he was fully inside her, she stroked her hands down his abdomen with an appreciative hum. "You're all muscle."

"One advantage of being a wayfarer."

"You grow hot muscles?" She trailed a fingertip down the ridges of his abdomen.

He chuckled. "We burn a lot of energy, and we're natural athletes." He moved his hips, enjoying how her pupils dilated.

"Ah." She leaned forward, set her hands on his chest and began to move. The milky quartz banged against his chest, and without breaking her rhythm, she dragged it off and dropped it on the cavern floor.

He caressed the smooth, golden-brown skin of her hips and ass. "That's it, love."

He moved his hands to her breasts, playing with her firm little nipples. He gave them a pinch and her breath hissed out.

He smiled. "You like that."

At her murmur of assent, he pinched them harder. She twisted his nipples in playful retaliation, and his balls drew tight.

He began to move, meeting her thrusts with his own. She ground her pelvis on his, and contracted around him.

"More," she husked. "I need it harder."

Oh, yeah.

Happy to oblige, he rolled over so she lay on her back on the sweaters. Bracing himself on his forearms, he gave her a deep, leisurely kiss and, when she wrapped her arms and legs around him, began thrusting again. Slow at first, and then, when she dug her fingernails into his ass and urged him on with broken cries, hard and fast.

Heated inner walls squeezed him. She breathed out his name and came, the pulsing of her sex almost sending him over the edge with her.

He gritted his teeth and slowed down, riding out her orgasm, and then pulled out. A few strokes against her abdomen, and a goddamned fireball exploded through him. He groaned and buried his face in her neck, breathing her in as he rode the searing wave.

In its aftermath, he curled over her body, breath sawing in and out of his lungs, careful not to put his full weight on her. When he could talk again, he pressed a kiss to each of her eyelids. "Thank you."

Her low chuckle did funny things to his heart. "No thanks necessary."

He heaved himself off her and then lay down beside her on the hard stone, half-off the sweaters. Somehow she found the energy to rearrange the sweaters so they made a small bed. He scooted over so he was fully on them while she rose to clean herself in the pool.

When she returned, she curled up next to him, head on his shoulder. He tucked her close to his side. He hadn't figured her for a cuddler, but he liked it. He looked down at where her eyes were closed, her face relaxed. She looked so damn young. Too young to be a clan second.

His heart filled. *I love you*, he thought, but knew he couldn't say it. She'd probably laugh in his face. Instead, he brushed his lips over her forehead.

Her eyes opened. "You didn't have to pull out. If I did get pregnant, the clan would welcome the baby. We have so few cubs."

"Even so. Since Evie, I've been careful."

She glanced away. "I guess I'm not mom-material anyway. I...I'll probably never mate."

He made a low sound of disagreement. "You'd make a great mother."

"How would you know?"

"Because you love with all your heart—your brother, your friends, your clan. And you've seen enough to know that life's precious. Any kid would be lucky to have you as a mother."

"Yeah?" She gave him a wistful smile. "Well, thanks."

She was silent for a time, and then she pressed a kiss to the underside of his jaw. She smelled of sex and her own earthy spice. "You're not what I expected."

"Neither are you."

"Mm. When I heard how Evie's dad was never around when she was growing up, I figured you for a selfish ass. But then she told me about how you always seemed to show up when they really needed you, and I wondered why."

"Don't kid yourself." He stared bleakly at the ceiling. "I *am* a selfish ass."

"Maybe. But you love Evie, don't you? I think you stayed away to protect her."

He moved a shoulder. "I couldn't be sure the king wouldn't use her against me. Or worse, someone like Lady B. And as long as I'm under the *geas*, my life's not my own."

"Oh, Fane." Her voice was sad. "You're in deep, aren't you?"

His stomach constricted. He hadn't allowed himself to want for a long time. Not another person, anyway. But he wanted Marjani, bad.

He could guess what her life had been like up until now. The Baltimore Earth Fada were a small, poor clan. Most of their elders had died in those bloody feuds she called the Darktime. She'd probably had to fight for every last scrap she owned.

He yearned to pamper her. Drape her in pearls and diamonds, buy her flowers and chocolate. Indulge her with expensive clothes and trips to exotic, sunny places.

Evie's mom had been a mistake, but he'd been good to her in his own way. When she'd found another man—one who loved her back and was willing to take on Evie—Fane had been happy for her. And he was older now, smarter.

But Marjani was her brother's second, and intensely loyal. She'd never leave Adric and Baltimore.

And even though Fane was allowed his own women, there was no fucking way Sindre would allow him *this* woman. Besides, he was under a *geas*. Even if Sindre allowed it, it would just give the king power over them both.

The words spilled out anyway. "You asked if I ever come to Baltimore. I've been thinking—this doesn't have to be a one-night thing. The king will forgive me." He hoped. "I'll wait a couple of months, and then send you a message. I have a condo on the Mediterranean—in Spain, near Barcelona. We can meet there. No one has to know."

"Yeah?"

Encouraged, he said, "Say yes, Jani. I'll buy you anything you want. Clothes. Jewels..."

She stiffened and he trailed off.

"Fane." That was all she said. But it was all she needed to say.

He took her mouth, pouring everything he knew about seduction into the kiss. "Think about it. That's all I ask."

She turned her head away. "If we do meet, it won't be because you fucking pay me."

He swore under his breath. "I'm sorry." He nudged her chin until she was looking at him again. "I didn't mean it that way. It's just that I want to buy you pretty things."

Because I love you, damn it.

"But you don't have to. I don't need them."

"Got that. Loud and clear."

The hell with talking. He had the sinking feeling that nothing he could say would change her mind. And she'd made it clear this was a one-time thing. He might as well enjoy it while he could.

He inserted his thigh between hers, wrapped his hand around her nape and gave her a deep kiss.

Their lovemaking this time was urgent, frenzied. The bittersweet coming together of two people who knew something was ending almost before it had begun.

Marjani let out a sigh and rested her head on Fane's chest. The second time had been even better than the first. She'd been able to enjoy it without worrying she was going to freak out on him and go clawed.

Now dawn was speeding toward them way too fast. If she could just stop time, have another day with him. But they had only a few hours.

She stroked a hand down the hard planes of his abdomen to where his cock lay nestled on a patch of wiry dark hair.

"Hold that thought, love." He pressed a drowsy kiss to her temple. "You wore me out."

She grinned. "I guess you *are* just getting over a fever." She wrapped an arm around his waist and drifted off, sure that tonight, there'd be no nightmares.

She was wrong.

Men. Stinking of alcohol and lust.

Grabbing her, so hard they bruised her. Throwing her down on the floor. Thrusting into her.

Hurting her.

Shame filled every corner of her...spilled onto the floor along with her cries.

Weak. She was so damn weak.

The aphrodisiac burned like fire in her belly...and lower. And after a while, she'd stopped fighting—and begged, instead.

They'd made her beg. That was the one thing she couldn't forget...or forgive. She'd held out for as long as she could—fighting them, and then when she couldn't fight anymore, closed her eyes and pretended it wasn't happening to her.

The drug racing through her veins...making her weak and needy. That was what an aphrodisiac did to you—made you crave sensation. Sex. Pain. Drugs. Alcohol.

And when they ordered her to beg for more, she did.

They just laughed and passed her from man to man, until she curled into a tiny ball in her mind and tried not to go mad.

From far away she heard whimpering and knew it was her. But her eyelids stayed glued shut.

Without Tiago do Rio, she didn't know what would've happened.

He'd killed one man and scattered the others. Then he'd passed out and she'd spent the night beside his unconscious body, trembling from the effects of the drug...wondering if he'd wake up and rape her too, because they'd both been given the same powerful aphrodisiac.

And the worst thing was, she might not have fought him off. The drug had made her crave sex like a cat in heat.

No. No. No.

She moved her head restlessly from side to side.

"Jani. Jani." Fane stroked a hand down her back. "Wake up, love."

His gravelly voice, his scent—she knew it was him, and yet she didn't. The arms cuddling her became a cage. Terror swamped her.

Never again.

She fought free of his grip and crouched on the stone floor, breath scraping in and out of her lungs.

"Hey," he said. "Calm down. It's only me."

She unpeeled her eyelids. Her fingers were claws. She laid her ears back on her head, hissing in warning.

She realized she'd shifted partially to her cougar.

They stared at each other. She knew what Fane saw: a monster—a woman half-covered in fur with a cougar's paws and ears and teeth.

A corner of his mouth lifted in a sympathetic smile. "Bad dream, huh?"

She hissed again. But the spell was broken. Because she scented absolutely no fear—just concern.

He patted the nest of sweaters. "Come here."

She ignored him to creep to her cargo pants and her quartz, still in a side pocket. She set her paw on it, drew a deep breath—and shifted back to woman. Taking out her quartz, she sat on the cold stone floor facing the pool, the quartz tight in her hand.

Breathe in, breathe out.

The water steamed around her. She'd almost gotten used to the stench of sulfur.

Behind her, she heard movement—Fane curling up on the sweaters. "I'm here," he said. Just that and nothing else.

She moistened her lips. "I'm sorry."

"Jani. You have nothing to be sorry for."

"Yeah? I nearly ripped your throat out."

"But you didn't."

"No." She chuckled darkly. "Give the woman a freaking gold star."

"I'm not afraid of you."

"You should be."

Rising to her feet, she splashed some water on her face and then went around the back to pee. While Fane took his turn, she washed up and pulled on her briefs and a T-shirt. When he came back, she was seated at the pool's edge again, feet dangling in the hot water, the quartz still in her hand.

Fane donned his boxers and sat down beside her. Not touching her, but close enough to feel his body heat. His scent wrapped around her. Familiar...reassuring.

"I've seen a hundred turns of the sun," he said. "Did you know that?"

She shook her head. "You don't look much older than me. Although if you're Evie's dad, I guess you must be."

He nodded. "For sixty of those years, I've been the king's envoy. In that time I've done a lot of things I'm not proud of. But the worst was giving you to him."

"No!" She whipped her head around. "I gave *myself* to him. I might as well have wrapped myself up in shiny paper and mailed myself to the ice fae court."

"I should've stopped you. Way back in Reykjavik."

"You really think you could've stopped me? Even my brother couldn't, and he's my alpha." She looked back at the shimmering black water. "I knew what I was getting into. And I didn't care, as long as I took Corban with me."

"I thought it might be something like that." He inched closer so his shoulder touched hers. "What happened, Jani? What did they do to you?"

"You don't want to know."

"Maybe. But I think you need to tell someone. An outsider."

She pulled her legs out of the water and wrapped her arms around her legs. Maybe he was right. The first month, she shared parts of her story with Suha and Adric, but for the past year, she hadn't talked about it all.

"They gave me an aphrodisiac," she told her toes, the images unspooling in her mind.

He sucked in a breath.

"These were old fada. Going feral. You know what that means?"

"Not exactly."

"When we get old or damaged somehow, the animal takes over. You fae call us animals, but we're not. Trust me, there's a difference."

He touched her back. "I have *never* called you an animal. Even in my thoughts."

She nodded against her legs. "The alpha was from Greece. He mixed the aphrodisiac himself from an old recipe. It was...incredibly strong. It drove me a little crazy. They slapped me. Hurt me. And I wanted it." She sipped a breath. "I even wanted the sex."

"It was the drug, Jani. Not you."

"That's what I tell myself. Sometimes I even believe it."

He started to put an arm around her.

"Don't." She hunched her shoulders. "Let me finish."

"All right." He brought his arm back to his side.

"I begged them, Fane." She forced the words past her lips. "Instead of fighting them, I begged them for more."

His swallow was loud in the quiet cavern. "I'm so sorry. If I could only go back and change things for you, I would. But I can't. All I can say is that you're strong. A warrior who should never have had to fight that kind of battle. But you survived, and I'm so grateful for that."

Sharp glass filled her throat.

"I'm broken," she managed to say. "I spent most of the last year as my cougar. Because it's safer that way. Now I'm afraid to shift. Afraid the cougar will take over once and for all."

"*No.* Not broken. A survivor." He reached for her again, and this time she went into his arms.

He pulled her onto his lap and pressed a kiss to the top of her head. She stared, dry-eyed, at the pool. She was so fucking tired. Most nights, she only slept in snatches.

Fane stroked her back. Slow, soothing caresses. He crooned a wordless tune in his rough, sexy voice. Gradually she relaxed.

He massaged her nape until her head drooped, then murmured, "Let's lie down."

When she nodded, he rose to his feet and carried her the few steps to their sweater-nest, where he lay on his back, her draped over him like a blanket.

Keeping the quartz loosely in her hand, she laid her head on his chest, grateful for the sound of his heartbeat. It made her feel less alone.

"I'm here," he murmured one more time. And for now, that was enough.

CHAPTER 26

Fane woke to find the thin light of dawn spilling through a crack in the cavern ceiling. But what had awakened him was the tug of the *geas*.

His heart sank. Guess Sindre knew he'd recovered.

A chilly white mist formed in his palm. Blue writing unfurled against it and then faded away: *Return to court. If the fada is with you, bring her, too.*

He drew a long breath. Such a long-distance command didn't have the same power as when Sindre addressed him directly, but he couldn't ignore it.

He turned to Marjani—but he was alone on the cavern floor.

He lifted up a little and saw her creeping fully dressed toward the exit, her boots in her hands. He felt a sharp hurt that after the night they'd shared, she'd sneak out without even saying goodbye. But how could he blame her?

The *geas* tugged harder. He dropped back on the floor and clenched his jaw, resisting. Let her go. That way, he could truthfully say he didn't know where she was.

Gods, it had nearly broken him to hear her story last night. The things the woman had survived. It was amazing she was still walking around.

Just before they'd fallen asleep, she'd curled into a ball on her side, wound tight as a watch spring. He'd followed, wrapping his body around her.

Somehow, he'd vowed as his eyes drifted shut, he'd save her from Sindre and Blaer.

Now he glanced at her again. Maybe he could use Sindre's order to help her? Because he *knew* she was going back to the court to save that damn friend of hers

—and the king would be waiting. That maze of his would snap shut on her like a wolf's jaws.

He sat up. "Wait."

She whipped around as he snatched up his clothes.

Her eyes blazed cougar-blue. "Let me go, Fane."

"You're going back, aren't you?" He zipped up his jeans and sat down to put on his shoes. "To save your friend."

"I'm not going to answer that. You're under a *geas*, remember?" She stepped into her boots and leaned over to tie them.

He winced but persisted. "He might have escaped."

"Then where is he? He's a wolf. If he got away from them, he would've followed our scent."

He blew out a breath and tried another tack. "You need me. You can't get through the portals without me."

"I did it once."

"And the goblins almost captured you."

She finished tying her boots and straightened up, arms crossed over the pert breasts he'd kissed just a few short hours ago. "Goodbye, Fane," she said in a hard voice. Then she scraped a hand over her shaved head. "Have...a good life, okay?"

She slanted him a crooked smile that arrowed straight to his heart—and slipped into the tunnel.

"Damn it, Jani." He strode across the cavern and inched his way after her.

She bared her teeth at him. "Stay the fuck away from me. Or is this a way to get back on the king's good side?"

His jaw set. "Look, you want back in, and I have to return—so why don't we work together? I'll escort you into the castle, and then you can give me the slip. That should give you a chance to do whatever you need to do."

"No fucking way." She kept going.

"Bloody-minded woman." He followed her as she made her way back to the surface. When the passage narrowed, this time he bent his knees so his shoulders wouldn't get stuck, and squeezed his way through.

When they emerged from the boulders, the rising sun washed the sky a pale pink and gold. To the north, Sindre's magic hid the castle from the human world, but as a member of the court, Fane could see it hunched on the tundra, dark and brooding.

He grabbed Marjani's arm. "Please don't go back there." He desperately tried to come up with an argument that would keep her safe, but he had nothing.

And the *geas* had sunk its talons deep now. If he walked in any direction but toward the castle, it would get stronger until he literally couldn't take another step except in the way Sindre wished him to go.

Marjani's eyes changed to blue frost. She bared her teeth. "Let. Me. Go," she said in a guttural, barely human voice.

Wariness slid up his spine. He loosened his grip, uncomfortably aware he was dealing with a woman who could change into a large, predatory cat. But some stubborn part of him refused to believe she'd attack him.

"At least promise you won't take the king's bargain."

Some of the brown seeped back into her irises. She set a hand on his cheek. "I can't promise that. Luc is clan, one of my brother's lieutenants. But more than that—we grew up together. I won't leave without him. Not when it's my fault he's here."

"The hell it's your fault. He's an adult; he makes his own choices. And I'd bet if he was here right now, he'd tell you to save yourself."

"Maybe. But..." She moved a shoulder. "He's in love with me. I knew he'd follow me, but I just had to prove I could do this."

Something dark made his fingers tighten on her arm. "Is he your mate?"

"No." Her gaze flew to him, startled. "I...don't feel the same."

That was something, at least. He blew out a breath. "Look, I have to go back anyway. At least let me get you safely inside. But we have to hurry. The best time to slip through the portals undetected is at dawn or dusk when the guard changes."

"No. Now let me go." She looked pointedly at his hand.

He hesitated, knowing he should let her go and yet unable to. And the awful thing was, he wasn't sure how much was him and how much was the *geas*.

"Goodbye, Fane." She wrenched herself from his grip and took a step back, her eyes sad but determined.

He opened his mouth and then shut it again as the truth struck him like a boot to the gut. She didn't trust him. And she was right, because he wasn't sure how far he could go before the *geas* made him betray her.

Sorrow stabbed through him. His throat felt too thick to breathe.

In accepting the *geas*, he'd lost her before he'd ever even had her.

He curled his fingers into his palms to keep himself from reaching for her. "Go, then," he said through numb lips.

She set off for the castle at a jog. He watched her go with the hungry eyes of a man who'd lost everything, including his self-respect.

Suddenly, she stilled, slim body taut, her eyes trained on a slight rise a hundred yards away. She'd never appeared so catlike.

His scalp lifted. "Jani? What is it?"

She slashed her hand downward. "*Quiet.*"

A high-pitched, excited shrieking came on the wind. *Goblins.*

What the fuck? Why would the king order Fane to return and then allow Blaer to send her little fiends after them? But there was no time to ponder that.

He raced across the grass, scooped up Marjani and turned to run back to the cavern. But they were surrounded, the small, fur-clad beings hurtling at them from every direction.

"We have to fight." She twisted out of his arms. "Here." She shoved the dagger into his hand and stood back to back with him, her switchblade ready.

"Hell." He looked from the dagger to the goblins racing across the tundra. "You think I know how to use this thing?"

"It's iron. Aim for the eyes. The poison will slow them down."

"I have a better idea." Gripping the dagger, point out, he reached back with his other hand, looped his fingers through Marjani's belt loops and made the two of them invisible, a shadow on the tundra. "They can't see us now," he whispered.

"Works." She kept her eyes on the goblins, who had slowed to a creep, chittering in puzzlement to each other.

Marjani lashed out, stabbing the closest ones in the throat. Unable to see her, they fell at her feet, dead. Even Fane managed to take out a goblin that had practically run straight into his dagger.

The rest fell back, muttering to each other. Fane and Marjani stilled, scarcely daring to breathe. But they were surrounded by the dead goblins' bodies. Even goblins—who weren't the brightest creatures on the planet—could deduce where they must be. With a gleeful roar, the remaining goblins piled on.

Razor-sharp teeth sank into Fane's arm. Black claws raked over his face. Behind him, he heard grunts as Marjani's blade found a few more of their attackers.

But ten more goblins took their place, dragging Fane to the ground. Marjani was torn from his grip. He lost his focus, and they both became visible again.

He glanced up to see Blaer had 'ported onto the boulders. The blond hair whipping around her face didn't hide her smug smile.

Then a rock smashed into his temple and everything went black.

CHAPTER 27

ane was down, his head bloody. Marjani's breath hitched.

Please let him be okay. Don't let me lose him, too.

Because walking away from him had been right up there with one of the hardest things she'd ever done in her life. But how could she trust a man under Sindre's *geas*?

The goblins kept coming, so she couldn't even check if he was still breathing. Snatching up the dagger, she grimly fought on, a blade in each hand.

But the vicious little creatures seemed to multiply like rabbits. For every goblin she killed, two more sprang forward to take its place. Biting and gouging her, until she was bleeding from multiple wounds and their sour stench filled her nostrils.

They climbed each other to leap at her until a blow knocked her to her knees beside Fane's prone body. Her knives went flying. She scrabbled for them, but the dagger was too far away, and she didn't know where the switchblade was.

A stir in the air made her lift her head. Blaer had 'ported in, although she chose to perch on the rocks above the fray. Marjani snarled and inched her way toward the dagger. It wasn't a throwing knife, but she thought she could still hit her mark.

There. She had it.

A shadow near Blaer's leg moved and became a wolf—a wolf with Luc's eyes and a quartz hanging from its neck.

The fae lady set a hand on his head—and smiled.

"*No.*" Marjani wasn't sure if she'd whispered or shouted. She leapt to her feet and aimed the dagger at Blaer's throat.

A small body slammed into her legs at the same time another landed on her back. Wiry arms wrapped around her wrist, pulling her arm down so that the dagger hit a boulder instead of Blaer. Long nails raked down Marjani's body, ripping through her clothes to dig into her skin.

Marjani spun in circles, trying to knock them off, but they kept piling on until she fell flat on her stomach. Maddened with pain and the goblins' high-pitched shrieks, the cat forced its way to the surface. Bloodlust filled her, hot and red. She shifted partway, teeth elongating and claws sprouting from her fingertips, and fought as her animal. Sinking her teeth into the goblins' squat necks. Ripping open their soft bellies with her claws.

Someone moved behind her. She tried to twist away, but there was nowhere to go—she was surrounded. Something hard crashed into the back of her skull and a white light exploded behind her eyes.

The next thing she knew, she lay curled on her side, looking through bars.

Shiny iron bars.

~

MARJANI SWALLOWED, her mouth still filled with the bitter taste of the goblins' blood. She scrubbed a hand over her lips and tried not to wretch.

She was fully human again and lying on a sheepskin. Not touching the iron directly, but she still felt like crap from the poisonous metal already seeping into her. Not to mention that her body was bruised and bloodied from the fight with the goblins.

From its place against her thigh, her quartz hummed a healing song, valiantly doing what it could, but with the iron surrounding her, the best she could hope for was to maintain.

And the decoy quartz around her neck was gone.

She lifted her head. Pain lanced her brain. The room swooped around the cage, leaving her shaking and nauseated.

"Jani." In the next cage, Fane crouched on his haunches, his clothing in shreds, his face a mass of bruises and an egg-sized lump on his temple. "You all right?"

She closed her eyes and concentrated on not throwing up. Even talking was difficult through her swollen mouth.

"Yeah," she managed to say. "And you?"

"I've been better." Even with her eyes closed, she somehow knew his mouth had kicked up in his trademark wry grin.

"Blaer?" She spoke the fae lady's name, because what did it matter if she drew her attention?

"We're alone for now, except for the black wolf. I'm not sure if he's still alive, though. He hasn't moved once in the last half hour."

Corban could go fuck himself. It was Luc she was worried about. She made herself ask. "Luc?"

"No. It's only us three."

"No. She has...him. I saw."

"Fuck. I'm sorry."

Her chest constricted. Luc had been there for her through thick and thin, patiently waiting for her to grow up and choose him as her mate. For a while, she'd thought maybe... But no. It had been some time since she'd known she just didn't think of him in that way.

But even though she'd told him that, he'd stubbornly insisted on waiting. Hoping.

Tears seeped from her eyes. She cried not because she loved Luc, but because she didn't—at least, not in the way a woman loves her mate. And now he was under Blaer's control. If only she hadn't been so hellbent on proving she still had what it took to be Adric's second, he might still be back in Baltimore.

"It's okay, sweetheart," murmured Fane. "There's a canteen next to you. Drink. It's just water."

Without opening her eyes, she felt for it. The first thing she did was rinse her mouth and spit out the water through the bars of the cage. Then she took a few small sips, needing the fluid but afraid her stomach would rebel. The water soothed her swollen mouth, and she managed to keep it down.

She capped the canteen and set it back down before lifting her hand to explore the bump on the back of her skull. It was caked with dried blood, but at least it was no longer bleeding.

Next, her hand went to her front pocket. Her stomach lurched as she confirmed that she'd lost both the switchblade and the dagger. Even her stiletto would've been something, but she'd tossed it to Luc. She was defenseless.

Panic clawed her nape. Behind her eyelids, black spots danced.

"Hey." Fane's voice. "You still with me?"

She dropped her hand back to the sheepskin. *Answer him.*

But she couldn't seem to summon up the energy.

He muttered something harsh. "Shift, damn it. You'll heal faster."

True. But there was a reason she shouldn't. She feared letting the cat out, weak and exhausted as she was.

She lifted heavy eyelids. This time, the room remained steady.

And at least her quartz was still safe in her cargo pants. The pocket's flap had ripped, but by some miracle, the zipper had held. She set a hand over the material covering it and concentrated on not throwing up.

Fane had dropped onto his hands and knees. His whole body spoke of his worry for her. "Jani. You need to shift."

"Can't," she said between swollen lips.

"Why the fuck not?"

"Not...in control."

His forehead creased. "What do you mean?"

"Cougar...wants to take over."

"So? You won't let it."

She gave a mirthless chuckle. "Not...that simple."

"Screw that." Blue eyes blazed into hers. "You *can*. I know you can."

For some damn reason, she believed him. She wriggled out of the tattered sweater first. Someone had removed her boots. She eased her briefs and pants down her legs at the same time, taking care with the deep slash on her right thigh, and then pulled off her socks.

Next came her T-shirt. Just pulling it over her head made her go blind with pain. A moan escaped her lips. She curled into a panting, agonized ball, and then gritted her teeth and dragged off her bra, too.

"That's my girl," Fane said.

She growled, low and mean, but he just winked back.

Sitting cross-legged on the sheepskin, she dug her quartz out of the pocket. Holding it to her heart, she opened herself to the shift.

Another wave of nausea rolled through her. She clenched her jaw and kept trying. Her quartz warmed against her chest, but the energy level was dangerously low. That was bad—she'd counted on drawing on the tiny crystals to help her through the shift. She estimated she had a fifty-fifty chance of succeeding.

She swallowed dryly. Should she risk it?

But for once, her cat's independence served her. It surged up, determined to be out. For a few frightening seconds she wavered between human and cat—and then she was crouched on the sheepskin as her cougar.

"Excellent," said Fane.

She twitched her tail, pleased with both herself and him.

Already she felt better. The shift had healed the minor cuts and bruises, including her swollen mouth. Even her head ached less.

Her sharp hearing detected a faint heartbeat to her right. Corban—alive, but close to death.

She gave her injured thigh a few soothing licks and then settled onto the rug, positioning her center over her quartz. The healing energy hummed through her, sinking into her very bones. If she could just get out of this fucking cage, she could go looking for Luc. But the iron continued to sap her energy.

Fane lay down on his rug with a sigh. She eyed him anxiously. He was hurt bad—worse than her. His heartbeat was slow and uneven, and blood seeped from cuts and gashes all over his body, its sharp iron-and-silver scent filling her nostrils.

The cat yowled and flexed its claws, frantic to go to him. It couldn't understand why it couldn't batter itself against the cage door until it broke.

Bad. Too much blood. The man needs help.

Marjani mentally stroked its head. *Iron*, she told it. *Bad magic.*

"Love you," Fane rasped.

The cat purred, liking the sound of that. Beneath Marjani's abdomen, the quartz hummed joyfully against her heart.

Love? She didn't know about that, but Fane was hers in some way she didn't want to examine too deeply.

Ours, the cat agreed.

But it was bad that the man was in an iron cage. He needed to get out, to heal.

And then the thing Marjani most feared happened. The cougar wrenched control from her.

CHAPTER 28

The cat whined and pushed itself up on all fours.

The human was too cautious. Maybe battering itself against the cage wouldn't help, but it couldn't just lie there and do nothing. And it might bring that fae bitch running, and then the cat could sink its teeth into her.

"Jani?" The blond man with the good smell lifted his head. "What are you doing?"

The cougar flung itself against the door. The iron bars seared its fur. It fell back on the sheepskin, wheezing.

"No!" He pushed himself up on his forearms. "It's okay—honest. I know you can smell the blood, but don't forget, I'm a quarter fae. The cuts are already closing up."

Rising back onto all fours, the cat swung its head in the man's direction. A deep inhale confirmed he spoke the truth. The terror eased.

"Rest, now." A soft command. "If you want to help me, you have to heal first."

Calmer, but still agitated, the cat snarled at the locked door. It still wanted to go to him. It *needed* to go to him.

"Please, Jani." His gaze snagged the cat's. "Calm down. I can't stand for you to get hurt any worse."

Jani? The name belonged to the human part. The woman.

The cat turned it over in its mind. A cougar had no name—or need of one.

It shook its head. The cage pressed in on it from every direction. Something wild and primitive screamed for it to beat itself bloody against the bars. But the man was right—it needed to heal first. Then when the woman who had dared put the cat and its man in a cage returned, it would be ready.

The cat settled back onto the rug.

"That's it," the man said. "Rest."

The cat *was* tired. So tired... Its eyes shut and it dozed.

Time passed. An hour, maybe two. The cat had little use for the way humans marked time.

"Jani. Jani? Wake up, damn it. Someone's coming."

The cat jerked awake just as the heavy oak door banged open. The cat snapped up its quartz, hiding it in the pocket of its cheek. No way was that bitch getting her hands on its real quartz.

But it wasn't Blaer, it was a big, bearded redhead with the acrid silver scent of a pureblood.

The cat lifted onto its forepaws, growling a warning.

"That woman has gone too far," the redhead declared in ringing tones. "Caging the fada is one thing. But my own bloody grandson?"

Words. But they might be important. The cat allowed its Marjani-part to surface enough to understand.

"I agree," said a silky voice. The fae king with the cold gray eyes followed him into the room. "My apologies, Roald."

Roald? From Marjani, the cat got a picture of a fierce redhead who captained the fae king's warriors. Another picture told the cat that the warrior could conjure fae balls, the fae version of grenades. Take a direct hit, and you were toast.

The Marjani-part blinked. Fane was Lord Roald's *grandson*?

The man—Fane—pushed up onto his knees and glared at both fae, his heart beating hard and fast. He was too hurt to be moving.

The cat rose, anxious to go to him. To make him better.

More talk from the two purebloods. Then the king snapped his fingers and Fane's cage opened. He half-crawled, half-fell out and then, with a pained grunt, drew himself up to his full height.

"The boy needs healing," snapped the redheaded fae.

The fae king inclined his head. A fog-message formed in his palm and then disappeared. Thirty seconds later, a tall blonde with the serene presence of a healer entered the tower. Clucking her tongue at Fane's injuries, she set a hand on his back and urged him to sit.

"I'll stand." Fane glanced at the cougar. It could *feel* him willing it to trust him. That he'd get it out of the cage.

The cat stilled, its gaze flicking between him and the cold-eyed king.

"As you wish." The blond healer kept her hand on the small of Fane's back. Magic hummed in the air.

Fane's eyes drifted half shut.

The king gave the cat a small, satisfied smile. He might not have ordered the cat's imprisonment, but he was happy to have it in his power.

The cat whipped its tail back and forth. *Come closer if you dare.*

But the iron sapped its strength. It rested its head on its paws and stared at the king, unblinking, knowing that made the fae nervous.

"She's got pride," Roald murmured to the king.

"Yes."

They examined the cat. It curled its lip, letting them see a sharp white fang. Roald just shook his head, and the blond king's mouth curved in amusement.

Fane murmured a thank you to the healer. The bruises on his face had faded and the egg-sized lump on his temple had gone down. The blonde must be a powerful healer.

Fane crossed the room to the cat. "Shift," he murmured. "Don't give them an excuse to treat you as an animal."

The cat shook its head. The animal was strong. A fighter.

"Jani," he said. "Shift. *Now.*"

The cat resisted.

Not Jani—cat.

The fae king and his warrior moved closer.

"Please, love." Reaching through the iron bars, the blond man smoothed a hand down its head.

The cat nuzzled his palm and without meaning to, let down its guard. Instantly, Marjani elbowed her way into its consciousness, saying, *Shift. I need to talk to Sindre. Bargain with him.*

Too much talking, the cat shot back.

Now, Marjani insisted. *Unless you want to be stuck in this cage until we die.*

The cat grumbled but conceded the point.

The shift this time was long and hard. It was too soon after the last one, and the cat was still recovering from its injuries, its quartz almost depleted of energy. Its head started to pound again.

Marjani surfaced in time to understand. Her entire body iced.

She wasn't going to make it. She was going to die, stuck halfway between forms.

CHAPTER 29

*N*o. Terror seared Marjani's spine.

She sucked the quartz dry, but there still wasn't enough energy. Black edged her vision.

The cat panicked and tried to stop the shift, but that only made things worse. She fought with the frightened cougar for control. They'd gone too far to stop now.

Fane crouched beside the cage. "Shift, my beautiful cat," he crooned. "You can do it."

Love poured from him. She *felt* it, like something she could touch, grab hold of. The cougar calmed, and Marjani saw her chance.

She lunged at that love like a lifeline to yank herself through the shift—and then she was crouched on the sheepskin as a woman. Her breath shuddered in.

Goddess, that had been close, and not just the shift, either. She scraped her hands down her face. For a while there, she thought she'd finally gone feral.

She stood up, Fane rising with her. Her knees wobbled. She locked them, hoping Sindre wouldn't notice.

On the plus side, shifting twice had gone a long way toward healing her. Only the knot on her skull and the slash on her thigh still hurt.

The king's gaze traveled down to her bare toes and back up, taking in every detail. If she'd had any doubts about what he wanted, that look erased them.

She lifted her chin and stared back. The fingers of her free hand twitched, yearning for the security of one of her blades. It was her worst nightmare: to be trapped in her human form with no weapons.

Like the night she was kidnapped.

She swallowed over the crater in her throat.

"Get dressed." Fane gestured at her clothes.

Clothes. Right. She glanced down at the tangled pile. The sweater was a lost cause, but the T-shirt was only ripped in a few places. She picked it up and stood, unmoving. Sipping breaths.

The bars of the cage pressed in on her. Her skin prickled.

Lord Roald muttered something impatient, but Fane gave her an encouraging smile. "Go ahead."

Yes. You're alive and healing. You still have a chance if you keep your head.

She didn't bother with her bra, just put on the black briefs. The T-shirt was next. She palmed the quartz as she pulled the shirt on, and as she stepped into the cargo pants, slipped the precious chunk of rock into her front pocket. But without her blades, she might as well be naked.

Naked and defenseless.

A cold drop of sweat slid down her spine. Her heart slammed against her ribs so hard she was sure everyone in the room could hear it.

The blond healer crossed the room to Marjani, her gray eyes compassionate. "She could use healing, too," she told the king.

Fane faced Sindre. "Let her out, and allow Ilka to heal her. You promised her no cages."

"So I did. But she didn't agree to the bargain, did she?"

"Fane," said his grandfather. "Stay out of this. It's between the king and the fada."

Fane ignored him to glare at the king. "Let her out," he insisted. "Or I swear I'll make sure her brother hears about this."

The two men locked gazes.

Marjani caught her breath. Was Fane batshit crazy? If he wasn't careful, Sindre was going to do that fucking frozen thing on him again.

Lord Roald cleared his throat. "The boy has a point. The fada before her were outcasts from their clans, or else had willingly entered into a bargain with Blaer. This woman is the Baltimore second. If she dies, her brother will stop at nothing to avenge her. You'll be fighting off assassination attempts for years."

The king considered that. "Very well. Blaer took her without my permission anyway." He snapped his fingers again, and the door swung open.

Marjani leapt out, and then wavered woozily on her feet. Immediately, Fane was there, wrapping an arm around her, lending her his strength.

He was warm and solid, and even covered in blood, had that faint scent of the outdoors she liked so much. She wanted so badly to lean on him.

But she saw a muscle in Sindre's jaw flex. Better not give him an excuse to hurt Fane again. She slipped out of his grip and put some space between them.

Ilka made a small, concerned sound. "You've used a lot of energy, between healing and shifting. If you'll allow, I can give you a boost."

Marjani hesitated, but the healer's scent held nothing but compassion. "Thanks," she replied. "I'd appreciate that."

Ilka ran a hand down Marjani's back, and her skin warmed as life-giving energy spread throughout her. Her pounding heart calmed, and her breath sighed out.

"That's better." The healer rubbed her back. "I wish I could do more," she said in an undertone, "but…"

Their eyes met. "Thank you," Marjani whispered back.

Ilka gave her a last squeeze before moving away.

Meanwhile, Fane had turned back to Sindre. "We were on our way back," he said in a hard voice. "You didn't have to set the goblins on us."

"That was Lady Blaer," the king returned.

"So she did it without your permission?" Lord Roald's lip curled. "God's balls, the night-fae woman grows bolder every day."

"Yes." Sindre's face seemed carved from ice. "She does."

Ilka stepped forward. "If I may speak, your highness?" When the king nodded, she said, "The fada is better, but she needs rest." She looked at Fane. "Both of them."

Sindre cut her off with a curt thanks. "That will be all, Ilka."

She inclined her head and glided out of the room.

"My tower." The king's gaze swept over Marjani, Fane and Roald. "Seven o'clock. All three of you. Consider this your invitation to dinner."

"We'll be there," Roald said.

"And Fane?" Sindre added. "Bring Marjani to the north tower first, and then return at seven for dinner. That's an order."

Fane nodded tightly, but Sindre had already 'ported out.

Dinner? Marjani thought. But then, the fae liked to think they were so civilized—as they forced you into unwilling bondage.

"You fool." Fane's grandfather scowled at him. "What were you thinking, to get involved with a fada?"

"Her name is Marjani."

The fae warrior raked his fierce hawk's eyes over her. "She's an animal, boy. And worse, the king wants her."

"Damn it, she's *not* an animal. She's a person—just like you or me. And the king can bloody well keep his hands off her."

Roald's heavy cinnamon brows lowered. "By the gods, you don't deserve my help."

Fane glowered back. "When have you ever helped me?"

"Who do you think vouched for you with the king?"

"That wasn't you, it was my dad."

"Aye, Arne brought you to the king's attention, but it was I who asked him to give you a chance. And this couldn't come at a worse time." Roald shook his head. "I've requested that the king declare you a full member of the court."

"A full member?" Fane got a funny look on his face. "You'd do that for me?"

Marjani looked from him to his grandfather. A full member of the court? She wasn't sure exactly what it meant, but it was obviously a big deal.

"You're my grandson, after all. And I have some small influence with the king."

"But you never said anything..."

"Well, what did you expect? You're a mixed-blood, and on top of that, you're too much like your father. Wayfarers, not warriors." Roald's mouth turned down as if that said it all. "But as I said the other day, I've been keeping an eye on you. You've made me proud. In your own way, you have courage. And you've proven your loyalty to the king."

Fane gave a short nod. "Thank you."

The big redhead raised a hand. "Let me finish. But this, this is an embarrassment. The whole court knows you snatched this fada from under the king's protection and ran away with her. You want to have a woman like her, fine. But not a woman that Sindre wants. Where's your common sense, boy?"

"The king's *protection*?" Fane's voice was coldly furious. "He wants Marjani as his plaything. He offered her anything she wanted—wealth, power. And when she turned him down, he tried to use her love for her friend to force her into accepting his *geas*. I saved her from him, damn it."

The two men glared at each other. It was Roald who looked away first. "The king awaits," he ground out, and stalked from the room.

Fane watched him go, his body rigid, before turning to her. "I'm sorry you had to hear that. He's old and set in his ways."

"I know." She twined her arms around his neck and gave him a crooked smile. "Thanks for sticking up for me. Here I thought you were just another fae asshole."

He smoothed the backs of his fingers over her cheek. "Do me a favor."

"What?"

"Don't lump me with those arses."

"You got it."

They grinned at each other, but it was the kind of smile you give when everything is about to go to shit.

"I have something for you." He pulled her switchblade out of his pocket.

Her jaw dropped. "How in Hades did you get that?"

"Wayfarer, you know. Quick hands."

"But you were unconscious. I saw you myself."

"I came to while we were still on the ground. It was just a few feet away. I managed to grab it before the goblins saw it." His throat worked. "I have to take you to the king's tower, Jani. The *geas*—it's pulling on me."

"I know. But this. I—" She slid the blade in and out a few times. Despite a few dents, it worked as good as ever. She clenched her fingers on the handle. "Thank you. It's the best gift you could have given me."

"Better than diamonds or pretty clothes?" He set his hands on her hips.

She lifted her eyes to his. His eyes were so clear, like falling up into the sky.

"Way better," she husked. "Light-years better."

His grip tightened on her. "I won't let him have you. I swear on my mother's grave."

"Oh, Fane." She came up on her toes to kiss his scruffy jaw. "I love that you said that. But—" She halted, but they both knew what she was thinking.

What could Fane do against one of the most powerful fae in the world? And there was the *geas*, too.

"I'll think of something. Promise me you won't agree to his bloody bargain."

"You know I can't promise that."

"Damn it, Jani." He pulled her hard against him, her face pressed to the crook of his neck. She heard his heartbeat beneath her cheek and it came to her. Like lightning on a dark night or a crack of thunder that rocked her to her soul.

Her breath snagged. This was why the cat had called him *Mine*. Why she'd felt his love and had been able to draw on it to finish the shift.

Because the mate bond had budded, fragile as a just-born rose. Her mom had told Marjani she'd know it when she felt it, and oh, she did. It made her hot and yearning and needful—and sad to the depths of her soul.

Because she couldn't let that beautiful, delicate bud grow into anything. For so many reasons, they weren't right for each other. She was a fada soldier. He was the stupid-rich, classy-as-fuck envoy of the ice fae king. She could never fit into his world.

And as for Fane fitting into hers? Yeah, right. She could just picture him living in a den in Baltimore. And what would Adric say? He might be more tolerant than Leron, but if his sister—and second—came back mated with a part-fae, it would cause trouble.

"Jani?" He set a finger under her chin and tipped up her face. What he saw there made him furrow his brow.

Then his face changed. His eyes crinkled and his lips curved. For once, she didn't see a trace of wryness or irony in his expression.

Just wonder and heat.

He said her name again, low and rough. "*Jani.*"

Mate. That was the cougar.

Her heart lurched. "No," she rasped and turned away.

Fane grabbed her upper arm. She stilled, and he wrapped his arms around her from behind. "When this is over, we're going to talk."

"No."

"Yes," he returned, soft but firm. Warm lips traced the side of her neck. "Do you think I'll let you go just like that? No fucking way."

And here she'd thought he was laid-back. But it made her smile, deep inside, to know he wanted her so much. Even if it would never work.

She pushed at his arms and got her nape nipped in retaliation.

"I want your promise." A growled demand.

She blew out a breath and gave in. Because really, what was she afraid of? Give the man a few days, and he'd see for himself how impossible this thing between them was.

"Fine." She let her head rest against his shoulder. "I promise."

"Good." He kissed the spot he'd nipped. "And now, we'd better go before the king sends someone looking for us." He urged her toward the door with a hand on her back.

She halted. Corban had lifted his head to watch them. She slipped out of Fane's grip.

"Wait for me outside," she told him. "I'll be right there."

"Leave him." Fane's gaze followed hers. "We don't need any more trouble."

"I can't."

"Then I'm staying right here."

She recognized that tone. He wasn't going to budge. Still, she tried one more time. "I don't want you to see this."

"Jani," he said, very patiently. "I've seen a hundred turns of the sun. Where do you get the idea you have to protect me?"

She dragged a hand over her stubbled head. "Stay then," she gritted, and crossed to her cousin.

Corban pushed himself up to stand on trembling legs, chest working like a

Her cousin closed his eyes.

She rubbed her nape. Why was she fighting with him? He was going to pass out without her learning anything.

"Tell me what you know about Luc," she said, "and I'll do it."

Beside her, Fane tensed.

Her chest squeezed. She didn't want him to see this. He'd probably never killed a man in his life, while she'd killed so many, their faces ran together in her mind.

"Go," she hissed. "I promise, I'll be there in a minute."

He crossed his arms over his chest. "I'll wait."

"*Please*," she said, but all she got was a shake of his head.

Then Corban spoke, and she turned back to him. Maybe it was better if Fane saw her as she really was—a killer. Then she wouldn't be forced to reject the mate bond, because he would.

"He's...with her," Corban said. "The lady."

"He went with her willingly?"

"Yes. She...told him...only way...to help you."

"She lied to him?"

"Don't know."

"It might not be a lie," Fane inserted. "You're alive, aren't you? That may be due to the bargain he struck with her."

Oh, Luc. Marjani briefly closed her eyes.

"So he's bound to her?" she asked. "He accepted her *geas*?"

"Yeah. She has a thing for fada lovers. Luc's probably even enjoying himself." Corban's lips stretched in a death's-head grin. "Until he...pisses her off."

"Is that what you did? Pissed her off?"

A shrug. "I told you...what you asked. Now...do it."

"One more thing. What did you tell her about our quartz?"

Her cousin's eyes slid sideways. That was all the answer she needed. Her breath caught at his treachery.

"Damn it, Corban. What the fuck have you done?"

"Couldn't...help it. She'd heard something. Figured...some of it out herself. I tried to...bargain with her. But I lost."

"Jani." Fane touched the small of her back. "We have to go."

"I'll be right there." She crouched next to the cage. Corban's eyes met hers through the iron bars.

"You don't have to do this," Fane said. "I know it's why you came, but he'll be dead by tomorrow anyway."

She shook her head. It wasn't about her revenge anymore, but how could she explain that to Fane? She barely understood herself.

"Do it." Her cousin crawled forward until they were just inches apart. He stared at her, his body trembling from the effort to keep himself on all fours. "Or are you too weak?"

Anger spiked through her. Not because he'd called her weak—she knew he was simply trying to goad her into doing it—but because she was going to have to kill her own cousin. Yet another death to haunt her.

"Fuck you." She pressed the catch releasing the blade. "I hope you go straight to Hades."

"Count on it." His mouth twisted. "Wondered if...you had...it in you."

"Believe it. I learned from the best, remember?" She slid her arm through the bars, careful not to touch the iron.

Corban gave a weak chuckle, before turning his head at an angle so she could slice his artery. He closed his eyes.

She took a deep breath, and then did it, quick and clean. It took a minute for him to bleed out. She set a hand on his shoulder and waited. She needed to witness this, so she could report to Adric that he was really dead.

And because even a bastard like her cousin didn't deserve to die alone.

Corban's eyelids fluttered. "Tell Adric...not doing...so bad."

She swallowed over a boulder-sized lump. "I will."

Air rattled in his emaciated chest—and then he lay still. His heart gave a few rapid, erratic beats and then lurched to a stop.

"Peace," she whispered and stood up. She wiped her blade on her pants leg and then shoved it into her pocket.

Her eyes met Fane's. She lifted her chin. Just let him look down at her. She refused to be ashamed.

But he held out his arms. "Come here."

Her mouth worked. She stared at him miserably, and then stumbled the three steps between them. His arms wrapped around her, strong and comforting.

"You did good," he said. "It was a kindness to put the poor man out of his misery."

Her breath rasped out. He was right. So why did her heart feel like a weight had been attached to it?

She'd hated Corban, but he'd still been her cousin. And a member of the clan.

She closed her eyes and breathed in Fane's clean scent. "I wish..."

He nodded against her hair. "Me, too."

"Why the hell did I have to meet you? I was doing just fine without you."

"I know you were."

"No, I wasn't," she contradicted. "I was going feral. I *am* going feral. It's just too fucking hard to be a human."

And then she was blubbering like a baby. Deep, wrenching sobs that felt like she was being turned inside out.

"Hush, now." Fane rubbed her back. "It's okay, love. It's okay."

She cried harder. Because it wasn't okay, and it hadn't been for a long time. The Darktime had taken her mom and dad, and good friends like Jace's sister Takira.

And although the Darktime was supposed to be over, bad things just kept happening.

"I'm...so tired," she said on a sob. "So fucking tired. Of all the killing. And I can barely control my animal anymore. It wants out, and I'm not sure why I shouldn't let it."

"Oh, love." Fane rocked her back and forth like she was a child. "I'm so sorry. Your cougar is beautiful, but so is the human part of you."

Her breath rasped in. "But it's so...hard to be human," she said to his chest.

The cat was so much less complicated. Straightforward. Basic. Mess with it, and it would rip out your throat and not lose a moment's sleep.

"I know." Soft lips brushed over her temple. "But you're not an animal, you're a fada. And I'm pretty sure that means accepting every part of you. Woman. Cougar. Even that small part of you that's fae."

She took another rasping breath and nodded. He was right. She'd just been trying to forget it.

"And you know what?" He pressed a kiss to each of her eyes. "I want to learn every part of you. Everything. Because that's what makes you who you are."

His words were balm to her broken soul. For so long, rage had been a bitter black knot in her chest.

Now, the knot slowly unclenched. Her sobs slowed until she hung in Fane's arms, drained.

"I love you." Fane stroked a hand over her head. "Whatever happens, remember that, okay?" He waited until she nodded before saying, "Stars, I hate to say this—but we have to go. The *geas* is pulling on me. And if we stay here much longer, that bitch might come back."

"Okay. Okay." She took a deep breath and then pushed away from him. She scrubbed at her face, knowing she must look like shit. And why did she care? But she did. Fane made her care about things like that.

He took her by the arm. "You all right?"

"Yeah." She took a last look at Corban. The lines of pain bracketing his mouth had smoothed. He looked almost peaceful. That was something, anyway.

Her jaw tightened. "You know what? I hope it pisses off Lady B to find him dead. The woman's a monster."

His smile held absolutely no humor. "It will. That, I can guarantee."

He reached for her, but she shook her head. "Let me wash first." Crossing the room to the kitchenette, she turned on the faucet as hot as she could stand and scrubbed her hands and arms.

As she watched the blood-stained water swirl down the drain, the shadows in the tower thickened. Her fangs pricked her gums.

She washed the tears from her face and strode back to Fane. "Let's get the fuck out of here."

"Yeah." He twined his fingers through hers, and together, they headed down the stairs.

CHAPTER 30

ates. As they exited the tower, Fane tightened his grip on Marjani's hand. He'd sensed the bond come to life, warming him from the inside out. Filling him with wonder—and hope, small but stubborn.

Through the bond, he'd *felt* her fear that he'd judge her for taking her cousin's life. But he'd known it was a mercy killing. He hurt for her, but he understood.

Gods, he'd hated seeing her cry. She might as well have reached into his chest and cracked open his heart. So much pain, his warrior woman had endured. Sometimes fate was one cruel son of a bitch.

When they got out of this—and they *would* get out of this—he'd spend the rest of his days showing her there was more to life than what she'd seen so far. Maybe that wolf fada would be better for her, but then again, maybe not.

A serious woman like Marjani needed someone to help her lighten up, make her smile. A man like Fane.

They set out for the north tower. Suddenly, the maze was nearly impossible to navigate, narrowing until they could barely squeeze through the tall walls, spiraling in on itself like a twisted skein of yarn and sending them down multiple dead-ends.

Marjani plodded alongside him, shoulders hunched a little. He hated to see her so subdued. He wracked his brains for a way to help her escape, even if it meant fighting Sindre's direct order. But the king knew she was here. How far would she get?

Anger churned in Fane's stomach. He felt so goddamned powerless.

"Cat's balls," Marjani muttered. "Does the man want us to get to his tower or not?"

"Oh, he wants us there." Fane glared at the towering white wall that had sprung up out of nowhere to block them. "He's just playing one of his fucking games." And messing with Fane's head. He was a wayfarer, a man always on the move. He hated small, enclosed spaces, and Sindre knew it.

At last, they came upon a familiar passageway filled with fae heading to dinner in the great hall. No one seemed surprised to see Fane and Marjani's fading bruises and tattered clothes. But then, gossip spread like wildfire through the court.

Most of the fae barely noticed them, uncaring what a mixed-blood and a fada were up to. Some shook their heads, their mouths in disapproving lines. A few smiled and nodded.

Fane kept a firm grip on Marjani's hand, proud to be seen with her. She was strong. Beautiful. Caring. And if she had a problem with you, she'd tell you straight out, instead of circling around the subject like these beautiful, two-faced creatures.

So he nodded back to the friendly fae, and ignored the rest.

"So." Marjani gave him the side-eye. "You're the famous Lord Roald's grandson. I had no idea."

"Trust me, he wants it that way. I'm a wayfarer, which means I'm a frivolous SOB who'd rather drink a beer with you than fight. Just like my dad. Roald blames it on my human grandmother—except humans don't have Gifts."

Her lips twitched. "If the shoe fits…"

He hooked an arm around her neck, glad she seemed to be feeling better. "We prefer to say we're well-rounded. What's wrong with enjoying life's pleasures?"

"Don't change, okay?" She reached up to squeeze his hand. "The world needs more people like you."

He nuzzled her ear. "I gave up trying to change a long time ago. Too much work. And I like me as I am."

She shook her head. "You're impossible."

"Now you sound like Roald." He released her to slip through a narrow opening.

"But you *would* like to be a full member of the court," she said when they were side by side again.

He lifted a shoulder and let it drop.

"Why? What would it mean, exactly?"

"The short answer? I'd be one of them. Right now, there are rituals I can't attend. Magic I can't access. And I have to smile and pretend not to see when one of them sneers at me."

"And that's important to you—to be accepted as one of them?"

He jerked his head in assent. "I'm one of Sindre's top envoys, but I'm so low in the hierarchy I might as well be dirt under their feet. If the king declared me a full member of the court, it would make me a pureblood in every way that counts. I could even mate with a pure—" He snapped his mouth shut. "Not that I'd want to. Not now."

Yeah, it had been his goal once. But not any longer.

She stopped and he did, too. The expression on her face made him reach for her, but she held up a hand. "Don't."

"Don't what?"

"Don't give up your dreams. Not for me."

"But I want to. Those dreams mean nothing if I don't have you."

"Fane." Lines formed between her brows. "This thing—it can't go anywhere. You know that, right? Nothing has changed."

Anger clogged his chest. Anger, and a touch of panic. "The hell it hasn't. You felt the bond, same as me. Don't try to tell me you didn't."

She looked at her bare toes.

"Go ahead," he growled. "Tell me we're not mates."

"I can't," she said in a barely audible voice.

"Then what's the problem?"

"You and me." She shook her head. "I'm my brother's second."

"So? What, you took a vow of celibacy?"

That almost got a smile out of her. "No, but I can't leave the clan. My brother needs me. The *clan* needs me. There are so few of us left after the Darktime."

"We'll figure it out." He reached for her, but she took a step back.

"You don't understand. Adric will never accept you. He can't."

He let his hands drop back to his sides. "Why the hell not? He accepted Evie, didn't he?"

"She's not under a *geas*. How could we trust you?" She shook her head. "I'm sorry, but it just wouldn't work."

"Okay." He dragged in a breath. Where was his so-called charm and negotiating ability when he needed it? But he couldn't seem to leave it be. "Maybe you're right. But after I serve out the *geas*?"

She stilled, her eyes searching his. "Are you asking me—?"

"To wait for me? Yeah." He stepped closer and framed her face. "Don't answer—not now. Just think about it, okay? I know it's a lot to ask, but you felt the bond, too. I know you did." He smoothed a thumb down the smooth butterscotch curve of her cheek.

She opened her mouth to speak, but he stopped her words with a finger.

"Later. Somehow, I'll come to you in Baltimore—or get word to you. I promise. Now come." He took her hand. "We must be almost there."

He was right. They turned a corner and there was the door to the north tower. It swung open and they stepped into the anteroom—and into a howling snowstorm that blew up out of nowhere, engulfing them in a blizzard of icy flakes.

"Bloody hell." He tightened his grip on her hand. "I'm not leaving you here," he shouted.

"You have to," she yelled back. "I'll be all right."

The wind whirled around them like a mini-tornado, jerking Marjani from his grip. The next thing he knew, what felt like a giant hand slammed into his chest, shoving him toward the outer door.

"*Jani.*" He tried to reach her but for every step forward, he was forced two steps back. The door opened and he was thrust into the hall. He clung to the doorjamb, bellowing her name.

The dark-haired Irish fada appeared out of the swirling white ball. The wind died, leaving just a few stray flakes drifting down, and a sudden, unnerving silence.

"Welcome, Marjani." The Irishwoman gave a dignified little bow. "I'm Jewel. The king has directed me to see to your needs."

Fane tried to re-enter the tower, but couldn't step over the threshold. Fury shook him.

"Damn you, Sindre," he yelled. "Let me in, you bastard."

Jewel clucked her tongue at him. "Don't worry yourself, now. She'll be fine. I'm to get her ready for dinner, that's all." She held out a hand to Marjani. "Come, *alanna.* You look like you could use a nice hot bath and a change of clothes. And perhaps a cup of tea?"

Marjani nodded at Fane. He knew she sensed the truth in Jewel's words, same as him. "Go ahead. I'll see you at dinner."

He hesitated. Gods, he hated to leave her. Still, what choice did they have but to follow Sindre's orders? The king had made it clear he wanted both Fane and Marjani at the dinner. Whatever he intended, it involved them both.

"She'll be fine," Jewel repeated. Her gaze caught his. "I promise."

He gave a curt nod and headed back to his room, hating how helpless Sindre made him feel. It was like playing cards with a hand you weren't allowed to see. But what could Fane do but play out the hand?

In his apartment, he dragged off his ruined clothes and threw them into the garbage chute. Unlike Marjani, both his shoes had remained on and somehow made it through the attack with only a few scuff marks. He left them on the floor next to the closet and headed into the bathroom. He'd have liked a soak in the tub, but he contented himself with a hot shower and a shave.

He racked his brains for a way to save Marjani. Maybe if he signed on to serve Sindre for another ninety-nine years? But he was afraid there was nothing he could offer that the king wanted more than her.

With a muttered curse, he set down his razor and strode naked out of the bathroom.

His father was sprawled on the easy chair, long legs stretched out, a beer in his hand. It was like looking into a mirror—the two of them had the same blond hair, dark brows and narrow face. A poet's face, his mom had said.

Arne grinned up at him. "There's my boy."

That was his dad. Always sure of his welcome. Fane hadn't seen him in years, and he acted like they'd just met last week.

"Hi, Dad." Fane glanced at the door, which apparently he hadn't locked. "Just come in and make yourself at home, why don't you?"

"I have, thank you." Arne raised the beer bottle to Fane and then stood up, arms open wide. "Now give your old dad a hug and act like you're glad to see me."

"You know I am." Fane hugged him back. "Where the hell have you been, anyway?"

"Oh, here and there." Arne slapped him on the back. "I hear you're having dinner with the king."

"You've been talking to Roald."

Arne waved his bottle noncommittally and settled back into the easy chair. "Why don't you get dressed and we'll have ourselves a chat?"

"I'd like that." Fane headed into his closet, emerging a few minutes later in clothes fit for a dinner with the king: black leather pants and a collarless shirt in a fae material that changed from navy to light blue when he moved. Clasping a gold bracelet around his wrist, he turned the wood chair to face Arne and sat down.

"So. Let me guess." He leaned back in the chair, fingers interlaced behind his head. "Roald ordered you to bring me to my goddamned senses. Give up the fada female, and stop embarrassing the family."

His dad chuckled. "Something like that."

"Consider it done. And the answer is no."

The skin around Arne's blue eyes crinkled in amusement. "Fair enough. Roald is breathing fire, though. Something about how you owe him and the Morningstar name. Oh, and he threw in something about diluting a bloodline that can be traced back to the first fae warriors."

"Like hell. I've been at the court for sixty turns of the sun, and in all that time, he's spoken to me less than a dozen times. I don't owe the man a bloody thing."

Arne's good-looking face turned serious. "Forget Roald. He's always growling about something or other. And he's a fine one to be talking about diluting bloodlines—he mated with my mother, after all. No, it's the king you should be worrying about. He makes a powerful enemy."

"You think I don't know that?" Fane sat up and leaned forward, hands on his thighs. "I love her, Dad."

"Lovers come and go. Life's too short—"

"And time goes by," Fane finished for him. "Yeah, I know. But..." He stared unseeingly down at his bare feet. "I think she's my mate, Dad."

"I see." Arne took a thoughtful sip of beer. "That changes things."

"No kidding."

"You can't hide from the king. It might take a decade, but he'll hunt you down."

Fane dragged a hand over his wet hair. "So we'll bargain with him."

"What can you offer that he doesn't already have?"

Fane's stomach sank. "I don't know, but I'll think of something. I have to."

A knock sounded on the door. Fane opened it to find three tall, stern-faced warriors—a woman and two men. The woman informed Fane that they'd been sent to escort him to the north tower.

Fane nodded. It was unnecessary, and the king knew it. He'd sent the warriors as a warning. "I'll be right out." They tried to object but he repeated, "I'll be right out," and shut the door in their faces.

He sat on the chair and put on his shoes and socks.

Arne rose to his feet. "I'm coming, too."

"Yeah?" Fane glanced up, surprised. He'd expected his dad to make some excuse and then get the hell out of there. "You sure?"

Arne shrugged. "I've known the king a lot longer than you. Who knows? I might be able to help. And besides, he always sets a good table."

CHAPTER 31

ewel led Marjani to a staircase of brushed steel and sparkling white granite that wound around the outside of Sindre's tower. When they reached the second floor, they crossed a glass skyway to a three-story wing and then continued up to the top floor.

"Here we are." Jewel ushered her into a large, airy apartment with sky-colored walls and long, narrow windows with a view of the windswept tundra.

The living room alone was three times the size of Fane's apartment. A couch and three chairs in an embroidered silver fabric were grouped around a glass-and-wood coffee table. Hanging from the ceiling were three ethereal silver chandeliers lit with flickering fae lights, and several thick, fleecy white rugs were scattered across the polished parquet floors.

Marjani's mouth slackened. She'd never been in a place half so gorgeous. "So this is how the other half lives."

Jewel gave a small smile and indicated a bedroom. "The bath's in here." She directed Marjani past a round pedestal bed into a bathroom with a pink marble bathtub the size of a small pool. Lush ferns, English ivy, and other green plants spilled from niches in the pink-and-beige tile, and the fixtures appeared to be solid gold.

Marjani's brows climbed. "I thought I was supposed to be the king's prisoner."

Their eyes met. "Oh, you are," the other woman said. "Don't mistake it for a moment. Would you like help with your clothes?"

It took Marjani a second to understand that the other woman was offering to help her undress. She gave a firm shake of her head. "No, thanks. I've got it."

"As you wish." Jewel crossed to the pink marble tub and turned on the faucets before sprinkling a sweet-smelling bath salt into the steaming water. "There are the towels." She indicated the thick white towels draped over a heated rack. "Help yourself to anything else you see. I'll be back in a few minutes with your tea."

"No tea for me. But I'd like a glass of water if you have it."

"As you wish." Going to a small cooling unit in the wall, Jewel removed a bottle of a fancy Icelandic water and poured it into a crystal glass before handing it to Marjani.

"Thank you." She took a sip and then inhaled slowly.

Even this close, the woman didn't have a scent. And there was that big, black-haired bodyguard who looked so familiar. Now that Marjani thought about it, he reminded her of Dion do Rio, the Rock Run River Fada alpha.

She narrowed her eyes. "Who are you, really?"

The other woman busied herself shutting the taps. "The fae call me Jewel."

"Which tells me nothing. You know I'm a fada, right?"

"I do." Jewel straightened. "From the Baltimore clan, I'm thinking."

Their eyes met. Marjani knew she should mind her own business, but something niggled at her. "You're a fada, too, aren't you?" And some kind of water fada, since she didn't wear a quartz.

Jewel tilted her head in assent.

"And that big bodyguard, he's your mate?"

The other woman's cobalt eyes flickered, telling Marjani she'd guessed correctly. But all Jewel said was, "Your bath is ready. Will you be wanting anything more?"

When Marjani said no, the other woman inclined her head. "I'll be in the living room. Call me if you need anything."

As soon as the door closed behind her, Marjani stripped off her ripped, bloody clothes. She hid the switchblade and her quartz beneath a towel on a ledge next to the tub where she could easily reach them, and then climbed into the bathtub.

The first thing she did was soap up a washcloth and scrub herself. Hard. When you shifted, the dirt and other stuff—like blood—got left behind. So she wasn't that dirty, but she still felt the need to clean herself.

It had been that kind of a day.

Maybe she *was* weak. She could just hear Leron sneering about her taking a mixed-blood lover. And mate with Fane? Her uncle would've run her out of the clan.

But it didn't feel weak, this thing she had with Fane. It felt like something that could make her stronger.

She finished scrubbing and reached for her quartz. Its song was barely audible, the crystals drained of energy. She closed her fingers around it and then sank beneath the hot water with a little sigh. The water was just the right temperature, and it smelled like a flower garden.

There was no hurry. Her internal clock told her she still had about a half an hour before she had to meet Sindre.

Above her, fae lights floated near the ceiling, their colors changing from pink to gold and back again. Her clenched muscles loosened. She set her quartz on her solar plexus, leaned back against the smooth marble and let her eyes drift shut.

She'd had time to come up with a plan while nursing Fane. She was starting to intuit the basic, underlying structure of the maze. She was pretty sure that with the help of her quartz, she could find her way to the portal Fane had taken her through the other day.

She couldn't open it herself, but a portal was like a fae ward, only instead of keeping people *out*, a portal allowed you to pass each way. And fae wards often had a fatal weakness—they couldn't detect the fada when they were in their animal forms. The wards simply didn't "see" the fada as people, but as animals.

So the plan had been to spring Luc, make their way to the portal, and then shift and go so deep into their animals that the portal allowed them to pass out of the castle—and back into the human world. It would have been a risk, since Marjani would've had to cede complete control to the cat. Still, for Luc, she would've done it.

But now Luc had accepted Blaer's *geas*. That fae bitch would make a pet of him, maybe even keep him in a cage.

Tears stung her eyes. *Damn wolf fada. Who asked you to sacrifice yourself for me?*

Luc tried to give her an out by removing himself from the equation so that Sindre couldn't use him to force his *geas* on her. But she was afraid the king would think of something else. The man was old and scary smart.

Her fingers tightened around her quartz. If only she could call Adric. Because she was fresh out of ideas.

Either she accepted Sindre's *geas*—or she got him alone and slit his throat. The tricky part would be escaping his bodyguards afterward and finding her way back to the human world. The only possible way would be to shift to her cougar and slip through the portal, but she wasn't all that eager to tangle with the cougar again.

Her breath sucked in as she relived those terrifying moments when she'd been sure she wouldn't make it through the shift. The cougar had almost won. Without Fane's help, she'd be dead—or feral.

Life was fucking strange. She'd come to Iceland prepared to die, as long as she took Corban with her. At least she'd go out with some honor.

Now Corban was dead, but she'd changed. She very much wanted to live, see where this thing with Fane went.

It won't be hard to get Sindre alone. All you have to do is flirt with him. Let him touch you.

A tremor raced over her skin.

To shift afterward, though, she'd need her quartz. She smoothed a thumb over the triangular amethyst conglomerate at the top. The crystals would take hours to recharge. Right now, they were only at ten percent of their normal energy levels, but she'd shifted twice in just a few hours. For her to safely shift a third time, they had to reach at least fifty percent.

She'd have only one opportunity to escape. So she'd have to stall Sindre until the quartz had recharged. Hopefully, the dinner would last several hours.

The bathwater had cooled. Marjani pulled the plug and stood up. She was drying off when Jewel knocked on the door.

Marjani palmed the quartz before calling, "Come in."

Jewel entered with an aqua-green dress draped over one arm. "The king sends this to you with his compliments."

Marjani fingered the flirty little skirt. She'd never owned anything so beautiful. Clearly fae-made, the aqua fabric was tissue-fine and shot with gold thread.

Releasing the skirt, she resolutely shook her head. "Tell Sindre thank you, but I'll wear my own clothes. I left a backpack when I was here before."

"I have it. But he won't like it."

"Just get me the backpack, please. Unless he'll be angry at you."

"He will." Jewel shrugged. "But it won't be the first time."

"Fine." Marjani stuck out her hand. "I'll wear the damned thing."

"You'll need this, too." The other woman produced a bra-and-panty set of gossamer gold.

Marjani couldn't help a purr of pleasure as she put them on. The silky material felt so good against her skin.

Next came the dress. It was simple but elegant, with spaghetti straps and a scooped neck. As she dropped it over her head, it fit itself to her curves as if it had been sewn just for her.

"I'll be right back with the shoes," Jewel said.

While the other woman was out of the room, Marjani stashed the switchblade and quartz in her bra. It wasn't easy finding a place where they didn't show under the dress, but she managed.

Jewel returned with a pair of gold satin pumps with tiny crystals scattered across the toes and a big bow on each heel. Marjani eyed them skeptically.

"Do I look like a high-heels-and-bows kind of female?"

"You don't. But you *do* look like one who knows that camouflage can be a good thing. Do you want them to see you as you are—or as a high-heels-and-bows kind of female?"

Marjani sighed. "Hand them over." She stepped into the heels and turned to look at herself in the floor-length mirror.

A stranger stared back at her. A classy stranger with long, toned legs and surprise in her dark eyes. The aqua-green was a pretty contrast to her skin, and when she moved, the gold thread caught the light so that she seemed to shimmer.

Yeah, she still had a few bruises, but she barely recognized herself. "Damn," she whispered.

"Don't you look beautiful?" Jewel's eyes swam with tears.

Marjani bit her lip. "You okay?"

"Don't mind me. It's just that my daughter is around your age. It's been so long since I last saw her. She was a little girl when—" She pressed her lips into a line and shook her head.

"I'm so sorry. Is there something I could do—take her a message, maybe?"

Jewel clutched Marjani's hand. "Could you?"

At a rap on the door, they sprang apart. A golden-skinned elf with big green eyes stuck her head inside. "The king requests your presence at dinner."

"She'll be right there," Jewel replied, and the elf nodded and shut the door again.

"Here goes nothing," Marjani muttered.

Jewel squeezed her shoulder. Suddenly, her blue eyes deepened to a navy that was almost black, and her face went dead white, so it looked like those scary midnight eyes peered through a mask.

"Jewel?" Marjani gulped. "You all right?"

The other woman seemed not to hear. "Make the wrong choice," she replied in a toneless voice, "and you'll never get home."

Marjani's nape prickled. Jewel was a Seer. Suddenly, the pieces snapped into place.

This must be Ula Gallagan, and the black-haired guard her mate, Nisio do Rio. Nisio and Ula were Dion's parents, and Nisio had been alpha until the couple disappeared about fifteen turns of the sun ago.

"What is it?" she whispered. "What do you See?"

Jewel/Ula looked right through her. "The end of the game is the beginning," she said in that low, eerie voice, "and the heart wins over strategy every time."

Marjani's hand went to her chest and the quartz she'd stowed in her bra. "I don't understand."

The other woman's breath whooshed out, and her eyes returned to their normal blue.

"Please." Marjani grabbed her. "Tell me what you See. What do I need to do?"

The river fada's expression was troubled. "I didn't See anything else. That came to me as a prophecy—words, nothing more. Every Sight is different. All you can do is think on it, and perhaps it will help. Then again, it might not make sense until it's too late."

"But…"

"I'm sorry, love." Ula moved a shoulder in a small shrug. "You're on your own. If I could help you, I would. When we first got here, I tried a couple of times. But the king always finds out. And it's not me he punishes, but my mate."

Marjani's heart constricted. "I understand. And it's okay."

The river fada gripped Marjani's arms. "You're a warrior," she said in a voice pitched for her ears alone. "But that switchblade you have in your bra won't do you any good here. You'll have to find another way to fight him I can tell you one thing—he'll try to use your greatest weakness against you."

Marjani swallowed. "My greatest weakness?"

"A person. A thing. Even an idea. You may not even know what it is, but trust me, the king will find it."

"But how can I fight that?"

"With us, he used the fact that we're mates. He hurts one to bend the other to his will. But he also promised us that if we accepted his *geas*, the clan would prosper, and he made it happen."

Marjani nodded. Even though Rock Run's territory was just thirty-five miles from Baltimore, the two clans had bad blood between them, so she didn't know much about them. All she knew was that less than two decades ago, the Rock Run River Fada had been in trouble, and then Dion had somehow turned things around—after his parents had disappeared.

"That's the king's weakness," Ula added. "He's never broken a promise. I think he can't—his fae blood is too powerful."

Marjani's gut tingled. "So if I can get him to promise the right thing…" She trailed off. Because she had to get Sindre to promise—what? Hopelessness welled up in her.

You've got a plan, remember?

But her plan had been admittedly crude, a last-ditch attempt to save herself. If she could somehow use this information to craft a better strategy...

Another tap on the door.

"Be right there," Ula called. She pressed her cheek to Marjani's. "You know who I am?" she whispered.

"I think so. The Rock Run alpha's mom."

Ula dipped her chin in assent. "If you do escape, all I ask is that you inform my children that we're alive and well. That's the hardest thing, knowing they believe we're dead." Her throat worked. "And tell them not to come to Iceland again. They're just putting themselves in danger for no reason. We're serving out a *geas*. Even if we wanted to leave, we couldn't."

She released Marjani. "You mustn't keep the king waiting," she said in a normal tone.

Marjani nodded and followed Ula into the hall where the elf awaited.

As they walked back down the spiral staircase, it occurred to her that Ula's daughter must be Rosana do Rio. The young woman Adric couldn't seem to forget, even though he knew that as alpha, he had to mate with another earth fada. He couldn't mate with a river fada—especially the Rock Run alpha's sister— without creating a huge rift in the clan.

Marjani had warned Adric to stay away from Rosana. "She's not for you," she said.

Now she mentally cringed. Goddess, she'd been a self-righteous ass. If she got home—*when* she got home—she owed Ric an apology.

Because she understood now how you could want someone all wrong for you. Logic didn't enter into it. What had Ula said? *The heart wins over strategy every time.*

On the tower's main floor, someone had swept the snow into white heaps against the walls. In the background, a high, otherworldly voice crooned a song in an ancient fae language, and magical fires that cast no heat had been lit in firepits scattered around the large, circular space.

In the center stood Sindre and Roald, deep in conversation. They made an imposing pair—the king with his long, almost feline body and coldly perfect face; and the fae warrior with his broad shoulders, wide chest and hawkish features.

The king had changed into a long-tailed, shimmering silver shirt and blue pants that fit like he'd been poured into them. His white-gold hair hung loose around his shoulders and hanging from his neck was a fiery diamond as big as Marjani's quartz. Other diamonds glittered on his fingers, and a heavy, diamond-studded platinum bracelet encircled his wrist.

Roald had secured his mane of copper hair with a leather tie. He wore a black tunic embroidered with sinuous red and green dragons, and three emerald-and-gold hoops ran up the outside of each pointed ear.

Ula squeezed Marjani's hand and dropped back. The perfect servant, when once she'd been an alpha's mate.

And she was the lucky one. What the king had in mind for Marjani was worse.

She squared her shoulders and headed toward the two ice fae.

CHAPTER 32

The click of Marjani's heels against the white marbled granite sounded loud in her ears. Sindre and Roald turned to watch her.

"That will be all," the king said to Ula.

"Very well." With a nod, she left Marjani alone with the two purebloods.

Marjani quelled the cowardly urge to run after Ula and beg her to stay. Instead, she kept moving, stopping a few feet from the men and inclining her head like the alpha's second she was. "Good evening, my lords."

"Good evening, Marjani *mín.*" Sindre looked her over with unmistakable satisfaction. "You look lovely. I thought that dress would suit you."

She wanted to growl that she wasn't "his" Marjani, but she forced herself to thank him. "So do you," she added.

He lifted a brow in question.

She smiled sweetly. "Look lovely, I mean. The silver brings out your eyes."

Take that, you condescending prick.

A beat passed, and then Sindre broke into the most genuine smile she'd yet seen from him. "Thank you," he returned, while beside him, Roald harrumphed.

Two elves bearing trays of appetizers emerged from one of the arched doorways. A third elf, a white-haired, dark-skinned man with a cheery smile on his round face, appeared at Marjani's elbow.

"Some nectar, Miss?" He offered her a sparkling gold liquid in a crystal goblet.

Marjani's eyes widened. She'd heard of fae nectar, of course. An army could travel for days on the sparkling drink, which magically provided both energy and necessary nutrients.

"Thank you." She accepted the goblet, no longer worried about eating and drinking Sindre's offerings. He wanted her to willingly accept his *geas*, which meant no tricks on his part.

Sindre touched his goblet to hers. "To a productive negotiation."

"I look forward to it, your highness." She let her lips curve.

His left brow quirked.

She'd surprised him. Good. That was the plan: Flirt with Sindre. Let him think she'd changed her mind so she could catch him off-guard—and then strike.

She brought the goblet to her mouth. The nectar smelled amazing, like ice wine and apricots, and tasted even better.

Fane arrived along with a man who looked so much like him that she blinked. Same lean good looks. Same blond hair, although the older man's reached halfway down his back. Same wry smile and gravelly voice.

"Arne," said the king. "I wasn't aware you were invited to dinner."

"My lord." The handsome blond fae inclined his head and then grinned. "I assumed it was an oversight, since both my father and my son were included."

Sindre's answering smile was indulgent. "I'll tell the elves to set another place."

Marjani barely heard as Fane gave her a slow, hot look that moved down the aqua dress to the silly satin heels and then back up.

"Hey, there." His deep voice was soft. Intimate. "You look like you're feeling better."

She couldn't control her body's reaction at that heated look and voice. Her nipples tightened and her stomach hollowed out. But her reply was cool because she had to convince Sindre she'd switched her interest to him. She couldn't even tell Fane why, because she knew he'd try and stop her.

"I am," she said. "And you?"

A small frown creased Fane's brow. "I'm good, thanks."

He edged closer, and she edged back. His frown increased. Just as he opened his mouth to say something, Arne turned to her.

"And you must be this Marjani I'm hearing so much about."

"Yeah?" She eyed him warily.

"Meet my dad," Fane said in a wry but affectionate tone. "Arne Morningstar, this is Marjani Savonett."

"Peace to you and yours," she said to Arne—and let out a squeak when he pulled her into a hug.

"Peace to you and yours." He kissed both her cheeks and murmured, "I'm here to help."

Their eyes met, and she nodded.

The five of them formed a circle. Roald was the only one not drinking nectar. Instead, he had his broad hand wrapped around a frosty mug of beer.

Lord Roald's grandson. She looked from Fane to the fae warrior.

She'd assumed Fane was basically a hanger-on at the ice fae court, but he had a powerful, high-ranking grandfather. It explained a few things—like why he was still alive. Sindre might punish Fane—she'd seen that up close and personal—but even the king would think twice before killing the grandson of the captain of his guard.

And on top of that, his father, Arne, was clearly a favorite of the king.

The five of them made small talk. Arne managed to bring the tension down a few notches, joking and telling stories until even Roald unbent enough to chuckle. It was kind of surreal—she'd gone from a cage to a freaking cocktail party.

Except one of the men wanted to steal her freedom and another—Roald—barely managed to be polite to her.

Still, that left her two allies, if Arne could be trusted. She'd been in worse situations.

She sipped her nectar, enjoying the little charge the sparkling liquid gave her.

Sindre waved one of the ever-smiling elves over. "Try the salmon tartare," he said. "It was caught just this morning and prepared with lime sauce."

The tartare was mounded on a tiny cracker. The salmon's fresh, raw scent made her cat salivate. She practically inhaled the first one, and the king urged her to have another as more fae arrived, decked out in designer clothes and expensive jewelry. The men ran their eyes over Marjani as if she were a T-bone for sale, and the women glanced knowingly from her to the king.

Marjani tightened her fingers around the goblet's crystal stem, fighting the urge to bare her fangs at them.

A few feet away, Fane exchanged air kisses with a statuesque redhead in a tight black dress that barely covered her ass. "Viktorie. You're looking beautiful, as always."

"How kind of you to say so. And you, love?" The woman ran a possessive hand down his arm. "How have you been?"

Ha. And he says he doesn't fit in.

Marjani clenched her teeth so hard it hurt.

Mine, hissed the cat. *Mate.*

No, she snapped back.

A tall blonde with skin a shade darker than Marjani's ran practiced eyes over her dress. "I love that green. Is it a Favreau?"

She shrugged. "Hell if I know."

"She's a fae designer," the blonde explained, a little too helpfully. "French."

"It is." Sindre touched the small of Marjani's back. "Specially made for my guest."

Another round of knowing looks was exchanged. Marjani set her jaw, the small pleasure she'd taken in the dress evaporating.

The blonde's mouth curved. She smoothed a hand down her own outfit, a slinky gold number with cutout shoulders. "I knew it. I absolutely adored her spring collection."

"I prefer Adèle myself," a silver-haired woman interjected.

"Adèle?" The blonde waved her hand dismissively. "She's so last year." She glanced at Marjani. "Don't you agree?"

She shrugged. "Never heard of her."

The silver-haired fae's look was pitying. "She's a fada, you know. The animals don't bother with fashion like us frivolous fae."

Both women laughed.

Marjani flashed on Corban's wasted body, and Luc, forced to accept the *geas* of one of these snobby females. She raised her chin and showed her teeth in a grin that had both women stepping back.

"No. I have better things to do."

"Of course," the blonde said hurriedly. With a muttered excuse, she and her friend slunk off to join another group.

"My sweet," Sindre said in her ear, "I'd appreciate it if you wouldn't terrorize the other guests."

She gave him the same toothy smile. "It's your fault for inviting an animal to dinner."

The corner of his mouth quirked up. "We'd better keep you fed, then. Here, try the caviar." He heaped a spoonful of shiny black eggs on a small round of bread and handed it to her.

She took a cautious bite. The briny flavor was unexpectedly good. "Not bad," she allowed. "Tastes kind of like the sea."

"Have another then."

The man was definitely going all out for her. If she didn't know he was a cold, scheming SOB, she might have even fallen for it. But she was hungry and she could travel a long way on a full belly, so she let him ply her with appetizers.

Fane had extricated himself from the redhead to chat with his father, but she sensed his growing tension—and hurt. It made her own shoulders tighten.

She sent him a pleading look and he shuttered his eyes. She let out a small sigh of relief until she realized the two of them were practically reading each other's minds. And they were definitely sensing each other's emotions...like mates did.

No. She deliberately gave him her back.

He didn't like that. She *felt* his disbelief and agitation.

This is so not good.

Lord Roald joined Arne and Fane and they started a low-voiced conversation that no one but a fada could've picked up. She sipped her nectar and unashamedly eavesdropped as Sindre greeted another guest.

"I've been in talks with Lord Hamar," Roald told Fane. "His daughter is interested in taking you as her consort."

Marjani's stomach constricted. From the corner of her eye, she saw Fane glance at the redhead in the black dress.

"Lady Viktorie?"

"That's the one. A lovely woman, and strong. She'll give you healthy children."

Claws pricked at Marjani's fingertips. *Like hell.*

"But what about the mate bond?" asked Arne.

Roald waved his hand. "Children will come as long as neither of them is bonded elsewhere. Fane has proven himself in that regard. There are no guarantees, but it's likely."

"It's likely," Fane repeated flatly. "And I'd be her consort, not her mate."

"Of course," said Roald. "You can't expect a pureblood to offer you more."

"Of course."

"Naturally," Roald added, "the offer is contingent on your becoming a full member of the court."

Marjani gritted her teeth. She was happy for Fane, she was. This was it, the thing he'd spent six decades working toward—full acceptance in the ice fae court. He'd even be the consort of a fae lady.

And Marjani had told him herself that the two of them didn't have a future. So why did she want to scratch out Lady Viktorie's tip-tilted brown eyes?

"Please tell Lord Hamar that I'm honored," Fane told Roald. "Deeply so. But I'm not interested."

"You'd choose the fada female over a pureblood fae?"

"I would." Fane swallowed. "I do."

Oh, Fane.

"Try these." The king appeared at Marjani's elbow with a small plate of appetizers.

"Thank you." She forced herself to smile and accept the plate.

A female elf in a flowing green tunic and striped leggings came forward and bowed to Sindre. "Dinner is served, your highness."

He nodded and flicked his fingers. A long wooden table materialized in the center of the room, its gleaming surface set with heavy silver chargers topped with paper-fine ivory porcelain. Down the center snaked an ice sculpture of intricately carved flowers and vines lit by cut-glass votives. The finishing touch was the tiny fae lights that drifted down to arch over the table in a sparkling bower.

Marjani gaped. She'd bet there were only a few fae in the entire world who could teleport an object that large without even touching it. Good lord, the man was powerful.

"Well," she muttered, "that's handy."

The king's lean cheek creased. "The elves prepare the table in the kitchen. I just 'port it in."

They took their seats, Roald to Sindre's right and Marjani to his left. Arne took the chair on her other side with Fane across the table next to his grandfather.

She met Fane's eyes. He lowered one eyelid in a wink, and she dropped her gaze to her plate.

"Prosecco?" asked the elf in the green tunic, and when Marjani nodded, the elf removed her empty goblet and set a glass of sparkling wine in its place.

The first course arrived, delicate spring greens topped with walnuts and cranberries. She ate the salad and sipped her prosecco as the fae gossiped about people she didn't know. Cat's balls, she just wanted this to be over with.

But she knew the fae. She might as well enjoy her dinner, because Sindre would get to things in his own good time. And the more time her quartz had to recharge, the better.

Arne launched into a story about his travels that had everyone grinning and shaking their heads. Sindre leaned back in his chair, smiling with the rest, but his glittering gray eyes kept turning to her. She felt like a rabbit staked out for a wolf.

The second course arrived, a dish with cod and berries and some other ingredients she couldn't name, but it was delicious. More wine was served, but Marjani switched to water. She needed to keep her head clear.

Roald murmured something to the king about Blaer, and Sindre said, "She's no longer at the court."

Roald lifted a brow. "She got away?"

Sindre's mouth hardened. "Lady Blaer has been stripped of her position as my advisor and banished from the court for a year and a day."

All around the table, brows shot up.

Marjani exchanged a look with Fane. That was good news. She concentrated on buttering a roll. "And the man from my clan?"

Sindre moved a shoulder. "I don't keep track of Blaer's servants."

Her fingers clenched on the butter knife. "He's not her servant. He's her prisoner."

"Is he?" Sindre sipped his wine. "He accepted her *geas*. I can tell you this—he's not in the castle. I assume he left with her."

"I see." She set down her roll and stared at her half-eaten fish.

Further down the table, a man laughed, and her stomach turned over, the rich food threatening to come back up. That these fae could sit here in their expensive clothes and jewels, and eat and drink and laugh as if Luc meant nothing.

Her fangs pricked her gums. The cat wanted to taste some fae blood—and she was tempted to let it.

Fane set down his fork. She shot him a fierce *stay-where-you-are* glance.

A hand touched her back. Arne, in a quick gesture of comfort. "Did I tell you the story about the human and the pot of gold?" he asked the king.

"Yes," said Sindre, "but I don't think our guest has heard it."

Marjani released her breath. She only half-heard the story, a long, involved tale of a man who'd do anything to get rich, even trap an elf, but she silently blessed Fane's dad for giving her a chance to calm herself.

The elves cleared away the second course and served the next, a small steak surrounded by mushrooms in a wine sauce. The meat was so tender it practically melted in Marjani's mouth, but she only managed to eat a few pieces.

A few more courses followed, interspersed with tiny glasses of sorbet to clear the palette, but Marjani couldn't even pretend to enjoy the food. It was funny, during the Darktime there'd been times when she'd been so hungry, she'd have done almost anything for a meal like this. Now, though, she just wanted this interminable dinner to be over.

She checked her quartz. The energy level had reached thirty-five percent, still too low.

At a nod from the king, the elves cleared the table. A cheeseboard was passed and after-dinner drinks served.

In an unguarded moment, she glanced at Fane. Their gazes snagged, and she *felt* his concern.

That's when it hit her. With Luc gone, Sindre had nothing to hold over her—except Fane. What if the king realized they were mates? Or at least, that the bond was a possibility.

He uses mates against each other. Hurts one to bend the other to his will. And it wouldn't be her that Sindre would hurt—it would be Fane.

She wrenched her gaze from Fane's, heart thundering in her ears. From somewhere far away, she heard Sindre say, "Are you finished?"

She nodded and they rose, followed by the rest of the company. They drifted to the couches and sat in small groups, but the king guided her to a more private spot near the leafless trees. The place between her shoulder blades itched—behind them, Fane was watching.

"Your dinner was satisfactory?" Sindre asked.

"Yes." She forced herself to focus on him.

"Good. Whatever you want, it's yours. Clothes. Jewelry. Just speak to Jewel or one of the elves. You'll find I'm a generous man."

"Are you?"

His gaze was on her mouth. She nervously moistened her lips, and he leaned close, his mouth a whisper from hers.

"Emeralds," he murmured. "Or rubies. They'd look stunning with your skin and eyes."

Arne and Fane approached from the side. Fane had that determined look on his face, the one that said he'd decided on a course of action and nothing would change his mind.

Her stomach lurched. She was running out of time.

She angled her body toward Sindre. "Emeralds?"

"Mm." He stroked a cold finger down her cheek.

She captured his wrist and made herself smile up at him. "Why don't we go somewhere less...crowded?"

Behind her, she heard Fane's sharp inhale.

Sindre's answering smile was smug. "You read my mind."

Fane pushed himself between her and the king. "Enough, Sindre. Let the woman go. She's done nothing to deserve this."

The room went silent, save for the hushed, otherworldly music. The temperature dropped. Goosebumps prickled Marjani's bare arms. "Fane."

His look seared her. "I'll be damned if I let you take his *geas*."

The king's eyes narrowed at his envoy. "I see you've decided today is a good day to die."

Her entire spine tightened. "*No*," she rasped.

Fane narrowed his eyes right back at Sindre. "She doesn't want you. She wants me."

"My lord." Arne slung an arm around Fane's shoulders and eased him backward. "I apologize for my son. He's still young."

Sindre's perfect features could've been carved from marble. "Not too young to know he shouldn't interfere with a negotiation."

Roald shoved his way into their little group. "By the Goddess, boy. Have you lost your mind?"

Fane shook off Arne's arm and glared back. "I'm. Not. A. Fucking. Boy."

"Enough." Sindre's nostrils flared. "On your knees. Apologize to me, and I may let you live."

Fane's knees bent. With an effort, he locked them. His mouth opened and shut as he fought the order to apologize.

"No," he gritted, tight-lipped. "I've done nothing to be sorry for. And I'll be damned if I ever go on my knees to you again. I, Fane Morningstar, am breaking the *geas*."

Roald's fair skin reddened. "Like hell."

"Fane!" Marjani said. "Stop this, damn it."

Neither he nor the king seemed to hear her.

"You'd break your sworn oath?" Sindre asked. The already cool room grew even colder. A light snow began to fall.

"I am. And Marjani Savonett goes with me." Fane grabbed her hand. "I'm claiming her. She's mine. My mate."

"And what does that leave me?" Sindre returned.

"You get everything I've earned since accepting the *geas*."

"But I'd get that anyway," he reminded Fane in silky tones. "Those are the terms you agreed to. No, I think I'll keep the fada."

Fane's chin lifted. "Then take my Gift as well."

CHAPTER 33

S hock reverberated through the room.

Marjani slowly shook her head from side to side. She had to stop this. She tugged at her hand but Fane tightened his grip.

"Trust me," he mouthed.

"Be very certain," Sindre said. "You'll have nothing. You might as well be a human. And your name will be known far and wide as an oath breaker."

Fane swallowed audibly, but when he spoke, his voice was strong. "I'm certain."

"*No*," Roald growled. "He takes it back. No grandson of mine breaks his word." He swung to Fane. "Have you no honor?"

"I can speak for myself," Fane retorted. "And I will *not* serve a man who would force my mate into his *service*." He glared at the king. "There is no honor in that."

"Honor?" His grandfather spat the word out. "Where's the honor in breaking a vow made to the king himself?"

"Sometimes," Fane returned, "you have to choose the lesser of two evils. Yes, I'm breaking a *geas*, and I'm truly sorry if that reflects on you and Arne. But Marjani doesn't deserve to be kept here against her will. Her only crime was to enter the ice fae court without permission. If the king is merciful, he'll accept my bargain and let her go."

"It's a tempting offer." Sindre tilted his pale blond head. "But doesn't the woman have to agree? According to fada tradition, the female must accept the claim."

"She will," Fane said. He raised his voice so it rang out in the huge room. "I, Fane Morningstar, am mate-claiming Marjani Savonett now, before all of you and the God and Goddess." He glared at the king. "Try and touch a mated fada and she'll kill herself rather than let you have her."

Marjani's mouth fell open. The man was mate-claiming her *now*? But he was correct. If they mated, her animal wouldn't accept anyone's touch but his.

Mate, the cougar agreed with satisfaction.

"But it's not up to you, is it?" the king responded. "It's up to our guest."

Everyone looked at her. Fane's grip on her tightened. "Jani?"

Gods, she was tempted. Her whole body yearned toward him. A fada might go centuries without finding her or his mate, and some never did. When you were fortunate enough to find your mate, you accepted it as the gift from the gods it was.

"You bloody fool," Roald ground out. "You'll lose everything. Your money. Your honor. Your chance to have children with a pureblood."

"Not everything." Fane didn't take his gaze from her. "I'll have Marjani."

"You leave me no choice, then." Roald crossed his arms over his massive chest. "If you persist in this foolishness, I'll disown you."

Arne made a shocked sound. "Father. You don't mean that."

"I'll not claim an oath-breaker as my blood," the fae warrior returned.

Fane whitened. "That's your decision, of course."

Marjani's lungs squeezed. She couldn't let Fane give up everything for her. It was bad enough that he'd lose all his money, but she refused to let him throw away his chance to be accepted by not only his grandfather, but the ice fae court.

Make the wrong choice, and you'll never get home.

What else could it mean but that she must make the sensible choice? Not the one she might want, but the one that was best for them both.

She gently extricated her fingers from his. "You're right," she told Sindre. "I haven't accepted his claim."

"Then accept it." That was Fane.

"I can't," she answered, her gaze on the king.

"Why the fuck not?"

She turned to face him. "I don't owe you an explanation. This is between me and King Sindre."

Fane's head jerked back as if she'd slapped him.

Her throat closed. She swallowed thickly. "I propose a game," she told the king.

His eyes sharpened. "A game?"

"Yes. A competition."

The king was bored, a weakness she could use against him. Fane had told her that right at the start. Fane had wrecked her chance to quietly assassinate Sindre, but the tingle in her gut told her this was even better. She just had to tempt the king into making a promise.

Fane grabbed her arm. "Damn it, Jani. Don't you see this is exactly what he wants?"

"Be silent," Sindre snarled, "or be gone. The choice is hers."

Fane jerked her around to face him. "Jani?"

She gulped. Inside, the cat lashed its tail in agitation. She dug her nails into her palms and ruthlessly forced it down.

Fane reached for her through the bond, but she slammed her heart closed to him.

He uses mates against each other.

"You and me?" She shook her head. "It would never work. No, I think I'll strike my own bargain with the king."

Fane's mouth twisted. He looked from her to the king and released her. "I see."

No, you don't.

But she didn't say it. Instead, she raised her chin. "It's what I want."

Sindre turned a slow, *I've-got-you-now* smile on Marjani. The falling snow glittered on his hair and shoulders like magic dust. "A competition, you said?"

"Yes." And suddenly, she knew exactly what to do, her Gift settling on the perfect strategy. "A test of my skill against yours."

"Explain."

"Me against your maze. If I find my way through the maze and escape the castle, I go free—forever. No tricks, no loopholes. And you give me a half-dozen of those diamonds you showed me the other day." Even six diamonds would go a long way toward getting the clan back on its feet.

"If you escape the castle," Sindre repeated.

He didn't think she could do it. It was clear he controlled that odd maze, but what he didn't know was that she could use her quartz as a GPS. Of course, she'd still have to make it through a portal. She'd just have to hope that her plan to escape as her cat worked.

"Yes," she said.

"Very well. But I have a condition, too. You will only have until dawn tomorrow."

Her palms were sweating. When she'd come up with her plan of escape, she hadn't expected to do it under the king's very eyes. She rubbed her palms on her skirt and opened her mouth to agree, but Fane interrupted her.

"What if I offer my Gift for her freedom?"

Sindre didn't even look at him, just flicked his fingers. Fane jerked and grabbed his chest. He doubled over, his breath juddering in and out.

This time, the ice didn't start at his feet. Sindre had gone straight for his heart.

Arne swung to face Roald. "Stop him, damn it."

The burly redhead set his jaw. "The boy has chosen his path."

Arne cursed and turned to Sindre. "My lord, please."

Fane gave a strangled moan.

Arne continued pleading with Sindre, but she didn't hear them. Something dark and red filled her head. Fane was dying. She felt the clench in her heart.

Mate.

And just like that, something inside her broke open.

Fane was right, and so was the cougar. It was Marjani who was wrong. She and Fane were mates. They did this together, or they didn't do it all.

In one smooth movement, she pulled her switchblade from her bra and launched herself at Sindre. Grabbing him by his long blond hair, she jerked back his head and pressed the tip to his carotid.

"Stop it—*now*. Or you're dead."

The king hissed in pain as the iron seared into his flesh.

Inside, the cougar snarled to be let out. *Kill. Death.* The man had attacked their mate, and it wanted blood.

She pushed the sharp point in a little deeper. "I mean it."

"Fine." Sindre flicked his fingers.

Fane's breath sucked in and she felt his pain lessen. She eased off the pressure of the point against Sindre's throat.

Roald made a move toward them, and she whipped her head around, teeth bared. "Come any closer and I'll shove this blade into his fucking brain."

Gripping her wrist, Sindre forced the switchblade a little away from his throat. At the same time, Fane staggered toward them.

Hell. He was going to just keep coming until he either died or got her away from Sindre. He was that determined to protect her.

She had to do something. Now.

"Change of terms," she gritted, her voice barely human. "Fane Morningstar goes with me. If we escape, then you free us both."

"And if you fail?"

"We'll both stay here and serve you. That is, if Fane agrees."

"I do," he managed to gasp out.

Behind her, she heard the hum of powerful magic. She glanced over her shoulder. A light glowed in Roald's palm as he conjured up a fae ball.

Arne stepped between her and his father. "Let them work this out."

"Get out of my way," the warrior ordered, "or I'll blast you, too."

"No," Arne drawled. "I don't think I will. She won't hurt the king. If she meant to kill him, he'd already be dead. This is her way of bargaining with him."

Sindre squeezed her wrist. Her fingers went numb and ice spread from her hand up her arm. Then as quickly as it had started, the ice melted, and she realized it had been a demonstration, a taste of what he could do if he really wanted.

She stared back, unblinking. She was fast, and almost as good with her left hand as her right. Maybe he'd win and maybe he wouldn't.

"Let me go," he said, "and we'll talk."

She jerked her head in assent and released him, switching her knife to her left hand. Her right hand prickled painfully as the feeling returned to it, but she ignored it, her gaze locked on the king.

"I accept your terms," he said. "But you both must escape the castle by dawn. If even one of you fails, you'll accept my *geas* for a fae year and a day, and Fane will serve out the rest of his term, plus an additional ninety-nine years."

She and Fane exchanged glances. Then Fane gave a firm nod. "Done."

"Done," she echoed.

"But Fane Morningstar still loses everything." The king turned an icy stare on his envoy. "His wealth—and his Gift."

"His Gift?"

"He offered, and I accept. It makes the game more interesting."

Her stomach sank to the soles of those stupid satin heels. "No! That's not part of the bargain."

"Then he stays with me."

Fane's body went stick straight. "Take it."

Sindre's lips pulled back in a smile that made it very clear he wasn't human. "I already have."

CHAPTER 34

The loss of Fane's Gift shuddered through him. He felt like a fucking limb had been torn off. He set his jaw and tried not to throw up.

His magic was gone, and with it, a vital part of himself.

A cold sweat pricked his forehead. Without his Gift, he was defenseless—and worthless to Marjani.

His intrepid mate closed her fingers around his. "If we escape the castle by dawn," she told the king, "you'll also restore Fane's Gift. That's nonnegotiable."

His abused heart punched in his chest. It was a chance. Sindre wouldn't bargain with Fane, but Marjani was a different story.

The king regarded her as if she were an interesting species. Fane could count on the fingers of one hand the fae who'd dare openly thwart Sindre when he had his heart set on something. The man who could buy and sell whole nations hadn't been able to buy this one woman.

No wonder the king wanted her so badly.

"You're in no position to be adding conditions," Sindre told her. "The bargain is set."

"No." Her chin jutted. "It's not. I did *not* agree to Fane losing his Gift, and neither did he until *after* the bargain was set. You talk about dishonor? Where is the honor in tacking on a new condition after a bargain is made?"

The temperature in the room dropped below freezing. The snow came down harder.

Fane locked his knees and tried not to look as weak and lightheaded as he felt.

It was Arne who broke the deadlock. "What's the harm?" he murmured to Sindre. "It adds another dimension to the game."

Thank you, Dad.

A long silence during which Fane held his breath.

Sindre gave a curt nod. "Very well. If you both escape the castle by dawn, I'll return Fane's Gift. *If.*"

Hope surged in Fane.

Marjani inclined her head, regal as a queen. Goddess, he loved this woman.

"That's acceptable." She stuck out her hand. "We have a deal."

Sindre pressed her fingers. "The bargain is set."

He raised his voice, repeating the agreed-upon terms for all to hear. "Witness my words: If both Marjani Savonett and Fane Morningstar find their way through the maze and out of the castle by dawn, they will be free to leave Iceland with no retribution from me. You, Marjani Savonett, will receive six diamonds worth at least two hundred thousand dollars in the human world, and I'll release Fane Morningstar from the rest of the geas and return his Gift."

Beside him, Marjani gave an audible swallow. "Two hundred thousand dollars," she whispered.

"But," Sindre added, "if either of you is still in my castle at dawn, you, Marjani Savonett, will accept my *geas* for a fae year-and-a-day, and Fane Morningstar will serve out his *geas* plus another ninety-nine years. And his Gift will be mine."

Fane squared his shoulders. "Agreed."

"Agreed," echoed Marjani.

Around them, the room was buzzing. Roald gave Fane a last, contemptuous look and then deliberately gave him his back. One by one, everyone but his dad and Sindre turned their backs on him, too.

Fane kept his head high. Let them scorn him as an oath breaker. He knew it wasn't so black and white. Sometimes a man had to choose between two opposing points of honor, and he'd chosen to protect Marjani.

But that didn't mean it wasn't hard.

He waited, tight-lipped, for his father to join the others. The king would expect a show of loyalty. Arne was his longest-serving envoy, and one of the few half-bloods granted full status in the court.

But his dad didn't turn away. Instead, he put a hand on Fane and Marjani's backs and urged them toward the door. "I hope you know what you're doing," he muttered to Fane. "Even the fae get lost in that bloody maze."

"You think I don't know that? But I had to do something."

The two of them exchanged a look, and then his dad moved a shoulder. "Hell. If it was your mom, I'd have done the same thing."

"Don't worry, I have a plan," Marjani said.

His dad looked skeptical. "You'll need it."

Marjani's backpack had appeared next to the oak door. When Fane asked where it had come from, she just smiled. "A friend."

Arne squeezed Fane's shoulder. "I'll keep the king occupied as best as I can. Go with the Goddess. Both of you." He winked at Marjani and strode back to the center of the tower. "Who wants to bet on the fada?"

An excited ripple of voices responded. "Me!"

"I will."

"I'll put ten thousand on the king."

Diamonds, the court's preferred currency, exchanged hands, with Arne keeping the bank.

Marjani shook her head. "They really don't see us as people, do they? They're betting as if it were a fucking horse race."

"Their loss." Another wave of dizziness hit him. He reached for her arm. "Let's get out of here."

But Sindre 'ported in front of the door, blocking it. He raised a glass of wine to Marjani, ignoring Fane as if he was less than dirt. "Dawn is at 6:17 a.m. I'll see you then, love."

His nephews—the blond twins—strode up to flank them, their expressions avid. They loved a good bet, and Fane suspected they hoped that if Marjani were forced to serve Sindre, they'd get a chance at her. Bastards.

Marjani's eyes flashed turquoise. "I'm not your *love*, and I plan to be long gone by dawn."

She slipped out of those fuck-me heels that Fane knew must be from Sindre, and tossed them in the powdery snow at the king's feet—first one, then the other. They landed with a puff of white.

"We'll see," he said with a little smile and moved aside.

She slung her backpack over a shoulder and slid an arm around Fane's waist. "Ready?"

Lightness filled his chest. Even if they did escape, he was out of a job and stripped of everything he'd earned since accepting Sindre's *geas*. But hey, he'd be with Marjani, and he'd still have his Gift—and he'd never again have to kiss Sindre's cold white arse.

Things could be worse.

"Ready." He wrapped an arm around her shoulders and together, they walked past Sindre and the twins. The oak door swung open and then slammed shut behind them with an ominous thud.

The maze stretched in either direction, the path wide but with no openings to be seen in either direction. He waited until they went around a corner before pulling her to a halt.

"Jani? I meant it. I'm mate-claiming you."

"Now?"

"Now."

A shadow crossed her face. She set her palm to his heart. "Fane—think. If we lose, he'll use the bond against us."

"Is that why you didn't accept my claim?" He heard the anger in his voice, but damn it, if the woman was still trying to protect him, he was going to turn her over his knee when this was over.

"He'll hurt you to control me. Like he did just now." She rose up onto her toes to whisper in his ear. "You know those river fada he keeps as servants? The woman and I talked while I was getting ready. She told me he hurts her mate to punish her. Do you think I could stand by and watch him hurt you?"

"Fuck that. I can take anything that SOB dishes out. At least if you're my mate, he'll stop trying to seduce you." He gripped the back of her head and tilted it so that her face was angled up to him. "Accept the claim. We'll do this together. If we lose, at least let me have that much. I'll know he can't touch you."

Her throat worked. Her mouth opened. Rather than hear another no from her, he covered those soft, dusky-rose lips with his own. Spearing his tongue into her mouth.

Prepared for a fight.

But she didn't fight him. Instead, her breath released with a sigh and her taut little body melted against him. He forgot how shitty he felt as his dick went iron-hard.

He kept his one hand behind her head, holding her mouth where he wanted, while his other hand went to her round little ass. He molded her to his body, pressing his insistent erection into her belly. Against his chest, her nipples pebbled through that sexy scrap of a dress.

She undulated her hips against his, and said something that sounded like, "All right."

He dragged his mouth from hers. "That had better be a 'Yes, Fane. I accept your claim.'"

A smile trembled on her lips. "It was."

"Say it. I want the words."

"Yes, Fane. I accept your claim." Her smile broadened and then she was beaming up at him.

Inside his ribcage, something warm and luminous bloomed, like a piece of the sun trapped in his heart.

He gathered her closer. "Goddess, I love you."

Her eyes widened. "I feel it. It's humming inside me like my quartz does."

"The bond?"

She nodded. "Not that you're getting out of the mate ritual, but we're bonded."

"You see me arguing?" He gave her another kiss to seal the deal. When he released her, another wave of dizziness hit him. He dragged in a breath.

Her brow creased. "You're hurting."

He massaged his chest with the heel of his hand. "I need a little time to recover, is all."

"And I have zero healing ability." She placed a hand over his and eyed him worriedly. "First he stole your energy and then your Gift. I'm surprised you're still upright."

"It was worth it to get you away from the king." He rested his forehead against hers. "I'm some bargain as a mate, aren't I? No money, no job, and an oath breaker on top of it."

"Yeah." She caressed his shoulders, her tone so tender. "You know you're out of your freaking mind, right? Giving up everything for me?"

"No, I'm not. This is the sanest I've ever been. But I wanted to spoil you—buy you things, take you places. Now, even if we get out of this, I'll have nothing except my Gift. Oh, and a house in Newfoundland. I'm pretty sure he can't take that; it was mine before I accepted the *geas*."

"Fane." She gave him a little shake. "You're all I want. And when we get home, I'll show you just how happy I am to be your mate."

Home. He liked the sound of that.

He hadn't had a home—not a real one—since his mom died. His chest warmed even more, Marjani's love pouring through the mating bond. Melting Sindre's ice and healing the pain.

"All right, then." He took her hand. "Let's get the fuck out of here."

Instinct had him drawing on his Gift to spirit them out of there. But it was gone. He set his jaw and started walking. He'd just have to get used to it.

They turned a corner—and halted.

They were outside the castle. Above them, the first quarter moon peeped above the horizon on a chilly September night. His breath hitched. He and Marjani spun around, looking at the jagged black castle behind them.

She spoke first. "He let us go—just like that?"

Uneasiness prickled Fane's spine. "This isn't like him."

Her eyes met his. "Maybe he has something else planned. Anyway, let's get the hell out of here while we can. Just let me change first."

She was already dragging off her dress. She knelt on the tundra to rummage in her backpack, covered in only a couple of silky gold scraps.

His mouth dried. He could just make out the shadows of her nipples, and when she leaned forward to dig deeper in the pack, the gold material stretched taut over her round behind.

She stilled and glanced up. "You're looking. I feel it."

"Yeah. Does it bother you?"

She shook her head. "I like it. I never thought I'd be so comfortable with a man again. But with you, I am."

"Good. Because I intend to do a lot of looking." He waggled his brows at her. "Among other things."

Her lips twitched as she pulled on her jeans. "Don't distract me."

"Sorry," he said meekly.

She just snorted and finished putting on her clothes—a T-shirt and a gray hoodie. She shoved her feet into a pair of sneakers and slid the switchblade into her front pocket.

The dress she rolled up carefully.

He scowled. "Leave it."

She hesitated. "I know *he* gave it to me, but it's pretty—and it must have cost an arm and a leg."

"Leave it," he repeated. "I'll buy you another one. Even if I have to save up for a year to do it."

She gave the dress a last regretful look and then with a shrug, dropped it on the grass. "I don't have anywhere to wear it anyway."

Fane slung the pack over his shoulder. When she objected that he should take it easy until he felt better, he said, "When it gets to be too much, I'll let you know."

"Men," she muttered, but stopped arguing.

He pointed west. "That way. We'll find a portal to the human world. From there, we can hitch a ride to Reykjavik."

"What about your SUV?"

"It's Sindre's now."

"Oh. Right."

They started jogging across the tundra. At least this side of the castle wasn't as boggy as the south side. Still, without his Gift, Fane felt like he was running through molasses. He grimly slogged on.

They'd gone about a mile when he realized nothing had changed in their surroundings. The moon was the exact same height in the sky, and the castle hadn't grown any smaller.

He muttered a curse and halted.

"What's wrong?" Marjani asked.

He knelt to finger a clump of weather-beaten grass. It felt real, but... "Sindre's Gift is chicanery. The man can create illusions so real you can touch them."

"You think we're still in the maze."

"Yeah. I do."

Her nostrils flared and then she let out a single pithy word. "You're right. I smell silver. Just a hint, but it's obvious now I'm aware of it."

"Damn it, I should have expected this." Fane rose to his feet. "I know what he's capable of, but I thought he'd use the maze itself to mess with us."

"He did. If we're still in the castle, then we're in the maze. We just don't know it."

He nodded grimly. "How in Hades can we get out of it when we can't see where it begins or ends?"

"Or when dawn comes."

They met each other's eyes.

And then the illusion faded, and they were in the maze, the pearly walls towering over them. Before them was a forked intersection with three options— left, center or right.

"Gotcha," Marjani murmured. "Or do you have us?"

Fane peered down each of the paths, looking for a landmark, but all three were blank as a sheet of paper. "I have no fucking idea where we are. The maze is impossible to navigate without Sindre's permission."

The adrenaline that had fueled his jog had dissipated. He leaned over, hands on his thighs, suddenly so weary he could barely keep on his feet. Beside him, Marjani slumped against a wall.

"Nothing is impossible," she said, but she didn't move.

Silence fell. A thick, watchful silence.

The walls on either side pressed closer, squeezing in, inch by slow inch. His nape tightened. He shook his head from side to side.

It's not real. It's an illusion.

Beside him, Marjani drew a jagged breath, and he knew Sindre was getting to her, too. A hot, cleansing fury swept through him. She'd been through so damn much, and now she had to survive Sindre's mind games as well.

Mind over matter, Fane.

He had to be strong for Marjani. He touched her hand, and damn if the encroaching walls didn't recede a little.

"We have to keep moving," he said. "Part of Sindre's Gift is that he can manipulate things to seem worse than they are. He tries to steal all your hope."

Her mouth tilted wryly. "He must not know what the Darktime was like. Okay." She let out a long breath. "Let's do this."

He nodded and straightened back up, and then reeled as the maze swooped around him.

"Take it easy." Marjani grabbed his arm, twin creases between her brows. "I wish I could help, but I have no healing Gift."

He swallowed dryly. "I'll manage. But now would be a good time to hear that plan of yours."

She touched his cheek, concerned, and then nodded. "Okay, here's what I think. An illusionist can only fool a living thing. He can't fool an inanimate object like my quartz. And I've been studying the maze every chance I got. I think I've figured out its underlying logic."

He shook his head. "I told you, that won't work."

"But north, south, east and west don't change. I can use my quartz as a compass to keep us on track."

He nodded slowly. "It's worth a try."

Setting her hand over where her quartz was concealed by her hoodie, she focused for a few moments. When she opened them, she said, "We're a little east of the north tower. Where's the closest portal?"

He dropped his voice. "The one by the east tower—the one I took you out of the other day."

"Okay." She pointed toward the left fork. "East is that way."

"Lead on."

CHAPTER 35

This time Marjani took the lead, since the maze had narrowed to where they had to walk single file. The path twisted and turned, but she simply consulted her quartz at each intersection. At first there were only a few openings, but then doors and forks in the path started appearing every few yards, forcing her to keep referring to her quartz.

Midnight came and went. Fane halted. "We should've reached the east tower by now. Hell, we've had time to walk around the whole damn castle."

She frowned down at her quartz. "As far as I can tell, we're basically where we started. It's like the entire structure has been twisted into a new form. It's not anything like it was last week." She scowled. "How the hell does he do that? Keep us walking but never going anywhere?"

"I don't know, but it's fucking brilliant. Even if someone breaks in, he can keep them wandering and confused for as long as he wants. Sometimes he doesn't bother to send the guards to get intruders, just waits until they collapse from hunger and exhaustion."

Her chest tightened. She raised her gaze to Fane's.

"It's almost one o'clock. We've spent close to three hours trying to get out already, and we haven't gone anywhere."

"Hey." Fane rubbed her arms. "He hasn't won yet."

"No? I feel like a fucking lab rat, running on a wheel as fast as I can without getting anywhere."

A low chuckle sounded from somewhere nearby. She whipped out her switchblade and turned in a slow circle, but there was no one to be seen.

Fane blew out a breath. "It's just Sindre, messing with your mind. You have to fight it."

Weak. You're weak.

"Sorry." She returned the switchblade to her pocket. "You're right."

Fane pointed left down yet another narrow passage. "I don't think we've tried this way yet."

Once again, they followed the path around what felt like the entire castle. She tried to key into the maze's underlying logic like she had before, but there didn't seem to *be* an underlying logic anymore.

Then things got worse. The tiled floor turned into a bog.

They slogged through it, feet sinking into slimy black muck, the icy water sloshing around their calves. Marjani frowned. Something seemed funny, and then she realized what it was. All she smelled was the faint scent of silver.

"Wait." She grabbed Fane's arm. "If it's really a bog, it should stink like a rotten egg. But it doesn't."

His nostrils flared. "You're right."

"It's not real," she said. "It's another illusion."

They continued walking, more confidently now. But the icy water rose higher until it was at their waists, then their chests. Fane shrugged out of the backpack and held it above his head.

"Just in case," he said.

When it reached her throat, Marjani had trouble convincing herself that the bog wasn't real. The cold seeped into her bones and her feet felt like blocks of ice.

She stumbled and knew a moment of stark terror when the black water closed over her head. She came up, choking and coughing. Fane grabbed her, and she clung to him, shaking with cold.

"Get on my back," he said.

She shook her head. "I'm okay," she said between chattering teeth. "You're... the one...hurt."

"Get on my back," he repeated evenly. "The man's a genius at illusions. If he convinces you that you're drowning, you will. It won't matter that it's all in your head. Your lungs will seize and you'll die anyway."

She gave a hard shiver and sucked in another mouthful of water.

"*Now,* Jani."

"Okay, okay."

He shifted her to his back. Slinging the backpack over a shoulder, she twined her arms and legs around him and Fane continued slogging his way through the water. He was half-walking, half-swimming now.

Then Sindre took pity on them—or more likely, he didn't want to actually kill them, just scare the crap out of them. After all, he couldn't enforce a *geas* on a dead person.

Whatever the reason, the land sloped up. When the water reached Fane's waist, she slid off and walked alongside him until they stepped onto the dry blue tiles again.

Marjani instinctively started to scrape the greenish-black slime off her arms and hands—and then swore under her breath. "I'm clean." She held up her hands for Fane to see.

"Me, too." He showed her his own unsoiled hands.

"Holy mother, he's good."

Fane nodded grimly. "What time is it?"

"Two-thirty."

"Less than four hours."

Their eyes met. She knew his thoughts must be running along the same lines as hers. What did it matter if they had four hours or four minutes? They were no closer to escaping the castle than when they'd left the north tower.

Weak.

She dragged a weary hand over her face, her mouth gritty. "I'd kill for a glass of water."

"Yeah." He squared his shoulders, but his lean face was gaunt. The man was running on fumes.

Then they both froze as a door opened in the unending white wall, but it was only Ula, dressed for bed in a plain cotton nightgown, her hair in a long black braid. In her hand was a large glass of nectar.

"You didn't get this from me." She shoved it at Fane.

He took it and handed it to Marjani. "You first."

"No, you."

"Hurry," the river fada hissed. "Arne's distracting him, but I don't have much time."

"We'll split it." Marjani drained half the glass. It was just what she needed, quenching her thirst and spreading warmth through her tired and chilled body.

She handed the nectar to Fane, and he gulped down the rest before returning the empty glass to Ula. He touched her arm. "Thank you."

"Yes." Marjani gave her a quick hug.

The other woman jerked her head in acknowledgement, and then slipped back through the door. It closed behind her and the wall smoothed out as if nothing was there.

Fane rubbed his forehead. "Was she really here, or was that just another hallucination?"

"She was here." Marjani rose on her toes to whisper, "We have a deal, me and her. When I get home, I promised to give a message to her family, but I think she would've helped us anyway."

He nodded. "She's a good woman," he whispered back. "And thank the gods for that, because I feel much better."

They kissed, and for a few seconds, Marjani forgot all about Sindre and the maze as a warm, needful ache spread through her lower abdomen.

The quartz was outside her hoodie, nestled on her chest between them. Fane lifted his head and traced his fingers down her neck. A lazy turquoise light swirled inside the smoky gray and purple, and he lightly stroked a thumb over it.

Marjani tensed, but it didn't hurt—it felt good. She lifted her gaze to his. "No one can touch our quartzes but close friends or family—or a mate."

"Sorry." He lifted his thumb. "I didn't know."

"Don't be." She moved his thumb back to the quartz. "When it's you touching me, it feels good, like you're stroking me."

"Yeah?" His grin was wicked. "Like I'm stroking you where?"

She slanted him a look from beneath her lashes. "Where do you think?"

Against her belly, his cock jerked and lengthened. "You're a bad woman to tease me right now."

"Am I?" She extended a single claw and scraped it down his cheek, shadowed with his night beard. "I think I like being bad."

"Hold that thought, okay?" He put his mouth to her ear. "When we get out of here, I'm going to fuck you, so hard. But right now we have a maze to solve. And I have an idea. The illusions are designed to trick our senses, right?"

She pulled back to look up at him. "Yeah. Why?"

"The eyes are easier to trick than the sense of touch. So why don't we try closing our eyes? Then we can feel our way along the wall and—"

"We should be able to tell what's really there," she finished, hope springing up in her. "Let's try it."

They agreed that Fane would lead while she held onto him so they wouldn't lose each other. She looped the fingers of her left hand through his belt, setting the other hand on the wall.

"Ready," she said, closing her eyes, and he started walking. Within seconds, the wall changed and straightened out.

She caught her breath. "I think it's working."

"Me, too." He picked up the pace.

Another ten minutes had passed when they heard a high-pitched gibbering. Goblins, and from the sound of it, headed straight for them.

Her eyes flew open.

"This way." Fane jerked her into a tiny alcove with barely enough room for them to stand side by side.

The gibbering grew louder. A small pack of the short, wild-eyed creatures streamed around a curve, animal skins draped over their shoulders and tied around their thick waists as loin cloths, pointed teeth gleaming. Their stench hit her like a shovel to the gut.

She slapped a hand to her mouth and tried not to wretch. "No illusion."

"Yep. Pretty sure those fuckers are real." He took short, shallow breaths.

"Take this." She released the catch on her switchblade and shoved it at him. "I'll fight clawed."

"Have I mentioned I haven't a bloody idea how to use this thing?"

"It's iron. You don't have to know how to use it." She kept her gaze on the screeching goblins. "Just cut them anywhere and it will hurt. Even better, aim for their eyes—or balls."

"Remind me never to make you angry."

The pack was almost upon them—only five goblins. Sindre was giving them a sporting chance.

She bared her teeth and took a fighting stance, knees bent, claws out.

Beside her, Fane mirrored her stance, the switchblade up and ready, his other arm bent at the elbow to block blows. He gestured with one hand. "Come on, you bastards."

In spite of their danger, she let out a huff of amusement. The man was a fast learner—or a talented actor. If she didn't know better, she'd think he was a trained soldier.

With a howl, the goblins were upon them.

But this time, Marjani and Fane had the advantage. The two of them might be outnumbered, but they had their backs to the wall, so the goblins had to attack them head-on.

And she had cat-fast reflexes. Even Fane was slashing the knife through the air lightning-fast, parrying each attempt to jump him. So he hadn't lost that part of his Gift, maybe because it wasn't magical, just part of his genes.

A goblin aimed his sharp teeth at her leg, but she slammed the toe of her sneaker into his balls and he collapsed with a groan. She tore out its neck with her claws—and then spun to the left and took out another goblin's eye.

A third jumped at her—a female, this time. She caught her in mid-air and wrenched her head to one side. Her neck broke with an audible snap. Two more goblins came at Marjani—the one with the missing eye and a new one, and she quickly and efficiently took them down, too.

She turned to the last goblin just as Fane got in a lucky jab to the goblin's throat. Blood spurted from the goblin's artery, and he wavered and then crumpled to the tiles. They'd won, with only a few minor cuts to show for it.

Marjani dragged in a breath as Fane shot her an exuberant grin. "How'd I do?"

"Not bad." She smiled back, amused at his elation. But that was adrenaline from the fight. "I'll make a fighter out of you yet. And now, if I can have my switchblade back?"

He handed it over, and she methodically stabbed the long, thin blade into the heart of each of the five goblins. When she looked up again, Fane looked a little pale under his tan.

"Sorry," she muttered. "But they have magical blood, same as us. I have to make sure they're really dead." She wiped the blood on an animal skin and slipped the knife back into her pocket.

"No need to apologize. You're right." He let out a long breath. "We're close. That's why he sent the goblins."

"The end is also the beginning," she murmured. "Make the wrong choice and you'll never get home."

"What?"

"It's just something Jewel said." She rubbed her arm over her forehead. "Have you noticed that as soon as we recognize an illusion, it disappears?"

He nodded as they started walking again. "But those goblins were no illusion."

"No."

She stopped in her tracks as it hit her. Sindre's illusions were designed for humans. If she shifted, her cougar might see through them where her human mind couldn't.

"What is it?" Fane frowned down on her.

Her gut tingled. This could work. She *knew* it.

But would her cougar cooperate?

He'll use your greatest weakness against you.

She dug her nails into her palms. *I can't go feral. I have too much to live for.*

But Fane was here to help if she had any trouble, the mate bond strong and steady between them.

And maybe her greatest weakness wasn't her cougar, but her *fear* of it. That the cat would take over, that she'd become a feral.

You're not an animal. You're a fada. I'm pretty sure that means accepting every part of you.

Fane was right. She had to stop fighting the cougar. To trust it, which really meant trusting herself—because her cougar wasn't a weakness, it was a strength.

"I have an idea." She grabbed Fane's arm. "I think if I changed to cougar, I could see through the illusion. The maze might not even detect me. Fae spells have trouble recognizing fada in their animal forms."

"So you're going to shift?"

She nodded. "When I'm done, grab hold of my fur and don't let go, even if it looks like I'm walking through a wall."

"Okay." No argument, just a confident nod. "Don't worry, I trust you."

He meant it. Through the bond, she *felt* his unquestioning belief in her. It both shattered her heart and healed it at the same time.

She dragged off her clothes and stuffed them in the backpack, keeping nothing but her quartz.

Fane shrugged into the pack and then pulled her into a kiss. A deep, thorough kiss—his hard body against hers, his shirt silky against her bare nipples. Through his pants, his cock nudged against her mound, thick and insistent.

Need curled through her. Deep within, the cat rubbed up against her skin, purring.

He lifted his head, blue eyes dark with wanting. They stared at each other for a moment, and then Marjani gave a little shake of her head to clear it.

"What was that for?"

"I just want you to remember that I love you."

"Oh, I will." She pressed a kiss to the soft hollow at the base of his throat, and then stepped back, fingers wrapped around her quartz.

"You got this," he said with complete confidence.

"Yeah." Because she did. She believed in herself—and her cat.

And I am not *weak.*

Taking a deep breath, she let herself resonate with the tiny crystals, but before she could shift, Fane disappeared. *What the fuck?*

"Fane?" Heart thumping, she aborted the shift. "Where are you?" She turned in a circle.

No answer.

"Fane?" she called louder. And then she screamed his name. "*Fane!* Where are you?"

Somewhere nearby, Sindre breathed a soft laugh. She didn't know how she knew it was him, but she did.

Anger blazed through her. "You can't do this, you asshole. We're supposed to solve the maze together."

Cool fingers touched her bare shoulder. She whipped around to find the ice fae king looking down at her.

His mouth curved. "That wasn't part of the bargain."

CHAPTER 36

"Jani?" Fane scrubbed his hands over his face and looked again, but she'd disappeared.

What felt like a giant fist squeezed his lungs.

"Jani!" he roared. "Where are you?"

But he was alone in a small room. No, make that an ice cave. No windows. No doors. And the icy blue walls reached twenty feet high.

"No," he rasped.

Because Sindre didn't want Fane—he wanted Marjani. In fact, the king might intend to let Fane rot in this small, confined space.

And Marjani would be forced to accept Sindre's *geas*, because the bargain said they *both* had to escape the castle by dawn.

Fane ran his hands over the icy walls, desperately searching for a hidden door or window, or even just a crack in the smooth surface. Anything that would get him out of here and back to his mate. But he worked his way around the entire room without any luck.

He eyed the wall. On a good day, he might be able to leap high enough to grab the top and then swing his legs up and over. But he was tired and Gift-less.

He *felt* Sindre smile.

His spine tingled. He glanced around, even though he knew he was alone in the room.

"You're a bloody prick, you know that?"

Silence, but snow began to fall.

He gave a savage grin. Damn, it felt good to finally tell Sindre what he thought of him.

Adrenaline surged through him. Backing up, he took a running leap at the opposite wall, but he only made it three quarters of the way up before he dropped back to the floor.

Hell.

Shrugging out of the backpack, he took a deep breath and tried again. The third try, he almost made it, his fingers just six inches from the top. He tried to scramble the last few inches, but the wall was too smooth. He slid back to the floor, losing a couple of buttons off his shirt in the process.

He tried again. And again, until he was bent over, hands on his thighs, sucking in oxygen.

Mind over matter.

He eyed the wall. Sindre had stolen his Gift, but as a former wayfarer who could make himself virtually invisible, Fane knew something about illusions himself.

As he'd told Marjani, they only worked if the viewer believed in them.

He heard the murmur of voices and stilled. Marjani and Sindre.

No fucking way.

She's mine, you bastard. My mate. My beautiful cat.

He took a deep breath to calm himself. Sindre was messing with his head.

Forget him. Think about Marjani instead. Focus on the mate bond—you can use it to get to her.

Warmth filled his chest, and he felt a strong but invisible thread connecting him to his mate. He straightened his spine and stared at the wall in the direction the thread seemed to be coming from. Was that an opening?

It disappeared.

Don't fight it. His strength was going with the flow. He needed to remember that.

He grabbed the backpack and let his gaze soften and relax. *Yes. There.*

Keeping that soft, hazy focus, he walked through the wall.

~

MARJANI GLARED at the ice fae king. "What do you mean, that wasn't part of the bargain?"

His chiseled lips curved. "The two of you solving the maze together. I don't recall promising that."

Marjani replayed the wording of the bargain in her mind. He was right. All he'd said was that both she and Fane had to escape the castle by dawn. Nothing in the bargain said they had to do it together.

Thrice-damned fucking fae.

Her growl actually had him backing up a step, but he recovered quickly.

"What would you give me for this, I wonder?" He raised a hand. Dangling from his fingers was the substitute quartz; the one Blaer had stolen from Marjani.

She swiped at it, just to throw him off.

"No, Marjani, *mín*." He closed his fingers around the milky chunk of rock. "I think I'll hang onto it for now."

She shrugged. "You do that."

The fae king eyed her. "I thought you earth fada needed your quartz."

"We do. But I can get by without it." She looked at the quartz in his hand as she spoke, so it was perfectly true. She could get by without *that* quartz.

Her own quartz was hidden against her side, her fingers holding it loosely so her hand appeared empty. Thank the gods Fane had suggested the substitution.

"Where did you get it, anyway?" she asked. "I thought it was lost."

"This?" The king tossed the milky quartz lightly into the air by its leather thong, catching it on the way down. "Lady Blaer gave it to me in return for shortening the period of her banishment. She tells me I can use it to control you." He gave it a squeeze. "Is that true?"

She met his eyes. "No."

His gaze probed hers. "So one of you is...mistaken." He muttered an incantation.

Marjani froze. Blaer must have shared the secret with Sindre.

The North African fae who'd help create the original earth fada had gifted the quartz and its special energy to them alone. But like most fae gifts, it came with an edge—with the right incantation, an earth fada's quartz could be used to compel him or her to obey a fae.

And the king had the complicated phrase correct in every particular.

She forced herself to shrug. She was damned if she'd help Sindre puzzle this out. "I guess it's Lady Blaer, then."

With a shrug, he pocketed the quartz. "I don't need tricks like this anyway." He moved closer, his voice deepening. "Marjani. Are you sure you want to do this?"

She opened and closed her mouth like a beached fish. The man was so beautiful, she couldn't tear her eyes away. His white-blond hair glimmered, his eyes a brilliant silver.

He smiled, and her knees went weak. Those chiseled lips promised so much pleasure. She could almost feel them tracing over her naked breasts, making their way down to her clit...

"Why do I want you so much?" he murmured, almost to himself. "I think it's because you're so serious. Life means something to you."

She somehow managed to find her voice. He might be beautiful, but he wasn't Fane. "And it doesn't to you?"

He moved a shoulder. "I prefer it to death."

She stared up at him. *This isn't real. You're not my mate.*

The bastard was using a glamour on her. She growled and the spell broke.

The wall across from them wavered. Fane stalked through, hair dusted with snow and deep smudges beneath his eyes. His shirt had lost a few buttons, and he was breathing hard. Dark stubble had sprung up on his jaw. He looked exhausted and primitive in a way that stole her breath—and not in the artificial way that Sindre had.

He hauled her up against him. "Get away from her, you bastard."

Sindre did a double take, then his brow flicked up. "You're more powerful than I realized. Perhaps I could still use you after all."

"Go to Hades. I'm leaving." He squeezed her shoulders. "With my mate."

The king's jaw loosened. His gaze swung to her. "You'd choose him over me?"

"I already have." She leaned into Fane. He was her man. Her *mate*.

Something cold whispered over her skin. Sindre was pissed off.

That told her more than anything that this was it, their final test. They had to pass it—or they were fucked.

"Get out of our way," Fane ground out. "Let the game play out—or forfeit."

Smart. Marjani could tell the king didn't want to appear a poor sport, especially since other fae had bet on the outcome.

Sindre inclined his head and then muttered a short incantation. The air around him warped in a dizzying way as he 'ported out of there.

"We're close." Fane nuzzled her cheek and then released her. "He wouldn't have interfered if we weren't. I think you're right—you need to shift."

With a nod, she brought her quartz to her heart. Fane winked at her, his confidence in her palpable.

Closing her eyes, she drew on the quartz's energy—and let the change take her.

It was a hard shift. She'd shifted too many times in too short of a period, but at least her quartz's energy level had reached seventy-five percent.

She determinedly maintained her focus. This wasn't just for her, it was for Fane. She couldn't stand the thought of him being in Sindre's power for another day, let alone another century plus however many years he still had to serve of the first *geas*.

Energy rippled over her, and then she landed on all fours. She stowed the quartz in the pocket of her cheek and looked around with her cat's keen vision. The maze was still there, but she could see a straight line to the outer edge, as if the maze were a patchy white mist overlaying the true path.

Gotcha.

Fane had donned the backpack while she shifted. He stroked a hand down her spine. "Did it work?"

She nodded—and then realized she was the old Marjani again—the Marjani where the cat and human worked together and shared thoughts and emotions.

He threaded his fingers through the fur at the scruff of her neck. "Ready when you are, beautiful."

The cat liked being called beautiful. It purred and rubbed its head against Fane's hip in thanks—and marking him as hers, just in case that redheaded ice fae female hadn't gotten the message.

They set off, Fane's eyes shut, one hand gripping her fur. They came to the first dead end, and the cat walked right through it.

The next dead end actually was the end of a passage, but now she saw the opening to the right. She walked through, Fane right beside her.

Around her, the maze shifted. Grew dark.

Stupid man. Didn't Sindre know cougars had incredible night vision?

With a lash of her tail, she paced forward, following the line as it zigzagged toward a portal, increasingly confident.

An icy mix of sleet and snow began to fall. A wind whipped crystals into her eyes. The cat snarled and kept going. They were almost to the portal.

They reached the end of a passage, and the maze became the inner wall of the black lava castle.

"You did it, love." Fane's grin split his face as he touched the rough black wall. "I know where we are now. Come." He turned left, still holding onto her fur.

They came to a portal. Marjani couldn't see it, but she sensed an opening in the wards.

Fane flicked his fingers and said the incantation that would allow them through. But the portal remained closed. He scowled and tried again.

Nothing.

Fane said something low and ugly. "I'm not a member of the court anymore. The portal won't allow me through."

She nudged him aside. Time to test her theory and see if her cat could pass through. Then she halted. What good would it do if she left—but Fane remained trapped on the ice fae side?

They'd lost.

Ice balled in her stomach. She pressed against Fane.

He crouched down and enveloped her in a hard hug. "I love you, Jani. I swear, I'll figure out a way to get him to release you from the geas if it's the last thing I do."

Suddenly, the wind and snow stopped as if a switch had been thrown. Into the silence came the crunch of footsteps on the snow. She and Fane whipped around.

Sindre was back.

Marjani's lip peeled back in a snarl. Fane took a step toward him, hands fisted. "Let us out. We made it through the maze. We won."

Sindre's head tipped to one side, considering. "Actually, I'd say it was a draw. You made it through the maze—but you're still on this side of the portal."

"Because you changed the fucking rules."

The king ignored him to speak to Marjani. "It's a pity you met that mixed-blood first. We would've made quite a pair, you and me."

No way in Hades.

"My congratulations," Sindre said.

Both their jaws dropped.

The king chuckled. "It was a most entertaining game—and that tips the balance in your direction." He snapped his fingers, and a blue velvet bag settled between Marjani's front paws. "There are your diamonds. And you," he said to Fane, "have your Gift back. Now get out of Iceland—and if I were you, I wouldn't ever return."

Fane recovered enough to thank him. "Trust me, we won't."

The king said a phrase in fae and flicked his fingers. The air around Marjani and Fane warped. She just had time to snatch up the pouch of diamonds in her teeth before her stomach lurched and everything went dark.

The next thing she knew, she and Fane were alone on a cliff overlooking the ocean. To the east, the breaking dawn sent a gleaming gold trail over the dark waves crashing below.

Fane threw an arm around Marjani's neck. "We did it!" He planted a kiss on her furred cheek.

She rubbed her face against his, purring loudly.

"And damn." His eyes widened. "I have my Gift back."

She let out a happy yelp.

"Thanks to you, my hard-ass negotiator." He gave her another hug and then rose to his feet. "But I don't think we're in Iceland anymore."

They were on a narrow dirt path scattered with lichen-covered rocks. A chilly wind ruffled her fur and whipped Fane's hair back from his face. A half mile to the south, colorful boats bobbed in the harbor of a small fishing village.

"Well, hell." He squeezed his nape. "That's the village where I grew up. He sent me back to Newfoundland. And I still have a house just outside the village. It's even empty—the renters left a few months ago and I haven't gotten around to finding someone else. You up for a run?"

Of course.

She passed the blue velvet bag to him, keeping the quartz in her mouth, and waited as he secured the diamonds in one of the backpack's pockets before setting off down the trail, her loping behind.

The path wound along the cliff before sloping downward through a sweet-smelling pine forest. Halfway down, they came across a stream. Fane dropped to his knees to drink in great gulps, while she crouched beside him, lapping as fast as she could. It was delicious, clean and cold. She felt like she hadn't had a drink in days, other than that half-glass of nectar. How long had they been wandering in the maze, anyway?

After drinking their fill, they set off again. Ten minutes later, they reached a windswept headland on which was perched a little blue saltbox house with white trim. The wide front porch held a couple of weathered Adirondack chairs and a trio of empty flowerpots. Fane felt under one of the pots and emerged with a key.

"The water and electricity should still be on. A woman from the village comes in every couple of weeks to clean." He unlocked the door and ushered her in. "Welcome to my home, love."

They were in a small foyer with wide pine flooring and a timber-frame ceiling that opened into the kitchen. Fane set the backpack on a kitchen table the same bright blue as the house. To their left was a living room with a large fieldstone fireplace and rustic wood furniture.

Marjani liked it. A lot. She bumped her head against Fane's leg to tell him so.

"The bedroom is upstairs," he said. "And there's a bath up there, too."

The refrigerator was turned off, the door left open to air it. "There's no food in the house," Fane said as he closed the door and plugged the refrigerator in. "But we can get something in town." He pulled out his wallet and swore. "Bastard even took my cash."

Marjani decided it was time she shifted. As she rose to her feet, naked, she removed the quartz from her mouth and set it on the table.

"Gods, you're beautiful." Fane's blue eyes took her in hungrily. A lean arm snaked around her waist, pulling her close for a kiss. When he let her up, he set his forehead against hers. "I'm sorry."

Her brow creased. "Why?"

He indicated the house. "This is all I have now. I owned it before I accepted the *geas*, so he can't take it from me. And I have a bank account in town—like the house, it's mine from before I worked for the king. I'm not sure how much is in it, but it's something."

"Fane." She framed his face. "I love it—and I don't even have this much. I share a den with my brother."

"But I wanted to give you—"

"Hey." She set a finger on his mouth. "This isn't the fae court. You don't have to buy my love."

He blinked and looked at her, arrested. "You're right."

"I know I am."

He sucked her finger into his mouth, and her inner thighs clenched. His mouth was so warm and wet, the eyes gazing into hers promising heated things. He released her finger and she swayed toward him.

He kissed her and then set her a little away. "Lord knows I want you, but I should feed you first. We can get something to eat in town."

"I *am* hungry." She slid her arms around his neck. "But I want this more."

Fane's hands moved down to grip her ass. He dragged her up against him so she could feel his erection through his leather pants. "I shouldn't. You..."

He trailed off as she rubbed her breasts against his shirt, the material rasping pleasurably against her nipples.

"Yeah," she said in husky whisper, "you should."

He lowered his mouth to hers again. It was a deep kiss, full of need and love. She took that love into herself and returned it, stroking her tongue over his, sucking it into her mouth.

He traced his lips down her throat. He was licking her nipple when her smartphone pinged from the kitchen table.

"Leave it," he murmured.

She drew a shaky inhale. "I can't. It's Adric. I should give him a call, let him know I'm okay."

"Right." He kissed his way across her breasts to her other nipple before releasing her. "Make it quick," he said as she reached for the quartz.

"I will." When she turned back, he was shrugging out of his shirt. The hand holding the quartz dropped to her side as she took him in: broad shoulders, an abdomen ridged with lean muscle. Curly hairs formed a dark T that arrowed into the waistband of the black leather pants encasing his long legs.

And he said *she* was beautiful... She swallowed, still not quite believing he belonged to her.

He dropped the shirt on a chair and rummaged in a cupboard for two glasses. She watched the play of his muscles across his back and shoulders as he ran the water and then filled the glasses.

That leather-clad ass was a woman's hot dream—firm, muscled. Perfect. She wanted to lean forward and take a bite.

He turned to hand her a glass of water and caught her staring. His mouth quirked, but all he said was, "You thirsty?"

"Thanks." She dragged in a breath and accepted the glass. "You know what? I'll just text Adric for now."

After taking a drink, she shot off a quick message to inform her brother she was safely out of Iceland and would call later. Then she sauntered the few feet to her sexy mate and stroked her fingers down the lean, hard muscles of his chest.

"Wanna show me the bedroom?"

His eyes glittered. "Fuck, yeah."

Setting a hand on the small of her back, he urged her toward the living room and the stairs leading to the second floor. She barely had time to snatch up her quartz on the way by the table.

Fane stopped at the foot of the narrow flight of stairs. "After you," he said with a gentlemanly nod.

She started up, and then realized his letting her go first had nothing to do with being a gentleman when he smoothed a hand down her ass. She laughed at him over her shoulder. "You're a bad man, Fane Morningstar."

He grinned back. "I like the view from back here."

Joy bubbled up in her. And that was so wonderful, to feel happy when she was naked with a man—happy, and turned on.

She swiveled to face him and just to tease him, moved up, one step at a time, her gaze locked on his.

The grin wiped from his face. He followed after, stalking her, slow and sexy, his face level with her breasts. His gaze went to her nipples, which had formed hard points of arousal, and then down to the nest of curly black hair at the apex of her thighs.

She walked up another two steps, but Fane remained where he was so that his head was now level with her navel. When she moved her foot to the next step, he reached out and snagged her by the hips, halting her. His mouth touched the soft skin beneath her navel, and then moved lower to brush over her curls.

She stilled, waiting. And then his mouth touched her clit.

Heat streaked up her spine.

He lapped at the swollen bud of flesh, his tongue warm and wet. Her thighs tensed. He nudged her legs apart so he could get deeper, swiping his tongue over her sex.

Her lungs jerked. With a moan, she grabbed the railing and locked her knees so she wouldn't fall down.

But he only took a few teasing licks before moving his mouth up her body again. He gave a hard suck to each nipple, leaving them moist and aching, and then turned her around.

"Keep going." He caressed her bottom.

She forced herself to focus. She was only three steps from the top. She took them a little clumsily, but Fane was right there to steady her. He put an arm around her, his long fingers spreading over her belly, his lower body pressed against her ass, the leather cool in an exciting way.

The second floor was narrower than the main floor. A slatted wood bed with matching end tables was at one end, and across the front wall was a row of four windows overlooking the ocean. A ladder-back chair was set next to a bookcase spilling over with books, and a red door led to a bathroom with black-and-white tiles and a clawfoot tub.

Fane opened a couple windows to let in the air while she drew down a pretty red-and-white quilt. She set her quartz on an end table and then sat on the bed as he toed off his shoes and tried to peel off the leather pants. They got stuck partway down his thighs, and she smothered a laugh.

He grinned back. "Damn leather. But the ladies seem to like it."

"This lady sure does." She watched as he sat on the ladder-back chair and pulled the pants the rest of the way off along with his socks before rising to his feet, fully aroused.

Her eyes went to his cock, flushed and hard, the tip curving toward his stomach. She tensed, her amusement draining away. Her heart raced in a panicked little rhythm.

"Jani?" He took a step toward her and she had to force herself to remain seated. "What's wrong?"

"I'm sorry. It's not you. But—" She shook her head.

"Oh, sweetheart." Sitting on the bed beside her, he set his hand on the mattress between them, palm up.

She dug her nails into the sheets. "I thought—"

"What?" he prompted.

She made a low, unhappy sound. "That I was done with this. You're my *mate*. How can I be afraid of you? And I was having fun, damn it."

"Take my hand." A low, comforting rasp.

She looked at his open palm.

This is Fane, she reminded herself.

Mate, the cat added.

She let out a ragged exhale and uncurled her fingers from the sheet to place her hand on top of his. It felt good: cool, but firm.

"I don't think it works like that," he said. "You won't be all better in a day. Or a month. Or even a year."

"But I *want* this, damn it. I don't want to be afraid. I'm so fucking tired of being afraid."

"It's okay." He threaded his fingers through hers. "I want to be with you any way I can. The sex is just icing on the cake. We can take it as slow or fast as you want."

The tightness in her shoulders eased. She took a calming breath.

"This helps. Just sitting with you. Holding hands."

"You *will* get over this. I know it." He leaned toward her. "Can I kiss you?"

Tears pricked her eyes. He was being so damn careful with her.

"Yeah," she said in a barely audible voice. "I'd like that."

He set his free hand on the side of her face and brushed his lips over hers. "I love you." His mouth touched one cheek. "I will always be there for you." He traced his lips across to her other cheek. "I will never, ever hurt you."

What felt like a boa constrictor wrapped around her chest. Her throat worked. "I know you won't."

His eyes held hers. "I want you to promise something. That if I ever do anything to scare you, you'll tell me. Or just smack me upside the head and tell me to stop."

She worried her lower lip. "Oh, Fane."

He smoothed a thumb over her cheek. "Promise me, Jani."

She gave a jerky nod. "Okay. Yes. I promise."

"Good." Releasing her hand, he lay back on the mattress, his erection mostly deflated, and patted the sheet next to him. "Come here. Cuddle with me."

She knelt next to him. His cheeks and chin were shadowed with stubble. He folded one arm beneath his head, his bicep bulging, a tuft of dark hair in his armpit.

Desire twanged through her. Only a hint—but she welcomed it, focused on that warm tingle instead of her fear.

She ran a hand down the washboard ridges of his abdomen, just to see if she could. It felt good, the touch grounding her.

She did it again.

The cat purred. *Mine.*

"You could be a model," she told him. "If you're looking for a job."

He let out a startled laugh. "I don't think so."

"Oh, you could be. But you know something? Never mind. I want you all to myself."

His cock twitched and lengthened, and this time, it just fed the warm tingles.

His smile was slow and intimate. "I know you're the only woman *I* want. The only woman I'll *ever* want."

"Good. Because if that red-haired fae lady starts rubbing up against you again, I just might have to take her down."

"Just so you remember it goes both ways."

"Of course. We're mates. And I don't get off on making men jealous." She toyed with the wiry nest of hairs encircling his cock. "You're dark here. Like your beard."

He sipped a breath, and she knew he wanted her to stroke him. But she didn't. It was more fun to tease. Instead, she circled her index finger around the base as he watched, heavy-lidded.

"You like to play, do you?"

She tilted her head, considering that. "Maybe I do. When it's you."

"Have at me, then," he said in the tone of a man sacrificing himself.

She couldn't help smiling—and the boa constrictor released its grip on her chest. "All right. But you can't move."

Placing her hands on either side of his hips, she leaned forward to lick him. Slow, languorous licks. He stilled, his free hand clenching, but he kept it on the bed.

"Mm." She pressed a kiss to his hard stalk. "I like how you taste."

She drew her tongue up and down him, swirling it around the cap. Tonguing the sensitive underside.

He groaned. "Jani?"

She hummed against his flushed skin. "Yeah?"

"You're killing me here."

She wrapped her fingers around him, lapping at the salty pre-cum coating his head. "Should I stop?"

"Gods, no."

She gave a soft hum against his cock and then took him fully into her mouth. As she relaxed and began to enjoy herself, the mate bond heated in her chest.

She felt his excitement, and it fed her own, turning her insides hot and liquid.

She played with him for long minutes, learning the taste and feel of him. And when he reached for her, saying, "I have to be in you," she was as ready as him.

She crawled up his body, kissing each male nipple, smoothing her hands over the dark, gold-tipped hairs on his chest. But when she reached down to take him inside her, he gripped her hips and lifted her higher—and then scooted down the bed, muttering something about "returning the favor."

She knew the man had a talented mouth, but this time was even better than the first time. He positioned her so she straddled his face, and then opened her with his thumbs so he could swipe his tongue along her weeping slit.

"God's balls," he growled. "You're so wet." He went to work on her clit, sucking and swirling his tongue around it in slow, incredibly arousing circles.

She arched her back and set her hands on her calves, opening to him.

"That's it," he husked, low and rough. "It's your turn to stay still. All you have to do is enjoy it."

Shivers tripped up and down her body. Her skin heated. She gripped her thighs and moaned his name. Close...so close, but not quite there.

"Take it, love."

He gripped her thighs, his thumbs brushing the soft skin next to her sex. Meanwhile, his mouth kept up its magic. He swirled his tongue through her juices and thrust into her, while his thumbs toyed with her clit. She felt like he was touching her everywhere.

He pressed a kiss to the sensitive skin of her inner thigh.

"Fane…" She shook her head.

He rubbed his lips over her other thigh. "Tell me what you want," he coaxed.

She brought her hands to her breasts and pinched them. "Please," she said. "Touch me. Take me." And had the brief, sure realization that there was no shame in begging. Not when it was her and Fane. This wasn't meant to break her, just pleasure her.

Then her whole body went taut as a wire stretched to its limit.

"That's it," he murmured. "Come for me, love." He gave a hard suck to her clit.

Her sex clenched. Lightning shot up her spine, flashed behind her eyes.

She grabbed the headboard and held on as the climax rolled over her in endless, searing waves. When she opened her eyes again, she was surprised to find the room was still filled with sunlight. She could've sworn a storm had broken over the bed.

He gave her a last lick and then slid out from beneath her. She rolled onto her back and he came over top of her. Setting his forearms on either side of her head, he captured her gaze—and slid into her.

"Fane," she moaned, the thick glide almost too much against her sensitized flesh.

He halted in mid-thrust. "Too much?"

"No." She wrapped him in a hard hug and they shared a kiss. She could taste herself on him, a salty musk. "I like it. Just like that—nice and slow."

"Then that's what you'll get." He stroked out and then back in. Sweet, easy strokes, parting her a little more deeply each time, until he was all the way in.

She squeezed around him, enjoying his moan of pleasure.

"Fuck." He stopped moving. "No condoms. You want me to pull out?"

Her eyes widened. *A cub—her?* She'd never, ever thought she'd be a mother.

The idea warmed her to her toes—but not today, or even this year. She pressed her lips to his stubbled cheek.

"Yeah. For now, anyway—I want you all to myself for a year or two. But some-day, yeah. I'd love to have a baby with you."

He met her eyes, his soft with affection. "Exactly what I was thinking."

He started to move faster, harder. Angling himself to stroke against the knot of pleasure on the upper wall of her pussy.

It seemed with every stroke, their bond grew stronger, so that she was feeling his arousal along with her own. She closed her eyes and tightened around him, and came again in another hot, bright explosion.

"That's it, love," he said on a groan. He thrust in hard and then pulled out to spend himself on her stomach.

His head rested on the pillow beside hers for a minute. Then he rolled onto his back, tucking her into his side. She set a hand on his chest. He was warm and a little sweaty, his heart thumping as if he'd run a race.

For a time, they were silent in the sunshine-filled room. Then Fane kissed her forehead.

"I'll do my best to be a good dad. I know I could've done better with Evie, but I was always afraid the king would use her against me. And yeah, some of it was me being an arse. I didn't want the court to know I had a kid with a human mother." He swallowed. "Gods, that sounds so fucking shallow. But it's the truth."

She tangled her fingers in the fur on his chest. "She loves you. You must have done something right."

"Yeah?" He looked at her, pleased. "You think so?"

"I do. But it's not too late—I think she'd like to get to know you better."

"I'd like that, too." He let out a breath. "Guess I'm coming home with you. You think your brother can make a place for an unemployed, penniless fae envoy?"

"He won't like it," she said, "but he'll come around. He loves me."

It wasn't Adric she was worried about so much as the clan. Everyone had expected her to mate with Luc. They wouldn't be happy when she brought home Fane instead, a part-fae who had been part of the ice fae court for six decades. Especially when they found out Luc had accepted a *geas* to save her.

She tamped down the guilt that flared in her. Now was for her and Fane. She'd worry about Luc and the clan when they got back to Baltimore.

"But what about you?" she asked, those doubts she'd had in Iceland returning. "You gave up everything for me. You'll never have a place in any fae court again. You sure you want to mate with a woman from a poor clan in Baltimore?"

He touched her face. "Forty, even twenty turns of the sun ago, that might have stopped me. But now, all I want is you. You're too good for me, Marjani. You think I don't know that?"

He meant it. She scented the truth in his words, saw it in his eyes.

"And besides," he added, "I didn't do it only for you. The last few years, I could barely stand returning to the court. I just didn't have anywhere else to go. But now I do."

He rolled on top of her and, capturing her wrists in his hands, pressed them to either side of her head. The hard ridge of his erection nudged against her stomach.

"We're mates, Jani. I'm not going anywhere. Get used to it."

She frowned. "I don't want you to go anywhere. I just want you to be happy."

"Then stop trying to convince me I'd be better off without you."

She gave a jerky nod, and then turned her head, offering her throat to him. Inviting him to mark her in a way her cat craved.

He might not be a fada, but he understood. He stilled, and then lowered his head and bit her. Just hard enough to leave a mark.

Her hips rocked up. Heat bloomed in her belly.

He laved the mark with his tongue, and while she was sucking in a breath, thrust inside her again.

Their loving this time was hard and fast. Marjani let her wild side out, and Fane met it with some wildness of his own. They ended with her on her hands and knees, him thrusting into her from behind.

"Touch me," she begged, and his long fingers stroked over her body, pinching her nipples and rubbing her clit until she split apart in another earth-shattering orgasm. He pulled out and came right after her, breath sawing in and out, spilling hot against her lower back.

After that, all she wanted to do was sleep, but she made herself call Adric first. He wasn't overjoyed to learn she was bringing Fane Morningstar back to Baltimore, but she was pretty sure he'd guessed they'd mated. She didn't tell him though. That news could wait until she was home.

"I heard from Luc," he said. "He told me what happened."

She gripped her quartz. "He's okay?"

"As far as I could tell. The fae bitch allowed him one call, and then he's not allowed to contact me for the length of the *geas*. I had to banish him from the clan, Jani. I can't have a man under a *geas* connected to me and the clan that way. She could use Luc against us."

"Oh, Ric." She rubbed a hand over her face. "I'm sorry."

"He understood. Hell, he suggested it. And he knows he's welcome back as soon as he serves out the *geas*."

"I tried to save him."

"I know you did. It's okay, Jani. He did it for you."

"That doesn't make me feel any better."

Adric blew out a breath. "What about Corban?"

"Dead."

Something about her tone made him ask, "What is it? He *is* dead, isn't he?"

"Yeah. I made sure of it."

"Good."

She sighed. "It's just...he was our cousin, Ric."

"That didn't mean he wasn't trying to kill us both. Corban could have accepted me as alpha. Hell, I made him a sentry. He would've made lieutenant eventually, if he'd just given me a reason to trust him."

"I know. You did what you had to."

"And so did you. You're...all right?"

"Yeah." She glanced at Fane. "Better than all right."

"Then get your ass back to Baltimore. I need you here. But keep an eye out for the night fae. The prince has eased off the pressure for now, but he's not going to let this rest."

"We'll get a flight as soon as we can. And Ric? I miss you. So much."

"Miss you, too," was the gruff reply.

She ended the call and crawled back into bed with Fane. Strong arms hauled her close to him.

"You're tired. Go to sleep."

"Kay." She curled up against Fane and fell like a stone into a deep, dreamless sleep.

When they awoke, it was early afternoon. After a long, hot bath in the clawfoot tub—and another round of lovemaking, this time tender and drawn-out—they hiked into the village.

It turned out Fane had close to a hundred thousand dollars in his bank account.

"I never touched it," he said with a shrug. "Just used it to pay for the house's upkeep. The interest kept compounding."

She snorted. "Must be nice to be rich."

"Well, I'm not rich anymore. But at least I won't be totally dependent on you. That would be one more black mark against me as far as your brother is concerned."

He withdrew enough to pay for their flights back to Baltimore, plus some extra, including some American dollars for after they crossed the border. Then they ate a chunky fish chowder in a pub and bought groceries, including a box of condoms. In a gift shop, Marjani even found a new leather thong for her quartz. She fastened it around her neck as soon as they left the store; the connection worked best when the crystals could vibrate against her skin.

Their errands done, they headed back to the cozy saltbox house and stole another night and day just for themselves. Adric would just have to understand.

To her surprise, Fane had a down-to-earth side. He pitched in with the cooking, chopped wood, took her on long hikes along the cliffs. When she mentioned it, he shot her an affronted look from where he was lighting a fire in the big fieldstone fireplace.

"I spent twenty years as a fisherman," he growled. "And working for the king wasn't all sunshine and rainbows."

She bit her lower lip. "I'm sorry—I didn't think. You had to be pretty fucking tough to survive as his envoy."

He wrapped a long arm around her waist and pulled her close. "I'm not weak, Jani. Don't make the same mistake that my grandfather makes about me and my dad. Just because we're easygoing doesn't mean you can push us around."

She slid her fingers into his hair and pulled him close. "I know," she said against his mouth. "I was there when you gave up your Gift for me, remember?"

"And I'd do it again in a heartbeat," he said—fiercely, as if she were arguing.

She traced the tip of her tongue over the seam of his lips. "I know."

"I love you." He didn't wait for her to reply, just wrapped his other arm around her and gave her a kiss that she felt clear to her toes. And after that, they stopped talking and just loved each other in front of the fire.

The second day, he rented a sailboat and took her out on the Atlantic, showing her a hidden cove. They made love on the deck, with the sun shining down on them and a cold breeze biting into their skin.

"This is fun?" She rubbed the goose pimples that had popped up on her naked body.

"You'll warm up," he assured her, and then proceeded to show her exactly how hot he could make her.

On the way back to the village, she couldn't stop smiling.

Fane would've liked to stay longer, but he understood that she needed to get home. And it turned out that during that night in the maze, another ten days had passed in the human world. It was nearly mid-September.

So two mornings after they arrived in Canada, they caught a flight to Toronto and then back to Baltimore.

CHAPTER 38

Marjani's brother was bloody scary.

A few inches shorter than Fane and cat-lean, with Marjani's warm brown skin and black hair dyed blond at the tips, Adric Savonett was younger than Fane had expected and good-looking, with a cocky smile. But his eyes were an opaque bronze that sized Fane up, looking for a weakness, like he was prey and not his sister's mate.

They'd landed in Baltimore around dinnertime. Marjani had taken Fane straight to her brother's den.

"You're back!" Adric met them at the outside door and dragged Marjani into a hug. "You're okay?" He held her a little away and scrutinized her face.

"Yeah." She slanted a smile at Fane. "Better than okay."

"Good. That's good." Adric gave her another hug and then turned to Fane. "This is him?"

"Yep." Marjani slid an arm around Fane's waist. "Fane Morningstar."

"Evie's dad." Predatory bronze eyes narrowed on him.

Fane decided it was time to speak. The fada respected strength. "Yes." He stuck out a hand. "Peace, and good to meet you."

"Peace." Adric gripped his hand firmly. His nostrils flared, and then his irises blazed a spooky blue like the flaring of a corona. "Fuck." He scowled at his sister. "Tell me you're not mated."

"Cut the crap," Marjani snapped back. "You know I am. *We* are."

"oath breaker."

Fane's jaw tightened. "I'm not proud of that. But if you've heard that much, then you know I broke the *geas* to save your sister. And in the end, the king officially released me from my bargain with him anyway."

"That's right." Marjani's chin jutted. "And you know what? I don't need your permission to mate with him."

"But we would like your blessing," Fane added.

"The alpha crossed his arms, biceps bulging in his green T-shirt. "How do I know you're not going to put a cub in her and then disappear like you did with Evie's mom?"

Fane drew a slow breath through his teeth. The man might be an alpha, but Fane wasn't a member of his clan and so was outside the hierarchy. And frankly, it was fucking irritating to be scolded by a man so much younger than him.

But for Marjani's sake—and because the man had a point, damn him—Fane replied calmly. "Because we're mates. And I *promised* her that if and when we have a cub, things will be different this time. And I give you that promise now, too."

"I have your word?"

"Yes."

Adric sneered. "But then, what does your word mean?"

Fane ground his teeth. But he'd known breaking an oath would put a black mark against his name that he'd have a hard time shaking. He'd probably have to spend the next century living it down.

"For Goddess's sake," Marjani burst out. "Like you haven't slept with half of the women in the clan, Ric. What would you do if you got a cub on one of them? Evie's mom wasn't his mate."

"I know one thing," her brother snarled. "I wouldn't leave the mother of my cub alone for years at a time."

"She took another partner," Marjani shot back. "Remember Evie told us that her mom remarried? Kyler's her half-brother. And later, after Kyler's dad died, Fane helped out when he could. He wasn't a free man—he was under the ice fae king's *geas*, and he didn't want the fae to know about Evie. Hell, I might've done the same thing if she was my kid. Those ice fae are cold bastards."

Adric turned back to Fane. "Exactly what did you do for the king?"

"I was an envoy."

"A spy, then."

"I was a messenger—a negotiator. But yeah, at times I spied for him."

Marjani bristled. "Look, Ric. Either you accept him, or I'm resigning as your second."

Adric's mouth hardened. Then he expelled a breath. "You know I don't want that."

She folded her arms over her chest. "Then stop the inquisition."

"Jani?" Fane gave her nape a light squeeze. "Let me talk to your brother. Alone."

"What?" Her look would've fried a lesser man. "You're going to send me out of the room so the men can settle this?"

He shrugged. That was it exactly, but he wasn't stupid enough to admit it. Instead, he brushed his mouth over hers. "Please, love?"

"Fine. See if I care if you ream each other a new one. I'll be at Suha's." She stomped out of the den.

Adric shook his head. "Hell, I guess you are mates. She wouldn't have left for me."

Then the alpha had him by the throat. Fane blinked. Damn, the man moved fast.

"If you hurt her," Adric grated in a voice that raised fine hairs all over his body, "I'll rip off your fucking balls and stuff them down your throat. I can't kill you—that would hurt Jani, too. But I can make you wish you were dead."

"Hey." Fane held up his hands, palms out. "I love her. I'll rip off my own balls if I hurt her."

He used his Gift to slip out of Adric's grip, because the alpha needed to know Fane wasn't powerless. He reappeared on the other side of the room.

Adric was right there. "Why? What could a man like you want with Marjani?"

His scornful gaze took in Fane's expensive rayon shirt and close-fitting jeans. All his old clothes had been left behind in Iceland, of course, but he and Marjani had done some shopping in Toronto during the layover between flights.

Fane's jaw clenched. "That's an insult to your sister. The better question is, *Why not?* She's smart, loyal. Beautiful, inside and out. And so brave she makes me ashamed. The woman faced down the ice fae king for me." Fane shook his head. "She struck a bargain with him, do you believe it? The man could crush her with the magic in his little finger, but she made him agree to her terms. I'm a wayfarer, but when I broke the *geas*, he didn't just take everything I earned while I was an envoy. He took my Gift, too. But she made him agree to a bargain that officially released me from the *geas*—and returned my Gift."

"Cat's balls." Adric looked a little sick. "I told her not to go to Iceland. But you can't stop my sister when she gets an idea in her head."

"I noticed." They exchanged a very male look of commiseration.

The younger man dropped onto the couch. Resting his forearms on his thighs, he interlaced his fingers and stared down at them. "I scented the mate bond. I know it's real."

"Yeah." Fane took a chance and sat on the other end of the couch.

Adric shot him a glance but allowed him to remain. "I thought I'd lost her," he said lowly. "She was going feral on me."

"I know. But I saw her shift multiple times. She was always in control."

"Yeah? That's good. And her scent has changed. It's not just the mate bond. She's calmer, more in control." He shook his head. "If that's due to you, then I owe you one."

"You don't owe me a thing. Maybe I can take a little credit, but she did most of it on her own. She killed your cousin Corban, you know. A mercy killing. Poor bastard was half-dead and locked in an iron cage."

Adric nodded. "She told me he'd died, but not the details."

"He was going to die anyway. She didn't have to kill him—she could've let him suffer."

"The prick deserved whatever he got."

"Yeah. Anyway, he begged her to do it. And when it was done, she cried her heart out."

The alpha's throat worked. "Jani never cries."

"I think," Fane said softly, "that was when she began to find her human side again."

"Tell me."

And so Fane sketched out the story of what had happened in the ice fae court.

When he was done, Adric shook his head. "Holy mother. I had no fucking idea."

"I'll tell you one thing. The ice fae are going to think twice before messing with the earth fada again."

"Because of Jani."

"Yeah."

Adric's lips curved. "That's my sister." He was silent for a few seconds, and then he sighed. "This mating. It comes at a bad time. The clan—I'm trying to bring us into the current century, but we were raised not to trust outsiders. Told that earth fada should stick with earth fada. When Jace mated with your daughter, there was grumbling, but Evie is hard not to like. And on top of that, she has a Gift that's useful to our healers, and that makes her an asset. You, though." The alpha shook his head. "A male, and one of the ice fae king's envoys? You're going to be a hard sell."

"Former envoy," Fane corrected. "And I may have more to offer than you think. I know details about every fae court, and most of the fada clans. I can give you a run-down on the people, who has the power, what their pressure points are...that sort of thing."

"Yeah?" Adric pursed his lips. "You're right, maybe we could use you. But you'll have to lay low for a while. The clan knew Marjani was struggling to stay in control of her animal. This could help—or be the final straw."

"Say the word and we'll leave."

"But Jani will go with you." The younger man scraped his hands down his face. "Fuck. I don't want that."

"You'll have to ask her, but—" Fane moved a single shoulder.

"You're mated. I know."

"It would tear her up to leave the clan—and you. I can tell you that much."

Adric jerked his chin in acknowledgment. "Then they'll just have to accept you."

He rose to his feet, and suddenly, Fane saw why Adric had won alpha at such a young age. His face was steely, his body language that of a man used to command.

"Marjani isn't just my sister, she's my second. With Luc gone, I only have three lieutenants. I need her. And if that means we have to accept you, we will." Adric stuck out a hand. "Welcome to the clan."

It wasn't the warmest welcome, but it was honest. After six decades at the ice fae court, Fane appreciated that more than the other man could know.

He gripped Adric's hand. "Thank you."

The alpha brought his left hand up to lightly clasp Fane's throat. When he stiffened, Adric said, "I'm marking you with my scent. The clan will know you're one of us now."

"Okay," Fane managed to say, although instinct urged him to knock the other man's hand away from such a vulnerable place.

Claws pricked his throat. A delicate touch, not enough to break the skin. Fane held steady. Something like approval shone in the alpha's metallic eyes. He raked the claws across Fane's skin, leaving a thin mark, and then clapped him on the back.

"Let's go give Jani the good news."

CHAPTER 39

"Your Marjani mated with Fane Morningstar." Blaer dropped her little bombshell at breakfast.

Luc continued chewing his toast, even though it suddenly tasted like sawdust.

Jani had gotten free, then.

"It's true," Blaer said when he didn't reply. "I heard it from a member of the ice fae court itself."

So she still had spies at the court. Not that Luc was surprised. The woman had her fingers in pies all around the world.

He chased the toast with a gulp of coffee and then smiled at the fae lady. "Good."

Surprise flared in her midnight eyes. "But you want her for yourself."

"I did. But here's the thing about love, my lady. I want her to be happy. And if he"—he couldn't bring himself to say Morningstar's name—"makes her happy, then I'm happy."

Blaer scowled. "I don't understand you fada."

"No," he agreed. "You don't."

It was mid-September, almost two weeks since Luc had accepted her *geas.* He'd stubbornly refused her offers—power, money. She'd even tried to tempt him with sex.

"I'll stay in the cage," he'd told her coldly.

But that asshole Corban Savonett had told her too much. She knew the secret words that gave a fae power over an earth fada, as long as the fae was also touching the fada's quartz.

She'd let Luc out of his cage and told him if he made one wrong move, Marjani was dead. Then she'd ordered him to remain still—like a fucking dog—and watch as her goblin horde attacked Marjani.

Just having her cold fingers wrapped around his quartz was painful enough. But he'd believed Marjani was going to die right before his eyes.

"Accept my *geas*," Blaer had said. "And I'll call the goblins off."

Luc had dropped to his knees there on the mossy black rocks and agreed. He just hoped Marjani knew he'd done it for her, not for anything Blaer could give him.

Blaer had kept her word. She'd called the goblins off—and then thrown Marjani into a fucking cage.

Luc had cursed himself for being an ass. If a fae could twist things to their advantage, they would. Now he was bound to serve Blaer for a fae year-and-a-day.

Still, he'd endure that and more, as long as Marjani was safe.

And the cages were gone, destroyed at Sindre's order—and Blaer had been banished from the court.

Now they were in Paris, along with a few of Blaer's closest allies—Jon and Krysten, and a golden-haired male named Jagger—and several fada who, like Luc, had accepted Blaer's *geas*.

He knew from Blaer's scent that she was a mixed-blood—half night fae, half ice fae. According to one of the other fada, her mother was a night fae priestess. The others suspected Sindre was her lover.

But Luc had scented something interesting; there was a blood connection between Blaer and the ice fae king. He'd bet good money that Sindre was her father, not her lover. It explained why the king had given her so much rope, until she'd apparently gone too far even for him.

Not that Luc had minded leaving Iceland and the ice fae. If he had to serve Blaer for ten years, he'd as soon not spend it at that cold, isolated castle. Just being surrounded by that many fae made his skin itch.

Jon entered the breakfast room and murmured in Blaer's ear. She rose to her feet. "We're leaving."

"Where?" Luc refused to act submissive. He responded like the lieutenant he was.

"Ireland. I've had word of something interesting. A water fada with something I want."

And Luc would probably be forced to help her ensnare the poor fool. He shoved back his chair and stood up. "Why?" he demanded.

"Why what?"

"Why trap fada? Put them in cages?"

"Because." She stalked around the table to him.

He stilled, keeping his face expressionless.

A cool finger traced his jawline, slid down to the hollow at the base of his throat. He couldn't help a hard swallow.

"I get off on your energy." She touched her lips to the side of his neck. "It's so...raw."

And then she bit him, just hard enough. His cock jerked.

He fisted his hands at his sides. "Get. Away," he said between clenched teeth. "Nothing in the *geas* says I'm your fuck-toy."

"Agreed."

Dark tendrils slid over his skin. Sucking on his helpless anger and humiliation.

Her smile froze him to the marrow. "I'm a night fae, darling. Yes, I want to fuck you, but this is almost as good." She patted him on the ass. "Now get ready. We leave in an hour. And Luc? That's an order."

The *geas* bit into him. "I understand," he gritted.

She took a step back. Her gaze dropped to the erection straining against the zipper of his fatigue pants.

A slow smile spread across her face, but she didn't say anything, just turned and strolled out of the room, hips swaying.

Smile all you want, bitch. It doesn't mean anything.

He'd use this opportunity to study Blaer. Learn her weaknesses. And the instant the *geas* was met, he'd have his revenge.

CHAPTER 40

The evening of Marjani and Fane's mate ritual dawned clear and cool. They'd chosen to have the ceremony on the first day of fall—the equinox, when night and day are in balance. That seemed perfect to Marjani. Balance was what she'd found in Iceland, the balance between her dark side and her light side.

She'd been so angry for so long. With Corban and the river fada. With her uncle Leron, who'd made a young girl feel like less than dirt. Even with her brother, who hadn't realized she'd been kidnapped until it was too late—and she knew that wasn't fair, but rage isn't always rational.

She'd aimed herself like an arrow at one goal—avenging herself upon Corban. Yes, she'd done it for Adric, but also for herself. To gain back some self-respect. But Corban was dead and she had to discover who she was today, this woman without that anger fueling her.

She was never going to be the same as before the kidnapping. She'd been broken and although she'd put the pieces back together, there'd always be cracks. But the cracks didn't have to make her weaker. Maybe they made her stronger, sturdier; like pottery pieces that had been cemented into place.

She and Fane had talked about it late one night. She'd cried a little, but they'd been good, cleansing tears. She'd finally been ready to share the darkest things with someone. Fane had listened without judgment—and then held her close as he crooned a sad song in his low rasp.

Fane's mate gift to her had been a gold heart with two jagged halves that fit together. When she'd opened the box, her throat seized up. He really did understand.

She wore one half of the heart next to her quartz, and he had the other on a leather cord around his neck.

"It's time," Suha murmured now. The two of them were alone in Adric's den, dressing for the ceremony.

Marjani examined herself in the bathroom mirror. For the ceremony, she'd chosen a fire-engine red dress with a form-fitting bodice and a skirt that flared around her legs. On her feet she wore caged heels the same red as her dress.

She ran a hand over her cropped hair and smiled at herself. It felt good to be wearing a bright color, like a flower that had been deep underground and had once again emerged into the sunlight.

"You look amazing." Suha gave Marjani's bare upper arms a squeeze. "That man of yours is going to swallow his tongue."

Their eyes met in the mirror. "So do you." She smiled at Suha, who wore a matching lime green dress.

"Thanks." Suha smoothed a hand down her skirt. "Beau likes me in this color." Beau was a big, laid-back bear whom Suha had been dating for the past few months.

Marjani turned to face her friend. "You really do like Fane, don't you?"

"Yeah. The man's a charmer."

Marjani chuckled. "He is, isn't he?"

"And he worships the ground you walk on, which gives him major points in my book. You're a lucky woman—but I think you already know that."

Marjani nodded. "I do." Her hand went to the gold half-heart next to her quartz.

Suha handed her a bouquet of bright, late-summer flowers, and together, they walked up the steps to the backyard.

Adric had closed off their street for the party and told the drug dealers to get lost for the evening. Evie and some of the other women had created a flow-ered arch of sunflowers, lavender, cosmos, zinnia and other flowers in the backyard.

As Suha and Marjani emerged from the den, the clan drummers beat out a slow, complicated rhythm. The small yard was full, the entire clan present.

Nerves jumped in her stomach. She knew some of them hadn't come will-ingly. The old prejudices weren't going to be swept aside that easily. But Adric had made it clear that she was going to remain his second, and they'd better support her and her mate—or else leave.

Dusk had fallen. A few fae lights wafted in air currents above the yard. All around her, earth fada eyes glowed in the fading light as an almost full moon rose above the rooftops. The five drummers sped up the rhythm.

Marjani bit her lower lip. If only her mom and dad could've been here—and Luc. But maybe her parents *were* here—in spirit, anyway—and she knew she had to let go of her guilt about Luc. He'd be okay. Adric would make sure of that.

The clan had formed a spiral for her to follow to the center of the yard where Fane waited along with Adric, who as clan alpha would perform the ritual, and Jace, who'd agreed to stand as Fane's best man.

With a last hug and a whispered, "You got this, girl," Suha started into the human labyrinth.

Stomach still tense, Marjani squared her shoulders and followed. Because even though Adric had laid down the law, that didn't mean people had to do more than tolerate her mating. And this was the first time she'd seen most of them since leaving for Iceland six weeks ago. She felt like everyone was looking at her extra hard, wondering if she'd really recovered.

But nearly everyone was smiling—real, genuine smiles. Voices thanked her for all she'd done for the clan and murmured congratulations. "Blessings on you both."

Marjani's throat clogged. She hadn't expected this show of support.

Then an old woman named Lily fastened a gnarled hand on her arm. "We're proud of you, girl. And your mama and dad would've been, too. You beat that fae king at his own game."

"Thank you, Lily." Marjani kissed her papery cheek and moved on, smiling now, her nerves gone.

She was almost to the center when she saw Evie. The pretty blonde grinned and bounced a little on her toes, overjoyed that Marjani and her dad had mated. Nearby, Kyler stood with a couple of the younger soldiers, legs apart and skinny arms folded over his chest like the soldiers beside him.

The last person she passed was an impassive Zuri. She knew he was suspicious of Fane, unhappy to have a former ice fae envoy so close to both Marjani, and by extension, Adric. Fane would have to prove himself before Zuri accepted him. But he politely inclined his dark head to her.

And then she rounded the last curve and all she saw was Fane. Her tall, blond and gorgeous mate, his lower face covered with the trim beard he'd grown since leaving Iceland. He held out a hand, unsmiling—and yet inside, he was so happy she felt it warming her own chest.

She took his hand. He squeezed her fingers, and together, they faced her brother.

Adric gave her a formal nod as the drums fell silent. Suha took her place at Marjani's side, and Jace stood next to Fane.

"Welcome to my den," her brother said in a carrying voice. "Please join me in blessing the bond of my sister and second, Marjani Savonett, and her mate, Fane Morningstar."

She faced Fane, and they recited the simple, beautiful words they'd prepared. First Fane, who spoke of his love and admiration for her, and then it was her turn. Most people had heard at least part of their story, but she made it clear Fane had been willing to give up everything for her—his money, his job, even his Gift.

When she said, "You gave me back my cat," she heard some of the women sniffing. But it was only the truth.

Adric's mouth edged up. He'd guessed her strategy—sway the clan to Fane's side. It wouldn't happen overnight, but already, Fane was making friends. As Suha said, the man was a charmer.

When it was Fane's turn, he first presented her with a new iron dagger, saying, "Because this is what you need to feel safe."

She bit her lip. "Thank you." She wanted to say she didn't need it, but that would be a lie. Then she noticed the blade, inscribed "Badass M," and laughter bubbled up inside her.

She reached up and gave him a quick kiss. "I love you, Fane Morningstar."

His breath jerked in, and then he gave her a broad smile.

For a few seconds they stared at each other, and then she realized she was smiling too, a grin so wide it almost hurt her face.

"Jani?" Adric cleared his throat. "Do you accept Fane's claim?"

"I do," she said without taking her gaze from Fane's. "For the rest of my life, and beyond."

"Congratulations," Adric said, and called the blessings of the God and the Goddess down on them.

Fane framed her face with his hands. He didn't say anything, just brought his mouth to hers in an achingly sweet kiss. When she surfaced again, the drummers had launched into a cheerful reggae beat. Other musicians joined them, including a steel drummer, and bright, happy music filled the air, a song that her Jamaican mother had loved.

Her eyes met her brother's. "Thank you," she mouthed, knowing he must've asked for it to be played.

During the big party that followed, she danced with Fane first. He wrapped his long arms around her. "Say it again."

"Say what?"

"That you love me."

"But—." She stopped dancing, arrested. "Was that the first time I said it?"

"Yep." He gently urged her to continue dancing. "I've said it, more than once. But you never said it back."

So that was why his breath had jerked in; he wasn't sure she loved him. "But you're my mate."

"That doesn't mean you have to love me. I know I'm not exactly the man of your dreams."

She came up on her toes to murmur in his ear. "Only because you're so much better than anything I could have dreamed up."

His grip tightened on her. "I love you, Jani. You're the best thing that ever happened to me."

They danced in silence until the song ended, their steps in perfect harmony, her heart so full it felt like it might burst.

The music changed, and Adric claimed the next dance. "I like that dress," he told her. "It's about time you wore something besides gray and army green."

She wrinkled her nose at him. "I was pretty hard to live with, wasn't I?"

He shrugged. "I could've lived with that Marjani, as long as you were happy. But you weren't."

"No."

Just then, Fane danced past with Evie. He sent her a quick smile, eyes crinkling at the edges, and then dipped his head to listen to his daughter.

She looked back at Adric. "I didn't even really know what happiness was. Not until Fane."

"Then I'm glad you mated with him."

The party lasted well into the night, but at last everyone went home. Adric left his den to them for the night, sauntering off with Zuri and four women. It was clear the six of them had plans.

Marjani just rolled her eyes and headed back inside with Fane. In the living room, she turned the quartz fire on low. The flames flickered, amber and blue.

"Well." Fane framed her face with his palms. "It's official, mate."

"Yeah." She smiled up at him. "I love you."

"And I love you." His voice had that sexy rasp that never failed to turn her on. Heat curled through her belly.

His mouth went to the turn of her shoulder. A tiny nip and her knees turned to jelly.

His hands were busy, divesting her of her dress. "Have I told you how beautiful you look tonight? And that you're fucking hot in red?"

She hadn't worn a bra. He pressed a kiss to each of her nipples, then crouched down to slide her tiny scarlet panties down her legs. "Lift your foot."

She obediently lifted each foot in turn and he pulled the panties over the caged heels. He touched the red straps. Heated blue eyes met hers.

"I think we'll leave these on."

Pressing a kiss to her inner thigh, he came back to his feet and lifted her up against his body. He was still dressed. She wrapped her legs around him, his clothes excitingly rough against her bare skin.

Between them, her quartz warmed.

"I can feel it." He gave her a slow, wondering smile. "Your quartz."

"Because we're mated. I think in some way, the crystals bonded with you, too."

"Yeah? Good. That way, you'll never leave me."

She sunk her teeth into his earlobe, a little harder than necessary. "Try and get rid of me."

His whole body shook in a belly laugh. "Damn, I love you. My own personal badass."

"Go to Hades," she muttered and dug her pointed heels into his ass.

Fane walked with her until her back touched the wall. "*My* badass," he repeated tenderly. "My sweet, sexy badass. I'm going to turn you around and take you hard. You'd like that, wouldn't you?"

Her womb constricted. She did like it hard.

And his words made her so hot and wet. Her mouth was suddenly filled with saliva. She swallowed and nodded, unable to speak.

He kissed her, long and slow. Sparks skittered up and down her body.

When he broke the kiss, she tore at his shirt. "Get this off."

Together, they peeled it off his shoulders and it dropped to the floor, forgotten, while she lightly raked her nails down Fane's back. Marking him in a way only the two of them would see.

Fane muttered something hot and dark. "That's it," he growled. "Scratch me, sweetheart."

He rocked his hips against her, making them both moan in pleasure. His mouth came to her throat and he gave her a love-bite, sucking hard so she'd bear *his* mark, too.

Her insides went liquid. She tightened her arms and legs around him and with a small, surprised cry surrendered to the heat as she came in a mini-orgasm.

"Love you," Fane said against her skin.

"Love you, too."

Still holding her high against his body, he walked with her to the bedroom. Someone had placed the flowered arch from their ceremony over her headboard to frame the bed. Three fae lights floated above the sheets, coloring the room a warm, sunset pink-and-orange.

Marjani caught her breath. "It's beautiful."

"Mm-hmm," Fane said, his mind clearly elsewhere. He set her on the bed, turned her around, and pulled up her hips so she was on all fours. "Stay there."

She heard the rustle of clothes being removed and dropped on the floor, and then he knelt on the mattress behind her. Cool fingers stroked her bottom.

"You have the sexiest ass...nice and curvy. And those red high heels are so bad."

She smiled over her shoulder at him. "I thought you'd like them."

"Oh, I do. A lot." He slid a finger between her thighs. "Sweet Goddess, you're wet."

With a moan, she went down on her forearms. "Don't tease me."

"I'm not. I'm very serious."

She gave a muffled laugh. "*Now* you're serious."

"And you're loving it."

"Mm."

He toyed with her, stroking her clit until she came in a hot rush. He didn't give her time to catch her breath, just rolled on a condom and thrust into her. Slow and hard and perfect.

Her sex tightened around him and he groaned her name. "That's it, love. Come around me. It feels so damn good."

Her inner muscles convulsed. Pleasure rolled through her in hot, endless waves. He was right behind her, pushing deep inside until she felt him at her womb, and then stilling as she moaned his name into the sheets.

Celebrating their mating in the oldest and best way.

EPILOGUE

Adric shoved his hands into his pockets and stared out at the Inner Harbor. It was almost midnight, a few days before the winter solstice. The docked boats were tricked out with holiday lights.

His lips twisted. The humans loved their Christmas celebrations. Even most of the clan had put up a little tree and a few strands of lights. Adric hadn't bothered, since he was living alone again. Marjani and Fane had moved into Evie and Jace's den, taking Luc's old room.

He rubbed a hand over his face. Gods, he'd hated to banish Luc. He wasn't just a lieutenant, he was an old friend. But Adric couldn't have a clan member under the control of a fae.

But Adric was left second-guessing himself. Could he have handled it differently? Sent more men to Iceland?

No regrets. When he made alpha, he'd told himself he'd do whatever it took to keep the clan together, and fuck regrets.

But holy mother, it had been some year. Two cousins dead. The night fae on the prowl in Baltimore again. And both Sindre and Lady Blaer in possession of the earth fada's secret incantation.

At least his sister was on the mend, and back at his side as his second. She'd even helped Evie decorate Jace's den for the holidays. Their mom had always made a big deal out of Christmas, too.

On top of that, the message that Marjani had carried from Ula to Dion had put the Rock Run alpha in Adric's debt. So count that as another win.

He smiled just as a burst of icy raindrops hit his face.

He cursed and wiped it away. If there was anything his cat hated more than a cold night, it was a cold, rainy night.

He should return to the Full Moon Saloon, or better yet, go home. But he was too jumpy to sleep. He'd just end up pacing restlessly around his den.

Letting his head fall back, he stared up at the dark sky. Gods, he needed to get laid. It had been months, and he was so horny it hurt. There were plenty of women in the clan who'd be happy to welcome the alpha into their bed for a night, no strings attached. And he could always find a human female in one of the bars behind him.

But his heart wasn't in it.

Heels tapped on the cobblestone street behind him. His whole body went alert. He turned to look at the woman strolling toward him in a red leather jacket and tight jeans and knew this was why he'd been drawn to the waterfront.

You.

The last time he'd seen Rosana do Rio, it had been early summer, and she'd been naked. But not, unfortunately, because he'd finally talked her out of her clothes.

No, it had been because Adric was on Rock Run territory. Rosana had been with another sentry, cruising the Susquehanna as her river dolphin, and she'd shifted to woman to confront him.

The sight of her naked body was burned on his brain: her breasts high and slick from the swim, her legs long and sleek. She knew as well as him that this thing between the two of them could never go anywhere, but when he'd taken her mouth in a deep, soul-stealing kiss, she'd let him—and then ordered him off her clan's land.

So what was she doing in Baltimore? And alone, when usually her brother Dion guarded her like a wolf with one pup.

His breath snagged. He covered it with a scowl. "Aren't you a little far from Rock Run?"

"I came to see you." Her long black hair hung in damp corkscrews around her heart-shaped face, and her big blue eyes were deep pools in the dim light, like a siren who'd emerged from the harbor to lure him to his doom.

"Yeah?" His heart gave a hard thump. He scraped his gaze insolently down her body—and tried to ignore his rapidly hardening cock. "Finally decide you can't live without me?"

"Screw you." She spun on her heel.

"Oh, no." He grabbed her arm. "You don't get to run away. Not this time. You're in my territory now."

She halted, lungs jerking. Too hard. She was pissed off, yeah, but beneath the anger he scented desire.

And because he wanted her so bad, his fingers bit into her arm. "Talk, damn it."

She whirled to face him. "Dion's right. You're an ass."

His smile was sardonic. "I love him right back."

Her hands balled, and he half expected her to take a swing at him. The gods knew, he deserved it.

But she blew out a breath and then with a visible effort, relaxed. "I'm here about Merry Jones."

So she wasn't here for him. Disappointment made his voice harsh. "She's okay?"

"Yeah. Except for the night fae prince demanding to know why Rock Run didn't inform him she'd died."

"What did Dion say?"

"That what happens at our base is none of the prince's fucking business. Of course, he put it more politely. The prince still hasn't responded."

Adric nodded. He might not like the other alpha, but the man was smart. "So what's up?" he asked, releasing her.

Rosana immediately put a little space between them. He had to force himself not to grab her and keep her close. Inside, the cat was damn near drooling, it was so thrilled to be near her after six long months.

She shoved her wet black curls behind her ears. "You know me and Merry are friends, right? I mean, I'm eight years older than her, but she's like the little sister I never had."

He nodded. "Jace told me."

"Well, Merry's scared." She lowered her voice to subvocal level. "We all know that someday the prince will learn the truth and come for her. She's terrified he'll force her to go back with him to Virginia. Dion and Cleia told her there's no way they'll let that happen, but she's still worried. After all, she *is* his granddaughter."

His eyes narrowed. *What did Rosana know?*

But she simply waited for his answer, an anxious crease between her brows.

"Tell her not to relax," he said, affronted at a primal level that a cub should have any worry other than the usual ones of adolescence. "If that S.O.B. tries anything, he's dead."

She scrutinized him. "You mean that, don't you? Even though she's part night fae herself."

He scowled, angry and a little hurt that she harbored even a tiny doubt. "She's

Jace's niece, which makes her clan, even if she lives with your people for now. And her mom was a good friend. I'll make sure Jace tells her."

"That's how Dion feels—that she's clan. But Merry's still worried. Look what happened to your clan when the night fae went after them."

He stiffened. "That was different."

"How?"

He hesitated, and then figured, why keep it a secret? "My uncle invited them in. The night fae didn't cause the infighting—they just fed on it, did what they could to encourage it."

"Oh. Is that why you—?" Her mouth snapped shut.

"Go ahead, ask." His lips peeled in a toothy smile. "Is that why I killed him?"

She shook her head. "Sorry. Not my business."

"That's right. It's not." He blew out a breath. "Look, you said what you came to say. I appreciate it. I promise, Merry's safe. If the night fae come for her, it won't be because of anything my clan did. And if her grandfather dares to steal her, I'll hunt him down myself."

She nodded her thanks. "If it comes down to that, Rui would go into Hades itself for her."

Which was only the truth. He studied her. "So why are you here?"

Even white teeth worried her lush lower lip. "Don't take this the wrong way, but I know you're planning something against the night fae—and I want to help."

He stilled. "And you know this—how?"

She moved a shoulder. "I get...hunches, that's all. And besides, everyone knows there's bad blood between you and the night fae. It doesn't take a genius to guess you might be planning something."

He prowled forward, erasing the space between them.

"Adric?" Her eyes widened, but she didn't step back.

He inhaled slowly, filling his lungs with her scent—rain and fresh spring flowers. Without his volition, his hand shot out, closing around her fingers.

Her breath hitched. As he brought her hand toward his mouth, her eyes came up to meet his. Holding her gaze, he traced his lips down the soft underside of her wrist.

Heat arced between them. Electric. Fiery. Speeding up his heart, making his whole being contract with longing. It had always been like this, from the moment he'd first seen her six years ago at Dion and Cleia's mate-bonding celebration.

She moistened plump red lips and he stifled a groan.

"One night," he said, low and rough. "We'll go somewhere out of town. No one has to know."

Her jaw set. "Answer the question. Will you let me help?"

He leaned closer so their mouths were almost touching. "No. Fucking. Way."

She growled and tried to wrench her hand from his. Then suddenly, she froze, her fingers gripping his as her eyes went black.

"No," she rasped.

His scalp prickled. "Rosana?"

"The Darktime isn't over," she said in an eerie toneless voice. "The prince will destroy your clan from the inside out."

A chill ran over his skin. *She was a Seer.*

He hadn't known, and there wasn't much he didn't know about the do Rio family. They must keep her Gift a secret from everyone, even the rest of the clan.

"What do you See?" He gave her a little shake. "Tell me."

She didn't seem to hear him. There was a fraught silence, and then with a shudder, she came back to herself. She snatched her hand from his and pressed it to her chest, face closed. Tiny tremors shook her slim body.

"Goddess," she whispered. "That's insane. You can't kill him. You'll set off something you can't stop."

"Yeah?" He raised a brow.

Tell her she's the one who's insane. That you have no fucking idea what she's talking about.

But he couldn't bring himself to prevaricate—not to Rosana. The woman his cat had decided was his mate, even if the man refused to accept it.

She grabbed his arm. He tensed, but this time, nothing happened.

"Promise me you won't do it."

He showed her his teeth. "I don't have to promise you anything, love. We're nothing to each other, right? Because that's the way we both want it."

She flinched and let him go.

"Go home to your big brother. It's not safe for you to be alone down here at night." He leered at her, hating himself, but he had to get her out of here—and out of his life. "A big, bad cat might snatch you and carry you back to his lair."

She shoved her hands into her pockets, her pretty mouth set. "You don't scare me, Lord Adric."

He just stared back at her until she turned and stalked back the way she came.

He gave it a minute and then followed her. She headed around the harbor and he waited for her to shift to her dolphin, but she leaned against a scrubby little street tree and stared out at the black water.

He waited downwind until with a muttered curse, she walked the few feet to where a sleek purple sportbike waited. Slinging a leg over the seat, she flung him an unreadable look over her shoulder and then zoomed off, leaving him standing there, scowling and clenching his fists...and hollow inside.

ADRIC'S HEART

A FADA NOVEL

To save his clan, the badass Baltimore alpha sacrificed everything—even his honor. Will he be forced to give up his mate as well?

The explosive conclusion to the Darktime Trilogy!

"A fun, rich read... **Fans of paranormal romance will devour this novel!**"
~InD'Tale Magazine

CHAPTER 1

SEVEN YEARS EARLIER, IN THE LAST DAYS OF THE DARK TIME

The kill was swift, silent...and without honor.

Honor was a luxury Adric Savonett couldn't afford.

He crouched on a dumpster in a dead-end alley. The alley was pitch-black, because he wanted it that way. While he'd acted as lookout, his sister Marjani had shimmied up the nearest streetlight and shattered the glass with the heavy handle of her dagger. Now she waited on the sidewalk while he squatted on top of the rusting metal container.

A human would've been nearly blind. But he was a fada—he picked up every detail. The dark pool of motor oil seeping into the cracked pavement. The sour-smelling garbage spilling out of the dumpster. The rumble of a late-night delivery truck barreling down the street.

And his uncle Leron as he stalked toward Marjani, brutal features displeased. "What the fuck are you doing here, girl? I ordered you to go to Jumar."

Adric's fingers clenched on his dagger. The blade was iron, honed to a razor-sharp edge. Inside, his cougar hissed.

Marjani lifted her chin. "And I said no."

They'd agreed to give Leron one last chance. If he rescinded his order that Marjani become his second's whore, Adric would let him live. For now, anyway.

Because everyone in the Baltimore clan, even their uncle, knew it was only a matter of time before Adric challenged him.

"I'm your alpha," Leron growled. "You don't tell me no." He backhanded Marjani across the face—and sealed his fate.

She reeled backwards into the alley, their uncle following. Unlike them, he was a wolf shifter with his animal's big, powerful body even when he was a man. The S.O.B. was easily twice her weight.

Rage ripped through Adric, clouded his vision with red. He took a calming breath.

Come on, motherfucker. Just a little closer.

"I won't whore for you," Marjani spat out. "Jumar can find his own damn woman."

Leron's eyes flashed wolf-gold. He showed his fangs. "You'll do whatever I fucking say. If I tell you to drop to your knees and suck off every single one of my lieutenants, then you will. Understand?"

Marjani snarled and backpedaled past the dumpster.

Leron prowled after.

Closer, closer. And...now.

Adric launched himself off the dumpster, landing on his prey's back. His uncle cursed and tried to buck him off, but Adric got him in a headlock. Leron ran backwards, slamming him into a brick wall. Adric grunted and grimly hung on.

One hard stroke of the dagger across his uncle's throat, and it was over. Leron made a terrible sucking sound and clawed at his neck. The coppery scent of blood filled Adric's nostrils as the iron blade poisoned his uncle, hastening his end.

Adric met Marjani's eyes over Leron's head. Her irises glowed cougar-blue in the dark. A sharp dagger was clenched in her hand. He said a silent prayer of thanks that she hadn't had to use it. Better it be him who killed their father's only brother.

He released Leron, let him drop to the pavement.

The dying man managed to turn over. His eyes widened. "You," he gurgled as his blood pooled on the asphalt.

"Me," Adric confirmed.

"Too much of a coward...to challenge...me."

Adric leaned forward. "Everything I know about honor," he growled, "I learned from you. Burn. In. Hades."

Reaching into Leron's shirt, he grabbed his quartz pendant and jerked it over his head. His uncle's face contorted. His mouth opened and shut, and then he shuddered and went limp. His eyes filmed over.

Adric found a rock, smashed the quartz. Leron was powerful. Adric was taking no chances he'd somehow heal himself.

A quiver racked Marjani's lean frame, but the look she turned on Adric was triumphant. "You did it. You really did it."

"Yeah." He stared down at his monster of an uncle and wondered why he felt nothing, not even elation. The man who'd made both their lives a living hell was finally dead. Surely he should feel something?

Together, he and Marjani bundled the dead man into the trunk of their car. By dawn, Leron Savonett was buried deep in a western Maryland forest.

Within a week, Adric had fought off a challenge from first Jumar, then one of his own cousins, and been declared alpha of the Baltimore Earth Fada.

Adric and Marjani immediately set about saving the clan that his uncle had all but decimated. The Darktime, the clan had called it, although only behind Leron's back.

Adric's first order of business was to gather the clan in a secret corner of Druid Hill Park and appoint Marjani as his second-in-command. Then he looked around at his hungry, hollow-eyed people. In the last ten years, the clan had lost nearly half its members. The elders had been especially hard-hit, caught up in the bitter infighting of the Darktime. And he could count the number of cubs born during Leron's decade-long reign of terror on two hands—and still have a few fingers left over.

"As of today, the Darktime is over," he declared, hard-voiced. "You can leave, if you choose. But fight me, and die. Those who stay will follow my orders. In return, you and your cubs will be fed if I have to grow the damn food myself. The elders will be honored again, and you will be free to mate as you wish. We *will* become a strong, healthy clan once more. That, I promise on the souls of my mother and father."

The clan took a collective breath, and then one by one, they dropped to their knees, accepting him as the new alpha. It was spring. In a nearby tree, a bird sang as the sun rose over the park, casting a pink glow on the kneeling crowd.

Adric allowed himself a thin smile. "Okay, then," he said, and watched as the clan rose back to their feet, some smiling, some—especially the clan's wolves—with set faces.

He hadn't asked for this, hadn't really wanted it. Hell, at twenty-six turns of the sun, he was barely an adult by fada standards. But he squared his shoulders and set to work rebuilding the clan, Marjani and a few trusted friends at his side, and he kept every damn promise he made.

Every promise but one, that is. The very first promise he'd ever made—to protect Marjani, no matter what. He'd saved her from Leron and Jumar, but five years later, she'd been lured into a trap by members of his own clan, who'd handed her over to a den of feral river fada. And Adric hadn't known until it was too late.

Leron might be dead, but the Darktime hadn't ended with him.

It still lived in the shadowed corners of the clan's souls—Adric's included.

THE PRESENT DAY

A human shrieked with laughter near Adric's left ear. He winced and fingered his lobe.

The Full Moon Saloon was packed tighter than a can of sardines. Mainly earth fada, but also river fada and a handful of humans slumming with the shifters. The dank air reeked of lust and stale beer, and the band had more enthusiasm than skill.

What in Hades was he doing in this crowded, noisy bar? But it was Saturday night, and he had nothing better to do. Which was fucking sad.

He glowered at his beer bottle.

Crowded around the table with him were two clanswomen and his friend Zuri, a big, smooth-talking wolf with a shaved head and a soul patch.

Zuri divided his attention between the women, and Dina and Cara flirted right back. Then Zuri reeled Dina in for a leisurely kiss.

Cara just smiled and hitched her chair closer to Adric's. "Hey, sweetie." She set a hand on his knee. "Wanna take this back to your den?"

He hesitated. The gods knew, he'd gone too long without, and all Cara wanted was a night with the alpha. No harm, no foul, and both of them free to go their own way in the morning.

But he simply wasn't interested.

Removing her hand from his knee, he kissed her fingers. "Not tonight, beautiful."

Cara leaned in, a worried pucker between her pretty brown eyes. She was a warm-hearted young deer, one of the few herbivores in a clan of big cats, wolves and bears.

"You sure? You seem—" She paused, rubbed her nose. "Edgy."

"I'm sure," he said in a tone designed to halt further questions.

Cara studied him another few seconds before nodding. She was low in the hierarchy. Just questioning him—her alpha—had clearly taken all her deer's courage.

Looping an arm around her shoulder, Adric nuzzled her cheek, offering reassurance in the way of their animals. She relaxed and turned back to Dina, who was now on Zuri's lap. The wolf shifter made a dry, Zuri-type comment and both women giggled.

Adric made himself listen, smile. But Cara was right. He *was* edgy, although he hadn't realized it was bleeding into his interactions with the clan.

He took a gulp of beer and forced his shoulders to relax.

One more drink, and he'd leave—or maybe check out the poker game in the back room. Because the only thing worse than this crowded bar was his solitary den.

The opening of the saloon's outer door sent a blast of icy air down the short hall. A woman sauntered inside, her lush body poured into tight pants, a red leather jacket and ankle boots the same scarlet as her jacket. Wavy hair the blue-black of a raven's wings framed her pretty, heart-shaped face.

One wide smile and Benny, the hulking earth-fada bouncer, fell over himself to wave her in.

Rosana do Rio.

Adric's heart gave a hard knock. His cougar snapped to attention, eyeing her with a cat's intentness.

What was she doing here?

And alone.

She headed toward the long wooden bar without bothering to remove her jacket or gloves. The woman didn't walk, she sauntered, hips swaying, all high breasts and long-legged beauty.

All around the saloon, males—shifter and human—pulled back their shoulders and puffed out their chests. Zuri muttered a curse and set Dina back on her chair.

Rosana hadn't gone ten steps when a human asked her to dance, a cocky blond college-type surrounded by three equally entitled wingmen.

Adric's back teeth clamped together.

Not your business.

Rosana smiled and allowed the blond human to take her gloved hand. He led her onto the microscopic dance floor and set his hands on her hips, drawing her closer.

A growl scraped Adric's throat. His claws slid out and he started to his feet.

No one touched Rosana but him.

"Easy now." Zuri's fingers clamped onto Adric's wrist. He wasn't just a good friend, but one of Adric's lieutenants. "Don't do anything you'll regret."

Adric snarled. *Back off.*

Zuri removed his hand but stared back steadily. Not challenging Adric, just reminding him of who and what he was.

He sank back onto his chair, aware people were turning to stare at him. His friend was right.

Rosana was a dolphin shifter, a river fada—and he was alpha of the Baltimore earth fada. Water and earth fada didn't mix. And Rosana wasn't just any river fada, she was the sister of Lord Dion, alpha of Adric's clan's biggest rival.

Which meant he could look but not touch.

Rosana did one of those evasive twists women do, forcing the human to release her, and danced away.

Adric's claws retracted.

"Drink your beer," Zuri prompted.

He picked up his bottle but didn't bring it to his mouth.

The lieutenant fingered his soul patch. "You want me to boot her sexy ass out of here?"

"For what reason?"

"Disturbing the fucking peace."

The Full Moon Saloon was technically a neutral space owned by a Brazilian river fada named Claudio. But Baltimore was Adric's territory; if he gave the word, Rosana would be banned from the bar.

But then he wouldn't get even these occasional glimpses of her. The Rock Run Clan's base was an underground fortress protected by fae wards impossible for him to break. And he'd tried.

He brought the bottle to his lips. Swallowed. "Let her stay."

Zuri leveled a look at him. "Maybe you should just take her," he said in a voice pitched for Adric's ears only. "She wants you. Even her brothers know it—that's why they try to keep her up at Rock Run. Bang the woman already. Get her out of your system."

Adric's fingers tightened on the bottle. "I'll handle my own damn love life, thank you."

"But you haven't been handling it. When's the last time you had a good, hard—"

He sliced Zuri a look. "Enough."

The other man moved a big shoulder in a shrug and shut up, thank all the gods.

Adric glanced around. In addition to Dina and Cara, there were five other unmated earth fada females in the bar, any of whom would be happy to take the alpha to bed for a night. And like with Cara, it would be no harm, no foul.

But he only wanted Rosana.

Who hadn't even glanced his way since entering the bar.

The song ended. With a nod at the cocky blond, Rosana wended her way through the tables to the polished oak bar. The man followed, his gaze glued to her ass.

Fuck this.

Adric moved, cutting off the human and squeezing in next to Rosana.

"Hey!" The man's fingers dug into Adric's arm. "She's with me."

Adric turned. "No," he said, letting his cat into his eyes. "She's not."

The man's Adam's apple bobbed. He released Adric and backed away. "Right. I—" He fled back to the safety of his wingmen.

Adric turned to Rosana. "Hello, love." Her lips were a slick crimson the same shade as her jacket. "What're you drinking?"

"Adric." In her faint, sexy accent, his name came out as *Ah-dreek* instead of Aaa-dric. The two syllables shivered deliciously over his skin. He could almost ignore the way she inclined her head like she was a princess and he a slimy green frog.

So she was still pissed off at him. He supposed he deserved it. The gods knew, he'd been an ass the last time they'd met.

Her deep blue eyes flashed. "I can get my own drink, thank you." She reached for her wallet.

He slapped a hand onto hers over the glove. "I asked," he said between clenched teeth, "what are you drinking?"

"Fine." She jerked her hand out from beneath his. "Buy me a Dos Equis."

He raised two fingers at Sophie, the motherly Mediterranean Sea fada tending bar along with Claudio. "Two, please."

While they waited for their beers, he put an elbow on the bar and angled his body toward Rosana. She had the fresh, clean scent of a clear mountain pool. Beneath his T-shirt, his quartz warmed, like it always did when she was near—seeking to complete their connection, as if they were two mated earth fada.

But Rosana wasn't an earth fada, she was a river fada. And the two of them could never mate.

Inside, his cougar hissed in disagreement.

A corkscrew of black hair had fallen forward over her shoulder. He itched to finger it, see if it was as soft as he remembered. Instead, he fisted his hand and gave her a mocking smile.

"Didn't expect to see you in Baltimore again so soon. Decided you want to tangle with a cat, huh?"

The last time they'd met, he'd told her to stay out of his city if she knew what was good for her. Said that if she wasn't careful, "a big, bad cat would carry her off to his lair."

Her long-lidded blue eyes narrowed. "You know what?" she asked sweetly. "Sometimes you can be a real *cabrão*."

A *bastard*, a *motherfucker*. That was one Portuguese word he knew. She wasn't the first Rock Run fada who'd tossed it at him. But with Rosana, he deserved it.

His gaze slid from hers. "It was for your own good."

"Oh, yeah?" Her look should've fried him where he stood. "Well, maybe I'm tired of other people deciding what's good for me. Maybe I want to decide for myself."

He raised his beer to her. "Then go for it."

When she shot him an uncomprehending look, he shrugged. "Hey, I'm not your brother or even a member of your clan. You want something, go out and get it. Just don't come to *my* city and try to mess in *my* business."

She leaned closer, dropped her voice. "And if what I want is you?"

He gulped. Took a swig of beer. Replayed her question in his head. "*That's* why you're here?"

A tiny nod. She looked out over the crowd, seemingly unconcerned, her slim frame was taut with tension. "I want to take you up on your offer."

His heart slammed in his chest. Hard, disbelieving beats. "My offer?"

He'd practically begged her for one night, had even offered to meet her out of town so no one would know. But she'd turned him down.

He shifted closer and she turned her head to meet his eyes. The noisy bar faded away until it was just the two of them.

He swayed toward her, his gaze locked on her shiny red lips. He could already taste them beneath his, feel their softness. Hear her gasp as he took her deeper...

"Here you go, *bibi*." Sophie's cheerful voice wrenched him to his senses. She set the beers on the bar behind them.

He dragged in a breath, handed the bartender a ten. "Keep the change."

"Thanks." Her gaze flicked between Rosana and him, and then she chuckled before moving on to the next customer.

Adric picked up both bottles and handed one to Rosana.

The other fada in the bar—both river and earth—were eyeing them.

He smoothed out his expression and lowered his voice to subvocal tones. "Just to be clear, you'll give me one night."

She dipped her chin in assent.

He rubbed a thumb over the bottle's two bright red X's. "And you changed your mind—why?"

Why the fuck was he arguing? She'd said yes, hadn't she? But he couldn't help being suspicious.

He'd wanted—no, craved—this woman for six and a half years. But it was like Romeo mooning over Juliet, and he wasn't the idiot Romeo had been. Besides, she'd been barely sixteen, too young and way too sweet for a cynical bastard like him. He'd contented himself with a dance the few times their clans had socialized —and a searing kiss or two. She was twenty-two now, and he was tired of pretending this thing between them didn't exist.

But he'd made a move—twice—and both times, she'd shut him down.

Then, a few weeks ago she'd come looking for him, said she'd had a "hunch" that he was planning something against the night fae, and she wanted to help.

He'd told her no fucking way.

They'd argued, and then he'd taken her hand. She'd gone stick-straight, her irises darkening to an eerie black. That was when he'd realized she had the Sight.

"The Darktime isn't over," she'd said in a Seer's toneless voice. "The prince will destroy your clan from the inside out."

A chill had run over his skin. *She was a Seer.* He hadn't known, and there wasn't much he didn't know about the do Rio family.

He'd shaken her, demanded to know what she'd Seen. There was a fraught silence, and then with a shudder, she'd come back to herself and whispered, "That's insane. You can't kill him. You'll set off something you can't stop."

But maddeningly, that had been all she could tell him.

His spine had iced. Nobody knew what he was planning. Not even his sister.

And Rosana didn't know. Not really. She'd Seen a possible future, that's all. So he'd sent her on her way, told her to stay the fuck out of Baltimore.

Now her fine dark brows scrunched together. "If you're not interested…"

He growled. "You know damn well I'm interested. I'm just wondering why now."

A shrug. "Maybe I'm curious."

Cat's balls.

His dick twitched, his dark side picturing all the things he could teach a curious virgin, because he *knew* she hadn't had another man. She was only twenty-two turns of the sun, and an alpha's pampered baby sister.

Unashamed, he reached down and adjusted his pants.

Her eyes tracked his movement. The tip of her tongue darted out to moisten her full lower lip. He stifled a groan as his dick went from half-hard to full, aching attention.

But the alpha in him was still suspicious. "Does this have something to do with that vision you had?" He lowered his voice even more. "Because I told you, there's no way I'm letting a river fada help in any way, shape, or form. Especially a Rock Run fada."

She blew out a breath. "*Deus*, Adric. I'm just looking for a little fun. But if you changed your mind, I get it."

And without giving him a chance to reply, she took her beer and headed into the crowd. A few seconds later, she was dancing with another man, this one a river fada.

Adric's nostrils flared. *No. Hell no.*

So Rosana wanted some fun? Then she'd damn well have it with him.

Still, he hadn't become alpha of a murderous, warring clan by playing his cards for all to see. And the other river fada in the bar were glaring at him with fire in their eyes.

He lifted his beer to them in a mocking salute and headed to the back room and the poker game.

But when she left the bar, he was waiting.

CHAPTER 2

*R*osana eyed the small bathroom window in the ladies' room, calculating she'd just fit. Locking the door—*Sorry, ladies*—she removed her jacket and gloves and eased up the window.

A hop and a slither got her upper body through the narrow opening, but her hips were stuck fast. She turned sideways, pushed hard against the frame and with a deep inhale and a little cursing, popped the rest of the way out. Twisting in mid-air, she landed on her feet in the tiny parking lot behind the saloon.

An icy January drizzle spattered her. She raised her face, drinking in the coolness against her heated skin, before pulling on her jacket and heading around the corner to her sportbike.

Built on the waterfront, Fell's Point dated to the time when Baltimore was a major port and shipbuilding center teeming with seamen and pirates. The road was paved in cobblestones, the streetlights an old-fashioned black metal. Trees pushed through miniscule squares of earth in the sidewalk to raise stunted branches to the moonless sky, and the buildings were a mix of shops, warehouses and brick rowhouses with gabled roofs.

Her hands were clammy. She wiped them on her pants and pulled on her gloves.

Elation filled her. She'd done it. Gone to Adric, the man she'd wanted since forever, it seemed.

But he didn't say yes.

Her steps slowed. Was he going to just let her leave?

He'd been so suspicious. She hadn't expected that. But then, that vision had shocked them both.

It had been last month, right before the winter solstice. She'd tracked him down because she'd been having maddening glimpses of the future. Her gut had told her he was planning something against the night fae, and she'd wanted to help.

He'd been suspicious then, too. But he'd taken her hand, kissed her wrist. His fingers had closed on hers, and...

Darkness. So much darkness.

Stomach churning, she pressed the heels of her hands to her eyes.

His touch had triggered her Sight. She'd Seen Adric crouched as his cougar in a tree, focused on a tall, black-haired man with pale skin and a fae's pointed ears.

Adric is slipping through the forest, a man now.

Something flashes in his hand—a dagger made of iron, the only metal that can kill a fae or a fada.

The black-haired fae turns around. It's Langdon, the night fae prince.

His gaze flicks in Adric's direction. A smile moves across his coldly beautiful face...and three night fae warriors converge on Adric.

The scene shifts to Baltimore, sometime in the near future. Adric's clan is hunkered down in their dens. The night fae are everywhere, and darkness slinks through his people like a feral wolf.

Cold. Relentless. Hungry.

And their alpha is nowhere to be seen.

She removed her hands from her eyes, stared at the gloved fingers.

Why had she let Adric touch her bare hand? She *knew* touching people could set off her Sight, and when she was in the grip of a vision, she wasn't in control. Things—prophecies—spilled out of her as if she were just a mouthpiece.

Her lips twisted. Wouldn't it be ironic if she'd scared off the man after he'd been chasing her for six years?

"Rosana." A thread of sound from a nearby alley, accompanied by Adric's scent, musky, a little earthy. The forest on a rainy day.

Her heart jumped.

The alley appeared empty until she looked up. The Baltimore alpha crouched on a warehouse roof like the cougar he was, blending into the shadows in dark jeans and a black leather jacket. She knew she'd only seen him because he'd let her.

Her mouth dried. Anticipation shivered up her spine.

A supple flex of his muscles, and he dropped soundlessly to the pavement.

He straightened, prowled nearer.

He wasn't as big as her brothers, but he was just as powerful, lean and hard-bodied. An alpha to the bone.

And gorgeous with tawny skin, spiked-up black hair bleached blond at the tips, and a face meant for sinning: long cheekbones, heavy-lidded eyes and a sensuous mouth just this side of mocking.

In the human world he'd have been a rock star. A badass, rule-breaking rock star.

He stopped so close she felt the heat of his body. Earth fada ran warmer than water fada; it was like standing next to a bonfire, hot and heady.

Her nipples pricked, pushed against her shirt. Her pussy clenched.

His nostrils flared, and she knew he scented her arousal. His odd bronze eyes darkened. "Tomorrow night. I'll book us a room on the Eastern Shore."

"And no one will know."

"No one," he confirmed. "There's a B&B on the beach. Owned by a human. He takes cash and he doesn't ask questions. Can you meet me on I-95?" He named a service plaza between Baltimore and Grace Harbor.

"What time?"

"Noon." His mouth edged up in a sardonic smile. "You sure this is okay with your brothers? I don't want to wake up with a knife to my throat—or..." He gestured at his crotch.

She shrugged, because it wouldn't be okay with them—if she told them. But Adric didn't need to know that. "No one followed me here, did they?"

A shake of his head.

"I'll be there," she told him. "Alone."

Fada had a hard time lying, but she didn't have to tell the whole truth, either. She'd explain to Dion and his mate, Cleia—who were more like parents to her—that she wanted to get away for a night or two. The Goddess knew, that was the truth. Sometimes she was so desperate to get away from the base and her well-meaning but overprotective family that she felt like screaming.

Adric stepped back. "Come here." He leaned against the brick wall and extended a hand.

Her stomach did a little flip. She moistened her lips.

I'm really doing this.

On the nearby sidewalk, several too-loud humans strolled past, but she barely heard them. Here in the alley, it was just her and Adric.

He cocked a mocking brow. "You in—or not?

She lifted her chin and took his hand. "I'm in."

He drew her closer and in one smooth move, had her crowded up against the wall. His eerie metallic irises were shot with blue now. His cougar was awake, intent on her like she was prey and it was starving.

He fisted his hands in her hair. His gaze went to her lips, and then his mouth was moving over hers. Softly, slowly. Teasing. Seducing.

The nerves in her belly fired up. Points of heat sizzled up and down her spine.

She moaned and opened her mouth, and his tongue slipped in, curling around hers. She sucked it deeper. He gave a low, exciting groan from deep in his throat.

He tasted of beer and his own dark male flavor. His body pressed hers to the wall, his erection hard against her belly. Heat came off him in waves. Stoking her desire, scrambling her brain.

She forgot that anyone could stumble upon them, especially those Rock Run men in the saloon who'd watched, narrow-eyed, the whole time she was speaking to Adric. They'd be out here now if she hadn't escaped through the bathroom window.

Worse, she completely forgot that she shouldn't touch him.

She jerked off her gloves and slid her hands under his jacket. She dragged up his T-shirt, seeking skin. Sliding her hands over his hard, dangerous body.

His hands were busy as well. One gripped her hair, pulling her head back so he could nibble at her throat. With the other, he unzipped her jacket and palmed her breast through her shirt.

She twined a leg around his thigh, urging him closer, rubbing herself against his erection. His chest flattened her breasts, the pressure easing her aching nipples.

He sucked on the tender skin beneath her jaw. Sensation speared from her breasts to her womb.

She gasped and writhed against him. "Adric. I—"

"Shh. It's okay. Just a little more..."

He moved to another spot, murmuring how beautiful she was. Telling her how much he wanted her. That he'd make it good, so good for her.

"*Sim, sim.*" She slipped into Portuguese and then caught herself. "Yes. Anything."

Adric was the one who called a halt. He lifted his head, breathing hard, and she gave another moan and tried to pull him back, but he set her a little away from him.

"Tomorrow." He brushed his lips over hers. "Tomorrow. Noon."

"Okay. Yes." Her voice sounded hoarse to her ears.

"I want your promise. You'll be there, no matter what."

"I'll be there. I promise."

"Good." He nipped her earlobe and then faded back into the shadows, watching as she zipped her jacket with fingers that felt thick, awkward.

He waited until she'd picked up her gloves before turning toward the wall. She watched as he leapt ten feet straight up, catching onto a gutter and swinging himself back onto the roof.

The man was a freaking human cat. Literally.

He remained on the roof, watching over her as she walked the half block to her sportbike.

She touched her tingling lips. The man sure knew how to use that sexy mouth.

She turned and walked backward. "Tomorrow," she mouthed and blew him a kiss.

Adric's eyes flashed an electric blue. His growl was soft, but she heard it. A thrill shivered over her skin.

She grinned and turned back around. She was halfway up I-95 before her body stopped humming.

~

BACK IN GRACE HARBOR, she parked the sleek purple bike in the clan garage and wiped the rain off the body. She didn't own the sportbike—the clan shared most vehicles—but she used it enough that she thought of it as hers.

That done, she tossed the rag into the bin provided for that purpose and headed into the passage that tunneled under Rock Run Creek to the base on the other side. The caverns were quiet, most of the clan in bed. An aqua-blue fae light wafted over to light her way through the labyrinthine tunnels.

She nodded at the few people she met without adding the usual hug. Since coming into her Gift as a Seer, she'd learned to avoid casual touches so as not to set off the Sight. People thought it odd, but fortunately, she'd always followed her own quirky drum. The clan expected her to be different.

Only her family—and now Adric—knew about her Gift, and she intended to keep it that way. She'd heard the stories of her Irish Seer mother. People might have liked Ula Gallagan, but they'd been wary of her, too. Everyone said they'd like to know the future, but when it came right down to it, no one wanted to be told their own death was barreling down at them like a great white shark, cold-eyed and relentless.

She turned a corner and stopped dead. She'd touched Adric without setting off her Sight. That was odd, especially after what had happened in December.

But not unexpected. One thing she'd learned was the Sight was erratic. It came and went at its own whim.

She continued walking until she reached the quarters she shared with Isa, her childhood nurse. Something else that had to change. She was too old to be living with her nurse, much as she loved the older woman. Everyone else her age had moved to the unmated warriors' quarters.

Easing open the door, she slipped off her boots and padded into the small *sala*.

"*Boa noite*," said a deep voice from the direction of Dion and Cleia's apartment.

Her alpha brother loomed in the doorway connecting their apartments, big hands gripping the doorjamb above him, his black hair loose around his shoulders, his only clothing a pair of cut-off sweats that bagged around his muscular thighs. Even fresh out of the bed, the man looked authoritative, in control.

She stifled a sigh as she set down the boots and stripped off her jacket and gloves. Yep, she definitely had to get her own place.

Dion was over one hundred turns of the sun, more like her dad than a brother. And like her *papai*, he'd been born and raised in Portugal with an old-world way of looking at things. He also had that whole alpha-protective-thing going on. He just didn't understand that at twenty-two, his little chick was ready to spread her wings and fly. And if she fell, well, that would be on her, not him.

"*Olá*, Dion. Sorry if I woke you up." She spoke in Portuguese, the language the clan used at home. She dropped onto the couch to take off her socks.

Dion sat next to her. "You didn't wake me. The little one was fussing."

"Brisa?" Rosana stopped in the act of removing a sock. Fada didn't often get sick, even the children. Their touch of fae blood fought off human viruses. "She okay?"

Brisa was the one thing Rosana and Dion agreed on. The tiny girl had them both wrapped around her plump little finger.

"She's fine. Just teething. Cleia gave her a shot of healing energy, and she went right back to sleep."

"*Bom*. I hate it when she's hurting."

Rosana pulled the sock the rest of the way off and wriggled her toes. *Deus*, she detested shoes, but even a shifter couldn't walk barefoot around Baltimore.

"Me, too." He exhaled. "I feel so fucking powerless."

She blinked. Her big brother had admitted there was something he couldn't fix? The man had balls of steel. Hell, he'd kidnapped the sun fae queen—one of the most powerful fae in the world—and not only had he survived, he'd mated the woman.

"She'll be fine." She awkwardly patted his leg over the cut-offs, careful not to touch his bare skin. "Kids have to go through these things, you know."

"I know." He gave her a lopsided smile. "I remember when you were teething —we all took turns walking with you at night."

"Yeah?"

"Oh, yeah. You were the cutest thing, and usually all smiles. But when you weren't happy, the whole family knew it."

She chuckled. "Sorry. At least Brisa has a mom who's a healer."

"*Sim.* And a full belly."

Their eyes met, and she knew they were both recalling the years when the clan was poor and hungry, the children too thin, sickly. Rosana might have been a pup, but she hadn't forgotten how hard Dion had worked to save the clan, even while their *papai* was still alpha.

And then their parents had gone missing, and Dion had had to step in and raise both Rosana and their brother Tiago while also leading the search for Nisio and Ula. Then, when it became clear their parents had either died or been ensnared by the fae, he'd taken over as the new alpha.

For the first time, she realized how hard it must have been on him. He'd become both a father and alpha, all within a few months.

"Brisa's a lucky girl," Rosana said. "She has you and Cleia for parents."

"You really think so?" A strange, almost diffident look crossed his face.

She gave an emphatic nod. "I know so."

"*Obrigado.*" Dion stifled a yawn.

"No need to thank me. It's the truth." She made to stand up. "But I should let you get to bed."

"Sit." A soft command.

She sank back onto the couch, spine stiff.

"You were in Baltimore."

She lifted her chin. "So?"

"Davi was here earlier. He said you were talking to Lord Adric. That the two of you looked...involved."

Her jaw tightened. On the way home from Baltimore, she'd toyed with the idea of telling Dion straight out about her and Adric. Now she was glad she'd kept her mouth shut.

"Davi should mind his own business." He was an ambitious young *tenente* who was only interested in her because she was the alpha's sister.

"He didn't have to tell me. I can smell Adric on you."

Her chin jutted. "So?"

"Rosana." Dion's tone made her feel like a pup again. "The man's a sneaky S.O.B. He wants Rock Run territory for his own clan. He tricked his way inside once—how do you know he's not trying to do it again?"

She stared down at her hands. They'd curled into fists. She straightened them out. She was *not* going to fight with Dion. He might have raised her from the time she was six, but she was an adult now.

"That was years ago. When was the last time you had any problems with him?"

"Doesn't mean he isn't planning something." Dion's mouth turned down. "The man doesn't have control of his own clan. In the last year alone, he and that sister of his have taken out two of his cousins."

She gritted her teeth. Dion was so certain he knew Adric, and sure, he'd done some bad things in the past. But Adric had changed. She knew he had.

"He's doing the best he can. It's not his fault he inherited a mess from that uncle of his. If he killed his cousins, then he had a good reason."

"And then there's his uncle. He didn't even have the balls to challenge him—Leron Savonett just disappeared. The man has no honor, and he wants Rock Run's territory. Don't forget Tiago. Adric played him like a fucking violin—and we almost lost the base because of it. The bastard will do anything to take me down, and you're my sister."

"So he can't want me for myself?" she asked evenly.

A muscle ticked in Dion's jaw. "That's not what I meant. You're a beautiful girl. You know that."

"I'm not a girl," she said between tight lips. "I'm a woman." Which was the whole problem. To Dion, she'd always be a girl, the little sister he'd raised from the time she was a pup.

"Rosana..."

She expelled a breath. "You were there for me after we lost Mama and *Papai* to King Sindre and the ice fae. I'll never forget that. But you're not my dad, Dion. Even if you were, I'm all grown up now. I love you, but you don't get to tell me who I—"

"And if he's just using you?"

The hurt nearly doubled her over. That the big brother she admired more than anyone in the world thought she was so stupid Adric could use her to harm the clan.

She came to her feet. "We're both tired. I'm going to forget you said that. *Boa noite.*"

"Rosana. Damn it, I—"

"No. Just...no." She walked into her bedroom and shut the door. Calm and controlled.

Then she fisted her hands, arched her back and let out a silent scream.

CHAPTER 3

dric tapped his quartz against the door to Jace Jones' den.

He'd been up since dawn, too antsy to sleep. After making the reservation at the B&B in Lewes, he'd headed across town to see Marjani, who, along with her mate Fane, roomed with Jace now.

The door opened—all the clan's dens were keyed to his quartz—and he slipped inside. Jace wasn't home. Another of Adric's lieutenants, the jaguar shifter was spending the winter in Grace Harbor with his human mate, Evie, and her brother Kyler while Kyler finished his senior year of high school.

Earth fada didn't gather in one base like water fada. Instead, the clan lived in underground dens scattered throughout the city. Everyone was still in bed, the living room empty except for the orange tomcat stretched along the couch's back. Tigger gave an ostentatious stretch—making sure Adric knew he'd interrupted his nap—and leapt to the floor. He butted his head against Adric's calf, one dominant feline to another.

Adric knelt to scratch Tigger behind the ears, his gaze taking in the homey clutter that spoke of the clan members who lived there. Jace, Evie, and Kyler when they were in town. Marjani and her mate, Fane Morningstar, an ice fae/human mix who was also Evie's father. Rounding out the group were three unmated males: a dreadlocked cougar named Horace; a burly tiger named Sam; and Beau, a big, slow-talking bear.

Sneakers and motorcycle boots were jumbled by the front door beneath the leather jackets and hoodies hanging from pegs on the wall. The couch was big and comfortable, and a sturdy coffee table held three empty beer bottles and a stack of cards. In the fireplace, chunks of amber quartz glowed cozily.

It made Adric's own den seem sterile. He frowned. Maybe he should invite someone to move into his sister's old bedroom. His den was too quiet these days, the two bedrooms more space than an unmated man needed.

But he was alpha. No one but his lieutenants and a few close friends were trusted with his address. And politics being what they were, he couldn't invite someone to live with him without appearing to be favoring one faction over the other. The cats would object if he invited a wolf, and the wolves would get pissed off if he invited a cat. And that didn't even take into account the dozen or so bears and deer. So for now, he lived alone.

The kitchen was large, welcoming. Jace had inherited the den from his parents, who'd always had an open door. Stop by for a meal or a few days, it was all the same to them. They'd never turned anyone away, even during the Darktime when they'd barely had enough food for their own small family. The stout plank table could seat twelve people, and the counter was tiled in a light green ceramic that Adric remembered from when he was a cub. A wood block held knives of various sizes, and pots and skillets hung over the elderly gas stove.

While he waited for Marjani, he boiled water for coffee. She would've heard the front door open, recognized his footsteps. Hell, she'd probably sensed him from a few blocks away. The two of them had grown up together, survived the Darktime and his uncle. She might be younger by a couple turns of the sun, but the two of them were more like twins, attuned to each other.

Which was the real reason he hadn't invited anyone else to take her room. He still hoped she'd move back in, even if it meant Fane came, too.

Still, he understood why she'd moved out. She was newly mated, and Adric and Fane weren't exactly good friends. The tall blond male was a little too slick, the kind of man who could charm your pants right off your ass. For his sister's sake, Adric had accepted Fane into the clan, but that didn't mean he trusted him.

Adric took out the French press, filled it with ground coffee. As he plunged the press into the glass carafe, Marjani padded into the kitchen in an oversized T-shirt that hung loosely on her spare frame.

"Ric. Whassup?" She smothered a yawn and stepped in for a hug.

"Morning." She'd gained weight, he noted with satisfaction, and stopped shaving her head. He gave her a hard squeeze and released her.

She really was better. He owed Fane for that.

Marjani got out two cups and he filled them with the coffee. She dosed both with half-and-half and handed one to him. "So. Why are you here?"

He took a gulp of coffee. It was perfect. Creamy, with a dark bite.

"I'm going to be out of town until late tomorrow." Gods, he hated having to inform someone every time he made a fucking move, but he was alpha. He couldn't just disappear for twenty-four hours.

"'Kay. Where?"

"Delaware. But unless the city catches fire, handle it. Anything else can wait until I get back."

"So this isn't business."

"No."

"You going to tell me what it's about?"

"No."

"Does it have anything to do with the little convo you and Rosana do Rio had at the Full Moon last night?"

He scowled. The clan grapevine had been working overtime. "And if it does?"

Marjani had told him straight up that this yen he had for the Rock Run alpha's little sister was insane. Hellfire, he knew that himself. But he couldn't let it go. His cougar insisted Rosana was his mate, but that *was* insane. Adric couldn't think of one single earth/water fada mating, anywhere.

What would their cubs be, anyway? Catfish?

"Because." Marjani set a hand on his arm. "If she's your mate, maybe you need to stop fighting it."

He almost choked on his coffee. He set down the cup. "Is this the same sister who's always telling me to forget about Rosana? That it will only fuck things up for me and the clan?"

Her dark eyes flickered. "I know, I know. It's the wrong thing for the clan, and we both know it. But Adric, this thing I have with Fane—I couldn't turn away from it if I tried. If either of us rejected the other, it would literally kill us both."

He wrapped his arms around her still-too-thin body. "That's because you accepted the bond. I haven't, and I never will. You know I can't. I'm alpha, and there are still people who are unhappy with that. I can't give them any more fuel for their fire."

She looped her arms around his waist and rested her head against his chest. "So you do feel the bond."

He stiffened. "No. Just the...possibility. And that's all it'll ever be. I promise."

"Oh, Ric. Don't make promises like that. Because if something changes..." She shook her head against his shoulder. "I just want you to be happy. You deserve it, more than anybody."

He pulled back and grinned. "Well, I intend to get very happy tonight."

Marjani chuckled, like he'd meant her to—and the sound went straight to his heart. These last few years, there'd been times when he'd wondered if she'd ever laugh again.

"Good." She gave him a squeeze and released him. "And don't worry, I'll cover for you. For the next twenty-four hours, forget you're alpha. Just be Ric."

CHAPTER 4

osana waited until breakfast was almost over before making her announcement.

They were in the spacious cavern that served as the Rock Run Clan's dining hall. It was the second breakfast shift—the fishers and marine workers were already out on the river or at the marina, their children in the creche. Now the warriors took their turn before heading off to their duties.

Dion sat at the table's head with her brother Tiago on the opposite end. Lucky her—Tiago had stopped by with his dryad mate, so she had not one, but two big brothers to deal with.

Across from Rosana, Dion's mate Cleia fed strawberries to little Brisa, back to her usual cheerful, high-energy self. On the bench next to Rosana, Tiago's mate Alesia dug into a bowl of yogurt and berries. Perched beside her was Tiago's otter friend Fausto, greedily downing a heaping plate of raw mussels.

Rosana took a deep breath. "I just wanted to let everyone know that I'm going to the beach." She spoke in English for Alesia's benefit. The dryad only knew a smattering of Portuguese.

"I have a couple of days off and..." Rosana trailed off as Dion and Tiago turned identical frowns on her. The only two of her four brothers still at Rock Run, they could be scarily alike. Same wavy black hair tied back with a leather string. Same steel-blue eyes. Same disapproving scowls on their good-looking faces.

Fausto paused in the act of cracking open a mussel to dart a glance at Rosana.

He might not understand English, but he could detect the abrupt change in atmosphere.

"Which beach?" Dion asked.

She hitched a shoulder. "I don't know. Somewhere on the Eastern Shore—Delaware, or maybe one of the Maryland beaches. I'll be back by tomorrow night."

"You're not going alone." That was Tiago.

She toyed with a piece of bread. She couldn't lie to them. Fada could scent a lie, and besides, it would make her violently ill. It had something to do with their fae blood, even though it was just a trace.

So instead, she went on the attack. "Look, I just want to get away, all right?"

"Not alone." Dion's stern look was spoiled by his tiny daughter wriggling away from her mama and onto the floor.

"Up, *Papai*." Brisa patted his thigh, a sprite in a pink-and-yellow striped dress, her fine gold hair caught up in two pigtails, her eyes the same warm amber as Cleia's.

His hard face softened. "Of course, *menina*." He cuddled her to his chest.

"You'll take a friend." Tiago again. "Davi would be happy to—"

"*Deus*." Rosana glared at him. "What part of getting away don't you understand? I'm going. *Alone*."

Most of the clan had cleared out by now, but those still in the dining hall glanced her way.

"Dion." Cleia spoke in her throaty voice. "It's only one day."

The sun fae queen was blindingly beautiful, with large tip-tilted eyes, shoulder-length hair in shimmering shades of gold, silver and copper, and a fae's pointed chin and ears. Rosana still wasn't sure how her hardheaded oldest brother had won Cleia's heart, but without the older woman to smooth things over, she just might've left the clan by now like her two middle brothers had.

Dion turned an irritated look on his mate. Their gazes locked, the two of them communing through their bond—not in words, but in some deeper way that only mated pairs could.

Alesia touched Rosana's back. "Take a breath, sweetheart."

Rosana sent her a guilty glance. The dryad was a solitary fae, more comfortable with plants than people, and she hated arguments.

"*Desculpe-me*," she muttered, and took a breath. Tiago's mate had that effect on people. Half-wild with an elfin face and mass of sun-streaked brown curls, the dryad radiated an earth-mama calm.

"Talk to them," Alesia added. "Please? Because they'll listen to you. Right, Tiago?" She reached across Rosana to squeeze his hand.

"*Sim, sim,*" he grumbled.

Rosana took another breath. Alesia was right. If she wanted Dion and Tiago to see her as an adult, then she had to show them she was calm. Mature.

And able to run her own fucking life.

Dion fingered a lock of his mate's sun-colored hair. "I'm her alpha," he told Cleia. "If I say she stays, then she stays."

"Of course," the queen agreed. "But it's just one day. And Rosana's a smart, capable woman. She's not a child anymore."

Dion shook his head.

Rosana gritted her teeth and helped herself to a slice of the thick peasant bread. She drizzled olive oil on it and tore off a piece to eat.

Calm. Mature. In control.

"I did you the courtesy of informing you where I'll be," she said. "But I'm not asking your permission. I'm an adult now. I don't need the alpha's okay to leave the base, as long as I fulfil my duties to the clan."

"Try it," Tiago invited, "and you'll find yourself with two bodyguards on your ass everywhere you go."

"Since when did you become my dad?" she snarled back. She'd expected better of him. Just five years older than her, they'd once been partners-in-crime, united against Isa and their three much older brothers when it came to childish pranks.

Dion raised a staying hand. "I just don't understand why you have to go alone."

"I'm twenty-two turns of the sun. When Tiago was my age, did you make him take a babysitter every time he left the base?"

"Of course not. He's a man."

Across the table, Cleia winced.

Rosana flung up her hands. "So this is because I'm a female? I made warrior with the rest of my cohort. You trained me yourself."

"No. Yes." Dion shook his head. "It's just..." He cursed under his breath, then shot a contrite look at a wide-eyed Brisa. "If something happened to you, I'd never forgive myself."

"For *Deus*'s sake, I'm going to the beach, not a war zone."

"There are people out there who would love to get at me through you."

"Like Adric," Tiago murmured.

Rosana stopped tearing her bread into pieces and reached for her orange juice.

Calm, controlled.

She itched to defend Adric, but her brothers weren't stupid. It wouldn't take much for them to connect her conversation with him last night with this sudden desire to go away on her own.

Cleia set a hand on Dion's arm. "I can give her a protection charm. One that will deflect both physical and magical attacks."

A muscle jumped in his cheek. When he'd mated with the powerful fae queen, he'd made it clear she wasn't to interfere in his governing of Rock Run, however well-meaning. He hated asking her for anything. But to Dion, family was everything.

"*Bom*," he agreed. "But only if you wear the charm all the time. And one day only, understand? I want you back here by tomorrow night."

Rosana shot Cleia a grateful look. "Sure," she said calmly, while inside, she was doing a full-out happy dance. "I'll be fine, you'll see."

"You'd better be," he returned, but his lips curved in a reluctant smile.

Cleia rose to her feet. "I'll be right back with that charm."

The air around her brightened and contorted so that it hurt your eyes to look straight at her. When Rosana glanced back, she'd 'ported out of the hall.

Brisa removed the chunk of bread she was gnawing on from her mouth and waved it at the spot where Cleia had just been. "Mama?" Her small brow knit uncertainly.

"She'll be right back." Dion set a cup of apple juice to her lips. "Here, drink."

Brisa took a sip and then wriggled off his lap to make her way around the table to Alesia and Rosana, one hand on the bench for balance. When she reached Alesia, she handed her the half-eaten piece of bread.

"Here, Tia Yesa."

"Thank you." The dryad gravely accepted it and set it on her plate. "I'll just keep it for you in case you want it back."

"Okay." Brisa continued to Rosana. "Up, Tia Wosa." She lifted her arms.

Rosa swung her up. "Well, hello, there."

Children were the one group she wasn't afraid to touch. She might get a glimpse of a possible future, but their lives had so many possibilities that it was like looking down a hall with a thousand doors.

"What's under here? A belly button?" She lifted her niece's striped skirt to blow on her stomach.

Brisa chortled with glee. Then Alesia tickled one of her tiny pointed ears, and she giggled even harder.

Cleia 'ported back with the charm, a silver Celtic knot inscribed on a plump heart. "It's not one-hundred-percent foolproof," she warned as she clasped the delicate chain around Rosana's left wrist. "But it should at least buy you time to get away."

"I love it." Rosana turned her wrist from side to side, admiring the shiny charm. She beamed at Cleia. "It's beautiful—thank you."

"What if she has to shift?" asked Dion.

His mate's smile was smug. "I've had my people working on that. This is a new design that will magically adjust and attach itself to her tail fluke."

"No kidding? We may have to buy some of those from you."

"You know I'd give them to you for free."

"But we'll pay the same price as anyone else," Dion returned.

Cleia sighed. "Pigheaded, that's you." But her eyes laughed at him as she reached for Brisa and set her on her hip.

"Come here, you." Dion pulled the two of them down on his lap and gave her a hard kiss, while Brisa flung pudgy arms around both their necks.

Cleia nuzzled Dion's cheek contentedly. She wore a yellow top and a short pleated pink skirt the same colors as Brisa's stripes. The two of them could have posed for a mother-daughter photo in a fancy human catalog. Once, Rosana might've rolled her eyes at their matching outfits. But Cleia had waited a long time to have Brisa, and the look she turned on her daughter was so loving that instead, Rosana's heart constricted.

She dimly recalled her Irish mom looking at her like that. Before that summer when her parents had left—and never returned.

They're alive. That's something.

For a long time, they hadn't known if Ula and Nisio were alive or dead, although they'd suspected King Sindre of the ice fae was behind their disappearance. Then their brother Nic had confirmed it, but it was Adric's sister Marjani who, on a mission to Iceland, had seen them at the ice fae court. Ula and Nisio were under a *geas* that bound them to Sindre himself.

But Rosana still couldn't see them, because apparently each time Dion or any of the do Rio brothers had come to court asking about Ula and Nisio, the king had punished their parents.

Rosana's throat worked.

She was lucky and she knew it. She'd had a brother who'd stepped in as a father, Isa to mother her, Tiago as a playmate. And then later, there'd been Cleia and now Alesia and little Brisa.

Ula and Nisio had never even seen their granddaughter.

But that didn't mean Rosana didn't feel an emptiness, a ragged hole in her soul that no one else could fill.

She rose to her feet. "I'd better get going."

Cleia smiled up at Rosana. "Have a good time, darling."

Their eyes met, and Rosana *knew* that the sun fae had guessed exactly where Rosana was going and with whom. But she also knew Cleia wouldn't tell Dion unless absolutely necessary.

"Thanks, I will." She blew a kiss at her niece, who puckered her small mouth back, and then strolled out of the dining hall.

Not hurrying, because that would make her brothers suspicious.

She waited until she was out of sight to speed up.

BACK IN HER ROOM, Rosana threw off her clothes. Fortunately, Isa had already left for the creche. Although officially retired, the former nurse still helped with the pups most mornings. With her round, comfortable body and graying hair, Isa might look like everyone's idea of a grandma, but she was nobody's fool.

Rosana shimmied into an ivory chemise and matching boy shorts, a birthday gift from Cleia. Soft and silky, the fae-made fabric magically molded itself to her body. Next were a black Henley, skinny jeans and the red kitten-heel boots, another gift from Cleia. She donned the matching leather jacket and headed to the clan garage.

The good news? There was a car available. The purple sportbike was too noticeable, and besides, she didn't want to leave it overnight at a busy rest area.

The bad news? The car was in for an oil change and wouldn't be ready for an hour.

By the time Rosana drove out of the garage, it was nearly noon, and she had no way to contact Adric, because she didn't have a cell phone. No one in the clan did. Something about a water fada's physiology shorted out small electronics.

He'll wait, she told herself as she raced the twenty minutes south to the rest area.

But she didn't relax until she saw him standing next to a sporty blue Mazda in a T-shirt, black jeans and combat boots, scanning the incoming cars. Their gazes met. His shoulders eased, and he gave her his trademark cocky smile.

But she'd seen that tense expression. He'd been worried she wouldn't show. She smiled to herself and pulled into a nearby parking space. Adric was right there, opening the door for her.

"Thanks for waiting," she said. "I'm sorry, I—"

"You're here." He stopped her apology with a kiss. "That's all that matters. This all you brought?"

He reached for her canvas overnight bag while she locked the car.

"That's it."

He set a hand on the small of her back and steered her to the Mazda. She dragged in a breath, released it.

"Trouble getting away?" His smile was knowing.

She lifted her chin. "Nothing I couldn't handle."

"Good." He dragged her to him for an open-mouth kiss, and while she was still catching her breath, helped her into his car.

He drove one-handed, wending his way through the Sunday afternoon traffic with ease. His mustard-colored T-shirt clung lovingly to hard, rounded deltoids. His forearms were dusted with soft dark hair, his hands strong, capable.

Anticipation churned in her. Those hands would be on her in just a couple of hours, and she could hardly wait.

But her stomach was jumping with nerves.

Her first time with a man. And she had the added worry of wondering if sex would set off her Gift.

Because sex was the most intimate touch there was.

She stared down at her gloved hands.

Adric reached across the console to brush the backs of his fingers over her cheek. A soft touch that shuddered through her like a promise.

She swallowed hard. *You want this*, she reminded herself.

Because she did want it, bad. If she had a vision, well, Adric would just have to deal with it.

She stripped off her gloves and shoved them into a pocket.

"Do you know Lewes?" he asked.

"Yeah. I go there with my—" She stopped, bit her lip. The last thing she wanted was to bring up Dion and Tiago. Adric didn't like her brothers any more than they liked him.

"So you like it?" Adric prompted as if he didn't know why she'd halted.

She nodded. "It's a pretty little town. But we go to swim in the ocean. Delaware has some of the cleanest beaches on the East Coast."

Some of her best memories were going to Lewes with her brothers and spending a few days cruising as their dolphins off the coast, following the currents and snacking on fish.

Adric took her bare hand, the one with the protection charm, and lifted it to his lips. "I like the beach this time of year. It's cold, but there's almost no one else out. You have it all to yourself."

She smiled at him. She hadn't expected tenderness, not from the hard-ass Baltimore alpha. But his lips were warm and soft as he pressed them to her skin, and his smile had a sweet, almost tentative edge.

He set her hand on his leg but kept hold of it. She tensed, but her Gift was quiet. Maybe, just maybe, she could get through the next twenty-four hours without freaking Adric out by going full Seer-mode on him.

Anticipation buzzed in her veins. She pressed her inner thighs together and concentrated on keeping her breathing even. But Adric was a fada. He could scent her arousal, spicing the small space.

His lips curved in a slow grin.

There. That was the Adric she knew. Sexy with an edge.

The kind of man your brothers warned you about—which only made you want him more.

She grinned back at him.

He responded with a hum that was almost a purr and released her to whip the little car around a semi.

Traffic was light. It wasn't long until they entered Delaware and turned south toward the beach. Adric fiddled with the radio while the flat terrain unspooled on either side of them, winter fields of tattered cornstalks and soybeans interspersed with shiny-new housing developments.

As they entered Lewes, the billboards and pizza places gave way to charming wood-shingled homes and hip little shops and restaurants. Crepe myrtle, bare for the winter, arched cinnamon-colored branches in front of painted Victorians with lacy trim. In the summer, she knew, the tiny yards would overflow with flowers and pots of fragrant herbs.

They took the drawbridge over the Lewes and Rehoboth Canal. The B&B was between the canal and the Delaware Bay. Three stories high and painted an eye-popping turquoise, blue and peach, it was as if a piece of Key West had levitated and flown north to Delaware.

Rosana slung her canvas bag over a shoulder while Adric took a leather jacket and a duffel bag from the backseat. The building was on stilts to protect against flooding. To reach the front door, they passed beneath an overhang guarded by a busty carved figurehead like the kind you saw on the prow of a ship, and wound their way through three kayaks, two surfboards and a stand of rusting beach bikes.

Inside, Adric led the way up a stairwell crammed with quirky art—an outsized pig in a red tutu, the head of a laughing cow, a seductive mermaid. They found the proprietor on the second floor in a small, open office, feet propped on his desk, watching a video on his computer.

He came unhurriedly to his feet. Solidly built with salt-and-pepper hair, he was dressed in pink board shorts and flip-flops despite the near-freezing temperature outside.

"Lord Adric," he said with an easy smile. "You're right on time. The room's all ready."

Adric inclined his head. "Mark. Peace to you and yours."

"And to you and yours." Mark turned his smile on Rosana. "Welcome to Lewes," he said as he took Adric's cash and noted something on the computer.

She smiled back. "Thank you. And peace to you."

"You've got the Hemingway Suite. Right down that hall." The innkeeper indicated the hallway to the left as he handed Adric the key. "There's only one other couple staying the night, and they're on the third floor. Other than me, you have the second floor to yourself."

Adric thanked him and, taking Rosana's hand, led the way down the hall to their room.

"He doesn't mind us being fada?" she murmured. Humans tended to be wary around shapeshifters, especially dominant ones like Adric.

"Nah. He says my money's as good as anyone's. I don't bother him and he doesn't bother me."

"So you've stayed here before."

"A couple of times. I mind my business, and he does the same."

Rosana quelled a twist of jealousy.

Who? she wanted to ask. *Who did you bring those other times?*

But she refused to go down that road. She'd known when she walked into the bar last night that Adric wasn't celibate.

Unlike her.

The Hemingway Suite was dominated by a king-sized bed covered with fake leopard-skin and flanked by two rattan lounge chairs. A photo of Ernest Hemingway presided over a hutch filled with copies of the author's books and an old-fashioned typewriter, and the sliding glass door was covered with blinds made of wood slats.

"Nice." Rosana set her bag on one of the rattan chairs and hung her leather jacket on a hook near the door. "I'm impressed."

She crossed the room, trying not to stare at the huge bed, to open the blinds on the sliding glass doors. Outside, a small terrace ran the length of the room, with steps leading down to a grassy strip behind the B&B.

"And private." Adric dropped his duffel bag by the door and hung his jacket next to hers.

She turned to face him. Picturing why they might need privacy made her shove her hands into her back pockets, and then take them out again.

Relax, damn it. You want this, remember?

Adric leaned against the door on the opposite side of the room, arms crossed, a small smile on his face. "Want a drink? Mark keeps wine and beer for the guests in the breakfast room."

"Water's good for now."

He nodded, and going to the small refrigerator near the door, removed two plastic bottles and held one out to her.

"Thanks." She forced her feet to unscrew from the floor. She took the bottle and gulped water, avoiding his eyes.

"Rosana."

She jerked her gaze to him. "Yeah?"

"It's okay." He set his water on an end table. "There's no rush."

"There isn't?" Oh, she was being such an idiot about this. But her insides were a big knot of tension.

"Of course not." He caressed her shoulders. "Are you hungry? We could go out for a late lunch."

"Not really. I had a big breakfast." Which was churning undigested in her stomach.

"Then why don't we go to the beach while the sun's still out?"

She sent him a relieved smile. "That would be nice."

"Okay." He brushed his lips over hers.

They walked the two blocks to the beach. It was a crisp, sunny day. A number of the houses were shut for the winter, but they passed a couple of humans out running, bundled up against the cold, and a woman pushing a baby in a stroller who took one look at Adric and made a wide circle around them. A pint-sized terrier barked at them from a covered porch, and a tomcat trotted across the road on its way to some important rendezvous.

They left their boots at the head of a path through the dunes and wended their way through the scrubby bushes and grasses to the water. They were on the Delaware Bay, a large estuary at the place where the Delaware River emptied into the Atlantic. An icy wind blew from the northwest, but the bay's winter-blue surface was calm. Long, low waves slid in, broke against the sand, and then slipped back out.

Adric took her hand. She tensed, and he brought her fingers to his mouth.

"Hey. I told you, there's no rush. I'm just happy to spend some time alone with you. If you've changed your mind, I'll live." He gave her a crooked grin. "I won't like it, but I'll live."

Her heart turned over. He was being so damn sweet. "It's not that. At least, it's not just"—she waved her free hand— "*that.*"

"Then what's the matter?" he asked as they started walking barefoot along the bay's edge.

"You know I'm a Seer."

"I figured that out when your eyes went all scary black on me."

She nodded. "Well, I never know when touching someone will set off my Sight, especially someone's hand."

"Even someone you know?"

"Yeah. At home, they think I'm a little strange."

He frowned. "Your clan doesn't know you're a Seer?"

"Just my family and a few close friends—but no one else." She lifted her chin. "I'm going to tell them. Soon."

"Good. You shouldn't have to hide your Gift."

"That's what Isa says. She's the woman who helped raise me after the ice fae captured my mom and dad."

"She's right."

"You didn't tell anyone, did you?" Rosana asked.

"Just Marjani, but she can keep a secret. I'll make sure she knows to keep it quiet. And if you don't want to hold hands, that's okay."

She tightened her grip on his fingers. "No. I want to hold your hand." She took a deep breath. "I want to do everything."

"Good." His smile was wicked. "Because trying to be nice about this is fucking killing me."

She chuckled—and her tension eased. After all, he'd seen her in the grip of a vision, and it hadn't freaked him out. Much. He still wanted her.

They continued walking in a companionable silence, the wind ruffling their hair, the sand damp beneath their toes. Overhead, seagulls wheeled and shrieked.

She slid Adric a look. She'd never seen him so relaxed, almost boyish, his spiky hair tousled, a slight smile curling his sexy mouth.

She knew so little about him. Oh, she knew he was the bad-boy Baltimore alpha, the man who gleefully provoked Dion every chance he got.

That he hadn't won alpha in a challenge, as honor demanded. Instead, it had been a sneak attack. And worse, the alpha had been Adric's own uncle.

Some of the Rock Run men, like Davi, sneered that Adric was a coward with no respect for fada *tradição*, tradition. But Leron Savonett had dragged Baltimore into the Darktime, an internal war that ripped his clan apart. Even Dion said Adric's uncle had been a self-centered, sadistic *cabrão*.

As far as Rosana could tell, if Adric hadn't killed his uncle when he had, his clan would've been wiped out.

Adric angled his head in a very catlike way. "You're frowning."

"I am?" She smoothed out her forehead.

"No, don't hide. Tell me—what were you thinking?"

She hitched a shoulder. "That I don't really know you."

"You know the important things."

"But I want to know the unimportant things."

"Like what?"

"Like...do you bleach your hair tips?"

"Nah." He shook his head. "It happened the first time I shifted to cougar, and never changed back. It grows spiked-up like that, too. My dad had the same hair."

"Huh."

"Here's one for you. What's up with the claws? Your animal's a dolphin, isn't it?"

She let the short but sharp black claws slide out. "Otter. We can shift to other water animals, you know. We're not limited like you earth fada. I just prefer my dolphin."

"Limited, huh?" He grabbed her, tickling her until she was breathless with laughter.

"I'm sorry, I'm sorry."

"You should be." He kissed her on the mouth and then released her, keeping an arm around her shoulders as they resumed walking.

"I have more," she said. "What's your favorite color? The one dessert you can't pass up? What do you do for fun? I don't even know how old you are."

"Peach ice cream. Music—I don't play an instrument, but I like to dance. And thirty-three turns of the sun—eleven older than you."

Of course, he knew her age. The man probably kept files on everyone in her family.

"As for my favorite color"—he swung her to face him—"that would be blue. The deep blue of the ocean out there, where the color is so intense you can almost feel it." He nodded at the horizon. "The blue of your eyes." He cupped her face, his fingers warm against her chilled skin. "Sometimes I forget how incredibly blue they are."

She swallowed. "Yeah?"

His own irises were a brilliant golden-brown. She swayed toward him, entranced.

"I mean it." His voice was a low rasp that reverberated in her body. "I love your eyes. Almost as much as I love your face, your body. Your smile."

Her heart gave a hard thump. "My smile?"

"Um-hmm." His fingers curled around her waist. He reeled her in, slowly, deliberately, until her body was flush against his. The firm muscles of his chest pressed her breasts, his erection hard against her belly. "Your smile is so wide and happy. It makes me...want."

"Want what?"

"You." His mouth whispered over hers. A barely-there touch that made her catch her breath.

Excitement skittered up her spine. Her breasts felt full and heavy, the nipples pushing against the silky chemise.

His tongue teased the seam of her lips, coaxing her to open to him. When she did, he tunneled his fingers into her hair, holding her still as his tongue explored the soft cave of her mouth—the sides, the sensitive roof.

She rose on her toes and twined her arms around his neck, sucking his tongue deeper. His groan made everything female in her clench.

Her leg was around his hip now, her sex rubbing against his.

Somewhere nearby, a seagull screeched.

Adric lifted his head, his breath uneven. "Let's go back."

She swallowed. "Yes."

ADRIC'S HEART WAS THUMPING, his dick so hard it ached.

Rosana strolled beside him, her mouth swollen from his kisses, her bare feet dusted with sand, her hair a silky black waterfall down her back.

She was a pagan priestess in red leather and jeans. The kind of woman who dropped men to their knees.

He shoved a hand through his hair. The woman shredded his control. She'd all but melted in his arms, making those needy little noises, rubbing against him. Driving him insane with her unpracticed, uninhibited moves.

He shouldn't even be here with her. This could never go anywhere. But Rosana just had to crook a finger and he was there.

Her very innocence was a beacon to a man like him. A man who'd seen so much darkness, done so many dirty things that he'd never be truly clean.

He set an arm around her shoulders, pulled her closer. Because he could. He had one night with her, and he was going to enjoy it to the fullest.

She came readily. Their hips bumped, and she giggled, a young, happy sound.

His heart twisted. If only things were different...if only she were a member of his clan, a woman he could claim as his own.

You couldn't claim her even then.

He was basically a dead man walking.

A less selfish man would stop this before it began, but he'd waited six-and-a-half years for her. He was damned if he'd turn back now.

He nuzzled her hair, breathing her in. His hand went to her round ass.

"When I get you back to the room," he murmured in her ear, "I'm going to strip your jeans off you. But I won't take your panties off. Not right away. I'm going to tease you first. Make you hot and wet. Make you beg a little."

She moaned his name. The spice of her arousal teased his nostrils.

He smiled and ran his hand over the curve of her bottom. "Then, I'll peel your panties off—but not fast. We'll go slow, because it's your first time. And I want to drive you a little crazy. And you'll let me, won't you?"

Her pretty mouth formed an O. Her breath sped up, and she hunched her shoulders. She nodded rapidly.

Gods, she was so young, and so much less experienced. On some level she'd been his since age sixteen, when they'd first met at Cleia & Dion's mate ball.

And so, she'd waited for him.

He didn't know why he was so sure, but he was.

I'll be her first. His chest squeezed.

No other male had touched her. The primitive part of him reveled in that. He wanted to take her, long and hard. Imprint himself on her so that she'd always remember him.

But he also wanted to take care of her. Show her how special she was. Caress her. Love her.

He was a hard man, some would say a cold-blooded killer. But he'd done what he had to, survived when a softer man wouldn't have—and saved his clan besides. For Rosana, though, he'd dredge up whatever tenderness he could.

They exited the beach and stopped to put on their boots.

The wind had picked up. It whistled through the dunes, whipped Rosana's long black curls across her face. She captured them in one hand and beamed at him, her irises a deep sapphire in the fading light.

"Race you back to the B&B." She took off down the street, surprisingly agile in the high-heeled boots.

He blinked, and with a predatory grin, loped after her. His cougar loved a chase.

He stayed behind her until they were almost to the B&B, because hey, watching that ripe, pretty ass wasn't a hardship. Then he lunged, grabbing her waist and swinging her into the air.

She gave a shriek of laughter and grabbed his shoulders. Long legs wrapped around his hips.

"Beat you." He gently closed his teeth on her full lower lip and continued walking. "What do I win?" He nibbled his way down her neck.

"No fair." She angled her head so he could taste the tender underside of her jaw. "We didn't agree to anything for the winner."

He reached around her to open the door to the B&B. The stairwell was silent, his animal-enhanced senses telling him they were alone in the building. He headed up to the second floor with Rosana wrapped around him like a sexy vine.

He let his cat into his smile. "Where the fuck did you get the idea I play fair?"

CHAPTER 5

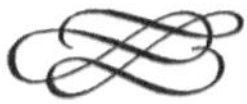

*A*dric set Rosana on the floor and reached behind him to lock the door. She had time for a single sharp inhale, and then he had a hand fisted in her hair. He tugged her head back, exposing her throat.

It was a very male, very dominant move. And damn, it turned her on.

Her pussy clenched. Her knees turned to jelly.

I'm going to tease you first... Make you beg a little.

Goddess, he'd almost made her come right then with those hot, dirty words rasped against her throat.

She set her hands on his chest. His face was still chilled from the cold, but the rest of him was all hot, tensile strength, his scent a mix of earth and the winter wind.

He fastened his mouth to her throat above the collarbone and sucked hard. Leaving a love-bite she'd have to hide, but right now, she just didn't care.

Heat shot from her breasts to her womb, pooled between her thighs. Her skin felt too tight. She moaned and gripped his shoulders.

Releasing her hair, he bent her over an arm and kissed his way down her neck to her breasts. Her nipples beaded against the thin barrier of her chemise and the cotton shirt. He pushed up the shirt and traced a finger down the V of the neckline to her cleavage.

"Pretty." He placed his mouth on the ivory material over one tightly furled bud and sucked.

Her lungs jerked. She dug her fingers into his shoulders and rasped his name.

"Mm." He swirled his tongue around her nipple through the silky cloth and then moved to her other breast. "I want to lick you all over."

Need twisted through her. "Right back at you."

That earned her a deep kiss. When he lifted his head, he pulled her shirt the rest of the way off so that she stood before him in just the chemise, jeans and boots.

His gaze locked on the wet fabric over her breasts. She glanced down to see her nipples dark against the pale material.

"Yeah," he said hoarsely, "I'm going to lick you all over. And maybe bite a little."

Anticipation coursed through her. She shivered and rubbed the goosebumps that popped up on her arms.

"Cold?" he asked.

"No. Just..." She shrugged a shoulder.

His smile was knowing. He dragged off his T-shirt.

Her breath jammed in her throat. In all the years she'd known him, she'd never seen him unclothed.

He was...perfect. Smooth, honey-brown skin stretched over firm muscles. Dark hair dusted his pecs, arrowed through washboard abs before disappearing beneath his waistband. Her gaze locked on the hard ridge beneath his zipper.

He didn't give her nearly enough time to look. Instead, his hands were on her waist, his mouth covering hers. He walked her backward until her thighs hit the mattress, then lifted her onto the bed and crouched at her feet.

Slipping off her boots and socks, he cradled one boot in his hand. "Later," he said with a wicked curve of his lips, "you'll wear these for me—and nothing else."

"I will?" She eyed the boot, intrigued. But it wasn't in her nature to submit easily. When you were the youngest child—and a girl—in a family with four large, hard-ass brothers, you either stood up for yourself or got crushed.

She moistened her lips. "Maybe if you ask nice." Her voice came out husky, seductive, in a tone she barely recognized as hers.

His smile increased. "You'll do it. That's my reward for winning the race."

She arched a brow. "What reward? I didn't agree to—"

"But you'll do it. Because I want you to." He set down the boot but remained where he was, crouched between her legs. Warm hands ran up her inner thighs. He rubbed a thumb over the seam of her jeans. "Won't you?"

She moaned, so sensitized that even that small pressure was almost too much.

Then he leaned forward and replaced his thumb with his mouth, and it got even better. He blew on the material, a hot, moist stream that nearly made her come out of her skin.

Gulping air, she dug her fingers into the fake leopard skin and arched her back. Pressing her pelvis toward him, unconsciously begging for more.

He undid the button of her jeans and eased down the zipper. Two long fingers slid inside. He worked them under the boy shorts so he could tease her clit.

"Say yes, angel. Say you'll wear the boots. To please me."

She studied him. His eyes glinted up at her, bright, devilish. Did he mean it, or was it a game? Either way, she wasn't ready to give in.

She smiled and twisted against his fingers. If he'd just apply a bit more pressure...

"More," she said in smoky tones that made him swallow. Hard.

He rose up to kiss her. His tongue swirled around hers, while inside her jeans, his fingers moved in a similar tantalizing pattern. Promising pleasure but holding it just out of reach.

"You're so wet." A low growl. "So ready for me. But I haven't heard a yes."

He withdrew his hand from her pants and brought his hand to his mouth, licking her juices from his first two fingers while he watched her from beneath his lids.

She blinked up at him. Somehow she'd ended flat on her back with him propped on an elbow next to her.

He peeled her out of the tight jeans, and then shucked his own pants. He crawled over her, heavily erect, his only adornment the big chunk of gray-and-orange quartz hanging from the leather thong around his neck.

His expression was hard with desire, his bronze irises shot with the blue of his cougar. They were gorgeous, mesmerizing, like cyan fireworks exploding against a dusk sky.

Both man and cat were making love to her.

A primitive thrill raced over her skin. She touched his cheek, letting her own animal into her eyes—and surrendered.

Because suddenly, she didn't want to play games. What mattered was that he wanted her, and that she wanted him back, clear to the wild, untamed heart of her.

"Yes," she rasped. "Make love to me. Any way you want."

His throat rumbled in a rough purr that vibrated in all her secret places. He tugged at the chemise's strap. "Take this off."

He helped her shimmy out of the sexy little top and then traced the edge of her jaw with his tongue before moving down to her neck. He pressed a damp kiss to the hollow of her throat and then continued licking and sucking his way to each breast. His hot tongue swirled around each nipple in turn, leaving them wet and aching.

Her body went taut with wanting, and maybe a touch of fear.

"Relax," he murmured.

She moved her head back and forth against the pillow. "I can't," she confessed.

He nuzzled her cleavage. "Maybe I can help with that."

He continued down her abdomen, leaving a trail of kisses in his wake. And then he was between her legs, a hand on each thigh. He held her gaze, unsmiling —and blew on her clit through the silky panties.

Her hips rocked up. She rasped his name.

He pressed her back down to the mattress. "Slow and easy. Remember what I said?"

Belatedly, she recalled his promise to take things slowly. "No..."

"Shh. This will feel good." He hummed against her clit. The sound vibrated through her whole body.

A groan escaped her throat. The fada were easy about their sexuality. She might be a virgin, but she'd fooled around with a few of the men in her cohort, especially the year before she met Adric. And then later, when she realized that any man but Adric left her cold, she'd touched herself, learned what she liked.

But nothing had prepared her for this.

A man between her legs, his eyes burning into hers. The hot swipe of his tongue on her most sensitive flesh. The strong hands holding her open for him. The teasing heat of his mouth against her sex through the barely-there fabric.

"Please," she said. "Please..."

A sexy growl. "I like it when you beg. I just may keep you here for the next hour." He gently bit her clit through the panties.

Her breath stuttered. Her hands fisted in the sheets. "No..."

His eyes glittered at her. "You don't like it?"

"No. Yes. I do, but I need..."

But he kept her there for another ten minutes, licking and sucking her through the silky material. Keeping her on a knife's edge of need until her senses felt overloaded. Then he slid his hands into the boy shorts from beneath, squeezing and caressing her bottom.

And even as she begged him to stop teasing her, a part of her wanted it to go on forever. But then he was easing the shorts down, an inch at a time. Her chest heaved. Her muscles went tight with anticipation.

At last the shorts were off. He tossed them away and came back between her legs. His hands gripped her ass, lifting her up like a special dish for his delectation —and then he swiped his tongue through her slick, needy sex.

Sensation rushed through her like an out-of-control storm. Overwhelming and a little frightening. She was going to break apart, lose herself to him.

From far away, she heard her voice, high and needy. She was speaking in Portuguese now.

"*Meu querido. Meu amor.*" My darling. My love.

She reached for his head. To pull him closer, to push him away—she wasn't sure which.

He turned his head and kissed her palm, and then continued licking her.

Her lungs constricted. She couldn't get enough air into them. "Adric. I—"

"What, love?" A husky murmur against her clit. "Tell me."

She licked her lips, tried to form the words in English. "I can't. I need..."

"What?"

She released his head, dug her fingers into the mattress and gave in to it. She wanted this. Sometimes she thought she'd been born wanting Adric.

"More. Please."

A low chuckle. "Like this?" He closed his lips around her quivering flesh and sucked hard.

Her breath hissed out. Her hips rocked up, seeking more.

"Yes," he said against her clit. "Come for me, baby. And then I'm going to fuck you, so hard." He sucked harder.

The hot, dark words mixed with the sweet suction of his mouth sent pleasure rocketing through her. She sobbed out his name and let herself wallow in the sensations. Exhilaration filled her. It was like diving off a high cliff. Standing on the edge, you couldn't help being afraid, but the surge of adrenaline as you leapt made it worth it.

Her climax coiled in her belly, spread up her spine, unfurled through her nerve endings...and then erupted in a burst of heat and bright color.

He stayed with her but lightened his touch. Soft, sweet licks until even that was too much. Then he kissed her belly.

"Beautiful," he murmured, and rose from the bed.

She rolled onto her side and watched as he took a box of condoms from his duffel bag and set it onto the night table. She closed her eyes against a pang of sadness. He was right to be careful, but it still hurt.

Fada rarely had children even with their mates. Most fada didn't bother with birth control, since STDs were almost unheard of and they knew that any child would be welcomed by the clan.

Unless it was a child she'd made with Adric.

Together, they pushed down the covers. He pulled her into his arms and kissed the top of her head. "You're so beautiful when you come."

She tilted her head, summoned a teasing grin. If they had just this one night, she wouldn't ruin it by crying for something she'd never have. "You're so beautiful when you're making me come."

"Is that so?" He crawled on top of her with a wolfish smile. "I'll be even prettier when I'm inside you, fucking you." He dragged his cock over her stomach.

A hot ribbon of desire curled through her. Goddess, she ached to have him inside her, filling her. "Prove it."

His mouth came to her ear. She could smell herself on him, a warm, oceany scent.

"I will," he whispered as if it were a secret for her alone.

He left the bed to roll on the protection and then came down over her. Taking her hands, he pressed them to the bed on either side of her head. Her thighs instinctively bent up to cradle him.

His tip nudged her sex and she tensed.

He stilled. "I'm the first."

It wasn't a question, but she dipped her chin.

His eyes flashed, the blue blotting out the bronze. "I thought so." He pushed a little deeper. "I promise I'll be...easy."

She moistened her lips, nodded again. "I know. I want this."

"Oh, angel." His voice was tender.

His mouth touched hers. He kissed her, slowly, voluptuously, like she was a feast he'd waited for months to savor. She felt surrounded by him, his body...his heated, earthy scent...the strong hands pinning her to the bed. Against her breastbone, his quartz was warm, almost alive.

Something in her opened, like a flower unfurling, petal by petal. He gave another nudge, and his thick head slipped inside her.

It burned, but in a good way. Like he was marking her as his.

Excitement built in her. She needed this. She needed *him*.

"Rosana," he said on a sigh and pressed deeper.

He was thick, hot, wonderful. Stretching her until she had the brief, panicky fear that she couldn't stretch any more...and then he was inside her.

Her eyes widened. He held still, but she felt his cock pulsing. Or was that her? The small pain of his entrance receded, replaced by a sense of rightness.

This was her man. The one she'd always known would be her first.

Her and Adric, joined together. His flesh deep inside hers. Their two breaths mingling, their hearts beating in time.

"You okay?" His mouth whispered over hers.

"Oh, yeah." She interlaced her fingers with his, uncaring that it might set off her Sight. Just needing to touch him.

When nothing happened, elation raced through her. She tightened her fingers on his and gave an experimental lift of her hips.

"God's cat." His groan was low and raw, ripped from his chest. "You're so hot...so fucking tight. You're going to kill me."

She narrowed her eyes. "Not until you finish."

He gave a bark of laughter, and she raised up to give him an openmouthed kiss. Their mouths were still joined when he began to move, easy, unhurried strokes.

She tried to pull her hands from his—she wanted to wrap her arms around him—but he tightened his grip and rose higher. Keeping her where she was, open beneath him, unable to do anything but accept his thrusts. Angling his body so that his hard flesh massaged her clit with every stroke.

Heat radiated from him. He lowered his head and sucked each of her nipples in turn. Pleasure streaked through her, tightening her womb.

She was melting. She was burning up.

She dug her heels into the mattress and clenched her inner muscles around him. "Adric..."

His lips moved to her ear. He tongued the outer edge, slipped inside. It was warm and wet, and so sensual.

"Take it." His thrusts grew harder, more powerful. Dominating her in a way her animal craved.

She dragged in a breath. "*Ohgod, ohgod, ohgod...*"

"Come for me, love." A low command in her ear.

It was too much. "No," she rasped.

"Yes. Take it. Take *me*." He pushed into her. "All of me, angel."

Deep, so deep.

Then again, and again until she broke into a thousand shimmering fragments.

He groaned her name and propelled himself in and out of her, over and over, and then stilled. A growl that was more cat than man vibrated in his chest.

She tightened her thighs around his lean hips as he pulsed deep inside of her. He dropped his head forward, his cheek against hers.

Only then did he release her hands.

ADRIC HUNG OVER ROSANA, breath jerking in and out of his lungs.

He felt emptied out—and yet somehow filled as well. Complete in a way he was afraid to examine closely.

His quartz rested between her pretty breasts. Now that he could think again, he realized it had heated as they'd approached their climax. He frowned down at it —and blinked.

The gray-and-orange crystals were lit deep within with a new color, a brilliant sea-green that spiraled through the center in a graceful twist. A green the same color as Rosana's dolphin's eyes.

What the hell? His brows drew together.

"Wow," she said. "Just...wow."

He shrugged mentally and decided to worry about his quartz later. He lifted up and she gave him a broad smile that warmed him clear to his toes.

He kissed her, wanting that smile against his lips. She was warm, her skin moist with exertion. She smelled like woman and sex—and him. He rubbed his cheek against hers, mingling their two scents even more. For this night, at least, she was his.

"Mm." She slid a languid hand down his neck, petting him in a way both man and cat craved. Fingering the gold stud in his earlobe. Tracing a finger over his jaw.

He licked her just beneath her ear. She tasted like the sea.

Inside her, his dick lengthened. He'd come hard. No, he'd fucking exploded— and still it hadn't been enough.

He had the sudden, sinking conviction that with Rosana, it would never be enough.

He wanted to thrust into her mindlessly. Imprint his body on hers so that she'd feel him all week. But she had to be tender, even though she'd been an eager, if innocent, partner.

Hell, he'd been too rough—at the end, his mind had blanked with pleasure and he'd forgotten he was fucking a virgin. But he was fully aware now, so he gritted his teeth and withdrew from her.

Her soft hiss told him she *was* hurting, at least a little. Guilt tightened his belly. "You okay?"

"Mm-hmm." She curled on her side, cheeks flushed, eyes half-closed, the picture of a well-pleasured woman.

His guilt eased. He kissed her cheek. "Be right back."

He made a trip to the bathroom to dispose of the rubber, returning with a warm, wet washcloth. "Let me." He bent up her top leg and, pressing the cloth to her sex, gently cleaned her.

She winced at even a soft touch, and he grimaced in sympathy. "Sorry, love. I was too rough. I—"

"Was amazing." She grinned up at him. "It's fine. I'm just a little sore."

A wave of tenderness rolled through him. Unexpected and unwelcome— because he couldn't let this be anything more than it was.

Returning to the bathroom, he rinsed the cloth and tossed it over the towel rack, and then slid back into the bed. He pulled the sheet up over them both and reached for her, but she was already there, tucking herself into his side, one hand on his heart, as if they'd done this a hundred times.

Her hair spilled onto his chest in silky dark tendrils. He pressed a kiss to her temple.

The tenderness mixed with something basic. Primal.

Mine.

He wanted to keep her. Lure her back to his lonely den. He might even be able to convince her it was her idea. Just for the next few days, until he left...

He fingered his quartz, considering. He had a rare, little known Gift—he could hypnotize people with his quartz, compel them to obey him. He could induce Rosana to come back to Baltimore with him.

It wouldn't be that hard to get her to do something she wanted anyway. Just a nudge would probably work.

But even the cat, primitive beast though it was, knew that was wrong.

And the man admitted that having Rosana move into his den—even for a few days—would be hollow if she didn't do it with her full knowledge and consent. If she ever came to him, he wanted her whole heart and soul.

His lip curled. Gods, he was pathetic. Next he'd be lighting candles and scattering rose petals on the sheets.

He tightened his arm around her. "Last night—why did you come to me?"

She traced a finger over his heart. "It was time."

What the hell—? He pulled back so he could see her face. "Are you saying you Saw something? Something about the two of us?"

"Not a vision, no."

"Then what?"

She expelled a breath. "Look, I wanted you and you wanted me. Isn't that enough?"

She was evading a straight answer, but he let it slide. "If your brother finds out, he'll skin me alive."

Once, that would've made this little getaway all the more fun, but not these days. Maybe at the beginning he'd gone after Rosana partly to tweak the other alpha, but he'd long since admitted to himself that he'd want her no matter who she was.

"Don't worry. No one knows I'm here."

He played with the pretty silver charm on her wrist. "What if he asks you straight out?"

She moved a shoulder. "I love Dion. He pretty much raised me and Tiago after my mom and dad disappeared."

Adric nodded. There wasn't much he didn't know about the do Rio family, including that Rosana's parents had been captured by King Sindre when she was just six, leaving Dion to raise both her and Tiago. There were two middle brothers, but they'd left Rock Run rather than challenge their oldest brother for alpha.

"And he's my alpha," she continued, "but that makes him my boss, not my master. If he asks straight out, I won't lie, but otherwise, this is between you and me. It's none of his business."

"We're rival alphas, love. What I do will always be his business, and vice versa."

"So this is it?" She pulled away and sat up. "One night and nothing else?"

He stared up at her. "That was the agreement."

But fuck, he wished it were different.

Hurt flickered across her face.

"Hey." He touched her hand. "You know it can't be more than that."

Rosana's mouth twisted.

He swallowed against the desire to apologize, to somehow take the words back. He owed her honesty, at least.

"Right." She averted her face. "I understand."

"Rosana..."

She cut him off with a sharp shake of her head, then rose up on her knees.

His hand fisted. She was going to ask him to take her home, and he'd have to be a fucking gentleman about it. But instead, she straddled him, brought his hands to her high, full breasts. She looked down at him, cobalt eyes unreadable.

He held his breath, but he couldn't stop his thumbs from caressing her pretty nipples. They beaded under his touch, and his dick twitched in response.

The corner of her mouth edged up. She traced two fingers down his forearm, and every nerve in his body felt the shock wave.

"Then we'd better not waste any time."

CHAPTER 6

Outside, the sun was setting. A hazy winter light slanted through the blinds, gilding Adric's skin a warm gold.

Rosana ran her hands down his rock-hard torso. Learning the shape of his muscles, absorbing the heat of his skin.

She hadn't lied to him. It wasn't worth it—it would make her sick, and besides, he'd scent the lie.

But she hadn't told him the whole truth, either. Because yeah, it was time.

Not time for them—she'd never Seen whether they'd eventually end up mates. That would be a glimpse into her own future as well as his, and she was as blind as anyone when it came to Seeing her own future. Still, you didn't have to be a Seer to guess that Adric was preparing to move against Langdon, and she didn't have another way of keeping him close.

She traced her fingers up and down his forearm. The hair covering it was soft, barely visible, the skin beneath warm. *Deus*, it felt good to touch someone, be touched back.

"I need you." She swallowed. "So bad."

But you need me, too. That's what I have to show you.

She hadn't Seen that, but her gut told her she was right, and Colm, the Irish Seer who was training her, had told her to trust her hunches. According to her Sight, Adric intended to assassinate Langdon, but instead, he'd be captured and executed.

She had to do *something*.

"Good." His smile was relieved—and a little devilish. "I like you all hot and needy." He cupped her breasts, squeezing and caressing.

Her breath hitched. She placed her hands over his and set her worries aside for the time being. These sensations were too new, too wonderful to ignore.

"More." She rubbed her breasts sensuously against his big palms. His hands were hard, calloused, with a couple of healing cuts. What did the Baltimore alpha do that gave him a laborer's hands?

"Like this?" He rolled her nipples between his thumbs. An electric pleasure stabbed to her womb.

"Yes..." She gripped his wrists. His eyes were dark with desire, his handsome face intent. Her core clenched. A hot, needful yearning slid through her veins. She wanted him so much it hurt.

Why you?

They'd met for the first time at Dion and Cleia's mate ball. To a teenager who'd grown up in Rock Run's rough-hewn, dimly lit caverns, the ball had been something out of a storybook. Outdoors on a bright summer day in two massive white tents overflowing with flowers, one tent for dancing, the other for dining. All seven of the sun fae clans had been present, their long, inhumanly perfect bodies clad in the finest fae couture, their hair all the fiery shades of sunshine: gold, silver, copper. One-of-a-kind jewels glittered in their ears and around their wrists and throats.

Rosana had been dancing with a tall blond sun fae when her nape had prickled. She'd glanced around, and there was Adric, lean and unsmiling and gorgeous in a colorful African-style tunic. Standing at the edge of the dance floor with his sister and watching her with a feline intensity.

Arousal had shivered over her skin, the first ever in her life. At sixteen, she was barely adolescent; a fada's life was measured in centuries. Too young to be thinking of love or finding a mate.

He'd sauntered across the polished wood floor, a cat on the prowl, and asked her to dance. She almost said no. His scent and quartz marked him as an earth fada, and she suspected he was just trying to piss off the Rock Run males.

Then he'd introduced himself, and she'd realized he was the new Baltimore alpha. The man who'd already managed to make an enemy of both Dion and Tiago.

"Well?" His expression was challenging.

A spark flashed between them—and she found herself saying yes.

He'd been polite, respectful, careful not to pull her too close, his hands light on her shoulder and waist. But for those few minutes, her nerves had tingled with excitement, her heart drumming crazily in her chest.

The moment the music stopped, two Rock Run men stepped in and suggested in hard voices that Adric find someone else to dance with. He'd left soon after.

Since then, she'd only seen him once a year or so. She'd told herself she wasn't interested, especially when she'd heard a group of warriors laughing a little enviously about what a horny dog the Baltimore alpha was. The man had a different woman every other week.

But the heat was always there, simmering between them.

Until Adric had changed the game. Stealing kisses whenever he had the chance. Making her want him. Daring her to come to him, when they both knew Dion would take it as a personal betrayal. And Adric didn't help. He seemed to take a special glee in seeing how far he could push Dion.

Well, she'd taken Adric's dare, and if it pissed off her brother, she'd just have to accept it. This wasn't some reckless, juvenile rebellion.

Adric was her mate, even if she'd resisted admitting it. How could he ever claim her? Their two clans barely tolerated each other. Mate with him, and the balance might tip, setting off a war or a series of challenges.

Hot tears stung her eyes. She inhaled, blinked them away.

Adric rubbed a thumb under her eye, confused and concerned. "You're crying?"

Her heart turned over. It was the uncertainty that got her. She guessed he didn't let many people see him looking anything but controlled, in charge.

She lifted a shoulder, let it drop. "It's just...so much." Which was the truth.

"Too much?" He curled up to cup her face, his gaze searching hers. "Just say the word and I'll stop. You want to go home?"

"No!" She clutched his shoulders. "I want this. So much."

He brushed his lips over hers, slow and sweet. "You sure?"

She gave a vigorous nod.

"Okay, then." His mouth nudged hers open, deepening the kiss. His tongue touched inside, teasing her, taking her deeper step by step until she was making low sounds of arousal in her throat.

He ended the kiss and lay back down, looking up at her with heated eyes while his hands played over her body, toying with her nipples, shaping her waist, her hips. Between their bodies, his cock pressed against her sex without entering her. She reached down and adjusted it so she could slide back and forth on its slick length.

His breath hissed in.

She felt an unfamiliar, very feminine sense of power. At least she wasn't alone in this neediness.

Setting her fingertips on his abdomen, she undulated her hips, pleasuring them both. He caught her hair in his hand, tugged her head back.

Craving contracted her womb, hot and liquid. "Adric."

"Ric." He rose up to kiss the side of her neck. "My friends call me Ric."

"Ric," she obediently repeated.

A sexy growl against her throat. "Lift up a little."

When she obeyed, he wet his thumb in her juices and then swirled it around her clit. The work-roughened pad made her suck in a breath. It aroused, and yet hurt.

And then the two mixed together, and she moaned.

His smile was feral, sharp-toothed. "That's it. Come for me, love."

He used the hand in her hair to control her, keeping her body stretched taut, her pussy rubbing against the edge of his erection, that erotically rough thumb on her clit. She had her own hands on her breasts now, both soothing her own ache and seducing him with an age-old instinct.

He muttered something dark and gave her hair a firm tug. Sensation rocketed down her spine.

"Come for me." A soft command.

She inhaled raggedly. He rolled her clit between his thumb and finger and the pleasure exploded through her. She moaned and let it take her, riding the waves as they crashed through her, over her, lifting her up and stealing her breath until she was wrung out and gasping.

She let out a slow exhale and hung over him, limp and satiated.

"Beautiful." He curled his hand around her nape, drew her close for a hard kiss.

Between their bodies, his erection pulsed. She slid a hand down to caress him.

His eyes sparked hotly into hers, but he set a hand on her wrist. "You're not too sore?"

Her heart constricted. He was being so considerate, even though he was hard as steel, his erection pulsating beneath her fingers.

"A little," she admitted, her gaze on his cock. It was smooth and a little sticky from her juices. She ran a thumb over the wide, flushed head, and he groaned.

But he continued, "If it's too much, we don't—"

She curved her fingers around him and squeezed, halting him in mid-sentence. "I'm fine," she said, and lifted off him long enough to grab one of the little blue packets. She ripped it open with her teeth and worked the condom down over him.

When she was done, he lifted her by the hips so she was poised over him, and then paused. "You do it. Take me inside you."

Setting her hands on his chest, she eased herself down. He slipped inside and she stilled. "It feels...different." She slid down the rest of the way, and then sucked in a breath as he touched deep inside, where she still throbbed. "Deeper."

"Good," he said hoarsely as he grasped her hips and started to move. "It feels... good. So fucking good."

"*Sim*..." She slipped into Portuguese without realizing it. Telling him how beautiful he was, how good he made her feel.

She skated her palms over his chest. His skin was heated, a little sweaty. She fingered his nipples, and his breath hitched.

She leaned down to rub her breasts over his chest. The wiry hair abraded the sensitive tips. Electricity jolted through her.

She closed her eyes, drinking it in.

This. She hungered for this.

Not just the pleasure, but the closeness. She'd been so starved for touch.

Wonder filled her, a wonder touched with sorrow. How could she have found this beautiful, aching closeness only to let it go? Let *him* go?

She slid her arms beneath his hard shoulders, set her face against his.

Mine, she thought fiercely.

She *would* save him. And then somehow, she'd force both their clans to accept them as mates.

At that moment, it seemed not just possible, but inevitable.

He moved her so her breasts were over his face and latched his mouth onto her nipple. A single hard suck and she was lost, sobbing out his name.

"Take it." He thrust inside her, firm and deep. Moved his mouth to her other nipple to suck that, too.

Mine, she thought with each hard stroke. *Mine, mine, mine.*

Her blood heated, flushing her face, pounding in her ears. She dug her nails into his shoulders and with a helpless sigh, shot over the edge.

He released her nipple to capture her mouth. Devouring her while he thrust into her, over and over, until he pushed up hard in her and stilled. Tearing his mouth from hers, he buried his face in her hair.

"Rosana," he growled against her ear, and came.

CHAPTER 7

Sometime after midnight, Adric jerked awake. He glanced around, shaking off a very pleasant dream. Rosana was sprawled on top of him, her breasts soft against his chest, her head tucked into the curve of his neck.

His mouth curved. So that part of the dream had been true.

After they'd made love the second time, they'd napped and then taken a hot shower together. Just a shower—he'd wanted to give her time to heal. But he'd never had such an erotic shower. They'd washed each other from head to toe, intermixed with slow, sensuous kisses, until the hot water ran out.

They'd toweled each other dry—and then she'd gone to her knees on the bathroom rug before him. Her mouth was warm and wet, and while a part of him registered her lack of experience, the rest of him muttered *who the fuck cares* and enjoyed.

Then it was his turn. He led her back to the bed and feasted on her, reveling in her sexy little sounds of pleasure and how she wriggled and bucked beneath his tongue and hands.

By then it was dinnertime. She put on her snug red jacket and those fuck-me boots, and he took her to a restaurant overlooking the canal. They had local beers and grilled rockfish as the stars appeared, one by one, over the canal's night-dark waters.

When they returned to the B&B, he had her strip and then helped her step back into the boots while she watched with those wide, ocean-blue eyes. They'd explored all the ways a man and woman could enjoy each other without full pene-tration before falling asleep, bodies entwined.

Now she snuggled closer, murmuring his name. He tightened his arms around her, nape tingling uneasily.

What had awoken him?

The outside door opened. Footsteps started up the stairs to the main floor. Three people, from the sound of it.

He lifted his head, straining to hear something. Anything. But they were dead silent. Yeah, it was late, but surely a group of three would speak at least a few words among themselves?

They reached the main floor and rapped on the door to Mark's private apartment.

"What the hell?" the innkeeper demanded in rough, just-woke-up tones.

"Where are they? The fada." A man's voice.

Adric tensed. Easing out from beneath Rosana, he crept to the door, setting his ear against the wood.

"I don't know what you're talking about," Mark returned.

"Yes," the man said in a cold voice, "you do."

"Get your hands off me," Mark snarled. "You've got five seconds to get out of here or I'm calling the cop—"

The thud of flesh against flesh was followed by an "oof."

"Talk," the man said.

The only sound was the harsh scrape of Mark's breathing.

Adric whirled into motion. "Rosana," he hissed.

She was already sitting up. Scrambling out of bed, she whispered, "What's the matter?"

He tossed her some clothes. "We're leaving," he replied in an equally soft voice. "Someone's asking about us."

She froze. "My brothers?"

He shook his head. The Rock Run men might be hard-assed S.O.B.s, but they wouldn't beat a man just for renting the two of them a room. No, they'd kick Adric's ass instead.

"I don't think so. Now, *move*."

She hurriedly pulled on her jeans and shirt while he dragged on his own clothes. He shoved an iron dagger into his back pocket. Iron was the only sure way to kill a fae.

"No shoes," he told her. "We may have to run for it."

"Got it." She crammed her things into the canvas bag, leaving her barefoot in the Henley and jeans. He silently blessed the tight operation run by Dion. She'd clearly been trained how to respond in an emergency.

"This way." Rosana jerked her head at the sliding doors. "Down the back stairs."

He gave her a silent thumbs-up.

In the hall outside their room, footsteps could be heard. Another person ran lightly up to the third floor.

Apparently, Mark hadn't given up their location. Adric would owe him for that. He just hoped the human would be alive to collect.

Rosana slung her bag over a shoulder and eased open the sliding door. He grabbed his duffel bag and followed, quietly closing the door behind him. Hopefully, that would buy them a little time before their pursuers realized they were no longer in the B&B.

Rosana ignored the stairs to sling a long leg over the wood railing. She worked her way hand-over-hand down the outside of the stairs before dropping the last few feet to the grass. The entire descent took five seconds, tops.

Despite the danger, his mouth edged up as he swung over the railing and dropped to the grass beside her. Damn, he liked how the woman's mind worked.

They glided around the enclosed outdoor shower and halted against the far wall where they couldn't be seen from the B&B.

Rosana set her mouth to his ear. "They'll be watching the parking lot."

He nodded. Why the fuck hadn't he parked the rental car somewhere else? But he'd believed they were safe. No one knew his exact location, not even Marjani.

Had he'd been followed from Baltimore?

He peered around the corner. The lights in their room came on, visible through the cracks in the wood slats. His nostrils flared, but he couldn't pick up a scent from that far away.

If only he knew who, exactly, was after them—fada or fae? Because a fada could track the two of them even if they ran.

His neck crawled. The backyard was too small, nothing but a narrow strip of grass between the B&B and the tall fence surrounding it. They had to get out of here before the bastards came looking for them.

He jerked his chin in the direction of the beach. "We'll go over the fence," he whispered in Rosana's ear, "and stick to the backyards. Make our way to the bay. You can go into the water, and I'll shift to my cougar and run along the beach. They won't be able to track us in the water."

Her mouth formed a shocked O. "You think they're fada? Not humans robbing the place?"

He shook his head grimly. "They asked Mark where the fada were."

And even if they hadn't, his itching nape told him he and Rosana were in danger. He trusted that itch. During the Darktime, it had saved his life more than once.

"Once you're in the water, head for Henlopen," he told her. "I'll meet you at the park."

The Cape Henlopen State Park was a good mile away, but in his cougar form, he could sprint as fast as fifty miles per hour. It would take Rosana a little longer to swim there, but unless one of their pursuers was a water fada, she'd be safer in the ocean than with him.

Not even a wolf could track her in the water.

She worried her lower lip with her teeth. "You want us to split up?" she whispered back.

"Just for a few minutes—maybe half an hour. I'll meet you at the Point. I'll be on the beach that faces the Breakwater Lighthouse. You know it?"

"Yeah, but—"

Footsteps on the balcony above made her snap shut her mouth. As one, they shrank deeper into the shadows.

Adric risked a look. The man was scanning the wetlands behind the B&B. Tall and dark-skinned, and dressed in a black leather jacket and pants, he would've blended into the shadows if not for his cropped silver hair. His pointed ears stood out in stark relief against his pale hair.

A fae, then. But Adric had been expecting a night fae, and the only fae with such light hair were ice fae.

His brow furrowed. What the fuck was an ice fae doing in Lewes, Delaware?

The fae turned his gaze on the backyard. Adric dropped his eyes so the fae wouldn't see them glowing in the dark.

"Ice fae," he mouthed at Rosana.

She gulped. Then she raised her left arm, the one with the silver bracelet. "Protection charm," she whispered back.

He nodded, relieved.

He fingered his quartz. A few months ago, he'd stumbled upon a new use for his Gift of hypnotism. He could somehow induce people to look right past him. It was similar to a cloaking spell, something the fae charged an arm and a leg for—if they'd even sell it to a fada.

But he'd never tried to cloak a second person as well. He wasn't even sure if he could. Plus, it drained energy at a rapid rate, energy he might need to shift.

Still, if it came down to it, he'd try. He was *not* letting that fae bastard get his hands on Rosana. At least she had that protection charm.

"See anything, Jon?" A woman's cool, aristocratic voice.

"No. But that doesn't mean they're not out here."

Adric risked another look as the woman joined Jon on the balcony. She was tall and curvy with long hair the color of moonlight, her scent a mix of silver and something acrid.

Every hair on his nape rose. Only a night fae had that distinctive scent of metal and decay. His heart clenched with pure, unadulterated hate.

But she wasn't a pureblood. No, that silver-blond hair spoke of an ice-fae ancestor, and the only ice fae/night fae mix Adric knew was Lady Blaer.

The woman who'd put Marjani in a cage.

His upper lip peeled back in a silent snarl. He wanted badly to sneak another look, but night fae could see in the dark as well as cats.

Gods, he wished he were alone so he could shift to his cougar, rip both fae into tiny pieces. He'd lost too many good friends to the night fae, been hunted himself too many nights. And Blaer had not only attacked Marjani, she'd forced his friend Luc to accept her *geas*.

Rosana bumped her shoulder against his. "Calm down," she mouthed.

He gave a tight nod.

She was right. Night fae were energy vampires, with a creepy sixth sense that allowed them to home in on negative emotions—fear, anger, agitation. The only way to hide from them was to stay calm, slowing your heart and breath so they couldn't track you.

Breathe in, breath out.

Retracting his claws, he pulled out the dagger and held it against his side. He forced himself to relax, blanked his mind.

In, out.

Beside him, Rosana slowed her breath to almost nothing.

The two fae continued scanning the backyard. Power brushed over Adric's skin, cold and black. A night fae questing for prey.

He stilled, sinking deep into his animal.

Next to him, Rosana drew a barely perceptible breath and gripped his left wrist. He turned his palm over, threaded his fingers through hers and gave her an encouraging squeeze. She lowered an eyelid in a slow wink.

He managed a small smile back, although he'd never felt less amused.

Inside the B&B, doors slammed. From the third floor came the sound of frightened human voices. The bastards had rousted the couple upstairs.

Adric's fingers tightened on the dagger's handle, but he remained where he was. The fae wouldn't do anything but scare the crap out of the human couple.

The humans hadn't even seen him and Rosana, so they'd be no help to the searchers.

Rosana's palm was damp with nerves. He squeezed her hand again.

Hold on, angel.

A minute ticked by. The tension wound tighter.

He took another deliberate breath.

Calm, cool, blank. A sheet of paper. A snow-covered field.

Serenity flowed from Rosana. Maybe it was her, and maybe it was the charm, but it helped.

At last the woman murmured in disgust. The dark tendrils withdrew.

"They could be miles away by now. All I know is they're not in this bloody inn."

The man murmured assent, and the two of them returned inside without bothering to close the sliding door.

Adric waited until their voices receded before jerking his chin at the fence separating the next yard from the B&B.

Rosana nodded, and together, they scaled the fence and sprinted behind the neighboring house. They continued that way down the street, sticking to back-yards as they aimed for the water.

When they were almost to the beach, Adric pulled Rosana into the shadow of an empty cedar-shingled house.

"*Mãe de Deus.*" Her breath whooshed out. "What was that about?"

He shrugged, although he had his suspicions. "You were perfect." He gave her a hard kiss. "Cool as could be."

She shrugged, but he could tell she was pleased. "My training as a Seer includes meditation techniques."

"Well, it worked, but now we need to get the fuck out of here." He indicated the deck behind her. "We can stash the bags under there and come back for them later."

His quartz was engineered to be a smartphone. While Rosana stowed their bags beneath the deck, he notified the Lewes police about the break-in at the B&B.

"A man's hurt. Send an ambulance ASAP."

"Your name, sir?"

"That's not important," he said, and ended the connection.

He and Rosana peeled off their clothes and tucked them under the deck, and then he dragged her long, lush body up against his. Her skin was icy, and even though he knew river fada had naturally cool metabolisms, he hated that she'd been pulled out of a warm bed because of him.

"The Breakwater Light," he reminded her. "Stay in the water until I signal you. Three flashes with my quartz."

She wound an arm around his neck. "'Kay."

He brushed a strand of her hair back from her temple and then frowned. Rosana was a river dolphin, not an ocean-going dolphin like a bottlenose. "The salt water isn't a problem?"

She shook her head. "The bay is actually an estuary—a mix of fresh and salt water. And I can take salt water for short periods of time. My mom's a bottlenose."

"Okay, then." He kissed her nose. "Watch for a blue light—I'll flash it three times in a row, then pause and repeat it."

"Got it—three blue flashes." She touched his cheek. "Be careful, okay?"

He blinked, bemused. When was the last time anyone besides Marjani had told him to be careful? He was the strong one, the alpha. Even as a teenager, he'd been the one his friends looked to for direction.

"Yeah. Sure."

He watched as she glided across the deserted street to the beach, sticking to the shadows, silent as a ghost. She sprinted across the sand and dove into the shallow water. Shining bits of green and blue and purple glimmered beneath the surface, so beautiful he caught his breath. A slender torpedo-shaped body sketched an arc against the night sky and disappeared beneath the waves.

Adric waited another minute to make sure she got away safely. Then he shifted to his cougar—and headed back to the B&B.

CHAPTER 8

"What's the use of being a Seer," Rosana muttered as she jogged into the icy bay, "if you can't See your own freaking future?"

She hadn't had a hint the fae were coming. They could've been in the room before she'd known they were there. Why couldn't she have a useful Gift, like being a healer?

"You don't choose your Gift. It chooses you. Lucky us." She could almost see Colm's mouth twisting in a self-mocking smile. *"And you know Seers almost never See what lies ahead for themselves."*

"Yeah, yeah," she snarled. "Can't forget Rule 1." She dove into a wave.

Colm had drilled several truths about being a Seer into her. Colm's Rules, she called them.

Rule 1: A Seer almost never Sees his or her own future.

Rule 2: The Sight is unpredictable. You can train it, but it's like trying to ride a tiger. You never know when it will turn on you.

Rule 3: Belief is as important as skill. To free your Sight, you must believe in its essential truth.

Freaking rules. As far as she could tell, being a Seer was worthless. People were wary of you, and they didn't want to listen to you even when you *knew* you were right.

You couldn't even use your Gift to save yourself. If Ula had Seen that King Sindre was laying a trap for her and Nisio, they wouldn't have left on that trip across the ocean and Rosana wouldn't have grown up without her parents.

She gave a hard kick and let the change take her. Magic shimmered over her skin. For a timeless few moments, she was neither human nor dolphin, but colorful fragments of light and energy. Then her legs fused, became a tail. Her face elongated into a river dolphin's beak, and her arms became flippers.

She sucked air through her blowhole and with a powerful thrust of her tail, skimmed through the midnight sea. She was Rosana, and yet not Rosana.

Stronger, more supple. Wild. Free.

She remained beneath the surface for several minutes, not resurfacing until she was a few hundred yards out, the shoreline curving behind her in a giant C. Ahead, the flash of the Harbor of Refuge Light marked Cape Henlopen and the Delaware Bay's western boundary. The Breakwater Lighthouse was a little before it, but unlike its sister lighthouse, it was dark, having been decommissioned years ago.

She set out for the Point on a path parallel to the shore.

That had been a night fae on the balcony. Or maybe the woman was a mixed-blood, because Rosana had never heard of a pureblood night fae with blond hair.

Fear tripped up her spine.

Somehow, that woman was connected to her vision. Nothing else made sense. But how?

She knew Prince Langdon was out for blood. His only living son, Tyrus, had gone missing last June after attacking Adric's clan. The Baltimore fada had clammed up about what really happened, but everyone knew Tyrus was dead, with Adric the chief suspect.

But without proof, Langdon had done nothing. Yet.

Still, Adric wasn't the type to wait around for the prince to attack. If he thought Langdon was a threat, he'd strike first.

But when? And more importantly, how could she stop it?

If only she knew more.

She gave a frustrated swish of her tail. Helpless, and hating it.

If what she'd Seen was true—and she'd never had such a clear, detailed vision before—Adric was going after Langdon soon.

And he'd die.

THE SWIM to the Point took about fifteen minutes. Rosana navigated with sweeps of her sonar, emitting sound and interpreting the echoes: the curved shape of the shore line; the fishing pier that jutted into the water; a school of Atlantic croakers; a shipwreck dating to the 1700s.

A stack of huge granite slabs loomed before her, the half-mile-long breakwater that gave the lighthouse its name. She surfaced on the inner side of the breakwater a safe distance from the rugged slabs. The sky above was clear, the stars white pinpricks in its dark cloth.

She scanned the beach. No sign of Adric.

She slapped her tail against the water a couple of times. The breakwater blocked the Atlantic to form a calm, quiet harbor. If he was nearby, he'd hear her.

She waited a minute and then smacked the water with her tail again.

Still no Adric.

Her stomach clenched.

Stop worrying. The man's an alpha. A big cat with teeth and claws.

A pod of three wild female bottlenoses appeared, drawn by the commotion. They were larger than Rosana's six-foot length, but friendly. They greeted her with a mixture of squawks, whistles and clicks.

Rosana replied in their language, and they circled her.

Who, who who? whistled the eldest female, a motherly sort with small, wise eyes.

Visitor, Rosana replied. *I mean you no harm.*

Why, why why? the motherly bottlenose asked.

Meeting a friend. But he's not here. Worried.

Sorry… We wait.

Their bodies brushed hers, offering comfort.

For the next quarter hour, the four of them swam back and forth in front of the lighthouse until Rosana had to face facts. Either Adric had been captured, or he'd returned to the B&B to sniff around some more. It was what her brothers would've done.

The smart thing, the *safe* thing, would be to head farther out to sea. No one but another water fada could track her in the ocean, and with the head start she'd had, even a shark would have trouble scenting her.

But fuck being safe. If Adric had been captured, it was three against one, and at least two of the others were fae.

Not just any fae. A night fae.

Damn, damn, damn. She didn't want to go back. She wanted to get as far away as possible from that scary bitch and her henchmen.

But there really wasn't a choice. She wished the wild dolphins a polite farewell and whipped around to head back to Lewes.

CHAPTER 9

*A*dric raced through the backyards, a shadow in the night.

He had a bad feeling about the second man with Lady Blaer, the one he hadn't seen. He couldn't leave without knowing for sure.

Sirens split the night. He gritted his teeth, the high wail excruciating to his shifter ears. At least it meant help was on its way to Mark.

The wood fence ran the length of the B&B's property. He peered through them into the parking lot. The two fae were just getting into the back of a glossy black limo. But it was their rangy, hard-faced driver who made Adric's lungs cinch tight.

His hunch had been correct. The second man was Luc, one of his lieutenants. No, make that former lieutenant.

Anger and guilt clogged his chest.

Late last summer, Luc had accepted a *geas* from Lady Blaer. For the next decade, the wolf fada was Blaer's man, not his. So Adric had been forced to expel him from the clan.

It didn't matter that Luc was an old friend, one of the small, close-knit group who'd helped Adric and Marjani take down Leron Savonett, their bastard of an uncle. It didn't matter that Luc had been imprisoned and tortured simply for being Adric's friend.

Adric had had no choice. As alpha, he was connected through his quartz to every man, woman and child in the clan. He couldn't allow a man under the control of a fae to remain part of that network.

"Get us out of here," the blond female ordered Luc.

Adric's lips peeled back in a silent snarl. He was sure now that she was Lady Blaer.

His muscles gathered, his whole body shaking with the need to attack.

Kill.

The woman had put his sister in a fucking iron cage. She'd forced Luc to accept her *geas*. And perhaps worst of all, Blaer had learned the secret of the earth fada's quartz. With the right words, a fae could control an earth fada through their quartz—and Blaer knew the incantation.

For so many reasons, Blaer needed to die. But attack now, and Luc would be forced to defend her. And while the two of them fought, Blaer would simply teleport herself and the ice fae male out of there.

"Where to?" Luc asked Blaer.

"Virginia—the New Moon Court."

Luc nodded and shut the limo door. His head swung to where Adric crouched, his eyes the amber of his wolf.

Adric froze, a sick feeling coating his stomach—because he wasn't one-hundred-percent sure that Luc wouldn't betray him.

The former lieutenant's face blanked. He opened the front door and slid behind the limo's steering wheel.

Adric released a breath.

The car purred to life and headed down the street. At the corner, Luc pulled over to allow two police cars and an ambulance pass by.

Adric waited until the limo was out of sight before racing back to the house where he and Rosana had left their things. There, he changed back to man and pulled on his pants and T-shirt, leaving the rest in the duffel bag for now.

Luc's face had been hard as stone, closed up tight. The man had always been grim, but now he looked like he'd been scrubbed clean of emotion.

Gods, it sliced at Adric, to leave a friend with the fae, especially Luc. During the Darktime, Adric had risked his own life to rescue Luc from Leron. If it would do any good, he'd do the same thing in a heartbeat.

But Luc had accepted Lady Blaer's *geas* of his own free will to save Marjani in Iceland. Now Luc was bound to her for the next decade, and Adric couldn't do a damn thing about it. Only Luc could break the *geas*, and his former lieutenant would never do that. The man would die before breaking his word.

Adric tightened his jaw. If only he hadn't sent Luc to Iceland after Marjani.

The clan needed you in Baltimore. And Luc insisted on going. You probably couldn't have stopped him if you tried.

But Adric was alpha. The final decision had been his—and because of it, he'd lost Luc to that fae bitch.

That's when it hit him. Luc was Blaer's man. He must have led the fae to Lewes—and Adric.

His lungs contracted. He pressed the heel of his hand to his chest, telling himself that it wasn't Luc's fault. He was under Blaer's control.

But it felt like Luc had shoved a knife into his heart.

He grimly set his hurt aside. Rosana was waiting for him. Rolling up his jeans, he jogged barefoot into the bay until it reached his calves before setting out for the Breakwater Light. If Luc did return, the water would erase Adric's tracks.

He hadn't gone far when he saw the river dolphin slipping through the waves, a sleek smudge against the lighter gray of the night sky. He should've known she'd come back for him.

He dropped the bags on the sand and signaled her with his quartz. She immediately headed in, shifting a few yards offshore. She rose from the bay, water streaming down her naked body, and everything in him stopped.

Breath, heart, even his mind.

All he could do was stare in helpless longing.

She strode through the waves toward him, all long legs and curves, wet hair snaking like seaweed over high, firm breasts. Water droplets shimmered on her skin, the charm a silver glint on her wrist.

She was a siren with ocean-colored eyes, come to land for one short night.

Sorrow squeezed his insides. She was so beautiful, so at home at the water.

So different from him.

They could never have more than these snatches of time.

But his feet were already moving, taking him to her.

CHAPTER 10

dric was okay.

Rosana's knees went weak with relief at seeing him unharmed.

Their eyes locked, and her spine tingled at the need and heat in his. She walked toward him, a moth to his fire.

He met her halfway, hauling her up against his lean, sinewy frame. The water sucked at their ankles. The icy wind whipped around them.

She had time to draw a breath and then his mouth crashed onto hers. One kiss spun into the next, and the next. Hard, drugging kisses that took her deep and whipped her around until she clung to him as if he were the only solid thing in the world.

His hands gripped her hips, molding her to his body. His erection pressed against her belly through the placket of his jeans. She rubbed against it and he groaned.

The wind picked up, scouring her exposed skin. She shivered and pressed closer, tunneling her fingers under his T-shirt, seeking his warmth. She might be a river fada, adapted to cool streams and caverns, but even she got cold on a night like this.

He lifted his head, swore. "You need to put on some clothes."

"Clothes." Dazed, she rested her forehead against his chest. "Right."

As she got dressed, Adric suggested they camp out in Cape Henlopen for the night and get the car in the morning. "Otherwise," he added, "we'll spend half the night answering questions for the humans."

"Sounds good," she said as she rolled up her pants.

They set off at a jog down the beach, running through the surf to hide their scent. In the park, they continued off-road through the pine-covered dunes until they reached the Point, a sandy spit of land that hooked into the bay, dividing it from the Atlantic. There, they made camp in a hollow beneath a loblolly pine, zipping up their jackets and pulling on socks.

Leaning back on his forearms, Adric stared grim-faced into the pine trees. Whatever he was thinking, it wasn't pleasant.

She sifted a handful of sand and pine needles through her fingers. "You went back without me, didn't you?"

"Yeah. So?"

She rolled her eyes. Typical alpha. Send the female to safety so he could investigate alone. "So it was three against one. I could've helped you."

"Rosana." His voice was so reasonable, she ground her teeth. "It wasn't your problem. They were after me."

"What makes you so sure? Maybe it was me they were after. I *am* the Rock Run alpha's sister, you know."

He turned his head to look at her. His eyes had gone night-glow, the irises the same brilliant blue at the heart of a flame. "Oh, I know. I don't ever forget it. Not for a single second."

She swallowed. "But something made you go back."

He heaved a breath. "You're not going to let this rest, are you?"

"Nope."

He shook his head, but said, "The other man, the one we didn't see? He was an earth fada."

Oh. "He's working for the fae?"

"Yeah."

"From your clan?"

His mouth set. "Not exactly."

She rolled a loblolly needle between her fingers, releasing its sharp, piney scent. "This has to do with what happened last summer, doesn't it? When Lord Tyrus died."

He lifted a shoulder, dropped it. Not confirming, but not denying either—which told her she was right.

"His father wants revenge." She was careful not to say Prince Langdon's name. Speak a fae's name, and you risked drawing his attention. "But Tyrus attacked you, didn't he? Merry said he almost killed her uncle Jace."

Adric snorted. "He's a fae. He doesn't need a reason. No, I was supposed to lie down, belly up, while Tyrus picked off my lieutenants one by one."

"What about that blonde we saw? She's not a pureblood, is she?"

A pause. "That's what I can't figure out. She's not a member of the New Moon Court. She's an ice fae/night fae mix. So is she working for the prince—or on her own?"

Rosana frowned. "In my vision, three night fae warriors captured you. One of them could have been a woman, but none of them had blond hair."

A noncommittal grunt.

To the east, the surf boomed. Above, the wind growled and snapped at the treetops. Rosana shivered and hugged her knees. She'd known Adric was in danger, but seeing those fae at the B&B had rammed it home.

He was in a fight for his life.

The Darktime isn't over. The prince will destroy your clan from the inside out.

She gripped her knees harder.

"That earth fada," she said. "He's someone important to you, isn't he? A good friend."

Adric stiffened. "How the fuck do you know that?"

"I don't read minds, if that's what you're thinking, but I can tell he upset you."

Her Gift made her more sensitive to emotions than most people, although Adric had always been hard to read. But since they'd had sex, it was as if they'd connected on some deeper level. Right now, she *felt* the anger and hurt radiating from him.

She furrowed her brow. Was it always like that?

"You're right," Adric admitted. "He's not a clan member—not anymore— but the two of us go way back."

"He's *hunting* you for them?"

A curt nod. "He's under a *geas* to the fae lady. I know he doesn't have a choice, that he has to obey, but he is—was—one of my best friends, a lieutenant. It—" He shook his head. "He must've tracked me to Lewes for her. I had to expel him from the clan—I had no choice. The way our quartzes work, everyone in the clan is connected to me."

Her heart ached for Adric. She touched his leg. "He understands."

"Maybe." Adric's mouth twisted. "When I went back, he saw me. But he kept quiet. Just got in the car and drove off."

"So he *does* understand."

"I suppose so. I know he has to obey her, but—"

"I'm sorry."

He moved a shoulder. "Not your problem."

"But I'm the only one here." She lay down, gave him a tug. "C'mere. Keep me warm."

He let her pull him down so his head was cradled against her breasts. He set an arm on her waist and moved his head, finding a comfortable spot.

She stroked his nape, excruciatingly aware she was almost out of time. In a few hours, they'd be returning to Maryland. Who knew when she'd have him alone again?

But *Deus*, this was fucked up—the fae at the B&B, the earth fada tracking them. And she sensed there was more to the story, that Adric hadn't told her everything.

But then, she hadn't told him everything, either. Because that vision she'd had in December? A few days later, she'd taken out her scrying bowl, hoping to See a different fate for him. But she'd Seen the exact same thing—and this time, the scene had played out to its conclusion.

She swallowed sickly. Because she *knew* she was right.

Adric intended to assassinate Prince Langdon. And if he went alone, he'd die.

"What's wrong?" He lifted his head to scrutinize her.

She took a deep breath and blurted, "You need me. When you go after the prince, you have to take me, too."

He pulled away from her. "Rosana. Please."

She swallowed. "I know it sounds crazy. But I have this feeling."

"A feeling," he repeated flatly.

"That I can help."

"How? I'm not saying you're right, but what help could you be against the night fae? Or any fae, for that matter?"

She shut her eyes. Goddess, it did sound crazy. The fada might be physically equal to the fae, but the fae had magic to call on. They even healed more quickly.

She might be a warrior, but she'd never seen actual combat. What help could she give a man who'd spent half his life fighting a vicious civil war?

"You know I'm a Gifted Seer. The fae who's training me believes that someday I'll be one of the most powerful Seers in the world. And he says sometimes you don't See something, you *feel* it—a gut instinct. And my gut tells me I should go, too."

"Yeah?" he said in that same flat voice. "Well, my gut says you should stay home."

"Listen to me!" She gave him a shake. "There's more. After I left you that night, I Saw it in my scrying bowl. You—"

"Forget it." He rolled onto his back and dropped an arm over his eyes. "I don't care what you Saw, I'm not taking you with me."

She let out a breath through her teeth. "You know, Dion says you're smart. A bastard, yeah, but a smart bastard."

"I love him right back."

"Well, a smart man would listen to a Seer's warning."

A charged pause. Then he lifted his arm. "Okay, then. Talk."

She hesitated. How do you tell a man you foresaw his death?

That night in December, she'd Seen him going after Langdon. But later, there'd been more. Something so raw that just recalling it made her lungs lock.

The night fae capture Adric, drag him to a clearing in a dark woods. Stake him, spread-eagled, to the ground.

A black-haired priestess in a silver dress steps forward, a gleaming knife in her hand. She raises the knife above her head, brings it slashing down...

Rosana squeezed her eyes shut, but that just made it worse. The image was burned on her retinas. She opened them and stared fiercely up at the trees.

"Hey." He rolled over, touched her arm. "Take it easy. I *did* think about what you said, okay? But a vision is just one possible future."

She started, focused on him.

He was still free. There was still time to change his fate.

"I—I Saw your death. You go after the night fae, and you *die*. I Saw you on the ground. I smelled the freaking blood."

His swallow was loud in the clearing. When he spoke again, his voice was gentle. "I'm sorry, but my mind is made up. I'm going. Alone."

Her heart sank. "But *why?*"

He shook his head. "It's the only way."

"Adric. You have to listen. If you won't take me, take someone else—one of your men, or Marjani. Yeah, a vision is only one possible future, but it can only be the changed if you change the path you're on."

His face shuttered. "Enough, already. You had your say. Consider me warned."

She growled. "*Deus*, you're pigheaded—even more than Dion. And that's saying something."

Colm had warned her in his sardonic way that being a Seer was a thankless task, saying you might as well piss into the wind for all the notice most people will take of you.

But *Deus*, she hadn't realized how hard it was to have your warnings ignored.

Adric scrubbed a hand over his face, and then with a sigh, rolled over to face her. "Thank you, love." He took her hand, pressed a kiss to her knuckles.

"For what?" she snapped.

"For caring."

She looked down at the calloused fingers wrapped around hers. Sadness washed over her. "Oh, Adric. You don't have to thank someone for caring."

His mouth contorted. "Maybe not in your world." He reached for her. "Let me hold you. Okay?"

She shook her head but allowed him to pull her into his arms. Above, the wind whistled over the dunes, but here in the cozy hollow, they were snug and warm.

He nuzzled her hair. "It wouldn't work anyway. You know that, don't you?"

"Don't," she whispered, tears burning her throat. "Just don't. Please?"

He nodded and nudged her chin up so he could rub his lips over hers. They fell asleep like that, mouths still touching.

THE FIRST RAYS of dawn had pushed through the trees when Adric brushed Rosana's hair back from her face. "Time to go."

The two of them crept back to the B&B and peered through the fence. The parking lot was empty except for two cars—theirs, and a white truck that she assumed belonged to Mark. The human couple must've checked out.

Adric motioned for her to remain hidden behind the fence. "Wait here until I pull out of the parking lot. Just in case."

When she nodded, he slipped into the parking lot and strolled up to the Mazda. A press of the keyless remote, and the doors unlocked. He drove it a few yards up the street and then waited as she slid into the passenger seat.

The streets of Lewes were nearly empty, the houses still dark. Streetlights glowed against the slowly brightening sky as they pulled onto the highway.

Adric slanted her a look. "You hungry? We could stop somewhere."

She shook her head. "I'll eat when I get home."

"You sure?"

"Yeah."

They drove back to Maryland in silence. Rosana stared out the window, dully aware she'd failed.

So this was how it ended. One night was all they'd ever have.

In a few weeks—or maybe even a few days—Adric would leave for Virginia and the New Moon Court, and be captured by the night fae. Maybe he wouldn't die—maybe he'd somehow avoid that slashing knife. Like he'd said, that was just one possible future.

But even if he survived, what would become of the two of them?

It wouldn't work anyway. You know that, don't you?

They were almost at the rest area where she'd left the car when something in her snapped.

No.

She was *not* going to lose Adric because she was too afraid to speak up. If he didn't want her, he could tell her straight out.

She turned in the seat to face him. "*Why* wouldn't it work?"

"Rosana," he said in a hard, don't-question-me voice. "Don't do this."

"But it *meant* something. You felt it. I know you did." He'd touched her with such tenderness. Held her all night in the park. "You...thanked me for caring."

"And I meant it. But you and me?" He shook his head.

Her breath felt heavy in her lungs, as if she were trying to breathe underwater. Adric started to say something else and she threw up a staying hand.

"It's all right. Really. I get it. You don't want me that bad."

"Fuck." He swerved to the side of the highway and stomped on the brakes, throwing them both forward against their seatbelts.

A car zoomed past, horn blaring.

Rosana looked at the arm Adric had flung across her chest. "What the—?"

He unbuckled his seatbelt and hers with shifter-fast speed and dragged her toward him so that she lay half over the console.

"The hell I don't want you." His fingers dug into her shoulders. "If it was up to me, we'd be halfway across the country, looking for a place to make our own den away from both our clans. But I'm the alpha. The clan needs me. Before I took over, we almost lost everything. You know how many elders we have?"

She shook her head mutely. Hurting for him. Hurting for herself.

"Five—three women and two men. Other than them, no one older than forty survived the Darktime. I lost my mom and dad. Jace lost both his parents and his only sister. And the list goes on and on. That man I saw last night?" His throat worked. "He was captured and tortured for close to a year just for being my friend. So don't tell me I don't want you. It's not a question of what I fucking want."

He kissed her. A hard, fierce kiss, his arms clamped around her.

She brought her hands up, instinctively stroking, soothing.

He groaned and tore his mouth from hers. His grip on her loosened. He brought his forehead to hers.

"I can't turn my back on them," he rasped. "And they'd never accept you."

"It's okay," she managed to say, even though her heart had fractured into jagged shards. "I understand."

"The only way we can be together is if we keep sneaking around like this. Just say the word, and I'm there. But do you want a man who can never claim you?

And what about your family, your clan? Do you really think Dion would accept me as your mate?" His laugh held zero humor. "God's cat. The man would probably try to carve off my balls if he found out we spent even one night together."

She shook her head, but in her heart, she knew he was right. A truck rumbled past, rattling their windows, but inside the car, the only sound was the harsh scrape of their breathing.

She pushed away from him. His hands tightened for a second as if he wanted to keep holding her, but then they opened, and she knew it really was over.

Adric regarded her moodily. "I'm not going to say I'm sorry. Last night was... special. I'll be damned if I regret it."

She pressed her lips together so he wouldn't see them trembling. Lifted her chin. "I didn't ask you for an apology." Returning to her seat, she fumbled blindly for the seat belt.

"I'll take you back."

She latched the belt and sat back. "Thank you."

Back at the rest stop, Adric turned off the engine. "One thing you can count on. I'm not going to die. He is. So stop worrying."

She just shook her head.

"So." He drummed his fingers on the steering wheel. "Take care of yourself —okay?"

"Yeah. Sure."

She reached for her canvas bag. Got out of the car. Shut the door.

Moving on automatic, because if she let herself think, the sobs locked in her chest might spill out.

Adric accompanied her to her car. After she unlocked the door, he reached around her and opened it. He didn't say goodbye, just touched her cheek and then closed the door for her. But he tailed her out of the rest area and up I-95. Making sure she got safely back to Grace Harbor, because that's who he was.

She watched through her rearview mirror as he followed her off the exit and then turned south toward Baltimore.

Her stomach was a hard, hurting knot. She pressed a fist to it and aimed the car for home.

~

ADRIC DROVE the thirty-five miles to Baltimore, foot heavy on the gas pedal, radio blasting. Just let the cops pull him over. Right now, he'd welcome the chance to pound on someone.

With every additional mile he traveled from Rosana, something inside him unraveled. Like his heart was attached to hers by some invisible thread, and with each mile, that wanting, needy organ was being shredded and left behind.

Mine.

His fingers tightened around the steering wheel. Her scent was still in the car, on him. Driving him insane.

He'd meant every word he'd said to her. The two of them together just wouldn't work.

Yeah, the clan had accepted Evie, Jace's mate, but everybody liked Evie. And she'd turned out to have a Gift that helped the healers, so she was an asset to the clan.

Marjani's mate, Fane, had been a harder sell, but Adric had made it clear the clan had better accept him or else. After what his sister had been through, she deserved to be happy.

But Adric was alpha. The clan needed him, and after the Darktime, they didn't trust easily. He'd worked his ass off to win over the doubters, convincing them that the only way forward was to work together. But choose a river fada as a mate—and worse, a Rock Run river fada—and that fragile accord could be blown sky-high.

Still, none of that mattered anyway. Because despite what he'd told Rosana, he didn't expect to get out of Virginia alive.

Inside his cougar lashed its tail, furious that he'd let Rosana just drive off. The cat was a simple beast. To it, Rosana was theirs and Adric was a fool for letting her go.

But he was a highly disciplined man, so he ruthlessly wrestled the cat under control, and then slowed enough to blend in with the human traffic.

CHAPTER 11

Rosana returned home to find Rock Run on high alert. A Baltimore fada had been seen near the base, a wolf. A sentry had given chase, but the wolf had evaded capture.

Dion was coldly furious. In recent years, he'd made concessions to the Baltimore clan, accepting the clan's mining operation on sun fae lands and allowing Jace Jones to visit Merry near the Rock Run base. In return, Adric had agreed to stop trying to steal Rock Run's territory.

Now Dion felt betrayed. He and Rui do Mar, his second-in-command, were in the war room, discussing the situation with his *tenentes*.

At least they knew it couldn't be Adric. Unlike water fada, earth fada took only one form and everyone knew Adric was a cougar. Rosana took advantage of the confusion to sneak through the back tunnels to her quarters so she could wash off his scent before anyone noticed.

She and Isa had their own bathroom, carved out of the wall between their bedrooms. The counter was marbled granite, the toilet a solid black ceramic. Two shelves chiseled into the granite wall held her and Isa's toiletries, and the shower spilled out of the rough gray rock like a waterfall.

Rosana turned on the shower, stepped under it. She washed her hair, and then soaped up and leaned against the wall, letting the cool water wash over her.

She felt empty. Scooped out, one big hurt beneath her ribs where her heart should be.

What did you expect? One night with you and Adric would start to trust you?

She blew out a breath. Because yeah, she supposed she had expected it.

Not because they'd had sex—she might've been a virgin, but she wasn't an idiot—but because the two of them had finally had a chance to spend some time away from the disapproving eyes of their two clans.

She'd learned better. For him, it was just sex. End of story. There was nothing else between them.

Oh, he'd said he wanted more, just not enough to put her before his clan. Rosana respected that; for an alpha, the clan should come first. But if he really loved her, wouldn't he work out a way for them to be together?

Everybody leaves. Rosana had learned that early.

She'd begged her mom and dad to take her with them on that last trip, but they'd gently but firmly refused. Then her *papai* had handed her to Isa and told her to be a good girl.

And that was the last she'd seen of them.

She turned off the shower and reached for a towel.

The mirror over the sink had steamed up. She cleaned a circle in the center and stared at herself. Nothing had changed—and yet, everything had. She expected to look different, older. In the twenty-four hours she'd been gone, she felt like she'd aged at least a decade.

But she looked exactly the same. Same black hair hanging in wet curls around her face. Same full lips and slightly pointed chin. Same deep blue eyes that everyone said were just like her mom's. Even the love-bite Adric had left on her throat was almost gone.

Chest aching, she touched a finger to the small red mark.

Her shoulders slumped. She hung the towel on a peg, light-headed with exhaustion, and stumbled into the bedroom.

When she awoke a few hours later, Isa was bustling around in their little *sala*, or living room, humming to herself. Rosana pulled on a tank top and shorts and joined her.

Isa was wearing one of her usual simple dresses, this one dark blue. Her thick, graying hair was wound into a crown braid that framed her round face, and her sturdy feet were bare.

"Boa tarde." She leveled Rosana a look. Isa might look like a kindly, cookie-pushing grandma, but not much got past her. "Are you hungry?"

"I guess." She listlessly eyed the fruit bowl in the kitchenette before helping herself to an apple.

"So," Isa said. "The beach, it was nice?"

"*Sim.* Hardly any humans. I even went for a swim." At night and to hide her tracks from the fae, but Isa didn't need to know that.

Isa set her hands on her ample hips. "And?"

Rosana took a bite of apple. "And what?"

"That's not all you did. You were with *him*, weren't you?"

"Yeah?" Rosana clenched the apple. "Well, if I was, that's my business, not yours, isn't it?"

The older woman's eyes flickered with hurt.

Rosana sighed. "I'm sorry. I didn't mean—"

Isa clucked disapprovingly—and then shocked her by saying, "You're a woman now, *bonita.* Your choices are your own. I just don't want you to be hurt."

A raw ache stung Rosana's throat. She set the half-eaten apple on the counter, hunger gone. "Isa." She reached out her arms, wanting a hug so bad, and then checked herself.

Isa crossed the room to gently rub Rosana's back over the tank top. She knew not to touch Rosana's bare skin. "Was it so bad? He was cruel to you?" Her dark brows snapped together. "I'll carve out his heart with a spoon."

"No, no. He was...sweet."

Isa snorted. "That one?"

"He was," Rosana insisted. "And it wasn't bad at all. It was...amazing."

Her cheeks heated, because after all, this was the woman who was like a second mother to her.

"Then perhaps I like him after all," Isa decided.

"It's just..." Rosana blinked back tears. "Me and him? It's never going to happen. He told me straight out."

"Sit." Isa's dark eyes were sympathetic. "I'll braid your hair. You went to bed with it wet, didn't you?"

Rosana ran a hand over her head. It felt like a bush had sprung up on her scalp.

"Thanks," she said with a sniff and allowed the other woman to guide her to the couch.

Isa shut the door between their apartment and Dion's, and then got a brush and sat on the couch next to Rosana. "Tell me," she said as she set to work on the tangles.

Rosana gave a small shake of her head. Once, she'd come running to Isa with every bruise and scrape, but this was one problem her former nurse couldn't solve.

"*Obrigada*, but I don't want to talk about it."

"It might help. And hold still." The tangles gone, Isa switched to long, soothing strokes.

Rosana let her head fall forward, eyes half-closed. How many times had Isa brushed her hair just like this? Nostalgia tugged at her, sharp and bittersweet, as if already, this was something she'd left behind along with her girlhood.

They fell silent, the older woman drawing the brush through her hair. When it was free of tangles, she began to plait one side into a braid. "Tell me," she repeated. "Perhaps I can help."

"I don't think so." Rosana's mouth twisted. "Unless you can turn me into an earth fada."

"Ah, *bonita*." Isa braided the other side. "Is that what you think it will take?"

"He won't have me any other way. And let's face it, Dion would disown me if I mated with a Baltimore fada. Especially Adric."

"Mated?" Isa joined the two smaller braids into a single plait at the back and wrapped a leather thong around the bottom. "You believe this is possible?" she asked as she tucked the end of the thong into the braid. "A river fada and an earth fada?"

Rosana turned to face her. "It must be. How could I feel like this if he wasn't my mate?" She pressed the heel of her hand to her heart. "I ache for him, Isa."

The old nurse's expression was troubled. "I've lived a long time, and I've never seen such a thing. I can tell you one thing, that one won't be tamed. He'll always be a little wild. Hard. You'll have to take him as he is."

Rosana lifted her chin. "He's hard because he had to be. He'd be dead by now if he hadn't been. And I don't want to tame him. I like him just the way he is." A smile tugged at her lips.

"It was good, *sim*?" Isa waved a hand. "No, don't answer that. There are some secrets a woman keeps close."

They shared a grin.

Isa tucked a stray hair behind Rosana's ear, serious again. "Your Adric is the alpha, not a man who can do as he pleases. The alpha is the leader of a clan, *sim*, but he's also bound by his duties, his responsibilities to the people he governs."

"That's what he said. And he's not *my* Adric."

"He hasn't mate-claimed you, then."

"No. And he won't."

"But if he did? You would accept his claim?"

Rosana opened her mouth, shut it. "I don't know," she admitted. "I'd have to leave Rock Run, my family, my friends. I—" She shook her head.

Adric's clan was so different from theirs. He seemed to be constantly fighting off challenges from his own people. Hell, just last summer, two of his own cousins had tried to kill him.

She heaved a breath. "It doesn't matter. He's never going to ask me."

"Then put him from your mind."

Rosana swallowed. Isa was right. Adric was an earth fada alpha, and she was a river fada from a rival clan. The two of them weren't going to have some fairytale ending.

But he needs me.

"You're right. I know you're right." She jumped up and paced across the *sala.*

"But I can't." She shot Isa a lopsided smile. "*Deus,* Dion would kill me if I mated with Adric."

"But it's not up to your brother, is it? Only you can choose the mate bond."

"You're right." Rosana stared at her, arrested, before shaking her head. "It doesn't matter. He told me straight out he'll never claim me."

"Bah." Isa clucked her tongue. "He's a man. What does he know? If you want him badly enough, you can convince him. But think about it. This is not a decision to be made lightly."

Rosana nodded slowly.

"Senhora Isa!" Brisa's voice piped from the other side of the closed door. "I-sa! Me here!"

"I'll get it." Rosana opened the door to find her niece standing wobbly-legged on the other side, one plump hand gripping the door jamb.

Her small face lit. "Tia Wosa!" She reached for Rosana with both hands and nearly overbalanced herself.

"Brisa!" Rosana swooped her up. "Just the girl I wanted to see."

She spun around in a circle as the toddler put her head back and squealed with glee. When she stopped, they were both laughing.

Rosana hugged her close, pressed a kiss to the little girl's sweet-smelling neck.

If she mated with Adric, she wouldn't get to see Brisa every day. Her smile faded. The thought made her a little sick.

She hugged Brisa closer until her niece squirmed to be put down.

Cleia appeared, Dion on her heels. Her brother had apparently been coached by his mate because he didn't ask a single question about her trip, just said, "I hope you had a good time." When Rosana said yes, he nodded, and with a glance at Cleia, turned the conversation to other matters.

So that was that, Rosana thought as she got ready for bed that night.

Even if Adric survived the night fae, he wasn't going to choose her over his clan. So it would be just like always. She'd see him maybe once or twice a year—at the Full Moon Saloon or one of the sun fae parties. Cleia usually invited Adric and his sister. She believed that if Adric and Dion just got to know each other, they'd realize they weren't so different after all.

Her mouth twisted sardonically. If she was lucky, she might even get to spend a few minutes alone with him without their respective clans breathing over their shoulders.

But Goddess, it hurt. A whole life stretching ahead of her without Adric.

CHAPTER 12

*L*angdon woke at dusk as the black-out shades slid up to let in the last feeble rays of the setting sun. He pushed the silk duvet down to his waist and folded his arms behind his head. Above the four-poster bed, a handful of fae lights glowed on in iridescent shades of lavender and blue. The colors within spiraled around each other in a slow, hypnotic dance.

At his side, Fleur stirred. Her attentiveness to his moods was one of her most attractive qualities.

She propped herself on a forearm and trailed a glitter-tipped nail down his naked chest. The duvet sloped across her hips, leaving her upper body bare except for the black star medallion that marked her as a priestess of the night.

"Good evening, my lord." Her carmine lips curved, the dark eyes above watchful. One of her small, moon-pale breasts sported a nasty crescent where he'd bitten her earlier before taking her, hard and rough.

He'd been in a vile mood for months, dating to when his son Tyrus had disappeared, his body never found. But then, Fleur liked it rough. When he'd closed his teeth on her soft, delicate flesh, she'd merely sucked in a breath and, when he'd commanded her to beg, crawled in a most satisfactory way.

"Do you require anything?" Her hand slipped under the duvet to his half-hard cock.

A lock of shiny black hair had fallen over her shoulder. Looping it around his fingers, he tugged her closer. "You pleased me this morning, love." He sank his teeth into her lower lip hard enough to draw blood.

She made a small sound, and then her eyes drifted shut. He *felt* her excitement, knew she wanted him. In her own way, Fleur loved him.

But right now, he wanted her distress. Because he *was* a night fae.

He released her and left the bed, strolling to the bathroom without a backward glance. He knew by the time he returned, she'd have ordered his breakfast and then left for her own lair. After all, he'd trained her himself.

After showering, he donned a black silk bathrobe embroidered with silver moons and stars. His coffee, croissants and a bowl of hothouse peaches awaited him in the breakfast room, a small octagonal space off the living room. Taking a seat at the linen-covered table, he unfolded his napkin and set it on his lap.

A flick of a finger and the silver coffeepot floated off the table to pour coffee into an eggshell-thin cup, followed by a dollop of cream from a pitcher. His croissants were still warm. He broke off a buttery piece and put it in his mouth.

The Baltimore alpha was cannier than Langdon had expected. Adric had managed to dance around the fact that an earth fada had killed Tyrus. But they both knew the truth.

Langdon sipped his coffee. Frankly, his middle son had needed killing. He'd poisoned his older brother, and then sent assassins after Langdon's half-human son, Silver. Tyrus's men would've also slain Merry Jones, the daughter Silver had had with an earth fada, if Rui do Mar hadn't saved the child and taken her back to Rock Run.

Langdon had been furious with Tyrus. That he'd dare kill children of Langdon's own body. If it had been anyone but his son—and only remaining heir—Langdon would've executed him on the spot. Instead, he'd banished Tyrus from New Moon, and set a protective spell on Merry's quartz.

But his son hadn't stopped there. He'd joined forces with an exiled Baltimore earth fada and tried to stir up trouble between Baltimore and the Rock Run Clan.

Which was why Tyrus was dead.

It had taken time for Langdon to unearth the truth. Adric had covered his tracks very, very well. But all trails led to Baltimore.

So Langdon had started to harry Adric, politely, relentlessly. The alpha hadn't broken, but a few months after Tyrus's disappearance, Langdon had finally Seen his son's death.

But not at Adric's hand, as he'd believed. No, it was Marjani Savonett who'd killed Tyrus.

Langdon knew damn well that his son had deserved it. Tyrus had come into Adric's territory, looking to stir up trouble. Sent assassins after Adric's people. Invaded Jace's den and kidnapped him and his mate.

Still, Langdon couldn't allow a fada to get away with murdering one of his sons.

Marjani Savonett had to die.

But Tyrus's death had left Langdon with a problem. He had no heir of his direct bloodline, and to the fae, blood was everything.

Blood, and tradition.

Picking up the slim silver knife, he cut a peach into six perfect slices and ate them before calling his butler to clear the table.

He stood before a window, hands clasped behind his back. Outside, his clan was emerging for the evening from their lairs. They glided among the winter-bare trees like elongated shadows, their tall bodies clad in black, their eyes dark holes in pale faces. The priests and priestesses wore shimmering silver—a dress, a shirt. A few of the more fashion-forward had added a splash of crimson—a scarf, high heels, a pair of gloves.

The New Moon Court was in a lush old-growth forest in Tidewater Virginia, spread across a peninsula that jutted into the mouth of the Potomac River. Each family or couple had their own home, built of granite or veined marble and set partly underground. The few feet that showed above ground were narrow structures with fanciful carvings at the apex—moons and stars, vining flowers, snarling wolves, bats with wings spread wide. English ivy ran rampant, crawling across the ground, over the roofs and up the towering trees.

To a human, it looked uncomfortably like a cemetery with above-ground tombs. To Langdon, it was home.

Tradition, he mused. His people had lived like this for thousands of years.

"Change is coming. The old traditions will be no more."

At the last full moon ritual, the Goddess had spoken through Fleur. The priestess had stared straight at Langdon as she channeled the prophecy, making it clear to whom the message was directed.

Langdon had inclined his head.

Later, when Quade, the captain of his guards, had asked what the prophecy meant, he'd replied, truthfully enough, "We must see what the Goddess has in store."

He glanced up at the immense oaks and tulip poplars that guarded the compound, their muscular branches stark against the dusky sky. The New Moon fae had established their court in this backwater country centuries ago, carving out a mile-square territory in the forest. It was dark, isolated, and yet easily accessible to the Chesapeake Bay and from there, the Atlantic Ocean. The indigenous peoples had been wise enough to give them a wide berth, and vice versa.

Langdon could still recall the arrival of the first European humans. His grandfather had been prince then, with Langdon's father the designated heir. The old prince had enforced their traditions with an iron hand. He'd arranged Langdon's mating with a high-born French fae, a beautiful, submissive woman. Langdon had been happy enough with her.

But she'd presented him with two sons and then died of a sudden, mysterious illness. Langdon had suspected poison, but he had no proof. The fae had ways of making poisons that left no trace.

Langdon had still been a young man—a hundred-and-ten turns of the sun. Youthful enough to chafe at the restrictions put on him by his powerful family. He'd buried his French mate and then fought with his grandfather over some ridiculous thing.

Looking back, he'd been grieving, but he'd only known he was furious with both his grandfather and his father, who'd taken the old prince's side. So he'd left his sons with his parents and spent the next few decades traveling up and down the Americas disguised as a human folk healer. If he could heal the patient, he did —and if not, he fed on the family's misery.

It was in New Orleans that he'd encountered a dark-haired, golden-skinned human. Marie-Josana, a Creole singer who performed in the city's opera houses and theaters. He'd fallen hard. Within days, he'd bought a house in the Garden District and settled down with his beautiful Josana.

He hadn't mate-claimed her. The heir to the night fae throne couldn't have a human mate. But he'd loved Josana with all the passion in his dark heart.

With her, *he'd* been the needy one.

An uncomfortable sensation, one he'd taken care never to repeat.

In the end, he and Josana must have mated on some basic, primal level, because he'd gotten her with child. Langdon had named the boy Quicksilver, since he had the Gift of wayfaring. Silver, for short.

Then Langdon's father had died suddenly, and he'd been ordered home by the old prince to take his place as the heir. His grandfather knew about Josana and Silver, of course. Very little escaped the old man.

But he'd made it clear that no one else could know about Langdon's half-blood son.

To this day, very few people knew about Langdon's third son, and even fewer knew Silver had had a daughter with an earth fada. Langdon had kept Merry hidden. To the pureblood fae, she was a mongrel, an embarrassment. His grandfather had sneered at Langdon for letting his seed be diluted.

But Langdon had loved his youngest son, even if he was a half-blood. Silver had been educated at the best schools, and Langdon had set up a trust that made his son a rich man in the human world.

He scowled into the rapidly falling night.

Ironic, that of his three sons, the half-blood Silver had been the best. The oldest, Dorian, had been weak, and Tyrus a ruthless, power-hungry S.O.B.

Langdon had cursed the tradition that didn't allow him to claim a half-blood as his heir. And then it was too late. Silver was dead.

But Silver's mixed-blood daughter lived.

The table had been cleared. His butler Olivier waited until his assistant left with the dishes, and then appeared at his elbow in his usual perfectly pressed black pants, pristine white shirt and natty bow tie.

"Will you require anything else, my lord?"

"No." Langdon dismissed him with a wave of his hand.

Crossing to an antique mahogany hutch, he removed a scrying mirror wrapped in soft cotton. He unwrapped the mirror and sat down again, the mirror cupped in his hands. The mirror was carved of pure obsidian, the edges beveled, a flowing white frame around the stone's glossy black.

He gazed into the dark center. The shiny surface threw back his own reflection, his mouth a line of concentration.

He slowed his breath. The reflection blurred, transformed to dark-edged clouds that raced across the obsidian's surface like a fast-approaching storm.

Change is coming. The old traditions will be no more.

Both Cleia and Dion had let Langdon believe his granddaughter was dead.

And Adric had told Langdon a flat-out lie, which must have made him deathly ill.

Langdon now knew differently. Merry was alive and still at Rock Run, as she'd been for the last seven turns of the sun. And soon, he'd bring her to Dark Moon to raise as his heir.

Centuries of tradition were about to be shattered. His grandfather would roll over in his grave.

Langdon's mouth edged up.

He tightened his fingers around the mirror, drew deeply on his Gift.

"Show me Merry Jones." He spoke her full name aloud to increase the power, his voice echoing in the small room.

On the mirror's shiny black surface, clouds swirled and piled upon each other into a towering thunderhead—and then parted to reveal his granddaughter.

CHAPTER 13

"Have a good trip?" asked Zuri.

He and Adric exchanged a look. They were at the Full Moon Saloon again, standing near the long wooden bar. It was Monday evening and the tavern was nearly empty. No humans. No river fada, even—just a few of his own men and a couple of visiting earth fada. Claudio was serving as the only bartender, and instead of a band, the TVs on either side of the bar were tuned to the replay of a soccer game in Madrid.

"I did." Adric took a gulp of beer. "Anything happen that I should know about?"

"Other than my alpha going A.W.O.L. for a night—and then nearly being captured by the night fae?"

Adric's fingers tightened on his bottle. "Everyone's allowed a fucking night off, even me."

The lieutenant acknowledged that with a tight nod. "You are. But as your head of security, I should have been informed."

"Jani knew."

Another short nod. Then his friend sighed. "Did it work?"

"Did what work?"

"Did you get the woman out of your system?"

Adric's mind went to the sea-green swirl in the quartz tucked out of sight beneath his T-shirt.

Hell, no. I only want her more and my cat's insisting she's the mate.

And I can't do a damn thing about it.

He took another swig of beer. "None of your fucking business."

"Hey, I'm the one who told you that if you wanted her, take her. But now you need to put her behind you. This thing with the night fae following you to Lewes? That's messed up."

"Yeah." Adric rubbed a thumb over the beer's glossy label.

He'd told his lieutenants about being tracked by the night fae. What he hadn't told them was that it had been Lady Blaer, and that Luc had been with her. Not even Marjani knew.

He just couldn't expose his old friend to the clan's condemnation. They might ask why Luc wasn't trying harder to fight Blaer's orders.

Adric wondered that himself. For instance, Luc could've taken his time tracking Adric so that by the time he and the fae arrived in Lewes, Adric and Rosana were gone. On the other hand, there was that moment in the parking lot when he could've given Adric away—and hadn't.

Zuri fingered his neat black soul patch. "Know what I think? Things are coming to a head. Something's about to happen. I can practically taste it."

Adric stilled. Had the lieutenant guessed his plans?

"And you think this, why?"

"Hell if I know. Things are quiet, but that's the problem. It's *too* quiet. For months, we've been seeing night fae every time we turned around. And then suddenly—nothing. Something's up. My wolf's so antsy I can barely sleep."

Adric relaxed. Zuri hadn't guessed.

"It's not just you. My cougar's antsy, too. Every time I'm out at night, my skin itches. I'm sure those bastards are still around, just hiding in the shadows."

"If only we had someone on the inside. If we had even a clue as to what they're planning, we could prepare a counterstrike." Zuri's lips peeled in a humorless smile. "A Seer, that's what we need. Although the old Seer wasn't much help. She didn't see her own death coming, did she? Or prevent the Darktime."

Adric blinked. "No," he said slowly. "She didn't. But she tried, remember? Except Leron didn't want to hear it."

A trickle of unease slid through his veins.

You need me.

What if Rosana was right?

Seers were rare. His own clan's Seer had met with an 'accident' during the Darktime when she'd refused to slant her prophecies to suit Leron's orders. Since then, no one else had shown signs of the Gift.

He reminded himself that no Seer was infallible. What Rosana had Seen was simply a strong possibility. She couldn't *know*. Not for sure.

The Darktime isn't over. The prince will destroy your clan from the inside out.
Adric's fangs pricked out. *The hell he would.*

"Step up patrols of the city," he ordered.

"Already did. But if a night fae doesn't want to be seen, we can run all the patrols we want and it won't do much good." Zuri shook his head. "Wish I knew how the motherfuckers slip in and out of the shadows like that. They can even hide their scent, which is just not possible."

"Except they do it."

"Yeah." Zuri took another slug of beer.

"Contact the alphas in each den, warn them that things are heating up. No one is to go outside without at least one other person. If they're younger than fifteen, they should have at least three people, including an adult. I'll make sure Jani knows to take extra care. It's her the prince really wants."

They shared a grim look. Langdon had somehow discovered it had been Marjani who'd killed his son, even though Adric had let everyone assume he'd been the one who knifed the prick.

His sister was a marked woman…unless someone took out Langdon first.

"I'm on it," Zuri assured him.

"Thanks, bro." Adric squeezed the other man's shoulder. "But watch your own back, okay? The prince knows you're one of my top men. If he can't get to me or Jani, he'll go after my closest people instead—and you and Jace will be at the top of the list."

Zuri's grin was all wolf. "He can try."

A commotion at the saloon's entrance made them both swing around. Dion do Rio stalked inside followed by his *tenente* Davi, both in black leather and jeans, their faces set in menacing lines.

The Full Moon went dead silent. Benny was on the door again. He moved to intercept them, but Dion snarled and the bouncer checked, his animal instinctively recognizing a dominant.

Dion's gaze swung to where Adric stood at the bar. His nostrils flared. He strode toward him, his eyes the pure silver of his animal.

"Uh-oh," muttered Zuri.

Benny recovered and stomped after Dion, but Adric shook his head. "Let them in." He set down his bottle, gave the Rock Run alpha a mocking little nod. "Peace."

"I'll give you fucking peace." Dion halted a foot away, Davi at his heels.

Zuri moved to block the *tenente*. The three other Baltimore fada present sprang up to form a semi-circle around them.

Dion didn't even bother to look at the other men.

Claudio moved out from behind the bar. Lean and charming, he had salt-and-pepper hair and the features of a Latin American aristocrat.

"*Senhores*," he said in his melodic Brazilian accent. "This is neutral territory. I must ask you gentlemen to take your dispute—"

Dion and Adric turned as one to bare their teeth at him, and he inclined his head and glided back behind the bar. "My apologies, *senhores*."

Dion's scent was hot with anger. His dark brows formed a furious slash across his forehead, and the look he trained on Adric was pure murder.

"I've tolerated your mining in my mate's territory. I've let your people mix with my clan in Grace Harbor. And I was happy to allow your lieutenant, Jones, onto our land to visit his niece. But—" His lips peeled in a snarl.

Adric tensed. *Here it comes.*

"*Deus* if I'll let your people come and go on Rock Run territory as they please."

"What?" It took Adric a full three seconds to realize the other alpha wasn't here to beat the crap out of him over Rosana. "One of my people was on Rock Run territory?"

"A wolf."

Adric's stomach bottomed out. He straightened from the bar, conscious of their audience. If it was Luc, he didn't want the whole damn world to know.

"Let's take this to the back room."

He led the way down the hall without waiting to see if Dion agreed. A poker game was in progress, but at a nod from him, the four men tossed their cards on the table and vacated the room.

Adric entered and faced off with Dion. Davi stood at his alpha's shoulder, while Zuri shut the door and leaned against it, arms folded over his broad chest.

"What color was this wolf?"

"Dark brown." The other alpha's lip curled. "Are you saying you didn't know?"

Hellfire. It sounded like Luc, all right.

He willed his heart and breathing to remain steady. "Yes. No one in the clan has my permission to enter your territory without your say-so."

Dion inhaled, testing Adric's statement for truth. He leaned forward, his mouth a hard line.

"Then get control over your own damn people. Because that wolf was in my woods. If we see him again, he's fair game."

Adric went rigid. In the six years since he'd become alpha, he'd thrown his heart and soul into healing his fractured clan. However, as Dion knew, he still had trouble from time to time.

Davi smirked at him over Dion's shoulder. The *tenente* was Adric's height, with the dark eyes and Mediterranean features of his Portuguese ancestors. On Davi, those looks were poster-boy gorgeous.

Adric narrowed his eyes. He'd seen Davi hovering around Rosana. If the other man wasn't careful, he was going to find his pretty face rearranged.

From the door, Zuri growled lowly, his wolf pissed at his alpha being challenged.

Adric made himself give Dion a tight nod. "I'll make sure my people know."

"You do that," was the grim reply.

Zuri opened the door, but Dion stayed where he was after ordering Davi to wait in the hall. To Adric he said, "Tell your man to leave."

Adric nodded at Zuri. "Okay," he said when the door closed behind him. "Talk."

"The room is soundproof?"

"Yeah." He folded his arms over his chest, ignoring the sinking sensation in the pit of his stomach.

Dion took a step closer. "Stay the fuck away from my sister. She's not for you."

It was what Adric had told himself for years, but he bristled. "That's up to her, isn't it?"

A muscle jumped in Dion's jaw. He drew a breath through his teeth. When he spoke, his tone was irritatingly reasonable.

"She's young. I know you're not that much older than her, but you grew up in a whole different world than she did. She's sheltered." The corner of his mouth tipped up wryly. "A little spoiled. I did my best, but when my parents disappeared, she was only six. For months, she woke up crying for her mama. Begging me to let her help search for them. I...it broke something in me."

Adric pictured a small Rosana crying for her mama and swallowed. "I'm sorry."

"I know you wouldn't mean to hurt her. I've been watching you. You've done a good job with your clan, and *Deus* knows, that wasn't easy. Tiago tells me that quartz factory you're trying to get off the ground just might be genius."

Adric's mouth fell open. Praise from the Rock Run alpha? The world must be ending. For some damn reason, he got a lump in his throat.

"Get to the point," he said gruffly.

"Even if you could make a safe home for her here in Baltimore, it wouldn't work. River fada have to live near fresh water—a river, a lake. She needs to be able to shift, to swim as her dolphin. Yeah, you have the Inner Harbor, but that's a cesspool of human shit and trash. She couldn't stay in it long."

A dull ringing filled Adric's ears. He uncrossed his arms. "Got it. Stay away from Rosana."

"Thank you. And I mean it. I know there's...something between you. But this is for the best. You'll see."

Adric jerked his chin.

Dion gazed at him for another heartbeat, and then inclined his head. "Peace to you and yours."

"Yeah. Peace. But Dion?"

"*Sim?*"

"For the record, I was planning on staying away anyway."

The other alpha turned to leave, and then hesitated. "I'm sorry. But you know I'm right."

For answer, Adric reached past him to open the door.

Zuri was waiting to escort the men off the premises. Not causing trouble, just sending a message that they were in Baltimore fada territory.

Adric sank down on one of the metal chairs vacated by the poker players and waited for Zuri to return. The dull ringing was joined by a suffocating sensation in his chest. Like his heart was being wrung out. Crushed.

She's mine.

He dropped his head into his hands. *No. She's not yours, and she never will be.*

Rosana couldn't live with him, and there was no way in hell the Baltimore alpha could move to Rock Run. The very idea made his lips peel in a humorless smile.

Zuri returned, closing the door behind him. He set his hands on the table. "The wolf was Luc, wasn't it?"

Adric grimaced. *Right.* Luc was the problem here, not Rosana. And since Luc was being controlled by Blaer, things had just gone from bad to worse.

Somehow he pushed a response past the obstruction in his chest. "That's my guess."

Zuri's dark gaze narrowed. "And you're not surprised."

"No."

"Care to explain? Or is this something else your head of security doesn't need to know?"

Adric heaved a breath. "I'll explain. But tomorrow. We'll meet at the Factory. Jani and Jace need to hear this, too."

CHAPTER 14

With the base on alert, Dion had ordered the sentries to double up, some to patrol the forests and vineyards, some to patrol the water. Rosana reported to the marina for duty early Tuesday morning to find she'd been paired with Chico Nobrega, her brother Tiago's best friend, and assigned to the section of the Susquehanna River north of Rock Run Creek.

The two of them walked to the end of a dock and peeled off their clothes with the nonchalance of old friends. Chico was frankly gorgeous, with cropped brown curls and soulful dark eyes. More than a few hearts had been bruised when he'd mated with a human named Jenny. But to Rosana he was just a man she'd known since she was a pup, almost a fifth brother.

"Beat you into the water," he said and leapt, shifting to his dolphin in mid-air. She landed in the river a second after him. Just so he didn't get too cocky, she waited for him to surface and then slapped her tail on the surface, splashing his face.

Chico wanted to talk about the mysterious brown wolf, of course. Everyone did. Their orders were to capture the wolf if he set even a paw on their land. If he resisted, they were to kill him.

You hear anything else? he asked as they dodged between two fishing boats.

No, she returned shortly.

The endless speculation was driving her crazy. Adric wouldn't have sent a wolf to Rock Run. Not when he was in Lewes with her.

But if he hadn't sent the wolf, then why had it been on their territory?

She had a bad feeling it was the same earth fada who'd led the fae to the B&B—which opened up more questions, like why look for Adric at Rock Run?

Or had the wolf been looking for her, Rosana? Which made even less sense.

Davi says Adric didn't know one of his own men was on our land. Chico shook his head. *What's up with the Baltimore fada, anyway? They have no fucking discipline.*

She moved her body in the dolphin equivalent of a shrug. *Maybe they had their reasons.*

If they do attack, it won't be from the river. Chico's disappointment was clear. *Adric's not stupid. Water's our element, and he knows it.*

She released a forceful exhale through her blowhole. *They're not going to attack, period. Adric told Dion straight out he had nothing to do with it. If he was lying, Dion would've scented it.*

Okay, okay. Chico gave her the side-eye. *Hell, you still have a thing for him, don't you?*

That was the problem with people who'd known you since you were a pup. They knew you too well.

So what if I do? She circumvented another fishing boat. *It's not like it'll ever come to anything.* She tried to sound matter-of-fact, but her bitterness must've seeped through because Chico brushed his flank over hers.

Sorry, Rosie.

She body-checked him. *I told you not to call me Rosie.*

For once, he didn't tease her back, just nodded.

With a powerful pump of her tail, she shot forward. *Beat you to the dryads' islands.*

And she did beat him, because he let her win. She, in turn, taunted him for being too slow because otherwise, he'd keep shooting her those concerned looks and she just might break down and embarrass them both.

As Chico had predicted, the river was quiet. They cruised around the trio of islands inhabited by Alesia and her two sisters. The trees were bare, their branches stark against the cloudy sky. Alesia waved at them from high up in an oak tree, but her sisters didn't leave the camouflage of their forests.

The rest of the day dragged on, the only excitement coming when they had to rescue a human fisherman who'd fallen into the icy river. Rosana steadied his boat while Chico shifted to human and heaved the half-frozen man back onto its shallow deck. They pushed him back to a Grace Harbor marina and then returned to Rock Run, where she left Chico at the operations room to make their report to the *tenente*.

As Rosana headed back to her quarters, Chico's mate Jenny waved from the other end of the stone corridor. "Hey, girl! I've been looking all over for you."

Rosana smiled and waved back. The two of them had become good friends in the year and a half since the human had moved into the base. "What's up?"

"I want to know what you think about that piece I'm making for Lady Olivia." Jenny's jewelry was rapidly becoming famous in both the human and magical worlds, but she'd been shocked—and flattered—when Lady Olivia, Cleia's intimidating older cousin, had commissioned a pendant.

"Sure." Rosana fell in beside the human. Anything to take her mind off Adric and the mysterious wolf fada.

"And you can tell me all about your trip to Lewes." Jenny's grin was knowing. "You met *him*, didn't you?"

"Yeah." Rosana grimaced. "Someday, I'll tell you all about it. But not today, okay?"

"That bad?"

"Worse."

Jenny shook her head, sending her long black braid dancing. "Men are asses. Except when they aren't."

"Yeah. The thing was, it was...incredible. Except when it wasn't."

They exchanged a look and burst out laughing. Maybe Rosana's laughter was edged with pain, but it still felt good.

"Just keep it quiet, okay? I'd rather not get into it with my brothers."

Jenny traced an X on her chest. "Cross my heart."

"Rosana, Jenny—wait for me!" It was Merry Jones. They halted as she loped down the hall toward them.

Rosana still recalled the night Rui do Mar had brought the orphaned earth fada back to Rock Run. She'd been all big eyes in a narrow, sharp-chinned face, her body too thin, her arms and legs brown sticks. At fourteen, she'd filled out some, but she was still skinny, with long legs and a lanky, boyish body.

Merry bumped her shoulder against Rosana's. "What'cha doin'?"

"Going to Jenny's."

"Can I come? Please?"

"Sure." Jenny slung an arm around the teen's slim shoulders. "I could use your opinion, too. You have an artist's eye." Jenny had been teaching Merry basic jewelry-making techniques.

"You think?" Her thin, mobile face lit up.

"Yep. In fact, I think you're ready to start that bracelet for your mama."

"Seriously? I can give it to her for her birthday."

Jenny's big gray tabby was waiting on a ledge near her apartment. He leapt off the ledge and brushed between Merry's legs, meowing in welcome. Merry's animal was a jaguar, and Max had apparently decided that as the only other feline at Rock Run, she was a kindred spirit.

"There's my sweetie." Merry scooped up the cat and rubbed her face against his. He butted his head into the space between her jaw and throat, purring loudly.

Jenny chuckled. "I swear that cat is crushing on you."

The teenager gave one of her rare, slow smiles. "Well, I love him, too. He's a handsome cat, aren't you, *meu querido*?" She cuddled the tabby closer, and his eyes slit in bliss.

Inside, Jenny prepared Max a small plate of sardines in her kitchenette and set it on the stone floor. While the cat made short work of his dinner, the three of them traipsed into the workroom that Chico and Tiago had built for Jenny off the *sala*.

A sturdy table had been installed along one wall, with shelves above for supplies. Every spare surface was cluttered: gemstones in all the colors of the rainbow, boxes of crystal beads, spools of wire, scraps of metal. Wire cutters in three different sizes lay next to pliers and calipers, and a ceramic brick held a jeweler's soldering torch. An idea board was covered with photos and sketches, and a slit in the cavern ceiling provided light and ventilation.

"Lady Olivia gave me a pink diamond to work with." Jenny took an object wrapped in cotton from a shelf.

"I didn't even know there was such a thing as a pink diamond," Rosana remarked.

"Right? She liked that necklace I made for Cleia, so she brought me this pink diamond, told me to see what I came up with." Jenny unfolded the cloth to reveal a thumbnail-size diamond set off-center in a hammered gold sun with wavy rays.

"Wow." Rosana's eyes widened. "Just wow."

"Genius," Merry breathed at the same time.

Jenny beamed. "I just hope Lady Olivia thinks so."

"She'll love it. Even Lady Olivia can't find any fault with *this*. May I?" Rosana stretched out a hand, and when Jenny nodded, fingered the pendant.

"You know," her friend said, "Cleia would give you a pink diamond—you just have to ask. Or any gemstone. And I'd make you a pendant for free. You'd just have to pay for the materials."

Rosana hesitated, tempted, and then resolutely shook her head. "I know she would, but I'm trying to be more independent, and that means earning my own way. But thank you—that's really sweet of you to offer."

Her friend nodded. "If you change your mind, let me know."

"You know I will."

Jenny rewrapped the pendant, and they returned to the *sala* for snacks and girl talk. It was exactly what Rosana needed. For the next hour she didn't even think about Adric—at least, not more than once every ten minutes or so.

Then Chico returned and pulled his mate into a kiss that made her heart constrict with envy.

She was happy for them, she was. Really.

She just wanted what they had.

Chico released Jenny, and they all chatted for a few more minutes until Rosana rose to her feet, saying she had to go. "I promised to meet Isa for dinner."

Merry jumped up as well. "I'll walk you to your quarters."

Rosana blinked. Her apartment was on the base's opposite side, while the do Mar's apartment was just a few minutes away.

But she waited until they were alone before slanting Merry a look. "Something wrong?"

"Not here," the teenager said. They were in a large, well-traveled hallway filled with people on their way to the dining room. Taking Rosana's hand, she pulled her into a side corridor. "I want to know what's up. Something's wrong, I know it is. They barely let me outside these days—and my *papai* won't tell me anything."

Rosana hesitated. "I'm sure they have their reasons."

Merry folded her arms over her narrow chest, but her lower lip trembled. "Don't you treat me like a baby, too. You're the only one I can ask. My mom and dad just tell me not to worry, they're handling it. Even Uncle Jace won't tell me anything."

"Oh, *querida*." Rosana's heart contracted. "You know it's for your own safety."

Merry had been born during the Darktime to an earth fada mother and Prince Langdon's half-human son. She'd spent her early life on the run from both the earth fada and the night fae. After her parents had died, she'd been adopted by Dion's second, Rui do Mar, and his mate Valeria—until Adric and her uncle Jace had discovered where she was and tried to kidnap her back. That had been sorted out, with the earth fada agreeing to let her remain with Rui and Valeria while Jace received visitation rights.

But now she had to hide again, this time from her own grandfather. It didn't make sense. Langdon had never formally acknowledged his mixed-blood grand-daughter. No one had expected him to suddenly start asking about her.

"Well, I don't like it," Merry said. "All Mama will tell me is that it's better if the night fae believe I'm dead." She dropped her head, stared at her feet. "Why do they hate me so much?"

"They don't hate you, sweetheart." Rosana reached for her. Merry needed to be held. If she had a vision, so be it, although she was careful to touch only Merry's clothing.

Merry burrowed into her. "Yes, they do," she returned in a sad little voice. "Because I'm a mixed-blood. I don't really belong here. Or with the earth fada, either. And the night fae just want to kill me."

"Hey. You do belong here. Dion adopted you into the clan. Did someone say different?" Rosana pulled back, scowling. "Because if they did, I'll—"

"No." She hitched a shoulder. "Not really. But I'm a jaguar. I like to swim, but I can't spend hours in the water like the rest of you. I can't even enter through the water entrances—they're too deep for me."

"So? Neither can Jenny, and that doesn't mean she's not clan. And you have friends. What about Trina and Marco?"

"That's what Mama Ria says."

"And she's right."

"But Anabella says I'm just a freak. Not fae, not fada. Even my own clan doesn't want me." Her voice dropped to a ragged whisper.

Rosana's jaw worked. She was going to have a long talk with Anabella.

"That's not true," she told Merry. "Lord Adric *did* want you. He'd take you back into his clan in a heartbeat. And your uncle Jace wants you, doesn't he?"

A small nod. "But that's just them. There are others who think my mom should never have mated with a half-blood."

"You heard earth fada saying that? From Adric's clan?"

Another tiny, miserable nod. "Last year at the Midsummer Ball. They said"— she swallowed—"that I stink like a night fae."

Rosana's chest knotted with fury. "Well, fuck them. You have the scent of an earth fada, and maybe a little river fada, because you spend so much time with us. And you know what? It's their loss, because you're special. Any clan would love to have you as a member. Dion was saying just the other day how smart you are."

"Seriously?" Merry's hazel eyes were hopeful.

"Truth." Rosana touched her heart. "Cleia thinks so, too. And you're not only smart, you'll probably have a really cool Gift because you have so much fae in you." That fae blood had already made Merry one of the most beautiful teenagers in the clan.

"Yeah? You really think so?"

"I do. I really do." She ran a palm over the teen's electric black hair and was rewarded by a bashful smile.

"Thanks, Rosana."

"Anytime. You can ask me anything, all right? Because you're clan. And because I love you, just the way you are. Understand?"

She grasped Merry's hands—and stiffened at the vision that flashed across her retinas. A man's black eyes, and nothing else.

"Rosana? You okay?"

She squeezed her eyes shut, and when she opened them, all she saw was the younger girl's anxious face. "Yeah. It's...been a long day, that's all."

They continued walking. They were almost to Rosana's quarters when Merry asked, "Do you think my grandfather—the prince—could've found out I'm still alive?"

"I don't know. But Dion and your *papai* will keep you safe, no matter what—and Cleia wouldn't let him take you against your will."

Merry nodded, her expression troubled.

Rosana's skin prickled. "Why?"

"Because." Merry ran a hand over her nape. "Sometimes I could swear he's watching me."

~

ROSANA WAITED until she heard Isa's soft snores before easing her bedroom door shut. To ensure she wasn't interrupted, she propped a chair under the door handle before retrieving a small teak chest from beneath the bed. A bottlenose dolphin was carved on the lid. She traced its curving back, sadness pinching her heart.

The teak chest dated to when her parents had first come to America, a gift from her Irish granddad to his daughter Ula. The bottlenose carving was a reminder of her mom's sea fada roots. Dion had gifted the chest to Rosana on her sixteenth birthday, saying their mom would want her to have it.

Opening the lid, she took out a cobalt scrying bowl. As part of her training, she'd experimented with different modes of scrying—a mirror, polished lava, smoke, tarot cards, even a crystal ball—but not surprisingly, the best focus for her was a bowl of water.

Now she unwrapped the chamois cloth protecting the deep blue glass and set the bowl on a small table next to a pitcher of water.

She'd walked Merry to her own quarters, had waited while the teen told Rui and Valeria about Prince Langdon. But there wasn't much her parents could do beyond the close watch they were already keeping on their daughter. To protect Merry, Langdon had spelled her quartz so that no night fae could touch her without dying. Unfortunately, the prince had excluded himself from the spell.

But Rosana was a Seer. Maybe she could See something that might help Merry. And what about those black eyes she'd glimpsed?

She poured the water into the shallow blue bowl, and then sat cross-legged on a sheepskin rug, the bowl in her hands. She took several slow breaths, calming and centering herself, and then let her gaze go soft.

At first, all she saw was the water. Then her vision shifted somehow so that she saw her reflection instead. She kept breathing, slowly, evenly.

She pictured Merry, adding details as she'd been trained. The teenager's sharp, lively face. Her serious hazel eyes and her rare but contagious giggle. The wiry, exuberant curls. Her lanky body and love of bright colors.

Rosana's mouth curved. Merry was adorable, the little sister she'd always wanted.

Minutes passed with nothing happening. Her mind wandered.

She dragged it back, focusing on Merry with a grim determination. But although she conjured up a photo-perfect picture of her friend that would've pleased even Colm, that's all it was—a picture conjured up by Rosana. Not a vision.

She expelled a breath and straightened up. Maybe scrying just wasn't her thing. Not every Seer could scry, right?

"Discipline, Rosana, it's all about discipline—and belief in yourself. If you think you can't, then you can't. Belief is as important as skill."

Her head snapped back. She cast a guilty look around. She could've sworn Colm had 'ported into her room to remind her of Rule 3. But it was empty except for her and the scrying bowl.

She set her back teeth and glared into the water. "I'm trying," she growled as if the sardonic Irish sun fae was actually present, shaking his mane of blond hair reprovingly.

She'd disturbed the surface. She waited for the ripples to smooth out and then focused again.

The water in the bowl grew dark and still as a deep-jungle pool, and then she saw Adric. On his motorcycle in a shadowy forest, his tires making a single track in the fresh snow.

Her eyes widened. She'd never had such a clear vision when scrying. She squeezed her eyes shut, re-opened them. Adric was still there, driving through the snow.

Her breath hitched. Snow was predicted for later that night.

Suddenly the water shivered as if touched by a finger, and she saw Adric-the-cougar slinking through the snow-covered forest. He reached the edge of the trees, stared at the fog-shrouded grounds beyond. At first, she thought he was looking at a graveyard. But the tombstones were house-sized, with lush ivy vines snaking over fanciful gothic arches.

She'd never been to the New Moon Court, but she recognized it immediately. And Adric was on his way to it.

Rosana's heart stuttered. The water shivered again, and she became part of the scene, slinking with Adric through the forest. She felt the frozen earth beneath his paws, heard an owl's mournful call, scented the musk of a deer herd huddled against the cold. The rising sun glimmered a pale gold, and then was hidden by a fast-moving cloud.

Once again, the water in the bowl lurched and swooped. When it cleared this time, a tall fae was strolling around a pond on a path of white pebbles, his black head bare to the falling snow, a duster swirling around his long legs.

Her bowels iced. It was Prince Langdon, exactly as he'd appeared in her vision in December.

His head swung to where the cougar crouched, and then his gaze flicked to her. He turned.

The scene shrank in on itself until his face filled the scrying bowl. It was a poet's face—narrow, dark-eyed, incredibly beautiful. Tiny diamonds outlined his pointed ears, glittered in his winged black brows.

She gulped. His eyes narrowed, looked straight into hers.

He can't see you, she told herself frantically.

Then he smiled.

CHAPTER 15

The Factory was in an abandoned grocery on the west side. The sign outside still read Allen's Stop-and-Shop; it worked as camouflage, and suited Adric's sense of humor besides. After they'd gutted the place, there'd been plenty of space for the shop that Jace Jones had set up to test and manufacture the clan's quartz-based smartphones. When Adric entered Tuesday afternoon, the jaguar fada was already there, deep in conversation with his small team of quartz-crystal techs.

Jace turned to him. A tall, rawboned man, he had cropped black hair and the same serious hazel eyes as his niece Merry.

"Ric." A smile lit his face. "We have something to show you."

Jace and the three techs spent a few minutes bringing Adric up to date on their current projects, including the quartz mine on Rising Sun Fae land which was the clan's hope for turning the smartphone technology into a money-maker.

"We could have them in production by summer." Jace handed him a prototype made from the mine's high-quality quartz.

Adric fingered the smartphone. Durable and waterproof, one side of the quartz had been ground down to mirror-smoothness so the user could access the technology. "You'll be able to make enough for every adult in the clan?"

"Absolutely. With enough left over to start selling them to other clans."

"Impressive." Adric included the entire team in his nod of approval. "Keep up the good work."

Zuri and Marjani arrived as the meeting broke up. The four of them climbed down the ladder to the war room, a chamber carved out of the bedrock that had been magically soundproofed so they could speak freely, even refer to the fae by name.

They took seats around the round table that Adric had carved himself from a massive slab of granite. He looked around at his three remaining lieutenants. "You know why you're here. Dion do Rio came looking for me last night, seriously pissed off. A wolf trespassed on his territory—a large brown wolf."

"Luc." Marjani's face remained expressionless, but Adric scented her distress. She'd probably always feel guilty that Luc had accepted Blaer's *geas* to save her.

The wolf had loved her since they were both teenagers. The problem was, she'd never felt the same way.

Adric nodded grimly. "That's my guess. And if he's here, then so's Lady Blaer."

"But why would she send him to Rock Run?" his sister asked.

Zuri's jaw hardened. "To piss off both clans, of course. If she's really lucky, she'll set off a war between us and Rock Run."

"Wouldn't be the first time a night fae tried that," Jace muttered.

Adric exhaled and came to his feet. He felt like he was banishing Luc all over again, but Zuri was right. His lieutenants needed to know the full story about what had happened in Delaware.

"What I say next doesn't leave this room." He waited until the other three nodded before continuing, "It was Luc who tracked me to Lewes. He brought Blaer and another fae—a male—straight to the B&B. They came in after midnight and tore the place apart. It was sheer luck that I got out of there with my hide intact. And Rosana do Rio, too. You may as well know she was with me."

Marjani drew a sharp breath.

"Yeah," Adric said. "He's not to be trusted. He's completely under that fae bitch's control. We have to consider him one of them."

Zuri's dark brows lowered. "Fuck, Ric. You should've told us this immediately."

"Maybe. But there was a minute, right at the end. Luc and the fae were in the parking lot, and I was on the other side of the fence. I know Luc scented me. He could've fingered me then, but he didn't." Adric lifted his shoulders, let them drop. "I didn't want the whole clan to know."

Zuri swore. "He knows everything we do. The location of our dens, the Factory. Our secret tunnels. He even knows about this room."

"He can't get through the ward," Adric said. "Any of our wards. I made sure of that when I expelled him from the clan. But—"

"—he could bring Blaer to the Factory," Marjani said. "Or even your den. He might not be able to bring her inside, but all they have to do is wait outside for you to show up. And Blaer knows the secret incantation. If she gets close enough, she doesn't even have to force you to accept her *geas*. She can control you through your quartz."

Adric growled. "Let her fucking try. I was this close to her." He held up his index finger and thumb, the pads almost touching. "*This* close. But I had to let her go. Luc would've fought me and given her time to 'port out. And I would've had to kill him."

"Plus, you had Rosana to think about," said Marjani. "You did the only thing you could. But you can't let Blaer get that close again." She toyed with the smooth ivory handle of one of her daggers.

None of them paid it any mind. Marjani's blades were as much a part of her as her claws.

She scowled. "I don't like this. You have to increase your security."

"Jani. I can take care of myself."

By tomorrow, it wouldn't matter anyway. He'd be on his way to Virginia. But no one—especially his sister—could know that.

A small whetstone appeared in Marjani's other hand. She began sharpening the already keen-edged iron blade. "We could buy you a protection charm."

"We don't have the money, and you know it."

"But—"

"No. The best defense is to eliminate the threat."

Marjani compressed her lips and swiped the blade viciously over the whetstone.

Adric set his hands on the table. "Lady Blaer is up to something, and thanks to my asshole cousin Corban, she knows the secret of our quartz. It's time to take her out."

Zuri's smile was all teeth. He and Luc had been close friends. "I'm your man."

"Agreed. But take your time, assemble a team—the woman's powerful, and she's smart. I'll be damned if I lose anyone else to her. And before you do anything, ramp up our defenses. You and Jani both."

Marjani jerked her chin in assent.

"I'll let the clan know that the cubs aren't to go out alone, and that even the adults need to take care." His jaw set, because Gods, he hated to do this. "I'll also warn them that Luc can't be trusted. Anyone seen talking to him will answer to me."

Zuri fingered his soul-patch. "The wolves aren't going to like it. One day Luc's a hero for saving Jani, the next, he's bad news. If you don't tell people about

Lewes, they'll say it's just another example of how the cats have taken over since you became alpha."

Jace scowled. "Ric appointed two wolves as lieutenants. What more do they want?"

"Hey, don't shoot the messenger. I'm just saying it looks bad. And then there are your cousins," Zuri said to Adric. "Two out of three of them are dead."

"Thanks to me and Jani." Adric blew out a breath. "I know. It's damn convenient that out of Leron's immediate family, only Nash is left. A suspicious man might think we planned it that way."

And everyone knew Marjani's Gift was strategy.

Zuri moved a big shoulder. "Nash says himself that it's Corban and Kane's own fault they're dead. But you gotta admit it looks shaky."

"He's right," his sister chimed in. "And I have an idea. You need a new lieutenant—why not Nash?"

Adric sank back onto his chair. "Nash Savonett?" he asked, as if she could mean anyone else. "I don't know, Jani."

"He's a Gifted tracker," she returned, "one of our best, and he's backed you since day one. If he wasn't Leron's son, you probably would've considered him before now. And he's a wolf. It keeps the balance."

"She's right," said Zuri. "The lupines appreciate that you appointed me and Luc as lieutenants. After the way Leron treated you, you could've turned on the wolves, but you didn't. You brought us into your inner circle. But these last couple of years have set some of them off again—too many wolves have died."

"Because they attacked me and mine," Adric shot back. "Every damn one of them would be alive today if they'd accepted that *I'm* the alpha now. Not Leron, and not any of his sons."

Zuri spread his large hands. "I know that. Even they know that. But..."

Jace had been sitting back in his chair, silently observing. Now he leaned forward. "Nash has my vote. Keeping the balance is important, and the man is smart. Plus, he doesn't have the prejudices his brothers had. Take Evie's brother, Kyler. Nash has gone out of his way to be a friend to him—a human. He's been working with Kyler, showing him how to defend himself."

"So it's unanimous," said Adric. The clan wasn't a democracy—the final decision was his—but these three were his lieutenants precisely because he trusted their judgment. "I'll inform Nash that he's my newest lieutenant. But he's on probation for the next six months. If it works out, we'll make it official."

"Fair enough," said Zuri.

"Anything else?" Adric glanced around the table.

When the other three replied in the negative, he adjourned the meeting.

Marjani fell in beside him as they left the Factory. "I keep telling myself that Luc's not responsible, that he doesn't have a choice, but he *knows* what that bitch is capable of. If she'd captured you…" She shook her head. "It's like I don't even know him anymore."

He set an arm around her narrow shoulders. "It hurts."

Her chest heaved. "Yeah."

"You sure you're okay with Nash making lieutenant?"

"I wouldn't have brought it up otherwise."

"Even though his own brother was behind your—" He halted.

They didn't discuss the attack on her. At first, it had been because she wasn't talking to anyone but Suha, the clan's head healer. Then, as the months passed, he'd let it go. Some things were better left buried.

"You can say it—I won't break. Corban Savonett was behind my kidnapping. And—" she swallowed, then lifted her chin—"it was because of him I was raped by those bastards."

Dragging in a breath, he forced the words past the hot ball in his throat. "I'm sorry. So fucking sorry."

"Damn it, Ric." She jerked away to glare at him. "You've got nothing to be sorry for. It. Wasn't. Your. Fault."

He kept his gaze on where they were going so he wouldn't have to meet her eyes. Heavy gray clouds had blotted out the sun, bleaching color from the Formstone rowhouses that marched up either side of the street. It was going to snow later.

"I'm alpha. I should've known what was going down."

"Stop it." Marjani punched his shoulder. Hard. "Just stop, already. They fooled me, too. I thought Shania was my friend. I agreed to meet her at that bar. I was stupid enough to get drugged."

"You would never have been attacked if not for me. Corban targeted you because I was alpha. That's the only reason." He drew a breath between clenched teeth. "And I didn't even know until the next morning."

By then, she'd been given by Corban and his people to a den of sick river fada. They'd smashed her quartz, leaving her hurting and defenseless, and then proceeded to gang-rape her. She might have disappeared forever if not for Tiago do Rio, who'd been kidnapped along with her. Somehow do Rio had resisted the drug enough to fight back.

And Adric hadn't known until it was too late.

"It's over." She gave him a shake. "I need you to accept that. It's hard, I know." Her throat worked. She closed her eyes, took a deep breath. "But it's over, and I'm okay. And I'm working on putting it behind me. Because I will *not* let those motherfuckers ruin my life. But I can't if you're still beating yourself up about it."

"I'm sorry." He smoothed his palms up and down her arms. "I'll try, okay?"

"You do that." She opened her arms and he came into them.

And then they had their arms wrapped tight around each other, rocking back and forth. Adric's throat ached with unshed tears. He gulped them down. For the first time in forever, he let himself take comfort from his sister instead of giving it.

When she released him, her cheeks were wet. She wiped them away with the sleeve of her hoodie. She sniffed. "They're happy tears."

He eyed her doubtfully. "Yeah?"

"Yeah." She gave a watery chuckle. "Come to dinner tonight? Beau's cooking."

He managed to smile back, because that's what she needed from him. "In that case, I'm there." The bear shifter loved to cook, and his Louisianan mama had taught him well.

She gave him another hard hug and then they separated—her to meet up with Fane, him to inform Nash of his promotion to lieutenant.

His cousin could barely contain his excitement. Like Corban, he was tall and good-looking with close-cut black hair. But the resemblance ended there. Corban had been a tight-lipped, calculating man, while Nash had warm brown eyes and a ready smile.

"You won't regret it. You'll see." Nash stepped toward Adric, arms outstretched, and then hesitated, head cocked to one side to expose his throat. His wolf demonstrating its complete loyalty and trust.

Adric pulled him into a hug and gently bit the offered throat, acknowledging and accepting that trust. "You have to pass the trial period first."

"Don't worry." Nash nuzzled Adric's cheek, marking him and being marked. "I will."

Adric gave Nash's head a rub, just like when they were kids and Nash was the little cousin who idolized him. "You know what? I think you will, too. Report to Jani tomorrow. She'll bring you up to speed."

After that, Adric crisscrossed Baltimore. Checking in with the various dens. Spreading the word about Luc and the night fae. Reassuring the cubs, who'd picked up on the adults' tension. At least he could throw in the good news about Nash, too.

Doing what an alpha did, because his conscience wouldn't let him leave without making sure everyone and everything was as ready as possible.

∼

DINNER WAS A ROWDY AFFAIR. A dozen clan members squeezed around Jace's big plank table. They laughed and talked over one another, drank beer, passed bread and salad. Gorged themselves on Beau's truly excellent shrimp étouffée.

Beneath the table, Tigger bumped his head against Adric's leg. He scratched the cat behind his ears and watched approvingly as his sister devoured a good-sized helping of the shrimp étouffée.

Fane had taken the seat by Adric. He glanced over to see the other man watching Marjani, too, a smile on his narrow, good-looking face.

Fane turned his head toward Adric, and their eyes met.

Adric drew a breath. He'd accepted the other man into the clan for Jani's sake, but that didn't mean he was happy about it. Not only was Fane a quarter fae, he'd been one of King Sindre's envoys, a trusted member of the ice fae court. The blond mixed-blood was as wily as they came.

But Fane was proving useful. His wayfaring Gift meant he could slip in and out of places as well as the night fae, and as an envoy, he'd been inside all of the major fae courts—sun fae, ice fae, and most importantly, the night fae. As a sign of good faith, he'd drawn Adric maps of all three courts, with key buildings and rooms marked.

Fane leaned forward, letting his long blond hair curtain his face from Marjani. "I'll take care of her," he murmured. "Lady B will have to go through me to get her."

Adric kept his expression blank. "Oh?"

"Don't worry—Jani doesn't know for sure. She just suspects. She *is* a Gifted strategist, after all."

Fuck. "She can't know. No one can. I want your word on that."

"I won't lie to her."

"I'm not asking you to. Just keep your mouth shut."

Fane inclined his shiny blond head. "Then you have my word."

Adric took a gulp of beer. "Thank you. And not just for keeping your mouth shut, but for being the mate she needs."

From the other end of the table, Marjani regarded them with narrowed eyes. Fane winked at her.

"I'm the one who's thankful," he murmured, and then asked Horace to pass the hot sauce.

Adric blinked. The thick stew was already spicy enough to burn a hole in a man's stomach.

An evil grin split Horace's broad face. "You sure?"

Fane stuck out a hand and the cougar fada placed the bottle in it.

While Fane recklessly risked his stomach lining, Adric took a thoughtful bite of shrimp.

Good thing he'd already decided that tonight was the night.

If Marjani suspected something was up, then he had even less time than he thought. Because he was going alone. His sister had a mate now, a chance at real happiness.

No way would he let her risk that.

He'd failed her once, let those river fada get ahold of her. He wasn't going to fail her again.

Fane got up and took Marjani's plate, filling it with another helping of étouffée before Adric could.

Something tightened in his chest. He had to admit Fane had turned out to be a good, caring mate. His sister was a lucky woman.

Their brother-sister bond would never be the same...and that was how it should be.

But it was a bittersweet feeling, knowing that it was now Fane she turned to, not him.

By the time Adric left for his den, an icy rain was falling. Cursing under his breath, he headed across town with a ground-eating lope. He didn't scent Luc or Blaer—or any fae at all—but just in case, he intermittently used his quartz to cloak himself. The energy drain was too great to use it constantly unless absolutely necessary.

He zigzagged through the concrete and granite towers of the business district, circled the Inner Harbor. As he left the harbor behind, the streets emptied, becoming an industrial wasteland of warehouses and parking lots.

To the south was the Seagirt Marine Terminal, its hulking cranes like metal giants backlit against the night. There'd been a time right after he made alpha when the clan had been so poor that some of his men had hired themselves out loading coal at the nearby CSX railyard.

Adric himself had worked for the fae. He was a Gifted tracker. Smart, dogged and with that magical something that meant if he wanted to find you, you couldn't run far or fast enough. The fae were willing to pay stupid sums for his services. He'd poured the money back into his hungry, impoverished clan, making sure everyone was fed and clothed. The remainder had gone to developing the quartz smartphones.

He could leave for Virginia with a clear conscience, knowing the clan was in a much better place than when he'd taken over as alpha. That his sister was healing.

His only regret was Rosana. He slowed, pressed the heel of his hand to his heart, which literally hurt for her...a constant, low-level ache.

Shaking his head at himself, he shoved the hand in a pocket and picked up his pace again. A few minutes later, he entered a neighborhood of shabby rowhomes with worn marble stoops. A couple more turns and he was on his own street of small detached houses, half of them boarded up with the rest locked up tight for the night.

His neck itched. He rubbed it, looked around, inhaled deeply.

Nothing unusual. Still, that eerie feeling someone was watching tripped up his spine. Luc? Blaer? Or just one of Langdon's warriors, here to harass Adric?

He peered into the shadows. But if it was a night fae, he or she remained concealed. Just in case, Adric bared his teeth at the darkest corner.

Footsteps sounded behind him. He whipped around, hand going to the switchblade in his pocket.

A wild-eyed human kid aimed a handgun at his head.

Cat's balls. He really needed to clean up his neighborhood like Jace had.

He let go of his switchblade, raised his palms. "Easy, now."

"Your wallet." The kid's throat worked. He clutched the gun in two shaking hands. "Give me your w-wallet and ph-phone, and you won't get hurt."

"I don't think so." Adric didn't bother going clawed, just aimed a booted foot at the fool's solar plexus.

The kid wheezed and folded in on himself, dropping the gun.

Adric snatched it from the air before it hit the sidewalk. He opened the chamber and shoved the bullets into a pocket.

The human was on the ground, sucking air like a beached fish. Adric shoved his fangs into the would-be robber's face. The kid's eyes went flashbulb. Terror scented the air.

"Yeah." His mouth curved. "You messed with the wrong dude. Next time you rob someone, make sure he's not a fada. This is my territory, asshole. I see you around here again, and you're dead. Understand?"

The kid's head bobbed. He tried to speak, couldn't.

Adric nodded at the gun. "And I'll be keeping this."

The kid's breath finally whooshed in. "Yes, sir." Tears filled his eyes. "I...just needed something to eat. I—I'm hungry. P-please don't hurt me."

Adric hesitated. The kid didn't smell of alcohol or drugs. He was just a skinny teenager scared out of his mind. His quilted puffer jacket was a size too large and his sneakers a size too small.

And Adric could scent the truth in his words. The kid was hungry.

He shoved the gun into the pocket of his jacket. "What's your name?"

"Shawn."

"Well, Shawn." Adric picked him up by the scruff of his coat and set him on his feet. "You know Bruce's Creole Kitchen?"

"Yes, sir."

"Tell the cook that Lord Adric sent you. He'll let you work for food. If you're a hard worker, he might even give you a job."

The kid's thin face lit. Then his eyes narrowed. "You're not shitting me?"

Adric growled.

"S-sorry, sir. Okay. I will. Thank you, sir." The kid bobbed his head several times. Then he gulped. "*Lord* Adric? Fuck. I'm really sorry. I—"

"Get going," Adric suggested.

"Yes, sir." Shawn scurried back the way he'd come. When he reached the corner, he shot a look at Adric over his shoulder and then broke into a run.

Adric continued down the street. He was almost to his house when his nape prickled again. He heaved a breath.

Maybe he should've slept at Marjani's den after all.

Without breaking stride, he scanned the shadows. A human wouldn't have seen the woman leaning against the side of his house, but his cat detected her just fine. She wore a baggy hoodie and a knit cap pulled low over her forehead. But he'd know that long, curvy body anywhere.

CHAPTER 16

$\mathcal{A}$dric's heart kicked into gear. Hard, slow, and damn it, needy.

Rosana's back was to the brick wall, one leg bent and her foot on the bricks as if she'd been there a while. A small backpack was on the grass beside her.

What was she doing in Baltimore? And how the hell had she known which house was his? His den was two stories underground and warded against intruders, its location on a need-to-know basis only.

Slipping into an alley, he circled through the neighborhood so that he came out in the backyard behind his. He vaulted the chain link fence, landing behind his shed, and peered around the corner. Rosana had her head turned toward the street.

He gathered his muscles...and leapt.

By the time she swung around, he was on her. He pushed her face-first into the bricks and touched a claw to the soft underside of her jaw.

"What are you doing here?" he growled against her ear.

She turned her head sideways and tried to shove off the wall, but he thrust a thigh between her legs, pinning her in place with his body. Her fingers curled against the bricks, but her answer was as calm as if they were having a friendly cup of coffee.

"Not out here."

Her ponytail was against his cheek. The fresh meadow scent of it tangled his thoughts. Below, his pelvis pressed against her firm ass, her inner thighs warm around his leg.

The gods knew he was no saint. He couldn't help reacting to the suggestive position. Her breath hitched, and he knew she felt him hardening against her.

He scowled and increased the pressure of the claw, careful not to break the skin. He'd cut off his own hand before hurting her, but she didn't need to know that.

"How did you find out where I live?"

Her mouth twitched. "Nice to see you, too."

"Don't mess with me, love." He pressed her a little harder into the bricks. "I'm not in a good mood. Now, how did you find this house?"

She expelled a breath. "I'm a Seer, remember?"

"You had a vision that showed you where I live?" he asked, incredulous.

A jerk of her chin. "I saw the street name, anyway. And then I followed your scent to this house. I can't find the entrance to your den, though."

"It's protected by a *look-away* spell." He let out a breath, thinking. "Does anyone else know you're here? Your brothers?"

A short laugh. "You think they'd let me come down here alone?"

She had a point. Especially after Dion had gone out of his way to warn him away from her.

"Fine. Swear you won't give the location of my den to anyone else, and I'll let you in."

"I swear it," she replied without hesitation. "I'm not your enemy, Adric."

He retracted the claw and released her. She spun around, the sharp point of an iron stiletto aimed at his balls.

He raised a brow, impressed. Not many people could get close enough to pull a weapon on him. "Careful, love. You might damage my junk, and then neither of us will be happy."

A pissed-off snarl. "Threaten me again, cat, and I'll make you into a rug."

A rug?

He let out a startled chuckle—and grabbed her wrist, lightning-quick. He dug his thumb into a pressure point until she opened her fingers and released the knife. They both lunged for it, but he snatched it by the blade just before it hit the grass.

The iron seared his palm and fingers. His breath hissed in. It was like grabbing a hot poker. He quickly transferred the knife to his other hand, this time careful to touch only the mother-of-pearl handle.

He straightened, and they stared at each other.

Rosana's chest heaved. Blue eyes seared into his.

He forgot about his burned hand. He forgot that a river fada shouldn't be able to locate his den so easily, Seer or not. He forgot that in the morning he was leaving for Virginia.

And most of all, he forgot that Dion had warned him away from her.

All he knew was that Rosana was here, and he craved her with a hunger that ate at his insides. It felt like it had been two months, not two days, since he'd had her.

His jaw set. Because he did *not* need a distraction, tonight of all nights.

He shoved the stiletto at her, handle first. "Stay away from my den, and I won't have to threaten you."

She snatched it from his hand and slid it into her back pocket. "So." She reached for her backpack. "Where's your den?"

"This way." He closed his fingers around her upper arm and marched her around the back to the small brick hut that concealed his den's entrance. He'd never actually lived in the house, preferring instead to rent it out to the locals as a smokescreen. No one expected the Baltimore alpha to have a couple of drug dealers living above him.

He muttered an incantation, and the *look-away* spell lifted, revealing the heavy oak door that led down to his den. As he tapped his quartz to the door lock, Rosana jerked her head at the purple sportbike propped against his shed.

"What about my bike?"

"I'll put it in the shed." No one around here would touch it—they knew better, Shawn excepted—but there was no sense advertising she was here. "Don't move," he added as he crossed to the bike.

"I asked to come in, remember?"

But she obeyed, arms crossed over her chest and a scowl on her pretty face, while he locked the sportbike in the shed with his own motorcycle and then opened the heavy steel door to his den.

"After you," he said with a mocking wave of his hand. He reset the spell and followed her in.

They were on the landing at the top of the steps his dad had cut out of rock. Set into the rise of every other stair were quartz-powered amber lights. As they started down, the tiny lights glowed on, illuminating the carvings that his dad had chiseled into each step—a leaping manticore, a fierce griffin, a soaring dragon. After his dad's death, Adric had doggedly continued, working the stone with a combination of chisels and magic, until only the bottom few steps were still unadorned.

"Wow." Rosana shot him a look over her shoulder. "Who's the artist?"

He shrugged. "Me. And my dad."

"You're kidding." She crouched to trace the raised outline of a phoenix bursting into flames.

"My dad did the first four, and we did the next few together. Then things... changed, and he was always gone. He was a soldier, although he really wanted to be a stoneworker."

"You must miss him." Her voice was sympathetic.

He gave a hard swallow. "Yeah." His father had been one of the first slain, executed by his own brother, Leron, over some trumped-up charge. Adric and Marjani had been forced to watch.

"And your mom, too. I'm so sorry."

"It was a long time ago."

"Not that long. And you never really get over it."

"No," he agreed.

They exchanged a look. He recalled that until a few months ago, she hadn't known herself if her own parents were alive or dead.

And she was right, you never really got over the death of a parent. The wound scabbed over, but it never really healed. You just tried your damnedest to live your life the way they'd have wanted.

"I guess you know how it is."

She gave a jerky nod. "Sometimes I wonder if it's even true. It's hard to believe they're really alive, since I can't see or talk to them."

"It's true." He crouched to squeeze her shoulder. "Marjani spoke to your mom herself. She was fine, and so was your dad. They just have to serve out the terms of their *geas* and then they'll be home."

"I know." She grimaced and touched his arm. "But hey, I know I shouldn't complain. At least I'll see them again someday."

"Yeah." He glanced away.

She fingered the carving. "These are really beautiful. I don't know anyone who can work stone like this." She stood back up, and he rose with her. They were crowded together on the same step. She met his eyes. "You're not what I expected."

"It's just a hobby," he muttered. He set a hand on her lower back, urging her to continue down the stairs. "Now, get going. I still want to know what the fuck you're doing here."

But he'd lost control of the situation, if he'd ever had it.

Rosana acted as if she were an invited guest instead of a not-so-welcome trespasser, exclaiming over each carving as they continued down the two flights to his den. He had to admit, he enjoyed showing his carvings to her. They even discussed possible designs for the last few steps.

And when they entered his apartment she didn't feel like a trespasser. She felt right. Like she belonged there.

Her eyes widened as the amber sconces in the foyer glowed on. "Those are powered by quartz?"

He nodded.

"Cool."

He guided her into the living room and tossed his jacket on a chair. The gun clattered to the stone floor. Rosana didn't even blink, but his cheeks heated.

"It's not mine." He set it on the mantelpiece. "I took it off a human kid before he hurt himself."

"I saw. And I heard you send him to that restaurant for food. That was nice of you."

"Yeah, I'm a real philanthropist. So. Why are you here?"

A secretive little smile. "Maybe I just couldn't stay away."

Setting her backpack on the floor, she peeled off her gloves, then removed her knit hat and hoodie and dropped them on his jacket. She was all in black. No high-heeled boots this time; instead, she wore short moto boots. He couldn't help noticing how good her ass looked in the tight black jeans. Almost as good as her breasts in the ribbed sweater.

He swallowed. Hard.

She turned back and caught him looking. Their gazes snagged. It was her turn to swallow.

"I'm sorry about your hand." She reached for it and turned it over to view the damage, and for some reason he didn't shake her off. She clucked her tongue at the blisters forming on his palm and first three fingers. "You should soak it in salt water."

He pulled his hand from hers. "It's okay. The blade didn't even break the skin." If it had, the iron would already be poisoning his blood.

She rolled her eyes and muttered something about hardheaded men. "Come on. I'll prepare a salt water soak for you."

Bemused, he followed her into his kitchen and watched as she prepared a solution of salt and warm water. She set the bowl on the table and ordered him to sit. "Put your hand in the bowl."

Why not? He shrugged and obeyed, and then sucked in a breath as the salt bit into the wound. But within a few seconds, the pain eased. To help it along, he pulsed some energy from his quartz to the injury. He wasn't a healer, but he had a minor ability to heal. The blisters began to recede.

"Better?" She took the seat across from his.

He nodded and reluctantly tacked on a thanks. "Now, about why you're here—"

She gave him a sunny smile. "Aren't you going to offer me a drink?"

"Would you like a drink?" he said between his teeth.

"Yes, please. But don't get up," she said airily when he started to remove his hand from the bowl. "I can get it." She opened the quartz-powered cooling unit and peered at the nearly empty shelves. "You don't entertain much, do you?"

He set his jaw. "I wasn't expecting company. There should be a couple of beers, though. Or I can make coffee."

"I'd rather have juice."

He winced. "I'm not sure how fresh it is."

She pulled out a carton of orange juice, took a sniff and poured it down the drain. "I'll stick with water. What about you?"

"Water's good. The glasses are to the right of the sink."

She found two mismatched glasses, filled them with tap water and set one on the table before him. But instead of retaking her seat, she moved back into the living room, glass in hand, examining the amber quartz sconces, taking in his thrift-shop furniture. A second-hand couch. A coffee table he'd scavenged from a dumpster and repaired. The only newish item was the soft orange shag rug in front of the fireplace, purchased because his cat liked to warm itself at the fire.

He felt a curl of shame. He and Jani had furnished the apartment right after he first made alpha, back when the clan could barely manage to feed the women and cubs. Things had improved enough that he could've bought some new furniture, but why bother? Plus, it sent a message that, unlike his uncle, he wasn't enriching himself at his people's expense.

But compared with what Rosana was used to, his den must seem cramped, shabby. The Rock Run Clan was three times the size of his, with a huge base and hundreds of acres on the outskirts of Grace Harbor. Not only that, they were allied with Queen Cleia and her powerful Rising Sun Fae Clan.

Still, Rosana didn't seem disdainful, just curious.

Taking his hand from the water, he tentatively worked the fingers. The blisters had almost disappeared. He set the bowl in the sink and joined her in the living room.

She was examining the foot-high geode on his mantelpiece. On the outside, it appeared to be an ordinary gray rock, but he'd split it open to reveal the amethyst crystals inside.

She ran a finger over the reddish-purple crystals. "Amethyst is a type of quartz, isn't it?"

"Yeah." Not many laypeople knew that, though. "You work with crystals?"

"A little. I study with a fae Seer. He had me try different crystals to see if any of them amp up my Gift. Amethyst, especially. He says it helps promote balance, calm, peace." Her mouth curved in a wry grin. "In my opinion, he's the one who needs it. The man's an arrogant pain-in-my-ass. But he knows his stuff—I'm already getting better at controlling and directing my visions."

"Did the crystals work?"

"Not really."

She moved to a basket of quartz crystals on the mantel that he kept as an emergency stash for the clan and fingered another amethyst, a six-sided chunk of purple that faded to almost white at its points. "Pretty." She held it up to the light.

"Keep it."

"Really?" A smile lit her elfin features.

"Yeah." He moved forward, closed her fingers around it. "I found it myself— it's a special, high-quality quartz with a strong internal energy. Maybe you've just been working with the wrong crystals."

"Thank you." She carefully pocketed it.

He remained close to her. Breathing her in. Taking in every detail from the jet-black lashes fringing her eyes to her lush lower lip to her slightly pointed chin.

A strand of hair had escaped her ponytail. He brushed it back behind her ear. "That must be a tough Gift to have. My clan had a Seer, but my uncle ordered her to remain silent when she didn't See what he wanted her to."

Her pretty mouth twisted. "Everybody thinks they want to know the future, but they don't—not really. And even when you tell them what you See, they do what they wanted anyway."

"Like me."

"Like you." She met his eyes, and he knew they were both thinking of her prophecy.

"We always have free will," he reminded her.

"I know." She sighed and moved away. "It's okay? Your hand?"

He blinked. "My hand?" He glanced at his injured limb. "It's fine."

"Good. Because you'll need it when you leave."

His heart thumped. "When I leave?" he repeated neutrally.

"For Virginia," she said, as if she was inside his head. Those ocean-colored eyes narrowed thoughtfully. "And soon, I think. Maybe even tonight."

CHAPTER 17

The stare that Adric turned on Rosana made her go very still.

Time had run out. A terrible urgency vibrated in her body, banded around her chest. She was convinced he was leaving for New Moon—soon.

And Langdon *knew.*

He prowled closer. *Deus,* he was beautiful, even with his face dark with suspicion. His gold-tipped hair was damp from the rain, his jaw shadowed with stubble. His long-sleeved T-shirt clung like paint to his body, and cargo pants hung low on his hips.

But it wasn't just his looks. It was the way he moved, the sexy growl of his voice, his aura of power.

"What do you know?"

She moistened her lips. This man had killed his own uncle for the good of the clan. She needed to remember that. "Nothing for sure. But I Saw something new."

"What?"

"You, alone in a forest. On your motorcycle." She closed her eyes to better picture it. "There was fresh snow on the ground. And then suddenly, you weren't on your motorcycle, you were a cougar instead. Staring at the night fae court. And Adric, the prince Saw you. He *knew* you were there."

"Did you tell anyone?" He was a foot away, his metallic brown eyes boring into hers.

That he'd even ask hurt. But she shrugged like she didn't care. "Who would I tell?"

"So you're here to try and stop me." He exhaled. "God's cat, Rosana. Enough already. Nothing you can say will change my mind."

"I'm not here to change your mind."

His eyes narrowed. "No?"

"No." She took a deep breath. "I'm here because I'm going with you."

He fingered her ponytail, so close the heat of his body licked at hers. "Are you?"

"Yes." She lifted her chin. "You need my help."

"What did I say in December when you told me that? And again last Sunday? Oh, yeah." He leaned closer, his breath hot against her face. "I said, 'No. Fucking. Way.'"

She gazed back steadily. She'd expected this. Colm had even warned her. It was the Seer's Dilemma: You could plead, argue, demand, but if someone was determined to stick to their chosen path, there was nothing you could do short of locking them up.

But damn, it was hard.

Because Adric *had* to take her. Everything in her screamed that she was right. Not just her Gift, not just a gut feeling, but her whole self.

She set a hand on his chest. Maybe she was going about this all wrong. The man was an alpha to his core, and when it came down to it, an alpha always put the cubs first.

"There's something you don't know—we just found out ourselves. The prince has been watching Merry. He has the farsight."

His head angled in that feline way. "You're sure?"

She nodded. "She feels like he's watching her, and we believe her."

Adric swore. "So he knows she's still alive?"

"He must. Dion tried to put him off, but he must've found out somehow."

Adric stepped back, shook his head. "Maybe she's imagining it. Jace told me she's been edgy, worried that the prince might kidnap her—or simply demand that Dion hand her over."

"He can demand all he wants. Dion would never give her to the night fae. And she's not imagining it—I Saw the prince myself." Rosana gulped and rubbed her upper arms. "And I'm pretty sure he Saw me."

Adric tensed. "What do you mean, the prince Saw you?"

"In my scrying bowl. I thought maybe I could See something to help Merry, and suddenly he was there in the bowl."

"You're sure it was him?"

She nodded. "I've seen him a few times at Rising Sun. Never up close—Cleia made sure of that. But he's not a man you forget—tall, with black hair and pointed ears, and diamonds outlining his brows and ears." She traced her outer ear with a fingertip. "Beautiful, the way a cobra is, so that you can't look away, even though you know it thinks you're prey."

"That's him, all right." Adric raked a hand through his hair, leaving the spikes sticking every which way like a furious cat. "Gods. How could you let him See you?"

She scowled back. "I didn't mean to."

"And you want to come with me? The night fae are happy enough to play with a fada. But a fada Seer? A young, beautiful fada Seer? The bastard must be salivating like a wolf over a fawn. If he captures you, you're fucked."

"So I won't let him know I'm with you." Because yes, Colm had warned her that the night fae got a special charge from tormenting a Seer, but it was a risk she was willing to take. "I'll stay out of sight, disguise myself somehow."

"What if he Sees you? You just told me the man has the farsight."

"I'll take my chances. He can't be looking all the time—no one can. And what about Merry?"

"She's safe enough as long as she stays inside Rock Run's wards. Hell, you have a fae queen on your side. Can't she do something?"

"I just found out tonight, and the queen wasn't at Rock Run. But Rui and Valeria know. Still, from what I've heard, it's almost impossible to block someone with the farsight from viewing you. There's nothing *to* block. The person isn't really there—it's like trying to stop a ghost from walking through a wall."

"Fuck." Adric clenched his fists. "So Merry has to put up with that prick watching her without her permission?"

"Unless we stop him."

"Rosana." Her heart sank at his hard tone. He was going to say no.

"Thanks for the intel," he continued, "but I can't take you with me."

"So you are going."

He lifted a shoulder, let it drop.

"But why do you have to go alone? That's the part I don't understand. Take me—or some of your people."

Adric's face closed up like he'd slammed a door. "Trust me, I've figured every angle, and this is the only way. And before you ask—I've tried to lure the prince to Baltimore. It doesn't work. He never comes without at least two bodyguards. No, I have to go to him—catch him alone."

She grabbed his shoulders. "But don't you see? That's just what he wants. He *knew* you were in the forest. You're heading straight into a trap."

He gently set her away from him. "I'll follow you until you're back in Rock Run territory. You shouldn't be down here after dark—not alone. Here." He thrust her hat and hoodie at her.

She batted the clothes away. "Will you listen to me? He. Knows. You're. Coming. If he has the farsight, then maybe Merry isn't the only one he's been watching. Maybe he's been watching you, too."

He just sighed and pushed the hat and hoodie at her again.

She snatched them and stared at him, hands fisted in the material, angry and defeated.

She took a calming breath. Time to switch tactics.

"What's the hurry?" She dropped the clothes on the chair and stepped closer. "No one knows I'm here."

By the time she'd decided to go to Baltimore, Isa had been fast asleep. Rosana had scrawled a note of explanation and then slipped out of the base. By the time anyone knew she was gone, she'd be on her way to Virginia with Adric.

Or at least, that had been the plan.

Adric's throat worked. "It's late, Rosana. I'm going to bed." But he didn't move away.

"Okay." She unwrapped the leather tie around her ponytail, tossed it onto the hoodie. Her damp hair tumbled around her shoulders.

His gaze tracked her movements. "Alone." It was more a growl than a word.

She slid her hands up his chest and out to his shoulders. Beneath the cotton shirt, he was all hot, smooth muscle. "You said yourself, it's not safe for me to go back tonight."

A muscle jerked in his jaw. "Did I say that?

"More or less." She lifted onto her toes to nibble his earlobe.

His breath hitched, but his arms stayed at his sides. "Fine. You can sleep in Marjani's old room."

"I'd rather be in your bed." She tongued the outside edge of his ear.

He groaned. "Your brother should've turned you over his knee when you were a cub."

Her mouth twitched. "How do you know he didn't?"

"I know."

"Adric?" She trailed kisses down his jaw, traced his full lower lip with the tip of her tongue. "Kiss me, you stubborn ass."

His body went taut, and then with a muttered curse, he hauled her up against him, his lean, powerful frame pressed to hers from breast to thighs. She had time to draw a breath and then his mouth was on hers.

Need jolted through her. She eagerly opened to him. His tongue swept inside, tasting every corner. She sucked on it, rocking her pelvis against his. He was hard, so hard, and she felt a thrill of triumph.

Until he dragged his mouth from hers and set her a foot away. "I'll show you your room."

"My...room?" She blinked rapidly, a little stupid from that kiss.

He guided her down the hall. "Bathroom's here, and you can sleep there." He pointed across the hall to a cozy bedroom with warm amber lighting and a colorful quilt on the bed.

She glanced around, dazed. "But I thought—we're not going to...?"

"No."

She swallowed her hurt. "You said that if I wanted you, I could have you. That we'd just have to sneak around. Well, here I am." She spread her arms wide. "Ready to sneak."

A shake of his head. "Not tonight, Rosana."

She brought her arms back to her sides, tilted her head. "I scare you, don't I?"

"Scare me?" A mocking smile curled his mouth.

"Yeah. You're afraid because you want me too much. I make you lose control, and you don't like that."

His eyes sparked blue. His primal growl set her spine tingling.

She took a step back before she realized it.

"You want this?" His body crowded hers, backing her to the wall next to the bathroom. "Fine. I hate to leave my women...unsatisfied." He slapped his hands to the stone on either side of her head.

She slit her eyes at him. "Your *women*? You *filho da puta*—"

"Shut up," he said gently, and captured her outraged gasp with his mouth.

His kiss this time was rough, demanding. Arousal jolted through her. He kept his mouth on hers, pressing her into the unforgiving stone. His heat surrounded her, his earthy male scent filled her nostrils. He didn't let up until she was clinging to him, knees weak.

He tore his mouth from hers, pressing hot kisses to her face, her neck, while she gulped in oxygen.

"Is that what you want?" he ground out. "A hard fuck?"

Somehow, she found the energy to straighten her legs and push him away. "Go. To. Hades. I am not just one of your women."

He grabbed her wrists and pressed them to the wall above her head. His burned hand was barely marked. She had time to think that he healed awfully fast, even for a fada, and then he was kissing her again.

Soft, sweet kisses that slid through her blood like wine.

She was lost. She could fight him when he was rough—maybe—but how do you fight tenderness from the man you want with everything you are?

She sucked on his tongue, drawing him deeper. His dick was a hard bar against her lower belly. She rubbed her mound against it, desperate to ease the ache between her thighs.

He tore his mouth from hers, took a jagged breath. "You're right."

"I am?"

"You're not just one of my women."

"Oh." She remembered that she was still pissed off and curled her lip. "Well, fuck you anyway."

She tried to wrench her hands free, but he easily kept them where they were, stretched above her head. And damn if that didn't make her hot, which just made her fury increase.

"Let me go." Her glare should've reduced him to a smoking pile of ashes. "*Now.*"

He nipped her lower lip. "I'm sorry, okay? It was an asshole thing to say."

"Yeah, it was."

"Forgive me?" A sheepish smile, but she caught the glint in his eyes.

Her lips twitched, but she continued glaring.

"I'd go down on my knees and beg," he murmured, "but I think you'd rather I did this…"

Transferring her wrists to one hand, he jerked her shirt up. Strong fingers cupped her through her purple exercise bra, sending another bolt shooting through her.

She arched her back against the wall and bared her teeth.

Daring him. Challenging him.

Somehow, this had become a game, and she was more than happy to play. "You'll have to do better than that. And I'd love to see you on your knees. Begging."

A dark chuckle. He squeezed her nipple, a little too hard. "But I'd rather hear *you* beg. Tell me, Rosana." He pinched her nipple. "Tell me you want a good, hard fuck."

Her smile was slow, knowing. If he thought he could scare her off, he was mistaken. She was a fada female. Her animal reveled in the rough play, understood it meant her male's need matched hers.

She lifted onto her toes to lick the seam of his lips, enjoying how he went taut. How his heart kicked into a pounding rhythm that matched her own.

"Yeah," she said against his mouth. "That's exactly what I want."

CHAPTER 18

$\mathcal{A}$dric's vision hazed.

That's exactly what I want.

He crowded Rosana against the wall. Drowning in her. The breast filling his hand. Her scent in his nostrils, fresh and clean as rain. The needy moans she made when he rocked his pelvis against hers.

He'd tried to be good. Tried to send her away. If she refused to go, well, he wasn't a fucking saint.

Besides, it wasn't safe for her to be out alone. Not tonight. The hours between dusk and dawn were when the night fae hunted. Better she stay with him until morning.

And yeah, he was grasping at straws, but tough shit.

Her tongue flicked at his closed mouth. He dragged in a breath, picturing what else she could do with that hot little appendage.

For an almost-virgin, she was sure catching on fast. He loved that she felt comfortable enough to challenge him. His cat adored a good game.

"*Ah-dreek.*" A husky murmur against his lips. "Kiss me back."

"Rosana..." He squeezed his eyes shut, struggling to remember why this was a bad idea. Why he should boot her sexy ass out of his den.

But he could barely recall his own name, and somehow his hand was on her other breast now, pinching that nipple into hardness beneath the purple stretchy-thing she wore.

She nipped his lips. "Kiss me."

Hunger crashed through him. He wanted, no *needed*, to spend this one last night with her.

Langdon had to be taken out. Marjani would never be safe otherwise. And he'd be damned if he'd let the prince tear Merry from the only family she remembered to raise her in the dark, twisted world of the New Moon Court.

When he left this time, not even his sister would know. Because she'd never let him go alone, and the plan called for one man—a quick, surgical strike. The problem was getting back out again after he'd made the kill. Frankly, he didn't expect to return.

Then here came Rosana, offering herself to him. And gods, he wanted her. Craved her more than life itself.

She wasn't just one of his women.

She was the only woman.

He released her to strip off her shirt and bra. The silver charm bracelet got tangled in the shirt sleeve and gave him a slight shock, so she removed it and pulled off the shirt and bra herself, shoving the bracelet into her pants pocket.

Meanwhile, he dragged off his own shirt, and then pressed her to the wall again. Her nipples were hard and aroused against his bare chest.

The knit cap had protected her hair from the rain. Only the ends were damp, curling wildly around her face. He filled his hands with her glossy tresses and brought his mouth to hers.

She made a sexy sound low in her throat and gripped his head. Heat leapt between their bodies, like they were kindling and someone had set a match to them.

They kissed each other, hungry and unrestrained, both their animals awake, greedy. Devouring each other's mouths. Raining kisses over each other's faces. Grinding their hips against each other.

His fangs pricked out of his gums. He drew back, wary of hurting her, but she just smiled and pulled him back to run her tongue over the tips.

Her hands were on his waistband, undoing the button and streaking inside. He'd gone commando, and she gave a hum of satisfaction before closing cool fingers around his cock.

His eyes rolled back in his head. He groaned and reveled in the squeeze and slide of her fingers.

She was right, he was a little afraid of how he was with her. Only with Rosana did he forget he was Lord Adric, an alpha with an entire clan depending on him. With her, he was just Ric Savonett. A man with his woman.

Grabbing for the last shreds of his control, he caught her wrist, stopping her.

For the first time, she looked unsure. "You don't like that?"

"I like it fine." He crouched to unbuckle her moto boots, tapped the right boot. "Lift your foot." When she obeyed, he removed first that boot, then the other one, slipping off her socks as well. Rising back up, he swung her into his arms. "But I want to get horizontal with you."

"Oh." Wrapping an arm around his neck, she smiled into his eyes. "So now you're asking."

"I'm not asking."

Her chuckle drew an answering smile from him. He realized he did a lot of that around her—smiling. They were still grinning at each other when he set her on her feet in the bedroom.

Their smiles faded, and they stared at each other. He didn't know what Rosana saw, but he saw a woman coming into her full beauty. Wavy blue-black hair tumbled around a heart-shaped face. Her nipples were a dusky rose, her waist a taut indentation above softly curved hips, and her skin the color of rich, warm cream.

Her chest heaved. "Adric?"

He traced a fingertip around each high, flawless breast. "I like how you say my name. *Ah-dreek*."

Her mouth edged up. "*Aa-dric*," she said with perfect American pronunciation. "I just like how it sounds in Portuguese better."

He huffed a laugh. "You're such a bad girl."

"Bad girls have more fun."

"Do they? Let's see..." Bending his head, he gave each of her nipples a hard suck. Her arms came around him, one on his back, one holding his head to her breasts.

For a few heartbeats, he allowed himself to remain there, cradled against her body. Just breathing her in.

His shifter senses picked up her pounding heart, but that was only fair, because his heart was beating just as hard.

"Definitely more fun," he managed to murmur.

He undid the button of her jeans, slipped a finger inside. She opened her legs a little as he teased the edge of her panties.

A fine quiver raced over her skin—and something inside him melted. Something so hard and tight and hidden, he hadn't even known it existed.

He felt sad and angry at the same time, that this was probably the last night they'd ever share. But it was one more night than he'd expected, and he was determined to make it good for her.

The amber sconces had glowed on when they entered the bedroom. He snapped his fingers and they dimmed to a warm, candlelight yellow.

Guiding Rosana to the bed, he pulled down the quilt. She sat on the mattress and he drew off her jeans. Her panties were the same purple as her bra, and damp with her excitement. Sliding them over her hips and down her legs, he dropped them on her jeans and then knelt on the floor before her.

He nudged her thighs apart. Her sex was a slick, rosy pink. Using his thumbs to open her, he swiped his tongue up the center.

Her breath hitched. She gripped the edge of the bed.

He raised a brow. "More?"

A jerky nod.

"Like this?" He licked her again, and again. Swirling his tongue around her clit, then sucking it into his mouth. Feasting on her. Inhaling the wild, musky fragrance that was Rosana.

When she fell back on the quilt, eyes closed and thighs clenching around him, he lifted her feet onto his shoulders and slipped a finger inside her.

"Yes..." Tiny muscles tightened around him. "Oh, Goddess..."

"That's it," he said against her clit. "Come for me, bad girl."

He ruthlessly sucked and tongued her until she was begging and pleading with him to come inside her. "Not yet," he said against her sex. "I want you to come for me first."

"Please," she rasped—and then arched her back and came with a low, animal sound.

He crawled up her body. Her eyes were closed, the lashes thick ebony crescents, her mouth turned up in a replete curve.

"I think I like being bad."

"You're very good at it," he returned, straight-faced.

Her smile increased. "I am, aren't I?"

Amusement rumbled in his chest. "But I bet you could get even better with practice." Rolling on a condom, he set his mouth to the tender underside of her throat.

"Oh, yeah," she said on a moan. "Lots and lots of practice..."

Her arms came around him. Their scents mingled, hot and aroused. She widened her thighs, making space for him.

He settled into that warm, welcoming place. Not entering her, but it still felt like coming home.

Be mine. I want you. Always.

He didn't say it. Fada mated for life. If he mate-claimed Rosana and then died in Virginia, she'd likely never mate again.

He'd seen how his mom had been after his dad's death. She'd tried to keep it together for him and Marjani, but she'd stopped caring whether she lived or died.

Rosana was too young to spend the rest of her life alone. At least this way, she had a chance at happiness. Kids.

Even if the thought of her with another male made him want to smash something.

Rosana smiled up at him, her eyes midnight-blue stars, her full lips kiss-swollen.

His throat constricted. "You're so fucking beautiful."

Her smile increased. "Yeah?"

"Yeah. Beautiful...and hot." Holding her gaze, he reached down and opened her, and then entered her in a slow slide, groaning as she closed around him like a hot fist.

He gave her an openmouthed kiss, and then rested his cheek against hers and began to move.

"Yes. *Deus*, yes." She wrapped her limbs around him.

Gods, he loved her. It wasn't just that she was his mate. He loved how she smelled, how she moved. How she was so damn open to him, in a way that had nothing to do with sex. He even loved her stubborn insistence on doing what she thought best.

"More." Her heels dug into the backs of his thighs, urging him on. "I need more."

He slowed even more, and she whimpered. "*Adric*."

"Trust me," he murmured against her ear. "This way is better. We don't want to rush things."

"No..." Her head moved from side to side against the pillow.

He pulled out.

"No!" Her hands came to his hips, urging him back to her. "Stay. Don't leave me."

He nipped her plush lower lip. "You'll like this, you'll see."

He turned her over, helped her up onto her knees. She blinked at him in surprise over her shoulder, so damn cute his heart contracted. Then understanding dawned and she came down on her forearms, her wild raven locks spilling over one silky shoulder.

He smoothed his hands over her ass. It was perfect: round and smooth, a luscious fruit that he wanted to lick, bite.

Own.

He played with her ass for a while, giving her light smacks, slipping his fingers into the slick, warm cove beneath to tease her. He even scraped his teeth over her soft skin until she was begging and pleading with him to come back inside her.

He took her by the hips and entered her with a firm thrust that made her moan his name.

"That's it," he told her. "Take it, bad girl. *My* bad girl."

He reached around her to play with her heavy breasts as he slid his cock in and out of her. Pleasure gripped him by the scruff of the neck. His nerves were heated, sensitized.

"Touch yourself."

"Oh." She gave him another adorably startled look.

He gently bit the turn of her neck. "You heard me."

Her hand slid down between her thighs. The fingertips grazed the root of his dick and he hissed with the pain/pleasure of it. He put his hand over hers, guided her to tease her plump little clit.

She groaned and pressed her ass into him.

"That's it. Make yourself come, angel. I want to feel that hot pussy squeezing around me."

The cougar surfaced, reveling in this most primal of mating positions.

So tight. So wet. So fucking hot.

He wanted to pound into Rosana, lose himself in her slick heat, but he also wanted this to last. For minutes, hours...as long as it took. Until she knew exactly to whom she belonged.

So he gritted his teeth and grasped her hips, setting a firm, steady rhythm until she keened out his name and constricted around him.

"Please, please, please..."

Flames streaked up his spine. His balls drew up, tight and hard.

At some point, she'd stopped touching herself. Reaching around her, he circled her clit with two fingers until she arched her back and with a little scream, went the rest of the way over.

He gave a few hard thrusts and followed her into the fire. Emptying himself into her until he had nothing left.

For a long minute, he stayed inside her, chest heaving, and then he somehow summoned the energy to withdraw from her. Flopping onto his back, he pulled her into his arms. She nestled against him, head on his shoulder. He dragged the quilt over them both and dozed for a few minutes before rousing himself for a quick trip to the bathroom.

After that, he didn't remember anything else until she left the bed an hour later to use the bathroom herself. When she rejoined him under the covers, she cuddled close, combing her fingers through the crisp dark hair on his chest.

His larynx vibrated in contentment.

She chuckled. "You're purring."

His mouth curved. "I'm a cat, love."

"I like it." She propped herself on an elbow to smile down at him. "You'll have to show me your cougar. I'll bet he's beautiful."

The purr increased in volume. Inside, the cat preened itself.

"He thinks so," Adric said dryly and tucked her into the crook of his elbow. "And yeah, he'd love to show himself to you."

He didn't add that it would probably never happen. For these few hours, he didn't want to think about what lay ahead, just enjoy being with her.

She resumed petting him, and his eyes closed. He hadn't expected to get much sleep his last night in Baltimore, but the sex had wrung him out in a good way.

He was drifting in that warm, comfortable place between waking and sleep when she murmured his name.

"Mm?" he replied without opening his eyes.

"There's something I've been wondering."

"Yeah?" he asked warily.

She traced a finger down his sternum. "You don't have to answer."

His wariness increased. He opened his eyes. "Just ask."

"Why did you kill your uncle?"

He went motionless. Even after all these years, the thought of Leron Savonett could still fill him with a murderous rage.

The hand on his chest stilled. "It's okay if you don't want to tell me."

He *didn't* want to tell her, but he wasn't surprised she'd asked—only that she'd waited this long.

"Because he needed killing," he said in a hard voice.

"I see."

"But what you really want to know is why I didn't challenge him for alpha in a fair fight."

A short silence. "Yeah. I guess I do wonder about that."

His teeth clenched. He put her away from him and sat up. "I know what your brother says. That I have no honor, no respect for tradition. That I murdered my own uncle in cold blood. Well, Dion knows *nothing*."

She sat up, too, the quilt clutched to her breasts. "But I'm not my brother. Tell me. Make me understand."

He eyed her. It occurred to him that this was his chance to push her away for good. To make her leave and never look back.

"Well, everything you heard was true. I lured my uncle Leron into a back alley and slit his throat because I wasn't sure that if I challenged him, I'd win."

She flinched. He waited for her to throw off the quilt, announce she would sleep in the other room after all.

But instead, she took his hands. "Oh, Ric. I know that. But that doesn't tell me why. Because I know you had a good reason. You *are* honorable, and your clan is so much better off ever since you became alpha."

He looked down at their clasped hands. So much for scaring her off.

The woman fucking *believed* in him.

And he found himself explaining further, something he never did.

"He...went after people I loved. He guessed that I'd grow up to challenge him, so he was especially hard on my friends. It got so I was afraid to even talk to someone, because they might end up locked in a cell—or dead. And it wasn't an easy death."

She squeezed his fingers. "Oh, Adric. I'm so sorry."

"So fuck honor. The man needed to die, and I was the only one who could take him out."

"You did the right thing."

"Not according to most of the world."

"Then they're wrong," she said fiercely.

"Maybe. But right or wrong, I'd do it again in a heartbeat."

He reached for her. He was done talking about his uncle. She had a red abrasion on her jaw—whisker burn.

"I hurt you." He lightly touched the mark. "If I'd known you were coming, I would've shaved."

"I don't mind." She captured his hand, held it against her face. "I kind of like it."

He leaned in to brush a kiss over the reddened skin. She turned her face so that he kissed her full on the lips instead, her mouth open, welcoming, as if he hadn't just admitted to breaking one of the fada's most sacred traditions.

"Me, too," he said. "I like seeing my mark on you, having you carry my scent." And that gave him an idea. He got out of bed and removed the amethyst quartz from her jeans. "I'll be right back."

He returned with the amethyst secured by a leather cord. The quilt had slipped lower, exposing her breasts. He dropped the cord over her head and settled the purple chunk of quartz between her cleavage.

"Thank you." She clutched the pendant with a starry-eyed look that made his heart clenching uncomfortably. "I love it."

"It's not much." Still, he liked seeing his amethyst there, over her heart.

"It is to me." She tugged on his hand. "C'mere."

"Is this where you show your gratitude?" He traced those pretty globes with a finger, teased the nipples into points.

A huff of laughter. "I thought it was a gift."

"Everything has a price." He crawled over her, pressing her back onto the pillows.

"And if I don't want to pay?" Sapphire eyes dared him.

He dipped his head to suckle a dusky nipple. "Then I'll just have to convince you it's worth it."

CHAPTER 19

$\mathcal{M}$arjani unlaced her combat boots and set them on the floor, frowning.

What was up with Adric? He'd acted odd all day. Calling meetings, visiting all the dens. At supper, he'd been almost sentimental, telling stories about when they were children, and then later, he'd actually pulled her aside to say how happy he was to see things with Fane were working out.

And when she'd boxed up some shrimp étouffée for him, he'd turned it down. Her brother never turned down food. The man hated to cook.

If she didn't know better, she'd think he was leaving town. But he wouldn't go anywhere without informing his second, would he?

Fane wrapped his arms around her from behind and kissed her nape. The jagged gold half-heart that hung from his neck pressed against her spine. She wore the other half—his mate gift to her—on a leather cord along with her quartz.

Long, clever fingers teased her nipples. "Did I tell you how hot you look in this tight little shirt?"

Pleasure slid down her spine. She told herself that Adric wouldn't do anything in the next few hours, and turned in Fane's arms.

"I don't believe you did." She threaded her fingers into his silky blond hair and heaved a sigh. "Mate with a man, and he starts taking you for granted."

He had the most gorgeous summer-blue eyes, made even more stunning by the dark brows and lashes framing them. Now the blue heated. "Oh, I'll take you all right."

Swinging her into his arms, he tossed her on the bed and followed her down. The T-shirt was deftly removed along with the rest of her clothes. She was still chuckling when his mouth covered her sex.

But she passed an uneasy night, gut churning, her Gift for strategy working overtime. Sometimes she knew what someone was going to do almost before they did.

Just before dawn, she bolted upright in the bed. "That *ass*. He's going after the prince."

Fane rolled over, his corn-silk hair tumbling around his bare shoulders. "Adric?" he mumbled sleepily.

"Who else?" She tapped her quartz, tried to raise him.

No response.

Which was suspicious in itself. Her brother *always* answered her calls.

"I'll kill him," she growled. "I swear to the Mother Goddess herself, I'll stick a knife in his big, fat ego."

She shoved off the cloud-soft feather comforter—Fane's purchase, not hers, although her cat was rapidly getting used to such creature comforts—and stalked down the hall to the bathroom.

She was back in under a minute. As she jerked on her clothes, Fane rose naked from the bed and headed to the bathroom himself. For once, she barely noticed his lean, beautiful body, just sent him a distracted glance as she slid an iron dagger into a sheathe in her boot.

When he returned, he reached for a pair of slim black jeans. "I'm coming with you."

Damn, she loved him. The man had her back—always. But she shook her head. "It's better if I talk to him alone."

"Then I'll wait for you outside." He pulled on a cashmere sweater. "I'm not letting you out there alone. The night fae have you in their sights."

She sheathed a second dagger in her other boot—her mate-gift from Fane—and laced the boot. Her custom-made iron switchblade was already in her pocket.

"They haven't caught me yet." She rose on her toes to kiss him. "And the sun will be up soon."

He caught her arm. "I'm not asking your permission, Jani. You're not going without me."

She narrowed her eyes. Her easy-going mate rarely put his foot down, but when he did, he was as immovable as a boulder. A large, house-sized boulder.

However, she was the Baltimore second and Fane was now a clan member. Which meant she outranked him, although his place in the hierarchy was...fluid. On the other hand, was it worth a fight? She hadn't been mated long, but she was learning compromise was key, especially with two people as different as her and Fane.

"I'll only follow you anyway," he added.

She expelled a breath. "I'm leaving in two minutes."

The corner of his mouth lifted. "I'm a wayfarer, love. I'll be waiting on the surface." There was a blur of motion, and then their bedroom door opened and she was alone in the room.

Her lips twitched. Sometimes she forgot how fast he was.

She grabbed her leather jacket. Time to stop her brother before he did something stupid.

CHAPTER 20

When Adric awoke just before dawn, Rosana was curled up in his arms, their bodies spooned together. He watched over her shoulder as she turned the amethyst pendant in her fingers, examining it like it was a fucking diamond.

He nuzzled her temple. "You really like it."

"Well, yeah." She rolled over to face him. "You gave it to me."

She had that soft, open expression that hit him like a fist to the chest. Didn't the woman know how to protect herself?

He swallowed and touched the pendant so that he didn't have to look at her face. "You're not what I expected either."

She circled his nipple with a fingertip. Petting him again. Like she couldn't get enough of him.

"What did you expect?"

He shrugged. "A brat. You're the alpha's baby sister." He only just stopped himself from saying *spoiled* baby sister.

The hand on his chest stilled. "Doesn't mean I got a free pass. I worked my ass off in the training cave, and I made warrior with the rest of my cohort."

"I know." He captured her fingers, kissed her knuckles. "That's what I'm trying to say. There's more to you than I expected. You're smart, tough. Good in a crisis. And sexy as hell."

A roll of her eyes. "Thanks." But she resumed petting him.

Tracing his collarbones, teasing his nipples, bumping a fingertip down each rib. He closed his eyes, drifting in a satiated haze, until she touched his pendant.

"Your quartz—there's a swirl of green inside."

His whole body jerked—an instinctive reaction. He yanked it away from her.

"Oh, gods." She clapped a hand to her mouth. "I'm so sorry. I wasn't thinking."

He gave a taut nod. Only another earth fada could know how bad it hurt—worse than a knee to the balls.

"It's all right. But nobody touches our quartz except family."

Or a mate.

Because Rosana's touch hadn't hurt. It had felt good, like she'd reached inside and caressed his heart.

His breath tangled in his chest.

No fucking way. We are not *mated.*

Both members of a pair had to agree to a mating. Words had to be spoken, a commitment made before the gods and the clan. But that sea-green thread was the same color as her dolphin's eyes.

She touched his arm. "You *are* hurt. I should've know better. Merry *told* me..."

He jolted, jumped out of bed.

"Ric?" She sat up, the quilt gripped to her breasts. "You sure you're okay?"

"Yeah, yeah." He shoved his fingers through his hair. "Sorry—I'm just....on edge. But don't touch it again, all right?"

"I won't. I promise. But I didn't know your quartz could change color. Merry's doesn't."

He wrapped his fingers protectively around the pendant. "It's...unusual."

In fact, he'd never heard of anything like it. Fada mates shared a special, mystical bond. Earth fada pairs connected through their quartzes—that warmth he'd noticed when Rosana was near—but he'd never heard of it appearing as a twist of color.

But then, he didn't know any water/earth fada pairs.

If only his parents were still alive. He needed to ask someone about this, someone he trusted. So few of the clan's elders had survived the Darktime.

Rosana was staring at him. Releasing the quartz, he got back into bed and pulled her back into his arms.

She rested her head on his shoulder, her hand carefully on his waist, far from his quartz. "You sure you're all right?"

"I'm fine. Really." He kissed her temple. "Go back to sleep."

She twisted her head so she could examine his face and then relaxed back against him again. Her breath sighed out, and a short time later she was asleep.

The fae lights dimmed to a muted peach. They floated above the bed like the last, glowing embers of a dying fire, painting Rosana's creamy skin a warm gold. Her inky hair tumbled over them both. He stroked it away from her face. Her mouth was slightly ajar, the full lips lax with sleep. Her eyelids fluttered but didn't open.

She looked so damn young, sweet...in a way he'd never been.

Mate.

His chest tightened, as the man recognized what his cougar already knew. The mate bond had already formed. A few fine-spun, hopeful strands, connecting his heart to Rosana's.

His stomach sank.

He couldn't let it happen, couldn't leave her behind to suffer as his mom had. He had to cut the link. He just prayed it wasn't already too late.

He slid out from under Rosana and rolled her onto her side facing away from him. She gave a discontented murmur, and he froze until she settled again, head pillowed on her hand.

He waited another few minutes. Then he set his jaw and rejected the bond. It resisted, more than he expected for such a tenuous connection. But the few strands were already intertwined, his a shimmering blue, hers aqua-green.

Behind him, Rosana mumbled unhappily. "*Não, meu querido, não ...*"

Sweat broke out on his brow. He pulled harder at his blue strands, but they just elongated as if they could stretch infinitely long. Without realizing it, his hand closed on his quartz, seeking strength, energy.

Rosana's strands wavered, tried to move around the barrier of his fist. And with that, he knew what to do.

He called on the power of his quartz. His cat clawed at him from inside.

Mate, it hissed. *Ours.*

He ignored it to ruthlessly throw up a barrier between his heart and Rosana's. There was an almost audible snap as the strands broke, severing the link.

He jolted. It hurt—bad. Like a crater had opened in his chest. The sheer emptiness made the breath whoosh from his lungs.

Rosana whimpered and flung out an arm as if warding off a blow.

He reached out a hand and then curled his fingers into his palm. He ached to touch her, to tell her it would be okay, but he'd lost that right.

He waited another few minutes before slipping out of bed. When he picked up his quartz, the sea-colored spiral had vanished. Sadness swamped him, bone-deep and grim, like the sun setting on his dreams.

He dropped the pendant over his head and glided soundlessly out of the room.

CHAPTER 21

R osana woke in time to hear the outside door shut. She blinked groggily —then sprang out of bed, snatching up her clothes.

Everybody leaves.

But Adric hadn't just left, he'd cut the connection to her. She'd felt the mate bond last night—a few fragile, delicate strands—but now it was gone.

Pain slashed her. She curled into herself, arms wrapped around her waist.

She was six again, begging her mama and *papai* to take her with them.

Ula had taken Rosana's face between her hands. "I'm sorry, love. We're traveling as our dolphins. You're too young—you couldn't keep up with us."

Her lower lip had trembled. "Please, Mama. I'm fast. I swear I am. I'm the fastest girl in the creche. See?" She dashed from one side of the *sala* to the other, then grinned up at her mom, triumphant.

"Oh, *alanna*. I love you. But not this time." Ula's eyes swam with tears.

"No!" Rosana hollered and clamped onto her mom's leg like a limpet.

Her father had had to pry her off. "Hey, now, *bonita*. We need you to be a brave girl, okay? No crying. I want your promise."

He waited until Rosana gave a tearful nod, then handed her to a grim-faced Isa, ignoring her panicked attempts to scramble out of the nurse's arms back to Ula.

"Keep her here," he commanded.

"*Sim*, Senhor Nisio." Isa held the sobbing girl in a gentle but unbreakable grip. Ula cast her a last, sorrowful look, and then the door shut behind the alpha couple.

"Mama!" Rosana let out a heartbroken wail and then shoved her fist in her mouth, because she'd promised not to cry. It had been months before she'd spoken again.

Now she hugged herself harder. Biting her lip so hard it bled.

She'd been left behind. Again.

She dragged the amethyst pendant off her head. Goddess, she was an idiot. She'd actually thought it was Adric's way of saying he loved her. Or at least, that he wanted her, wished things were different.

Hot tears stung her eyes. She went to fling the pendant across the bedroom— and then hesitated, unable to do it.

Everybody leaves.

Her fingers tightened around the chunk of purple quartz. *Not this time.*

Dropping the pendant back over her head, she hurriedly donned a fresh shirt and pants and shoved everything else into her backpack before sprinting barefoot up the stairs.

A wet snow covered the grass with more flakes drifting down. She peered around the side of the house as Adric wheeled a black motorcycle down the short driveway.

She dashed to the shed, jerked on the quartz handle.

Locked.

With a muttered curse, she dragged a boot from her backpack and hammered the handle with the heel.

Adric sent a startled glance over his shoulder. For a long moment, they stared at each other.

She took a step toward him. "Take me. *Please.*"

He shook his head, donned his helmet. "The lock will open for you in an hour." He snapped down a dark visor.

She gave the handle one last thump before looking around for a better tool. Her gaze lit on a rock. She dropped her stuff and lunged for it, but it was larger than it appeared, the bottom two-thirds lodged in the semi-frozen ground.

Adric zoomed off.

Her breath sobbed in. "No, no, no. You can't leave without me."

She was never going to catch him, but she clawed at the dirt until the rock loosened. She snatched it up and started to her feet.

Something slammed into her from behind, knocking her to her knees on the snow-covered grass. The rock flew out of her hands.

A man's rough fingers closed around her throat. A knee shoved into her spine.

She tried to buck him off, but he was bigger, heavier. He easily controlled her.

The blunt fingers tightened. She scrabbled frantically at them but the steady pressure didn't let up. Squeezing the breath from her.

Black edged her vision. Her hands felt strangely numb.

"*Adric*," she rasped.

A small, broken sound.

But in her head, it was a scream.

The fingers squeezed harder. The blackness rose up like a rogue wave and sucked her under.

CHAPTER 22

Luc had waited outside Adric's den most of the night. He'd noted Rosana's scent, of course. Fresh, as if she'd been there recently.

His mouth flattened. First Lewes, now Baltimore. Adric had finally gotten lucky.

Luc had never approved of his friend's obsession with the do Rio female. Adric was the alpha; he should know better. Earth and water fada didn't mix. Adric could never mate with the woman, and fucking her was asking for trouble. Dion would love an excuse to come down hard on Adric and the clan.

The rain changed to a wet snow. It clung to Luc's hair, melted on his face. His pants were soaked through, his feet blocks of ice in his boots. He started to shiver but didn't shift to his wolf.

He'd need his hands for what came next.

Still, snow was good. It would cover his scent.

He stationed himself upwind anyway. No one knew better than one of Adric's former lieutenants how sharp the alpha's senses were.

Dawn came late in January. The sun was just a glimmer on the horizon when Adric emerged from his den, a duffel bag in hand. He sniffed, glanced around.

On the opposite side of the house, Luc plastered his back to the bricks. Inside, the part of him that Blaer could never touch implored his alpha: *See me. Kill me.*

Death was preferable to being enslaved to a fae.

But his friend seemed distracted. Getting his motorcycle from the shed, he donned his helmet, shoved the duffel bag into a saddle bag and pushed the bike down the snow-covered driveway.

The *geas* pulled at Luc. *"Bring Adric Savonett to me."*

No. He resisted Blaer's order, shaking and sweating like a goddamn addict needing a fix.

Blaer would be furious, especially since it was at his suggestion they'd gone to Rock Run first. "Adric will take the river fada straight home," he'd told her. "We can capture him there."

But of course, Adric had never showed—which was what Luc had been counting on. Disgusted, Blaer had left Luc the car and 'ported herself and Jon back to their hotel, with instructions for him to meet her in Virginia—with Adric.

If he didn't return with the alpha, Blaer would want to know why. And she had ways to drag the truth from him.

Then the woman came out—a river fada.

Luc did a doubletake. But yeah, it was Rosana do Rio, with Adric's scent all over her. Not hard to guess what the two of them had been doing last night.

Even though he'd known she'd visited recently, he was shocked that the alpha had taken a river fada into his den—the same den that was a closely guarded secret from most of Adric's own clan.

The man was in deep. Way deeper than Luc had realized.

He eyed Rosana. A river fada, and the Rock Run alpha's sister. For Blaer's purposes, Rosana do Rio was just as good as Adric. In fact, she might even be better.

And Adric would be safe.

His gaze swung to the do Rio female. Better her than his friend.

Luc might no longer be a member of the Baltimore clan, but Adric would always have his loyalty. The man had rescued him from a living hell. That year Luc had been Leron's prisoner, he'd been tortured by not only Leron and his lieutenants, but his night-fae allies. He'd barely escaped with his sanity intact.

On the other side of the house, Adric started his bike. Luc took a step toward the street, the *geas* dragging at him.

No.

Crouching down, he dug his fingers into his scalp and resisted with everything he had until the motorcycle's engine faded into the other city sounds.

Behind him, Rosana was still in Adric's backyard. Apparently, her transportation was locked in Adric's shed.

He rose to his feet.

A female, argued his conscience. *A young, innocent female.*

Slapping it down like an irritating fly, he loped soundlessly across the lawn—and pounced.

~

Rosana groaned.

Her throat *hurt*, both inside and out.

She moved her hand to touch it, and then jolted when she realized her wrists were bound together in front of her. She popped her eyes open.

She was in the backseat of a car. A moving car.

She swung her feet to the floor and struggled upright.

Fuck. Her ankles were bound, too.

The world swung queasily around her. Bile coated the back of her sore throat. She squeezed her eyelids shut and tried not to vomit.

When the world righted itself, a long-limbed, dark-skinned man was regarding her in the rearview mirror with fierce gold eyes. A leather jacket and hoodie lay on the seat beside him, leaving him in a maroon T-shirt that exposed lean, ropey muscles—and the chunk of quartz hanging from his neck.

"Who are you?" The question came out as a rasp. She swallowed and tried again. "And where the fuck are you taking me?"

"There's water in the pocket in front of you," he replied, ignoring her questions.

She threw a wild-eyed glance around her. They were on a highway she didn't recognize, and according to the dashboard clock, it was a little after nine a.m., which meant she'd been out a couple of hours.

They could be almost anywhere, and she was trussed up like a pig on a spit.

Her lungs seized. Drawing up her knees, she slammed her bare heels into the back of his seat.

"I want to know what's going on. *Now*."

A rough growl. "You'll find out soon enough."

"Do you know wh—?" She clamped her mouth shut. She'd been about to threaten him with Dion, but if the earth fada didn't know who she was, it might be smarter to keep it that way.

She surreptitiously tested her bonds, but the rope was bespelled. The more she struggled to get free, the tighter it got, biting painfully into her wrists and ankles until she gave up, exhausted. Bile burned her throat again.

Water.

She worked the bottle from the seat pocket with her bound hands, awkwardly removing the cap and bringing it to her mouth.

Her throat felt too swollen to swallow. But she craved fluids. Water fada needed hydration more than other species.

She took a small, painful sip. The cool water slid down her throat. She took a few more careful sips before returning the bottle to the seat pocket.

Now that she was calmer, her internal GPS told her they were heading south, with the Chesapeake Bay ten or twenty miles to her left. So they were on their way to southern Maryland, or possibly Virginia. Not on I-95, though—this was a narrower highway with only two lanes in each direction. They passed through a small town and she tested the door, but her captor had removed the inside handles.

If only Adric would ride up on that black motorcycle of his... But he'd been gone before the earth fada had attacked her—or had he?

Her fingers curled into her palms. For a breath-stealing instant, she wondered if Adric was behind this.

No. He might be a hard, take-no-crap kind of guy, but he'd always been straight with her. He wouldn't kidnap her in this underhanded way.

Hell, he'd left her sleeping in his bed, which hurt, big time. Still, it wasn't the action of a man who intended to kidnap her.

She inhaled slowly, sifting the air for the driver's scent. Definitely an earth fada, but his scent had an unusual overlay of silver, like he was mated to a fae...or under a fae's power.

Fear scrabbled up her spine. She gripped her hands in her lap.

Nobody knew where she was. That note she'd left for Dion and Cleia? All she'd said was that she was going to Baltimore to be with Adric, and that they shouldn't worry about her.

She glanced at her left wrist and groaned. Cleia's protection charm was in the pocket of the jeans that she'd shoved into the backpack along with her boots and other clothes.

The backpack she'd dropped outside the shed.

She briefly closed her eyes, and then opened them to kick the backseat again. "Your alpha won't like this," she snarled. "I was in his den with his permission."

The driver's jaw worked. The pungent scent of anger filled the small space.

"He's not my alpha—not anymore. And some river fada bitch doesn't belong in his den anyway." His mouth turned down contemptuously. "Especially the Rock Run alpha's sister."

So he did know who she was.

She frowned. "You're not a Baltimore fada?"

"I am. But—" His fingers clenched on the steering wheel. He shot her a single, burning look in the rearview mirror and then shook his head, tight-lipped.

"Cleia won't like this, either." She spoke the sun fae's name clearly and distinctly. "If you know who I am, then you know Queen Cleia is my brother's mate."

They were out in the countryside again, with farmland on either side of them. The earth fada swerved onto the grassy berm, slammed on the brakes. "Don't say her name."

She lifted her chin. "Cleia! Help!"

"Shut the fuck up." He lunged over the seat, catching her jaw in powerful hands.

She glared back. "Cleia," she said indistinctly from behind his covering palms.

"You want to play with me?" He shook her—hard. Her head snapped back and forth and her teeth clacked together. "I could break your neck right here."

Her heart raced. He meant it.

But what did she have to lose?

Her preferred animal might be a dolphin, but river fada could shift to any river-based animal—and some of them had teeth and claws. Now she brought her bound hands up and sliced her claws down the inside of his arm. The metallic scent of blood filled the air.

His face hardened. "*Bitch.*"

He surged the rest of the way into the backseat and flipped her onto her stomach. Pushing her face down into the vinyl, he shoved a knee into her spine between her shoulder blades. She was trapped, her hands caught beneath her chest, her nose and mouth squashed against the seat.

She couldn't breathe. Spots swam before her eyes. She tried to buck him off, but he pressed her deeper into the seat.

Strong fingers closed around her bruised throat. A strange calm descended on her.

She was going to die. But at least she'd gone out fighting.

But as she started to black out, he lifted her enough to take a gulp of air—and then pressed her face down again.

"Listen, you crazy bitch." A harsh growl against her ear. "I took you instead of Adric. You make me kill you, I'll have to go looking for him. I'm under a *geas*."

She stilled.

This was the earth fada lieutenant Adric had told her about. The man who'd broken into the B&B along with the fae.

"Yeah," he said grimly. "I thought that might change your mind. His scent is all over you. The choice is yours. Come with me willingly—and that means no tricks. Or I'll slit your throat and leave you here for a farmer to find, and then go after Adric."

"Mmph."

"Say it." He lifted her off the vinyl. "I want to hear the words. You'll come with me willingly. No tricks, including calling the queen's name."

She sucked in a breath. "Yes," she said as clearly as she could, although it came out as a rasp.

"Yes, what? And use your name. Your full name."

It would bind her to keep her promise. But she wasn't going to try and escape now anyway.

"Yes." She pushed the words out as best she could through her abused throat. "I, Rosana Marie do Rio"—she sucked in another breath—"will go with you willingly. No trying to escape or calling Cl—I mean the queen's —name."

"Okay, then." He released her. "I'll just take this, too."

Sliding her stiletto from her back pocket, he returned to the front seat with a fluid twist of his body. As he pulled back onto the highway, Rosana rolled onto her side and lay there, lungs heaving. A tear trickled down her cheek. She knuckled it away and then pushed herself back up to sitting again.

With shaking fingers, she reached for the water, took a few gulps. She put it back in the seat pocket and then leaned back.

During their struggle, the leather cord of her pendant had twined around her throat. She unwound it and tucked the amethyst back into her shirt.

Too bad it wasn't one of those quartz smartphones. She could use it to contact Adric. But the six-sided stone was a comforting weight over her heart.

The earth fada eyed her in the mirror. "Ric gave you that?"

She moistened her lips. Would knowing the truth help her, or piss him off even more? But a lie would exact a cost, too.

"Yeah."

The earth fada shook his head in disgust. "The clan will never accept you. You can't be anything to him but a piece of ass."

That hurt. But she was damned if she'd let this *cabrão* see it. "Go to Hades," she said wearily and closed her eyes.

She must've drifted off again, because when the car stopped again, she jerked awake. They were deep in the forest on a narrow dirt track.

The earth fada rounded the car to open her door. "Out."

She grabbed the water bottle and downed the rest of it before swinging out her legs.

"Hold still." Flicking open a switchblade, he cut the rope around her ankles but left her hands bound. He grabbed her arm and helped her from the car. Not gently, but not roughly, either.

She stumbled forward, stiff and aching from their two clashes. As he righted her, his hand slid into her back pocket and she tensed.

Really? He was going to grope her—now?

Then she felt the stiletto he'd slipped back into her pocket.

Her heart bumped. She slid a sidelong glance at him, but he marched her into a small clearing and halted.

A tall blond female emerged from the shadows between a pair of towering maples. It was her. The mixed-blood fae from Lewes.

Rosana's right hand twitched, itching to go for the stiletto, but she forced herself to remain still. Adric's life might depend on it.

The earth fada inclined his head. "My lady."

The fae sauntered out of the trees on strappy high heels, long legs bare under a short silver dress, hands in the pockets of her black leather jacket. She was model-thin with a fine-boned face and a sharp chin. Pointed ears poked from pale shoulder-length hair and coffee-colored brows arched over large eyes so unnervingly dark you couldn't tell where the pupils ended and the irises began.

"What's this, Luc?" She eyed Rosana as if she were a piece of day-old fish. "Your orders were to bring me Adric."

"Yes, my lady. But this is Rosana do Rio. I believe you'll find her even more useful."

"The Rock Run alpha's sister?" A single dark brow flicked up.

The earth fada—Luc—nodded.

The fae pursed her full pink lips. "And you brought her instead of your alpha because—?"

Luc held himself soldier-stiff, but Rosana scented his uneasiness.

"Adric has escaped me. Twice. But his scent is all over this woman. Take her to the prince, and chances are, Adric will walk right into New Moon." Luc's mouth twisted. "I know him, you see."

Rosana's fingernails dug into her palms. *Devious fucking bastard.*

"Ah." The woman's mouth curved in a cold smile. "A man who thinks for himself."

He gazed steadily back without saying anything.

The fae lady paced forward, circled the two of them. "But your orders were to bring me Adric Savonett." Her voice was icy. "Weren't they, Luc?"

He released Rosana, took a step away. "Yes, my lady."

The fae homed in on him. Dark magic crackled in the air.

Rosana gave a hard swallow.

Luc clenched his fists at his sides and stared stonily at his fae mistress. She grabbed his quartz, and he jolted. She murmured a few words and a cold white energy crackled around it. Luc jolted again, sinking to his knees with an agonized groan. The blond fae bent with him, the pendant held tightly in her hand.

Rosana gasped as frost covered his torso, spread out to his limbs. Only his face was left untouched.

His claws slid out. He glared up at the fae, chest heaving.

She gazed back, a smile on her lips. Darkness slithered around the two of them as if the very shadows had come alive.

Rosana growled and took a step forward. "Are you *feeding* on him?"

The woman pinned her with an icy midnight gaze. "Come any closer, and I'll freeze you, too."

Rosana stilled until the fae turned her attention back to Luc. Then she twisted her arms around her body, trying to reach the stiletto in her back pocket. Luc might be a *cabrão*, but she was damned if she'd stand by while the woman tortured him.

But before she could work the stiletto free, the fae released the pendant and straightened up. Luc's head dropped to his chest. His breath sawed in and out, the sound harsh in the quiet clearing, as the frost slowly receded.

Rosana brought her hands back in front of her body.

"You *will* bring me Adric Savonett," his mistress said. "That's an order, Luc."

The earth fada's head came up, eyes blazing with hatred.

The fae lady only smiled before turning to Rosana. "The Rock Run alpha's sister, hm?"

Rosana swallowed queasily. Then she pulled back her shoulders.

"That's me. And if you're smart, you'll let me go, because my brother will come after you with everything he has. Hang on to me, and you're a dead woman."

"I'll let the prince worry about that. Come." She held out an imperious hand.

Rosana found her feet moving. Long fingers clamped around her arm, cold even through her hoodie.

Ice fae, Rosana realized. The woman was an ice fae/night fae mix, her scent a swirl of snow and decay.

"Go," the fae told the still-kneeling man. "Find Adric and bring him to me. And this time, don't fail me."

He rose slowly, painfully, to his feet as if every bone in his body ached. "To New Moon?"

"Yes. I'll instruct the wards to allow you both to enter."

Rosana swallowed. If only she could warn Adric somehow. But she could do nothing but stand by helplessly as Luc trudged back to the car.

Blaer murmured something in fae and the air around them *bent* in a dizzying way. Rosana braced herself to be teleported, and then the bottom dropped out of the forest. For a vertiginous moment, everything went black, and then the two of them reappeared inside a large, dimly lit room.

Rosana's eyes went night glow.

They were in a large, quietly elegant library. The walls were lined with books, the floor a cold white marble veined with black. The tall, narrow windows were covered with dark shades, the only illumination a few fae lights the color of black opals floating near the ceiling.

At one end of the room was a graceful Art Nouveau sofa and two chairs in a blue burnout velvet, and at the other end, a wide mahogany desk gleamed. Museum-quality statues of smooth black stone were scattered on pedestals around the room: a snarling panther, a feathered raven, a winged woman with flowers spilling from her hands. A table near the window held a silver vase with a single red rose.

Rosana's heart jittered. She could've sworn the room was empty—she hadn't even scented him—but now a man was seated at the table near the window. Like Blaer in the forest earlier, it was as if he'd coalesced from the shadows themselves.

A night fae, casually dressed in a loose white shirt and black pants, his pale, elegant feet bare. One long-fingered hand toyed with a pair of black dice.

Prince Langdon.

He tossed the dice on the table. She watched, stunned, as they transformed into two iridescent blue butterflies and flew away to perch on the snarling panther's head.

The prince rose to his feet. Onyx eyes examined Rosana.

Power emanated from him. Cold. Dark. And so strong she could literally feel it, like an icy black ocean sucking at her.

"Lady Blaer," he murmured without taking his gaze from Rosana. "What have you brought me?"

CHAPTER 23

A few tardy snowflakes sifted down as Cleia and Dion slipped out the back door of her mansion for a morning stroll, leaving Brisa to eat breakfast under her nanny's watchful eye. Cleia loved Rising Sun in the summer, when the gardens were a mass of colorful blooms, fruit swelled in the trees and the surrounding meadows were a soft, fecund green. But the overnight snowfall had touched the grounds with a sparkling wand, turning the gardens into a sugared wonderland.

Dion steered her onto a little-used path and pressed her up against a tree. His mouth took hers in a lazy kiss. She slid her hands under his leather jacket and kissed him back. Even with a nanny to help, a busy toddler meant they didn't have much time alone.

A low, sexy growl. "I could take you right here," he said against her throat, "if it wasn't so cold."

"Who's cold?" Her hands went to the zipper of her own jacket...and then fell away.

Rosana's in trouble.

Cleia clutched Dion's shoulders, ears straining.

His hands tightened on her waist. "What's the matter?"

She held up a hand, silently asking him to wait. A full thirty seconds ticked by before she gave up.

"It's Rosana." She swallowed hard. "Something's wrong. She called my name —four times."

"Where?" he bit out.

"Not close by." She scrunched her brows, focusing. "Somewhere south of here. Virginia, or maybe southern Maryland. It was quick—a brief touch, and then nothing."

Their eyes met. They'd spent the night at Rising Sun. Neither of them had seen Rosana since yesterday afternoon.

Dion muttered a nasty Portuguese curse. "She's supposed to be at the base."

"I'll 'port to her."

"Take me."

She nodded and took Dion's hand and teleported to the approximate location she'd sensed Rosana.

They were on a narrow country road, although that didn't stop cars from hurtling past. A field of dormant winter wheat stretched along one side of the road, and on the other, stubbled cornstalks marched off to the horizon.

Dion turned in a circle, scanning the area. "We're still in Maryland, about five miles from the Potomac River. What in Hades is she doing down here?"

"I don't know," Cleia said. "But she hasn't tried to contact me again."

His nostrils flared. "I can't pick up her scent. But if she was in a car, she wouldn't leave one."

Cleia narrowed her eyes to the south, as if she could somehow see where Rosana was now. "New Moon is right across the river in Virginia."

"I know." Dion glared in the same direction. "If that fucking *cabrão* thinks he can use my sister as a bargaining chip..."

Cleia's stomach hollowed. It was exactly what a night fae would do.

"We'll go after him with everything we have. Rosana isn't just your family, she's mine."

"I know. And I'm grateful, *querida*." Dion squeezed her hand. "But first, let's make sure that's where she is. Take me back to Rock Run. I need Rui—his shark can track anything."

"At least she has my protection charm. It'll give her an edge."

He nodded, expression grim. Humoring her.

Because they both knew Rosana might not be wearing the charm.

They found Rui in the training cave. The shark fada had once been Rock Run's top assassin until the job had taken its toll. These days Rui spent his time training the younger warriors, a position to which the hard-faced, taciturn man had taken like a duck to water.

"Be right there," Rui called over his shoulder, his gaze on the two young males he was sparring with. Another seven young men and women stood in a circle, observing.

The man on the left lunged. In a few swift, scarily efficient moves, Rui dropped him by hooking a heel behind his knee and then spun around to kick the other in the chest. The man flew backwards.

Cleia winced, but the two males bounded back to their feet.

"Good work," Rui said with a nod. The younger men beamed as he turned to the observers. "The rest of you, form groups of three and practice the sequence I just showed you."

He strode across the cavern to Dion and Cleia, big body naked except for a pair of shorts. "What's up?" he asked as he pulled on a T-shirt.

Dion tipped his head at the exit. "In the ops room."

"*Sim.*"

The operations room was in its own private corridor near the base's center. A couple of warriors were always on duty to sift through communications and respond to emergencies. Like most of the base, it was a utilitarian space with a handful of chairs and a sturdy plank table, the only lighting a handful of watery blue and green fae lights.

By the time they arrived, Dion had brought Rui up to date. Dion jerked his chin at the pair manning the room. "Wait outside."

They nodded and exited, but before they could close the door, Isa bustled down the corridor, her round face anxious.

"My lord, my lady. I need to see you, *por favor.*"

Dion nodded for the men to let her pass and then shut the door behind her.

Isa thrust a folded piece of paper at him. "I found this on Rosana's pillow."

Cleia read the note over his shoulder.

Dion, Cleia, Isa—

I'm on my way to Baltimore. But don't worry. You might as well know, I'm with Adric. I'm tired of hiding it. I love him, and he loves me (even if he hasn't told me yet).

More, he needs me. I'll be back in a few days—please, don't worry. Hugs and kisses, Rosana

"I'll kill him," Dion said calmly. "I'll wring his goddamn neck."

Cleia eyed her mate warily as he passed the note to Rui.

"If he's hurt her," Dion continued. "Forced her to go with him against her will—he's dead."

She set a hand on his arm. The bicep was balled tight. "Let's not jump to conclusions," she murmured.

"No?" The eyes he turned on her were the cold silver of his animal. "She goes to Baltimore and somehow ends up in a car a hundred-fifty miles south of here.

She calls on you for help—which she's never done in her life? Tell me, what am I supposed to think?"

"I agree it looks bad, but I've seen how Adric looks at her. We've all seen it."

Dion snarled. "Like a fucking cat stares at prey."

"No. Like a man who wants a woman with everything he has—but knows he can never have her. He's stayed away from her for her own good. And she feels the same. If he'd wanted, he could've lured her away years ago."

Beside her, Isa murmured agreement.

"Then why is he taking her to Virginia?" Dion demanded.

"We don't know it's him."

"Who else could it be?"

"I'm just saying, keep an open mind."

"Of course," he surprised her by saying, and then spoiled it by adding, "as long as you keep an open mind when I tear his lying, cheating throat out."

He turned to Rui. "I'm leaving ASAP. Who's available?"

"Three men plus the two of us?"

"*Sim.*"

"Then Ed and Jaxon can come." Ed was an older, canny *tenente*, and Jaxon a young, hard-driving warrior. "And Tiago—he's at the marina right now."

"That works. Tiago would want to come anyway. I'll tell Davi he's the *tenente* in charge."

Cleia chewed her lip, wishing she could help. But she wasn't strong enough to teleport even Dion and his motorcycle to Virginia, let alone four other men. They'd have to get themselves to southern Maryland.

Dion nodded at Isa. "Thank you. You did the right thing, bringing this straight to me."

His former nurse inclined her graying head, fingers twined tightly in front of her waist. "I don't know when she left. I didn't even know she was gone until after breakfast. For that, I beg your pardon."

"Senhora." Dion gently took her hands. "You have nothing to apologize for. You're not Rosana's keeper. Now, go back to whatever you were doing, but let's keep this between us, okay? Until we know exactly what we're up against, I'd rather the whole base didn't know."

"Of course," the woman said, and with a dignified nod to all of them, left the room.

"If that's it, then?" Dion asked, clearly impatient to be off, but Rui held up a staying hand.

"I'm afraid we've got another problem."

"It can't wait?"

"No," Rui said bluntly. He closed the door behind Isa. "Merry believes her grandfather's been watching her."

"The hell you say. Is that possible?"

Both men looked at Cleia.

She spread her hands. "Anything is possible. Our wards can block him from entering the base physically, but if he has the farsight, that wouldn't stop him from keeping a watch on her."

"Valeria knows?" Dion asked.

"*Sim*," said Rui. "She'll keep her inside the wards."

Dion squeezed his nape. "So the prince knows she's alive."

Rui nodded, his strong, sculpted face set in grim lines.

Dion swore. "I don't like this. There is no way to keep him out?"

"He can't do it constantly," Cleia said. "Only intermittently. Using any kind of Sight requires your whole attention. But I'll talk to Olivia, see if there's anything she can do to block him." Her cousin was a spell-worker and ward-maker. "Maybe a *look-away* spell would work."

"Good." Dion wrapped a hand around her nape and gave her a hard kiss. "Go home. Stay close to Brisa. Just in case."

Cleia's breath snagged. "He wouldn't dare."

"I don't think so, no. But I don't want to take any chances." He turned to Rui. "Have the men at the garage in fifteen minutes."

"Will do."

Cleia waited until Rui left before telling Dion, "Let me know the minute you find out anything. And if there's anything I can do, you'll call on me."

His black brows lowered, but he nodded reluctantly. "Fine. If it will make you happy."

"It will. And I want your promise that when you do catch up to Adric and Rosana, you'll hear them both out before you do anything. If she's his mate, and you hurt him..."

His chin jerked back like she'd hit him. "She's not his mate. That—it's not possible."

"But if she is, and you hurt him, she'll never forgive you."

"I can handle my own sister," he growled, and stalked after Rui.

Cleia pinched the bridge of her nose—and 'ported back to Rising Sun and her baby girl.

There was only so much a woman—even a powerful fae queen—could do. Some things her mate had to work out for himself.

CHAPTER 24

The New Moon Court was in a densely forested state park near the mouth of the Potomac. A powerful *look-away* spell meant the local humans didn't even know they had a night fae compound in their midst. The court didn't appear on maps or satellite scans, and if hikers somehow managed to bumble too close, they couldn't penetrate the court's wards.

Adric downed a plate of sausage and eggs at a local diner without tasting them. His chest still felt like a black hole had opened where his heart used to be. He ground the heel of his hand into his breastbone, trying to rub the ache away.

He kept seeing Rosana's face when she'd realized he was leaving without her. Anguished. Betrayed.

You did the right thing.

He couldn't mate with her, not when he might be dead before the week was out.

He forked up a bite of egg and stared at it. *She's back at Rock Run by now. Safe.*

So why did he feel like he'd left something vital behind?

Don't think about it. Do the job. You can make it up to her afterwards.

If there *was* an afterwards...

He grimly shoveled down the rest of his meal. Ten minutes later, he was checking into a cheap motel a few miles from New Moon, paying cash and requesting a room facing the strip of trees at the back. He wheeled his bike around back and went inside.

The room was a beige box. A king-sized bed vied for space with a flimsy armoire and a desk with one chair. Dropping his helmet and duffel bag on the bed, he stripped to the skin and then sheathed his iron dagger in a leather case with its own cord before dropping it over his head next to his quartz.

He cracked open the door. Other than his motorcycle, the only vehicle in the back lot was a dirty white sedan, and the sole sign of life was the humming of a vacuum cleaner two rooms down.

He locked the door and jogged into the trees behind the motel. He'd researched the area around New Moon until he could've navigated it blindfolded. The narrow strip of trees connected with other wooded patches, enough to provide cover for his cougar until he could disappear into the state park.

On the deserted country road, a truck rumbled past, accompanied by a belch of oily fumes. From the fenced-in yard of a nearby house, a dog barked, its scent a tart mix of bravado and fear.

Adric snarled, and the dog gave a startled yip before cowering next to the back steps.

He tucked the key card into the crook of a crepe myrtle, then closed his eyes and opened himself to the change. Hot sparks danced over his skin. Power surged through him, obliterating his human form. For a time, he was both Adric and not-Adric; pure, formless energy. And then he was on all fours, the wet brown leaves cool beneath his tawny paws, his senses a hundred times sharper.

He gave himself a shake, settling his fur into place, then set out for New Moon, intermittently cloaking himself. He hadn't forgotten Rosana's warning that Langdon had Seen he was coming to the court. The bastard might know Adric was on his way, but he couldn't know the exact moment. No Seer was that powerful.

A half hour later, he entered the state park. He was in a stand of sharp-scented longleaf pines, the sun high in the pale blue sky. He aimed for the park's center.

As he neared the New Moon compound, gray clouds blotted the sun, and the pines changed to menacing hardwoods that loomed over him like grim soldiers. His fur bristled. He crept forward, scanning the dark spaces between the trees.

Gradually, he became aware of the *look-away* spell pressing at him.

Turn away. There's nothing here.

When he continued, shadows gathered, and the warnings grew more foreboding.

Danger. Run...while you still can.

He closed his eyes, drew on his tracking Gift. The compulsion to look away passed. When he opened his eyes, the shadows parted to reveal a shimmering trail winding through the trees, the kind of path only a fae—or a fada with their touch of fae blood—could see.

Gotcha.

He avoided the shimmering fae path. The *look-away* spell was just the first layer of security around the court. The trail would be watched, possibly even booby-trapped. Instead, he ducked deeper into the woods, taking a parallel course to the trail.

A gravel road barely wide enough for a single car intersected the trail. He dropped to his belly and slunk forward to investigate.

The scent of rainwater and woman.

His nostrils flared. *Rosana?*

No fucking way. She was in Baltimore, or more likely, safely back at Rock Run.

Unless she'd followed him.

He shook his head. Impossible—he'd have noticed her and her motorcycle.

But she could've come straight to Virginia. After all, she'd guessed he was going after Langdon.

He inhaled, sifting through the forest scents. There, to the west. It was Rosana, all right.

He clenched his jaw so hard his molars hurt. He should've known she wouldn't return tamely home.

He muttered a cougar's equivalent of a curse and faded back into the trees, following the gravel road to the west.

Rosana's scent grew stronger, entwined with the scents of two others—Luc and a fae.

His heart stuttered. His curses changed to a low, continuous growl.

He entered a clearing. In the leaves and mud were the tell-tale prints of three people. The sharp indentation of a woman's high heels. A man's lug soles. And a single imprint of a long, narrow bare foot.

He sniffed. It was Rosana, all right, her pores leaking fear.

His body went taut as a stretched wire. He already knew the man was Luc, and he suspected the high heels belonged to Lady Blaer.

He could think of only one reason Rosana would be with them.

Luc had captured Rosana for Blaer. The fae who put fada in cages.

Rage blasted through Adric, a fury edged with panic. His claws dug into the mud. But the rest of him remained icy-calm, cat and man fusing into a single cold-eyed predator.

First, he'd rescue Rosana. Then he'd take revenge on those who'd dared to abduct her.

He scrutinized the foot prints. The story they told was clear. Luc had returned to a nearby car, but the women's tracks ended in the clearing. The only explanation was that the fae lady had 'ported out with Rosana.

He stilled, drew on his quartz. Tracking Rosana with every ounce of power he possessed.

But it was as if the earth had opened up and swallowed her whole. Still, that in itself was a clue. If she was at New Moon, the wards would shield her from him.

He raced back along the gravel road to the shimmering fae path and then turned north again, following the trail as closely as he dared, torn between the need for speed and concealment. He was closer than he'd realized. Within a few minutes, the half-buried, vine-covered buildings of the New Moon Court were visible through the trees.

He took to the treetops, leaping from branch to branch. Even another fada would have trouble tracking him high in the forest canopy. A few yards from the perimeter, he halted in a sturdy oak and crouched on a branch, a shadow in the trees.

The clouds dissipated, allowing the sun to melt the last patches of snow. The compound was arranged as Fane's map had depicted, with Langdon's lair near the center. Fog snaked around the eerie, cryptlike building. Walking paths of smooth white pebbles meandered through a lush landscape of azaleas, crepe myrtle and southern magnolia, and huge willows wept over the still black pond.

Adric's gaze returned to Langdon's lair. The tallest building at one-and-half stories, it was draped in the same ivy as the others, with vines and flowers chiseled into the creamy granite beneath. At its apex, a giant bat flew past a crescent moon.

He narrowed his eyes at the windows. If only he could see in…

At this hour, the prince was probably asleep, but Adric couldn't be sure. The powerful old fae was one of the few night fae who could tolerate the noonday sun.

And was Rosana with him, or elsewhere, with Blaer?

His stomach twisted into icy knots.

There was no choice but to hunker down on the branch to wait for someone to open a portal into the court. If possible, he'd slip inside before it closed, using his Gift to cloak his presence from the guards. But if not, he'd use his quartz to compel the person to allow him to pass through the portal.

Long minutes ticked by with nobody entering or leaving. In fact, it had been at least an hour since he'd seen anyone at all, even a human servant. Adric frowned. It was as if the shadows had thickened to conceal the court's inhabitants. Could the wards have sensed him and reacted accordingly?

If only he knew more. But the night fae were the most secretive of the fae. He was lucky to have Fane's intel; without it, he'd be going in completely blind.

He settled deeper into his cougar, drawing on its patience. Only his twitching tail betrayed his growing agitation.

More time passed. He'd been on the branch an hour now.

How long had Rosana been inside?

A fist squeezed his bowels. He knew—too well—what the night fae did to their prisoners. And it wouldn't be quick. The motherfuckers liked to toy with their prey.

Don't think about it. She's smart—she'll play for time.

Something rustled in the forest below.

Very slowly, he turned his head, scanning the undergrowth.

The big brown wolf was almost as good as Adric at concealing himself. But he couldn't hide his musky scent...or his gleaming amber eyes.

CHAPTER 25

*I*n person, Prince Langdon was even more beautiful.

Tall and lean, with silky black hair framing his narrow poet's face. Against his pale skin, his lips were a dark, sensuous red, and the diamonds that outlined his ears and brows sparkled like tiny stars.

Rosana realized she was gaping. She closed her mouth with a snap.

"My lord." Blaer dipped her shining blond head. "Peace to you and yours."

"Peace, Lady Blaer," the prince returned in a low, rich voice.

He paced forward, quiet as death, his gaze on Rosana. Distantly, she noted a night fae's unpleasant scent, but against his unearthly beauty, it somehow didn't matter.

He inclined his head to her. "And to you, Senhorita do Rio."

So he knew who she was. She jerked her chin in acknowledgement. "Peace."

"I offer her as a gift," Blaer said.

"Do you?" The prince lifted a winged black brow.

A gift? Rosana forgot how gorgeous he was and narrowed her eyes. There were rules about these things. The fae couldn't just snatch you without your permission.

"I agree to nothing," she said. "I'm here against my will, and I demand to be returned to Rock Run immediately. My lord."

Blaer just smiled.

Langdon stopped in front of Rosana. He was at least a foot taller. She had to tip her head back to meet his eyes.

He stared back, growing more beautiful by the second. Power enfolded her, as if he'd sprouted black wings and embraced her.

Her gaze snagged on his full mouth. She could almost feel his lips against hers, soft, caressing.

The dark wings tightened around her like a warm cocoon.

Her breath sighed out.

The prince's mouth curved in a faint smile.

Uneasiness skipped up her spine. She dragged her gaze from his mouth, pulled back her shoulders. "My lord? I repeat, I'm here against my will."

"She speaks the truth, Blaer?" Langdon asked, his gaze still on Rosana. "She didn't enter my court willingly?"

The fae lady's smile faded. She shot Rosana a dark look. "Yes, my lord."

"A miscalculation, no doubt," the prince returned silkily. "But perhaps I can convince her to stay." He smiled into Rosana's eyes. "What do you think, my dear? Would you like to spend a few days with me?"

That unearthly beauty tugged at her again. Was he using a glamour on her?

She scowled and wrenched her gaze from his. "I already gave you my answer," she said to his chest. "I want to leave. *Now.*"

"Is there nothing I can do to change your answer to a yes?" He fingered one of her curls. The dark power constricted.

Tighter, tighter.

Her heart sped up. She took short, rapid breaths, unable to fill her lungs. She fought the urge to thrash wildly at the invisible cocoon. He'd only use her fear to ensnare her further.

Instead, she stared stonily at the V of his shirt. "No, my lord."

Langdon *knew* she was afraid. So did Blaer. They had both stilled, their bodies vibrating with a greedy hunger.

But the prince nodded and to her surprise, released her hair and stepped back.

Her breath whooshed out.

Blaer glanced between the two of them, frowning. Rosana edged away from her.

"You're hungry." Langdon waved his hand and a steaming bowl of fish stew appeared on the table with the silver vase. "I've had my cook prepare something." Another flick of his fingers and a basket of crusty brown bread settled beside the stew, along with a bowl of fruit and a plate of small, perfect chocolates.

Rosana eyed the food, her mouth watering. He was right. She hadn't eaten since dinner last night.

It could be a trick. Eat his food, and you'll end up "owing" him.

She swallowed and looked away. "No, thank you."

"Then perhaps some wine?" A crystal glass appeared in her hand.

She stared down at the pale gold liquid. *Maybe just a sip?* She moistened her lips. It looked so good, and her throat still ached from Luc's attack.

Her fingers tightened on the stem. She set the wine on the table. "Not right now."

The prince shrugged a shoulder. "As you wish. But please, sit." He indicated a black burned-velvet couch on the other side of the room.

Rosana fingered the stiletto in her back pocket. For courage.

Because using it was a last resort. Even if she managed to escape this room, she'd still have to evade any guards and somehow open the portal to the outside world.

"With respect, Lady Blaer brought me here against my will. She admitted it herself. Now, either let me leave or I'll call on Queen Cleia." She spoke the sun fae woman's name loud and clear.

Langdon picked up the wine she'd refused, sipped it. "I should tell you that the queen can't get through our wards. In fact, it's unlikely she can even trace you to the court."

"She might surprise you," Rosana returned, but her heart sank. She was on her own, then. Even if Cleia had heard her earlier cry for help, she had no reason to suspect that Rosana had been taken to New Moon. And Dion might have a hunter's Gift, but Luc had made sure she couldn't leave a trail. She'd been closed up in his car until they'd reached the forest.

Blaer shifted impatiently on her sky-high heels. "My lord?"

"You did well," Langdon replied. "I accept your gift."

Rosana glared at them both. "I am *not* a fucking gift."

The two fae ignored her. "So I've won a place at your court?" Blaer asked.

The prince inclined his head. "Olivier will assign you an apartment. You will, of course, refrain from any attempts to influence my court. You'll find I'm not as forgiving as King Sindre."

Blaer's face set into a pleasant mask. And it *was* a mask. Rosana scented her anger, mixed with a cold determination.

"I understand, my lord." She sketched a small bow.

The prince studied the tall blond mixed-blood for a moment. "Do you?" he murmured, and then turned to Rosana, effectively dismissing Blaer.

Behind him, the fae lady's eyes blazed, twin red fires flaring to life inside obsidian pupils. But she meekly murmured, "Peace to you and yours," and strode to the door, silver heels clicking on the marble floor.

A portly human with deep brown skin and a shiny bald head appeared in the doorway. "If you'll come with me, my lady. I believe we have an empty apartment near the north gardens."

Rosana eyed Langdon, tight-jawed. "You won't get away with this."

"You're angry," he said—and smiled. But of course, to a night fae, anger was like catnip.

Her hands balled at her sides. "You know who I am," she said evenly. "Keep me here against my will, and my brother will come after you with everything he has."

"You're the woman I saw in the scrying glass," he said as if she hadn't spoken.

She stilled. "Am I?"

"Oh, yes." A tilt of his gorgeous head as he examined her, a wolf with an intriguing—and very tasty—rabbit. "Which brings me to an interesting question: why were you looking for me?"

Oh, Lord. She did *not* want to bring Merry into this—or Adric, for that matter.

She spread her hands. "It just…happened." Which was true enough. "Is that what this is about? You're pissed off that I accidently spied on you?"

"Pissed off?" he repeated. "No, merely curious. I assure you, I had nothing to do with Lady Blaer bringing you here."

Somehow, he was just a foot away again, that dark, seductive power licking at her. And gods, it was tempting to give in to it.

No. I love Adric.

But Adric doesn't want you. Not enough anyway. He cut the mate bond, and then he left you. You begged him to take you along, told him if he didn't, he'd die—and he still left.

Her heart squeezed.

"You're distressed," the prince murmured. "But there's no need. As you say, you've agreed to nothing." He paused. "Yet."

She shook her head and slipped around him. Putting some distance between herself and that seductive aura.

She picked up the wine glass, toyed with the stem without drinking.

Stall for time. Think about Dion, not Adric.

Because Dion would come for her. That she knew, as surely as she knew the sun rose in the east and set in the west.

Just picturing her large, very capable brother heartened her.

"It's you who was spying on Rock Run," she said. "If I happened to See you, that's not my fault. We just—intersected somehow."

Langdon nodded without confirming or denying that he'd been spying on her clan, or at least, on Merry.

"So you're a Seer."

Rosana's spine prickled. "I didn't say that."

"No," he agreed. His black eyes scrutinized her like she was an insect under a microscope. "I seem to recall your mother is, too. But then, her mother was a quarter fae."

Rosana swallowed. She didn't like that this dark prince knew so much about her family. But that was the fae; they collected information like dragons did treasure, hoarding it on the chance it might be useful.

"The question is, why were you scrying for me?"

She couldn't tell Langdon about Merry. Rock Run had never officially confirmed that the teenager was still alive. It didn't matter that he knew differently. Admit it straight out, and the night fae would have grounds to retaliate, resulting in open war between New Moon and her clan.

She saw only one option—admit she was a Seer.

"I was curious." She threw his own words back at him. It was the truth, after all. "I didn't expect to See anything."

Least of all, Prince Langdon himself. The most she'd hoped for was some clue that might help Merry.

"You're quite Gifted for one so young. You're being trained?"

"Yes." She set down the wine glass, nerves shrieking at all these questions. But he was a powerful fae, and she was in his territory. Answer his questions, and maybe he'd be satisfied, let her leave.

Yeah, right. And jellyfish can fly. But she had no choice but to play along.

"Odd, that I haven't heard of you before now." He sank gracefully onto the burned-velvet couch, crossed one long leg over the other. "I could work with you. It's been many turns of the sun since I encountered a Seer with such a strong natural Gift."

Oh, no. Hell, no.

"It's good of you to offer," she returned smoothly, "but the sun fae are overseeing my training."

"With me, you wouldn't have to hide who you are."

She flinched. What did he know?

A tiny nod. "I thought as much. Others so rarely understand what it is to be a Seer. They fear us, ridicule our Gift. Or worse, ignore our warnings."

Like Adric.

"Yes," he said with a commiserating smile. "That's the hardest of all, isn't it? When the people we love simply won't listen."

Rosana moved to the panther statue. The butterflies were still perched on its snarling black head, their fragile blue wings opening and closing.

She stared at them unseeingly. *Don't agree to anything.*

But, a sly voice countered, *Langdon's an old, powerful fae. He's probably forgotten more than Colm ever knew.*

"My people would honor a Seer with your Gift," the prince purred from the couch. "You could name your price. You'd be a wealthy woman—you could buy and sell your own brothers. But more, you'd have their respect. They don't see you how you really are, do they?" Soft, seductive tones. "They think you're still a child who doesn't know her own mind."

Her hand fisted.

"I'm right, aren't I?"

She shook her head, not because he was wrong, but because it hurt to admit he was right.

"Think about it. That's all I ask."

Temptation tugged at her. She swallowed around the constriction in her throat. "No," she rasped.

On the couch behind her, Langdon made a sharp, irritable movement. "Consider what you're turning down. Imagine the power you'd wield as an honored Seer."

She closed her eyes. Because she *could* picture it.

She fingered Adric's amethyst through the shirt. If she stayed at the court, she'd lose him.

Her mouth twisted. *So? He doesn't want you. Even your own clan doesn't know who you really are. Here, you could be yourself.*

Her fingers tightened around the pendant.

No. That's Langdon's darkness talking.

Beneath her shirt, the pendant warmed, almost as if Adric had infused it with a spark of his own energy.

Adric had given the pendant to her, attached it to a leather thong so she could always wear it. In that instant, she saw something very clearly—with her heart, not her Sight. The warmth expanded to fill her chest.

Adric did want her. He just didn't *want* to want her.

And suddenly, she wasn't tempted at all.

She turned around. "And if I say no? Will you let me leave?"

The prince moved an elegant shoulder. "Perhaps."

Anger balled in her stomach. "You can't keep me here."

"No? Try to leave without my permission and the portals will slam shut. I'm told it's like running full speed into a stone wall."

"You think you're safe behind your wards?" She stalked toward him. "Keep me here against my will and my brothers will carve out your fucking liver and feed it to the fish."

The prince's mouth curved. "You're a bloodthirsty little thing, aren't you?"

"Yeah." She smiled back, drew the stiletto—and leapt over the couch. She instinctively avoided touching his skin with her bare hands. Instead, she grabbed his long black hair, jerked his head back and touched the needle-like point to the hollow of his throat. His flesh sizzled, the acrid scent stinging her nostrils.

Langdon stilled—and then he raised a diamond-studded brow, that irritating half-smile on his lips again. "Now what?"

She pressed the blade a little deeper. "This isn't a joke, asshole," she said in her animal's guttural voice.

His hand shot out, quick as a striking snake, to grip her jaw.

"Careful," he gritted. "Right now the fact that you amuse me is all that's keeping me from returning you to Blaer. She's rather primitive in how she treats fada. She seems to consider you animals to be kept in cages. Perhaps you heard what happened to the Baltimore alpha's sister?"

"Marjani Savonett?" She sucked in a horrified breath. *Adric's sister had been shut in a cage?*

But she'd gone too far to back down now. "Go to Hades. I'm not here to fucking amuse you." She pushed the stiletto deeper, piercing the skin.

Blood slid down Langdon's throat, soaking the V of his pristine white shirt.

Cold fingers dug into her jaw. "That, my pretty little fada, was a mistake."

A red flame flared to life deep in his pupils.

She swallowed and tried to wrench her gaze away. But she was caught. The dark power that had been pulling at her surged to life. Tentacles wrapped around her like an invisible octopus, latching on to her skin with eager, mindless mouths.

Terror swamped her. "Stop it!"

She knocked Langdon's hand from her jaw and slapped at the writhing tentacles. But her hands slipped through them as if they weren't there.

Langdon rose from the couch without taking his gaze from hers. Her lungs seized. Her fingers opened and the stiletto clattered to the floor as she stared helplessly into his fire-touched pupils.

Yesss. The mindless tentacles drank up her fear, *enjoying* it.

She shook her head from side to side. Her knees felt like jelly.

Look away.

But she couldn't. She was ensnared, helpless as a trout in a net.

Breathe in. Breathe out.

A sharp rock of fear lodged in her throat.

I can't. Hopelessness welled up inside her.

Yes, you can. This isn't you—it's him. He's making you feel this way.

Somehow, she managed to drag her gaze from Langdon's. Her breath shuddered in. She stared at the floor, chest heaving, and stopped her useless slapping at the tentacles.

"Get them off me," she said. She tried to make it a command, but it came out more like a plea.

He stalked toward her. "I want you." A cold statement, spoken through set lips.

She blinked. "What? No."

"You still think to fight me?" His brows bunched in a baffled frown, and the sucking sensation receded.

She took a deep breath and lifted her chin. "I won't bargain with a man who's attacking me."

A considering pause. Then he nodded. "Very well." As suddenly as the tentacles had appeared, they disappeared.

She backpedaled, getting as far from him as she could. When her back hit a bookcase she halted, sucking in oxygen, skin crawling.

Langdon picked up her stiletto, tossed it into the air. It transformed into a small brown bat and with a high-pitched squeal, shot across the room straight toward Rosana.

She stilled. What kind of Gift did Langdon have, that he could bring inanimate objects to life?

The bat circled her head, its tiny face inquisitive, its scent wild, earthy, and then flapped away, curiosity satisfied, to perch on a window valence.

The prince stalked toward her, hand outstretched. "Come."

She forced herself to take it. His fingers were cool, firm.

He drew her toward the table. "Sit," he said, and it wasn't a request. "Eat my food. Drink my wine. And then we'll talk."

She moistened her lips. The best thing was to buy some time. Dion would come for her, and Cleia.

And then there was Adric. He'd left before her.

Which meant he was probably already in Virginia.

Ice sheeted down her spine. What if her being at the court somehow set off the timeline that led to his death?

The prince pulled out a chair for her. She sank numbly into it. As he took the seat beside her, an ornate silver spoon appeared on the table next to the fish stew.

"Eat." Langdon nudged the bowl in her direction.

CHAPTER 26

$\mathcal{D}$ion practically flew south, Rui and the others fanning out to either side so that their motorcycles formed a five-man arrow with him at the point. Just let the humans try and stop him.

Fortunately, it was a Wednesday morning in January. Even I-95 wasn't that crowded.

He clenched the handlebars, white-knuckled, trying not to picture all the ways a young female could be hurt. If he was going to save his sister, he needed to stay calm, in control.

But this was Rosana. The pup who'd owned his heart from the day Nisio do Rio had emerged beaming from the bedroom he shared with Dion's mom and announced that after four boys, Ula had finally blessed them with a girl. Dion and his three brothers had eyed the tiny bundle with awe.

Nisio had passed her to Dion first. "We're calling her Rosana Marie."

"Rosana Marie," he'd breathed. She was so light, like a handful of flowers. He'd held her so carefully, terrified of somehow hurting her, and cautiously touched his lips to her petal-soft brow. She'd scrunched up her little nose, scenting him, and they'd all chuckled.

"You'll take care of her," Nisio had stated. "If anything happens to her mama or me."

He'd met his *papai*'s silver eyes. "Of course."

She's smart, he told himself now. *And she knows how to handle herself.*

Cleia was always telling him not to underestimate his sister.

As they neared the exit for downtown Baltimore, Rui moved up beside him. "I vote we get off here," he called above the roar of the motors. "Check out Savonett's den." They both knew its approximate location, even though a spell kept it hidden.

Dion frowned, not wanting to stop for even a few minutes. "Why?"

Rui rolled a big shoulder. "A hunch. But we're flying blind here."

Dion hesitated. He'd grown up with Rui, the two of them brothers in all but blood. He trusted the shark fada's instincts.

The Baltimore exit loomed ahead. "Let's do it," he called back, and veered right, Tiago and the other two men following. They rumbled through the eastside until they came to Adric's street.

Leaving the bikes in a vacant lot that smelled of garbage and piss, they strode down the sidewalk, Dion and Rui in the lead. The few people they encountered took one look at their faces and moved aside. One man did an about-face and walked rapidly in the opposite direction.

Rui stalked forward, nostrils flared. The shark fada could pick out a single person's scent in a crowd of hundreds.

"There." He indicated a run-down brick house with three concrete steps leading to a faded green door. The bushes needed a trim, and a rusted porch swing took up most of the narrow porch.

"You scent Rosana?"

"*Sim,*" was the terse reply. "And Savonett, both recent."

Behind him, Tiago cursed.

They strode down the driveway. The first thing Dion saw was Rosana's backpack on the ground near the shed. Crumpled nearby were her hoodie and a knit hat, and a single black boot lay a few yards away.

He gave a hard swallow. He'd known something was wrong, but seeing her belongings scattered forlornly on the grass brought it home in vivid, terrifying color.

Rui touched his arm. "It doesn't mean anything. We already know she's not here."

"But it proves she didn't go with that bastard willingly." Dion pawed through the backpack, Tiago at his side, hoping for some clue, but all it held was the other boot, a pair of socks, a change of clothes—and the silver charm bracelet.

Hades. His fingers tightened on the charm. He and Tiago exchanged an apprehensive look.

Rui jerked a dagger from a hip sheath and leapt in front of Dion. "Up there." He indicated the shed roof.

Dion let go of the backpack and grabbed his own dagger. Tiago and the other two men ranged themselves at his back, knives ready.

Marjani Savonett dropped lightly to the ground in front of them. She took a fighter's crouch, a knife in each hand, lips peeled to reveal lethal canines.

"What the fuck are you doing in my brother's backyard?"

Dion pushed in front of Rui. "Looking for my sister."

Marjani's gaze flicked to the backpack, and he knew she scented Rosana. "She was here? With Adric?"

He nodded. "She left a note saying she was coming to him. That was last night. But this morning, she called on Cleia for help. We traced her to southern Maryland and then lost her."

"That's a good two hours from here. Even if she was with Adric last night—and I'm not saying she was—why would he take her that far from Baltimore?"

"That's what I'm trying to find out."

"Look somewhere else, then. Adric would never hurt her."

"Then why leave her backpack here? And her boots?"

A bewildered look crossed Marjani's catlike face. "I don't know," she admitted.

Rui sheathed his knife to sniff the grass. "The scent—" He shook his head. "Adric's scent on her is strong, but there's another, more recent scent. And Rosana was afraid. There was a fight, I think."

Dion pushed past Marjani to crouch beside him. "An earth fada."

"The brown wolf," Rui confirmed. He looked up at Marjani. "One of your brother's lieutenants—Luc."

She sheathed her knives and dropped to all fours, scrutinizing the slight depression the backpack had left in the wet grass. She inhaled deeply. They all heard her breath catch.

Dion grabbed her arm. "What is it?"

She shook her head. "I have to think," she said, tight-lipped.

"Damn it." He gave her a shake. "If you know something, tell us."

Her eyes flashed with the blue of her cougar. "Get your goddamn hands off me."

Suddenly, a tall blond male appeared out of nowhere—Fane Morningstar, Marjani's quarter-fae mate. He shoved his face into Dion's. "You heard the woman. Let her go."

Rui clamped a hand on Morningstar's shoulder, but Dion shook his head, and he let the other man go.

Dion released Marjani. "My apologies," he told her as he and Rui came to their feet. "You understand, I'm worried about my sister."

Marjani and her mate rose as well. Tiago and the other men closed in, and she bared her teeth. "Back off."

Dion raised a hand. "Let her talk." To Marjani, he said, "I would consider any help you can give me a personal favor. Rui is correct—my sister is with this wolf?"

She exchanged a glance with her mate.

They know something.

Fear for Rosana chewed at Dion's insides, but he forced himself to wait calmly. Adric's sister wasn't a woman you could push.

"Do Mar is right," she said. "It was Luc. But he's not a lieutenant—not anymore."

"He was demoted?"

She gave an unhappy shake of her head. "Not really. He accepted a fae's *geas*. Adric had to expel him from the clan, at least until he serves out his term. But Luc shouldn't be in Baltimore. We've been looking for him ourselves."

"So you're saying that if he took Rosana, it wasn't with your brother's permission."

"That's right. But—" The cougar fada scraped a hand over her wiry black hair.

"Tell me. Please."

"You say you traced her to southern Maryland?"

He nodded. "A few miles from the state line."

"Fuck." She dropped her hand back to her side. "Adric's gone, too. And I'm pretty sure he's on his way to Virginia. To the New Moon Court."

"He didn't tell his second where he was going?" That was Rui.

"No." Her mouth flattened. "He knew I'd never let him go alone."

Dion frowned. What was the Baltimore alpha mixed up in now? "But why go to New Moon in the first place?"

"To protect me, damn it."

"Jani," warned her mate.

She hitched a shoulder. "What does it matter if they know?" she said. "In fact, maybe it could help." She turned back to Dion. "It's me the prince really wants."

Rui made a small sound.

They knew, of course, that someone in the Baltimore clan had slain Langdon's only surviving son, but they'd assumed it was Adric. Now, the pieces of the puzzle rearranged themselves in a way that made perfect sense.

Dion lowered his voice to a sub-vocal level. "It was you who killed Tyrus."

She jerked her chin in assent.

"To save Jace Jones and my daughter Evie," Morningstar added in equally low tones. "And it was Adric who made the bastard's body disappear."

"Doing all of us a huge favor," muttered Rui. He'd argued for years that Merry would be safer with Tyrus dead.

"But what the fuck does this have to do with Rosana?" Tiago demanded.

"Nothing," Marjani said. "Unless…"

"What?" Dion said. "Please, tell us. Even the smallest piece of information could help."

The cougar fada met his eyes. "Unless the prince knows how Adric feels about her."

"And that is—?"

"She's his mate."

No. Deus, no. "Not if I have anything to do with it," he grated.

Beside him, Tiago shook his head, although he seemed unsurprised.

"Take it easy." Marjani glowered back. "He hasn't claimed her. He doesn't want this any more than you do."

Rui set a hand on Dion's arm. "Whether he's claimed her isn't important. What's important is what the prince believes." To Marjani, he said, "You think the wolf took her to New Moon?"

"I don't know. He's not under a *geas* to the prince, he's under a *geas* to a fae lady. But she's half night fae—she might be at New Moon."

Dion's stomach tightened. He had a bad feeling about this fae lady. "What's her name—this half night fae?"

"Lady B," Morningstar said, confirming Dion's suspicions. "I believe you've had some trouble with her yourself."

"We did," Dion replied grimly. Blaer had tried to kidnap his brother Nic's young daughter for some sick purpose of her own.

Morningstar spread his hands. "I'm afraid that's all we know."

"My thanks," Dion said. "I won't forget this."

Fear beat in his blood. If Adric's sister was right, then Rosana was at the night fae court…or worse, Blaer's captive.

The fae who amused herself by capturing fada and forcing them to live out their lives in iron cages.

He spun on his heel, rapping out, "Let's go," in Portuguese to his men.

"*Sim.*" Rui was right with him. "I know a way inside New Moon."

"Wait." Marjani raced after him. "Take me, too."

"No." He kept moving. Adric's sister was an unknown quantity—who knew what she'd do once they were in Virginia?

She kept pace with him. "My bike's on the next block. It will only take me a minute to get it." She grabbed his arm. "You owe me, my lord. Remember?"

His stride checked. The den of river fada who'd kidnapped her had included two former Rock Run men, and Dion would always wonder if he could've somehow prevented the attack. He'd promised then that if Marjani ever needed anything, she had only to ask.

"Come, then," he growled. "But you'll be under my command, understand? You'll do nothing without my express permission."

"Understood." She hurried down an alley, her mate following.

"I'm coming, too," he declared, and a low-voiced argument ensued.

Dion didn't wait to hear the outcome. He broke into a jog for the motorcycles, the other men at his heels. Let Marjani keep up if she could.

But as they turned onto the I-95 ramp, she zoomed up on a slim black bike built for speed, her long-limbed mate's arms wrapped around her waist, and with a terse nod at Dion, fell in behind him and his men.

CHAPTER 27

S he was in.

Blaer's mouth curved as she followed Olivier down the wide staircase to the starkly elegant foyer.

No windows, but the fae lights had been shaped into disembodied torches. They floated near black marble walls, their imitation flames flickering purple and blue. The floor was a white-and-black checkerboard marble, and in a far corner, a lush arrangement of creamy flowers and vinca spilled from an onyx bowl on a stainless steel stand.

A lean, black-haired woman with a face like a fox's—all high cheekbones and pointed chin—stepped out of the shadows. "Welcome home, daughter."

Blaer's smile warped into something dangerous as the butler faded discreetly into the background. Now, Fleur claimed her. The woman who'd sent her to live with the ice fae when she was just a child, tearing her from everything she knew with no warning.

"Mother." Blaer descended the last step to the foyer and they air-kissed.

Fleur wore heels and a chic silver shift that showed off her long legs. Funny. Blaer had never realized that she'd unconsciously emulated her mother's signature style.

Unlike Blaer, though, Fleur wore the high priestess's black star around her neck. So her mother's scheming had paid off.

"How kind of you to greet me," Blaer murmured as she stepped back.

A shrug of her mother's bare shoulder. They both knew kindness had little to do with it.

Fleur tipped her head to one side. "How is your father, anyway?"

It was Blaer's turn to shrug. "Sindre suggested I...leave." As her mother surely knew. "So here I am. And you?" Her gaze raked over her mother's slight body, taking in the bite mark just above the silver dress's low neckline. "How is the prince?"

As a ten-year-old child, she'd clung to Fleur, begged to be allowed to stay. But her mother had been adamant that she leave. It hadn't been until Blaer was an adult that she'd understood why she'd been sent to Iceland. Her mother had caught the eye of Prince Langdon, and she wanted no reminder of her half ice-fae child at the court.

Especially a child sired by the ice fae king himself.

The ice fae hadn't known what to do with Blaer, and her father had taken only a slight interest in her. When she'd tried one too many times to feed on the other fae at his court, Sindre had forced her into a tower with only goblins and the occasional elf for company. The fae governess he'd provided to educate her had only 'ported in for a short period each day.

For a decade, she'd only been let out of the tower for occasional visits, until she'd grown old enough to play Sindre's games and he'd decided it amused him to let her rejoin his court.

Fleur brushed a cool finger down Blaer's cheek.

Blaer stiffened. Even as a child, her mother had rarely touched her. She hadn't needed to. A night fae could inflict a world of pain without any physical contact.

"You've grown," Fleur murmured. "Become a beautiful young woman...and a powerful one."

So that's what this was about. Blaer's mouth twisted. But she'd play along, see what her mother wanted.

"And I see you've been appointed high priestess. You must have...pleased the prince."

Fleur's full lips lifted in a catlike smile. "He seems satisfied." She glanced at Olivier, standing at attention by the front door. The butler was doing his best to resemble a blank-faced statue, but they both knew he was listening.

"Langdon has granted you a place at the court?"

"He has."

"Good." Her mother nodded at Olivier, indicating he should precede them out the door. "Come, I'll walk you to your new lair."

"As you wish."

Outside, the temperature was just above freezing, but to a woman who'd spent two decades in Iceland, it was practically balmy. Her mother, though, concealed a shiver. She must have rushed to Langdon's lair the instant she heard Blaer had arrived.

And how *had* she heard so quickly?

Blaer eyed Olivier. No, the elderly butler wouldn't risk his well-paying position to spy for Fleur. But that didn't mean someone else in Langdon's household wasn't a spy. She filed that away for possible future use.

More interesting was that her mother appeared unaffected by the noon sun. She donned a pair of sunglasses but didn't seem concerned that the skin on her face and arms was exposed. Blaer recalled a time when her mother wouldn't have been able to face even the weak winter sunlight except at dusk or dawn.

Blaer wasn't the only one who'd increased in power in the years she'd been away.

"You came from France?" Fleur asked.

"Paris," Blaer confirmed, unsurprised at this evidence that her mother had had her watched.

"Such a lovely city, especially this time of year. Short days and lights everywhere. Did you pick up that dress there?" Some of the world's top fae design houses were located in the French capital.

"I did."

"It suits you."

Olivier took a path through a grove of towering oaks. They followed, discussing fashion as if they'd been separated for only a few days instead of two decades.

Blaer's new home was located on the compound's outskirts, Langdon's way of letting her know she was here on sufferance.

Fleur looked on as Olivier showed Blaer around. Her new lair was smaller than the tower she'd had at Sindre's court, with just two bedrooms, a living room and a small kitchen, but it would do. She didn't plan to remain on New Moon's outer edges for long.

"You may decorate how you wish, of course," the butler murmured as they returned to the living room.

Blaer glanced around. Like the prince's lair, the walls were black Italian marble with narrow windows covered by black-out shades. The furniture was Art Nouveau, all sinuous lines and plush burn-out velvet, and the rug was a dramatic swirl of black and white. The rest of the apartment was decorated in a similar style.

"This will do." The twins would have to sleep in the second bedroom, but Jon was often gone on assignments anyway. He was her eyes and ears in the fae world, while Krysten stayed close.

And Luc would sleep in her bed—or on the marble floor. The choice was his.

Her mother eyed her thoughtfully. Then her mouth curved. "I'll see you at dinner. Introduce you around. They'll be dying to see how you turned out."

They shared their first genuine smile.

"I look forward to it," Blaer returned.

CHAPTER 28

*A*dric *knew*, even as he fought admitting it. He'd have taken a blade to the heart rather than believe Luc would betray him like this.

But the wolf fada knew the location of Adric's den, even if the *look-away* spell prevented him from finding the entrance. If Luc had been outside when Rosana emerged...

Adric was moving before he realized it. He dropped from the tree, shifting in mid-air to land directly in front of Luc.

The wolf fada was much larger than an ordinary lupine. His head reached Adric's chest, and his canines were a good two inches long. But Adric was the dominant and they both knew it.

He grabbed Luc by the scruff of the neck, shook him. "What the fuck have you done?"

Orange tinged with gold glittered over the wolf's coat, and then Luc stood before Adric. He was thinner, all bone and sinew, his eyes burning holes in his craggy face.

His chin jutted out. "I gave that do Rio female to Blaer."

"Rosana?" Adric gaped at him. Even in the face of the evidence, he'd hoped it wasn't true. That Luc would have an explanation.

A black fury filled his head. His heart exploded into frenzied beats.

The cat clawed to be free. *Stole the mate.*

Blood.

Kill.

Adric's hands shot out, wrapped around Luc's throat. "You thrice-damned bastard."

Luc stared back proudly, not even trying to fight. "Did it...for you," he gasped out. "Lady B...ordered me to...capture you. When I saw Rosana...took her instead."

"For me?" Blood pounded in Adric's temples. He gave Luc a hard shake. "You traded an innocent female for *me*. What kind of a goddamned excuse for a man are you?"

Luc's eyes flared. "A man...under a *geas*."

He didn't add that he'd accepted the *geas* to save Marjani. He didn't have to.

Adric forced his fingers to unpeel from Luc's neck. Killing the other man might satisfy his blood lust, but it wouldn't help Rosana, and the wolf had intel that he needed. With a frustrated growl, he shoved Luc away from him.

The wolf stumbled back a few feet before catching himself. He brought a hand to his throat and eyed Adric, breath sawing in and out.

"Where is she?" Adric rapped out.

"Inside." Luc jerked his head in the direction of New Moon. "Lady B took her to the prince. An offering. She's trying to buy her way into the court."

Adric's lip curled. "I don't fucking believe it. You gave Rosana to that fae bitch after what she did to Jani. To *you*."

Blaer had caged not only Marjani, but Luc. And then she'd enslaved him.

"I did it for the clan, too," the wolf retorted. "If the fae get hold of you, the clan would never recover. We—they need you."

Adric's fingers flexed. Gods, he wanted to wrap them around Luc's throat again.

"Fuck what the clan needs. There are some lines you don't cross. Ever."

Luc's gaze slid from his, but he didn't apologize. He clearly believed he'd done the right thing.

Adric shook his head in disgust. He'd known Luc since they were both cubs, but now he wondered if he'd ever truly known the other man at all.

Inside, his cat crouched, a concentrated ball of rage. Aching to sink its teeth into Luc's throat, to drench the earth with his blood.

Easy. We need to find out what he knows.

"Why?" he ground out. "Why would the prince want Rosana?"

"He's a fae." The wolf shrugged a shoulder. "Since when do they need a reason to be S.O.B.s?"

It wasn't a lie, but Adric recognized evasion when he heard it. He scraped a hand over his spiky hair. Luc wasn't telling him everything, but maybe he couldn't.

"You say Lady B wants to join the New Moon court?"

A shrug. "She can't return to Iceland—the ice fae king banished her from his court for a fae year-and-a-day."

Adric nodded. "Jani told me."

"The night fae are her mother's people, but they don't want her, either. They pawned her off on the ice fae when she was still a kid."

"Figures." Adric snorted. The night fae would devour their own young if they didn't need them to pass on their precious bloodlines. "But that doesn't explain why the prince would want Rosana. Me, I can understand. Take me, and Jani will come running."

Their eyes met. They both knew the prince would do just about anything to get his hands on Marjani.

"But Rosana?" Adric shook his head. "He must know it will bring Rock Run down on him. They're a powerful clan, and everyone knows the sun fae queen has a soft spot for Rosana."

Luc gave a noncommittal grunt. He seemed distracted. A drop of sweat trickled down his face. At his sides, his fingers twitched.

Suddenly, he lunged. Adric flung himself to the side, but Luc's fingers closed on his quartz.

Adric jerked. It was like Luc had plunged his hand into his chest and wrapped his fingers around his beating heart. He couldn't think, couldn't breathe, his whole being consumed with a deep, visceral agony.

He shoved at Luc, but the other man held on grimly.

"Sorry." His old friend's face was a stony mask. "She gave me a direct order. I can't disobey." He gave the quartz a hard squeeze.

Adric bit down on a scream as more pain jolted through him. His eyes locked on Luc's own quartz, just inches from his face.

He scrabbled for it, missed. Tried again.

Claws slid out on Luc's free hand. He slashed at Adric's forearm, ripping him to the bone, but Adric was in too much pain to register it.

There.

His fingers closed on Luc's quartz. He glared into the wolf's eyes, using all the dominance at his command. Praying it would be enough to overcome the *geas*, at least temporarily.

"Release my quartz. *Now.*"

Luc shuddered. Sweat poured down his face. But he gripped the pendant even tighter.

Pain lashed at Adric like a fiery whip. Scorching through his veins in an unending shriek of agony.

His body jerked, but he kept up the pressure. "Let. It. Go."

Luc's gaze slid sideways—and then he released the pendant and stumbled back.

The absence of pain was stunning. Adric sucked in a breath. Another breath, and then he realized he'd let go of Luc's quartz.

Fortunately, the other man was in no shape to fight. He bent forward, hands on his thighs, chest heaving.

Adric didn't wait for him to recover. Jerking his dagger from its sheath, he slammed Luc to the forest floor. Straddling his abdomen, he touched the sharp iron edge to the soft place beneath the jaw where Luc's right carotid pulsed.

"Don't move. Don't even *breathe*. Understand?"

Luc hissed as the poisonous metal seared his skin. He stilled, resignation sketched on his face.

"Speak." Adric pressed the sharp edge a little deeper. "Tell me you understand. You won't move until I say so."

"Yes." Luc swallowed. "My lord."

Adric sheathed the dagger and dragged off his quartz, dangling it from his fingers. Blood ran down his arm. He ignored it to swing the stone back and forth on its leather cord. Deep within, a fiery bronze mixed with blue flared to life.

"Look at my quartz."

"No." Luc squeezed his eyes shut.

Adric growled. "Look at it, you son of a bitch. *Now*."

Luc shook his head, but Adric was still his alpha, even if he was technically no longer a member of the clan. His wolf wouldn't let him fight too hard, especially now, when Adric's command didn't interfere with Blaer's *geas*.

He opened his eyes. They were dull gold. Flat, hopeless.

Adric gave a hard swallow. For a few desolate seconds, he was back in the abandoned den where his uncle had imprisoned Luc for twelve long months.

By then, Adric and Marjani were on the run from their uncle. Leron Savonett had tortured and starved Luc for months, but he'd never given up their hidey-holes. Adric knew he'd have died rather than betray them.

When Adric and Marjani had finally tracked Luc down, they found him manacled to the wall with an iron cuff around one wrist. The constant exposure to iron had weakened him, making it impossible for him to heal. He lay curled up on the stone floor, his body a rack of bones on which to hang his skin. Open sores on his manacled wrist. His back bloody from a recent beating.

The eyes Luc had lifted to Adric and Marjani had held that same bleak hopelessness. Even as a teenager, the wolf fada had rarely smiled.

But at the sight of them, a corner of his mouth had lifted. "About time you showed up."

"Don't do this," Luc rasped now. "Just kill me."

Adric's throat worked. "I can't," he whispered.

Back and forth.

Luc might hate Adric for hypnotizing him, but at least he'd be alive.

"Damn you to Hades." The wolf's gaze locked on the quartz swaying, pendulum-like, above his nose.

Adric pumped energy into the crystals. Inside, the flames flared brighter until they were reflected in Luc's pupils, eerie blue flames in the glistening black circles.

"You'll take me to Lady B."

"Yes," Luc said in a flat voice.

"Can you get me through New Moon's wards?" He'd planned to use his Gift of hypnotism to trick a guard into sneaking him inside, but entering with Luc was even better. The wards would open for Luc, and Adric could slip inside with him.

"Yes."

"I want your promise on your honor as a wolf."

"Yes. On my honor as a wolf, I will get you through the wards."

Gotcha. Adric's mouth curved in a feral smile. "Where are your clothes?"

"There." Luc's arm swung up, pointed into the trees.

"Take me to them."

Luc immediately started to his feet. Adric had to scramble out of his way.

The wolf fada walked in the direction he'd pointed, halting in front of an oak tree, where his clothes were bundled into a leather jacket and wedged into a crook of the tree. He stood at attention, awaiting instructions.

Adric was surprised at how easy Luc was to control; it was as if he'd surrendered completely to Adric's will. But then, he was Luc's alpha, whether or not he'd been expelled from the clan. When a man like Luc gave you his loyalty, he'd walk through hell or high water for you.

"Give me the clothes," he told Luc, "and then shift to your wolf."

While the other man obeyed, Adric used his quartz to heal the slashes on his arm. After they'd scabbed over, he dropped the leather cord over his head and took the clothes from Luc.

They were a little big, but they'd do. He tucked the sheathed dagger beneath the T-shirt and laced on the lug-sole boots. If a fada came across their tracks, they'd see Luc's prints, not his. Lastly, he put on the black hoodie, pulling up the hood to hide his distinctive hair. The leather jacket he returned to the crook of the oak. It would only be in the way if he had to shift—or fight.

Weak as he was, Luc took a long time to shift. Too long.

Adric stood helplessly by as his old friend wavered between man and wolf, sparkles flickering anemically over his skin. If Luc couldn't complete the shift, he'd die, his body a grotesque mass of incompatible organs.

He growled. "Focus, damn you. You can do this."

A weak glimmer of orange, and at last Luc's huge brown wolf appeared. He was too thin in this form as well, his fur dull, patchy. At this rate, he'd never survive his decade with Blaer.

"Fuck, I'm sorry." He touched Luc's head. "When this is over, I promise I'll do what I can. There's got to be a way to break the damn *geas*."

The wolf's breath sighed out. Then he gave Adric's hand a firm nip. The message was clear: *Stay out of this.*

Adric scowled down at him. "I'm the alpha, remember?"

Luc growled lowly.

It was Adric's turn to sigh. "At least let me give you a shot of healing energy."

At Luc's nod of assent, he ran his quartz over the wolf's body. He was still thin—there wasn't much Adric could do about that, but his fur grew shinier, the patches closing over until he had a thick coat again.

Luc nuzzled his chest in gratitude.

Adric grimaced. "Don't thank me yet."

He lifted his quartz, dangling it in front of the wolf's face.

He paused, sorting his thoughts. He had to get the command just right. Once they were inside, and especially if Blaer caught sight of them, he had to make sure the compulsion to obey him, Adric, was stronger than the power her *geas* exerted on Luc.

When he was ready, he infused his voice with dominance. "Take me to Rosana do Rio. *Now.* No detours, except whatever's necessary to keep the night fae from detecting me. Understood?"

The wolf whined...and then turned and trotted out of the trees. Adric dropped his quartz back over his head, tucking it into the T-shirt along with the dagger, and strode after him.

Luc didn't take the shimmering fae path, confirming Adric's suspicion it was booby-trapped, or maybe even an illusion. Instead, he veered right.

They circled the compound, Luc padding stiffly beside him, his will under Adric's command. Adric swallowed something acrid. He'd promised himself he'd never compel any of his lieutenants or close friends.

The Darktime isn't over. The prince will destroy your clan from the inside out.

Was this how it started? With Adric himself?

As they passed through two longleaf pines, a small circle shimmered into being, widening into a wolf-sized portal. Luc stepped through it, Adric glued to his side.

His spine tingled. He pulled back his shoulders, his stance tough, as if he were a fada bodyguard. Someone who belonged. Meanwhile, his gaze roamed the compound, his body poised for anything.

A second ticked past, then another and another. From a nearby oak, a raven studied Adric with beady brown eyes. Finally, the portal behind them contracted shut.

He was in.

He blew out a breath, took a cautious step forward. It was darker in here—too dark—the weak sunlight barely penetrating the forest canopy. Something rustled behind him. He spun around, but nothing was there. Then it was in front of him, although he still couldn't see anything.

Until he realized the shadows themselves had come alive.

They blotted out the sky, slithered over the vine-covered buildings, morphed into nightmarish creatures that grew larger until they loomed over him and Luc before dissolving, only to reappear somewhere else. The worst were the faces, their eyes wide, their mouths stretched into predatory howls—or worse, smiles.

It was the Darktime amped up ten times over.

Breathe. Stay calm. Think of something good, something that makes you happy. Making love to Rosana, or playing soccer with the cubs.

Then it got worse. Magic shivered over Adric's skin...black, cold magic.

His nape tightened. Memories pricked his skin like sharp, painful darts.

Luc hadn't been the only one tortured to feed the night fae's craving for negative emotions. After he and Marjani had sprung Luc, Leron had finally captured them. They'd been lucky, though. His uncle had only let the beatings and torture go on for a few days, because he still had a use for them.

Marjani, he hadn't touched at all. No, she'd been chained to the wall, forced to watch as Adric took the beatings for them both.

When he'd deemed them sufficiently broken, he'd had them brought to him. Adric had been told he was leaving the country to fight as a mercenary for the fae, and Marjani had been ordered to whore herself to Jumar.

It was Leron Savonett's final mistake.

Adric's knees locked. Caught in the dark memories, he couldn't make himself continue moving forward.

Beside him, Luc seemed unaffected, probably because unlike Adric, he had permission to be here. He continued forward alone until he realized Adric was no longer following. Turning his head, he yipped a question.

"Right behind you." Adric steeled himself to walk into the nightmarish shadows. For Rosana, he'd enter Hades itself.

Luc sniffed the air and then aimed for Langdon's lair.

The shadows sucked at Adric, but the darkness lessened. His whole body slumped in relief.

Time to hide.

Adric removed Luc's boots and hid them under a bush. Then he touched his quartz, drawing energy from the tiny crystals to cloak himself. But he'd have to be careful—the energy drain was tremendous. He had fifteen minutes, maybe less, before the crystals ran out of power.

Luc swung his head from side to side, nostrils flared, clearly wondering where Adric had gone. Then he must've picked up Adric's scent because he gave a wolfy shrug and turned down a path of smooth white pebbles.

This time, when the darkness sucked at him, Adric twisted his fingers through Luc's ruff, and as he'd hoped, whatever protected the wolf spread to him as well. Together, they followed the path through the trees and around the still black pond.

The entrance to Langdon's lair was down a short flight of granite steps. Ivy spilled down either side of the tall door, a dark, polished wood with a triple moon carved into the top.

He stilled, inhaled. Lady Blaer had come this way.

And even though he couldn't scent Rosana, she was also nearby. He knew it with the same certainty that he knew the location of each of his clan members at any given moment.

"You go first," he told Luc in an undertone. "Distract the prince so I can get Rosana out. And Luc? If someone asks, you'll say you never saw me. That's an order."

The wolf's head swung up and down.

Adric tried the door handle. He wasn't surprised when it moved—Langdon had little to fear in his own compound. But as the door swung open on silent hinges, uneasiness crept up his spine.

This had been too damn easy.

Rosana's warning played in his head. Was he walking into a trap?

He can't see you. He doesn't know you're here.

The foyer stretched two stories up, and was completely empty except for an extravagant arrangement of white flowers in a large black bowl.

He hesitated, his uneasiness increasing, as Luc stepped across the threshold.

Then he scented Rosana. Faint but distinctive, and with an underlying tang of fear that made his chest clench.

His lips drew back in a silent snarl.

Thrice-damned, fucking fae.

He followed Luc into the foyer. Behind him, the wood door thudded shut.

CHAPTER 29

On the level below, a door opened and closed. Claws clicked on a marble floor.

Rosana's gaze flew to Langdon, but he didn't seem to have noticed. Instead, he set cool fingers on her wrist and urged the spoon toward her mouth.

"Eat." So soft, almost gentle, but steel edged his tone.

The portly butler appeared in the door. "My lord."

"Yes, Olivier?"

"There's a fada in the foyer."

No. Rosana froze, the spoon clenched in her hand. *You stubborn ass.*

Langdon's mouth turned down. "Deal with him."

Olivier inclined his shiny bald head. "As you wish. However, I believe he is one of Blaer's people. A wolf."

Not Adric, then. Rosana let out a breath.

The prince flicked her a look, no doubt detecting her agitation with those eerie senses of his. He rose to his feet.

"Alone?" he asked his butler. "You saw no one else?"

"No, my lord."

"I see. Well, let the wolf upstairs, and then inform Captain Quade that our wards have been breached."

Olivier gave a discreet cough. "The wolf has permission to pass through the wards."

"But the man with him does not."

The butler's eyes widened slightly. Then he nodded. "Very good, my lord." He made his stately way out of the room.

Rosana was still holding the spoon. She set it back on the linen napkin and stared unseeingly at the table.

The man had to be Adric. But why hadn't Olivier seen him?

Langdon pushed his chair in but remained behind it, his long, elegant fingers curled around the seatback. She felt him eyeing her downturned head.

When she glanced up, he arched a single diamond-studded brow. "Nothing to say? Perhaps you know why Lord Adric is here?"

She blanked her face. She couldn't let him know what she'd Seen. It could be the very information that tipped the balance and led to Adric's death.

"I don't speak for Lord Adric," she parried. "But I can tell you his animal isn't a wolf."

Langdon sighed. "I'm aware of that. And I didn't say Adric *was* a wolf. He's the man who entered with the wolf."

Rosana spread her hands in genuine confusion. "I'm sorry, but I don't know anything about a wolf."

Or did she? She stilled.

The wolf had to be Luc. And more, she'd bet a month's pay that he was Adric's former lieutenant, the fada who'd been with Blaer in Lewes. In fact, it was probably Luc who'd been seen at Rock Run earlier this week. The question was, why was Adric with him?

The wolf was outside the door now. Langdon strolled across the room to a bookcase and removed a small packet from an inlaid ebony-and-ivory box.

Rosana came to her feet as the wolf entered the library. She'd never seen Luc as his animal, but the scent fit. And damn, he was big. His head was almost level with hers, his eyes a deep amber just a few shades away from the gold of his man-form.

Her nostrils twitched. Adric *was* here. But why couldn't she see him?

Langdon's mouth turned down. "Does Blaer know you're here?" he asked Luc.

The wolf peeled his upper lip in a tooth-baring snarl.

"And you, Adric," the prince added. "Did you think I wouldn't know the instant you crossed through the portal?"

No reply.

But in the silence that fell, Rosana detected slow, almost-imperceptible breathing to Luc's left. Without moving her head, she slid a look in its direction. There was an odd, man-size disturbance in the air that made it difficult to see the bookshelf behind it.

Her heart jumped—and then sank. She smoothly turned back to Langdon. "All I see is a wolf, and I told you, Adric's not a wolf."

"Yes," the prince returned with a chilly little smile. "You did tell me that." He tore open the packet and tossed an acrid-smelling gray powder right at the man-sized disturbance.

Luc surged forward, aiming for Langdon's throat, but the prince threw up an arm to block him. The two fell to the floor, Luc on top, his teeth sunk into Langdon's forearm.

The gray powder outlined Adric and the dagger in his right hand. Swiping the powder off his face, he stalked across the library floor. Langdon was on top now, his hands wrapped around Luc's muzzle, the gash on his arm spattering blood everywhere.

"*Go,*" Adric growled at Rosana as he circled the two combatants, searching for an opening.

"I don't think so," she muttered. She shot a longing glance at the brown bat that had once been her stiletto and then grabbed the raven statue from its pedestal instead. It made a nice, solid weight in her hands.

She eyed the fighters. Adric was completely visible now, his body coated in the bad-smelling gray powder. He sliced at Langdon with his dagger, but the night fae rolled, shoving Luc in front of him. The blade slashed through the heavy muscles of the wolf's left shoulder.

Luc turned and snapped at Adric, and then froze.

A horrorstruck look crossed Adric's face. "Fuck. I'm sorry, bro."

He eased the knife out just as the prince grabbed Luc's ruff and slammed him headfirst onto the floor. The wolf made a final, jerky movement before collapsing, motionless.

Langdon flowed to his feet and faced Adric, taking a martial arts stance, arms raised and knees bent with one leg forward.

Adric prowled forward, the dagger loose and ready in his hand. His eyes were a cougar-blue, his expression hard, predatory. Rosana could almost see the big cat overlaying the human.

Langdon stepped backwards. He was at his desk now. Reaching behind him, he grabbed a paperweight and flung it at Adric. It turned in mid-air into a thick, hissing snake with a copperhead's distinctive hourglass markings. With a growled curse, Adric slapped it away. The snake landed on the floor, and he bent and chopped off its head with a single stroke of his knife.

Langdon's eyes flickered red and Rosana growled.

Oh no, you don't.

She regripped the raven, palms sweaty, and moved to the prince's left.

Adric indicated her with his chin. "Let Rosana go. This has nothing to do with her. She's not even a member of my clan."

Langdon tilted his head. "A trade?"

"What kind of trade?"

"Your sister for Rosana."

Her head jerked back. "No!"

Neither man looked at her.

"And if I say yes," Adric asked, "what would happen to Marjani?"

"That's between me and her. But I swear, she'll have a chance. More than she gave my son."

What were they talking about? Rosana clenched the raven, her gaze darting between the two men.

Adric's jaw clenched. "No fucking way. You get me, not my sister. And no matter what, Rosana goes free. That's non-negotiable."

Rosana had heard enough. She lunged, swinging the statue like a club at Langdon's head, but he ducked and flowed sideways so the blow glanced off his shoulder instead. A long leg swept out, knocking her own legs from beneath her.

She landed on her ass, the raven clattering to the marble next to her. But she'd given Adric an opening, and he pounced, dagger aimed at Langdon's throat.

The prince threw up an arm to block him, and with an agile twist of his body, used Adric's own momentum to throw him into a bookcase. Rosana scuttled backward as books showered down around her.

Catlike, Adric turned in mid-air so that his shoulder hit the bookcase instead of his head and landed on his feet, still holding the dagger. He stalked back toward Langdon, and the two men started circling each other again.

Rosana scrambled back to her feet.

Adric jerked his head at her without taking his gaze from the prince. "Get out of here already." To Langdon, he said, "You're dead. Nobody touches my sister. Nobody."

The prince went whiter, if that were possible for such a pale man. "Olivier!" he called.

Adric lunged, slashing the dagger through Langdon's shirt, drawing the poisonous iron across his torso.

Langdon sucked in a breath and danced backward. His eyes narrowed. "Kill me, and you'll never get out of here alive."

"You think I fucking care?" Adric shook his head. "You fae just don't get it, do you?"

The prince took another step back until he could reach his desk again. This time, he grabbed a handful of pens to fling at Adric. They turned into hornets and swarmed his head. Shoving the dagger into his pocket, Adric caught and crushed them with shifter-fast speed, one after another.

Meanwhile, Langdon had circled around Adric. He aimed a kick at Adric's knee cap from the side, which Adric only just evaded. Catching the prince's arm, he jerked him forward and down. His hand chopped down on the back of Langdon's neck. The night fae rolled with it, coming smoothly back to his feet.

The two men turned in a tight circle. Langdon flicked his fingers at the dagger and it turned into another bat that dove for Adric's head. He grabbed it in mid-air, flinging it to the hard floor where it lay, dead.

Adric let his claws and fangs slide out. With a guttural growl, he backed the prince into a corner.

Langdon's eyes narrowed. Shadows gathered at the room's edges.

Despair crawled over Rosana's skin. Hopelessness descended on her in a suffocating cloud. *You can't escape. Why even try?*

Adric gave a hard swallow.

Rosana clenched her fists. "Breathe," she whispered, speaking for herself as much as Adric. "It's him, not us. Don't let him win."

The shadows receded. She sidled along the bookcases, watching for a chance to help Adric. Her foot slipped and she looked down to find the hornets had changed back into pens.

Olivier rapped on the door. "My lord? Is everything okay?"

"Send for the guards!" Langdon called back.

"Pardon me?" The elderly butler opened the door, blinked.

"Send for my guards," Langdon gritted.

"Immediately, my lord." The door closed with a decided click.

Oh, no, you don't.

Rosana sprinted across the room, throwing open the door. She caught Oliver right before he reached the stairs and shoved him face-first against the wall.

"Don't move." She wrenched his arm up, ignoring the pinch of guilt at manhandling an elder. "I don't want to hurt you, but I will if I have to."

Beneath the natty yellow bow tie, the butler's throat worked. "Yes, miss."

"This way." She urged him back down the hall. "What's in there?" She jerked her head at the door opposite the library.

"The prince's bedroom."

Behind her, she heard grunts and a crash. She shot a glance over her shoulder, but all she could see was the still unconscious wolf. If Langdon managed to get a message out to his guards, they were fucked.

"Open the door," she snapped at Olivier, then waited impatiently as he turned the knob with agonizing slowness. "Inside." She punctuated the order with a small shove. As she kicked the door shut behind them, her gaze lit on the sturdy four-poster bed. Perfect.

"Take off your belt."

Olivier undid the buckle, slid the belt from its loops and handed it to her.

"Hands together."

A pained expression crossed the butler's broad face. "Is this necessary, miss?"

"Yes," she snapped. "Now do it."

His mouth thinned, but he presented his hands, palms together. Quickly, she wound the belt around his wrists a couple of times and then looped the rest around one of the bed's thick black posts.

"It's better this way," she told him as she cinched the belt. "You can tell the prince you had no choice."

His mouth lifted in a wry arc. "Next you'll be saying I should thank you."

Their eyes met. So the man had a sense of humor hidden behind that stone face.

"Sorry," she said with a shrug and shot out the door.

Downstairs, the front door crashed open. She darted down the hall long enough to see what looked like an entire cadre of warriors pouring inside.

Langdon had gotten a message out.

She sprinted back to the library, slamming the door shut and turning the key.

The entire room was roiling with shadows. Luc was still unconscious, but Adric and Langdon were in another corner now. Langdon was bleeding from the torso and favoring the arm the wolf had savaged, but he looked better than Adric, who wavered drunkenly from side to side.

He had the dagger again. A quick glance at the floor told her the bat had disappeared.

Unfortunately, the dagger wasn't doing Adric any good. He had it gripped in both hands but could barely keep the point turned up. Blood dripped from a gash in his temple, mixing with the gray powder streaking his face. He looked like a crazed clown.

He glanced at her, scowled. "You're s'pposed...to be gone."

She snatched the dagger from him. "Someone has to save your ass, cat."

She advanced on Langdon. He faded back into the darkest shadow—and disappeared.

With a frustrated growl, she shoved the dagger into her pocket and ran her hands over the wall, just in case Langdon was still there. But the bastard was gone.

The warriors banged on the locked door, demanding entrance.

"Now what?" Adric asked Rosana with a lopsided smile.

"We get the hell out of here."

"Sounds...like a...plan." He walked several unsteady feet and sat down hard next to the wolf. He stroked his friend's fur. "Luc?" When the other shifter didn't move, Adric looked up at Rosana, a perplexed line between his eyes. "He's hurt."

"So are you."

"Oh." He touched his head and then stared at the blood on his fingers.

From across the hall, Olivier was shouting for help.

She gripped Adric's shoulder. "We have to get out of here. The window."

"'Kay." He came onto his hands and knees and then just stayed there, staring at the floor as if he'd never seen marble before.

Outside the door, she heard Olivier explaining the situation to Langdon's guards. There was short silence, and then a loud explosion shook the library.

Hellfire. They were using fae balls.

The door shuddered on its hinges, but the thick wood held. For now.

Rosana crouched next to Adric, trying to lift him up. But he was heavy, with a fada's extra solid bones. She stifled a sob.

"Adric." She tugged on his arm. "Get up, damn it. If they find us here, we're dead."

"Yeah." He nodded sagely—and collapsed. She barely managed to catch him before his head hit the marble. She eased him the rest of the way down onto his stomach. He lay still, head turned to the side, blood seeping out of the wound.

"*No.*" She pressed a fist to her mouth. What was she going to do now?

Next to him, Luc's eyes fluttered open. He whined and nuzzled Adric's shoulder.

The door shuddered with a second explosion, and then another.

Bang. Bang.

The hinges shrieked as they started to give.

She lurched into action, grabbing Adric's wrists and dragged him toward the nearest window. Jerking the blind open, she ran her hands around the sash, frantically searching for a way to open it. But the window was one long oblong of glass with no latch that she could detect.

Giving up, she snatched up the poor, abused raven one last time and swung it as hard as she could at the center of the window. The glass didn't even crack. Instead, she watched, incredulous, as the statue broke instead, its stone head careening sideways and almost landing on Adric.

The door broke from the wall and crashed to the floor. She tossed the raven's body aside and whipped out Adric's dagger. Five night fae stormed into the library. One set a foot on Luc's neck, stilling his weak, half-conscious movements, while the others surrounded her and the still-unconscious Adric.

She moved in front of him, dagger out. "Stay where you are."

The man who'd led the charge regarded her with icy eyes. "Where's the prince?"

"He 'ported out of here. Or whatever you call that disappearing-into-the shadows thing he does."

The warrior jerked his head at one of his men. "Find Prince Langdon. The rest of you, take these two."

"Yes, Captain." The three remaining men closed in on her and Adric.

She bared her teeth. "Come any closer, and I'll rip your goddamned hearts out." She knew she wasn't being rational—she was surrounded, with no way out —but her animal wouldn't let them get any closer to Adric. Not while he was injured.

The captain swirled his hand, magician-like, and held it, palm up, fingers spread wide. A purple spark appeared in his palm, expanding into an orb of dark, pulsating light.

A fae ball, night-fae style.

She swallowed sickly. One of those could burn a hole right through you.

"Surrender," he said, "or I'll throw this at your mate, there."

"He's not my mate," she returned dully. But she brought the dagger to her side.

They swarmed around her. The knife was wrenched from her hand. The captain took her arm in a firm grip while two others lifted Adric like a sack of potatoes and carried him toward the door.

Langdon appeared in the doorway.

"My lord." The captain inclined his head respectfully.

"I see you finally realized there were intruders."

The tall warrior's spine went ramrod straight. "My apologies, sir. We didn't detect him when he came through the portal."

Langdon gave a cold nod. "We'll discuss your failure later, Quade. For now, confine the earth fada below. The woman you can leave here."

"No!" She jerked against the captain's confining hand. "You're not taking Adric anywhere without me."

Langdon tilted his head to the side. "You prefer to go with him?"

She raised her chin. "Yes. In fact, I insist on it."

The prince's lips stretched in a chilling smile. Too late, she realized she'd given him permission to imprison her.

"Then we'll be happy to accommodate you both."

CHAPTER 30

Captain Quade marched Rosana out of the library and down the marble stairs. The two warriors followed with Adric.

It was the first she'd seen the foyer. She had a brief impression of a large, dimly lit space, and then the captain urged her through an open door and down another flight of stairs.

They were in an underground warren with rooms and halls spearing off in multiple directions. As with the foyer, the only lighting came from a few torch-shaped fae lights. She glimpsed a cavernous wine cellar with hundreds of dusty bottles, and a room with an ancient brick hearth that she guessed had once been a kitchen.

Their destination was a short hall with just three doors, all constructed of a thick wood reinforced with iron straps. The men carrying Adric opened the door at the end and tossed him inside.

She flinched as his body thumped against the stone floor.

The captain gestured her after Adric with a mocking smile. "Be my guest, senhorita."

Her throat constricted. The three steps into that small, windowless room were the most difficult of her life, but the need to protect Adric drove her forward.

She had time to see a long wood bench against the far wall and that to her left, there was a rough toilet alongside a metal spout with a thin stream of water flowing into a narrow trough before disappearing down a drain. Then the door thudded shut behind her.

A key turned in the lock, and she was alone in the dark with Adric. The only light came from a slit at the top of the door.

Her eyes went night-glow, but all she could make out were dim gray shapes—Adric, the bench. Her chest tightened.

It felt like a tomb. Small. Airless.

She stumbled to the door, lungs pumping. Not sure what she was going to do, just knowing she had to get out. *Now.*

This side of the door had no handle. She ran her hands over the wood anyway, hissing when her fingertips brushed one of the iron bands.

Behind her, Adric groaned.

She leaned her forehead against the wood.

Calm the fuck down. He's hurt—bad. He needs *you.*

She took a deep breath.

Okay, then.

She'd make Adric as comfortable as possible and then trust that his natural healing ability would take over.

She made her way to the trough, rinsed her burned fingers. The water was ice-cold, fresh from an underground stream. She splashed it on her face and then stuck her head under the thin trickle, gulping water until the dryness in her throat eased.

She was pretty sure she'd glimpsed a cup near the trough. Calmer now, she felt around until her fingers closed on the cool metal. She filled the cup and took it back to Adric. Using a combination of touch and sight, she cleaned the gash on his head before returning to the trough for more water, which she used to rinse the gray powder from his face and hands. She was afraid the powder's bitter smell meant it was poisonous.

Adric moved restlessly, and she touched his cheek. "Adric? You okay?"

He mumbled something and then went limp again.

"That's it, *meu amor.*" She rubbed his shoulder. "Rest. Let yourself heal."

His lips moved, but all that came out was a croak.

"You must be thirsty. Hang on—I'll be right back." She made another trip for water, and then wet a finger and moistened his lips. He tried to suck her finger, so she trickled water into his mouth, but he murmured fretfully and turned his head away.

"Just a little," she said, and kept at him until he took a few sips. Setting the cup down, she sat next to him and eased his head onto her lap. "Rest." She stroked his cheek. "Everything is going to be all right."

It didn't matter that he probably couldn't hear her. Just saying it aloud made her feel better.

She was silent for a time, but that made the darkness creep closer, almost like it was a living being. Like when Blaer had tried to feed on them in Lewes—or Langdon just now.

She shuddered.

It's just your imagination.

At least, she hoped it was. She pulled Adric closer.

"Know something?" She nuzzled his hair. "I love that I can touch you without setting off my Sight. Although right now, I wouldn't mind Seeing how to break us out of here. Because I have to tell you, I just *knew* that I had to be here with you." She grimaced. "Just don't ask me why, because I haven't been much help so far."

She stilled. Not only had she not helped, she was probably why he'd been captured. Because she had the bad feeling that if not for her, Adric wouldn't have rushed into the library like that. He'd have waited to catch Langdon off-guard.

"No." A sick feeling seeped into her belly. "My being here does *not* set off the timeline leading to your death."

In her vision, Adric had been alone. She had to believe that somehow her presence changed things, although that didn't mean she could sit by and let things play out. She had to *do* something. But what?

She resumed stroking him. *Think, Rosana.*

But she was fresh out of ideas. Her only hope was that Cleia had heard her cry for help, and that she and Dion would realize Rosana had been taken to New Moon. If they didn't find her note and blame Adric for her disappearance...

She blew out a breath. *Deus*, what a mess.

She rested the back of her head against the wall. The rush of adrenaline that had carried her through the fight had worn off, leaving her feeling like a deflated balloon. Her eyelashes fluttered down. She forced them open, afraid to go to sleep.

The cell smelled musty, the floor covered with a layer of dust as if no one had been here for a long time. How long would Langdon leave them down here in the dark?

And what if Adric got worse? She was no healer. She could scream herself raw and no one would hear.

Fear clogged her throat. Her breath shortened. Were the walls closing in?

Stop it. That's just what Langdon wants. If you freak out, he wins.

Her chest heaved, shifting the pendant Adric had given her. She pulled it from her shirt, fingered it. As in the prince's library, the amethyst was oddly warm.

Her jaw set. "You do love me. You're just afraid to admit it."

"Mmph."

She glanced down. Adric looked back at her, eyes gleaming a brilliant blue in the gloom.

CHAPTER 31

From far off, Adric heard Rosana arguing with Langdon. Was aware of other people in the room, too, all men.

Get the fuck away from her.

His vocal cords vibrated in a growl that only he heard. He tried to rise but couldn't.

Rough hands lifted him, conveyed him down first one flight of stairs, then another. Pain jolted through his head, down his spine. He gritted his teeth and bore it. He would *not* give them the satisfaction of hearing him groaning.

The movement halted. The hands released him and he fell to the floor. His head bounced. A white light exploded behind his eyes. The pain reached a screaming pitch and he passed out.

For a time, everything was blissfully dark. But gradually, sensation returned, and with it the knowledge that Rosana needed him.

He clawed his way back to consciousness.

Cold. Dank.

Hard stone beneath his body.

The musical trickle of water.

Rosana's scent, and the murmur of her voice.

A soft thigh beneath his head...and his head pounding like a motherfucker.

"You do love me," she said. "You're just afraid to admit it."

"Mmph." He wasn't sure if he was agreeing or disagreeing, but he did know that he needed to see her.

He forced his eyes open. He was on his back with his head on Rosana's lap. The room was so dark he could barely see a foot in front of his face. His eyes went night-glow.

Rosana gave a tremulous smile, her own irises a luminous aquamarine in the shadowy light. "You're awake."

He grunted, the only sound he could manage right then.

He hurt everywhere. His muscles. His bones. His fingers. His face. Even his toes twinged when he gave them an experimental flex.

But the worst was his head. He fingered his right temple. He vaguely recalled Langdon slamming him face-first into the desk. The blow had reverberated through his skull and down his vertebrae. He was lucky the prick hadn't broken his neck. Thankfully, the wound had already scabbed over, his body drawing on his quartz to speed his healing.

But after that, he didn't recall much. In fact, he couldn't remember exactly how Rosana had come to be involved.

"How long...was I out?"

"About fifteen minutes."

"Fuck." He tried to lift his head off her lap and froze as the dull throbbing in his brain spiked.

"Shh. Don't move." Rosana guided him back onto her thigh. "Rest."

She smoothed a palm over his eyes and nose, down to his chin. The pain eased. His eyelids drifted shut. He nuzzled her hand, both man and cat wanting nothing but to drift off again.

He forced his eyes to open. "Where?" he asked through swollen lips.

"Still in Langdon's lair—a level below the foyer. A prison cell. The door is solid wood reinforced with iron, and there are no windows, just a slot at the top of the door. They didn't bother with a bed, either. Or heat."

His throat worked. "Sorry."

It was coming back to him now. Discovering that Rosana was the night fae's prisoner, rushing to her rescue. He'd have pulled it off if the prince hadn't tossed that damn powder at him. Its bitter scent still clung to his skin.

How the fuck had Langdon known he was there? He'd been careful to stick close to Luc. But he'd been angry with Luc and terrified for Rosana. He must've been leaking emotion, especially when he found Rosana alone with the bastard.

And now they were locked in an underground cell. His heart punched at his rib cage. A cold sweat prickled his skin.

The Darktime.

A dank cell concealed beneath Leron's den. The clanmates who disappeared below never to be seen again. The pervasive scent of fear, as if it had soaked into the very stones.

And the growing conviction that it was only a matter of time before Leron found an excuse to throw him in the cell...or worse, Marjani.

The teenage Adric had tried to appease his uncle, but Leron had seen how the younger clan members turned to his nephew. Hell, he'd known before Adric that he was alpha material.

So Leron had set out to break him.

One by one, everyone Adric loved had been stolen from him. His dad. His mom. Jace's sister. Until the only ones left were a few stubbornly loyal friends like Zuri, Jace, Luc—and Marjani.

That was when his uncle had made his fatal mistake. Go after Adric, and he would've endured it until he was strong enough to challenge for alpha.

But go after Marjani, and all bets were off.

"It's not your fault." Rosana's voice yanked him back to the present. "You've got nothing to be sorry for."

He unclenched his jaw, forced himself to inhale.

"Yes, I do. Luc...was ordered...take me, not you. But when he saw you... figured he'd save me...give you to Blaer instead. Last night...should've made you... go home."

The caresses stopped. "So you knew Luc was outside your den."

"What?" His brow lowered. "No."

"Then this is on Luc, not you. You didn't tell him to take me instead of you, did you?"

"Of course not."

"Then how is it your fault?"

He set a hand to his head. He *knew* he was right. Rosana wouldn't be here if not for him. "You...my guest, in my territory...and...I'm alpha."

"Which makes you the leader, not a god. Luc isn't even a member of your clan anymore."

He blinked. Nobody but Marjani took that no-nonsense tone with him.

"Now shut up and rest." Rosana touched her lips to his forehead. "Concentrate on healing. Because we need you better if we're going to get out of here— and we *are* getting out of here."

His mouth quirked despite the swelling. "Yes, ma'am."

She was right. Beating up on himself wasn't helping anything.

He drew more deeply on his quartz to increase the rate of healing. It would drain the crystals, rendering them useless for a few hours, but it couldn't be helped. In this condition, he was no use to anyone.

He dozed, catlike, relaxed yet aware of his surroundings. Rosana was quiet, too, her hand resting on his shoulder.

An hour or two passed before he opened his eyes, cautiously lifted his head. This time, the pain wasn't so bad.

"Luc?" His gaze skimmed the cell, confirming what he already knew. The wolf fada wasn't with them.

"He's okay," Rosana assured him. "When they took us away, he was just coming around. But I don't know what they did with him."

"Probably sent him back to Blaer."

"Oh." She grimaced. "I'm sorry."

"Yeah. Woman's not right in the head." Still—"Not right to drag you into this. When I found out...could've hurt him myself."

Rosana resumed stroking his face. He let out a grateful sigh. It felt so good.

"It's okay," she said. "If I was under a *geas* to Blaer, I might've done the same thing. I saw how she treats him. She grabbed his quartz and it *hurt*. And she just smiled. She was feeding on his pain."

"Fuck." His stomach clenched. Gods, he hated feeling so damn powerless. "If I could break the *geas* for him, I would."

But Luc had given his word. He'd serve out his time, or die. That's how he was.

Rosana squeezed his shoulder. "I'm sorry," she said again.

Taking her hand, he brought her fingers to his lips in silent thanks.

She leaned down to brush her lips over his. "Thirsty?" When he dipped his chin in assent, she eased his head from her lap and reached for the cup. "Be right back."

Just moving that tiny amount sent another jolt through his skull. But he made himself turn over, then pushed himself up to sitting, slowly, painfully. Halfway up, his stomach rebelled at the change in position, and he had to pause to ride the nausea out. He set his teeth and breathed through it.

By the time Rosana returned, he had his back against the wall, legs stretched in front of him. That was better. He felt more clear-headed. Less vulnerable.

Taking the cup from her, he drained it with small, careful sips. "Thank you," he said, handing it back.

"Let's see how that goes down," she replied. "Then you can have more if you want."

When he nodded, Rosana got herself a drink and then sat beside him, arms hugging her bent legs. Outwardly calm, but her scent was sour with fear.

He turned toward her, set a hand on her arm. That's when he noticed the finger-sized bruises on her throat.

He touched one of them. "Who did this?" he growled.

She shook her head. "Doesn't matter."

"It was Luc, wasn't it?"

She jerked a shoulder.

A dark rage balled his stomach.

Rosana shot him an uneasy look. "They're already better. If I could've shifted, the bruises would be almost gone by now."

He swallowed his anger, nodded. This was between him and Luc. But the man was going to pay for every mark he'd put on Rosana.

For now, they had other worries, like the fact that Rosana was a river fada who'd been forcibly removed from her home waters. And on top of that, she couldn't shift in this cramped, underground cell.

"You need your river. How long—?"

"I'm fine. The Chesapeake Bay isn't far from here, and we're right by the Potomac River. And this water"—she indicated the trickle coming from metal spout—"is spring water. Just splashing it on my face helped."

He frowned. She wasn't lying, but he recognized a half-truth when he heard it. "Why not shift to your otter?"

"If it comes to that, I guess I'll try. But the dolphin is my preferred animal. I haven't shifted to otter since I was a pup."

"So how long?"

She groaned. "You're like a pit bull sometimes, you know that?"

"Rosana."

"Okay, okay. I need to immerse myself in fresh water, and even if I shifted to otter, I'd still be too large for that little trickle to do any good."

His stomach knotted. "How long?" he gritted. "One day? Two?"

"I honestly don't know." She gave a half laugh. "It's not like I've ever been locked up before. But I'm not going to shrivel up overnight. I have at least a few days, maybe longer, although I'll start to feel it in a day or two." She opened her mouth, shut it.

"What aren't you telling me?"

"I have a feeling we've been in here longer than we realize—maybe even a day already. You know how time runs differently in a fae court."

He swore. "So you're already feeling it?"

Another jerk of her shoulder.

"Just hang on, okay?" He gathered her to him. "Your brothers will come for you."

Dion and Tiago would tear apart heaven and earth to save Rosana.

Like Adric would have for his sister—if he'd known those bastards had kidnapped her. But they'd smashed her quartz so she couldn't call for help. By the time Adric had found out, it was too late. They'd had a whole night with her.

He swallowed.

Let it go. Jani's okay, getting better all the time.

A silence. Then Rosana said, "About that..."

An icy finger traced down his spine. "What did you do?"

She lifted her chin. "I told the prince I wanted to stay with you."

"You did *what*?" He winced as pain squeezed his head. "Why the hell would you do that?"

"Because. I wasn't sure how hurt you were, and—" She swallowed audibly. "I didn't know what else to do."

"You should've demanded to leave. This is between him and me. Having you here just fucks things up."

"Maybe. And maybe not. In my vision, you came to the court alone—and you died, damn it." Her voice broke. She took a jagged breath. "You *need* me, Adric Savonett. Why won't you believe me?" Tears glimmered on her face.

Hell, now he'd made her cry. "Rosana..." He touched her wet cheek, but she growled and buried her head in her knees.

"Hey." He set a tentative hand on her back. "I'm sorry, okay? Just...don't cry."

"For your information," she said to her legs, "I did demand to leave—more than once. The prince wouldn't give me a straight answer. He was playing with me. Then you got here and you got hurt—bad. You were out cold, for *Deus*'s sake. And you think I should've just left you with them?"

He heaved a breath. "C'mere."

She scowled but allowed him to guide her back to his shoulder.

"I'm sorry, love." He kissed her temple. "I just hate like hell that you got dragged into this."

She gave a tight nod. "There is something," she said, low-voiced. "On the way here, I called on Cleia for help, and I'm pretty sure she heard me. We were still in southern Maryland, so they may not realize Luc was bringing me here. But at least they'll know I'm not in Baltimore."

"That's good. But why would they think you're in Baltimore?"

"I left Dion and Cleia a note saying I was coming to you."

His brows flew up. "You *told* Dion? About us?"

"Yep." Her full mouth set in stubborn lines. "I'm not going to sneak around to be with you."

"Rosana..."

"I mean it. If you want me, it's got to be out in the open."

"But I told you—"

"You want me. You're not going to tell me last night didn't mean something."

"No." He tightened his arms around her. He just couldn't do it. It would be a lie, and besides, he couldn't hurt her like that. Not when she was locked in this fucking cell because of him. "You know it did."

"Okay, then." He hadn't realized how stiff she was holding herself until she relaxed and curled closer, one arm resting on his stomach, the other around his back in a loose hug. He sucked in a breath when she pressed a tender spot on his lower abdomen.

"Sorry." She tried to pull away, but he kept her where she was.

"No, stay. I like you close."

"Me too." A pause, and then she added in a small voice. "It makes me less scared."

His heart lurched. "Don't be scared. You'll get out of here—soon. I promise."

"Not without you."

He tugged a long black curl. "Are you this much trouble to Dion?"

He felt her grin against his shoulder. "More."

"Never thought I'd feel sorry for the man."

She chuckled, and then laughed aloud when her stomach rumbled immediately after. "Sorry."

"You're hungry." He stroked his palm down the delicate knobs of her spine. "Why didn't you grab something this morning? There was cereal in the cabinet."

"I didn't have time," she said sweetly. Too sweetly.

"Oh."

"Yeah. You snuck out on me, asshole."

He moved uncomfortably. "You were asleep. I figured we'd said our goodbyes."

"Yeah, right. You were afraid I'd talk you into taking me with you."

"Not because I don't want you. It's because *I don't want you hurt.*"

A low growl. "Stop trying to protect me. I can take care of myself."

"Against another fada, maybe. But these are fae. You saw the kind of power the prince has."

"So what makes you think *you* can beat him? You're a fada, too."

"Because, damn it, I don't care about me." He gripped her shoulders, gave her shake. "But if something happened to you, I'd fucking break. I've lost too many people. I can't lose you. I *won't* lose you."

Her eyes widened. "You *do* love me."

His gaze slid from hers. His mouth opened, closed. Because he couldn't bring himself to deny it. What else could this hot ache crowding his chest be?

"That's okay." She snuggled closer again. "I can wait for you to say it."

~

AFTER THAT, they fell asleep, spooned on the bench together, his front to her back. But sometime in their dreams, they turned to each other. Adric woke with his hand on Rosana's breast, his tongue deep in her mouth. He was much better, his battered body nearly healed.

Rosana's eyes were closed but she was sucking on his tongue.

"Angel?" He nuzzled her neck. "You awake?"

"Mm-hmm." She tugged at the hem of the borrowed shirt.

He dragged it off and removed his pants while she wriggled out of her own clothes. He made a rough bed of their clothing on the stone floor and laid her down on it before coming over her. She moaned and bent her legs up. But even with their clothes as a cushion, he was conscious of the hard rock beneath her. He rolled onto his side, taking her with him.

She bent up a leg, rested it on his thigh. His cock brushed against her warm nest of hair, and he closed his eyes in pleasure.

"You're better?" She touched the bump on his temple.

He nodded. "I have a small healing Gift. I had to draw on my quartz, though, so I won't be able to shift for a few hours."

She traced the scruff on his jaw. "You know, I still haven't seen your cougar."

"He's here." And wide awake.

"He is?" She looked deep into his eyes before giving a satisfied nod. "So's my dolphin."

"Did I tell you how pretty she is?" He turned his head, sucked her wandering finger into his mouth.

Her breath hitched. "Uh-uh."

He rolled his tongue around her finger before releasing it to wrap his arms around her. "She's strong, graceful. Like you."

"You think?" She scooted closer, plastering that long, curvy body against his.

"Yeah." He smoothed a hand down her ass. Damn, she had a fine butt, round and firm, the skin like satin.

She nibbled on his earlobe, teasing the gold stud with her tongue. "In the summer," she said, as if there was no doubt whatsoever that they'd both escape the night fae, "we have to go for a swim together. My dolphin's skin is very sensitive—she'll want to rub all over you. You wouldn't mind, would you?"

His dick jumped. *Mind?* The thought of a wet, naked Rosana rubbing all over him sounded like his idea of paradise.

"No," he managed to say. "I wouldn't mind at all. As long as you promise to swim with me as a human, too."

"It's a deal."

"Naked."

A throaty chuckle. "Oh, I will be. I love to feel the water flowing over my bare skin."

He swore. "Have mercy, woman."

She gave a gleeful laugh—and pressed her mouth to his. When his lips parted, her tongue slid in, just a bit, sending a hot shiver down his spine.

She teased him with small tastes and nips until he groaned and sucked her tongue deeper. Kissing the breath out of her—and himself as well. Even in the dank, musty cell, her scent had a hint of fresh water.

When he finally came up for oxygen, she drew a serrated breath. Her eyes seared into his, the deep blue streaked with sea-green. "I love you."

His heart stumbled. "Rosana. I can't—"

"I'm not asking you to mate-claim me. But I wanted you to know. In case—" She moved a shoulder.

His stomach fisted. "Nothing's going to happen to you," he bit out. "You'll be out of here in a day, maybe two. I'll *make* it happen."

He speared his fingers into her hair, drawing back her head to press love-bites to her throat. She moaned and angled her head to give him better access. One hand came up to his nape, urging him closer. Her back arched, pressing her pelvis into his.

Electricity danced over his skin. He felt feverish, needy.

"Come into me," she murmured. "Now."

His throat worked. "Can't. No protection."

"Adric. I love you. And I would love any pup—or cub—we made."

She reached down and guided his cock into her, and the gods help him, he didn't stop her.

Because he felt the same way.

She was slick, hot. She gasped and clenched her inner muscles around him. Pleasure rocketed to his balls.

He clamped his teeth together, resisting the urge to pound into her. Instead, he dragged her bent leg higher on his hip so that he was rubbing right against her clit and rocked slowly in and out.

Drawing out the pleasure. Teasing them both.

Her arms tightened around him. "I love you," she repeated in a fierce whisper.

He faltered, swallowed.

Never had he heard those words from a lover.

While Leron was still alive, he'd stuck to casual, no-strings-attached hook-ups.

He couldn't risk anything more—Leron would've used any woman he cared for against him.

After he'd become alpha, he'd been too busy, his hold on the clan too shaky. Especially that first year, when he'd not only been working day and night to heal his fractured people, he'd had to fight off multiple challenges.

And then he'd seen Rosana at the sun fae ball, a vision in a sexy little dress the brilliant blues and greens of a peacock's feathers, her shiny black curls tumbling down her back...

Her eyelids drifted down. Her soft lips parted as she sank deeper into pleasure.

His cat bristled restively, hungry to lay its wild heart at her feet.

My woman.

My mate.

Mine.

He swallowed the words, although it *hurt* not to let them out. He was a killer, a man who'd cornered his own uncle in a dark alley and slit his throat. So what if he'd done it to save Marjani? It still shadowed his soul.

Someone like Rosana deserved so much better than him.

But too fucking bad.

Deep inside him, something moved, opened. In that moment, he understood what the cat had known for years. Some things were meant to happen. A man could only fight fate for so long.

If they got out of this alive, he was mate-claiming Rosana do Rio.

Whether her brother liked it or not. Whether his clan agreed or not.

Sinking his fingers into her hair, he tugged her head back and set his mouth to the silken skin of her throat.

"Mine," he rasped. "I'm not claiming you—yet—but when I do, you'll say yes."

Her full lips curved. "Haven't you figured it out? I already have."

CHAPTER 32

The Rock Run men rode fast and hard. Marjani grimly kept up, fear for her brother a live creature gnawing at her insides.

Behind her, Fane maintained a loose grip on her hips. She was thankful now he'd insisted on coming. She'd never needed his calm, steadying presence more.

As they pulled onto I-95, she tapped her quartz, calling Jace.

"Hey, Jani." He raised his voice to be heard over the sound of drilling. He must be at the quartz mine. "Whassup?"

"It's Ric. He's not at his den. I think he's going to New Moon."

"Alone?"

"Yeah. I tried to get ahold of him, but he's cut off all communication. And it's deliberate. I can tell."

"He didn't give you a heads-up?"

She ground her teeth. "No."

"Fuck." They both knew that if Adric hadn't told Marjani he was leaving, it was because he'd wanted to sneak out of town. Whatever he was up to, it was dangerous.

"And somehow Rosana do Rio got mixed up in it. I found Dion, Rui, Tiago and a couple of other Rock Run men outside Ric's den. They looked ready to tear him apart with their bare hands."

"His den? What the fuck?"

She explained how Rosana had apparently been kidnapped from outside Adric's den.

Jace swore. "They don't think it was Ric?"

"No. But it looks like it might've been Luc. His scent was all over Ric's backyard."

"Hell." Jace's tone matched the sinking sensation in the pit of her stomach. "So Lady B's a part of this? But what the fuck would she want with Rosana?"

"Good question. But Cleia traced Rosana to southern Maryland. I'm on 95 south of Baltimore, along with Dion and his men. Fane's with me."

"On my way." The sound of drilling faded as he made his way to the surface.

"I'll keep you updated on our location, but figure on going to Virginia. And Jace? Call Zuri, tell him what's up. Until he hears otherwise, he's in charge."

"Cat's balls, Jani. Give me the hard job, why don't you? Zuri's going to be royally pissed if we leave him in Baltimore."

"He'll just have to deal," she returned in a hard voice. "He's chief of security. With Adric and me both out of the city, he's in charge. And if the night fae catch Adric, we'll be at war—he'll have more than enough to keep busy. And Jace? No secrets." The clan had had their fill of that during the Darktime, and even since. "Tell Zuri to let everyone know what's up. Ric's going in there for me. Every den needs to decide once and for all if they're with the two of us—or against us. If not, they should leave now, or I will personally kick their asses out of Baltimore."

"Understood."

Fane leaned forward to mutter in Marjani's ear. "Tell him to send Evie and Kyle to Baltimore. They're not safe in Grace Harbor alone."

Marjani nodded. She relayed Fane's message, adding. "If she asks why, tell her the healers will need her."

It was the one argument guaranteed to get Evie back to Baltimore. If it came to war, the healers would be stretched to their limits, and Evie's ability to add her energy to theirs would be desperately needed.

"Already planning on it. Horace is with me—he'll make sure they get there okay. You heard that?" he asked the cougar fada.

When Horace said yes, Jace instructed him to shut down the mine and send everyone back to Baltimore, ASAP.

Marjani heard the rumble of Jace's motorcycle coming to life. "I'm right behind you," he told her, and ended the call.

The city fell away. The highway was lined with trees, giving the impression they were in the country, but she knew it was an illusion. This section of the East Coast was a string of towns one after another, with a continuous stream of traffic traveling the I-95 corridor.

"Don't worry." Fane squeezed her waist. "Adric will be okay. Your brother's bloody hard to kill."

She growled. "He shouldn't have gone without me."

"Mm." Her mate wisely refrained from pointing out that she'd gone to Iceland without Adric for the very same reason—to protect him.

She heaved a breath and cast Fane an apologetic smile over her shoulder. "Thanks for coming."

He shrugged. "I know the court better than any of you. Besides, I spent sixty turns of the sun with the fae. I might even be able to help. Envoy, remember? I was one of the ice fae's top negotiators."

"You're right. I'm sorry."

He wrapped his arms more securely around her waist, his hard-muscled body warm against her back. Despite her worry, her cat gave a little purr of contentment.

Fane brought his face as close to her as their helmets allowed. "You need to remember something, love."

"What's that?"

"You're not alone anymore."

~

DION WENT with his gut and aimed straight for New Moon.

Three hours later, they entered the forest surrounding the night fae court. They slowed their motorcycles to a crawl. A *look-away* spell pressed at them, but he drew on his internal GPS to keep moving forward, even when the pressure grew so strong it was like slogging through invisible quicksand.

Rui somehow picked up Rosana's scent. "This way." He jerked his chin at a narrow gravel road.

They bumped down the rutted lane until they reached a clearing. Rui engaged his kickstand and swung off his bike. He crouched, nostrils flared, to scrutinize the prints in the moist earth.

"Rosana was here," he said without raising his head. "Along with the wolf and Adric. And a night fae—a mixed blood, I think. Lady B?" He glanced up at Dion.

Neither of them had met Lady Blaer, although they knew from Dion's brother Nic that she was a night fae/ice fae mix.

Dion inhaled. "That's my guess." Beside him, Tiago grunted assent.

Marjani pushed her way through the other men to his side, her mate following. She drew a slow breath. "That's Lady B, all right. I'll never forget her scent. And the other two are definitely Adric and Luc."

Rui circled the clearing, still in a partial crouch, gathering further scraps of data. "Adric's trail leads out of here—I believe he was following the wolf." He pointed down the narrow road. "But Rosana's scent ends here, along with the fae."

Dion's stomach constricted, the small hope that they'd reach his sister in time crushed. "So she teleported out of here with Rosana."

"To New Moon," Marjani added.

"That's what I believe, *sim*. But if she's behind their wards, we can't know for sure."

"*I* know." The cougar fada's hand went to where her quartz rested beneath her leather jacket. "At least, I'm sure Adric's there."

"You can't contact him?"

She hesitated, shook her head.

He took a step forward. "What aren't you telling us?"

"He cut off contact with me. But I could still feel him, up until a couple of hours ago. Then—nothing."

"And that means?"

"He's behind a ward or—" She compressed her mouth.

"Or what?" he demanded.

"Dead."

Morningstar scowled at Dion and wrapped a lanky arm around his mate's shoulders. "So best guess is, Adric's inside the court along with Rosana. That's good news, right? She's not alone—and neither is he. Because if there's one thing I know about the night fae, two people together can fight their emotional assaults better than any one person alone."

Marjani nodded, firmed her chin. "What now?" she asked with a penetrating glance around at the dense forest.

"I'm going to contact my mate." Dion stared into the trees, his gaze unfocused. "Cleia, *minha reina*? Can you join us?" To them, he said, "She's on her way."

While they waited for the queen to arrive, he told Marjani, "Rui is going to track Adric and Luc to their last known location."

She nodded. "I contacted Jace Jones, too. He'll be here in an hour or so." To Rui, she said, "Fane and I will go with you."

"I can show you the approximate location of New Moon," Morningstar offered.

"Thanks, but we know," Rui replied. "I've been inside the court myself. But don't tell the prince." Rui's smile was thin. "He wasn't aware he had a fada guest."

The shark fada had taken the form of a smaller fish and entered the compound through a stream.

Morningstar flicked up a single dark brow. "I see."

Rui turned his hard green eyes on Marjani. "Ready?"

"As soon as I shift." Returning to her bike, she removed her clothes and shoved them into a saddlebag, and then shifted to a sleek cougar with startling turquoise eyes.

Before they could leave, Cleia 'ported into the clearing. One glance around and her full mouth compressed. "You tracked Rosana this close to New Moon?"

He jerked his chin in assent. "It appears she was kidnapped by an earth fada under a *geas*. We have to assume she's inside the court."

Her beautiful face set. "It appears I need to have talk with Prince Langdon."

CHAPTER 33

*R*osana pulled Adric closer, angling her body to take him even further inside.

He was hot, lithe, powerful. He fucked her with slow strokes that shot sparks up her spine, out to her fingers and toes.

Her pleasure built. She instinctively tightened her inner muscles around him and discovered that made it even better.

He liked that, too. His whole body went taut, and he muttered, "God's cat, you feel good," and thrust harder.

"Yes," she gasped. "So good."

His mouth captured hers, sinking his tongue deep, kissing her breathless. When he released her, he curved his body to kiss his way down her throat. His tongue rasped over each of her nipples in turn. She moaned and pressed against him, and he gave each a hard suck.

She hissed and clenched around him. It was like he'd pulled a string leading straight to her clit.

He continued moving. Deliberate, sensuous strokes that were a language in themselves.

I love you.

And I love you.

Between her breasts, the amethyst heated until it felt like another heart.

He pulled out, tapped the side of her hip. "Turn over."

She took a deep breath and then flipped onto her stomach.

"Lift your hips." He positioned himself behind her.

Yes... She immediately obeyed. Her ass was canted up, her breasts pressed into their shirts.

He grasped her hips and resumed thrusting into her. Filling her in a way she hadn't known she needed.

She'd told Adric she didn't know him, but she knew all the important things. That he was strong, confident, scary smart. A natural leader who didn't follow any rules but his own. Ruthless and ambitious, but not for himself. What drove him was bettering his clan.

Beneath that bad-boy façade, the man cared.

He twined his fingers in her hair and gave it a tug, gently urging her to lift up on all fours, her back arched. Kisses seared the side of her throat while his other hand slid between her legs to do magical things. Stroking, rubbing, circling until she was sobbing with need and want and wonder.

He released her hair to grasp her hip so he could piston into her hard and fast.

The two of us together.

Yes. Always.

They climaxed at the same time. She dropped to her forearms, moaning his name into their shirts. Behind her, he growled lowly and stilled, spurting into her, hot and urgent.

For a few seconds, he hung over her, lungs working, and then he disengaged from her and came down on the clothes, bringing her with him.

She curled into his chest. "Guess you're feeling better."

"Mm." He ran a palm down her spine. In the silence that fell, this time it was his stomach that rumbled. "And hungry," he added wryly. "But maybe no food is good news. Could mean they're not planning to keep us down here long."

"Maybe." She scooted closer. "The prince—he kept trying to get me to eat his food."

Adric's hand on her back stilled. Beneath her, his body locked up like a fighter's. "He wants you to stay, then."

"He knows I'm a Seer. He offered to help train me."

He swore. "I knew you'd be like catnip to that prick. But you told him no." It wasn't a question.

She thought uneasily about how tempted she'd been. "Oh, yeah."

"Good." He resumed caressing her. "So. Any ideas about getting out of here?"

She shook her head. "They took your dagger and the door's locked up tight. It doesn't even have a handle on the inside. The only thing they left us was your quartz."

"And that's low in energy right now. I drew heavily on it to heal myself. I probably couldn't even shift right now."

"You can't use my amethyst for energy?"

A shake of his head. "I have a magical bond with my own quartz. In an emergency, I can draw any quartz, but the energy doesn't have the same quality. I couldn't use it for something so tricky. But—" He fingered her pendant.

"What?"

"It's warm. And I can hear the crystals singing, louder than I'd expect."

"And that means?"

His brows squashed together. "I'm not sure, but... I think you've bonded with it. Not like an earth fada, but you've formed a weak connection. Don't ask me how, because I've never heard of anything like it. The good news is that if we get separated, I can use it to find you."

She gripped his wrist. "We have to stay together," she said fiercely.

He cupped her nape. "I'll do my best, okay?" He stopped there, but she heard the *but*. If it came down to it, he intended to sacrifice himself for her.

She set her jaw. *Not if I can help it.*

"I can tell you one thing," he added. "They won't take my quartz from me, not at first."

"Why not?"

He shrugged a powerful shoulder. "They're not stupid. They know it hurts like hell to have my quartz touched. They'll use it to torture me."

"*Deus*," she muttered, then brightened. "Can't you use it to call for help?"

"The wards would block it. But"—he jerked upright—"Marjani's close."

"How do you know?"

"I just know. As alpha, I'm connected to everyone in the clan through their quartz, but with her, it's even stronger. Fuck." He scrubbed his hands over his face. "This is bad."

"It is?" Rosana sat up as well. "She's here to rescue you, isn't she?"

"Gods." He drew a harsh breath. "She *knows* not to come anywhere near him."

"But why? I don't understand."

"Because. It's her the prince really wants. Not me."

She opened her mouth to ask why, but he shook his head. "I can't say any more, but take my word for it. He'd love to get his long, cold fingers on her."

And suddenly, Rosana *knew*.

Marjani had killed Langdon's son, not Adric—and Langdon had somehow found out. No wonder Adric had been so determined to assassinate the prince.

She grabbed his arm. "Tyrus," she mouthed. "It was her. And he knows it. That's why you came alone."

An infinitesimal nod. He set a hand on her mouth, warning her not to say more.

She dipped her chin, telling him she understood, and he lifted his fingers. "So that's why you wouldn't listen to me," she whispered.

"I told you not to come. But you just wouldn't listen."

"Maybe because I'm supposed to be here."

He made a small sound, half laughter, half groan. "Know something? I'm starting to believe you."

She watched as he rose to his feet and crossed to the metal trough. He took a drink and then used handfuls of water to rinse the rest of the powder off.

Adric was here to save his sister.

He wasn't here only for his clan. He was here for Marjani.

This changed everything.

She washed up herself, and they took turns using the toilet. She pulled on her clothes and sat on the bench, mind working.

Yeah, her gut told her she was supposed to be here, but why? She was a Seer, not a warrior. Until today, she'd never even seen combat. And without an iron weapon, she was helpless against the night fae. Even with their iron, the prince had fought off both her and Adric.

Adric got dressed as well and prowled around the small space, clearly unhappy at being confined. At least he was better. Seeing him so battered had hurt at a primal level, like she'd shared his pain—and she'd known the instant he'd come back to consciousness.

Which was strange, come to think of it. She furrowed her brow, unconsciously massaging her breastbone.

The realization hit her like a fist to the heart. The mate bond had formed on her side. Not just a few threads, but a shining ribbon of sea-colored light. She *felt* it, stretching from her to him. But before it reached his chest, it slammed up against something bright and hard, as if he'd thrown up a shield.

Blood roared in her ears. She gulped, the breath literally knocked out of her.

Adric fingered his quartz and slid her a look. But he didn't say anything.

The bond had formed, but he was blocking it from his side.

He's doing it to protect you.

It still hurt, but she understood—until she recalled he'd started blocking it even before he'd left Baltimore. Which meant he'd come to Virginia expecting to die.

The last piece of the puzzle thunked into place with an awful, stomach-drop-ping sound.

He'd told her himself, right before they'd fallen asleep: *Because, damn it, I don't care about me.*

This was a suicide mission. His life for Marjani's.

If Rosana hadn't been at New Moon, he might already be dead.

She moved her head slowly from side to side. "You...no. There has to be another way."

He didn't pretend not to understand. "Rosana." He sat next to her, took her hand. "I didn't want this to happen."

"But it has."

"No, it hasn't. The bond—it's not complete. I'm still hoping I can take down this bastard and escape, but.... At least this way, you'll be able to find another mate."

"That's up to me, isn't it?"

His glance was a brilliant mix of bronze and blue. "I need to know you have the chance, at least." He took her hand between both of his. "Promise me some-thing. If you get another chance to leave, you'll take it."

"No." She jerked her hand free. "Don't even ask."

"Please, Rosana. You say you love me. Do it for me if you won't do it for yourself."

She growled. "That's not fair. If you were me, would you leave?"

He exhaled. "No. But this is my fight, not yours."

She just shook her head and stared out at the room.

Adric eyed her. She *felt* his will beating at hers, demanding she give in. Her body tightened.

It wasn't easy to refuse him, not when she sensed how much it meant to him. How much *she* meant to him.

The tension in the cell ratcheted up until she could've screamed, and then he said something low and vicious and resumed his restless pacing.

"There's one thing I'd give a big fat diamond to know. How in Hades did the prince know I was here?"

She slumped against the wall, relieved he'd given up—for now, anyway. "I was there when Olivier—the butler—told him Luc was in the foyer. He knew then that you were with Luc."

"He did?" He shook his head in disgust.

"What was that invisible thing you did, anyway? I thought only wayfarers can disappear like that, but you're a tracker, aren't you?

"I have another, secondary Gift that I can use like a cloaking spell. The prince shouldn't have known I was there."

"I told you, he has the farsight. Maybe he Saw you before you entered the court."

"I was cloaking myself on and off. I mean, come on—the man can't be watching all the time, can he?"

"No. He has to sleep, eat, go about his business. And he can't hear you—just watch."

Adric swiped a hand down his face. "Gods, I made it easy for him. He just had to wait for me to arrive like a spider with a stupid-ass fly."

"He couldn't have Seen exactly what you had planned. Seers almost never See their own futures. I had no clue Luc was outside your den."

She raised her hands, palms up, and swallowed. Twice.

Adric crouched before her. "What?"

"My visions—I have to touch someone to See their future. And in the last week, I've had my hands all over you. My *bare* hands. But it hasn't set off my Sight."

"So?"

She brought her hands down, met his eyes. "So a Seer can't foretell her own future. That's why I can touch you without setting off my Sight—my fate is tangled up with yours now."

CHAPTER 34

A hesitant *tap-tap* on the bedroom door dragged Langdon from a sound sleep. Pushing himself up on his forearms, he bit back a groan. By the dark gods, he hurt. Even with his powerful blood, it was going to take a day or two to completely heal.

He could almost admire Adric and that river fada female of his. They'd fought hard and well. Not that the alpha wouldn't pay for attacking him.

Another apologetic *tap-tap*.

"What?" he growled.

The door opened. Jessica, Olivier's new assistant, peeked into the darkened room, her anxiousness palpable. A recent human hire, she regarded Langdon as a cross between a monster and a god.

At all that delicious dread, his mood improved. He pushed himself up on his forearms. "Come in."

She took a single step and halted, her slender body framed in the light from the hallway. Just for fun, he nudged her fear up a notch and then sipped at the luscious, panicky emanations.

Her dark eyes rounded. She wrung her narrow hands. "I beg your pardon, my lord. I know you gave orders not to be disturbed, but this can't wait."

He shoved off the duvet and strode naked across the floor. Sensing movement, a handful of fae lights glowed on, casting a deep aubergine light over the bedroom.

Jessica froze and blinked rapidly, her gaze jumping from his half-hard cock to his bare chest and back again before settling on his face. He caught a spark of arousal mixed with the fear. Interesting...

"Speak," he commanded softly.

"Yes, my lord." Her head bobbed up and down several times.

A pause as he waited for her to enlighten him. When she remained silent, fingers tangling nervously in front of her body, he stifled a sigh. Olivier was going to have to hire another assistant. Although she had possibilities as a toy...

"Jessica. What is so important that you disturbed my sleep?"

She started. "I beg your pardon, my lord." She licked soft, coral-colored lips and finally got it out. "The sun fae queen is here. She wishes to speak to you."

"Cleia? She's *here*?"

"Yes, my lord. Uh...not here, exactly. She's outside the wards, of course, but..." She shifted from foot to foot and added in a rush, "She's demanding to see you, my lord. Captain Quade tried to put her off, but she refuses to leave without seeing you."

His mouth pulled down. He'd expected Cleia, of course—the queen had an inexplicable fondness for her mate's young sister—just not so quickly.

"My clothes," he said. "Now."

"Yes, my lord."

Jessica scurried to obey, rushing into his walk-in closet and reappearing with a shirt and pants in a shimmering blue-black fabric. Meanwhile, he sent a message to Quade, agreeing to meet the queen in a pine grove outside the compound. Cleia might be young for a fae, but she was too powerful to allow within his wards.

That done, he selected a few pieces of jewelry—a glittering diamond pendant the size of a walnut, a couple of hand-worked platinum-and-diamond rings, a platinum watch. Jessica returned with a pair of Italian leather shoes and knelt on the floor so he could step into them.

He touched her curly brown hair. "Thank you, my dear."

"My pleasure, my lord." Her head bobbed in a way that had his mind picturing lurid acts.

He set them aside—for now—to head for the portal nearest the pine grove.

Cleia hadn't come alone. Quade and his warriors relieved her fada companions of their weapons before permitting Langdon to step through the portal. Langdon allowed it, but he couldn't help being amused; the queen was infinitely more dangerous than all the fada put together.

Time ran differently in a fae court. Inside his wards, it was early afternoon, but outside, a new day had dawned. As he stepped into the forest, the rising sun sifted pale gold through the pine branches. He donned a pair of sunglasses and took in his visitors.

The queen had planted herself in a shaft of sunlight, her statuesque body clad in a snug yellow T-shirt and bronze moto pants, her bright hair braided into a single over-the-shoulder plait. Lord Dion stood close beside her, his black hair in a ponytail, his eyes like silver flints, his broad shoulders straining at his leather jacket. A barbarian in human clothing. The fae world had been appalled when Cleia took a fada mate, but the Rock Run alpha had a certain primitive appeal. A pity the queen wasn't into threesomes.

Rui do Mar, Dion's second, stood a step behind along with Dion's brother Tiago. Next to them were a slim woman with short dark hair and large, catlike eyes, and a lean blond mixed-blood whom Langdon recognized as one of Sindre's former envoys.

There were other fada present, too, all men, but his gaze lingered on the woman.

Welcome, my pretty little cat.

He inclined his head to Cleia. "Your highness, you honor my court." He touched a hand to his chest in a gesture of respect. "Peace to you and yours."

He nodded at Dion and his stone-faced second-in-command, and then turned his gaze back to the Savonett female. This time, he let his mouth curve.

"Marjani Savonett. What a pleasure to meet you at last."

The blond male—Farr? Fern? Finn?—set a protective hand on her back and glared at Langdon.

Marjani stared back unblinking. She appeared unaffected, but he sensed the cauldron of fear and anger roiling inside her. It touched off an answering darkness in him. For a few seconds, the temptation to feed was almost irresistible, but he reined it in.

"Peace." Cleia's curt greeting made it clear she was unhappy with him. "I believe you have my mate's sister. A misunderstanding, I'm sure."

His brow lifted. She'd gone straight to the point, skipping over several pages of the polite thrust-and-parry that every fae learned at their mother's knee.

The queen wasn't just unhappy, she was furious.

"A misunderstanding?" He steepled his fingers and tapped them against his mouth. "No, my lady. Rosana do Rio is a guest."

Lord Dion made a sharp, angry movement. Cleia set a calming hand on his arm. "Then invite me into your court," she said.

Langdon considered that. But no, the queen too powerful to risk it.

He shook his head. "I'm afraid that's not possible."

With a growl, Dion lunged at him. Langdon simply faded into the shadows while Quade and the other guards surged forward. It took three of them to subdue the enraged river alpha. Meanwhile, do Mar, Marjani, and the other fada rushed to his aid.

Cleia raised her hands to the rising sun. A white-hot flame flared to life at the center of each palm. The queen didn't produce fae balls, she simply drew on solar energy to reduce an enemy to ashes.

"Let my mate go," she said in a low, terrible voice.

Langdon's guards flinched at the bright light, even Quade, the oldest and most powerful. This was getting out of hand.

Langdon emerged from the shadows. "Then tell him to control his temper."

The queen's tawny eyes slit.

Fane—Langdon had recalled his name—cleared his throat. "My lady. My lords." He glanced around at Cleia, Dion and Langdon. "If I may speak?"

Langdon inclined his head. "Go ahead."

The sun fae queen waited until Dion gave a curt nod and stopped struggling against the guards' hold. The flames winked out, and she brought her hands to her sides.

"We'll listen," she said. "After you release Lord Dion."

Langdon gestured at Quade to release the big fada. "But I'll have your word— all of you—that you'll respect this negotiation. Attack again, and this meeting is over."

When everyone had assented to Langdon's terms, Fane slid his hands into his pockets and gave Langdon an easy smile. "If I heard you right, Rosana is a guest at your court."

"Yes."

"So as a guest, she's free to go, yes?"

"She is."

Fane gave Dion a significant look.

The river fada alpha regarded Langdon skeptically. "My sister is free to leave New Moon?"

"She is."

"Say the words," he growled.

"Your sister, Rosana do Rio, is free to leave my court whenever she wishes."

Dion briefly closed his eyes. Then he gave a short nod. "See that you inform her."

"However," Langdon continued, "she has requested to remain."

"What? You lying *filho da puta*." The big river fada stepped forward, murder in his eyes. Wicked black claws sprouted from his fingertips.

"*Dion.*" Cleia gripped his bulging bicep. "You know the fae can't lie. Explain," she snapped at Langdon.

"I simply granted her request. Lord Adric was being conveyed to a cell, and the young lady wished to remain with him. I was happy to oblige."

Marjani gave a muted hiss, and Langdon's nape prickled warily. The cougar fada might be small, almost delicate in appearance, but he hadn't forgotten who'd killed Tyrus. He raised a challenging brow, daring her to break her word and give him grounds to capture her.

But she remained where she was, slender body strung tight, hands balled at her sides.

"Let Rosana go," Cleia told him. "And Lord Adric, too. You have no right to keep either of them against their will."

"No? Lord Adric attacked me in my own home. That gives me the right to exact any justice I choose. And the do Rio female is with him at her own request. Not a prisoner, but a guest."

The queen's eyes sparked dangerously. "You dare hold my mate's sister? A woman under my court's protection?"

He spread his hands. "I'm not an unreasonable man. For the right incentive, I could be persuaded to expel her from my court."

"Name your price," Dion said.

Langdon permitted himself a small smile. He jerked his head at Quade. "Leave us. All of you."

The captain's brows shot up, but he duly ordered the other warriors back through the portal. "I'll be waiting on the other side," he said with a warning glance at Cleia and Dion before following them.

Langdon drew the shadows around them like a thick cloak. What he was about to say was for no one else's ears.

"You have my granddaughter at Rock Run. She's not, in fact, dead as you and Lord Adric would like me to believe."

Dion's head jerked back. Beside him, do Mar's fists slowly opened and closed. The two men exchanged a look.

"She's alive," the Rock Run alpha admitted.

At last. Langdon's heart sped up. He slipped his hands into the pockets of his duster, kept his face impassive. "It's time she take her place at my court."

"No." That was do Mar. "Absolutely not."

Langdon eyed him. "She's not even of your blood. Why do you care what happens to her?"

"She's my daughter," was the terse reply.

Langdon scowled. He'd never understand the fada and their primitive ways.

"She's *my* granddaughter, the blood of my blood. At New Moon, she'll be treated as the princess she is."

Another man stepped forward, the earth fada lieutenant who was Merry's uncle. "She's my blood relation, and I say no as well."

"Those are my terms. Rosana do Rio for my granddaughter."

"No," Dion bit out.

Fane cocked his head. "You said yourself that Rosana is free to leave. Why should we bargain with you for something you've already granted?"

A wise man didn't bargain when he held the upper hand. "As you say," Langdon returned. "Peace, my lady. My lord."

With a nod at the queen and her mate, he moved back, retreating into the shadows layer by layer until only his face was visible, a pale glimmer.

"You son of a bitch." Dion stalked forward, matching him step for step. "I demand to see my sister. *Now.*"

"She's made her choice."

Dion swore and tried to grab him, but his fingers slashed impotently through the gray mist.

"Wait!" Marjani sprang forward. "What about my brother?"

"That," Langdon said, "is not negotiable. His execution is set for the night of the new moon."

Her honey-colored skin went ashen. "For trespassing?"

"He didn't just trespass. He was here to kill me."

"But—"

"More than that, the death of my son requires an equal sacrifice."

"No! We were only defending ourselves. Tyrus came into *our* territory, stirring up trouble. Sent assassins after our people."

"Invaded my den," growled Jace Jones. "And kidnapped me and my mate."

Langdon kept his gaze on the cougar fada. "The sentence hasn't been finalized. You can still take your brother's place."

When she opened her mouth, he knew he had her—until her blond mate slapped a hand over her lips. "No!" he whispered urgently. "At least give us time to find another way."

She hissed and twisted out of his grip.

"Marjani," her mate said. "I'm begging you. Wait. You don't have to decide right now."

She gave him an agonized look. "I'm sorry, Fane. But I can't—"

"Enough!" The white-hot flame flared in the queen's palms again. "The earth fada speak the truth. Our own investigations have confirmed that your son attacked the Baltimore fada. His death is no one's fault but his own. And in the months since, you've been seen multiple times in Baltimore. If Lord Adric attacked you, it was because you provoked him into it. Self-defense is not a crime. Moreover, you have no grounds to hold Rosana do Rio."

He sneered. "I should've known you'd take the fada's side," he said with a knowing glance at Dion.

The flame in Cleia's palms burned brighter. Even with the sunglasses, he had to squint to protect his sensitive eyes. He receded deeper into the shadows.

"I'm warning you," she said in a soft, dangerous voice. "Keep Adric and Rosana, and it will mean war."

He let his mouth curve. "But to us, my lady, war is food."

CHAPTER 35

*A*dric's stomach dropped. He sprang to his feet. "You—no." He paced away, then back again. "You could be wrong. Everyone knows the Sight is unpredictable."

Rosana spread her hands. "I'm not sure," she admitted, "but my Gift is strong, and I've touched you over and over in the last few days without even a glimmer—except for this gut feeling that if you came here alone, you'd die."

He stared down at her, lungs jerking. This wasn't how it was supposed to go down. If he died, Rosana was supposed to be safely back at Rock Run, free to mate with some other male.

My fate is tangled up in yours now.

He'd learned control in a hard school. But for the first time in a long time, rage got the upper hand. Rage at his uncle. Rage at Langdon and his thrice-damned son, Tyrus. Rage at the river fada who'd raped his sister, and at the members of Adric's own clan who'd set the whole thing up.

But most of all, rage at the world that wouldn't let him have the woman he wanted more than life itself.

He turned, slammed the side of his fist against the stone wall. Rosana flinched.

He exhaled, forced himself to speak calmly. "We can't bond. Not yet. I—you know why."

She jumped up as well. "I'm not asking you to choose me over Marjani," she said in a subvocal voice. "I'd never ask that. But what if you're wrong? What if the mate bond is the only thing that can save you? And don't forget what I Saw—you could set off another Darktime." She quoted her own words: "*The prince will destroy your clan from the inside out.*"

"Not if I kill the motherfucker first," he snarled.

"Don't you see?" She grabbed his arms. "It could mean *you*, not him. That you dying is what sets it off. You're the glue holding your clan together. If they lose you, the Darktime will rise again."

He stared at her, arrested. Could she be right? But if she was, where did that leave his sister?

He shook her off and backed away. "Marjani could lead in my place."

"Could she? Or would there be another series of challenges? Your clan is finally getting its shit together. Do you want to risk that? All I'm asking is that you stop fighting the mate bond. Maybe this is meant to be. Together, the two of us are stronger than either of us alone."

"Damn it, Rosana. This isn't your fight, it's mine."

"It's mine now."

He growled and dropped onto the bench. He leaned forward, head clutched in his hands.

She sat beside him. Her hand came to his nape, stroking in that way that made his cat want to lay its head on her lap and purr. He stiffened his spine against the temptation.

"I love you for so many reasons," she murmured.

"But?" There was always a *but*.

"No *but*. That you love your sister so much..." She rested her cheek against his. "It just makes me love you even more. I want you to know that."

He squeezed his eyes shut. Inside, the mate bond battered invisible fists against the barrier he'd erected.

He slid down the bench, away from her and that petting hand. "He came to me, you know. Your brother."

"Dion?"

"Yeah."

Her brows snapped down. "When?"

"The other night. After we went to Lewes."

He distinctly heard her teeth grind together. "What did he say?"

"That you and me just wouldn't work—and not only because you're his sister and my clan would never accept you. But because you're a river fada. You need water. Clean, fresh water to swim in as your dolphin."

A slash of her hand. "You think I don't know that? We could figure it out."

"You'd move to Baltimore? Leave your family, your clan? Because I sure as hell can't move to Rock Run."

She raised her chin. "Yes."

He shook his head.

"It could work," she insisted. "If we both want it to. Baltimore has fresh water —Herring Run, Jones Falls."

"They're filled with trash. And when it rains, there's run-off from the pavement. Raw sewage, when it rains hard."

"Then I'll go north every few days. I wouldn't have to go all the way up to Grace Harbor. I can swim in the Chesapeake north of Baltimore."

He ran some options in his mind. If he survived the next few days—and that was a big if—maybe they could work it out. There was still his clan, of course, although Marjani seemed to think they'd fall in line.

He wrapped his fingers around his quartz. It had warmed, the crystals humming an eager, yearning song.

Inside, the cougar snarled and scratched.

Mate. Our *mate.*

He released the quartz. "Tell you what. We'll talk, okay? When all this is over."

Her smile was wide. "Okay. Sure."

He could've left it at that. She was happy. He'd all but agreed to mate-claim her. At least if he died, she'd know he'd really wanted her. But somehow his mouth was moving again.

"You wanted to know why I didn't challenge my uncle for alpha."

"No." She squeezed his hand. "I know you, Adric. If you didn't challenge him, then you had a good reason."

He glanced at her. Tempted to agree, and then drop it. He didn't explain himself to anyone, even Marjani. But he wanted Rosana to know the truth.

"Yeah," he said with a bitter laugh. "I had a good reason."

He stared out at the shadowed room, his fingers intertwined in hers. The silence thickened. When he spoke, it was with a low rasp.

"My dad was the first. After Leron killed him, he sent my mom to fight in South America in some stupid war between two fae. And then he took me and Marjani in, and we were supposed to obey him. Like we didn't know what the fuck was going on. When I fought back, he beat me."

She sucked in a breath. "Marjani?"

"He never touched her—which is why he lived as long as he did. But he treated her like shit. Both of us. By then, I think he'd realized I was alpha material." His jaw set. "We never had enough food. We had to stay out all night spying on his so-called enemies. No schooling except what we picked up on our own. He even went after my friends. Fuck, I was counting the days until I was strong enough to challenge him. Then"—he swallowed hard—"he came to Jani, ordered her to whore for his second."

"Holy mother," she breathed.

"Yeah. His own niece."

"Did—?"

He shook his head. "She'd have killed herself first."

"Thank *Deus* she had you."

He grunted. "It was the only thing that kept us going—that we had each other. You know what that S.O.B. did? Invited the night fae into Baltimore. He let them feed on us so he could stay in power. What kind of monster does that?"

He was gripping her fingers too tightly, but he couldn't let go. He stared at their two hands, unseeing, caught in the nightmare of the Darktime.

His throat closed up. He pushed the words past it. "I was the only one strong enough to take him down."

Her swallow was audible.

"I live with it every single fucking day. The Darktime. The friends I lost. My mom and dad. But killing my uncle Leron?" His lips twisted. "I haven't lost a single minute of sleep over it."

She didn't speak, didn't try to tell him he'd done the right thing. Just opened her arms.

His breath shuddered out. Then his hands clamped on her. He dragged her onto his lap and buried his face in her hair.

"I love you, all right? I fucking love you. May the Goddess help us both."

CHAPTER 36

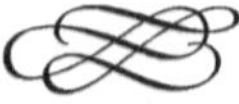

laer watched Langdon's maneuverings with interest. The Rock Run alpha and the Baltimore alpha had both come to him. And now the sun fae queen herself was involved, along with the powerful Lady Olivia and most of Rock Run and Baltimore's top people.

The prince was a master schemer. A woman could learn from him. Maybe she'd allow him to live—for now. For one thing, she was curious to know what his endgame was.

Her gaze turned to Luc, in his wolf form as he'd been ever since he'd brought his alpha to the prince. Her secret weapon. The prince knew Luc was under her *geas*—that was impossible to hide from other fae. But no one, not even Jon and Krysten, knew she could control the wolf fada through his quartz.

If she ordered Luc to kill Langdon, he would.

She wondered if Adric knew she'd learned the secret from his own cousin, Corban. Not that it mattered—Corban was dead. The fool had sought to control *her*.

Her lip curled.

She and Luc were alone in her new living room, she on a red velvet chair, the wolf fada on a rug before the hearth. A real fire burned in the fireplace. She'd learned to appreciate such things while shut up in her solitary tower in Iceland.

The solitary tower to which Langdon had helped banish her.

Luc's eyes opened. They stared into hers, an inhuman yellow-orange. The sheer hate on his furred face made her draw back. She covered her instinctive response by shifting her body on the velvet chair.

Luc had proved hard to tame. He'd lost weight, become increasingly resistant to her commands. She'd expected him to surrender to her more powerful will by now, but she was beginning to think he'd break first.

That...hurt.

She frowned. Fada were lower forms of life. Weaker than the fae, slaves to their emotions. To be used and then discarded when their purpose was served.

Why should she care what happened to Luc?

She rose to her feet. "Shift," she ordered. "And dress in the clothes I've provided, not those stinking rags you seem to prefer. We'll dine at the great hall tonight."

Luc immediately obeyed. It took longer than normal, and she wondered if she'd been wise to demand it. The stubborn ass was wasting away before her eyes.

At last, he stood before her, proudly naked. Too thin, yes, but with broad shoulders and sculpted muscles covered by smooth brown skin. By fae standards, his face was just this side of ugly: rugged and roughly formed, with a dark scruff on his jaw and bushy eyebrows jutting over deep-set eyes.

A wolf in a man's body. Wild, dangerous.

And Goddess, she craved him.

She moistened her lips. His gaze went to them, lingered, and his mouth twisted. The hate was there again, this time on a human face.

Instinct made her want to step back. So instead, she moved forward.

They were nearly the same height, with him just an inch or two taller. She was close enough that she could feel his breath on her mouth. Her lips tingled hungrily.

She ran her fingers over the black stubble on his jaw, traced a hard pectoral. "I know you want me."

His cock twitched. He stared back, his face a mask of disdain. "I'd rather fuck a viper."

Hurt twisted through her, followed by fury. She whirled away before he could see either.

"Get dressed. And Luc? You *will* eat, if I have to force-feed you myself."

His voice was expressionless. "Yes, my lady."

CHAPTER 37

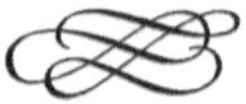

*D*ion and Rui set up a temporary ops center along with Marjani and the Baltimore fada at the motel where Adric had taken a room.

Neither Langdon nor his guards had been seen since that first afternoon, but that didn't mean their little group wasn't being watched. Every single one of them had felt ice creep up their spine, sensed eyes and ears on them. To keep the night fae at bay, Cleia conjured up fae lights for each of their rooms. They left them on low all night, shedding light on the treacherous shadows.

Marjani and Jace spent the nights as their cats, and they all took turns at watch, aware that if the night fae attacked, it would be in the hours between midnight and dawn. But Langdon refrained from attacking, clearly believing he had the upper hand as long as he remained behind his wards.

He was right. As things stood, they couldn't touch the man—or get to Rosana and Adric.

They all took a shot at breaking into the night fae compound. Cleia brought in her cousin Olivia to help shatter the wards. The two worked long hours, but each time they thought they'd done it, they hit a new barrier. At least Olivia had neutralized the *look-away* spell so they weren't constantly fighting it.

But he worried about them both. It was winter, when the sun fae were weakest. Cleia and her cousin should be home, curled up under a shaft of sunlight, not pushing themselves to the limit in this dank, cold forest.

Meanwhile, the fada tried to sneak into New Moon as their animals. Rui and Tiago changed to fish to try to enter the court through a stream, but the night fae had strengthened their wards to keep out anything larger than a minnow. And while fada could adjust their body size to a certain extent, they simply couldn't compress a man-size amount of matter into that tiny of a body.

Jace Jones didn't even get that far. He spent hours as his black panther, sniffing around the court's perimeter. But the wards repelled him with increasingly violent results. When he'd returned from his last foray with his fur singed, Marjani had drawn him aside and, after a heated argument, extracted his promise not to try again.

As for Marjani herself, she grew edgier with each day that passed. Dion kept a wary eye on her, afraid she'd slip off to exchange herself for Adric. It was what he'd do if he were her.

But where would that leave Rosana?

Sunday arrived with heavy clouds and snow flurries. They'd been in Virginia four days already. Five days until Friday and the new moon.

Dion spent the day prowling the forest around New Moon along with Tiago and Rui, daring the night fae to confront them. But the court remained maddeningly silent, concealed behind an opaque white fog.

Late that afternoon, he returned to the motel to find Marjani alone in the parking lot, gazing at the trees where they'd found her brother's keycard.

He left Tiago and Rui to approach her. "Walk with me?"

She nodded and fell into step with him. "Something wrong, my lord?"

"Please. Call me Dion."

She shoved her hands into the back pockets of her cargo pants. "Dion, then. What's up?"

The sun was low in the sky, but it was still daylight. Still, he waited until they reached the center of the lot, far from any shadows where the night fae could lurk.

"I'm asking you to be patient. Give us a little more time to work this out."

She bristled. "What do you mean?"

In the few days they'd been in Virginia, he'd learned Marjani was a Gifted strategist. Even afraid as she must be for her brother, she coolly examined a problem from all sides. Now he chose his words with care, knowing his only hope was to appeal to the strategist.

Because the sister knew that if she didn't do something soon, her brother would be executed.

"As it stands, we're even, more or less; the prince has Adric and Rosana, but we have you and Merry. So I'm asking you not to do anything on your own. We *will* bring them both home. That's a promise."

The cougar fada's gaze slid sideways. So he'd guessed right—she was planning to barter herself to save Adric.

"If they capture you," he added, "Merry will be our only bargaining chip, and I swore never to turn her over to the night fae."

"So you'll have nothing the prince wants bad enough to trade for Rosana." Marjani stared up at the darkening sky. The moon hadn't risen yet, but each night, the shadows took another bite out of it. "Even if he takes me in exchange for Adric, he'll still have her. Gods, you don't ask much, do you?"

He squeezed his nape, hating the bleak look he'd put on her fine-boned face. They both knew if things went south, her brother was dead.

"I have no choice. The night before Rosana was kidnapped, Merry Jones told Rui that she believes the prince has been watching her. Apparently, he has the farsight."

"He knows she's alive then."

"*Sim.* We think he's just waiting for his chance."

Marjani's head dropped. Her whole body hunched in on itself. The silence stretched, and then she blew out a noisy breath.

"Fine. I'll hold off for now. But only because I know if it was up to Adric, he'd sacrifice himself for Rosana in a heartbeat." She must have seen something in Dion's expression, because she snarled, low and mean. "You don't believe me? You think my brother would leave her with those sadistic S.O.B.s? And that goes double for Merry."

Dion hesitated. "I believe he'd willingly give his life for Merry, or any pup."

Adric might be a ruthless S.O.B., a man Dion didn't particularly like or trust, but he had to admit the other alpha was a good leader, one who put children and elders first. Everything he did, he did for his people.

But Rosana wasn't a member of his clan.

"You just don't get it, do you?" Marjani said. "He loves Rosana. He only kept his hands off her because he believes he's no good for her, that bringing her home to Baltimore would be a step down for her. If she didn't mean so much to him, he'd have taken her years ago."

"Maybe," he shot back. "But we both know your clan would never accept her. What kind of life is that—a pariah in her own mate's clan?"

"Merry has made a life in your clan, and she's not just half earth fada, she's a quarter fae. What makes you think we'd be any different? My own mate is a quarter fae, and Adric accepted him into the clan. He'd make damn sure Rosana was treated with respect."

He snorted. "Your brother can't even control his own people. *Mãe de Deus,* the very first night Rosana spent in Baltimore, she was kidnapped."

"That had nothing to do with Adric. That wolf—Luc—was working for the fae and you know it." Marjani leaned in. "You think you're so much better than us, but you're wrong. I've seen how my brother hurts, wanting Rosana, *loving* her —and not being able to claim her because he's too fucking noble to come between the two of you."

"She would never have him."

Then he recalled the note Rosana had left and scraped a hand over his hair.

I'm with Adric. I'm tired of hiding it. I love him, and he loves me...

Marjani gave Dion the look women reserve for clueless men. "What d'you think she was doing in Lewes last week?"

Dion rocked back on his heels. "What do you mean?"

A jerk of her shoulder. "Forget it."

"You're saying she was with Adric?"

When Marjani dipped her chin in assent, his jaw hardened. So that Tuesday night in Baltimore hadn't been the first time. In fact, that talk he'd had with Adric at the Full Moon Saloon? Apparently he'd already been too late—and the devious son of a bitch had neglected to inform Dion of that little detail.

"How long have they been meeting?"

"Overnight? That was the first time." She eyed him warily. "Look, forget I said anything. But I wanted you to know that Adric would do anything for Rosana. That's why I'm so worried about him." Her voice hitched on the last few words.

"No. You were right to tell me."

His claws pricked his fingertips. Adric, it always came back to Adric. He should've taken the *cabrão* out years ago.

But Dion didn't kill for no reason. And while Adric might be a cocky pain-in-the-ass, he'd also done things that had left Dion in his debt—like rescuing Tiago's mate from a pair of rogue river fada. Plus, he was ten times the alpha Leron Savonett had been. Take Adric out of the equation, and the situation in Baltimore would only get worse, and before you knew it, Rock Run could be dragged in.

If Dion was honest, this wasn't about Adric, it was about Rosana.

Shame squeezed his chest. That his own sister believed she had to sneak around to be with the man she loved rather than tell him, Dion, straight out.

So he can't want me for myself? she'd asked, and he'd brushed her question aside.

He withdrew his claws, stared unseeingly into the trees.

"Hey." Marjani touched his back. "She'll be all right. You'll see. Adric will make sure of it."

He jerked his chin in acknowledgement. "It's dark. We should go in."

～

WEDNESDAY MORNING DAWNED. Dion woke from a restless sleep with a sense of dread. Time was running out. The new moon was just two days away.

Cleia had spent the night at Rising Sun with Brisa while Dion bunked down with Tiago, both of them tossing and turning for those hours they weren't on watch, their worry for Rosana a constant, clawing thing.

He glanced at where his brother lay staring at the ceiling and threw off the sheet. "I'm going for a swim."

Tiago rose as well. "I'll come."

When they exited their room, Rui was waiting. They left Jaxon and Ed on watch at the motel and headed for the Potomac. Dion and Tiago swam as their dolphins, with Rui joining them as his bull shark. When they returned, Dion sent Jaxon and Ed for a swim while Tiago opted to make another attempt at slipping through New Moon's wards by water. Meanwhile, Rui held a convo with Marjani and Fane to determine if there was anything they were missing.

Dion took up a position in the forest near the court. The temperatures remained just above freezing, with a chilly wind rattling the bare branches. He paced a path through the trees, straining for a glimpse of Rosana, but the unnatural fog prevented him from seeing more than a few yards.

A black rage filled his head. That his sister was trapped underground in one of those cryptlike lairs. Upset, afraid, unable to shift.

With those perverted bastards enjoying her fear.

His claws pricked out. He dropped his head back, fangs bared. His animal wanted to slash and burn, to tear out Langdon's heart and feed on it.

The air nearby shimmered and then twisted as Cleia 'ported onto the grass between the woods and the court. She walked to him, a pretty peach-colored dress whipping around her long legs, her bright hair in a businesslike braid. Her only concession to the January cold was a soft cashmere shawl.

"My love." She touched his unshaven cheek. "You have to eat. Starving yourself isn't helping Rosana. And when was the last time you slept?"

Dion raked a hand through his hair. He hadn't tied it back for days, and his only clothing was a T-shirt and the leather pants he'd been wearing when Rosana had gone missing. His animal was too close to the surface to accept such human restrictions as shoes or a coat.

"I slept last night." For an hour or two. "And I'm not hungry. How's my Brisa?"

"She's good. She misses her *papai*, of course, and Rosana."

He ran a hand down Cleia's silky braid, needing to touch her. "Tell Brisa I miss her, too. With all my heart. And that I'll be home as soon as I can—with Rosana." He glared at the night fae compound.

"I already did." Cleia 'ported in a thick ham-and-cheese sandwich and a cup of coffee, and thrust them both into his hands. "But you still need to eat, and sleep more than a few hours a night."

When he just stared at the food, she sighed. "Dion. I'm as worried as you are. But you can't give up hope. We *will* get her back. And meanwhile, she's with Adric. From what the prince said, that was a condition of her remaining at the court. Adric won't let them hurt her."

Anger fisted in his chest. He hadn't forgotten that Rosana had been sneaking off to see the Baltimore alpha right beneath his nose. Even Tiago had known, or at least suspected. The sensible part of him knew his anger was misplaced, that it was just that he was so damn afraid for his sister, but he didn't care.

"If it wasn't for him," he growled, "she'd never have been there in the first place."

"You don't really believe that."

"No?"

Her lush mouth set. She started to argue further, but he shook his head.

"*Querida.* Not now. *Por favor?*"

She expelled a breath. "You're right. When they're safely back home, then we'll argue about whether they're mates or not."

"*Mates?*" That fist of anger tightened around his heart. "Who said anything about them being mates? It would never work. She can't live in Baltimore—I told Adric myself."

"Did you now?"

"And he agreed."

"Ah." Cleia opened her mouth, closed it.

"Go ahead. Say it."

"We made it work when no one—even you—thought we could. A sun fae and a river fada."

He just shook his head. He was still holding the food. He took a bite of the sandwich and followed it with a gulp of coffee.

"You *are* hungry," she said, and to please her, he kept eating until it was gone.

As he was finishing up, Lady Olivia 'ported in. They turned to her hopefully. She strode toward them, her long, fire-colored dress draped like liquid flame over her slender body, her penny-bright hair twined in a coronet around her head.

"Peace to you and yours," she said, and then gave a rueful shake of her head. "I'm afraid I haven't made any progress on the wards."

"By the Goddess," Cleia bit out. "How is he keeping us out? You're the best spell-breaker we have."

Dion briefly closed his eyes.

Olivia touched his arm for the first time ever, as far as he could recall. "I'm sorry, Dion. I've tried everything I can think of."

"I know. And I thank you for it."

"We *will* break through," she said. "And when we do, I've prepared a few helpful...aids, shall we say?"

"Oh?" murmured Cleia.

"One moment." Olivia conjured up a blazing fae light. A nearby shadow made a small sound of pain and hurriedly withdrew. With a little half-smile, she held the glowing orb higher so they stood within a shaft of light.

Dion narrowed his eyes. He didn't have the sun fae's love of bright lights, but he accepted the need for it.

"You have the protection charm?" Olivia asked him.

He wordlessly held up his wrist. The delicate silver bracelet encircled it.

"Good," she said. "Get that back to Rosana as soon as possible. It won't block a fae as powerful as the prince forever, but it will buy her time." She handed Cleia a small silk bag. "I made a charm for the Savonett female as well."

Cleia frowned. "That's good of you, but you've expended so much energy trying to break the wards. Are you sure this wasn't too much for you?"

The other woman raised a fine sable eyebrow. "I know my limits."

Which didn't really answer the question.

Dion eyed the fae lady. Her narrow, pointed face looked gaunt. Magic at the level she'd been wielding it sucked life-energy right out of you.

Cleia sighed and pursed her lips. She might be queen, but Olivia was her top adviser, their relationship one of near-equals. "Just remember we'll need you when we do break through."

Olivia inclined her head.

"What if he's convinced Rosana to accept his *geas*?" Cleia voiced Dion's deepest fear.

A chill prickled his skin. He was fairly certain his sister wouldn't accept Langdon's *geas* for herself, no matter what the prince offered her. But she might accept it to save Adric.

"Then we'll have to encourage him to break it," Olivia replied.

"How?" Dion demanded. "A *geas* is almost impossible to break."

"By the person who accepted it, yes," Olivia said. "But not by the fae who set the terms."

Dion's mouth twisted. "Why would he break it? He'd love to have a Seer in his power for the next ten turns of the sun."

Olivia moved a slim shoulder. "Then we'll offer him something he wants more." She pulled a gleaming iron dagger from a hidden pocket in her dress. "Meanwhile, I had one of our smiths make you this. It's bespelled."

Dion set down the coffee cup and took it by the ebony handle. Energy shivered up his hand. "A powerful spell."

Olivia inclined her head. "It will slice through any spell the prince casts at you."

He slipped it into his back pocket. "Thank you, my lady."

Dion pulled Cleia closer, and the three of them gazed at the fog-covered court.

His fingers tightened on Cleia's waist. A sun fae's metabolism burned hot, and *Deus* knew, he needed heat right now. He was chilled to the bone.

"Tell me she's getting enough to eat," he rasped. "Tell me he's allowing her to shift to her dolphin." According to Rui and Fane, New Moon was crisscrossed by creeks and streams. There was even a pond big enough for Rosana to swim.

"Of course, he is," Cleia said. "He knows a water fada will die if she's kept from the water."

Olivia made a small sound of dissent.

"What?" asked Dion.

"He may not consider that to a fada, time in a fae court can pass differently."

Cleia's gold-touched skin paled. "It depends on the fada."

Olivia inclined her pointed chin in that cool manner she had, but Dion had seen her with his sister. In her own way, the fae lady loved Rosana. "Some adjust to our time, but others find it difficult."

"She's fine," Cleia stated firmly. "He wouldn't dare harm her."

Dion's growl came from the darkest, primal heart of him. "I hope you're right," he said in a carrying voice. "Because if Langdon hurts her, he's dead."

CHAPTER 38

*I*n the never-ending twilight of the cell, day and night blended together. Adric had no idea how much time had passed—one day? three days?— before the night fae finally 'ported them some food.

He fell on it, his starving body needing calories, and watched, worried, as Rosana just picked at hers. But after that, meals came on a regular basis: fish chowder for her, steak for him, fresh fruit and vegetables, crusty homemade bread.

They slept, woke, plotted. He paced the cell, nerves stretched taut at their continuing confinement in the small, dark space.

His quartz had completely recharged—another clue that in the outside world, more time had passed than they knew. He gave Rosana what healing energy he could, but it was her life-energy that was fading, and he wasn't healer enough to fix that.

She grew weaker, edgier. She took to pacing the cell along with him, and when they curled up to rest, she felt warm, which was all wrong for a river fada.

And when was the last time she'd eaten?

Then the day came when she didn't get up at all, just lay curled up next to the water trough, fingers playing in the meager trickle, her breath so light, it was almost inaudible.

He bent to stroke her cheek. It was dry, feverish. Even though he'd blocked the bond, he *felt* her receding from him.

"Angel," he said brokenly.

"*Amo-te*," she whispered. *Love you.*

He briefly closed his eyes—and then rose to his feet.

"Prince Langdon!" He stood in the center of the cell, spine erect, hands clenched at his sides. Prepared to do anything, even accept the bastard's *geas*, in exchange for Rosana's life. "Come to me—please. I'm begging you."

Rosana lifted her head to hiss, "No, Rick!"

He ignored her to loudly repeat the prince's name. "Langdon! Are you there?"

A whiff of metal and decay.

Adric scanned the cell.

There. In the corner to his left, a shadow coalesced into a man-shape.

He whipped around. Hot, angry words crowded his throat, but he forced himself to speak calmly. "Prince Langdon?"

A whisper from the shadows. "You called me."

"Yes. Rosana"—his voice broke—"she's sick. She needs her river. You have to release her."

"So you're ready to negotiate?"

A muscle in Adric's cheek worked. Inside, his cat crouched, ears back, tail swishing angrily.

"As long as you let her out of here. She has to get in the water. Even that pond outside would work."

A dark chuckle. "Soon." The shadows settled again.

"No! Wait, you thrice-damned bastard!" He pounded his fists against the stones. "She needs out, *now*." But Langdon was gone.

Adric flung himself at the door. "Somebody, please!" He hammered on the wood between the iron straps. "Let Rosana out. She's going to die in here."

When no one came, he threw his whole body against the door, slamming into it again and again, uncaring of the iron straps. But the heavy wood withstood his battering, and when it was over, all he had to show for it were several burns on his arms and hands.

And he was still alone in the cell with Rosana.

He bit out a vicious curse and stood there, hands fisted on his hips, head hanging.

Rosana moved restlessly. "I'm so thirsty..."

"I'm here, baby." He rinsed the burns in the cold water and then sat down, easing her head onto his lap. "It's going to be all right, you'll see. Just hold on a little longer. Here, drink."

Dipping the cup in the trough, he brought it to her dry, cracked lips. She murmured something unintelligible and sucked at the cup's lip like a baby, tiny sips that had half the water trickling down her jaw.

But he heard her swallow.

"That's it. Drink some more." He urged water on her until she shut her mouth and turned her head.

~

ROSANA DREAMED she was a small girl again, floating in Rock Run Creek. Water flowed around her, cool and silky. She sensed her mama and *papai* on either side of her, but her eyes were glued shut.

And she was so dry, like she'd swallowed a desert.

"Shift," her *papai* said in Portuguese. "You can do it, *minha pequena*."

My little one.

Nostalgia cramped her stomach. How long had it been since anyone called her that?

And then something twisted and she was an adult again, watching her younger self play with her parents in the creek. Her father, big and black-haired like her brothers, his strong, proud face marked by the jagged white scar he'd received from a fae. Her mother, fine-boned and creamy skinned, with a heart-shaped face and blue eyes that always seemed to be smiling.

Rosana's throat burned. "I miss you, Mama," she whispered—and just like that, she was back in her little girl's body again.

"You can do it," Ula encouraged in her lilting Irish accent. "Shift, Rosie darling."

She whimpered. "I'm thirsty."

"I know. But I can help," her mama replied. "Just open your eyes."

But instead, Rosana opened her mouth to gulp down the river's fresh, clear water. It didn't help—she was drier than ever.

Her heart sank. "This is just a dream," she said sadly. "Because I need to shift and I can't."

Her dad faded away and now she only sensed Ula.

"It is a dream," she agreed. "But I'm really here. Now open your eyes, *alanna*."

"Mama?" In the dream-river, Rosana's eyes popped open. To her surprise, it was nighttime. The water flowed silver around her. On the nearby bank, bare trees scratched at the rising moon.

But her parents were nowhere to be seen.

Don't leave me. Please, don't leave me.

Hot tears clogged her throat. She squeezed her eyes shut, willing them not to spill out.

Gentle fingers brushed her face. "Not those eyes, *alanna*. The eyes you use to See."

"Go away." Rosana shook off her mother's hand. "You're not really here. This is just some night-fae trick."

"Oh, Rosie. You still haven't learned the most necessary lesson."

"Oh, yeah? And what's that?"

"Trust," Ula whispered.

"I do trust him. He loves me." Her mouth curved. "He told me."

"Ah, sweetheart. That's wonderful. Trust between mates is a beautiful, necessary thing. But you also must trust yourself, trust your Gift."

Rosana's brows snapped together. "You sound like Colm. '*Believe in yourself. If you don't believe you can do it, then you can't.*' But what good can my Gift do? It isn't a weapon."

"Oh, but it is. Touch *him*."

She turned her head away. "*Touch* him? But I can't See anything when I touch him. And how would it help anyway when we're locked in this freaking cell?"

Hopelessness settled over her like a dark veil.

Ula moved uneasily. "I have to go now—I shouldn't even be talking to you. But remember, Rosie. When you wake up, remember these words: *Touch him*."

Then she was gone, and when Rosana forced her eyes open, she was in the cell with Adric pleading for her to drink.

To please him, she took a couple of sips. But she was so tired.

She closed her eyes, telling herself she'd only rest a minute...and slipped back into the dream-river.

CHAPTER 39

*D*ion spent another almost sleepless night. Tossing and turning. Staring at the ceiling. Listening to his brother do the same.

By morning, he'd decided to trade himself for Rosana, to hell with the consequences.

The instant the sun peeped above the horizon, he was out of bed. He pulled on his clothes, sliding Olivia's bespelled dagger into his pocket.

Tiago raised his head to peer dully at him.

"Go back to sleep," he said and his brother dropped his head back on the pillow.

Overnight, the wind had dropped and heavy clouds had moved in. A storm was coming, rain this time. A daylong downpour from the air's scent and feel.

His mouth curved dangerously. Water was his element, the more the better.

This time, he didn't hide in the forest. Instead, he stalked back and forth on the grass in full view of the fog-covered court.

Daring Prince Langdon to make a move.

A movement behind him made him spin on his heel.

Rui strode out of the forest, scowling. "What the fuck do you think you're doing?" he demanded in Portuguese.

"Go away," Dion snarled in the same language. "That's an order from your alpha."

"Not when he's acting like a crazy man." Rui folded his arms over his chest, a rock-faced, stubborn-as-hell statue.

Dion ground his teeth. He knew Rui. If the shark fada had decided Dion needed him, an army wouldn't move him.

"Then don't interfere," he bit out.

Rui shook his head. "This all started when I brought Merry back to Rock Run."

Dion growled. "When are you going to stop beating yourself up about Merry's father? You took that job with my blessing. The clan needed Lord Tyrus's diamonds. You think I don't ask myself why I didn't dig a little deeper before letting him hire you? But unless you can turn back time, we both have to live with it. Merry is clan now. The night fae go after her, they go after all of us."

Rui drew a breath. "With all respect, I'd take Merry, Valeria and the girls and run before I'd let her anywhere near those dark bastards. That doesn't change the fact that this all comes back to me. I'll go to the prince. Offer myself for Rosana."

"No." Dion clamped a hand on his shoulder. "You, Tiago, Jaxon, Ed—I know every single one of you would trade yourself for Rosana. But that's not the way."

Rui regarded him through hooded green eyes. "Then why are you out here all alone?"

Dion simply looked back at him. But Rui knew him too well.

"Exactly. If you go to the prince, I go at your side. I demand this not only as your second, but as your friend."

Dion exhaled.

"I'll go." Tiago stepped out of the trees, jaw set, hands balled at his side. "As alpha, you're not expendable, and neither are you, Rui. I am."

Before Dion could draw a breath to argue with him, Marjani, Fane and Jace were there as well. They took up a stance next to Tiago. Jace was in his black panther form. He fixed emerald eyes on Dion, while Marjani folded her arms over her chest, a shorter, wiry imitation of Rui.

"This concerns us too," Fane said.

Dion shook his head. "It appears we have a mutiny," he muttered.

"I'm going with you," Marjani said in a tone that brooked no argument. "The new moon is two nights away. If Adric is executed, the clan goes down, too. He's the only one who can hold us together. And we won't survive another Darktime. You don't have the right to ask that, even to save your sister."

"You're right. I don't." His heart clenched for Rosana, but he made himself continue. "I apologize, I should've come to you first. I'm not...thinking too clearly these days. What do you want to do?"

She blinked, taken aback, but quickly recovered. "Not here," she said with a glance around. "Back at the motel."

As Dion nodded, the air shimmered and Cleia 'ported in. "By the Sun

Goddess." Her amber gaze raked over the six of them. "I hope you're not planning what I think you are. Because the prince would like nothing better for you all to go charging in there. If he captures even a few of you, he wins. He won't even have to negotiate with us."

Marjani growled lowly.

Cleia took her hands. "I know, my dear. It's your brother's life on the line. But don't forget, he has Dion and Tiago's sister—this is personal for everyone here." She released Marjani to speak to all of them. "I've talked things over with Olivia and a couple of my top warriors. They agree with me that the prince is playing a deep game, manipulating us so he gets what he wants. And we all know what he really wants."

"Merry Jones," whispered Marjani.

Jace's tail whipped back and forth.

"Yes. And I agree, it's an impossible choice. But I promise you"—Cleia's beautiful face was fierce—"I won't let him execute Adric. Now, let's all go back to the motel. I have news for you. Good news. We've got some planning to do."

Marjani, Jace and Fane exchanged looks, and then the cougar fada lowered her chin in assent. "We'll listen. But I'm not making any promises."

A key scraped in the lock. Adric lurched into action, snatching up Rosana and scrambling to his feet.

He waited with bated breath as the door swung open to reveal a tall silhouette with a pair of gleaming eyes. The shadows arranged themselves into a night fae female in a warrior's trim black uniform, her jet hair slicked back in a perfect ponytail.

He shoved past her, Rosana cradled to his chest. "She needs to get in the water. *Now.*"

Two more warriors, both males, waited in the hall.

"The prince has granted your request," the female said. "If you'll follow me..."

"I know the fucking way." His inner GPS would get him to the surface.

"As you wish." The men flanked him, and she followed behind.

A few twists and turns, and he was at the stairs leading up to the black marble foyer. He took them at a run. In the foyer, the tall door once again opened as he approached. He jogged up the steps leading to the outside and sprinted the fifty yards to the pond, the long-legged warriors loping alongside him.

Dusk had spread its gloomy fingers over the compound. A few night fae had already emerged from their lairs, but although he caught them eyeing him and Rosana with interest, they stayed out of his way.

He lowered Rosana to the grass beside the pond and stripped off her clothes. The three warriors hovered over him until he snarled at them to back off. "She's not going anywhere." Shifters were used to being naked in front of one another, but he was damned if he'd let these cold-eyed fae ogle his mate's naked body.

The female inclined her head, and they all moved a few steps back.

Dragging off his own clothes, he picked up Rosana again and strode into the icy pond. When it reached his waist, he lowered her into the water.

She shrieked and flung out her arms like a startled infant. One hand latched onto his shoulder in a death grip.

He frowned. "Easy now. It's okay. You're in the water now. You can shift." He bent his knees, submerging her to the chest.

"No!" She shook her head wildly. Both hands clamped around his neck.

"Shift, angel." He lowered her a little deeper, but she clawed at him, climbing his body like he was trying to drown her.

What the fuck—?

"Rosana." He gave her a shake. "Shift. Change to your dolphin."

Her eyes popped open—and looked right through him. "Go away," she hissed. "You're not really here."

Panic coated his throat. He lifted her out of the water and brought his face close to hers. "Rosana! Look at me."

"*No...*" She squeezed her eyes shut. "Why won't you leave me alone?"

"Because," he growled, "if you don't shift, you'll die." But he had the bad feeling she didn't hear him.

As he lowered her back into the pond, she flailed her arms and legs, frantically trying to escape. Her breath came fast and hard. He heard the frenzied beating of her heart, saw the frightened flutter of the pulse at the base of her throat. Worse, he *felt* her blind, unreasoning fear.

He stood it as long as he could, and then rose back to his feet with her. In her weakened condition, she could die of sheer terror.

He cuddled her to his chest. "It's okay, baby. It's okay."

At the pond's edge, the three night fae warriors gathered like a flock of tall black vultures. Watching and waiting.

He snarled over his shoulder at them. They stared back, blank faced. The eyes of the male on the left flickered red; he was eager to feed. But he didn't, no doubt under orders from his superiors.

Rosana locked her arms around his neck and burrowed her head into his throat. Like she was trying to crawl right inside him.

In desperation, he tried to pulse life-energy through the mate bond. But he was blocked by the shield he himself had erected between them.

He dropped back his head to stare up at the darkening sky. If he were a wolf, he'd have howled in anguish. Rosana was dying, and taking his heart with him.

Her breasts pressed against his chest. By some odd coincidence, their pendants had lined up side by side, his quartz touching her chest, her amethyst against his breastbone. He felt her reaching out to him—mate to mate—and knew what he had to do.

He'd rejected the bond to protect her. Now he had to accept it.

In the end, it was easy. He simply let the shield drop.

The shining strands leapt toward each other, his blue intertwining with her sea-green.

Rosana jerked. Mumbled something.

His stomach dropped. Her thread was so thin and weak. A shimmer so fragile, it hurt him to see it—and yet also incredibly beautiful, glowing with Rosana's very essence.

He poured his love into that fragile green strand. Willing her to feel how much he cared.

Willing her to *live*.

To his astonishment, a new thread shimmered into being, a gossamer gold that belonged to both of them. Together, they twined into single bright cord.

Rosana's breath shuddered in.

Hope leapt in him. He pressed kisses to her face. "That's it, love. Come back to me."

Her eyes opened. As she focused on him, a wondering look spread over her face.

She touched his cheek. "Ric. You—we—"

"Hey there, angel." Rubbing his lips over hers, he pulsed life-energy into her. This time, it worked, moving right to the deepest parts of her, healing her from the inside out.

She heaved a breath. They remained like that for a long minute.

When her lips curved in a smile, he felt it clear to his soul. "We're mate-bonded. But—" She frowned, shook her head. "I don't understand."

"I'll explain later. Can you stand now?"

When she nodded, he set her on her feet in the pond. She blinked around her. "We're outside. In the water."

"It's a pond at New Moon. Big enough for your dolphin."

"Oh. How—?"

"Go ahead." He gave her an encouraging squeeze. "Shift."

She blinked again—and then released him to sink beneath the surface.

She barely had enough juice to shift, but he remained connected to her, urging her on. That and sheer grit got her through. The dark waters glittered, and then she was a river dolphin with a long beak and charcoal gray body.

He watched tensely while she lolled in the water, sucking air through her blowhole, until she revived enough to give him a feeble nudge with her beak.

His whole body sagged in relief. He set his cheek against her smooth gray face. "Go. Swim. Catch some fish for me."

She cast him a worried look, clucked a question. Somehow he understood.

What about you?

"It's okay. You can find me later." He pressed a kiss to the edge of her beak. "I love you."

She hesitated, but she must have seen the wisdom of that because her body brushed against his and she was off.

The last thing he heard was a short series of clicks. *I love you, too.*

He watched until she was across the pond. Already she seemed stronger. She was going to be all right.

He turned and walked out of the pond.

The night fae warriors surrounded him. A fiery purple fae ball glowed in one of the male's hands, but he didn't need it.

Adric knew that if he didn't cooperate, Rosana would be back in that cell so fast his head would spin.

"Here." The other male tossed Adric his T-shirt and pants.

"The prince is waiting," added the female.

As soon as Adric was dressed, the three warriors marched him back to the prince's lair. Just before he walked down the steps, he caught a glimpse of Luc watching from a stand of trees, his too-thin face unreadable.

Adric expected to be taken to the prince, but instead the warriors took him back underground. He resigned himself to being locked in the cell again, but they kept going, navigating through a series of long, twisting corridors.

He gazed around, awed in spite of himself. The earth fada were considered master miners, but this beat anything he'd ever seen. The buildings aboveground were the tip of the iceberg. The night fae had an entire city down here. It must have taken centuries to carve out.

And still, they fucked with his clan, sucked its resources.

He shook his head, disgusted.

At last, they exited in an immense, windowless hall with soaring Gothic arches. Fanciful columns shaped like giant palm trees supported the ceiling with curved stone fronds. The only lighting was a handful of darkly shimmering fae lights ranging from purple to forest green.

Adric strode barefoot to the hall's center, the warriors on his heels.

"Well?" he demanded of the shadows. "I'm here, Prince Langdon. Now what?"

Olivier appeared in a nearby archway clad in his butler's uniform of black pants and crisp white shirt. His bow tie this time was lavender dotted with tiny white skulls.

"My lord. If you'll follow me."

He turned to go back the way he'd come, but Adric leapt forward and grabbed his arm. "Where's the prince?"

The guards clamped cold fingers on him, yanking him away with superhuman strength. Furious, he fought against their hold, but the two men dragged his arms behind his back.

An iron dagger flashed in the woman's hand.

He glared at her. "I demand to see Prince Langdon."

"Be still, fada." The blade hissed across his T-shirt, slicing through the material to his chest.

He jerked. It felt like she'd drawn a line of acid on his skin.

Her dark eyes flashed an unholy red. "I can bring you to the prince whole," she said, "or I can bring you carved. Your choice."

Adric narrowed his eyes. "Bite me."

"If I may, Neoma?" Olivier stepped between them, forcing her back a step. To Adric's surprise, she allowed it. He clucked his tongue at Adric. "My lord, there's no need for this. My orders are to make you comfortable, provide you with dinner. The prince will see you tonight."

Neoma sheathed the knife. The corners of her mouth turned up in a way that sent icy water down Adric's spine. "Yes. Tonight."

"Fuck that," he snapped back. "I want to see the prince now."

The warriors released him. Adric's neck tingled. He spun around.

Langdon stood a few feet away, dressed in a simple black outfit much like his warriors wore, his only jewelry the diamonds glittering in his eyebrows and ears. On his narrow feet were supple leather sandals.

He inclined his head. "My lord Adric."

"Lord Langdon," he returned. He about choked on the next words, but if kissing ass helped Rosana, then he'd kiss away. "My thanks for allowing Rosana to swim as her dolphin."

"She's a guest. I don't wish to see her harmed."

Then why the fuck keep her underground all this time?

But Adric knew the answer. The prince had used Rosana to break him. To save her, he'd promise the bastard anything.

His stomach clenched. He was more afraid for Rosana than ever. They were mated now. He wasn't fighting just for himself or even Marjani.

He was fighting for her.

If he accepted Langdon's *geas*, Rosana might have to do the same. A *geas* was typically for a fae year-and-a-day, or ten years in the human world. Mates couldn't live apart for that long. She might literally pine away, and it wouldn't do him any good, either.

But to Hades with that. He wanted her far, far from here.

"You have me," he said in a hard voice. "Let Rosana go."

The fae lights wafted lower to circle the two of them, the lustrous purple and green gliding like an oil slick over his skin. Or maybe it was just that standing this close to Langdon made him feel like he was covered in something foul and greasy.

Langdon spoke. "Senhorita do Rio is here at her own request."

Adric swallowed sickly. That was the truth—she'd said so herself.

"As for you, you've broken a number of our laws. Your punishment is set for the night of the new moon."

Adric's chin jerked up. "What are the charges?"

"Trespassing, attempted murder. And let's not forget your part in Lord Tyrus's death."

Adric's heartbeat thundered in his ears.

Oh, Rosana.

He could guess what his punishment would be—execution. Or if Langdon was feeling lenient, he might invite Adric to accept his *geas* instead—and not for the fae year-and-a-day. This would be a life sentence.

He'd accepted the mate bond to save Rosana's life. But in doing so, had he condemned her to spend the rest of that life alone?

He moistened his lips. "And Marjani?"

"She'll be punished for her own part in the death of my line."

"Your own fucking son ended your line," he growled back. "He ordered Silver's death, and he got within inches of killing Merry, too. Then he went after Jace just because he's Merry's uncle. Tyrus would be alive today if he hadn't attacked us."

"So you say." Langdon's lids lowered, concealing his thoughts. "Now go with Olivier or I'll allow Neoma to play with you."

The warriors tried to grab Adric again, but he was ready this time. He sidestepped, circled to the prince's other side.

"What about Rosana?"

"She must choose her own path. But you have my word she won't be harmed."

The fae lights darkened. Shadows danced over the room. Langdon didn't seem to move, but suddenly, he blended with them, part man, part wraith.

Adric leapt after him, but Langdon just…flowed away. This time, the guards didn't even try to stop Adric. They knew he couldn't touch the prince.

"The night of the new moon," Langdon said. "In our time, that's tonight at midnight. Tomorrow at dusk in the outside world."

"To Hades with your charges," Adric bit out. "Everything I did was in response to acts of war—on myself, my clan, or my…woman." He barely stopped himself from saying *mate*. It would just give Langdon another weapon to use against them. "You might be able to kill me, but my clan won't rest until you're dead."

"That's their prerogative, of course. However, they'll find I'm not an easy man to kill." Langdon receded deeper into the shadows. "As for Rosana, New Moon could use a Seer of her power."

Fury flooded Adric, hot and red. His fangs pricked his gums, his cat quivering with the urge to tear Langdon into bloody pieces.

The three warriors surrounded Adric. Fae balls burned in the men's palms.

"You're insane," he growled. "She'll never agree to that."

"No? When you've lived as long as I have, you find that everyone has their breaking point." The prince smiled. "Don't they, Lord Adric?" And he was gone.

Adric snarled and spat on the marble floor. "Stand and fight like a man, you thrice-damned prick."

The guards raised the fae balls threateningly. Neoma fingered her dagger.

From the archway, Olivier spoke. "If you'll follow me, my lord."

ROSANA SWAM.

For a time, there was nothing but her and the dark, life-giving water. She glided through it, instinctively mapping the pond's dimensions with echolocation so that within a few passes, she knew it and its aquatic inhabitants intimately. The school of minnows that scattered at her approach. The fat, whiskered catfish and the bluegills and carp. The snails, crayfish and leeches. The turtles hibernating in the soft black mud, and the frog slowly swimming in the deep water at the center.

She understood she'd almost died. Her body needed time to heal.

But her heart was singing—no, *shouting*—with joy, its every beat an ecstatic cacophony.

Adric had mate-bonded with her.

He loves me. He loves me. He loves me.

His amethyst hung around her neck, the cord a little too tight with her dolphin's thicker proportions—she'd have to fix that—but there, warm, comforting.

An hour passed, maybe more. She swam and healed, healed and swam.

As her energy returned, she became aware that Adric wasn't on the bank waiting. She surged out of the water in a long arc, scanning for him.

It was a murky, moonless night. Her eyes went night-glow as she anxiously searched the bank. He was gone, replaced by two night fae warriors, their eyes shining in the dark. She raced for the shore—and shifted without thinking of the cost. Her body could barely handle it. As depleted as she'd been, she shouldn't have tried to shift for another twenty-four hours.

For an awful, stomach-churning moment, she wavered between forms. She grit her teeth and powered through it. The next thing she knew, she was on all fours in the shallow water. She came up on her knees and bent forward, hands on her thighs, lungs working.

The night fae moved closer—one man, one woman, neither of whom she'd seen before. The female had Rosana's clothes.

Rosana pushed herself to standing and walked out of the pond, wobbly-kneed but determined. "Where's Lord Adric?" she demanded as she got dressed. "What have you done with him?"

"Jessica will explain."

"Who?"

They herded Rosana forward without speaking, and she allowed it, because it was clear she wouldn't learn anything from them.

It was the first time she'd been outside since arriving with Blaer. The compound was exactly as she'd Seen it: the large pond, the pebbled paths, the vine-covered lairs. The dark forest towering over cryptlike buildings.

The night fae drag Adric to a clearing in the woods and stake him, spread-eagled, to the ground.

A black-haired priestess in a silver dress steps forward, a gleaming knife in her hand...

She inhaled sharply, gave herself a shake.

The night fae walked her down a short flight of granite stairs, then led her deeper. But she balked as they approached the hall leading to the cell in which she and Adric had been imprisoned.

"I won't go back in there."

"Hello." A young woman in the same uniform as Olivier—white shirt, black pants and a bow tie—stepped forward. She gave a tentative smile. "I'm Jessica, Olivier's assistant."

Rosana blinked. "You're human." Of course, Olivier had been human, too, but Jessica was young to be living at a fae court.

"That's right, Senhorita." The woman gave another nervous smile. "Come with me, please. I promise you're not going back into a cell."

She led Rosana down another hallway and then opened the door to a roomy apartment with dark Art Nouveau furniture and large, brooding paintings. "This way."

She ushered Rosana into a bedroom with more beautiful furniture and a hand-woven rug so plush Rosana's bare feet left footprints. The black lamps on either side of the bed were in the shape of a naked woman holding a glowing moon above her head, and an intricate design of lilies and vines was carved on the mahogany headboard.

Laid out on the blood-red comforter was a sleeveless party dress in a shimmering purple so dark it was almost black. She fingered the short pleated skirt. The dress was clearly fae-made, with invisible stitches and a magic fabric that would fit itself perfectly to her body. Next to it were a bra and panties in a cobweb-fine lace, and on a rug were matching purple heels in a butter-soft leather.

If the outfit was from anyone but Langdon, she'd have been thrilled to wear it. Instead, she wanted to stuff it in a trash can.

"I'll order your dinner," Jessica said. "Meanwhile, the prince thought you might like to take a bath and change into clean clothes." She turned to go, but Rosana put out a hand, stopping her.

"Where's Lord Adric?" He was near, she sensed that much through the bond.

The human glanced uneasily at the room's darkest corner. "He's fine."

"Say the words. Tell me Adric's unhurt."

"Adric is unhurt." Her scent held the purity of truth. "Like you, he's being fed, made comfortable."

Rosana's shoulders sagged in relief.

"I'm to come for you a half hour before midnight."

Her head jerked up. "Why? What happens at midnight?"

"The new moon's tonight," Jessica said. "You'll be at the ritual. That's all I know."

A ritual. On a dark, moonless night.

A black-haired priestess steps forward, a gleaming knife in her hand...

Shaken, Rosana sank onto the edge of the bed.

Jessica edged toward the door.

"Wait!" Rosana sprang to her feet. "Please. Take me to Adric. Nobody has to know. I just need to see him for myself."

The human looked down at her feet. "I can't. But he's fine. For now," she added in a small voice.

"What do you mean, for now?"

Jessica shook her head.

Rosana dropped her voice. "Can you get a message to Lord Dion? He'll pay you—anything you ask."

"I'm sorry," the human whispered as she backed out of the room. In a louder voice, she said, "Your dinner will be in the kitchen. I'll be back for you in a few hours."

CHAPTER 41

Friday morning, they slipped out of the motel in twos and threes.

The meeting place was a little-used portal Fane had discovered on New Moon's west side. The plan was to go in at noon, when most of the night fae would be fast asleep. Olivia and Cleia would hit the portal with a one-two punch: first, Olivia would weaken the portal with a counterspell she'd concocted, and then Cleia would draw on the sun's energy to jab a hole through it.

Once inside, some of their group, including Marjani, Jace and Fane, would spread out to find Rosana and Adric. Meanwhile others, including Cleia, Dion and a cohort of sun fae warriors armed with fae balls, would mount a direct attack on the night fae.

Marjani, Jace and Fane reached the portal first. The *look-away* spell was powerful here, even with the counterspell cast by Olivia.

Look away. Danger. Runrunrun...

Rubbing her prickling nape, Marjani glanced away. But when it pressed her to leave, she set her teeth and pushed back.

The Rock Run men arrived and hid in a nearby marsh, while Marjani and Jace took positions high in the forest canopy. Fane simply used his wayfaring Gift to blend into the trees.

Marjani hunkered down in the branches of a maple to wait for noon. Her stomach was a tangle of nerves, her cougar edgy. For Rosana's sake, she'd kept her promise to Dion, but with every day that passed, her fear for Adric increased.

Her brother had sacrificed everything for her, even his honor. And now he was going to lose his life. Because of her.

She was *damned* if she'd let that happen.

A clot of silver-gray clouds shrouded the sun. She scowled at the shadows that raced across the forest.

Zuri arrived, along with several of the clan's top soldiers, all wolves. He'd demanded to come, pointing out that for now, the action wasn't in Baltimore, but in Virginia.

Marjani had hesitated and then given her okay. If they lost this battle, the clan might not survive anyway.

The last to arrive were the sun fae warriors, a dozen long-limbed, beautiful men and women. Marjani eyed them skeptically. In her experience, Cleia's people were the fae's version of Hollywood A-listers: all about the fun and glitter. This group looked like sexy models playing at war in their combat boots and camo gear, knit caps pulled low over their bright hair. But they silently disappeared into the surrounding forest.

Marjani glanced back at the portal. The ever-present fog made it impossible to see into New Moon. Were the night fae waiting on the other side?

She fingered Lady Olivia's protection charm, strung on the leather cord along with Fane's mate gift and her quartz. The silver charm was shaped like a prowling cougar. She'd been surprised—and touched—that the sun fae lady had bothered to make her a charm.

Her hand went to the sheathed iron dagger also hanging from her neck. Another two iron knives were tucked into her boots and her front pocket held a switchblade.

The protection charm had been a kind gesture, but Marjani wasn't here to be protected.

She was here to kill.

～

A STEADY DRIZZLE had begun to fall by the time Cleia and Olivia 'ported in, both in long-sleeved tees and camo pants, their hair in French braids.

Marjani swung off her branch and dropped the twenty-five feet to the ground. Fane and Jace trotted up as she tucked her leather jacket into a crook of the tree, leaving her in a slim-fitting, easy-to-fight-in turtleneck. The men shed their jackets as well.

Dion, Rui and Tiago appeared from the marshes, also dressed for a fight.

Dion kissed Cleia. "Are you sure about this?" he murmured, a frown creasing his forehead.

Sun fae were strongest at noon on the summer solstice—and this was the middle of winter. Night fae, on the other hand, were at their most powerful once each month when the new moon ruled the sky.

Which would be tonight.

Cleia cupped his cheek. "I'll be fine, love. Stop worrying." Her pointed chin went up. "It's time the prince learned he's not the only powerful fae on the East Coast."

Together, they formed a semi-circle around the portal. Behind them, Zuri and the other wolves formed a second row along with the sun fae.

Olivia glanced around. "Ready?"

At their nods, she faced the portal. The forest fell silent except for the steady *drip-drip* of the rain.

Raising her arms, Olivia took three deep breaths and spoke a phrase in an ancient fae language. Her palms shimmered. She traced a circle in the air and the portal became visible, a round door into the New Moon Court.

On the other side, fog snaked through the trees. Marjani gulped to see that inside, it was already night. How much time did they have before midnight?

"We'll find him," Fane murmured. "I promise."

She nodded and pulled a dagger from her boot. Around her, knives appeared in the other fada's hands as well. Dion gripped the bespelled dagger by its carved black handle. Even Fane had armed himself, and the man never carried a knife.

The barrier thinned slowly, almost imperceptibly. Olivia's face grew taut with strain. Her arms began to shake, but the shimmering light never wavered.

"*Now*," she said.

Cleia raised her own arms, calling on the sun's power. Her palms glowed. She chanted an incantation, over and over. The heat intensified and fire danced over her body.

"Holy cat," muttered Jace.

Mesmerized, Marjani stared into the unearthly fire along with everyone else. A warm breeze blew through the trees, tugging at their clothes, ruffling their hair.

Cleia gathered the fire, shaping it into a white-hot ball and flinging it at the portal. The ball stuck in the center as if it had been captured in a net.

"Fuck," whispered one of the sun fae men.

Marjani clenched the dagger.

"Steady." Dion set a hand on the small of Cleia's back. "You can do it." The fire danced over him as well, as he somehow aided her to control the energy.

"Yes," Cleia whispered. The ball brightened until the light was unbearable to look at.

Marjani averted her gaze. A sizzle and a pop, and suddenly, the light was gone.

Cleia lowered her hands, chest working.

Dion rubbed her back. "You're okay?" he asked anxiously.

"Go," Olivia hissed. "Before they realize we're here."

"Yes." Cleia gave Dion a small push. "Go. Olivia can only hold the portal open for an hour, maybe less."

He glanced from his mate to the opening, clearly torn, and then sprang after Rui and Tiago, who had already slipped into the night fae compound.

Lurching into motion, Marjani followed him through the portal along with Jace and Fane.

CHAPTER 42

The hours until midnight passed with agonizing slowness.

Olivier showed Adric to a large, comfortable apartment, but refused to answer any questions before locking him inside.

By then he was lightheaded from the iron poisoning his blood. He found salt in the kitchen, peeled off his shirt and cleansed the wounds as best as he could. The burns on his hands and arms had almost healed, but the knife wound on his chest seared like a red-hot brand. The salt solution burned almost as much as the iron itself, but he grit his teeth and rinsed the cut flesh repeatedly, then pulsed healing energy into it until the wound scabbed over.

He paced into the living room and sank onto a pricey antique couch.

Thrice-damned, fucking fae.

Langdon's sick bastard of a son had pushed Adric until he had no choice but to fight back—and the prince had the balls to blame him?

Worse, Marjani wasn't any safer from Langdon than she'd been before this all started, and now Rosana was enmeshed in this fucked-up mess, too.

His *mate.*

His claws pricked out. With a snarl, he slashed them through the couch's blue velvet cushions, sending stuffing flying around him.

Kill, hissed the cat.

Destroy.

Protect the mate.

He jumped to his feet and prowled feverishly from room to room, searching for a way out. The apartment was windowless, and the only exit wasn't just locked, it was warded, because when he tried the door handle, it buzzed warningly in his hand.

He was trapped again. Just in a larger cage.

With a low growl, he took a gilded chair from the dining room and smashed it against the heavy wood door, again and again, until it lay in broken shards at his feet.

He stared down at the pieces, chest heaving, and then resumed his restless pacing, half-cat, half-man.

Burning up from the iron poisoning. Furious at being confined. Terrified for Rosana.

A half hour passed, maybe more, with him only half aware of his surroundings.

When he surfaced again, he was in the opulent black marble bathroom.

He set his hands on the counter. In the large round mirror, his cougar's fiery blue eyes stared back. His fangs had lengthened, his claws fully extended to their two-inch-plus length. At some point he'd ripped off his shirt, and his pants were unbuttoned as if he'd started to remove them as well.

He hadn't come this close to losing control of his animal since his dad had been executed by Leron.

He drew a breath and then shrank his fangs, retracted the claws. His eyes changed back to bronze with just a few slivers of blue.

At least he hadn't reopened the wound on his chest. But his face was flushed with fever, his breath coming in rapid pants.

Sticking his head under the faucet, he took a long drink to flush the iron from his system. Then he got in the shower, scrubbing off the stench of the cell. He ignored the razor on the ledge with the shampoo and soap. Let Langdon see the rough-edged, dangerous animal he was dicking around with.

By the time he got out, his fever had receded. He felt weak but clear-headed again.

He dressed in the clean clothes he found laid out in the master bedroom and began a methodical search for a weapon. But the apartment held nothing that would damage a fae.

Food appeared in the dining room. A fat, juicy hamburger. Thick-sliced fries. Spicy coleslaw and a frosty glass of beer.

His skin creeped. How did they know his favorite meal? But he ate, even though it galled him to accept food from Langdon. He'd need fuel for the coming confrontation.

Belly full, he resumed his restless pacing, increasingly anxious to see Rosana. At least he sensed through the bond that she was healing, growing stronger.

He *would* break them both out of here. He was damned if he'd submit tamely to whatever Langdon had planned.

But without a weapon, it was up to his cougar.

Yes... hissed the cat.

His claws slid out again. He stared down at the wicked curved nails. Maybe he couldn't kill Langdon, but he could do some serious damage. That should buy him enough time to grab Rosana and then cloak them both so he could spirit her out of New Moon.

Langdon might be able to sense Adric's location with those Spidey-senses of his, but Adric would bet his entire collection of quartz that the prince couldn't actually see him. Get Rosana away from Langdon, and the two of them would have a fighting chance at escape.

If the wards let us out.

Adric had always known he might not get out of New Moon alive, but it had been a chance he was willing to take. Now, though, he had Rosana to consider.

His mate.

His jaw set. Failure was not an option. He *would* extricate her from this mess, or die trying.

That decided, he curled up onto the undamaged couch to wait for midnight. Not sleeping, but resting in the way of his cat with ears wide open.

The moment he heard footsteps in the hall outside, he was up and springing across the room. He kicked the remains of the chair out of the way and waited impatiently for the lock to disengage before jerking the door open.

Olivier took in the damage with a pained look and then gestured for Adric to follow him. "If you'll come with me, my lord."

Adric grabbed his arm. "Where's Rosana?"

"Right here, my lord." The butler led him around a corner before opening another door.

Rosana stood there, legs braced apart, claws out. At the sight of Adric, she broke into a smile and retracted the claws.

He shoved past Olivier to pull her into his arms. "You're okay?" He ran his hands over her. "How do you feel? Should you be out of the water?"

"I'm fine." She touched his cheek. "What about you?"

"I'm good." His hands trembled as he cupped her face. "But I was worried. About you. I—" His throat worked.

Worried was too tame a word for how he'd felt, but Rosana seemed to understand. She rose on her toes to brush her lips over his. "I'm okay. Really."

She was. He could see it, scent it. He breathed a prayer of thanks to the gods and pressed kisses to her eyes, her cheeks, her throat.

He'd almost lost her.

He had to touch her. Taste her. Assure himself she was really okay.

Olivier coughed.

Adric growled without lifting his head.

Oliver cleared his throat. "The prince—"

"Can fucking wait."

Adric pressed a last kiss to Rosana's soft mouth and released her. This time, he registered the sassy little purple dress. He swallowed hard. "Damn. You look beautiful."

The short, sleeveless design showed off her toned arms and legs, and dipped low over her full breasts. Her hair had been braided into a single inky plait, and like him, she was barefoot.

His mouth quirked. That was his Rosana, ready for anything.

Mate, the cat whispered in satisfaction.

"They took my other clothes," she said with a shrug.

He fingered her amethyst pendant. It was warm, the crystals humming a contented tune. And the sea-green thread was back in his own quartz.

Mate.

This time, he didn't even try to fight it. No, he welcomed it.

He snaked an arm around her waist. "You're beautiful—and you're mine. Don't forget that for a fucking minute."

"I think that's the key," she whispered in his ear. "You and me, together." She inclined her head at Olivier like the alpha's sister she was. "You may take us to the prince now."

They followed the butler down another corridor and into a hall of ornate black mirrors half-covered by the lush ivy which snaked over the walls.

Rosana glanced at her reflection and jerked.

Adric halted. "What?"

"I see Dion and your sister," she said in an excited whisper. "And Cleia, and Merry's uncle, Jace. In the woods."

His brows shot up. "Together?"

"Yes." She pointed to a point on the black glass. "And there—I can see night fae lairs through the trees. They must be here—in Virginia."

Olivier spoke directly behind them. "I believe they've been in negotiations with the prince."

Adric's stomach dipped. "Marjani, too?"

"So I hear," the butler replied. "However, I haven't been privy to the discussions."

Adric glared at the mirror, but all he saw were their three reflections. "She wasn't supposed to get anywhere near the prince," he growled.

"Come," Olivier said impatiently.

"Think, Adric," Rosana murmured as they followed the butler. "Your sister and Jace aren't here alone. She's with Cleia and my brothers. *You're* not alone. You have all of us fighting on your side. This changes everything."

"It's too dangerous," he bit back. "She knows it's her the prince really wants."

"Oh, Adric. Do you think that matters to her? How do you think she'd feel if you died because of her?"

He shook his head, still trying to wrap his mind around the fact that Marjani was right outside New Moon. The prince must be rubbing his hands in glee.

But a part of him couldn't help be warmed that she and Jace had come after him. And probably Fane—the man wouldn't allow Marjani to get this close to Langdon without him. Hell, there were probably some other Baltimore fada skulking around in the woods, too.

His step hitched. Every hair on his body raised. Even his scalp lifted.

Rosana had been right all along.

Her being here changed everything.

~

As they followed Olivier up the last flight of stairs to the outside, Rosana took Adric's hand. The fae-tailored clothes—a deep green button-up shirt and black pants—outlined every muscle on his hard body. His face was stubbled with night-beard, his eyes a flat bronze.

Mated.

Despite the danger they were in, a delicious shiver went up Rosana's spine. This beautiful, dangerous man was *hers*.

She took his hand, grateful for once to be a Seer. She'd *felt* hope surge in him when he'd realized they had a chance of rescue.

Outside, a soft rain was falling over the foggy grounds. A couple of fae lights wafted near, shimmering like opals in the mist.

Adric brought his mouth to her ear. "Be ready to run."

She squeezed his hand. "Together."

"Together," he agreed as a half-dozen guards emerged from the fog, a tall female at their head. Olivier nodded at them and headed back underground.

Adric stiffened at the sight of the woman. He moved to put himself between her and Rosana. "Neoma." The word was a growl.

Clearly, he'd encountered her before—and it hadn't been a happy encounter.

"Lord Adric." Neoma inclined her sleek black head. The guards surrounded them. Two grabbed Rosana, jerking her away from Adric.

Adric snarled and went clawed, but a fae ball appeared in the hand of a third warrior. He brought it close to Rosana's face. She swallowed, trying not to flinch from the dark fire.

Adric froze.

"Your quartz." Neoma held a silk pouch out to him. A cruel smile curled her lips. "Just in case you had any idea of trying to escape the prince's justice."

"No!" Rosana whispered.

Adric hissed, his eyes pure blue flame. But he immediately dragged the chunky gray-and-orange pendant over his head and dropped it into the silk pouch.

"Wise choice," Neoma said. "Now, get going." She jerked her chin at a path of smooth white pebbles.

The warriors released Rosana, but kept her separated from Adric.

The trail wound through the trees and past the pond before plunging into a garden that was, impossibly, blooming in the dead of winter. A moon garden of lush white flowers: creamy azaleas, snowy peonies, roses of pale ivory. Even when they passed back into the woods, lilies of the valley carpeted the forest floor like living pearls, and the smooth pebbles beneath their bare feet were as warm as if it was a balmy summer night.

In the distance, they heard shouting, saw bursts of light above the trees. There was a crack like thunder and the entire sky lit up.

Rosana's heart leapt. "They're here!" she said in subvocal tones.

In front of her, Adric nodded without looking back.

"Keep going." The guards herded them forward.

The path ended in a clearing. A frisson slid over Rosana's skin as they entered, indicating they'd passed through a ward.

The sights and sounds of the battle were instantly erased. Instead, shadows reigned, dark, menacing. Even the rain stopped, the ground beneath their bare feet cold but dry. Neck prickling, Rosana edged closer to Adric.

One by one, a circle of night fae emerged out of the gloom, each more beautiful than the previous—but in a cold, untouchable way, like perfect, polished statues. Their faces first, gleaming palely like the ivory sheen of the moon behind a cloud, even the darker skinned among them. Next to appear were their spare, elongated bodies: three females in short silver dresses and eight males all in black.

At the circle's apex, Langdon shimmered into sight on a solid silver throne topped by a triple moon: a full moon flanked by two crescent moons. Like the other men, he was dressed in unrelieved black except for the circlet of diamond-studded platinum leaves vined around his head.

Standing at his side was the thirteenth member of the circle, a woman with ebony hair and Blaer's fine-boned face, but older, harder. Diamonds glittered in her pointed ears and on the platinum bands twined around her upper arms. A single black star hung from a heavy platinum chain around her neck.

A priestess.

Rosana's lungs locked. She dug her bare heels into the soil, tugging them both to a halt.

"Adric. *No.*"

He pressed her fingers. "It's okay."

"No, it's not." She shook her head frantically. "It's *her.* The woman in my vision. They're going to kill you."

"Come." Langdon beckoned them with a single pale hand.

"Be ready to run," Adric muttered. He released Rosana's hand and strode forward. "Well?" With a sneer, he folded his arms over his chest. "I'm here."

Rosana looked frantically around for Neoma. At least if Adric had his quartz, he could shift—or cloak himself and escape the circle. But Neoma and the other warriors who'd brought them had disappeared.

She moved up beside Adric. But he put out an arm and moved her behind him without taking his gaze from Langdon.

Still trying to protect her when they were face to face with one of the darkest, most powerful fae on the planet.

Her heart clenched. "*Amo-te,*" she whispered. *I love you.*

She remained where he'd put her. Guarding his back.

Langdon eyed them without speaking. The circle of night fae went motionless along with him, their eyes gleaming darkly like a pack of wolves.

Rosana gulped, and then pulled back her shoulders. They might sense her fear, but she wouldn't give them the satisfaction of showing it.

Adric's scent was hot with fury. He stared back at Langdon, cat-quiet.

As the tension stretched, the priestess drew the tip of her tongue over her full lower lip like she could taste their fear and anger.

Langdon broke the silence first. "Lord Adric. Senhorita do Rio. Welcome to my court. Peace to you and yours."

"Fuck your peace," Adric snarled. "We're here against our will. I demand you release us."

"It was you who trespassed," the prince returned in silky tones. "As for Senhorita do Rio, I merely granted her request to remain with you."

Adric raised a brow. "Did I trespass? Or was I brought here by Lady Blaer? It was the wolf under her *geas* who brought me through the wards."

Langdon frowned. "She told me you forced the wolf to let you into the court."

"True. But the wolf led me straight to your lair, and no one stopped us—almost as if you wanted me here. Or was it actually Lady Blaer who wanted me here?"

Rosana made a small sound. Adric had practically accused Blaer of manipulating things so he could assassinate Langdon. Viewed from a certain angle, it made sense.

Langdon turned to the head priestess. "Fleur?"

Her pale throat worked. She moistened her lips. "This is speculation, your highness. The fevered imaginings of a desperate man. Surely you don't think my daughter is working with this fada." She shot a dark look at Adric.

"No," Langdon replied, "I don't think Blaer is working *with* him. That doesn't mean she's not using him to cover her pretty ass."

The circle of night fae rustled in agitation.

"However," the prince continued, "none of this matters. The facts stand. My son is dead—"

"Because he attacked my people," Adric said between set teeth.

Rosana set a hand on the small of his back, willing him to remain calm.

"As you say." Langdon inclined his head. "But that's not the issue. It's not even important whether you killed Tyrus yourself, or whether it was your sister. The issue is restitution."

"What restitution? I can't bring your goddamned son back from the dead."

"No. But you owe me, Adric Savonett." The night fae rose from his silver throne, prowled toward them.

Beneath Rosana's hand, Adric's body quivered like a stallion itching to attack. "I owe you *nothing*. Your son got what was coming to him. Your clan has persecuted mine for years. My own parents died to feed your taste for darkness."

"Your alpha—your *uncle*—invited us in."

"Fuck that. Yeah, my uncle Leron was a sick S.O.B., but he would never have stayed in power for so long if not for you."

"And Lord Tyrus was in Baltimore at your cousin Corban's invitation," Langdon added as if Adric hadn't spoken.

"And that was his mistake." Adric stood toe-to-toe with the prince. "Unlike my uncle, Corban was *not* the alpha, and Tyrus didn't have my permission to be in Baltimore. I owe you *nothing* for his death—and every fada in the world will back me up on that."

"You still think I want your sister, don't you?"

Adric's chin jerked up. "Then what's this about?"

"I'll admit I desired your sister's blood. 'An eye for an eye. A tooth for a tooth. A life for a life.' Those ancient humans had it right. Harsh, but effective. However, I've reconsidered. Perhaps we can resolve this to everyone's satisfaction. A bargain."

Adric's eyes narrowed. "What kind of bargain?"

"Due to your sister, I lost a son. In fact, all three of my sons are dead."

Another rustle went around the circle. The night fae muttered among themselves.

Langdon ignored them to say, "I had a third son by a human woman." A muscle flexed in his jaw. "I should've brought him up in the court. But instead, I hid—" He shook his head.

"Had, my lord?" murmured Fleur.

The prince gave a tight nod. "As I said, all my sons are dead. But my youngest son left a daughter."

Rosana's blood chunked with ice. Her mouth formed a soundless *no*.

Adric's face hardened. "No fucking way."

"Yes." Langdon's eyes were gleaming pools of midnight. "*A life for a life.* Have your clan bring Merry Jones to me and you'll go free. In fact, I'm feeling generous tonight. Bring my granddaughter to me, and I'll free not just you, but Rosana."

CHAPTER 43

$\mathcal{B}$laer was livid at being excluded from the new moon ritual. She stood at the living room window, staring out at the rain.

Luc's nape crawled. The fae lady was at her most dangerous when completely still.

A quarter mile distant, a pitched battle was being fought, but she seemed unaware of the light and noise. This wasn't just fada. From the bright bursts of color, the sun fae had joined the battle.

For the first time in days—no, weeks—hope sparked in Luc. Not for him, but for Adric. Maybe the alpha would get out of this alive, after all.

He flashed on Rosana's bewildered young face and swallowed, shame a hot stone in his belly. Just when he'd thought he couldn't go lower, he had. He'd given a woman—a girl barely out of her teens—to the night fae.

Adric had been right to be furious. He should've just slit Luc's throat and been done with it.

At least Marjani was safe. Luc didn't know what he'd have done if the prince had gotten his hands on her.

Blaer turned her dark eyes on him. Sensing his distress in that spooky way night fae had.

"Your alpha and the do Rio woman are at the ritual."

"What?" Luc scrubbed a hand over his face. Why would Langdon invite Adric to a private ritual?

And then he *knew*. His stomach lurched.

Blaer prowled across the marble floor. Her dress today was an ice-blue scrap of material that barely covered her ass. Sapphires and diamonds dripped from her throat and glittered on the pointed ears peeking through her platinum hair.

"The fada attacked the prince in his own lair. You didn't think he'd let them off with just a slap on the wrist, did you?"

Luc grabbed her bare arm. "Why are you telling me this?"

She tilted her head. "Why do you think?"

He narrowed his eyes. "You want me to get you inside tonight's circle. But why?"

"Can you?"

He knew when he was being used. But who the fuck cared? Adric needed him. Luc had no compunction using Blaer right back.

He released her. "Take me to the circle. I'll get us inside."

PASSING through the portal turned out to be the easy part. Marjani had only gone a few steps into the woods on the other side when she realized the shadows had deepened to pitch-black. Her eyes went night-glow, but she still couldn't see more than a couple of yards in any direction.

She tightened her grip on her dagger and peered around, growling lowly.

"It's okay," Fane murmured. "It's a different time of day in here, that's all."

She nodded tightly. The mechanics of fae vs. human time always made her dizzy. You could spend a few days in a fae court and go home to find a whole month had passed.

What made her heart falter was the realization that in here, the new moon might be just an hour, not five hours away.

"You feel Ric yet?" That was Jace.

"No," she admitted. She'd hoped that her quartz would relink to Adric's as soon as they passed through the portal, but it hadn't. She couldn't even say for sure if he was still alive.

"Me, neither," Jace said.

"He's here." She picked up the pace. "I know he is."

That's when the skies opened up. Rain sluiced down as if someone had turned a fire hose on them. Her black turtleneck was instantly plastered to her body. Within seconds, she'd lost sight of everyone but Jace and Fane.

She dashed the water out of her eyes and kept moving.

The deeper they went into the woods, the thicker the shadows grew. With the rain sheeting down, it was like fighting your way through a waterfall. They were soaking wet, and beneath their feet, the forest floor had turned into a gluey black mud.

The shadows grew thick enough to touch. The nearest one began to slowly spiral.

They all froze.

Marjani put out a hand to see if it was as real as it looked. The shadow—or whatever it was—tried to curl around her, but recoiled from the protection charm.

"Careful!" Fane jerked her back. "It's some kind of dark magic."

The three of them eased around the mini black cyclone, but all the shadows were swirling now.

"What the fuck?" Jace snarled, his eyes the bright green of his jaguar.

The shadows spun faster, coalescing into hairy vines that slapped at their faces, dragged at their clothes.

Marjani dodged between two vines. As before, Olivia's charm repelled them. But a third vine twined around Jace's legs and threw him to the muddy ground. In the next breath, he was being dragged through the forest, his body slamming into trees and bouncing off rocks.

"Jace!" She and Fane sprinted after him.

He managed to snag an arm around a tree trunk. With the other, he hacked at the vine with his iron dagger. As they caught up to him, the vine disintegrated into ashes.

She dropped to her knees, brushing the ashes off him. "You okay?"

Jace's chest heaved. He gingerly tested his arms and legs. "Yeah."

"Here." Fane held out a hand, pulling him to his feet.

"God's cat." The jaguar shifter swiped a hand over his face. "What the fuck are those vines?"

"Hell if I know," said Fane. "Some kind of ward? Or maybe even an illusion?"

"It was no illusion," was the grim reply. "I've got the bruises to prove it."

Fane shook his head. "With the night fae, it's hard to tell what's real, what's not."

"Look out!" Marjani slashed at a vine snaking at them from around a nearby tree. As before, it crumbled into ashes.

She took a second dagger from her boot so she had one in each hand. "Whatever it is, we have to get out of here. Stick next to me. The charm seems to repel them."

The men nodded, mouths set, as three more vines dropped around them. Together, they hacked their way forward for several endless minutes.

Just when she wondered if they'd ever get out of the woods, there was an intense flash, followed by two more in rapid succession. Through the trees, they glimpsed a group of sun fae hurling fae balls at the vines, forcing a large patch of shadows around them into retreat.

Fane swore and slashed through yet another encroaching vine. "The bloody things are multiplying faster than we can fight them."

"The sun fae." She stabbed a vine right before it wrapped around Jace's neck from behind. "They're our only chance."

The three of them continued slogging through the mud, dodging the shadow-vines when they could, and fighting them off when they couldn't, but the sun fae warriors kept moving, too. They couldn't seem to reach them.

They fought doggedly on. First Fane, then Jace were thrown to the ground. She helped cut the vines off them, and they continued forward, but they were all tiring. On top of that, they were soaked to the skin, and if there was anything Marjani's cat detested, it was being cold and wet.

Then they lost sight of the sun fae. Although they could still hear sounds of the battle, it was impossible to tell exactly where it was coming from.

"Fuck." Marjani turned in a circle, hopelessly lost. The shadows had somehow messed with her internal GPS. "Where'd they go?"

"I have no idea," Jace muttered, while Fane just shook his head.

The shadows seemed to sense their confusion. The vines twisted around them. Not trying to touch them now, just weaving an inky cage.

Marjani hissed and shrank back against Fane. It was like the vines *knew* she was terrified of being caged—any fada was, but her own recent experience with Blaer's cages had amped the fear up to near-panic level.

Her chest compressed. She snarled, her animal brain telling her to run like hell. She sprang forward. But the vines caught her, throwing her back against Jace and Fane.

Her terror ratcheted. "The charm isn't working anymore," she croaked.

Jace gave a low growl. She scented his own fear of being trapped, and it amped up hers.

"Easy, love." Fane squeezed her shoulders from behind. "Try focusing the charm on one section."

Yes. She gripped the charm, shoved it at the vines in front of her. To her relief, they parted. She moved the charm in a circle until she'd cleared a large enough opening in the vine-cage for her to pass through, then squeezed through sideways, unable to wait any longer.

Fane and Jace were right behind her—which gave her an idea.

"Form a single line behind me," she said and moved forward, the charm held out in front of her. Fane hooked his fingers through her waistband, and she heard him direct Jace to keep touching him.

As before, the vines parted to let her through, and Fane and Jace were able to pass through as well before they closed again. She increased her pace, and the vines and trees merged into each other, twining into a narrow passage with walls of a dank, murky fog that was nevertheless too solid for them to pass through.

She was growling continuously now.

"Keep moving," Fane ordered. "Don't stop, whatever you do."

They continued to what looked like the end of the passage, but wasn't. The shadows had formed a maze, forcing them to turn first right, then left, then another left and a right, and so on, in a seemingly random pattern.

Marjani lost all sense of direction and time. All she knew was that somewhere nearby, her brother awaited his execution—and she was trapped in this thrice-damned forest with its living shadows.

She was running now, her feet beating out a frenzied rhythm.

Hurry, hurry, hurry.

At last the walls of the maze thinned so they could see the trees again. Marjani checked, unsure which way to go.

Another explosion lit the night.

The three of them sprinted toward it—and exited the trees at last.

CHAPTER 44

Give Merry to Langdon?

Rosana didn't even have to look at Adric to know what his answer was.

"No," she growled. "We don't accept."

The prince turned to Adric. "And you?"

Adric's eyes were that flat bronze that was somehow more scary than the blue of his cougar. "You heard her. We refuse. In fact," he said, slowly and precisely, "you can take your bargain and shove it where the sun don't shine."

Langdon's mouth tightened. "Then you die. You've been informed of the charges against you."

"Which I don't accept," Adric shot back.

Langdon continued as if Adric hadn't even spoke. "I could demand you accept my *geas*, but as long as you're alive, your clan will plague me. I'll be fighting off assassination attempts every time I leave New Moon."

The other night fae murmured agreement. It was the simplest way to break a *geas*—kill the fae who'd set it.

"No," the prince decided. "Better to execute you."

A flick of his fingers, and Neoma and three other warriors appeared out of the shadows to grab Adric.

Rosana's lungs squeezed. It was her vision, her nightmare, come to life. Her feet seemed stuck to the ground. She watched, frozen, as they dragged Adric's arms behind his back and forced him to his knees.

Fleur stepped forward, the knife gleaming in her hand.

And Adric allowed it. He didn't even try to fight them off.

She understood why when he glared up at Langdon. "Kill me, then. But I'm begging you, let Rosana leave unharmed." To her, he mouthed a single sentence: *I love you.*

"No," she rasped.

"I have no interest in harming her," the prince replied. "But neither am I inclined to let her leave without receiving something in return. My offer stands: my granddaughter for your lives. Although Senhorita do Rio may, of course, bargain to live that life out as a Seer at my court."

Fleur stiffened and shot a dark look at Rosana, while the other night fae eyed her with renewed interest. She could almost see them rubbing their hands in glee at having a fada Seer to play with.

Langdon leaned toward Adric, his voice darkly persuasive. "Think, my lord. Without you, your clan will fall to us. Fleur has Seen it. Is one mixed-breed's life worth so much to you? I promise, the girl will be well treated at my court. Raised as the princess she was born to be."

The prince will destroy your clan from the inside out.

Ice trickled down Rosana's spine.

No. Adric *couldn't* die. Not only because she wouldn't survive his death, but because his clan wouldn't.

Adric glowered up at the prince. "Go. To. Hades."

Together, her brain shouted.

Instinctively, she reached out to Adric through the bond. The bond was still so new that she was shocked when he reached back. The connection between them hummed and sparked, and her amethyst warmed.

It was like he'd enfolded her in a full-body hug. "Together," he murmured— and slammed his head back into the night fae directly behind him while he twisted away from the others in a single lithe move. He leapt for Langdon, bearing him to the ground.

Rosana's mouth dropped open. Then her feet unstuck themselves from the ground. The guards were already moving. She threw herself in front of the nearest one, felling him with a couple of down-and-dirty blows. When your life was at stake, you went for the balls.

Her claws sprouted. She scratched them across another warrior's face. He swore and clapped his hands over his face.

Adric had his fingers wrapped around Langdon's throat. The prince's eyes bulged as he desperately sought to throw him off.

"Run!" Adric rapped out at her. "I'm right behind you."

But the night fae had surrounded her. Fae balls burned in two of the guards' hands.

She stepped back—and fingers latched onto her hair from behind, jerked back her head. An iron blade hovered over her throat. "Don't move," a voice gritted next to her ear. "Not a single muscle."

She froze.

"Release the prince," her captor barked at Adric. "Or your woman dies."

He glanced up, snarling—and stilled.

"*Now*," snapped the warrior holding Rosana. "Or I'll slice her fucking throat."

"Okay, okay." Adric rose to his feet. "I'm off, see?" He raised his hands, palms out. "Just let her go."

The warriors surrounded him and shoved him back to his knees. Neoma slammed her dagger hilt into Adric's solar plexus. He grunted and doubled over, chest heaving.

Rosana's lungs closed. Her mate was hurt. She felt his pain like it was her own. Her heart sped up and bile rose in her throat.

She dug her claws into her captor's arm, uncaring of the sharp blade an inch from her jugular vein. Just knowing she had to get to Adric.

"Be still!" the night fae hissed in her ear.

Langdon pushed up on his knees, gasping for breath. "Let her go," he ordered as two men helped him to his feet.

"My lord?" Neoma said. "Are you sure?"

"*Now*," was Langdon's reply.

"Try anything else," Rosana's captor hissed in her ear, "and I'll slit your pretty throat. Is that clear?"

"Yes," she said without hesitation. Anything so she could go to Adric.

"Listen well, then. You're going to kneel beside the earth fada. No touching him. No talking. Is that understood?"

"Yes, yes."

"Go, then." The fae released her, and she flew the few yards to Adric and lowered herself to her knees beside him. He was still bent over, chest working. She yearned to touch him, to reassure herself he was all right, but kept her hands at her sides as ordered.

Adric managed to straighten. He even gave her a reassuring smile. "You okay, angel?"

She nodded and summoned an answering smile.

Meanwhile, Langdon was already almost back to normal, his powerful fae blood healing any damage Adric had done.

As he turned toward Adric and Rosana, a warrior stopped him. "Begging your pardon, my lord, but Captain Quade has sent a messenger."

"Let him in."

The messenger bowed and drew Langdon aside. The two murmured, low-voiced, while Rosana strained to listen.

The snatches she heard made her heart leap. "The sun fae have breached the wards" and "we've suffered several casualties."

She exchanged a hopeful look with Adric.

"Withdraw underground, then," Langdon said more loudly. "And seal off all the entrances. Even if the queen finds her way inside, she'd spend days trying to find you, and she can't be away from the sunlight for that long. As for the circle, she'll never breach these wards—not during the most sacred hour of the most sacred night of the month."

The warrior looked doubtful. "The queen's powerful, my lord, and she brought a dozen sun fae warriors with her. And what about the fada?" He shot Adric and Rosana a look of dislike. "They're...devious."

"Let them run around in the darkness all they want. They won't find their way here unless I allow it."

"But—"

"Go," the prince commanded. "Before the hour of our Goddess is past."

"As you wish." The warrior inclined his head and exited the clearing.

Fleur walked to the center of the circle. "Start the moon fire."

A wide, burnished metal bowl appeared on a low stand. A night fae priest stepped forward, a silver triple-moon pendant around his neck. He pointed a finger at the bowl and a purple flame sprang up in the center.

The guards latched onto Adric's arms and legs, forcing him onto his back. He fought back, twisting and kicking in their grip, until Neoma took his quartz from the silk bag and wrapped her fingers around it.

"Be still, fada."

He jerked and let out an agonized groan.

Rosana glanced frantically around for rescue. *Where was everyone?*

The night fae formed a circle around her and Adric. Fleur raised her shiny iron knife to the moonless sky. "We are reborn with this New Moon."

"We are reborn with this New Moon," the circle chanted.

Rosana's stomach bottomed out. *No.*

It couldn't happen like this. Not when they were so close to being rescued.

Her mom's cryptic words flitted across her mind. *Touch him.*

She stared helplessly down at her hands. What good would touching Adric do? Even if she did See something, it would be his death.

Everybody leaves. That hurt, abandoned part of her dropped back its head and shrieked a primal *no* at the midnight sky.

If they took Adric from her, she might as well let them stick a knife in her heart, too. Because this was one loss she wouldn't survive.

The prince raised his hands. "May the Dark Goddess bless our circle tonight."

She glared up at him, her whole being consumed with a dark, burning hatred. She should've killed him the library when she'd had the chance. If only she still had her stiletto, she'd plunge it into his iceberg of a heart. Her fingertips literally tingled with the desire to kill the man.

She curled them into her palms—and suddenly, she *knew*, with a Seer's gut instinct. Her mom hadn't meant Adric, she'd meant Langdon.

And everything *wasn't* happening exactly as in her vision. Because she, Rosana, was present.

She was the key.

"Wait, your highness!" She scrambled to her feet. "Perhaps we can make a bargain after all."

"Quiet." A priest loomed over her, his impossibly beautiful face set in cold lines. "Or the Goddess will gain another sacrifice."

But Langdon beckoned her forward. "Let her speak."

She pushed past the priest. "You want a Seer," she told the prince, "you've got one. But execute Lord Adric, and you lose me, too."

Adric groaned. "Rosana, no!"

She turned her face so she wouldn't have to look at him. She *knew* this was the right thing to do. But she couldn't risk even a whispered "Trust me," to Adric.

"We're mates," she told the prince. "Kill Adric, and I won't live for more than a few days after him."

"Mates?" Langdon glanced at Adric. "An earth fada and a river fada?"

She raised her chin. "That's right. And I'm willing to join your court as a Seer. But Lord Adric lives—or we both die."

Fleur sneered. "You lie, fada. You won't die along with your mate. I've seen fada live for years after."

"Truth," Rosana snarled back. She touched her hand to her heart, sealing the vow. "Kill my mate and I'll *will* myself to die."

Adric let out a blood-curdling growl and fought like a wild man to get away from his captors, but they had him stretched out now, their hands clamped around his wrists and ankles.

He rasped her name beseechingly, his torment vibrating down the mate bond. "Don't do this, Rosana. *Please.*"

She swayed on her feet, his pain nearly dropping her to the ground.

Langdon scrutinized her. "She's not lying," he said, almost to himself.

She wiped her sweaty palms on her pleated skirt. What if she'd imagined that whole scene with Ula? It could've been some kind of fever-induced dream.

Trust your Gift.

She straightened her spine and held out her hands to Langdon. "Well, my lord? Do we have a deal?"

CHAPTER 45

Marjani, Fane and Jace were on a hill, the compound's grounds spread out before them, the low, vine-covered buildings barely visible through the pouring rain.

Up until now, the shadows had been doing all the fighting. Now, Marjani saw night fae warriors for the first time, engaged in a fierce battle with the sun fae, Cleia at their center. Fiery explosions of silver, copper and gold vied with bursts of dark purple, green and blue as the two sides hurled fae balls at each other.

The sun fae were holding their own, but they were outmatched, four or five night fae for every one of them. Shadows surrounded the sun fae's circular formation, creeping closer with every second.

Dion, Rui and Tiago were nowhere to be seen, no doubt searching for Rosana, but she glimpsed Zuri and his wolves slipping in and out of the trees, harrying the night fae.

But no Adric.

She closed her eyes and went deep into her quartz. She didn't have an alpha's ability to locate a clan member through their quartz, but Adric was family—her only brother.

But the darkness swallowed the connection like a stone dropping into a black bog. Her chest closed up. She'd been so sure she'd be able to find Adric once she got inside the wards.

She gripped Jace's arm. "Where is he? Can you feel him?"

A muscle worked in his jaw. He shook his head. "I'm sorry, Jani."

"Let's try the prince's lair." Fane pointed to the building nearest to the pond.

They started down the hill at a jog. The heavy rain had turned the grass into a muddy, slippery mess. If Marjani hadn't been a cat, she'd have face-planted halfway down.

As they neared the warring fae, Cleia raised her arms. The black sky lit with a burst of gold. Bright sparks streamed out from the center as if she'd set off a firework. The night fae screamed and slapped their hands to their faces, shrinking back into the shadows.

Marjani, Jace and Fane were temporarily blinded. Fane grabbed her hand and Jace glued himself to her other side. Together, they felt their way forward, skirting the battling warriors.

"Holy Mother," Jace muttered as another bright burst lit the night.

"Yeah," said Fane. "The queen's a one-woman war machine."

They were back in the shadows again. No obstacles this time, just a deep, unrelenting black. There was a hunger to the gloom now that reminded Marjani of the Darktime. A chill slid over her like a snake brushing past her skin.

Fane squeezed her fingers. "Use the charm." A pulse of love came through their bond.

She nodded, and with a whispered *fuck you*, lifted the charm and ran directly into the shadows' dark heart. As before, they parted seemingly at random, forcing her into a zigzag run. She soon lost track of the prince's lair.

She kept going because halting wasn't an option—that's how the night fae won. If she stopped, she'd lose first hope, then the motivation to keep moving... and then despair would set in.

Minutes passed. Her heart was in her throat. Was it midnight yet?

Hurry, hurry, hurry.

She darted left, then right. Cold and miserable from the monsoon-like rain, but determined to find her brother or die in the attempt.

Hurry, hurry, hurry.

Miraculously, a path opened before her, its white pebbles gleaming.

She couldn't sense Adric, and yet she *knew* this was the right direction. She pelted down the path.

Heart pounding, mind chanting: *Hurry, hurry, hurryhurryhurry...*

She slammed into a ward. Pain jolted through her. She reeled backward into a tree and leaned against it, sucking oxygen.

Her quartz twanged, the crystals humming with joy at reconnecting to the alpha's quartz.

Adric.

She'd found him, and he was still alive—but she was trapped on the wrong side of this fucking ward.

The air in front of her shimmered, and right before her eyes, a portal opened. A Marjani-size portal.

The hair on her nape lifted. She eyed it suspiciously. Still, what choice did she have? She pulled the dagger from the sheath around her neck and inched forward.

Footsteps pounded up behind her. She raised a hand, signaling Fane and Jace to halt as she peered through the opening.

What she saw there made her entire body ice.

Adric was on the ground in front of Prince Langdon. Several black-garbed night fae had pinned him down while others loomed nightmarishly over him. Rosana do Rio had her back to Marjani, her hands stretched out to Langdon. Nearby, a dark fire flickered.

Marjani shot a glance over her shoulder and then gulped as her brain caught up to what her nose had already told her. Fane and Jace were no longer behind her. Somehow, in her mad dash to reach Adric, she'd lost them—and picked up Lady Blaer and Luc instead.

Luc grabbed her arm. "Play along," he muttered, and stepped forward with her through the portal. "Your highness. Here's the fada that murdered your son."

CHAPTER 46

$\mathcal{A}$dric had resigned himself to dying. He'd never surrender Merry in return for his own life.

But gods, it hurt to die leaving Rosana still trapped at New Moon. He had to believe that her brothers and Cleia would get her away from the prince.

Then Rosana made her offer. Let Adric live, and she'd join Langdon's court as a Seer.

No. Fucking. Way.

Adric's muscles bunched. If only he had his quartz… But without it, he couldn't shift—or cloak himself.

Langdon's gaze went past Rosana to a point behind Adric. His smile made Adric's insides ice.

"Marjani Savonett." The prince deliberately spoke her full name in an attempt to establish power over her. "Welcome to my court."

Adric flung a look over his shoulder in time to see his sister enter the circle along with Luc and Blaer. And instead of helping her, Luc gripped her arm, urging her forward.

"No, Jani!" he said in a low, urgent voice. "Get the fuck out of here."

Blaer came up on Marjani's other side. A chill slipped up Adric's spine. This woman knew the secret incantation. If she shared it with Langdon, his clan was well-and-truly fucked. With Blaer's knowledge and Langdon's resources, the night fae could enslave every single member.

Horror gripped him as he recalled Rosana's prophecy.

The Darktime isn't over. The prince will destroy your clan from the inside out.

"Peace to you and yours, my lord." The tall blond fae lady bowed to Langdon. "I apologize for interrupting the ritual, but I believe you've been looking for this woman."

No.

Adric bucked wildly, fighting to get free of the night fae pinning him down.

Neoma tightened her grip on his pendant. The pain was almost unbearable, but he gritted his teeth and kept fighting. He had to get free. Had to somehow stop this.

The prince jerked his head at Marjani. "Take her," he commanded.

Twisting away from Luc, Marjani dropped into a crouch, a dagger in each hand. Two warriors broke from the circle to approach her, their own blades out, but she slashed about her, keeping them at bay.

At the same time, Luc saw Adric pinned down in the center of the circle. He growled and started forward.

"No." Blaer slapped a hand on his chest.

Luc halted. He sent a shamed look at Adric. At his sides, his fingers flexed and unflexed.

Then Rosana grabbed Langdon's hands. As her fingers closed around his, her body jolted and her braid lifted. The tie wrapped around the end slid off and the plait unwound itself to twist around her face in a sinuous black cloud.

"The old ways are no more," she said in a low, eerie voice. "Change is coming."

Everyone in the clearing froze, even the warriors attempting to capture Marjani.

Rosana moistened her lips. "Merry," she said in a scratchy voice.

"Yes?" Langdon turned his hands so he was gripping her. "What do you See?"

"Merry's a princess." She faltered. "I See a crown."

"Go on," he urged.

"Your granddaughter will rule. But not in darkness. In light."

The prince's diamond-studded brows snapped together.

Rosana's slender body shook. Adric could hardly bear to watch her, but she'd drawn everyone's attention. Even the men trying to corral Marjani were distracted.

Now was his chance to get his quartz back.

"And you," she told the prince. "Your life is a fine-spun web. Tear the wrong thread and you're dead. *Deus*, no." Her breath sobbed in.

Langdon's handsome face hardened. "What?"

Rosana shook her head and tried to pull her hands away, but he tightened his grip on her. "Tell me, damn you!"

"Death," Rosana whispered. "Death to your line...at the new ruler's hand."

"What new ruler?"

Rosana snatched her hands from the prince's, backed away. He reached for her and then checked as if she'd burned him.

Her body shimmered as if lit from inside by starlight. The night fae shrank from her. She swung around, pointed.

"Her. Lady Blaer."

Blaer straightened. "You lie," she hissed. "You'd do anything to escape." She motioned Luc forward. "Kill her. Kill the river fada."

Luc's hands fisted but he didn't move.

Blaer grabbed his quartz, squeezed. "I said, *Kill her.*"

Luc growled, eyes wild. The man was near the breaking point—and Blaer either didn't know or didn't care.

The night fae pinning Adric down were still intent on the drama. He forced his body to relax completely, and as he'd hoped, their grip on him loosened.

Now.

Jerking out of their hold, Adric lunged at Neoma, ripping the pendant from her hand and dropping it over his head. His body shuddered with relief at having his quartz back. As the guards dove for him, he drew on its power with everything he had, leaping straight up so they passed beneath him—and shifted while he was still in mid-air.

He lost precious seconds during the change. When he came back to himself, he was a cougar, his clothes in shreds around him. The warriors tried again to grab him, but with a slash of his claws, he was free.

Luc had apparently started for Rosana at Blaer's command, but Marjani had put herself between them. The two men who'd been trying to capture her were on the ground, bleeding from multiple wounds.

"No, Luc. You can't! She's his mate."

"Get out of the way," Luc said in a dull voice.

"No." Marjani took a fighting stance, daggers at the ready. "You want to kill her, you'll have to go through me."

Adric went invisible. The three warriors circling him swore. One of them shot a fae ball at the spot where he'd been standing, but he'd already slipped between two of them. He reached Rosana right as she came out of her trance.

She glanced around, blinking. "Adric?" she asked on a rising note of fear—and collapsed to the ground.

In an instant, he was standing over her, ready to protect her at all costs.

He nuzzled Rosana's neck, sending reassurance through their bond. To his relief, her eyelids fluttered and then opened.

"You're here," she whispered, sinking her fingers into his fur.

He rumbled in response.

"What—?" Her gaze went past him and Marjani to Luc. She sucked in a breath and tried to stand but could only manage to bring herself to sitting. She leaned against Adric, lungs working, face as drawn as if she'd run a marathon.

Luc's claws slid out. "Don't make me hurt you," he told Marjani in flat, emotionless tones. "Just get the fuck out of the way."

"*No.*" She jabbed a dagger at him, forcing him to back off. "I won't let you do this."

Langdon stalked toward Blaer. Adric could almost see the prince recalling his earlier insinuation—that Blaer had manipulated events so Adric could assassinate him.

"A Seer in the grip of a vision doesn't lie," Langdon stated. He seemed to grow taller, darker as he spoke.

Blaer licked her lips. "She's a fada Seer," she said with a scornful glance at Rosana. "Who knows what she can do?" She looked at Luc. "I gave you an order —kill Rosana do Rio. If the Savonett woman is in the way, then kill her, too."

Luc's irises turned pure wolf, twin orange embers in the dark clearing. He glanced from Blaer to Marjani, and then he withdrew his claws and turned away. "No."

Blaer cast him an incredulous look. "What did you say?"

"No," Luc repeated.

Blaer lunged. "I said, *Kill them both.* Now!" She squeezed Luc's quartz, her lips moving, adding the power of the incantation to the *geas.*

Luc jolted and dropped to his knees, his body a man, his scent all wolf. He was seconds from going feral, and Blaer either didn't know, or she just didn't care. He dropped his head back and howled at the sky, a sad, lost song that had even the night fae tensing.

Blaer bent with him, tightening her grip on his quartz. "Kill. Them. Both."

It was a fatal mistake. Luc had accepted the *geas* to save Marjani's life. By ordering him to kill Marjani, the fae lady had broken their bargain, releasing Luc from the *geas.*

Luc tore off his clothes and shifted. Blaer went stick-still as the brown wolf's fierce, half-mad growls filled the clearing. She threw up her hands and began to call on some other kind of magic, but it was too late. Luc sprang, slamming her to the ground.

With a muttered incantation, the prince raised a long-fingered hand. The leaves and twigs scattered around the clearing levitated off the ground and streamed toward Luc and Blaer.

The other night fae edged to the clearing's outskirts, giving the prince a wide berth.

Marjani inched back to stand by Rosana. A brief caress of Adric's back told him that she knew he was there, too, but her gaze was glued on Luc and Blaer and the debris swirling around them.

"What the fuck?" she breathed.

A twig formed itself into a wolf that knocked Luc off Blaer, tossing him three yards away before falling back to the ground, a twig again. Langdon rotated his wrist and the other leaves spiraled around Blaer, faster and faster, before morphing into ravens that flew around her in tight circles.

Blaer scrambled to her feet, but it was too late. She was enclosed inside a living cage of ravens.

Luc got off the ground and gave himself a shake. He bounded back to Blaer, lips peeled in a furious snarl—and then stopped short. He prowled around the circling birds, searching for a way to get at Blaer.

She locked gazes with Langdon. "You want a fight, my lord?" Her chin jutted. "You forget I'm half ice fae."

"No," was the prince's reply. "I haven't forgotten."

The ravens' harsh caws filled the clearing.

Blaer raised her hands. Frost crept up Langdon's shoes.

He flicked a finger and the birds dove, pecking at her eyes and face. She shrieked and dropped to her knees, arms flung up to protect herself.

At a murmur from Langdon, the ravens backed off but continued to twine around Blaer so she was forced to remain crouched on the ground.

Luc crept closer, eyes burning.

She tossed her head, the cuts on her face already healing. "Go," she told him bitterly. "The *geas* is broken. You have your freedom."

But he didn't leave. Instead, he paced a circle around her, not attacking the ravens, but clearly guarding her.

Adric frowned at that—and then set it from his mind, because the prince had turned back to Rosana and Marjani.

Adric changed back to man but remained invisible. He rose to his feet, drawing Rosana up with him. Marjani shoved a dagger in his general direction, and he took it with a murmured thanks as she retrieved another dagger from the sheath around her neck.

Neoma conjured up a fae ball and aimed it at Marjani. "Stand down, fada."

Adric sprang at Neoma, slashed her forearm. The fae ball winked out of existence as she hissed and twisted away.

Meanwhile, Marjani had slipped Rosana the third dagger. The two of them stood back to back. Rosana blinked down at the iron blade, still shaky from her vision.

Adric's heart clenched. She needed food, rest.

He moved up beside her. "Leave," he whispered. "We'll cover you."

She tightened her grip on the dagger and lunged at a night fae approaching from her other side, slashing it across his knife arm. "Together," she growled as the warrior danced backward.

"Nice," murmured Marjani.

"Thanks," Rosana returned.

Adric's mouth twitched. "Together," he agreed. "Jani. What's the plan?"

"Get the fuck out of this warded circle. There's help on the other side."

He nodded. "You two go first. I'll keep them busy until you're out. The night fae might be able to sense me, but they can't be sure exactly where I am, especially if I keep moving."

"Works," said Marjani.

Rosana was more suspicious. "Promise you'll come with us."

He touched her cheek. "You have my word," he said, and then sprinted across the clearing to kick over the fire pit. The dark fire blinked out as it hit the ground.

The night fae hissed and snarled. Fae balls appeared in more warriors' hands. Adric slashed at the nearest one's arm and darted away.

The two women edged toward the portal while Adric bedeviled the night fae, dashing from one side of the clearing to the other, slashing at arms, legs, faces—anything to draw attention from Rosana and Marjani.

A crack of lightning split the night. Wind whipped through the clearing, but the wards—or whatever was protecting the circle—kept out the rain.

"Capture him!" the prince commanded. "You can't see him, but he's bleeding emotion. Focus on that."

The shadows deepened. Tendrils snaked through the night, seeking Adric. He instinctively froze. A glance over his shoulder told him that Rosana and Marjani had almost reached the portal.

He doggedly continued to zigzag through the night fae. But he was moving slower now, his limbs strangely heavy, as if the shadows had somehow taken on weight and were tugging on him.

Another bolt of lightning forced the shadows to retreat. Or maybe it wasn't lightning, but the sun fae.

Hope surged in Adric. He slipped around a couple of night fae warriors to join Marjani and Rosana, but the prince had realized the two were about to escape.

He flung up a hand. "Marjani Savonett and Rosana do Rio!" he commanded in a voice thick with power. "Halt!"

Rosana checked, but Marjani spun around, one hand on a silver charm that hung from her quartz. For the first time, he realized she was wearing a protection charm.

A warrior started forward, fae ball in hand.

Adric rushed back to Rosana and his sister. "I can cloak all three of us," he said. "Get ready to run like hell." He slipped an arm around each of their shoulders.

The portal wavered.

"Hurry!" he said. "Before it closes."

The shadows surrounded them. Tendrils snaked toward them.

Marjani shoved the protection charm at them and they retreated. But the portal had closed.

"Fuck," she muttered.

Then the sky lit like someone had torn back a curtain to let in the noon sun. As the night fae hissed in pain, the wards broke with an audible crack, sending a surge of energy that forced the three of them to stagger back.

Rain sluiced down.

"Go!" Adric urged the two women forward again.

More bolts of light slashed through the night. Queen Cleia strode into the clearing, her body a sunlit column, bolts of gold shooting from her fingertips.

For a few seconds, everyone—even Prince Langdon—stared at her, mouths ajar. Then the night fae snapped to life.

But more people poured into the clearing behind the queen.

Sun fae. River fada. And Jace, Fane, and a pack of Baltimore wolves with Zuri at the head.

"Now these kind of odds I can live with," his sister said.

Adric dropped the cloak so the three of them were visible again. The earth fada surrounded them, and they prepared to fight as fae on each side armed themselves with fiery balls of light.

Cleia planted herself at the center. With a wave of her hand, a fireball exploded at Langdon's feet. "I warned you to set the fada free, my lord. Now I'm here to demand their release. And think before you answer. I have two hundred more warriors itching for a fight."

Langdon conjured up a seething mass of shadows and doused the fireball.

"Shadows blot out the sun," he returned. "It's the night of the new moon. Do you think you can beat me?"

Cleia raised her hands. Behind her, Dion placed his hands on her shoulders. Something flashed between the two of them. Twin suns sparked to life in her hands.

"But sunlight chases away the shadows." The glowing balls in her hands grew brighter.

Langdon recovered first. He took two steps forward, face pale and eyebrows glittering. Two black-clad warriors flanked him, fae balls glowing in their palms.

Cleia raised her hands higher. An unearthly flame danced in her palms, lighting her gold, silver and copper hair so that it shone like living fire.

"Tell your guards to stand down," she gritted, "or I'll turn them into ashes."

"Try it." Langdon pointed a finger at Cleia, but the rest of them had had time to shrug off whatever spell he'd cast.

Dion leapt to block him. In his hand was a dagger shimmering with magic.

Langdon flicked his fingers at the dagger, trying to change it to something else, but the bespelled dagger remained just that—a dagger.

Dion lashed out at Langdon, fada-fast. The prince only just managed to leap clear of the slashing blade.

Dion stalked after him, his eyes pure, molten silver.

The prince conjured up a whirling wall of twigs and leaves, but Dion slashed his way through them.

Meanwhile, the priests and priestesses had melted into the shadows so that only their eyes were visible.

Two wolves came at Langdon from either direction, but he evaded them by sinking into the shadows himself. More twigs and leaves swirled around Cleia, but before they could turn into anything, she incinerated them with another bolt.

A second, more powerful explosion ripped the night fae from the shadows. This time, Langdon was ready. He threw up a shade of leaves and other debris to protect him and his people from the worst of the light.

But Adric and the other fada had engaged them, he and Marjani fighting neck-and-neck with Rui and Tiago, while nearby, Zuri and the other wolves took down another couple of night fae.

Adric could see the moment Langdon realized that even if he survived, he was going to take heavy casualties, including losing most of the court's priests and priestesses.

He threw up his arms and a powerful wind blasted everyone except Cleia to the opposite side of the circle. But when they jumped to their feet, he ordered his own people to stand down, and then turned to Cleia.

"Peace, my lady." He kept his hands by his sides, palms out, in a proudly open posture. "Rosana do Rio is yours. I ask only one thing in return—that you grant me the rights I'm owed as a grandfather."

Dion moved next to Cleia. "A grandfather?"

"Yes. I demand the right to know the daughter of my youngest son. You and your clan have no right to keep me from the blood of my blood."

"Fuck your rights." Adric shoved his way next to Dion. "You'll have to go through me and every member of my clan first," he spat.

But Dion nodded as if he was considering it. "You'll release my sister without obligation?" While he was speaking, Dion undid the silver bracelet around his wrist and tossed it to Rosana, who quickly clasped it around her own wrist.

Adric shot him a furious look, but something in the other alpha's expression made him hold back.

"Yes," Langdon said. "She's given me an invaluable piece of information. I consider any debt between us paid in full. That is," he said to Rosana. "If I can't persuade you to remain as court Seer?"

Rosana couldn't conceal a shudder. "No," she said curtly. "But I refuse to leave without Marjani and Adric."

"Rosana," Dion said with a scowl.

Her jaw set. "He's my mate."

Cleia spoke. "You owe the fada a boon, Prince Langdon."

"My sister's life," Adric said.

"And Lord Adric's," Rosana quickly added. "We'll accept nothing else."

"Come," Cleia said. "That seems reasonable. After all, this was started by your own son."

Langdon eyed Adric coldly. Adric had a sudden insight—the prince was searching for a way to save face in front of his people. But more than that, he truly wanted to get to know Merry.

And it *was* Merry's birthright. She had the right to make her own decision.

"As for your granddaughter," Adric added, "as far as I'm concerned, the choice is hers. Not yours, and not Lord Dion's."

Rui do Mar made a sharp movement, but Dion nodded at Adric. "Go on."

Adric dropped his voice so that only Langdon, Cleia, Rui, Dion and Rosana could hear.

"When Merry comes of age, then you'll invite her to visit the court. I'm sure Lord Dion will agree that the choice at that point will be hers. But for now, leave her where she is. She's safe, happy. The river fada have done a good job of protecting her, and the queen keeps an eye on her as well. Too many people are interested in her."

A muscle in the prince's cheek worked. His gaze slid to the nearby night fae, straining to hear the low-voiced conversation.

"Very well," he said. "If you and Lord Dion both swear that when my granddaughter comes of age, the choice is hers."

"No tricks or coercion," Adric said. "She must be given a true choice."

Dion waited for Rui to nod, and then said, "That's acceptable to us."

Langdon inclined his head. "You have my promise."

"And my promise as well," first Adric, then Dion said.

Langdon hesitated. "I would like the chance to get to know her, though. Perhaps a meeting or two a year."

"That's up to her father," Dion said.

Rui crossed his arms over his broad chest. "No."

"And that goes double for me," said Jace from behind Adric's shoulder. "You had your chance to get to know her when she was on the run from Tyrus. Now, she stays with us."

The prince's mouth tightened. "Very well. But perhaps you can ask if she wishes to meet me. I promise, I want only to become acquainted with her."

Rui's dark brows lowered. "We'll see," was all he'd say.

"Thank you." Langdon stepped back. "Let them leave unharmed," he told his warriors. He bowed to the queen. "Peace to you and yours, Cleia."

"And to yours," she returned with a gracious bow of her own.

Adric and Marjani exchanged an incredulous glance. But that was the fae. Polite even as they slipped a knife into your rib cage.

In the exodus that followed, Adric sidled up to Langdon. "Just so you know," he murmured, "if you take Merry, I'll know. Every earth fada in the clan is connected to my quartz."

"I see." Langdon's eyes dropped to Adric's pendant.

Adric fingered it just to make sure his point was taken. "You can hide her, but eventually, I'll find her. And I wouldn't advise looking for a way to break the connection. It might work—or you might kill her. We're not the enemy," he added. "Your own people are."

Langdon's gaze flicked at a priest setting the metal bowl back on its stand. Others had faded back into the shadows, so that only their faces were visible. Watching. Waiting.

"I'm aware of that," the prince said, and striding back to his throne, settled onto it with his legs sprawled in front of him as if he hadn't a care in the world.

Adric's chest heaved. It was over.

He reached for Rosana, but she was already there. She took his head between her hands and gave him a smacking kiss, uncaring that her brothers, Cleia and the upper hierarchy of both their clans were watching. Or maybe, that was the point.

"You did it!"

"No, we did it," he corrected, enfolding her in his arms. "I love you, you know that?"

"Right back at you." She buried her face in his neck and they stood there, arms tight around each other, rocking back and forth. "I was so scared," she muttered.

"I'm sorry, angel."

She pulled back. "You should be," she said with a crooked grin. "Now take me home."

He glanced at where Marjani was crouched next to Luc, speaking in a low voice. The wolf growled and shook his head.

"You go," he told Rosana. "I'll be right with you."

Her gaze had followed his own. "Of course." She hugged him again and then turned to Dion, who was waiting to wrap her in a hug of his own.

Marjani looked up at Adric, biting her lip. "He won't leave. I think he's bonded to her somehow."

Adric scowled down at Luc. He'd thought the next time he saw the wolf, he'd rip off his face for what he'd put Rosana through, but now he just felt sorry for him. Besides, if he knew Luc, the wolf would punish himself more harshly than anything Adric could do.

He set a hand on Luc's head. The wolf pushed into his palm, taking his alpha's scent on himself.

"Luc. Come with us. The clan misses you. I miss you."

The wolf turned his head to look up at Adric. His eyes had lost their madness. He gave Adric a decided nudge toward the exit. *Go.*

Adric's throat tightened. He wanted to argue further, but almost everyone had left now. Besides him and Marjani, only Fane, Cleia and a couple of sun fae warriors waited, and it wasn't fair to ask them to stay in this nightmare of a court any longer than they had to.

"Okay. If you're sure that's how you want it." He rubbed his cheek against Luc's. "But when you return, your place in the clan will be there. That's a promise."

Luc dipped his head in acknowledgment.

There was still one thing left to do. Keeping a wary eye on the circling ravens, Adric thrust his quartz toward at the woman trapped within. "Lady Blaer," he commanded. "Look at my quartz."

She glanced up and dully shook her head.

He let the fire flare inside. "Lady Blaer," he repeated in a hard voice. "Look at my quartz."

This time, her gaze caught on the quartz. Held.

Maybe it was because he was so determined, or maybe it was because she'd been weakened by her fight with Langdon, but when he said, "You *will* forget the secret words. You'll even forget they exist," she gave a jerky nod.

"Say it," he ordered.

"I will forget the secret words. As if they never existed."

"And you'll never use them against a fada again," he added.

"And I'll never use them against a fada again."

"Good." He bared his fangs at her. "Because if you do, the next time we meet, I'll carve your fucking liver out."

He rose back up.

A tear ran down Marjani's mud-streaked cheek. She touched Luc's shoulder, then turned and stumbled toward the portal, where Fane wrapped an arm around her shoulders. Together, she, Fane and Adric exited the clearing, Cleia and her men behind them.

Dion and Tiago waited on the other side of the portal, along with Rosana, who had an arm around each of them.

"You came." She was laughing and crying at the same time. "*You came.*"

"Of course, we did," Dion growled and handed her off to Cleia for a hug.

"You were awesome," Rosana told her. "Totally kickass."

The queen grinned—and swayed on her feet. Her skin was pale under its dusting of gold. Dion was instantly there, sweeping her into his arms.

"Let's get the fuck out of here," he said.

Together, he, Tiago, and Rui hurried the two women through the forest. Rosana cast an apologetic look over her shoulder at Adric, but allowed it. But when she stepped through the second portal, she halted to wait for Adric.

He immediately set an arm around her waist. Staking his claim in front of her brothers.

Dion cast Adric a dark look. "You really mated with this *filho da puta*?"

"I was dying." Rosana moved closer to Adric. "He saved my life. We're bonded now. You can't undo it."

"But we would like your blessing," Adric added.

Tiago sneered. "What about your clan?"

"They'll treat my mate with respect, or they'll find a new clan." Adric touched his quartz. "I swear on my mother's grave."

Beside him, Marjani and Jace nodded agreement.

Dion gave curt nod. "I'll hold you to that."

Rosana beamed. "It will work," she assured her brothers. "You'll see."

As they started forward again, she lifted her face to a ray of sunshine. With a shock, Adric realized it was morning, the sun rising in a winter-blue sky.

His lungs expanded. Inside, his cat gave a luxurious stretch.

A dizzying exhilaration filled him. This was happiness, he realized. This light-as-air feeling.

The night fae had been defeated—for now, at least. His sister was free of the death sentence hanging over her, and he'd neutralized Lady Blaer. They'd even bought Merry some time before she'd have to deal with Prince Langdon.

And not only had he survived, he'd somehow won this smart, beautiful, caring woman as his mate.

Rosana turned to look at him. Curious at first, and then she broke into a wondering smile.

"You're happy. I feel it. Here." She pressed her fingers to her breastbone.

"Hell, yeah." He touched his lips to hers, taking that smile inside him. "Let's go home."

"Yes," she murmured against his mouth. "Let's go home."

CHAPTER 47

The mate ball was held at the Court of the Rising Sun.

Queen Cleia had offered, and Rosana had been so thrilled that Adric had agreed, even though he'd assumed they'd hold the ceremony out of his den. Still, at the end of the night, she'd be going home with him, and that was all he cared about.

The ritual was scheduled for sunset on the spring equinox. Adric slid a finger under the collar of his bronze button-up shirt as he waited for Rosana in the crowded, flower-filled tent. A fae light drifted by, a soft pink dotted with lazily spiraling bits of gold. More fae lights cast a hazy rose hue on the assembled clans—his, hers, and a sizable number of sun fae.

At his side were Zuri and Jace, and nearby were Rosana's attendants, Merry and Jenny. Dion and Marjani were joint officiants.

Dion was imposing in a deep blue shirt and dark slacks, his long hair flowing over his shoulders, his big feet bare. His pint-sized daughter was cuddled in one arm, her bright eyes taking in everything.

"Savonett." The other alpha nodded, unsmiling. "All the best on your mate-day."

He nodded back. "Thank you."

He turned to Marjani, stunning in an African wax-print dress with cheerful red poppies splashed on a green background. It was still a shock to see his sister in something besides brown, gray or camo-green.

"Jani." He embraced her. "You look—"

"Gorgeous?" She hugged him back. "Glowing?"

He grinned. "Yeah. All that." He stepped back to scan the meadow for Rosana again, but she was closeted with Cleia and her former nurse Isa in the queen's fanciful, four-tiered white mansion.

After they'd left Virginia, Dion had taken Rosana back to Rock Run to rest and prepare for the mating celebration. She'd visited Adric every few days, but at his request, it had been a week now since he'd last seen her. He'd spent the time making his den ready for her.

But damn, he ached for her. And not just his cock, which had been half-hard all day. No, it was his heart that ached. It *hurt* to be separated from his mate.

He shoved his hands into his pockets and scanned the tent again. This mating stuff was for the birds. It made you weak, vulnerable—and he wouldn't trade places with another man in this tent for any amount of riches.

The sun was painting the sky a spectacular peach and purple when Rosana and her entourage finally emerged from Cleia's mansion. An excited murmur rippled through the crowd as Tiago and the queen escorted her across the meadow to the tent, with Isa following, a proud smile on her elderly face.

Adric craned his neck, but after a brief glimpse, all he saw was the top of her black head as she wended her way through the crowd, greeting and being greeted.

It seemed like hours before Rosana finally came into view—and stole the breath right out of his chest.

She was gorgeous in a calf-length gown of ivory and gold that clung to her upper body, showing off her high, firm breasts and nipped-in waist before widening to an airy froth around long, sleek-muscled legs. Her only jewelry was his amethyst pendant, the charm bracelet, and a pair of dangling earrings, and she wore short lace gloves on her hands.

But what made him grin were the red kitten-heel boots on her feet.

"Breathe, Ric." Marjani slanted him a teasing smile.

Breathe. Right.

Adric sucked in a loud inhale that had everyone nearby chuckling.

Tiago took his place with the other men, and Cleia took little Brisa from Dion before joining the other women.

Zuri stepped forward to take Rosana's hands and thank her before everyone for saving Adric's life. Marjani and Adric had made sure everyone knew what Rosana had done at New Moon, starting with how she'd refused to leave him alone at the court after he'd been badly injured. It had gone a long way to reducing the clan's antagonism against her.

It didn't hurt that they had a healthy respect for Rosana's Gift. Some of them were even a little afraid of her, which was a good start. Fada respected strength.

True acceptance would take longer, of course. But he had a feeling Rosana would win them over. She'd already won over Zuri, and he wasn't an easy sell.

As for the hardliners, the ones who muttered their alpha shouldn't mate with the enemy?

Adric had made sure they knew that Rosana was his mate—period—and they'd treat her with courtesy, or find another clan. He'd only had to shove a few of the more dominant up against a wall to make his point.

Now, he stepped forward and extricated her from Zuri.

"Ready?"

She took his hands. "You know I am."

The ceremony passed in a blur. All he could see was Rosana, blue eyes smiling, a constant smile on her lips. Crazy in love, and unashamed to show it.

He no longer wondered if she'd ever learn to protect her heart. Instead, he thanked the gods that she'd given it to him. It was a gift he intended to treasure the rest of his life.

He spoke his vows to her loud and clear, proudly claiming her as his before everyone present. She accepted his claim in the same clear tones.

His mate gift to her was a three-strand bracelet of semi-precious stones— amethyst, lapis and green jasper—with a silver cougar and dolphin intertwined at the center.

Her mouth rounded in a soft *Oh* as he clasped it around her wrist next to the charm bracelet. "I love it," she said, leaning in for a kiss.

But he stopped her, removing his quartz. "Take off your gloves."

When she did, he wrapped her bare hands around the chunk of gray and orange. The earth fada sucked in a breath, understanding the symbolism.

Rosana was truly his mate.

Taking back the quartz, he cupped her face and kissed her as Dion and Marjani pronounced the last few words of the ceremony, asking for their mating to be blessed by the gods and goddesses, the sun and moon, and everyone present.

When he released her, her eyes were a deep, saturated blue.

"I love you," he said, and they turned to accept the congratulations of their clans.

HOURS LATER, Dion and Adric ended up side-by-side, watching the dancers. Their two clans had managed to get through dinner and the dancing that followed without any incidents. They were even intermingling. Zuri was currently charming a sexy older river fada, and Davi was dancing with Suha.

A tall, golden-haired sun fae spun Rosana in a circle and then bent her back over his arm. She laughed up at him and pivoted away, the skirt swirling around her slim legs.

An almost noiseless growl escaped Adric at seeing her so close to another male.

Mine.

It was primal, primitive—and he didn't give a damn. He was a newly mated fada male, and he wanted his woman all to himself. But he folded his arms over his chest and stayed where he was, because he also wanted his woman to be happy, and Rosana was clearly enjoying herself.

Dion's look was knowing. "It isn't easy watching your mate with another man."

He scowled and shrugged.

"You kept her alive. I owe you my thanks."

Adric snorted. "Like hell you do. I almost got her bound to the prince in a *geas*."

"You did what you had to do. I know the whole story—how she went to Baltimore, tried to get you to take her with you. And then when she had a chance to leave, she refused."

Adric met his eyes. "If this is the part where you say be good to my sister or I'll bust your balls, don't worry. I know I don't deserve her—but I love her. I'd burn down the fucking world for her."

A short nod. "I know you would. Do I trust you? You still have to earn that. But in this, I do—you won't hurt her because it would hurt you too much."

Adric moved uncomfortably on his feet. "She's my mate," he muttered. "Don't make me into some kind of hero."

Dion grunted. "Believe me, I'm not. I'm a mated man myself, remember? I know how it is." A feral grin. "And if you did hurt Rosana, I wouldn't have to do a damn thing. She'd bust your balls for me."

Adric gave a bark of laughter, watching as Rosana danced by with another man—Jace, this time. "You're right."

"But I have a proposition for you. I want to see my sister more than once every couple of weeks, and I know you're never going to be satisfied until you have more land for your clan."

"Go on."

"Here's the deal. You need a place for your people to run free as their animals. Rock Run might be able to help you there."

Adric's heart sped up. "Yeah?"

"I'll rent your clan the portion of our territory farthest from the base. I'll give you a line that you'll tell your people not to cross, but you'll still have a few hundred acres of forest to run in. Maybe down the road, you can buy up some of the nearby land, expand. When that Factory of yours finally gets off the ground, you'll have some extra cash."

"I see."

"Well? You interested?"

"Very," he returned with a cool nod, although inside, he was leaping for joy.

"We'll have to work out the details," Dion said, "but I'd say we have ourselves a deal." He brought his fist to his heart, and then offered his hand to Adric.

Adric touched his heart as well, and the two of them shook on it.

"Thank you," he said. "You won't be sorry."

"See that I'm not."

Adric nodded—and then grinned. "But for the record, I'm not done being a pain in your ass."

Dion smiled back. A white-toothed, frankly evil smile. "You just took on my sister. I figure we're about even."

CHAPTER 48

At midnight the celebration was still going strong. That was the sun fae for you; they'd still be partying until midnight tomorrow. Not that the fada looked ready to go home anytime soon, either.

But Adric had had enough.

He found Rosana near the dance floor with Jenny, their dark heads together, chuckling about something.

"Time to go." He put a hand on the small of Rosana's back.

"Already?" She glanced at him, surprised. Whatever she saw in his face had her sharing a grin with Jenny. "Guess we're leaving."

The two women hugged. "Don't be a stranger," Jenny said.

"I won't, I promise," said Rosana. "And you can come see me. Right?" She cast Adric an uncertain look.

He frowned. A Rock Run fada's mate in his den? The very idea raised his fur.

But that was the old Adric, the one who'd had to be suspicious of everyone and everything to survive.

So he smiled at Jenny. "You're welcome anytime."

The human's dark eyes lit. "Thank you, my lord."

"Please. Call me Ric."

"Ric," she said, her smile increasing.

He turned to Rosana. "Ready? I have a surprise for you."

Jenny smirked, and he winked at her as he took Rosana's hand. "Not that kind of surprise," he said.

Rosana's mouth twitched as they walked around the tent to thank Cleia and Dion for the party. "No? Now I'm curious."

He patted her round bottom. "Be good."

She nipped his earlobe. "But you like me bad," she murmured—and smiled at her brother and Cleia, leaving him to hide his erection. "This has been the best day of my life," she told them.

He set his mouth to her ear. "You'll pay for that," he promised, and added his thanks to hers.

THEY RODE BACK to Baltimore on Adric's motorcycle. Rosana wrapped her arms around his lean waist, still in her dress and red boots.

She slipped her hands under his leather jacket, toying with his ridged abs beneath the bronze shirt. "Did I tell you how good you looked today?"

"Mm." He took her hand, bringing it to his lips before setting it back on his waist again. "You were the hottest woman there."

She leaned her cheek against his jacket and slipped her fingers lower to the ridge beneath his zipper. "Keep talking, and you might get lucky tonight."

A wicked chuckle. "I'm counting on it, mate."

Her dress came off as soon as they walked in the door. Her only underclothes were a wispy white bra and panties.

Adric shrugged out of his jacket. "The boots stay on," he said and pulled her into his arms.

Her whole body thrilled at the low command.

He filled his hands with her ass and lowered his mouth to hers, tasting her with slow, knee-weakening sweeps of his tongue. She pressed against him.

He was still cold from the ride, the shirt soft and cool against her bare skin, his pants slightly abrasive. He pushed his thigh between her legs as he kissed her, rubbing against her sex through the flimsy panties.

She moaned and sucked his tongue deeper.

He eased up on the kiss and rested his forehead against hers. "It's been too damn long."

"A week."

"It felt like a year. Ten years." Suddenly, her feet were swept out from beneath her. She squeaked and looped an arm around his neck as he headed down the hall with her in his arms. "But first, your surprise. Close your eyes."

She obediently shut them. "What is it?"

He nipped her throat. "If I told you, it wouldn't be a surprise. No, don't open them yet." He set her on the floor and covered her eyes with his hands, nudging her through a doorway.

She gripped his wrists. Was that water she heard?

He took his fingers away. "Go ahead. Look."

She clapped her hands to her mouth. Amber quartz sconces lit a stone grotto twice the size of his living room. A waterfall fed the pool in the center—a pool large enough for her dolphin with a few yards to spare—and a narrow stream exited from the opposite end, providing further room to swim.

"It's beautiful," she breathed.

He caressed her shoulders from behind. "There are crystals set in the walls of the pool to purify the water, but it comes from an underground spring, which is about as pure as Baltimore water gets."

She turned in his arms. "I love it. I—" She shook her head, throat tight. "How—?"

A shrug. "We worked around the clock—me and three other stoneworkers. We didn't carve it all by hand. I blasted out the main cavity, then we went from there."

"It's incredible. I can't believe you did this—and so fast."

"You're my mate. I want you to be happy."

She took his face between her hands and kissed him on the lips. "I love it, and I love you. Thank you." She knelt to trail a hand in the water.

It was cool, clean-smelling. Perfect.

He smiled down at her. "Go ahead. Take a swim."

"I will." Rising to her feet, she set a hand on his chest and walked him backward until he was against the wall. She started undoing his shirt buttons. "Later. First, I have to thank my mate properly."

A slow grin. "I think I'm going to like this."

She helped him out of the shirt and dropped it on the stone floor. Removing her bra and panties, she sank to her knees before him.

His breath rasped in. "In the red boots? You know this is my fantasy, right?"

"Yeah?" She eased his zipper down over his erection and freed him from his boxers. "Tell me more." She licked her way around the rim, delicate, teasing touches.

His cock jerked beneath her touch.

Adric fisted his hands. His hips strained toward her.

She gripped one hip with her hand and wrapped the other around his hard stalk. It was so thick, her fingers barely made it around. She swiped her tongue over the smooth head, and he groaned.

His hands threaded into her hair, holding her in place as he stroked into her mouth.

"In my fantasy," he said, "you come to me, wet from the water, wearing those fuck-me boots and nothing else. I order you to get on your knees and take me, and you do. Because you like it as much as me."

The hot, dark words sent a jolt of excitement to her already soaked sex.

"You say you like my taste. My scent."

"Mm." She moaned around him. "I do."

"You say, *I See a lot of sex in your future.*"

She chuckled, causing him to jerk.

"Gods. When you laugh, I feel it vibrating clear to my balls." He pressed deeper into her mouth. "Take me, Rosana. Take me all the way."

She eagerly sucked, loving the salty-sea taste. He fell silent, letting her pleasure him. Even better, she could *feel* his enjoyment through the mate bond.

She slid a hand between his thighs, cupping and caressing his balls. He groaned and rasped, "And then, you say you love me. Tell me, Rosana. Tell me you love me."

But when she opened her mouth to obey, he lifted her from her knees, turning with her still in his arms and pressing her up the wall.

His tongue slipped into her mouth. "I can taste myself," he muttered. "And you. You and me, together. Now say it."

She wrapped her arms and legs around him. "I love you. I love you. I love you."

He started to press in, then halted. "Condom."

She dug her heels into his ass, keeping him where he was. "It's okay. If it happens, it happens. I want a big family like my mom and dad had."

"Yeah?" His eyes were a gleaming mix of bronze and blue. "That sounds pretty good to me."

He stroked in the rest of the way, and for a long while, the only sounds in the cavern were the waterfall's musical trickle—and an earth fada and a river fada making love.

Together.

ALSO BY REBECCA RIVARD

Thanks so much for reading! Want to be the first to hear about my upcoming releases and other fun stuff?

Sign up for my newsletter: rebeccarivard.com/newsletter

THE FADA SHAPESHIFTERS

Stealing Ula

Seducing the Sun Fae

Claiming Valeria

Tempting the Dryad

Lir's Lady

Shifter's Valentine

Sea Dragon's Hunger

Saving Jace

Charming Marjani

Adric's Heart

THE VAMPIRE SYNDICATE

Tempted

Pursued

Craved

Taken

Fallen

Hunger

The Vampire Kingpin

ABOUT REBECCA RIVARD

USA Today bestselling author Rebecca Rivard read way too many romances as a teenager, little realizing she was actually preparing for a career. She now spends her days with vampires, shifters and fae—which has to be the best job ever.

Her stories have been awarded multiple prizes, including the prestigious PRISM, the RONE, and the Paranormal Romance Guild Reviewers' Choice Award. Additionally, eight of her books have been honored with *InD'Tale Magazine*'s coveted Crowned Heart Review.

When she's not writing, Rebecca walks and bikes in the Chesapeake Bay area with her guitar-playing, storytelling husband. She loves traveling and delights in seeking out mysterious castles, cobblestoned streets, and eerie cemeteries—scenes that often inspire the settings of her novels.